Tiger Heart:
A Business Love Story

Tiger Heart:
A Business Love Story

A Novel

By
Robert E. Wescott

Strategic Book Publishing and Rights Co.

Strategic Book Publishing and Rights Co., LLC
USA | Singapore
www.sbpra.com

For information about special discounts for bulk purchases, please contact Strategic Book Publishing and Rights Co. Special Sales, at bookorder@sbpra.net.

ISBN: 978-1-68181-687-6

DEDICATION

To my brother, Don, who taught me to be funny
To my father who thought I'd never finish anything
To my mother who taught me grace and good grammar
To her mother who taught all of us about love and sacrifice
To my brother Gerry who lives ethically, religiously and still loves me
To my wife who teaches me to relax – or tries to
To my children who have shown amazing strength and talents I never had
And to my grandchildren who prove that the Universe is operating as intended

ACKNOWLEDGEMENT

This book is an odd project and not the first one started, God knows. It began as a short story about shenanigans among residents of a neighborhood that I could see in my minds' eye, the image one of a gritty street near the Lehigh Valley tracks in Stroudsberg, Pennsylvania, a town I've driven through. The time frame, would be late winter when the sand and gravel and bits of pavement are strewn across the street – literally gritty.

However, as most authors can relate to, in the first few lines I wrote "… in the old foundry building on Iron Way." and my world shifted to Pittsburgh and Blatchford Steel Services and a whole host of unanticipated characters showed up and I was off and running… for tens of thousands of words!

Way over 300,000 at first. Lots of those are gone, now, and I must thank the publisher, SBPRA, for prodding me and prodding me to clean it up; I do thank them. In the writing phase of "Tiger Heart" I was able to add to the story every time I sat down. I met and understood the characters enough to know what each would do – it was fun. Making it actually readable was drudgery. I appreciate more and more how good truly good authors are.

I owe great credit to my long passed mother, Barbara. Almost until her last day she was correcting poor grammar in her grandchildren, great-grandchildren and, yes, her children, God bless her. Both my parents were word-meisters and our house was full of books and multiple periodicals and two newspapers. There were Christmas Days when we couldn't touch the presents until my father and one of us boys had gone "uptown" to the "Paper Store" (not its name, but its function) to get a "Globe" and a "Herald." We survived, despite his careful installation of a scarf for 23 minutes.

I appreciate, too, my grandson, Jon, who accompanied me on one of the research trips to Pittsburgh for a weekend of total boredom – for him, not for me.

I had to see the intersections and bridges and houses and buildings that are the backdrop to what became, I hope, a good story.

YOUNGSTOWN

Henry Brill drummed his fingers on the steering wheel. He twisted his torso to make another sweep around his position amidst dozens of truck trailers in the make-up yard in Riverbend. The last half-inch of black coffee was cold and bitter. If McIlhenny didn't get here in the next few minutes…

Abruptly the back passenger door opened and McIlhenny rolled into the back seat, rocking the small sedan.

"Christ, Mickey, took ya long enough!"

"Keep your jock on. I gotta do this without drawin attention. That's a good plan for you, too." McIlhenny rocked himself back and forth to get comfortable, his three-hundred pound bulk not suited for Malibu back seats. "And get yourself a bigger car."

"Maybe I will when you start to come across." Brill turned to partly face his back-seat guest. He saw the big man shifting a pistol into his left coat pocket.

"What the fuck are you carrying for? What is this?" Brill was suddenly much colder than the night deserved. He stared at the pocket flap where the gun had been secreted.

"Take it easy, f'crissakes, will ya? This ain't Playskool, ya know." Mickey pulled open some rolled and folded papers as he glared back at his nervous host. "What? You getting chickenshit on this? Give me the word and you can be floating down the Ohio. We ain't fuckin around here!"

Hank Brill fought to contain his bladder, the last swig of cold coffee now heavy. This was supposed to be simple graft. A few doctored EPA records... twenty grand in untraceable cash. He could bury twenty thousand. And God knows he needed the dough if Marny was going to say "yes" to his imminent proposal.

"Take it easy. I'll do my part. Just gimme the plot data and I'll get the signs up like I said. We don't have to meet again."

"I ain't givin nothin. You read these things and memorize which blocks. Nothin on paper. Got it?" He handed the rumpled pages over to Brill who was happy to concentrate on something else. A total of two-hundred and eight acres of developable land above the Mahoning, slated for new retail, offices, and mid-rise luxury apartments. The wrong people were seeking permits.

Brill committed the lot numbers to memory and tossed the poisonous sheets back at the City Councilor. "I'll have the signs up Monday," he growled, "and there'll be papers on file. But anyone goes lookin too deeply and this won't hold, you know."

"It's only gotta hold through the election. I gotta protect that part of the district from the awful traffic and congestion, see?" McIlhenny gave Brill a rounded envelope without speaking.

He squeezed it a couple of times and dropped it on the front seat as the corpulent councilor struggled out of the back seat. Brill didn't follow the man's return to his own car. He pulled out and caught the Madison Avenue Expressway headed downtown. Outside a pub near Youngstown State he counted the sixteen hundreds and stuffed them into his front left pocket.

PROLOGUE

I like to cook. When I was eighteen and for a few years I thought I'd be a chef, and I had the good fortune of actually learning from a real second-chef. Over the years I tried out interesting recipes and some of my culinary victories were greatly enjoyed by my boss, Jack Jackson, and an occasional fellow worker at Blatchford Steel Services in the old foundry building on Iron Way.

When LTV closed Jones & Laughlin Steel, the huge buildings were left without their vital organs, blood supplies and nerve centers. Planning committees tossed ideas around about use of the land and buildings that once were the economic strength of Pittsburgh. Finally the city tore down the big open-hearth ovens and the quarter-mile building that housed them. The open spaces and new roads among the remaining buildings got companies looking seriously and Blatchford Steel Services took a chance on the foundry building because it had a big overhead crane that ran on rails near the roof line.

Blatchford doesn't make steel. We cut it and weld it and put holes in it so our customers can build bridges and buildings and hundreds of other things I never worried about because I had no good reason to. I approve invoices that come in and internal requisitions we issue and make cost projections twice a month. Blatchford won't start customizing I-beams and plates until the costs were known, and not until most of the price was paid, either. Made sense.

This doesn't prepare my story, really, except to show my days were each similar to the one before and the one to come with the exceptions of Mondays being a little down and Fridays up. Wednesday, of course, was league night.

To break the routine I created interesting dishes. Jackson, expected a gourmet lunch every Tuesday, and was grumpier and more critical should I fail to produce one. It became a de facto part of my job and I fulfilled it to maintain a reasonably cordial relationship. I did say I like to cook.

My wife, Linda, and I live in a small "Cape" that we'd raised the roof on to make two large bedrooms for kids we couldn't seem to have. Early on she devoted herself to the perfect family image her parents had engendered, designing and decorating the two bedrooms for one boy and one girl, a couple years apart, healthy and obedient. But it didn't happen, for all our efforts, delightful at first and more drudging later on until she suspended that mission and started spending more time in her "clubs." God had ordained that her children would be born to someone else and there was no point in trying to change His mind.

For my part I accepted sex for fun and for mission, and I bowled with the Blatchford Steel team at the Brunswick Bowladrome over in West Mifflin, that had a full thirty-two lanes. Our team, the "Iron Tigers," has a nifty symbol of an embroidered tiger carrying a couple of I-Beams. We bowled five other teams. There were five Iron Tigers. Other teams had four members. We had a dispensation, we thought, from the Professional Bowling Association, but it just meant we could suit up as many teammates as we wanted so long as only four of us bowled on any night. One of us was always substituting for another.

We had great attendance, thanks to Katy Mellon, who worked in Human Resources for Blatchford. Katy was nicely stacked, you might say, as we often did – the men, anyway. She went out with groups from Blatchford, like on Friday nights, properly demure, never flirting too much with any one guy. Rumors held that more than one co-worker had enjoyed taking Katy home, but nothing was, well... known.

Still, those stories kept the male Tigers showing up – those and the wonderful tits that Katy advertised demurely. She also bowled well, with excellent form, as our research proved about sixty times every Wednesday night and sometimes on Saturdays. This generated a pattern, since I seemed to want sex more on Wednesdays after "league" and sometimes on Saturdays.

Sex aside, Linda – Mrs. Walter Anton – and I, who lived at 7 Mapleledge Street in Penn Hills, in a neat brick Cape with a raised roof, were good neighbors. We shared cookout hosting, babysat for the Maxwells, across to the left, and later, for Penny and Bob Simpson who had just moved into their first home, closer to Jefferson than ours. It was pale blue, but they could afford it. They were the "kids" in our neighborhood.

Farther away from Jefferson lived Axel Johnson with his two children Sasha and Axel, Jr. who were both away more than home: Sasha in college and Junior with Xerox doing training that had him traveling quite a bit. Axel was not black, exactly, but his skin was a dark tea with milk which made him more handsome than if his features were molded in pure white. He could fix anything and he had the right tools. Women liked Axel more than their husbands did, but he was a gentleman, even reserved. I got along with him fine – he could fix small engines like the one on my hand-me-down snow blower.

I had imagined loving someone like Linda before we met, and she seemed perfect to me when we were dating and engaged. Her mom looked good at fifty and her parents enjoyed their marriage and flirted in gentle ways, portending a good life for me with their daughter. They liked my stable employment. I think they were as distraught about grandchildren as Linda was, but that was one of those areas of private grief I learned to keep away from.

***

Our honeymoon trip was a Caribbean cruise. We've got pictures, but I couldn't tell you which island was which. Those were the best days. Linda was determined to have babies and willing to try positions on the chance that penetration this way produced boy babies and that way might favor girls. I was equally accepting of either gender and positions related thereto, and the honeymoon and the following four years or so, were excellent. She even ordered a book and we carefully tried its suggestions in every room: cooking, taking showers, designing the kids' bedrooms and moving furniture in the living room. I rushed home for the two weeks we were painting the bedrooms to see how we would wind up in both intercourse and paint.

The last month of intentional procreation was highlighted by a week of underwear-less cooking and cleaning that had me ready for action every night and weekend afternoons. But it ended.

We took another cruise in the fall, five years and a few months after our April, '78 wedding. She had a lot of headaches that summer and seemed burdened leading up to the cruise. We drove six hours to a parking garage in Fort Lee, New Jersey where a big, air-conditioned bus gathered proto-argonauts and took us to southern Manhattan to board. The ride had been pretty quiet and I was oblivious to any storm clouds. We didn't chat. It was okay with me.

Through the serpentine lines of boarding procedures we were excited. Organized Linda knew what the steps were and seemed happy to get through each, holding my hand to encourage me to the next, even to having our picture taken going up the gangplank. I was thinking of skimpy bathing suits, hot tubs, warm weather and our private balcony. This trip held some promise.

Topside, a nautical term, we watched the mast on our liner just clear the Verrezano Bridge. Waiters served drinks with umbrellas and strawberry daiquiris with whipped cream. None suited us and the evening chill exceeded our clothing, so we descended to a small lounge. A pretty good songstress massaged some standards as we watched the lights of New Jersey.

"How are you feeling, Lindy?" I asked, looking for her eyes to center on mine for the first time that day. "Glad to be underway?" The still relatively newlywed Mrs. Walter Anton kept her eyes fixed on some point outside.

"Yes, I guess. It's relaxing."

"I thought if you were upset and I did something, just tell me. Okay?"

"No, no, we're fine. Just tired I suppose. Long day, today." Linda tightened her lips and nodded agreement with her own assessment. Almost as quickly she looked up with a flash of brightness but not quite the trademark grin I needed.

"So we might not start our second honeymoon tonight, huh?" I tried to make light of something I knew nothing about, still hoping to get laid. And if so, I might be able to make her relax and grin once in this twenty four hours.

"No, honey. If that's alright."

"Oh, no problem, Lin. We can use a little rest." I gulped my Manhattan and ordered another round, hers being Pinot Grigio – I knew that much.

The little chime sounded first seating. I carried her glass and felt good that she held my right arm as we entered the dining room, but this was Celibate Sunday. It would be warmer tomorrow.

***

By morning temperatures were pretty balmy. Most passengers were in the breakfast buffet or on the deck around the pool. Piles of food were disappearing quickly: the best way to get your money's worth.

Linda got toast and tea, while I went for fruit and fruit juice. I was determined to not gain weight. It was one of those high falutin resolutions that would last until dinner or the afternoon sundae buffet.

I had no plans; Linda had a plan for every port, places to see, and notes of historic and cultural fascination we needed to know if we were going to be right there, for Heaven's sake. I'd go where she said and try to not cause trouble. But, I didn't know what to do when she wasn't bubbly and funny and flirty. Here she was, un-Linda-like, and it was uncharted ground.

"Whaddayawannado t'day?"

"Oh, I don't know. Maybe try the slot machines. They have a Bingo at three. Do you want to do Bingo with me?"

Bingo I hated, but I put on my best can't wait to get there face and said, "Yeah, that might be fun. Could be our lucky day, I suppose. Sure."

"Are you sure, Walt? I can go alone. You don't have to."

"No, I want to. It's a chance to rub our thighs together."

"Oh, that's all you think about. We'll have to see. But it's only nine – what are you doing now?"

"I can read for a while. I thought I'd swim a while, too. Do you have something skimpy to swim in?"

"I brought a suit. I don't need to show off. If I see you in the pool I might join you. Or in the hot tub maybe."

"Okay. I'll leave a note if I go to the pool."

"Okay, good. Do you want to meet up for lunch? We could try that Art Deco diner."

"Well, I'm not going far. I'll be reading or swimming or looking for you." I liked this conversation: normal Linda. This cruise was a good idea and I wouldn't spoil it.

"Awright. I'll see you." Lindy went down a deck. I thought about our first five years and what might be eating her.

She had subjected herself to gynecological exams. Something had happened to her mother at a "womens' doctor" and that distrust of gynecologists was conveyed to Linda. But she went, believing that our lack of conception was a female thing. I went to a urologist once to check my own potency and testing had indicated that I was holding my own. Everything was always fine after her visits, too. For whatever reason, we couldn't click in fertility terms, though sexual compatibility seemed near perfect… to me. I wound up feeling depressed, sitting on the deck of a big, beautiful cruise ship, holding a paperback book. Thinking of positions we'd tried was nice.

***

After dinner on the second night Lindy held my hand and we walked hip to hip on the fifth deck, where we'd learned about lifeboats. The night was warm and movie-quality. The next day we'd be in San Juan.

"Walt, let's make love tonight." My mouth went dry. This was like the first time she'd agreed to sex before we married. Stunning. Eventually I found some saliva.

"Sure! I'm bursting to make you happy. Let's go now." I knew this wasn't the sexual abandon of before. Linda had a message to be conveyed with lovemaking and, despite my physical abilities, it wasn't my mother tongue.

"No. Let's walk a while. I have something to say." *Uh-oh, I thought. I knew it was something like, like... whatever it is.* She slipped her arm in mine and held it against her breast.

"I don't think we're ever going to have babies."

"Well, we don't really know that. I can get more tests. Maybe some clinic can figure it out. We don't have to give up!" I stopped walking and Linda swung around to embrace me. She was crying.

"No. I am not going to be poked and experimented on. You're okay, I'm okay, but we don't make babies," she sniffled. "But I've decided that it's all right. And you won't have to try so hard. I've thought it through."

"Hey! I'll try *harder*. Let's don't quit on my behalf!" Now I was worried. We were too young to stop screwing and, truth to tell, my Lindy was great in bed.

"No, no, no. I don't mean stop. I just don't have the same urgency for it. That's all. It's okay, really." She looked up at me as beautifully as ever and my heart pounded I loved her so much. I stroked her hair and pushed it back in place.

"Let's get to our cabin before you change your mind," I said. "You never know what might happen. God works in mysterious ways, and I do too." She grinned.

"Okay. I want to make love tonight. I don't love you less. We're still married and all that." She walked along a little ways and looked back. "Aren't you coming?"

"Yeah, but the room is the other way."

"I want to get the blood flowing with a walk. Come on."

"It already is flowing. I hope we don't bump in to those women who've had their eyes on me for the last two days. They'll see the blood flowing, too."

"Who is that? You think women are ogling you?" Then she saw my 'let's see how long she'll believe this' face and that the blood was, indeed, flowing. "You are impossible. Can't you control yourself?" She had her certain smile that had leashed me to her years ago.

"I am controlling myself. Find a short cut."

"Ohh, men," she said. "Take these stairs and we're only a few cabins down the hall." She pulled my hand and started down.

"Now we're talking." We practically ran down the stairs, through the double doors and down the hallway. She started fishing for a key but I had mine already pointed phallicly at the slot.

Inside, I swung her over my shoulder. She started pinching my butt with her nails, giggling. I spun around making my caveman sounds and plopped her on her bed. Her shoes had fallen off and her skirt was thigh high. She held the material to prevent my promised attack.

As I stood over her she grabbed my boner through my pants and pulled it one way and the other. "We'll see about that, mister. I'll scream!"

"Go ahead, no one will come," was my line.

She gritted her teeth as she yanked my penis left and right in cadence. "If… I… scream… we BOTH… will… come," she panted with a determined face. With the other hand she undid my belt buckle while I slipped my loosened shirt, tie and sport coat over my head together. Her knees were bent up, holding her skirt tightly. I kneeled over her belly in my underwear and unbuttoned her blouse as she tried to keep my hands away while again holding on to my erection as hard as she could. "No… you… don't," she grunted.

But, as always happened, yes… I… did. We made love as happily as we'd ever done and showered in the tiny stall. She was acutely appealing, soaking wet and small, hair clinging to her head. We kissed and kissed and Old Useless stiffened up again in the spray, but she said I really would have to control myself. She was exhausted from carrying her no-babies message for the past several days – or weeks – and was asleep within minutes.

***

About two months after the reformation Linda decided to go back to work, not that she'd worked more than part-time since we married, but she once worked for a textbook publisher and within a week a publisher loosely associated with Duquesne University called her in. Her pay enabled us to take some excellent vacations. She saved a lot, too, for a "scholarship fund."

Lindy worked four days a week with "*englishclass publishing*" in a building on the edge of Duquesne's downtown campus. "*englishclass*" was so special that it didn't waste ink on capital letters. Their books were education related, most authored by Duquesne and Pitt academics. Here and there was a book of poetry or a thesis turned into a well-edited treatise. Former Masters and PhDs from Duquesne also found *englishclass* to be suitable for scholarly writings. Evidently Linda was good at editing such dry stuff. She met some famous people and loved to tell me about them.

On her off days, Fridays, Lindy attended Quota Club meetings at lunchtime. They met at the Marriott. Now and then a project would involve gift baskets or food drives I could help with.

She also gardened. Across our street, Jack and Elly Maxwell had expanded their gardens bit by bit, even pushing into the scrubby woods behind their house. If there were green thumbs, this couple had four. I appreciated their work from a distance. Linda liked to dig right in, though. I'd come home in the spring and summer and find new flowery improvements to our yard and across the street would be two shapely butts, owners digging and cultivating to a fare-thee-well.

Jack Maxwell was an odd duck. He smiled and kept smiling regardless of what we talked about. At cookouts he maintained a mask, in a smile. I thought the smile got wider when a topic or question was bothersome. His conversation was friendly, though, and he would end a line of discussion with an unanswerable question or a bland statement about waiting to see what the future might bring. The rest of us guys learned to avoid meaningful chats with Jack Maxwell. You'd feel hollow, failing to learn anything while giving up something Jack had absorbed. It was odd. When neighborhood invitations went out we always included the Maxwells. Maybe Jack would express a like of something, a hatred of something else, or a desire for this or that to happen. He never did that I know of. Elly saw something in him. Maybe he talked with her.

Still, Jack knew mulching and composting. He built a composting shed that had shutters for a roof. He would adjust the slats to allow sunlight, rain or snow, but not too much. In dry weather he would close them up so that his pile of clippings, leaves, garbage, manure and ordinary dirt would not get too hot or too dry. Every Spring he had piles of incredibly rich soil to add to his beds of flowers and vegetables. His blooms were bigger, zucchinis more robust, tomatoes larger and redder. He didn't opine much, but he and Elly ate well.

He gave produce away, too. I think he brought us cucumbers and tomatoes to prove superiority, but they were tasty. Lindy made creative salads and cold soups with Jack's veggies. I would come home and say something like, “Oh, that salad looks great for a hot day!” I have a way with words.

Linda ascribed vegetables to Jack, not to Elly, not to the Maxwells. “Yes. Jack’s veggies make it so much nicer.” It was clear the roles in the Maxwell’s gardens were delineated. To the best of my knowledge we never ate any of Elly’s flowers.

Like I said, Lindy and I – mostly Lindy – babysat for the Maxwells. They had two boys who were six and eight when we moved in. They were Jack’s kids and Elly’s stepchildren. When they got a little older I hired them to shovel where the old snowblower couldn’t reach, or to rake or sweep. Nice kids, and they got along like twins. I never saw one without the other and the older boy, Teddy, was careful to treat Ronnie like an equal. I paid them equally, too.

When the boys were twelve and fourteen the Maxwells divorced and they left. I don’t think any of us had judged the Maxwell’s marriage as less than okay. Jack was odd, but he was probably odd when they were engaged, too. None of us ever heard about a fight or argument. Axel Johnson knew them better than the rest of us, although Lindy was pretty close to Elly. He couldn’t add anything to our surprise. He often fixed things for Jack and I’d see Axel walking home with a tool kit. He could fix anything.

Linda visited Elly daily in that first week. She even took a day off from *englishclass publishing* to stay with Elly and called me at the office to pick up something for dinner. She was more broken up than I knew.

I got a ham from “Buckler’s,” a butcher shop that became a tony market when it moved into a new building. Every kind of upscale mustard, horseradish and teriyaki glaze was available, along with brands of coffee picked by left-leaning, left-handed

Buddhists who earned a fair price while guaranteeing that no coffee trees had been harmed in the harvesting of the fabulous product we zhlubs now contemplated. But the meat quality had stayed high.

Bucklers smoked hams, sausages, and even venison and other game. Lately they'd started smoking turkeys, which were a special treat. I picked out a smoked ham and Franz Freundt wrapped it for me. I was looking forward to giving Elly a gift from my own hands.

Ham can be easy. I liked easy, but done right. I got home at five: maybe an hour and a half to get ready. Usually with a smoker I like to cut the smokiness with a rinse in boiling water, sometimes flavored with beer or ginger. I chose ginger root, and left the meat in the water a while since there wasn't time for full oven treatment.

I gathered up the ginger root and squeezed it into a frying pan with a garlic press. The meat I covered with cloves and spicy brown mustard, stuffed it into a roasting bag and set the oven at 375. It was cheating, but the bag was faster.

I changed into nicer than cookout and less than church. I thought about exciting some vegetables to go with the ham. I cared about having dinner with the bereft Mrs. Maxwell.

I like color, so green beans, especially next to sweet potatoes. Pink ham, green beans, orangy potatoes. I liked it. I also like simple, so I didn't mess with flavors on the veggies. A little butter sauce for the beans and some cinnamon and butter for the sweets. I set the beans in water and put the sweets in the oven with the ham. Timing is everything.

With ten minutes to go on the ham I put a couple tablespoons of molasses in the frying pan and some ginger ale and set it simmering. As it cooked down I added water. I kept stirring.

The oven dinger went off and I pulled the sauce off the heat. The sweet potatoes were just soft enough. I set them on a plate and lifted out the bagged ham.

I warmed square casserole dishes in the oven. The beans were boiling in one of my heavy steel pans. I spooned them into a dish. Then I put about a third of a stick of butter into the cook water and started stirring with a small whisk. I added a bit of white pepper and stirred until the liquid was fairly homogenous. Then a flash: I juiced a lemon and put half into the butter sauce and whisked it some more. I gently turned the beans over to coat them with the lemony sauce. I dumped the whole thing into a warm casserole, put a lid on it and wrapped it in a towel. The sweet potatoes I split in half and put some soft butter on each half as I stirred the pulp with a fork. I sprinkled some cinnamon on top and covered each with foil. These I put in the other warm, wrapped, casserole dish.

The ham temperature checked out. I left it in the bag and wrapped it separately. Lastly I poured the ginger sauce into a jar and tucked it beside the ham and veggies in a cardboard box. A quick check in the mirror and I was off.

Figuring I was welcome, I called out, "Dinner's here! Gourmet to you is what we do!" The dining room table was set with nice china and glasses: a real dinner. My hunger sharpened as I carried my "gourmet" into the kitchen. The girls had a salad sitting in a pottery bowl. I put my box on a kitchen chair and started lifting out the warm dishes. "Hellloooo!" I called out.

"Oh! Hi, Walter. Just a sec." It sounded like Elly. Moments later Linda opened the back door from the breezeway between the house and the garage.

"Hi, honey," she smiled. "That wasn't long. Smells great."

"Thanks. I think we'll like this: smoked ham." Elly Maxwell bounced into the kitchen from a back room. She gave me a quick hug and a kiss sound and gave Lindy a quick hug, too.

"I'm starving. Whatever you made, Walter, it smells terrific. We're all set for you. Do you need some serving things?" With a little flurry of drawers opening and dishes clinking we got everything served. Linda and Elly were on one side of the oblong table and I was not quite evenly across from them. I sliced the ham. The ginger sauce was a hit with Miss Maxwell. "Oh, Walter, you'll have to give me this recipe. I've never tasted anything like this. Umm – mmmnh – uhnn."

Linda remained quiet, just nodding and smiling while we ate.

"How are you doing alone, Elly?" I asked in my most deeply concerned voice. "I mean, I can't imagine losing Linda. I can't begin to imagine how it is for you…" I tilted my head a little to convey deep concern. It may have.

"Well, I don't know, Walter. Everyone has been so nice since Jack, um… left." Elly looked right at me and smiled as if to keep me from worrying too awfully much. "I know there won't be as much compost next year. So, the vegetables might not be as good, I suppose. Things like that." She smiled and looked down at her plate. It wasn't tearful, surely.

Linda and Elly had been baking. We topped off our meal with turnovers filled with cherries from the Maxwells' own tree. Nothing better. We helped clean up amidst Elly's protestations that she could handle it. I left enough ham, sweet potatoes and beans for at least two more meals. She packed up some salad and a couple of turnovers for us and everything seemed fair. We left Elly singing to herself as she cleaned.

***

"Well," I posited to Linda in our own kitchen, "Elly doesn't seem too broken-hearted about the big split, does she?"

"She's holding up. Nice of you to notice." I looked up at that.

"What? I'm just saying. I'm sure I don't understand these things. She just seems as happy as ever, that's all."

"Well, it's an embarrassment, you know? I mean, it looks as though Jack dumped her, but it's not like that at all. She's only sad about the boys. Although, not as sad as I'd be. I don't think either of them really wanted children. The lawyers are juggling the details and she's not sure where the boys will wind up."

I was about to say something not very pithy when Linda leaned against me and put her hands on my butt and pulled me into her. "How about we don't think about Elly just now. I've been thinking about you, mister. Come on – bring your boner." She pulled my hand and headed toward the bedroom but pulled me past it, and to the bathroom at the end of the hall.

"This is new."

"New, and improved." Lindy had already slipped her slacks off and had her blouse over her head by the time my shoes were off. She was wearing a stretchy half-T-shirt rather than a regular bra, and that was off quickly, too. I couldn't believe that I hadn't noticed the difference at dinner. I could recall the shape of Elly Maxwell's abundant breasts, though.

"Hurry up, silly," Linda complained. She was fixing the temperature in nothing more than thin panties. My boner had shown up and I was nude moments later. I grabbed her about the waist and lifted her into the spray of warm water. I was figuring to lift her up onto me as usual.

"Hey, hey, Speedy. Hold on a minute. I want new... and improved." She hung her dripping panties on a handle. She faced the shower, arching her pelvis toward the spray. Her hands cupped the water, rinsing liberally, then turned to face me. "Kneel down, Wally. Use your mouth."

My mouth was abruptly dry. I coughed. "What? Really? I didn't know you liked that... this." I had read about cunnilingus, and seen pictures. Women supposedly liked it more than anything, but I thought only certain kinds of women – women without men – actually did it. My hard-on was pretty soft, as I worried.

Tentatively I pushed my nose between her legs. Linda adjusted her knees, opening the mysterious valley and shifting her hips toward me. I was thinking about mouthwash. "Try it," she whispered. "Use your tongue. Start near the top. I'll tell you when you've got it right."

I started to put my hand up next to my nose, to push the folds of skin away.

"No! No fingers... no fingers. Just try your tongue. You can do it. Push a little. Mmmm. Move it around." Her hips were moving slightly to emphasize my tiny explorations. I tried sticking my tongue out as far as I could.

"Ooouuh...that's the idea. Work that bump... there. There. There. Uhh-huhn."

Okay, I thought. *It must be this structure. I feel it! She likes it when I fiddle right here.* Her hips pushed a little harder when I moved across the hard bumpy thing so I tried to stay on that. The taste wasn't what I had expected. *Maybe the mouthwash won't be necessary. If Linda likes this I can do it. She always satisfies me. I could do this. I could do... THIS.*

"Ohhh, my God, Walter. Whew, boy. Ohhh..." Linda was moving her body in waves with firm hip pushes. Her legs parted further leaving me plenty of room to lick and breath. I realized I had held my breath but now I breathed through my mouth. I wondered if licking like a dog would feel as good as what I was doing. I tried licking upwards the way a puppy might. Linda was right over me, propping her hands on my shoulders, her noises very encouraging. I realized my missing boner had found itself, hard and throbbing, while I puppy-licked over that hard lump I'd found, so long ago. She was pounding with her little fists.

"Ohhh…God, God, God. Walter, Walter, Walter. Ohhh… oh…oh…oh-oh-oh-ohhhhhh, ahhhh…mmmnnhh mmm ohhhh." Linda collapsed onto me, dislodging her puppy. "Get inside me right now, Walter. Right now."

I clumsily stood up, my hard-on a towel peg. I pulled her small body up and she wrapped her legs around me, slipping in so easily I hardly felt it – deeper than ever. With my hands under her buttocks I slid her up and down three times and shot off without warning. Lindy was poking her tongue inside my lips, breathing in deep pants. She rested her head on my chest and hugged me tightly with her arms and legs. I was happy. My legs cramped and started shaking. I let her slide down, my willie as soft as a washcloth. We hugged in the shower.

I pumped shampoo one-handedly and started to wash her hair, my hands making long sudsy caresses. She was rubbing my chest where the shampoo dripped. Then she grabbed the soap and lathered me top to bottom, literally. I did the same for her. She moved her breasts against me and I started to harden. This was terrific. I knelt again. "No, thanks. I can't do that again. Lets go to bed." We toweled off and I swung her over my shoulder and carried her into our bedroom.

"Me Tarzan," I announced. "You Jane. If you scream no one come. Ugh."

Linda giggled, "If I scream, we'll both come!" How right she was. With very little deviation we enjoyed comfortable, almost immediate orgasms. I collapsed and awoke to find her on top of me, her head not quite at my chin. Her hair smelled like a flower.

With some urgency I simply had to roll on my side. I tried sliding my legs out, but this awakened her.

"Oh, hi, honey," she breathed. "I'll get on my own side…"

"No, no, Lin. Stay warm. I'll be right back." I got up and did my business and brushed my teeth. I climbed back in and spooned against my lady.

WEDNESDAY, MAY 15, 1985

I was supposed to bring a special dish to Jack Jackson. There was enough ham. I called a buffet deli and asked them to pack up some of their famous au gratin potatoes and some big yellow lima beans with tomato sauce. It wasn't the first time I'd cheated with their help. I re-packed their food into my own glassware and carried it in to the office with a flourish. It passed muster with Jackson... a good thing.

Wednesday was bowling night. I cruised through my day without incident, really looking forward to bowling with the "Tigers" and Katy Mellon. It would be at least 10:30 before I could try licking Linda, again, and it just felt important to contemplate a finely stacked body as soon as possible. By quarter of six we four guys had ordered food and drink, talking about sports, weather and Katy. We were concerned about whether the 'mellons' was going to show. We rolled at seven and had decided I would sit out in favor of Katy's fluid, flexible deliveries.

At three before seven she trotted in, to our relief. Our opponents were from Osten Chevrolet-GMC over in Etna. They always ogled Katy, to the detriment of their own games, and we really didn't want to bowl against them without her.

"Hey, Katy, you had us worried there." Bobby Campbell kissed her hand.

"I wouldn't miss this, guys. We need to beat these bums. Ran a little late." Katie carefully folded her blazer and laid it on the back bench next to her street shoes and big, floppy purse. She was shoed and ready when the lanes turned on. It was neat how the machinery whirred and clunked, the polished lanes reflecting the Brunswick crown. Things were quiet as a couple of house balls finished their subterranean journey to the long channels at our end, thumping together to announce their energy. We all had our own balls, except for Katy. She did fine with house balls while the guys proudly polished their own custom-drilled, specially balanced and nurtured orbs. We knew every good score was due in part to how carefully we handled our personal ball – every missed shot was due to our lack of concentration and failure to adhere to the basics. It was bowling law.

Katy had a great sense of humor. A pretty woman could never survive amongst steel workers, warehousemen, truck drivers and horny office help, without being immune to innuendo and off-color stories. She gave as good as she got. The whole activity of bowling lent itself to dumb comments.

"You can see if our balls work better for you, honey," was the theme of helpful statements and questions from other teams. The Iron Tigers got that bullshit out of our systems early on, but banter with our opponents seemed to create little hiccups in their skills as they paid attention to Katy. We laughed but never joined in. Katy could give it right back to the other teams, and she realized what kind of effect she had on most men, and was happy to add that advantage to her decent scores.

We were really happy Katy was on time.

Katy never led off. That was Wil Guerin's position. For some reason, on the nights that I bowled I would go second and Katy third. When I sat out, she was second roller, followed by Bobby Campbell and then Tom Kotzinski. There was no science to what we did and we weren't going to change it. We usually got a couple of metallic-plated plastic trophies at the annual banquet and twice had our names on the big trophy that Playmore Bowladrome kept in the display case. Our league was called the 3-River Wednesdays. There were six teams and seven o'clock on Wednesdays was our battleground, lanes 27 through 32, against the wall.

The best trophy I ever received was for highest score in one game: 275. I can't explain it. It was a singular event. I remember it being rainy and warm. The air conditioning was having problems and we were sweating like pigs. Katy couldn't come that night and Wil Guerin had to leave halfway through the first string with asthma problems. League rules allowed one member to roll twice to cover a missing member. We flipped a coin and it was me. We were playing the Steamfitters and there was nothing exciting for either team until the last string.

The Steamers took the first game, 214 to 190, 221 to 209, 222 to 200 and 205 to 204. I think the Tigers were thrown off a little with Wil's leaving, and feeling flat. We'd lost every string, which was rare. Second string, I bowled first and second, two frames in a row. It felt good. I won the first string and lost the second by a single pin. Bobby won his line and Kotzinski lost by two. The Steamers each had a beer, but the Tigers had only Coke and NeHi. Our habit was no alcohol during a match. Every little advantage.

Both the Steamfitters and the Iron Tigers were very deliberate – never rushing shots. When we were head to head we'd be last to finish. In the last string I again bowled first and second, changing lanes between. By the seventh frame we were the only ones bowling and some of the other guys had congregated behind us. In our league a 250 was a headline, 300s only dreams. A hot night for anyone was something over two twenty-five. In my first line I was at 194 in the seventh frame, several pins ahead of Cam somebody of the Steamfitters. My second line was making history. I was already at 217 going in to the seventh, with no open frames. The Steamers were making comments to throw me off my game but the Tigers were quiet, offering encouragement when I sat down. Most of the growing audience was murmuring or making catcalls, but I didn't pay attention.

I had a strike in the seventh, the fourth one so far. In the eighth I had a spare with another strike to fill in the ninth. Two forty-seven. My opponent finished with a 230, one of his best strings. I had a strike riding into the tenth, ready to make history. I rolled a nine and clipped the single 7-pin for a spare, buying me one more ball for total. I hit eight for the 275 total. My knees were shaking as I turned around with a big shit-eatin grin. The other Tigers were jumping and cheering. For a non-athlete, it was a night to remember. Even the other teams were congratulatory. It was cool.

***

On this night, though, the air conditioning was fine and I was just hoping we outscored the "Hump-Day Drivers." The "hump" guys had a repertoire of stupid comments to aim at Katy Mellon. She played it cool while we guys would usually advise them to hump one another if they couldn't wait to get home. But there was no big enmity.

All day I had been a little horny, not fully down from the sexual high of the night before. By afternoon my mind drifted to what had gotten Linda to try oral stuff. She had kissed my boner before but I never even asked for a blow-job. I kissed the area right above her mound of Venus, but I never tried to do what I did in the shower. Why now? Who's she been talking to, I thought? Maybe she got a new manual. I was looking forward to making her feel good again, don't get me wrong. Still, it seemed out of left field. And all that thinking just kept me ready to stand at attention. I did my best to concentrate on requests for materials, comparison of invoices to packing lists and similar excitements.

Getting this Wednesday's match finally under way was a relief. I was relaxed and tense at the same time. I cheered my bowlers, of course, but my gaze lingered on Katy more than usual. She wore Capri pants that were not too tight, and a satiny blouse that could alternately cling and hang loosely. By a mysterious process her Capris could tuck into her cheeks, drawing a glance from our guys, and outright leering from the Hump Day Drivers. Their games were shaky, which I attributed to Katy's well-selected bowling outfit.

I sat at the scorer's table when I wasn't bowling. Scores projected on an angle of the ceiling, but bowlers still looked at the transparent scoring sheet. It was especially rewarding this Wednesday as Katy would check on her score after every "box" and her amazing satiny blouse would hang low, providing a sly scorer with voluminous looks at Ms. Mellon's melons. I found myself anticipating her every trip to the line, and every confirmation of her scores. "Wow, look at that score!" I would say. Wil, Bobby and Tom were well aware of this pattern and its rewards, but tonight was better than ever. I even held off taking a leak until the end of a string, lest someone else take the scorer's chair.

Being an accomplished lover, familiar with orally stimulating beautiful women to their greatest possible orgasms, I couldn't help thinking that an appropriate step would be to become conversant about my lingual skills. Mentally I heard myself discussing cunnilingus with Katy, a daydream that ended when someone said, "That's a nine on the spare, Walt." A perversely pleasant consequence of my little daydreams was that everyone, including Katy was more careful than ever to check what I recorded.

We won three out of four games. One of the winners was Katy and she was a little flushed after the last frame, making her cheeks pink and her light blue eyes more sparkly than usual. I wondered if she'd ever been treated to excellent oral sex, although it was certainly none of my business. Katy's blouse showed perspiration near the bottom of her back and between her breasts, which drew the eyes if you weren't careful.

"Well, you were great out there," I observed. "I guess a shower will feel pretty good, tonight!" That was the first time I had ever opined about Katy's bathing. For her part she made no acknowledgement of this change in our relationship. She never acknowledged our lack of relationship, either, but now that I knew how to please a woman like her, and she being a woman like her, we had a new connection. I took the score sheets up to the counter where the night manager racked up all the red and green bowling shoes. Wil joined me there and wrote out a check for $56.00 for our sixteen lines of bowling. We had a pretty good deal, saving fifty cents a line as part of a league. It probably meant more to the house to rent the shoes every Wednesday.

As I reached my car I was elated to see Katy parked near me. Her skin looked shiny in the parking-lot lights. "Hey! I thought I missed you, there."

Katy turned with a half smile. "Where?"

I fumbled my answer. "Well, inside. I… I mean we didn't say good night, like."

"Oh, well... goodnight then." I caught up to her and stood across the trunk of her Dodge.

"I know how to do oral sex," I said. Instantly I knew that there were better lead-ins. I also knew, in a distant, hazy way, that I had just said what I had been thinking for the past several hours. Katy had an odd expression.

Her face was pinched, as if she couldn't get enough air. "Umm, that's very nice, Walt. Have you… ahh… for a long time?" She was turned toward the front of her car, keys in hand, looking at me sideways.

"Ahh, no, no, not long really." I was over a precipice of dumbness. "I don't really, ahh, know that much, really, very much. No, I think."

"Another time, I guess. See you tomorrow." Katy stepped to her door and had the key in and the door open in one move. She slid in and locked the door. When her headlights came on I stepped back and she backed around and drove forward a few feet away from me. She rolled down her window. "You're a funny man. I always wondered about you. I'll think about you in the shower."

"Yeah. Good. Sure." Her car was rolling away, the window sliding upwards. I gave a half-wave and couldn't see if she waved back. Finally I moved to my car and dumped the ball bag . I sat for a minute. *Did I say what I said? You dumb fuck; what was that? That was stooo-ooopid. She'll never look at me again. Maybe she'll drop the Tigers. Jesus. I really said that? Unbelievable. Still, she didn't spit at me.*

I drove automatically, barely recording how. That Katy did have nice breasts. Quite similar to Elly Maxwell's, it occurred to me. I pulled in and shut off the motor. It was after ten, later than usual. I thought about how I could never discuss Katy's breasts with my ever-trusting Linda. But, then, I would never discuss Linda's breasts with Katy, either, and they were just as delightful. The main thing, I remembered, was that it was Linda's vagina only, that I had permission to lick, which memory got Old Useless stirring a bit, spurring me into the house. Looking at tits could not compete with showering.

The house smelled like ham and dish soap, the kitchen as clean as a whistle. I called out, "Linda? Lindy? I brought my tongue home!" It sounded funny.

I stowed my ball in the hall closet. Quiet. I turned on the ceiling light and looked in the fridge for I didn't know what. I grabbed the orange juice. As I put it back Linda came in the front door with a cheery "Hellooo..ooo!"

"Hey, Kiddo. Where were you?" I slurped some juice and looked over the rim of the glass.

"Oh, with Elly. Her bastard husband sent her divorce papers, today. I was…"

"Ouch! Is she okay?" I kissed Linda on the neck – both sides. She held me in a hug for a few moments and then started wiping invisible spots off the counter.

"She's hurt. Not really upset, except they came by a process server. She thought Jack would call or something. Whatabastard."

I tried to gauge her mood, hoping showering was on the menu. "Well, I don't know. Having the papers served is pretty standard. What would they talk about?" I got a glare in return. The sisterhood was another thing I didn't understand. It felt as though my tongue would rest, tonight, and I abruptly didn't care. "Hey. No disrespect or anything. I have no idea how she must feel. Maybe I'll make a roast beef."

"She's angry, not hungry." Trouble.

"Okay, okay," I held my hands up in defense. "I will never put you in her position. Let's relax, now. I was feeling really good when I got home. I'm going to take a shower to wash off the winning-team bowling smell, and I won't be locking the door, if you catch my drip…"

"Yeah. Sorry, honey. I'll be in'n a sec." I couldn't see any undone chores, but what did I know? I left Linda leaning against the sink, arms crossed. My legs felt like sand.

I showered, brushed, flossed and rinsed, alone. I killed the light and turned up the hall to the bedroom. Linda was lying on the bed in her briefs. She sat up as I came in the room. I reached for her, just in case, but she slipped by me and went down the hall.

I lay on my side in as welcoming a position as I could imagine, with the covers thrown back. She took longer than normal. She hadn't looked dirty, but cleanliness is next to Godliness, and no basis for complaints from me. I had nodded off when Linda finally slipped into bed. As she pulled the covers over us, I woke up. "Hi, again, sweetie. You okay?"

"Oh. Sorry I woke you. Let's go to sleep." She gave me a quick kiss and brushed my hair with one hand. I tried sliding my hand down her side, finding that she still had panties on, which was always a signal that tonight wouldn't be the night. She brushed my hand away before I could get to the good parts. After the night before I figured tonight would be a perfect time to continue our delicious sex. Not to be. I guessed that Elly's upset was more affective than me, a mere male. I wondered what I'd said. Nothing. I concentrated on keeping Linda's image in my dream-shower until I succumbed.

THURSDAY, MAY 16, 1985

I was careful to do everything normally. I said normal things. Maybe if I forced us into normalcy the effect would align the other minutes of the day and Linda and I would shower that night. When we kissed goodbye, I had no inkling of what was eating her from the night before. Wasn't that my job?

I drove in a cloud, again. As I anticipated how to say good morning to people I met every morning, I remembered my weird declaration to Katy Mellon. Man, what would she say? Probably she'd never talk to me again, so I didn't need to worry. But then, what could I say when Katy quit the team? Still, though, she had told me she was going to think about me... in the shower, no less. Maybe she'd be okay. Wow.

"Hi, Paul. Good day, huh?" Paul checked in the employees and had an official badge. A wide black belt zigged across his gut and some serious-looking keys hung from his belt. There was a covered holster but not a gun. Our guard service wasn't armed during business hours.

"Sure is, Mr. Anton, sir. Sure is." Paul smiled his genuine, ultra-wide smile. He enjoyed even a small interaction. Most people breezed by with little more than a glance. I liked him. He looked elegant in his careful, competent-enough way.

"The Iron Tigers whipped the Drivers last night, Paul. Katy Mellon was bowling and they never knew what hit em. We're tied for first place, now. I'm telling you, you should get on our team!"

Paul's big head swung back and forth. "Heh, heh, heh, Mr. Anton. I ain't no bowler. Shit. I was a baseball player in my little years, but I never done no bowlin, no sir. Sides, my wife be needin me most nights. You know how it is. Heh, heh, heh."

"Oh, boy, I sure do, Pauly, Most nights. The other nights I go bowling; see how it works out?" I was already walking past the little counter behind which Paul Lemay ruled the front door. If he answered something, I missed it.

I greeted fellow drones as I continued to my cubicle-almost-office. I had honey-colored walls like the other cubicles, but mine were topped with about three feet of pebbly glass that made it impossible to see my desk. It felt special, although my pay was not much higher than anyone's else "on the floor." I had a door, but I still shared the ceiling and the rows of finned florescent lights that brightened all our days.

Thursday is a day to get through to Friday so the weekend is closer. Today, though, there was tension. Blatchford had reached the last stage in a huge bidding process for a new-design bridge in Denmark. Our sales department had convinced the designers that Blatchford had the skills and, fortunately, an overhead crane, to handle the key girders specified as one piece, rather than bolted, riveted or welded on site. Adding to the tension was our claim of rail access to the Ohio River, where these large pieces could be barged to the Gulf and transshipped to Denmark. The whole bid would collapse if we couldn't ship them.

When Jones and Laughlin had been pouring and rolling steel in Pittsburgh, they had their own railroad. Steel is heavy and sold in dollars per ton. You had to have the ability to move many, many tons to make the kind of money that paid for the huge mills like that of which Blatchford occupied but a tiny portion. We already shipped by rail from our own siding. What we never had to do was transport by barge. The old spur that went directly from J & L to their own Monongahela Connecting Railroad sidings off Sidney Street was in rough shape. No maintenance had been done for years and the cost to rebuild it was in the realm of a quarter of a million dollars that Blatchford didn't want to shoulder.

I had to create projections for costs based on the accumulating pile of requests for King Frederik Bridge stuff we'd never purchased before. This caused me to make reports directly to some upper managers while Jack Jackson sat by, since he didn't want to answer for a mistake that I or he might make. He was a great leader.

I was preparing reports from our cumbersome MRP software for the mid-month meeting when Jackson walked in to my office.

"I need an analysis of costs on the King Frederik. Can you pull it together by, say, eleven?" Jackson was leaning toward me with his hand on the doorknob. At some management seminar he'd evidently learned that a stance like that indicated urgency and should result in faster action by underlings. I don't know that it did.

"I'm in the middle of mid-months, Jack... and, uhh… hey! It's five-of! What are you talking about? How about right after lunch?"

"Nope. Five minutes if not sooner. Drop what you're doing." Jack now stood flatfooted with his arms crossed, projecting his power stance, I figured, plus, I couldn't escape. He squinted at his big Seiko watch.

I swung back to my terminal and typed some commands that closed me out of the report program. I'd have to run the procedure all over again and it was more than a little irritating. I breathed loudly and frowned, a reaction I'd perfected on my own. "Four minutes," Jackson said.

"Hold on, Jack, hold on. I screw up everybody if I don't close out properly. Your stuff is on paper, anyway." My terminal screen returned to a blinking cursor in the lower left corner and I stood up and walked past Jackson to my big oak table. Several 14 by 17 ledgers were there, along with newsletters for products Blatchford had never needed before. The reports were up to date, although only two copies.

"Give me one of those." Jack held his hand out. He was more bossy than normal and if I had to guess, worried. *Something big is going on.* "C'mon, Walt. They're waiting on us."

"Who?"

"The big chiefs. We even got a Congressman. It's all about that railroad thing. Let's go."

Well, this might be interesting. I'd never met our Congressman. Maybe we were actually going to buy all this stuff I'd been cataloguing. We ran up the wide, wooden stairs to Hal Blatchford's anteroom, and went in to the office without asking, a place I hadn't been five times before – a combined board room and office. There were six people at a long table that made a "tee" with Blatchford's desk. I nodded to Harold Blatchford at the end of the table, and shook hands with his son, Peter, whom I spoke with often enough to call, "Peter."

Jackson was like a politician, shaking hands with everyone. Already seated was Tom Wittenauer, Representative to the 97th Congress from Pennsylvania's 14th district. He was smiling as if on TV. I nodded and reached across the table to shake hands just as Jack sidled up to do the same. He flashed a dagger of irritation.

Before I could sit a hand touched my shoulder and I looked directly into Katie Mellon's nicely made-up face. In a flash I realized that the rest of her was nicely made up, as well, including better exposure of her delightful melons than was customary around the office. "Coffee, Mr. Anton?" she asked without inflection.

"Uh, well, yuh. Thanks, Katie." I sat quickly and placed my spreadsheet in front of me, still rolled. The Blatchfords were chatting with the two vice-presidents who were already seated when I arrived. Jack Jackson had pulled a chair up next to Peter and his father. He was somewhat familiar with the figures, but I'd do the basic explaining. I could surmise why the congressman was here. We had to make our case for some kind of a grant for work on the old spur. Well, okay… I could do my part.

Katie came back with a tray of coffee cups and two pots of black coffee. There was cream, sugar and some butter cookies. Everyone had coffee, but no one touched a cookie. Katie sat next to congressman Wittenauer. She didn't have even coffee, but sat up straight and businesslike, projecting her attractive breasts over the edge of the polished table. I found myself regarding her between attempts to look as concerned as everyone else about the serious matters at hand. Aside from old man Blatchford, everyone else also managed to confirm his first, second, third and fourth impressions of the one female at the conclave, Wittenauer leading the pack.

One of us was in the dark, apparently. Katie's regular duties, so far as I knew, involved human resource paperwork, new applications, coordinating Blue Cross coverage and tracking supervisory reports on individual union employees. It was not a set of responsibilities that she could discuss with others and none of the Tigers ever did, I think. Bobby and Wil were union members, themselves.

Still, there Katie was, obviously with the Blatchfords' blessings. No one else seemed surprised. She listened quietly to the mix of self-serving justifications that each of us contributed. My own statement was simply that I had been keeping close track of proposed new costs and that I was happy to be able to share the information as requested.

Wittenauer gave a little campaign speech that made his interest clear. "Gentlemen ...and lady ...I am here to see if we can't create some new jobs in the fourteenth district. It sounds like your winning this contract will add up to fifty new positions for highly skilled employees and that is good news. Whatever the Congress can do to... to help, is why I'm here. American skill and productivity is why we are number one and this is being recognized in the awarding of this huge contract by the Danish government. Working together we can bring Pittsburgh back to full employment. So, thanks for letting me be a small part of this venture." He'd stood to make his speech and turned this way and that before sitting back down, grabbing a pleasant look down Katie's cleavage as he did so. Katie kept looking toward old man Blatchford and toward my side of the table, and didn't seem to notice.

I had not heard anyone say how many new employees we would hire, but no one showed skepticism when the congressman said fifty. Maybe that was why Katie was here. Peter Blatchford was spokesman for the company.

"First I want to thank Representative Wittenauer for taking time to meet with us, today. We all know that the congressman has been a friend of business here in Pittsburgh as the city rebuilds its manufacturing base. That's why we called on his office to look into ways to help us secure this big contract on the King Frederik Bridge. He has helped already, tremendously. Now we hope to hear that the federal government can help with the reconstruction of the old J & L spur line that will enable us to move these oversized structural pieces to the Mon. Congressman?"

"Thanks, Peter, I'll do the best I can." This time he remained seated. "I've already sent a letter to the EPA to see how they might help us clean up the two questionable spots along the line. If we don't push too hard they may help clean up the land and leave you with a useful railbed. By bringing them in first you won't wind up having to tear up track you've repaired when they suddenly wake up later. They have file numbers on that land."

"Yes. We know. It wasn't Blatchford that polluted that ground." Old man Blatchford, who rarely looked happy, was fully pissed, evidently.

"No, Hal, it wasn't. But trying to get a long-term lease on that right of way has stirred up the City, and the Three Rivers Trust wants to add that strip to park land. I think that's where the complaints have come from. We have to head them off. You may have to buy some land along there that you can donate to the city with some good press and pictures. Just an idea."

"Ahh, shit. None of those people ever created a job in their damn lives. Who do they think pays for all their damn parks? Three Rivers Trust... hummph." Harold Blatchford Stood up and walked over to the only window that looked outside. "How much will that cost, Anton?"

I didn't react. I was looking at Katie who was looking at the old man. She abruptly turned toward me when Blatchford asked his question, and made a head gesture to me to answer. I just stared for a couple of seconds and then realized two things: I had to answer... and everyone was looking at me.

"Ahh, well. At this point, Mr. Blatchford, no one has asked me to pin that down." Now no one was looking at me, except Jack Jackson who was afraid of the consequence of what I'd said. "However, sir, I will have some good estimates for you later today or first thing tomorrow. Jack and I already had some feelers out but the info just didn't come in as quickly as we hoped." Jackson displayed a dozen emotions. Finally he realized his fat might be out of the fire thanks to me, but his last expression was more suspicion than anything else. For my part I was shaking like a leaf, but everyone seemed to accept that Jack Jackson and his chief underling were on top of costs up and down the line. Old man Blatchford looked at Jackson and then at me, but I couldn't guess his thoughts.

Katie Mellon looked at me sideways. She knew I had just created some bullshit.

"What else we got, Anton? How much are we looking at for new costs on this fucking bridge deal?" Hal Blatchford probably always used rough language. No one else made note of it, including our congressman. I knew, though, that I'd better be good with my numbers.

"These costs break out in three areas, gentlemen. New tooling for our current machines, new equipment altogether, and a fairly large estimate of costs to install and reconfigure. That includes some significant bucks for installing a new winch on the overhead crane. Now Jack Jackson and I have been trying to squeeze these costs as much as we can without having an actual purchase authorization to bargain with. But, some of this work, and the new hoist, ...well, there just aren't any competitive sources for these and they are almost a million by themselves." Most of the guys took a few notes. Jack Jackson was pointing out the figures I was summarizing to Peter Blatchford. "I apologize for not having extra copies of these sheets for everyone. I'll have them for the mid-months on Monday."

"Peter," harumphed the old man, "what's the projected spread again on this with these new costs?"

Without missing a beat the younger Blatchford immediately replied, "nineteen-point-eight, minus the land cost we talked about."

"Okay, everybody. We can also *lose* over six million if we screw this up. That'll cost us jobs, Congressman – not add them.

There's a lot of risk, but a possible boost to Blatchford Steel that will put us in a bigger game. I want every penny looked at from both sides. And Anton! Get me those land costs. That Three Rivers Trust mess is the big question mark. I don't like it."

"Yes, sir," was all I had. Katie Mellon finished her notes and handed them to Wittenauer. I didn't understand that. She stood and collected the coffee cups. Blatchford was standing again. "Peter, Tommy, let's go. Thanks everyone." Wittenauer – 'Tommy' – stood and walked out with the Blatchfords, which was a signal to eat cookies and the plate was empty when I looked again.

I expected to find my own way to my big cubicle, but Jack held me back.

"That was pretty creative, Walt. You don't think he bought it?" I was looking around for Katie, but she had disappeared with the coffee things. "Walt?"

"Huh? Blatchford? Yeah, I don't know. I didn't want Wittenauer to think we weren't up on every aspect of our costs. It was spur of the moment, you know?" I wasn't very interested in speaking with Jack but what I had done was obviously important to him. He wouldn't let it go.

"Well it came out pretty smooth. Like toothpaste. I should say thanks for trying to make me look good but I don't see you getting those figures in the next few hours. You might have fucked us up." Jackson looked angry. Probably to mask nervousness. He often feigned being serious and critical to cover his own weakness. A leader through and through. I thought he was upset because Blatchford had spoken to me directly about the land costs. I was more nervous than Jack was, but damned if I was going to show *him*. Still, there was the matter of the cost of land along the rail spur and I knew next to nothing about real estate.

"You have your work cut out for you to negotiate with the Three Rivers Trust and the city and the EPA." He was staring at me.

"I'm going downtown right now, Jack. Don't worry. I'll start with the Development Commission. They got us the building and they must know what's up with that land, I would think." We were next to Jack's real office that had its own ceiling and lighting fixtures. "I'll call you with whatever I find out if you want to take it to the old man."

"Oh, sure. Yeah. Call me right away. I can't let this slide, Walt." Jack was looking more nervous than ever. His hand was on the doorknob but he was just staring at the door. I headed to my own sort-of office and closed the door.

I sat like a visitor, facing my desk. I was never political and certainly not about Pittsburgh. I knew big bucks were involved whenever the Pittsburgh Development Commission cleared the way for mill land, especially along the waterfront. I knew the spur we needed went right through some of that area. I knew that the professional beautifiers had clout with politicians as they tried to pretend that there never had been any steel industry, coke ovens, coal-fired power plants or those ugly railroads in their pretty city. Suddenly, now, I had to find a path through all of it to get a do-able price for several acres of industrial land near 'our' spur. I thought and thought.

The office was quiet – lunch hour. I could hear Jackson speaking forcefully on the phone but I couldn't make out any words except for a sharp "no, no, no!" His conversation continued for a bit longer and then he left, closing his door firmly. I stared, unseeing, at a bird's-eye-view of the old J & L factories on the wall behind my desk. I was imagining the rail spur. I decided to take a look before I went to the PDC, and had a rare flash of sense.

I crossed the 32nd street bridge and took the eastbound ramp toward my house. We had a Polaroid camera. It was almost one o'clock but it was only three exits. It seemed like a good idea to offer photos with the costs. Whether I would use them to make Jack Jackson look smart, too, I wasn't sure.

I got home in less than twenty minutes. When I turned onto Jefferson I caught a glimpse of a Toyota that I thought might be Linda's but the driver didn't wave. There are lots of beige Toyotas. I pulled into my driveway and let the driver's door hang open.

Axel Johnson was coming around the side of Elly Maxwell's garage. It was funny that he could be doing free home repairs in the middle of a workday, but I didn't know what flexibility he had at work. I dashed into the house, opened the front hall closet and put my hand right onto my camera bag. There was one full pack of film. I was all set for an afternoon's investigations.

I grabbed a cold Pepsi and locked the front door deliberately. I caught Axel's eye as I stepped around my car door.

"Hey, Axel! What's up? How ya doin?"

"Oh, good, Walt, good. You?" He kept walking toward his house.

"Yeah. Good, good." I stepped down the driveway a little to keep him in sight. "So watch'a got? Plumbing or electrical?" I smiled as I called out.

"No, no. Coupla door frames, few sqeaks is all. See ya!" Axel waved and was too far away by then to ask anything else. I looked up at the Maxwell house where all was still. It seemed funny but not my priority. I was on the interstate again in a few minutes, heading west.

***

The rail spur ran slightly downhill toward the Monongahela. A few hundred yards away it turned west to join the CSX which had sidings on quays along the river. I snapped a shot toward the river and one back up the slope. As I walked toward the river I took shots left and right. Both sides were wide open fifty or sixty yards from the tracks.

On the east the land was strewn with old railroad ties, steel drums and other junk, amidst scrubby bushes and grass, right up to a newer fence guarding the highway. On the west the land was fairly clean up to the backs and sides of multi-family housing units. Approximately halfway along the row of buildings there was a wide space that opened into a courtyard. I thought this might be where Blatchford wanted to buy land to convert to parkland. Made sense as I took a picture of it.

Blatchford needed this spur because the oversize structurals we were going to fabricate could not fit on the regular rail line. On the spur we could move them directly to the dock area with no tight turns and without being too close to any other buildings or signal bridges. Upgrading the spur was pretty important. I could see that.

I took pictures of the little white and red EPA signs on both sides of the tracks. I looked up the slope toward our building, about a quarter-mile. I couldn't see why anyone cared a whit about this land, but I wasn't hired for real estate expertise. I walked back to my Jeep and drove to the City-County Building on Grant.

The PDC was in the old Hall. I took the cage elevator to the fourth floor. Their office had three doors on the hallway that ran down the center of the building. Two of them opened into the same long counter area. One door was labeled "Commissioners." At the counter I put my palms on the black linoleum-like surface and looked for a helpful clerk.

After a few minutes a black woman looked my way. I couldn't guess her age, but she was approaching sixty as she got closer. I anticipated her competence.

"You looking for permits, Honey?" I liked her already. Her eyes looked accustomed to smiling, magnified by her glasses.

"No...ahhh, actually I need to get some information about some land. I don't know what to call it, but I can point it out on a map." I gave her as bright a visage as I had.

"We got lots of maps, Honey. Do you have an interest in a contract? Do you need to see the pollution sites? Or maybe you want to see plots that are already granted for development. What is it?" Her name tag said "Jasmine."

"Well, Jasmine...is that right? Jasmine?" She nodded.

"Call me Jesse, Mr....ahh..."

"Anton. Call me Walt, Jesse. Walter Anton. I work for Blatchford Steel, in the old J & L site?" I raised my voice like a question. Jesse nodded. Her hands were clasped in front of her on top of the counter, keeping her eye level closer to mine. "I need to see what is known about this land, here." I spread a half-dozen Polaroids in front of her. "There's an old rail line there. Do you know where I'm talking about?"

"You're south of the Mon." She was now looking below the counter and side-stepping to her right. She stopped and slid out a wide, shallow tray with giant plans lying flat in them.

"Yes. That's right. It's next to that Birmingham Bridge interchange. There's public housing on the other side of the track."

Jasmine slid out another drawer. I moved to where she was. "Ooo-kaay," she said to the open drawer in front of her, "this should be covering your land, Walter. Point out the area you photographed." She carefully pinched two opposing edges together. She made sure the counter was clear and let down one edge and gently rolled the rest of the drawing flat. "Please don't lean on it and don't touch it more than absolutely necessary. We can print new ones but most of these have been marked up like these lines here and like this outline and like these notes. So we're very careful with them."

"Okay, I'll be careful. It looks to me like the area I need to find out about is all in this lined area, here. Why is this designated like this? Do you know?"

"That's Trust land, Mr. Anton. They have filed plans for that parcel. You'll have to talk to them."

"What kind of trust? Do you mean they own that land?" My afternoon was becoming tedious.

"Like I said: You'll have to talk to them. They're not my department. I know what these maps say and I help people like you find out what they say, too. See?" Jesse started to pick up the edges of the big plan.

"Wait a sec Jesse, can you?" I was damned if I was going to leave with no more knowledge than this look imparted. She rolled the drawing out flat, again, and pushed her glasses up the bridge of her nose.

"Yes, Mr. Anton. Something else?" Jasmine was clearly finished with what she wanted to accomplish and seemed to have given up the cooperative warmth we'd shared moments earlier. "I do have other tasks."

"Thank you for helping me, Mrs… ahh, Mrs. …?" I had my most friendly face on.

"Lincoln. Jesse Lincoln. Now how can I help you further?" Mrs. Lincoln was dreaming of something… her desk, maybe.

"Do you see here in my pictures? There are little signs from the EPA. Are there any notes on the map about those?" I hadn't seen them with the map out flat, but didn't think of it until she started to roll it up again. "Do you know what the numbers on the little signs mean?"

"Well, Mr. Anton, I don't and I don't see those notes. But I do see a reference number, right here. See it?" She pointed at a string of numbers I had missed. They were angled along one side of the cross-hatched area. They certainly didn't jump out.

"Okay, I see it. What is it referring to?"

"Well, we have a bookcase full of books that are referred to on the maps. I suppose you want to look at the book with this reference?"

"That would be very nice, Mrs. Lincoln. Thank you." She ambled off to a center island that had thick post binders lined up on three shelves down to nearly floor level, identified by labels in plastic sleeves. She touched several in a row and finally pulled one out and carried it over to where we had been looking at the map, awkward for the small woman. The binders must have weighed twenty pounds.

"In here," she said, clumping the book onto the counter. "Take all the time you need." She sang the "you need" as she scurried back to her desk, clearly through with this part of Thursday. I stared at the binder for a few moments, then at Mrs. Lincoln's back. With a deep breath I pulled the book around and opened the cover. There was a two-column list of documents in government abbreviation code. I wrote down the number on the edge of the "Trust" parcel, "1983-840-SSF." I used the edge of the paper to follow the tiny characters of each entry. I checked all the "1983" listings and there were dozens with an "SSF" entry, but none with a "TRT" that I could see. There were several that said "840."

The covers of the binder had hinges and the book actually lay fairly flat, but the pages I wanted to see disappeared into the binding. I needed copies. I looked up to see if I could catch Mrs. Lincoln's eye but she was far too busy. At one end of the counter another woman was finishing a cash transaction with a man who was leaving with three rolled-up documents that were about the size of the map I had been looking at.

"Excuse me, ma'am. Is it possible to buy these drawings?"

She turned her tired eyes toward me. "You can buy copies. Copies of drawings are $25."

I tried not to be surprised, as if I did this all the time. "I need some copies of pages from those books, too. How much are those?"

"$2.00 apiece. Whaddayagot?" She made no move to change her location. I scooted back to the book and brought it to her, open to the first "840" page.

"I'm not sure of which page I need, so, all the 840's. And I need the map that's on the counter, there. Should I bring it here?"

"No! No! I'll get it." Now she moved. She came back with the drawing rolled up. "Just one copy?" I guessed that the pro's usually got more than one.

"Let me have two of everything. Thanks." I looked around for machines that could copy a big drawing but there were mostly desks and the big center island book case. The woman took the drawing and the book over to the linoleum-topped island. She took the book apart and lifted out several pages and disappeared through a door at the far end of the room. After a while I sat on the hard wooden bench provided for customer comfort.

"That's a hundred and twenty-two dollars, mister!" I stirred awake from my slump, stood up and half fell toward the counter.

"A what? Again?" I shook my head.

"One twenty-two. No personal checks." She stood impatiently, looking at me as though expecting me to walk out on the bill. It was a matter of luck that I had even a hundred dollars with me. I paid her as though this were normal, too. Being angry can wake you right up. I grabbed my copies and escaped the Pittsburgh Development Commission.

On the ground floor there was a small sign sticking out that said "COFFEE SHOP." It was run by a blind veteran. I sat at a café table. There was no space for the big drawing, but I was able to sift through the copies of the "840" pages. "840" referred to the parcel of land, itself. Probably 839 parcels numbered before it. In any event, there were eighteen pages about 840.

There were pages describing condition of the soil, chemical analysis of said soil, depth of the water table, former uses of the land and railroad track, and who the abutters were. I couldn't take time to study them, but I didn't see anything about a "trust" relative to the parcel. It was just one of hundreds of PDC parcels. I speculated that nothing had been done with it because of the pollution, but there weren't any notes about whatever polluting materials were there. Nor did anything indicate that transfer of the land was imminent.

I stretched my arms behind my head. I had almost nothing to bring to the Blatchfords about buying any of this land or even if the PDC would allow the railbed to stay. My thoughts turned to Brightman Partners, the commercial realtors who had helped Blatchford buy the foundry building we occupied. Then I wondered why I was on this goose chase instead of Little Blatchford or one of the V. P.'s. I had never met Brightman and I certainly was no expert on real estate. Finally I thought about how irked Jack Jackson looked when I was given this task. It was a weird day.

I had to move my car. Brightman was only two blocks from City Hall but I couldn't park here after four o'clock and it was already after three. I drove around the block where Brightman's offices occupied space in the Union Trust Bank. Ten bucks to park.

Brightman had half of the ninth floor. The elevator opened across from the reception desk, a modern glass construction with the skyline of Pittsburgh etched onto its various planes. The name "Brightman" shone out from thick glass behind the sweet young thing who smiled every time the elevator opened.

"I'm from Blatchford Steel. I need to speak to one of the partners." I was out of patience for this afternoon.

"Do we know you were coming, Mr. ahhh...Blatchford?" the smile was perfect.

"No *we* don't. I met with Tom Wittenauer this morning and that's why I'm here." That ought to get some action, I thought.

"I'll see if one of the partners is available for you, Mr. umm... is it Blatchford?"

"My apology. It's Anton. Walter Anton. Thanks." I stood still, looking out over the city. Perfect smile turned toward a set of angular panels on her desk and I was abruptly unable to hear what she was saying. Very slick.

"Mr Schumann can see you, Mr. Anton. May I get you some coffee, or a soft drink?"

"Thanks. No. I'm fine."

"Just a minute, then." The tiny receptionist turned to put on a set of earphones and resumed typing.

John Schumann had a fifty-year-old head on a thirty-five-year-old body. His bald stripe was as wide as his face, from his eyebrows to the back of his skull. The sides and back were almost shaggy and free of gray hairs. Maybe he colored it. He seemed normal. We shook hands and he guided my elbow into a magnificent conference room with windows on two sides. You couldn't help but look out over the city. I didn't. Schumann gestured to some plush chairs. Another cute assistant brought in a tray with coffee and tea service. I took some coffee.

"How can we help you, Walter? Is Blatchford looking to add a building? Or moving? No, I can't imagine that."

"No, Mr. Schumann. Can I call you John?"

"Sure, sure." Schumann was eyeing the rolled-up drawings.

"Well, John, I was in a meeting this morning with Harold and Peter Blatchford, some other big-shots and even Congressman Wittenauer. I was out of place, I think, but the upshot was that we need to buy some land so that... ahh... well, land you might be able to help me with. But, I need your confidence on this. I need you to be our agent, if this goes anywhere. You will represent us? I mean, Blatchford Steel?"

"Let me get a basic agency contract, Walter." He picked up a low, curved phone I hadn't noticed. "Tracy, bring me an agency agreement representing Blatchford Steel Services – all the details. Thanks." He turned to face me more squarely. "What's going on? You seem quite concerned about this transaction."

"I took some pictures of the old railbed Jones & Laughlin had. Do you know it?"

"Yes... I know where that is. Is that what you're interested in? There's pollution there."

"So I've heard. I went to the PDC and learned a little, but they didn't answer the real questions, so here I am."

"Brightman is pretty much up on PDC parcels. Let's see if we can answer those questions." Another aide slipped into the room and dropped two papers on the table next to Schumann's elbow. She left without a word. I thought I should ask old man Blatchford for one of those... with the same tight butt. Schumann signed the agency agreement and pushed it toward me. I looked at the beginning of the paragraphs. It was pretty standard, but committed Brightman Partners to represent the interests of Blatchford Steel Services in any realty transactions of purchase or sale, provided there were no legal conflicts restricting such agency, blah, blah, blah. I signed both copies with a flourish.

"Take a look," I said. I slipped the elastics off the drawings and rolled them out, one on top of the other. Schumann placed a couple of heavy magazines along the edges.

"I see your parcel...with the cross hatching. What about it? You want to buy this?" He placed incredulous emphasis on "this." The EPA has this all tied up, as far as I know. We can get you this much space without those problems..."

"It's the rail line we really need, John. The tracks. It seems we have to pay off some tree-huggers to facilitate our ability to use this track for about a year. Wittenauer suggested, or *recommended* that we try to buy a piece of this land so that it could be converted to a park or a playground or something. I don't really know, but I know we need to buy what is needed to use this track again. Supposedly it's connected to ahhh... a river trust of some kind. What do you know about it?"

"The Three Rivers Trust? They're complicated." John Schumann was now animated for the first time. "Why do you want to get involved with them?"

"How the fuck should I know?" Schumann sat back like I'd pushed him. "I just heard of this trust today. I just saw this plat an hour ago. I got these pages copied but I still don't know what I need to initiate a transaction. What does the Trust have to do with it? Do *they* own it?"

Schumann was shaking his head, partly in answer to my question and maybe in disbelief. "That group owns some sites but not this one. What they do is leech on to open parcels and start holding community meetings about wonderful uses for this or that site. They submit plans, get budget projections, do traffic studies and write up supposed community pressure for this or that form of improvement. Inevitably there are 'green' spaces, 'viewscapes,' and here and there a boutique. When a parcel is finally released for development these folks have all their ideas on file. Oftentimes they are invited to take part because their involvement is pure and democratic and already partly approved. They get paid for planning and testifying – the developer gets his project approved. Everybody makes money. Some of the projects are real gems the city is proud of." His head shook "no" as he spoke.

I thought about what Schumann had just laid out. The "TRT" could facilitate projects in ways that developers took advantage of. Maybe we had to kiss their asses to get something done. Maybe Wittenauer needed to kiss their asses. But what could I do right now, today, to get things going?

"Wittenauer seemed to say that he could help with the EPA, somehow, if we could purchase some land along the railbed that could be turned into parkland, or something like that. Make sense?"

"Hmmnnh...I don't know. Humph." Schumann's face was a mask of frustration. "It might work. We aren't without some influence with the PDC, and we have worked with the Trust, too. Might work." He wrote some notes.

"Basically, then, Walter, you need two things...no, THREE things: one you need the EPA to accept as is or do a cleanup on the site, second you need to upgrade the railbed which means you need a right-of-way agreement with somebody, and then you need to identify a portion of this land that would be adequate to satisfy the Three Rivers Trust who may be able to facilitate the whole thing? Have I outlined that correctly?" He waited for my answer.

"Pretty much, yes. But I need a number to plug into budgets. What is this kind of land going for?"

"I have some digging to do before I can give you a number on this parcel. You'd be surprised how fluid land values can be with so many players and politics involved. Do you want something to speculate with? For now?"

"That would be helpful. A good guess, anyway." I pursed my lips and blew out a deep breath. It was almost five o'clock.

"I've seen other odd parcels and I can guess based on a recent deal that had both the PDC and TRT involved. We got squeezed out on that one, but, in any case, it came to about three million for the land. It was a big development, the Penn Plaza, you know it?" I shook my head. "Well the Trust had all kinds of ideas for green zones and bicycle trails on old railroad lines – stuff like that. Their approval came after the developer promised land and the work to realize some of their dreams. Worked out. About three mil." Schumann's two hands were flat on the shiny tabletop. He looked like he wanted to stand up to end the meeting, but was too polite.

I sat, looking at the cross-hatched plot plan of the land beside the old railroad spur. I wanted to appear intelligent about the real estate game. I couldn't think of anything else to ask, nor could I explain what I'd learned. And how would what I now knew fit in with the line of bullshit I dished out that morning? Maybe they hadn't paid that much attention. I realized Schumann wasn't speaking.

"Uhhn…sorry, John. I was thinking of how to make this number sound good. What can you, or what can Brightman do about the Trust people?"

"Let me work on that. I suspect they will be happy to know someone is interested in that land. That means there's a payday up ahead for them."

"How long? Can you learn something by tomorrow sometime?" Schumann looked directly at me, his eyes a little squinted. He turned his head slightly.

"I'll see. I'll call you. Give me your extension."

"Two-forty. Take my home number, also." I gave him the number and stood up.

He jumped up even faster. "Can I keep one of these plats?"

"Yeah, sure. I though you might. Do you need copies of these pages, too?"

Schumann nodded. "Yes, absolutely. You saved me a lot of time."

I rolled up the remaining map and stacked my copies. We shook hands and Schumann guided me out to Miss Perfect

Smile's desk, but no one was there. He waited while the elevator responded. After a few pleasantries about Blatchford's business the doors slid open and we shook again.

As I crept toward the the Penn-Lincoln I felt drained. On a day I would have normally been buried in month-to-date expenditures and big spreadsheets, I had been thrust into negotiations on vacant land and old track. Why it became my job I couldn't fathom. I had never done anything like this for Blatchford. Why dump it in my lap? Work never left me this tired. Maybe Linda would be a little horny and I could relax. I drove to exit 81 automatically.

I was beat by the time I turned into our driveway... drained. If I were going to make love I'd better be cheerful when I walked in. No point sharing my irritation. I brushed my hair back, shook my head and climbed out with a bounce in my step. I thought of saying something silly like "Hi, Honey! I'm ho...ome!" Instead I just said, "Hellooo-oo! Linda?" But I sounded happy. No answer, although a few lights were on. The kitchen displayed no signs of supper. I dropped my briefcase in the front hall closet where I'd grabbed my Polaroid earlier in what felt like a different day.

Suddenly Linda was at my side, helping me with my suitcoat. "There you go," she said, "you're late, today. I was across with Elly. If you're wondering where dinner is it's waiting for us at *Fishwives*. I've been dreaming of some seafood all day so I'm ready to treat you to dinner. If you want to freshen up or something, there's no hurry. So, how was your day?"

"Take a breath, Lindy. Wow!" I looked at her sideways. "You're all wound up, aren't you?" I hugged her tightly and planted a big kiss. I still dreamed of some good slippery sex and if I had to eat fish to get it, that was okay too. I leaned back and looked at her. Her face was turned up and she was smiling just a little. "We could just jump in the shower right now, how's that sound?"

"Sounds interesting, but I'm hungry. Maybe later, hmnnh?" She touched my cheek with one finger and sashayed out to the car. What was I going to do? Stay home? Late sex is better than none. I locked the door and followed.

Fishwives is nicer than it sounds, and casual. We liked it for its excellent, always fresh fish. They claimed to fly it in. Prices were reasonable and the staff knew the regulars. We ordered wine and our meals. The wine hit me and I realized I hadn't had lunch. I ate bread.

"Sorry I wasn't in the house when you got home, Sweetheart. It just seems like I'm the only person who keeps an eye on Elly. She's doing fine by all appearances, but it must be hard to go through a divorce like that. I don't want to see her get all depressed, you know?"

I thought for a moment. "Well, Axel Johnson seems to keep an eye open for her, too. He was over there at lunchtime." Linda choked and coughed. "You okay?"

"Swallowed wrong." She took a sip of water. "You say Axel was over there? At lunchtime? How did... do you know that?"

"I had to get my Polaroid from the closet and we said 'hi' to each other. He was fixing some doors I think." I kept my face blank. I didn't want her to think I was spying on Elly or something. "He was surprised to see me."

"Well, I guess so. It wouldn't seem he could be around in the middle of the day."

"No, right? He must have a pretty good job." I sipped my wine.

"Some kind of engineer, isn't he? You talk to him."

"Never really got into it. He sure is handy with tools. I'm sure Elly finds him convenient."

"Ahh, what? Oh... Axel. Yes, I suppose she must. He's a handyman for sure."

We sipped wine until our meals arrived, steaming and fragrant. I dove in to my swordfish and rice pilaf. Lindy had her baked scallops with baked potato. We ate silently for a few minutes.

"Did I see your car on Jefferson at lunchtime? I couldn't tell if it was you."

"Me? Why would I be home?" She studied her dishes as she carefully took a bite of scallops, a bite of potato and a bite of green beans in proper order.

"Yeah. Must be a million beige Toyotas." Did she answer me? No sense arguing now. Maybe I could get dessert in the shower. "Do you, umm… need a shower tonight? I could use a shower." I looked at her, waiting to see her eyes.

When she looked up she was holding in her lower lip. After a moment she took another bite and tilted her head in that funny, calculating way she always did when deciding whether to "do it" or not. I liked it. "A shower? Tonight? Aren't you tired?" Her eyes looked down again.

"Not that tired. In fact, the way you chew those scallops is giving me a boner. We better hurry."

"You're ridiculous. Can't you control yourself?" She was smiling.

"I'm letting you finish, aren't I?" I'd finished my swordfish and she had only a few scallops left. "Want to take those home?"

"Lucky thing we don't pass a drive-in on the way." Her face was down but she was looking up at me. If the table were bare I would've put it to her right there.

"I'll get the check… my treat, not yours." I signaled to our waitress.

"Somethin else for you folks tonight?" I shook my head.

"No, thanks. I think my wife is going down with something. Can you put hers up to take home? That'd be great." I fished out my wallet and remembered that I had forked over a hundred and thirty bucks that afternoon. I counted carefully. I had enough to pay and leave a tip but no more. I took out all the bills and got some coins from my pocket and plunked them on the little tray.

"You better be good, lady," I growled, "that's my last five hundred." Linda shook her head and stood up to accept the bag with her leftovers.

"Geez, folks. I sure hope the missus feels better. You take care of yourselves, now. Thank you!"

"Oh, she will, I'm sure." I took her hand and pulled her past the other diners and out to the car. I even opened the door for her and helped find her seatbelt, dragging my hand across both breasts. "Watch your dress, Honey," I said as the door closed.

I gunned the engine, pulled away and signaled my turn up the old William Penn Highway.

"Is this car a… STICK shift?" Linda breathed. She grabbed my groin on 'STICK' and found what she wanted. It made it hard... to concentrate, but I kept my eyes on the road. We did some awkward feeling-up all the way to Penn Hills.

I whipped into the driveway and killed the engine. Linda jumped out and ran to the door. I exited carefully, but right behind her. I tried to swing her up to my shoulder.

"Hey! We just ate. Let me get undressed."

I had my suit-coat and shirt mostly off. I kicked off my shoes and undid my belt, letting the pants drop where I stood. Linda was in the bedroom being careful with her dress. "I'll meet you in the shower," I shouted. My penis was still at half-attention as I pulled off one sock then the other as I hopped toward the bathroom.

I warmed up the shower and started to wash. A minute later, Linda stepped in behind me. She wrapped her arms around me and hummed a loud "hmmmnnnhh…"

"I have a surprise for you."

"For me? I can't wait. Is it too big to hold in one hand?" I could feel her face rubbing my back as she shook her head no. I stood up as straight as I could. Old Useless did, too. "I have a surprise for you, too, lady. And, it is too big to hold in one hand."

"Well, turn around and see what you think." She let me go and stepped back a step. I turned and looked at her empty hands. I turned my eyes with a questioning look.

"Do I have to search for it? I don't mind…"

"Just get on your knees and see what you think."This was too technical for a guy with a boner. I knelt.

Linda came up to stand over me as on Tuesday night. During cunnilingus it is my habit to keep my eyes closed. I pushed in to get busy with my tongue and it was only then that I realized there was no hair – none – not even fuzz. I almost sat backwards. I grabbed her thighs and leaned back to get a good look. Bald as could be. I looked up across Linda's belly and between her breasts to her face. Old Useless got even harder. She looked back with her eyebrows up as if to ask, "How do like that, you horndog?"

The shower spray caused me to tilt my head back down. "I like it. I like it. When…?" I didn't wait for an answer. I started licking all around and up and down the little folded valley. I had never really had a good look at what was a very cute, ahhh, place, all soft and bare. I licked around until I found that bumpy thing. Linda grabbed little handsful of my upper back and pushed herself into my face. I had to breathe through my mouth as I continued my delicious work.

Abruptly the taste changed and Lindy collapsed on top of me. I straightened up and grabbed her around her waist and lifted her up. She slipped down over my penis and wriggled around for a moment. I shot off and pulled her tighter. My legs went weak and I leaned against the wall. We were fused together. She was chewing gently on my shoulder. I was sucking the water off her neck and shoulder. We stayed there for a minute. My hard-on became a soft-off and I let Linda slide down to stand on her own. I remembered the surprise and stood back to look, again.

"Do you like me... like that?"

"I guess I do. It's so smooth... it's cute." I placed my hand over her vagina and my middle two fingers slipped in automatically. She jerked her hips back but I was locked in. "I do like the feel of it. Not scratchy for you too. Mmmmnnh." I started to get hard again and she grabbed me and pushed and pulled my skin back and forth. Then she pulled my hand away and turned around in one quick move. She leaned down and guided me into her again. I pulled her hips into me and we screwed for about half a minute and I let go again and a few seconds later she came, too, her little hand helping. We were panting.

I squirted some shampoo into my hand and started to wash her hair. She just stood and closed her eyes. I ran my fingers through her hair and every stroke was a caress I desired to give her more than anything. Linda took the bar soap and lathered me up, meticulously around my crotch. I actually started to stiffen a third time.

"Oh, control yourself, you animal."

I tightened my muscles and made Old Useless jump up and down a couple of inches. "I am controlling myself!" I pumped a couple more times.

"I'm not paying any attention," she grimaced. I had the soap now, and I gently lathered her body. Her nipples hardened as I made sure they were as clean as a whistle. I carefully ran my hands up and down her thighs and from front to back, back to front, front to back. I was hard as a rock. "Oh, you," she said. She grabbed me firmly and made sure we both rinsed completely.

"See if you can hold off long enough to brush your teeth. Can you?"

I had no choice. We stood side by side, brushing. I looked at her in the mirror while she brushed seriously. I bumped her hip, causing her to look up. I held up my middle finger. She rolled her eyes and shook her head. We bent down to spit, and collided. "You first, my queen." She finished spitting and rinsing. I tried to slide my hand up her butt. She yelped and tightened up so effectively that I could hardly pull my fingers out. She wiped her mouth, rinsed and dried her hands, stepped back and started to brush her hair.

I looked at her in the mirror and then finished my own rinsing, wiping and drying. I pushed the towel through my hair. She was gone and I was soft as a marshmallow. By the time I got to the bedroom I realized how exhausted I was. I pulled on some briefs... admitting I was through. We hugged.

FRIDAY, MAY 17, 1985

I could see the time, 5:33, seventeen more minutes. I thought about Linda's interesting cosmetic change. *She must have read about it in the oral sex book. It sure was a change from the old days… 'old days!' Holy cow! We were too young to have 'old' days. Still, before we came to the understanding that children were not the reason, sex was great, but not nearly as inventive as the last two times. And now the shaved pubes. That must be awkward to do safely. I could help her the next time, I thought. I'll have to ask.* The alarm brought up the radio. The remote controller shut it off. Linda was off Fridays, so why not let her sleep? She had sent me off to dreamland. I got up quietly.

It wasn't until I pulled a coffee to my lips that I recalled the rest of Thursday. How much trouble was I in, getting real estate estimates to Blatchford senior? I remembered drinking pretty good coffee when I was handed the task of researching Congressman Wittenauer's suggestion.

And another thought: *Wittenauer seemed to be in on the whole project of refurbishing that piece of railroad. Yesterday couldn't have been the first time he and Blatchford had discussed it. Yesterday sure wasn't Katy Mellon's first meeting with the good Congressman. No one else was surprised to see her there. Big and Little Blatchford were both at ease. Naw… couldn't have been the first time she was in attendance.*

So, okay, I'd been collecting manufacturing projections for about three months since Blatchford won designation from the

Bridge architects – for the time being. All the pieces had to be in place and production ready to start by January first, seven months from now. But I'm no engineer. I didn't know until a couple of weeks earlier that the triangular girders we had to fabricate were too big for regular rail. If they traveled on their side, three flatcars long, they could not make the turns back into Pittsburgh after traveling almost two miles down the line, plus the railroad would need to change its schedule to clear the other tracks as the pieces went by. But in any case, the girders would have to be stood up on edge to make the tightest turns and bridge abutments coming back into the city, and they were too high to pass under bridges. The old J. & L.spur down to the main line, however, had room for upright transport with just two minor fixes: a few wires we could relocate, and one signal bridge we could modify.

Yet our expense projections hadn't considered railroad issues. In fact, I thought Blatchford knew a lot about the railroad costs long before, and Jack Jackson probably did too... so did Tom Wittenauer... and, son of a bitch, so did Katie Mellon! So, why the fuck is it my problem?

I'm not the fastest thinker. I had wandered through Thursday without connecting all those dots, including my own... the one with the circle around it.

My coffee was lukewarm. I poured more. Linda came into the kitchen.

"I'm sorry I woke you, Honey," I said as we hugged. "Thought I'd let you sleep."

"That's okay. I was done sleeping, anyway. Besides, I told Elly I would come over for coffee and then I've got a meeting for lunch, too." She took a half-cup. I still had to shave and it was a little late.

"Time for a shower?" I was smiling but, oddly, Linda turned bright red, and she rarely blushed. Her eyes looked wet, all of a sudden. "Hey, Sweetie, I didn't mean anything. I was being funny... unless you do have time...?"

"Oh, go shave, will you?" She dabbed her eyes and blew her nose. I followed orders.

When I finished, Linda was dressed as nicely as ever, and just waiting to leave. "Well, there you are. Okay. Listen, I'm going over for, ahh, coffee with Elly. Will you be late, tonight? You were late yesterday."

"Don't get me going on yesterday. What a circus! I was lost in the high-rise jungle."

"What? Downtown?" She faced me squarely and smoothed my collar.

"Yeah, goddamned Blatchford had me chasing real estate, of all things. Certainly not what I started my day doing."

"Real estate? You? What on Earth for?"

"It's all part of that King Frederik Bridge contract. I told you about that, didn't I?"

"Well, yes, but more accounting you said." Linda was itching to get across the street.

"I'll tell you the whole story of the PDC and the friggin TRT some other time." I placed air-quotes around "TRT." Linda was wide-eyed.

"The TRT you said? TRT?"

"Yeah…so? The Three Rivers Trust, I think it is." I was staring at her. "TRT" had made an impact. "Have you heard of it?"

She nodded with her eyes boring into me. "I can't believe it," she said.

"What?"

"I'm a member of the Trust!" Now she shook her head. "It's one of the things I do for *englishclass*. How weird that it'd be connected to Blatchford, somehow."

My mouth hung open. Linda was on the Trust? What a twist. "Hey! Maybe you can help me!" I was staring at her.

"Me? How?" Her look was incredulous.

"We, I mean, I... need to work with them, um... you, I guess. We need to talk about this."

She nodded slightly, but looked out the door and across the street.

"I'm late and you've got to go," I said. "That's okay. Please call me around eleven or so, can you?"

"At eleven. Yes, I can. What for?"

"We need to talk before I meet with the big boys again. Be sure you call me. Make a note or something." I was nervous.

"Don't worry, for goodness sake! I said I'll call. Gracious." She was on her feet. "You're gonna be late if you don't get going. I'll call you, okay?" She stepped up and gave me a kiss.

"Yeah, okay. See you." I tossed the rest of my coffee and swished some mouthwash. Linda was out the front door and almost to Elly's by the time I locked up. She and Elly waved as I rolled down the street. I tooted and turned the corner to Jefferson and then slid onto 791 and down to the interstate for the short ride to Blatchford Steel. Morning traffic made the ten-minute ride a thirty. I listened to KDKA's blather all the way.

As I parked and put my hand on the key it hit me! *Son of a bitch! They KNEW Linda was on that Trust. Son of a bitch! Every politician in town must kiss the ass of the TRT. They knew! They're stuck on this land and they figure I can get to the board because of Linda. Son of a bitch!*

Of course, that means Big and Little Blatchford both knew I was bull-shitting when I glibly told them I would have the pricing by this morning at the latest. Son of a bitch! My car was still running. I looked to see if anyone had heard me shouting to myself, but I was alone. I killed the engine and stared.

They're not only stuck on the land, there's serious trouble with it and it might fuck up the whole contract. Why didn't the old man just give me the story in the first place? Maybe they didn't think I could do it unless I felt responsible… pressured myself. Maybe they're right. That fucking congressman must have known Linda was involved. What a sly prick... probably his idea to hold that meeting and bring me in. Jack Jackson knew it all, too. Another prick, and all my special lunches, too. Sonofabitch!

I locked the car and looked at the old building with new feelings. I was supportive of Blatchford Steel Services, generally – like a sports fan – but I know I came to work in neutral most days. I had no stock options in *my* pension. I either somewhat liked or didn't pay much attention to most of the other employees. I was genuinely fond of my Iron Tigers teammates and I got along well with everyone I had to, I think.

But now… now… it seemed like Blatchford was ready and willing to put me in a bad position, even screwing with my relationship with Linda. I knew the profits on the King Frederik were big. I didn't want to hurt anybody, but I didn't get paid to take risks… I added up numbers, for crying out loud.

I consciously decided to be happy old Walt, though, as I walked into the guard-room. "Hey, Pauly. Get much last night?"

"Why yes, sir, I believe I did, heh, heh, heh. Best I can remember, Mr. Walter. The best."

"Me, too, Pauly. I can't remember that far back either!" We laughed as I breezed through.

Taped to my door were two papers folded together. I pulled them off as I opened it. I had only glanced at the fresh piles of receipts and requisitions in the two catch-baskets when Jack Jackson walked in, closing the door.

"And good morning to you, too," I said, not looking up.

"You're late, you know. Didn't you see my note?"

"I just got here, for chrissakes! I had a tough time yesterday that made me pretty late, and I've already been thinking about that land shit this morning. So don't worry – you're getting all the hours out of me." I looked at him with a sour expression. "I haven't opened your note so I didn't even know it's yours. What's so important?"

"I just wanted to see you first thing. You never called me."

My happy old Walt demeanor was long gone. I glanced at the pencil-written note: *Come to my office when you get this. Jackson.* "Well, I'm gonna get some coffee. Sit down and I'll fill you in." I started out the door.

"No, Walt. Bring your coffee to my office. It's quieter." Jack went directly to his real office with door, walls and independent lights. I got my coffee and purposely chatted with a couple of secretaries before I ambled down to Jackson's real office. He looked at his watch when I sat down.

"Who'd you see, yesterday, Walter? Is there actually a price you can estimate? You went downtown?" Jackson's eyes were shifting back and forth, catching mine only briefly.

"You know what, Jack, what the fuck am I doing with this project?" I never swore at people in the office… never. But I was irked at his attitude and he was acting like I had been on some espionage mission to the PDC.

"Easy, Walter. You said you would have a price and I need to report some progress. So let me have it. Get anywhere or not?" He was looking right at me.

I looked back with my mouth clamped shut. He stopped fidgeting with papers and wound up staring at me. "Do you want the story? I have a few questions for you, too, before I go any further with the whole project. I have a call at eleven, but I doubt I'll hear a real price. There's a story to tell."

"All right. Tell me. We're in this together, after all." Jack's face was as friendly as ever.

"Together? Really? Okay, here it is." I gave him a rendition of taking pictures, looking at the drawings at City Hall and consulting with Brightman later. He took notes on a yellow pad. "Brightman's worked with the Three Rivers Trust on similar political deals before. You probably already know how political this is, don't you?"

"I don't do politics, Walter, we just need to buy that land and get our railroad running. Should be simple, right?" His smile was working overtime. I knew he didn't believe it.

"Look, Jack, this stupid project was handed to me so smoothly I didn't see it happening. You've known about the problems getting this land long before that meeting, right?" My whole face tried to look questioning. "Right?" I waited.

It didn't take long. Like I'd observed before, Jack Jackson was a powerful leader-type. "Yes, I've known they needed land." He looked up at the ceiling and then at me. "So what?" He looked like he'd caught a mouse.

"Well, I'll tell you what, you're so curious. Something stinks about getting that land, it seems to me. Old man Blatchford and the great Tom Wittenauer probably figured they would grease the skids and do this with a few phone calls. Good ol' boys, huh?"

"I'm sure they worked together to get it done the fastest way possible. We need it for the big contract, don't forget."

"Oh for crissakes, Jack! I was born at night but not last night! That whole meeting was set up to hang this problem on little old Walter Anton, wasn't it?" He shrugged as if that were not specifically so – not necessarily. Maybe not. "C'mon, Jack. We've worked together for years and you have been able to trust me. Can't I trust you, too? Not anymore? When did that end?"

"That's not how it is, Walt, and you know it. We, umm… they just need your dedication on this to wrap it up. Our Rep is going to help with the pollution stuff and you're a damn good cost controller. That's it."

"Nothing to do with Linda, then?"

Jack buried his head in his hands on top of his desk. "Ahh, shit. I knew you wouldn't like this."

"Well that sounds honest. Why couldn't you... they, just bring me up to speed and tell me they needed leverage on the TRT board? Of course, the fly in that ointment is that I didn't know she was on that board… not until this morning, anyway." I sat and shook my head. "Listen, Jack, I support my employer and I am glad to see growth and I grasp the scope of this. But this could have had very bad results… I could have been very loud and pissed off about this. I could have quit and gone to the newspapers. Who knows? Why did they… or *you*, take that risk?"

"You're taking this whole thing the wrong way, Walt. We hit a roadblock with the Trust – that's true. When I spoke to Brightman it looked…"

"You what? You spoke to Brightman? Aaron Brightman? Then you sent me down there like a goddam flunkie? Jesus Christ, Jack! Son of a bitch!" I was standing and walking back and forth.

"Quiet, Walter, will you? Shhh, shh, shush. C'mon. Siddown. I know how it looks. Lemme explain. C'mon, now." Jackson was standing too, waving his hands downward to calm me. I slid my chair farther back and slumped in it.

"I'm all ears."

"All right, then. Do you want fresh coffee?"

"Cold is fine, let's go."

"I got this about two weeks ago. Apparently the congressman had figured to sweet talk the city into a long-term lease for the land just as it sits. Blatchford contributes a lot to him and he owes us. So, we were hoping we could slip this past all the agencies and just work with the city. Get the lease, fix up the tracks and do our business for a year or so and walk away from it. That was the best solution for us and Wittenauer acted like he had enough juice to get it done."

"And his bullshit was on par with mine." I was slowly shaking my head. The plan was actually a good one... good-sounding one. And it would have been cheap to do. I had to appreciate that.

"Trouble was," Jack went on with a nod, "the damn Three Rivers Trust ladies had a hair across their ass about this deal. The old dame, Roberta McGillvray, distrusts our fair mayor. He screwed up some greenway project they had already cut the ribbon on. There's an office building on part of the land now, and she has never forgiven him. I guess he can be a bastard. Someone's gears got greased on that deal – lot's of someone's, probably, including the mayor's. Anyway, she gets wind of this lease deal and hits the roof. The city figures it's got a couple million coming in for basically doing nothing and there's some jobs on the track and for Blatchford and Mayor McKay thinks he's put a cherry on his sundae. But, Hell hath no fury like a garden club scorned, I guess."

I thought how the mess had developed. It seemed innocent, or as innocent as anything political might be, but had been hung on the petard of other enmities, other screw-jobs, other politics. Probably involved plenty of graft and payoffs – it was an industrial, unionized city, after all.

Overall, Pittsburgh had been shrugging off the loss of its steel-making base about as well as it could. Aside from East Liberty and the Lower Hill, the pain was distributed city-wide. Those neighborhoods had been destroyed and "renewed" for the good of everyone else. Now, twenty five years later, Pittsburgh was much more genteel about its urban tinkering. Here and there it managed to cooperate with neighborhood groups, minority agitators and a variety of "development" commissions and agencies, the Three Rivers Trust being the grand dame of them, all. Without their blessing, nothing big within sight of the city limits got done. Because of them, many projects cost more and included renderings of slender people walking down spotless paths under neatly trimmed basketball trees.

"So what did they expect you to do, Jack? How could you succeed where the great U. S. Rep could not?"

"I had no plan when young Blatchford brought me in on it. All I could think of was to call Brightman and have them straighten things out for us. Of course, Wittenauer had already tried to work with them. They told me I would have to get it approved by the Trust. They alluded to problems with City Hall but didn't give me details. I went down there and the mayor actually met with me. He tried to explain how the Trust was a roadblock to many of his great ideas, but he didn't tell me how he had screwed em over on the Lyman Building.

"Anyway, we needed a key to the TRT and that's what I came back to Blatchford with. He told me that Linda Anton was on the Trust and I wondered why you never mentioned it. I figured if I got you on the team you would automatically offer to work with Linda to help us. That's why we had the meeting, and you played the part, except you never said anything about Linda and the Trust. The old man was pretty upset about that. I told them after the meeting that I had not mentioned Linda to you. But you took off with a mission and I hoped that you would come to find you were married to a great ally and things would work out. I had no way to go forward without you." Jackson held his hands out appealingly. I sat and just looked at him.

Finally I spoke. "It's a wonder this fucking outfit even does business." I held my chin in one hand and propped the elbow with the other. "I'll take this a little further, Jack. Everyone's been playing me like a sucker, but I am now interested in this labyrinth of double-deals. It might help my resumé to put some merengue on this pile of shit. I want some authority to act for Blatchford and I'll tell you what I think my bonus should be for pulling this off. First I have to see if I'm still a married man after I talk to Linda. Will that work?" I raised my eyebrows and looked wide eyed at him.

"I expect that will be okay. I'll talk to them. I'll tell them. Count on it." He nodded his head for emphasis.

"I'm sure. I'll get back to you." I walked back to my office. I sat facing my desk, again. Behind the desk I was afraid I'd lose my train of thought… I'd be Walter Anton, cost accountant. In the front chair I could stay Walter Anton… what? Real estate secret agent? Real estate marriage counselor? More like Walter Anton, real estate garbage man. I was in a corner. If I fucked up one way, I might lose my job. If I fucked up the other way, I might lose my job and my reputation. However it went, there was a good chance Linda would be upset to a point of changing our relationship. How the Hell could they play with my life this way?

I had to map out what to do next. First of firsts, I had to ease into my situation with Linda, and be careful to obtain her help with the Trust for my own benefit and to Hell with Blatchford... if I could even do that. The more I thought about the pickle I now owned, I realized this was exactly where all the King's horses and men had got to: unable to put pieces together without squaring things with the Three Rivers Trust. Until I spoke with Linda, I had nothing. It was only ten and Linda was calling at eleven.

Okay, I had a first step. More than the shit pile I had at quarter of nine. I shifted to my desk chair and started to catch up.

I cleared forty items by ten-thirty. Time for fresh coffee, and maybe someone had left a donut. I found less than a cup of java in the pot so I took the time to make fresh. Even I could make coffee in a Bunn-O-Matic. I poked around while it dripped. No donuts, english muffins or even pretzels. One of the guys from contracts came in with his mug.

"Hey! Valter! Thought I could smell a fresh pot. Do accountants make the coffee, now?" He was laughing in that superior way of high-end sales people. Most people wouldn't recognize our "sales reps." They were four guys who looked like they came out of a machine shop, but they wore nice suits. In fact, they each had a lot of steel-work experience. Two of em were precision welders in their former lives. I know one guy cut steel in our own shop. They could speak in 'steelworker,' pretty smooth English and four other languages among them. Their prospects needed to speak to knowledgeable reps – no bullshit. What our four contracts people knew could not be learned from books. They were how we won the King Frederik job.

"It's Dieter, isn't it?" I asked.

"Ya. German. But I drink coffee, same as you. What can I do for you?"

"Are you involved in the King Frederik contract?" I stirred some sweetener into my black coffee.

"Well, young fella, I belief I vas." He shifted around like a Teutonic John Wayne. "Actually, there were two of us on dat vun. I was the on-site man and Casey – Casimir – worked with the design engineers in their office. Worked out good dat vay."

"I'll say. You got everybody running around making sure we perform on time. Nice job!" I was genuinely impressed. They did what I could never, nor want, to do. "Is there some time when you, me and Casey can grab a coffee or a beer? I'd love to talk to you... might help me figure out the costs on the contract."

"Well, ahh, sure, I guess. Why not? Don't know what we can add to the details you have. When's good for you? Mondays are tough, but any other day?"

"Sooner is better," I offered, "so let's try for Tuesday. Can you both do Tuesday? Hit a steakhouse somewhere? Whatever you like is fine with me." I had to get back to my desk.

"I'll check with Casey and leave a note in the in-box."

"Great, Dieter. Thanks for fitting me in. It'll be great... an education." I tipped my cup toward him as I backed out. He nodded as he sipped, probably wondering what sort of mental illness I'd contracted from dusty ledger papers.

***

About five minutes before eleven my phone warbled and I knew it was Linda. "Hi, Honey," I declared.

"Lucky it's me, I guess." Linda was not laughing.

"Don't be silly, Lindy, I can feel these things."

"Okay, Houdini. I called as requested. Is this about a Trust problem?" She sounded fine, now.

"No, no problem, I don't think. But I suddenly need info about the Trust and rumor has it that you might be in possession of some. It would really help me a lot if I could meet you for lunch. Is your meeting closed or can I be your guest? I don't want to mess you up."

A few beats went by soundlessly. "Umm... does it have to be today, Walt?" She let out a long sigh I wasn't supposed to hear.

"It could be extremely helpful. I can't overstate that, Sweetie, just can't. Can we work it out? I'll give you the whole story when I see you." I shut up.

"I can't imagine what is so crucial but you think it is so let's find a way. Tell you what: meet me in the lobby of the Duquesne

Union building – on the campus. Do you know where I mean? You can park in the lot by the expressway. No later than ten of twelve… it'll be tight. Can you make it?" I let out the breath I'd been holding.

"I'm rolling right now. It's not far. Thanks a million, Lindy. You're my life-saver. I love you!" I hung up in her ear. Thank God I said "I love you." I started toward the front but trotted to Jack Jackson's real office, first.

I popped the door and started talking before he could stop what he was doing. He looked up like a deer in the headlights. "Tell em to be prepared for as much as three million, Jack. I'll have more info later. And have a good weekend." I turned and hustled toward the front. He may have called out but I kept going. Let him stew on that. I wasn't coming back this Friday.

The entry ticket said eleven-forty. I went up and down the rows. Ultimately I was in one of the last spaces, as far from Boulevard of the Allies as could be. I ran up to street level and huffed and puffed to the Union building. I spotted Linda waiting on the broad steps outside. She gestured for me to hurry, but I was slowing down.

"I didn't waste a minute, Honey. Thanks for waiting." I pecked her cheek and she squeezed my hand and led me to the elevators. She brushed my hair and flattened my jacket as I caught my breath.

"You're fine, Honey. We have guest speakers today so outsiders are fine. I should have told them forty-eight hours in advance, that's all. Let's get you a name tag." I stood a step back while Linda spoke to a well-dressed woman she obviously knew. After a few seconds she turned back with a clip-on badge that said simply 'WALTER,' with a small, but legible, *Blatchford Steel,* underneath. I felt licensed. We walked into the Duquesne Room and a huge brown banner with a map of the three rivers that made Pittsburgh, Pittsburgh, punched me in the eye. The words, "Three Rivers" arched along the Ohio and Allegheny rivers; "Trust" followed the Monongahela down to the right.

Linda led me to a table two rows back from the head table. It wasn't a big room but there were a dozen ten-seaters. Linda found her place-card between two occupied seats. Across from her was an open seat. She smoothly asked if folks would shift so she could seat a last-minute guest. Everyone adjusted as if waiting to be asked. Linda started speaking with the woman to her right. I walked around and introduced myself to our eight tablemates, three officious looking men and five women. I read their badges and forgot the names before I sat down. Linda patted my leg as a well-turned-out matron clicked a gavel on the podium.

"Good ahhfternoon everyone, and thank you for being on time, today! Today is our tenth annual *National-Local Cooperation Conference*. The Three Rivers Trust is proud to work with our city of Pittsburgh leaders," here she nodded toward the right side of the head table, "and with our Federal Representatives," nodding to the left, "to help the people of Pittsburgh make this great city the gem of Pennsylvania!" Applause greeted that. To her left, was an empty place. I could see the carefully coiffed Tom Wittenauer, representative to the 97th Congress, next to that open seat which I assumed was for Senator Fahnstahl.

"My name," the matron went on, "is Roberta McGillvray and I have the honor of chairing this Conference and the Board of Trustees of the Three Rivers Trust. For those of you who are first-timers to our Conference, the mission of the Three Rivers Trust is a simple one: the Trustees work with all interested parties to make certain that neighborhoods, governments, businesses and visitors to our city all enjoy the best and cleanest access to our beautiful land and resources. That is why we are here today..."

I tuned her out. She introduced the grand personages at the head table of whom I took almost no note until she mentioned the mayor, Harry McKay. Him I had to meet. The mayor appeared less than thrilled. I turned to Linda and whispered, "I had no idea your luncheon was with the Trust. I didn't mean to put you in a funny spot."

"For this meeting it's really fine. Everyone is encouraged to bring a guest to puff up the numbers. The lady to my right works with me at *englishclass*, so I have two guests. It's good," she whispered back.

Dame McGillvray completed her introductions. Apparently Senator Fahnstahl was delayed flying up from Washington and expected any moment. She thanked us all for caring about Pittsburgh and invited us to enjoy our lunch before we heard from our guests of honor. Immediately there was a clatter of service and repressed conversations.

Linda was careful to say something to everyone at our table. Anton Chiemelski was a CPA with connections of some kind to the city or to the Trust or to both; his wife was actually his wife and about the same age as he. She had one of the "TRT" ribbons on her name badge. Very nice to meet you. Next to him was Forrest Akers, president of Liberty Bank, the first black community bank; his wife was rather younger than he, but again, his wife. Next to him was a black state assemblyman, obviously a friend. The assemblyman was with his aide, much younger and quite attractive. Next to Linda was Maryanne something, her co-worker, and next to her were two women who must have come together. Carol had a tag that said 'Pittsburgh Development Commission'; Doris's simply said 'Pittsburgh City Hall.'

Table by table everyone received salad, rolls and beverages. When we touched the salads, the main course arrived. In short order we all had some kind of chicken, wild rice and vegetable medley, and not too much of any. I ate mine. Linda chatted amiably with her guest and the others chatted with one another. I studied the head table. The only black up there was the president of the City Council. He sat next to the mayor and they seemed at ease. The mayor did his best to chat up the Vice-President of the Trust. She smiled a lot, but it was evident that her topics of interest were not of the city, or of the TRT, or deep. On the other side of the podium Roberta McGillvray, having planned to sit next to a U. S. Senator, was forced to lean across the empty seat to chat up a mere Congressman. Wittenauer fawned over her every word and soon moved to be closer to her. Facial muscles said the great lady had little use for proximity, but could not be seen to have no one caring what she said. And Wittenauer did care. The others on the head table were all executive members of the Trust and relatively non-conversational.

A minor commotion signaled the arrival of Senator Fahnstahl. He took his time greeting everyone he could, shaking hands and clapping backs along a circuitous route to the dais. As he finally broke free, Roberta McGillvray stood up and banged her gavel. "Ladies and gentlemen, clearly our friend, Senator Hugh Fahnstahl has arrived...," she started the applause, "...Senator Fahnstahl!"

The senator climbed up the one step to the head table and touched the hand or shoulder of everyone as he walked to the podium. He gave a quick buss to the grand dame of the Trust and reached over to shake hands with the mayor and the Trust VP. The city council president took a step closer to be seen shaking his hand, too. Finally Fahnstahl turned back to Dame McGillvray and they shared a few words. She gestured to the microphone and said something to Wittenauer and then sat down. All in all, Fahnstahl managed to gain the maximum attention and completely upstage the congressman without breaking his smile. Very slick, I thought, and it didn't bother our hostess.

Linda and I listened politely as first Fahnstahl and then Wittenauer extolled the virtues of the Three Rivers Trust and the wonderful work it does, how beautiful Greater Pittsburgh was becoming with their guidance...and on and on. I didn't pay much attention until Mayor McKay took the podium. I knew his advocacy of "neighborhood revitalization" had borne fruit fixing up pockets of decay here and there; I also knew he'd tried to engineer larger projects that had been tied up for months. Suspicions existed that it was the Trust that was the impediment, but he never, to my knowledge, stated so publicly. There was some tension.

"Madame President, Madame vice-President, Senator Fahnstahl, Representative Wittenauer, Council President Jefferson, members of the Three Rivers Trust and friends of Pittsburgh, thank you very much for welcoming me to your annual luncheon. Let me begin by making clear that the City of Pittsburgh's goal is to work with all interested parties to make certain that neighborhoods, governments, businesses and visitors to our city all enjoy the best and cleanest access to our beautiful land and resources." There was a momentary pause as he allowed everyone to recognize the statement that Roberta McGillvray had made earlier. "I believe the goals of the City and of the Trust are that coincident. I believe that every group – and this Trust, absolutely – or person, that is constructively working toward the betterment of Pittsburgh is an ally of the City and, therefore, an ally of mine and this administration.

"A city government can do only three things, fundamentally...," and here he held up his hand and counted them off, "... clean streets, safe streets, good schools. These three key elements of a successful community are symbiotic; none stands alone. You've heard that speech before, I know you have. What we, all of us," here he looked at other elected officials very obviously, "are doing here, is loosely grouped under the heading of "clean streets." And it's not just streets. It's the empty lot that attracts trash, grafitti and junked cars; it's the odd alley or strip of undevelop-able land that could be turned into greenspace making adjacent businesses more attractive and more successful; it's the huge tract that could be developed for good or ill, with good or bad impact on abutters. I have told you nothing you do not know. But I do want you to know – make no mistake – that the City has not wavered in its commitment to see the best use and best impact of every inch of land within our limits. I and my administration are ready to roll up our sleeves and work with you, all. Thank you very much for listening!" He raised one hand to wave and smiled as he reclaimed his seat. The audience seemed to love him and a few stood in their applause. Dame McGillvray looked like her lunch disagreed with her. She clapped long enough.

I had never paid attention to the mayor. Pittsburgh was where I worked. When I went home to Penn Hills, the city and its problems were in my mirrors. But I decided I liked this guy and his three-part distillation of what city government should actually do. I liked that he was direct, to the point... and brief. I really wanted to talk to him about my real estate problem. Before the applause ended Roberta McGillvray reclaimed the podium.

"Ladies and Gentlemen, I am always afraid to do this but I promised Stan Waletski he could have FIVE minutes." People were chuckling, knowing of the Chamber of Commerce President's ability to pack a ten-minute speech into five. Waletski was already up from his seat and bouncing up to the podium.

"Madame President, Senator Fahnstahl, Representative Wittenauer, Mayor McKay, Council President Jefferson, members and officers of the Three Rivers Trust and fellow believers in Pittsburgh." Here, he took his first breath. "I will hold to this outrageous limitation on my oratorical profundity..." he got a few laughs as he paused for effect, " but I can't overlook the presence of our 1984-85 Chairman of the Board, attorney Brad Waterman, winner of the Steel Citizenship Award for 1983 and a great servant of the business and commercial communities of Pittsburgh and a great leader of the Chamber and a strong friend of the Trust." Another breath, thank goodness. "How am I doing on time, Roberta?" She just nodded. From the audience, someone called out, "Hey Stanley, you can always save these minutes for the next time!" More laughter.

"No, I can't Billy. You should know better than to come between Stan Waletski and the rest of his time! The Pittsburgh Chamber of Commerce is a voluntary association of more than two thousand manufacturers, retailers, professionals and involved people – involved organizations – who all work every day to make our city stronger and more attractive to smart employers. And businesses are moving to Pittsburgh because of the working relationships we have. The Chamber is there for all of you. It's where you can get things done if you want to grow and where you can get your questions answered when things get complicated in permitting or financing. Your Chamber is your facilitator to progress. Let me reiterate the steady and strong support we have for the Trust. It is always a pleasure to work with people who are committed to making Pittsburgh the most attractive economic area on the Ohio River!"

Waletski gave Damc McGillvray a quick hug, touched hands with the senator and the congressman and waved as he bounded to his seat. The room let out a sigh. I made a mental note that he might be useful. Our annual dues were high enough.

Now the Trust President was explaining a series of slides as they projected above her head. First came Trust renderings, followed by photos of improvements here and there. Many were simply photos of big shots – and Roberta McGilvray – cutting a ribbon or posing before a sign about the project. She ended by making a pitch for the next Council hearing the Trust would be attending, hoping for support. Then she invited everyone who was not a member of the Trust to speak to a Trust member before you leave, and that members had brown ribbons on their name tags and each was excited to answer your questions. "Thank you to our guests,..." I couldn't listen to another rendition of the head table. I placed my hand on Linda's arm.

"Linda, this was very illuminating. Thank you for getting me in. This is the first time I've ever heard these people. But I've gotta tell you what I'm involved with and what it has to do with the Three Rivers Trust. Can you break away?" I gave her my most appealing face.

"First let me introduce you to Roberta, Honey. Don't you want to speak to her? Before she disappears?" She had my hand and pulled me toward the head table where the great lady was disposing of conversations and greetings, one after another. We stood to one side so we'd be last. The matronly executive walked along the low stage and stopped to speak with her VP. Finally she stepped down to the floor and invited Linda and me to sit near her.

"Ohh, Roberta," gushed Linda, "I think your conference went wonderfully, don't you?"

"I am very pleased with the turnout, yes. I think we had the right leaders here. We'll have to see if we can manage to dissolve any of the log jams we've been experiencing, dear. Then we can say we had a good meeting. We'll have to see." She spoke to

Linda like a child and Linda seemed to expect it. Dame McGillvray's hand was on top of Linda's in reassurance. "So, my dear, who have you brought me today?"

"This is my husband, Walter Anton, Roberta. He works for Blatchford Steel here in town."

The older lady's face transformed from mildly interested to coldly distrustful in about one eye-blink. I might not have believed the two emotions could intertwine had I not witnessed it. To her credit, however, she did hold out the royal hand for me to touch... or something.

"Thank you for giving me a few moments, Mrs. McGillvray," I offered gentlemanly. She pulled her hand away. "I enjoyed your conference immensely. I am really glad Linda was able to get me in to hear it." I didn't think it possible to lay it on too thick.

"Hmmnnhh," was all she replied, but her face melted slightly.

"May I speak directly for a moment?" Buck private, Anton, was requesting permission from his C-O. She nodded.

"I don't know if you are familiar with Blatchford..."

"I have been aware of your company, Mr. Anton. You are in the old J & L foundry building."

"Yes, yes. Building 18. We've been there for twelve years, now, and we work hard at environmental responsibility, let me assure you." I paused to see if this tack meant anything.

"Yes. Good. I really am on a schedule, Linda." The old dame knew how to marginalize. I was learning to dislike her.

"In any case, madam president, I do have some serious matters to discuss with the Trust, and I think that means I need to discuss them with you. I am not attempting to waste anyone's time." I glared at the regal old broad. She seemed a little taken aback, but also to be sizing me up, not just dismissing me. I waited.

"Mr. Anton, it would seem that your issues would not be appropriate for the few minutes I have left, here. If you care to make an appointment to speak with me, call my office and my assistant will fit you in. How will that be?" She put both hands on her thighs to end the discussion.

It was my turn to size her up. I turned my head to one side and put my hand over my chin. She glared right back at me, but stayed to hear what I might say. "I think we need to set the time right now, Mrs. McGillvray, and I apologize for not being able to allow a lot of leeway. How late could we get together today?" You'd have thought I had jabbed her with a salad fork. Few spoke so directly to her, evidently. Linda's eyes were down.

"I like to schedule my appointments in advance, Mr. Anton. This is very difficult."

"I truly appreciate that, ma'am, I truly do. I would not push for your time if I were not in a very difficult position, myself. You will be doing a great service, and not just for me. A great service. Thank you in advance for helping me with this." I smiled as confidently as I could. The president of the Three Rivers Trust had softened a bit. I now put my hand over hers. She looked at it.

"My last appointment is 3:30… with Senator Fahnstahl." She couldn't help dropping that one. "That may run late; I won't know until then. If you can wait, why not come to the office at four o'clock and when I'm free we can talk."

"That's perfect. I know I've asked for a lot, but after listening to your conference, here today, I know I will be speaking to the right person. Thanks very much for agreeing to meet me." I pumped her hand repeatedly. She was back to her superior frame of mind. I stood and gently pulled Linda to stand with me. "Are you able to leave, Honey?"

Linda nodded. She said softly to Dame McGillvray, "I hope we haven't intruded too much. You're very kind. I'll see you at the next business meeting. Wonderful conference, today.

Wonderful." They hugged just so and Linda walked out with me. As we pushed through the heavy doors she started to give me what-for.

"You were awful to her. Why do you have to be like that when you just met? I was uncomfortable in there, in case you didn't notice." She pulled her elbow away from me. I pulled my lips between my teeth and guided her down the stairs. When we got to the entrance level I led her to a couch-settee thing.

"I know this is weird, but I have been thrust into straightening out some real estate problems for Blatchford and the land is a parcel the Trust is interested in. I'm in a pickle with a tight time frame. I just started yesterday and I already know your Roberta is crucial to my problem. So, I'm sorry... I really am. But I don't think I will disturb your relationships on the Trust. I'll be careful. I appreciate what you did for me."

"I didn't mean I don't want to help you. It's just that most people don't speak to Roberta like that. I'm surprised she will even see you. You're not into real estate stuff! And this is commercial real estate. Why did they pick you, of all people?"

"Honestly? I am still not sure. Let me explain why we even care about real estate…" I gave her the outline of the transfer problem for the oversized bridge components, the importance of upgrading the spur that ran over some empty land that the Trust had some concern about, the PDC, the EPA, congressman Wittenauer and the rest of it.

Linda was shaking her head. "Walt, I've seen these issues move like molasses when everybody thought they were a good ideas! I don't have a part in Trust decisions. *englishclass* likes to have a representative because the head of *englishclass* fancies herself a great urban Utopian. Having me there lets her hobnob with Roberta and other powerful people who back her – people I don't know, frankly. She doesn't want me involved in policy."

"But, Roberta seemed to make allowance for you."

"I make the meetings. I say nice things to everyone; I clap when she does something for which she expects applause. I've never mentioned the Trust because I never do anything important. It's all social, like a perk."

"Well, you did a big favor for me, today. I think your Roberta has enemies, including the mayor, and I need help from the city, too. Hopefully I can find a way to work with the Trust where others at Blatchford have not… even where Wittenauer has not, but I'm on my own. Others scorched the earth ahead of me. Jackson knows how angry I am… how this was dumped on me. But I'm more determined to win this battle than anything I've done at Blatchford. I may not stay at Blatchford after this or I'm going to get a hell of a bonus."

"Well, you're serious." Linda smiled. "I don't know the players in all this, except Roberta… but I'll keep my eyes and ears open. If I think of anyone... Anyway, you've got work to do. If you don't need me with you…"

"No. I mean, that would be nice, but I don't know what I need yet, or where to go next. I'm going to go see if I can talk to the mayor and I may be meeting with Brightman, if I can squeeze it in." We stood up.

"Did you say, 'Brightman?'"

"Yeah. *Brightman Partners*. They're big in real estate. They helped Blatchford get the building we're in, now. So what?"

"Well, Anna Shriver, *englishclass* president… her middle name is 'Brightman.' Maybe there's a connection. That's downright Machiavellian! I love it!" We walked outside.

"I'm going over to *englishclass* before I head home. I'll let you know if I find anything." Linda was agitated for the first time since lunch began. I felt like Mr. Alice-In-Wonderland. Nothing was as it seemed.

I checked my watch. "It's already two o'clock, Lindy, and I've got to see the mayor, if I can. How much trouble will leaving my car cause?"

"You don't have a sticker and there's a two-hour limit without one. Might be a ticket, but it's not a city ticket, so it's up to you. They'll tow you, but usually not until the second time, sooo..."

"I'll chance it. I can walk to City Hall faster." I gave her a big kiss. She pushed me away, but not too firmly. "I know, I know. You are just the greatest. Let's shower together later. It saves water, you know."

Linda smiled and pointed at her watch and toward City Hall, then blew me another kiss. She headed across Forbes Avenue toward *englishclass*. I started down Forbes, speed-walking.

***

"No, miss, I don't have an appointment, but he just left me at the Trust luncheon a half-hour ago. I need to see him about what he said there, so please?" I was plainly exasperated. I learned it from Jack Jackson. The Mayor's office was down a hallway past a conference room. The perky young thing whose job was keeping people away from the mayor, disappeared in that direction after failing to get rid of me.

She came back in minutes with her eyes looking daggers while her lips smiled, sort-of. "He'll see you, Mr. Anton, but he says he doesn't remember you from the luncheon, so your visit might be pretty brief. Good luck... you'll need it." She waved me down the little hall.

The double-doors and frame leading into the mayor's office were much nicer than standard issue. Light blond, fine-grained wood and beveled glass panes were framed by stainless steel light fixtures, a nice touch for the mayor of Steel City. I walked through the doors like I owned the place, but, for all I knew, Blatchford had pissed this guy off, too.

I wasn't in the mayor's office... quite. A carefully primped woman stood from her pristine desk to greet me. She held out her hand. "How do you do, Mr. Anton? Blatchford Steel Services, isn't it?" I was impressed she knew that.

"Yes, in fact, I'm fine; how did you know I work at Blatchford?" She shook my hand firmly. The brass name plate said "Maureen Bailey."

"Oh, well, Blatchford is an important employer and important to Pittsburgh and we are always open to help our major businesses. I know Harry wants to be available. He is managing to see you in the midst of a very tight schedule, so please realize there are others who need his time today, as well." Her smile was like a stainless steel trap. I was happier to be meeting with the mayor. She sat but didn't offer a chair... there wasn't one. When you were waiting to see the big man you obviously did it in the outer lobby.

Suddenly the solid, blond, tight-grained and plainly heavy door to Mr. Mayor's office swung open and Harry McKay's smile lit up the ante-room. "Walter, I'm busy but not too busy to help Blatchford! C'mon in, c'mon in, for Heaven's sake." He grabbed my hand and pumped it firmly. "So," he continued, "how in hell are ya? Nice luncheon, I thought today, huh?" The door closed with a soft 'thunk.'

"So, have a seat, have a seat. Take a load off, we used to say, huh?" This guy was an old asshole buddy that I'd simply never met. "You want a coffee? No? Or maybe something more suited to a Friday afternoon? Believe it or not, I've got Old Overholt, here. Smells just like the freshening woods in Springtime. It sure does. Or a soft drink?" I was slow to commit to a beverage, which seemed to trouble him somewhat. "C'mon, Walter, join me with some Overholt. If you've never tried it I know you'll love it. It's bonded, ya know. They first made it in Broad Ford, just south of right here."

I smiled and nodded. "Straight up... maybe a Coke chaser?" Sometimes it was good to accept refreshment. Restored old friendships you hadn't yet made.

"Sure, absolutely. I wouldn't let you put Overholt *in* a coke. Just take a little sip and sniff the aroma. In fact I'll put it in a wine glass. Swish it around. It's the best rye whiskey made." He poured it out and handed me a can of cold Coke. "You need another glass?"

I shook my head and lifted the wine glass toward him in a salute of thanks. He did the same and downed his shot in a blink. He poured another and carried it behind his desk and sat down. He spread his large hands flat onto the leather-trimmed blotter. "So, what is so damn crucial we had to meet right now, today? It's Walter, isn't it? What do you do for Blatchford, Walter?"

"I add up numbers, Mr. Mayor. It's Harry, isn't it?" His face blanched but his expression stayed friendly. "Yuh, Harry. Call me Harry. Sure."

"The reason I'm here, and in a severe hurry, I'm afraid, is that Blatchford has the primary option on a big, job-creating contract that we might lose, believe it or not, without your very crucial help. I can't overstate the importance and value of this contract for Blatchford now and into the future. There are upwards of fifty... fifty new jobs, Mr. Mayor, but I am forced by circumstances to move quickly. That's why I pressed to see you. After your very lucid speech at the luncheon, I knew that you were maybe the only speaker worth talking to. Here I am." I sipped my whiskey and smelled the fresh woods in Springtime. The son of a gun was right about that. The mayor's hands were fidgeting.

"What circumstances, Walter? You are in a hurry to do what, exactly?" He'd stopped fidgeting and his hands were steepled in front of his face, keeping them still, perhaps. He sat back in demand of an answer.

"I've got to clear a path to upgrade the rail spur that runs from the mill building we're in, down to a quay on the Monongahela. Do you know where I mean? Next to a new housing project? The land is just sitting there, empty." McKay's lips were compressed to two thin lines.

He sat forward. "Just what the fuck are you up to?"

I sat back as if offended. I tried to not change my expression, but I could feel my skin blushing. I waited to speak until I processed his sudden mood. I swirled my drink and looked at the glass. I took another sip.

"I really admire your choice of whiskey, Harry," I said, "but I don't feel very good about your being pissed off at me, all of a sudden. Maybe you can tell me what I stepped in and we can work together from there." I sipped again. McKay sat back but his whole expression changed. He was back to fidgeting. Probably his harsh obscenities usually got people to bend to his will, at least once. He was unsure what to do with me. He certainly had some history with Parcel 840. I hoped he was as straightforward as he'd sounded at lunch.

"How much do you know about this land, Walter? What have you had to do with negotiations, so far?" His words were measured. He downed the second shot of Overholt, clunked the shot glass down and crossed his arms.

"Yesterday, Harry, I attended an unusual meeting at Blatchford. Our great Congressman was there along with the two Blatchfords, my boss and other top dogs. I reported on potential expenses of preparing to execute the contract and the idea of buying a piece of land near the spur came up – from Wittenauer

– and I claimed that we would have a number for the cost of obtaining that land by today. Clearly I didn't know what in Hell I was talking about, but I was trying to make my boss look good to his boss. The next thing I knew, Old Man Blatchford was telling me to get on that number right away and to get back to him. So, I chased around the city and found out the Trust is involved somehow. This morning I figured out that I was at the tail end of some kind of screw-up, but I am determined to solve this. It's not my job, but it is my job. I do believe this contract is good for everyone, including the city, so I've got to find a path to upgrading that railbed. I very much need your help and here I am." I finished my whiskey, too. Then I folded my arms behind my head and waited.

Harry McKay stood up and walked over to the windows that overlooked the new Downtown and the Point beyond. "You're a sonofabitch, you know that?"

"I don't buy that, Harry, but what is your history with these negotiations? Must be a doozy." I stood up, too, but I stayed near my chair.

"How well do you know our wonderful U. S. rep?"

"I shook hands with him yesterday, didn't speak to him, and listened to him at lunch time. I've never paid a lot of attention to politics, tell you the truth."

"He's a Republican. Did you know that?"

"Well, I must have heard that, but, like I said, I don't know him. What difference does that make?"

"He thinks he shits pink marshmallow fluff."

I laughed in spite of myself. "You have a way with words, mayor. I guess you have history with him?"

"Look, Walt, when we run for office in the city it's basically non-partisan. But I'm a Democrat, I don't hide it and frankly I don't think a Republican could get elected mayor here. Wittenauer thinks he pulled some kind of coup by getting elected in Allegheny County as a Republican. Big damn deal. Trouble is, instead of working with the city to solve problems, he spends too much effort pushing us to go along with him. No matter what we need from the feds, Wittenauer tries to impose his ideas on how to run the city. He can pull a lot of strings and we are forced to accommodate him. Sometimes in very picayune, niggling pain-in-the-ass ways… stuff that helps him pad his relationship with big supporters. At worst, it screws up applications we have for federal funding that we ought to be able to take quick advantage of. He's a shit, if you ask me." McKay was clearly frustrated. He looked angry.

"Wow. Well then, okay." I looked around trying to find an idea about how to proceed. "Harry, if I had to guess I would say that the Blatchfords are tight in our congressman's corner."

"I believe you are correct about that. I haven't done much that involves the Blatchfords. I gave the old man a proclamation when the Chamber gave him the Steel Citizenship Award a couple years ago, but I don't think he's ever needed me for anything." He stopped walking around and sat down again. Maybe he was ready to talk business. "What are you, yourself?"

"Me? What?"

"Democrat, Republican, Independent? You must be something. You do vote, I hope."

"Oh, sure. Of course I do. I grew up in a Republican home and I registered that way and have never changed. It hasn't meant a whole lot to me, although I usually vote for Republicans."

"All right, we understand each other. My dad was a union man. Probably forged steel in the building you work in. I felt the pain of every union man who lost his job over the past thirty years. When I got out of Central Catholic in 1970 it was clear that my generation wasn't going to follow its fathers in the steel business. My parents were adamant that my brother and I were going to college. First generation in my family. You wanna know how my father ended up? As a night watchman at a shopping center. Part of the land it sits on was mill property. He died about a year after retiring for the second time, bitter to the end. The world he knew had disappeared. Whether it was foreign steel, environmental regulations, he didn't really know or understand. He just saw his city dying and his friends losing their jobs and homes. When they tore down East Liberty it broke his heart. Those were Democrats pushing urban renewal and he couldn't understand why they weren't watching out for the little guy anymore."

I shook my head, unable to add anything.

"After college I went to law school at Pitt. Then I went to work for Mellon Bank as a staff attorney on commercial lending projects. It was scary listening to these people carving up pieces of cities and towns and people's lives. I hated it. When the chance came to run for city Council, I took it. I made it and made what I think were the right associations and with lots of help and some very good luck, I became mayor. Most days I love this job. I've been able to guide changes for the better, I think. When I look at businesses I don't see the business, itself, I see jobs. If I can get Pittsburgh to make it possible for more people to have a good job, that's what I'll do." He leaned back and stretched. I had just heard his basic stump speech, I thought. But I also thought I might have an ally in my battle. He continued, "So fuck all that stuff. Here we are. You have a rather sticky piece of business and right now I'm not clear on what you – or I – can do about it.

"Your buddy, Wittenauer, was in here a month ago trying to pull that rabbit out of *his* ass. He was going to get some deal out of the EPA if I would just get the Development Commission to let him work his magic so Blatchford could run his railroad. Part of the deal also involved some UDAG grants that we were slated to get, that could be delayed until after the next mayoral election if he, Wittenauer, wasn't able to engineer free access to that strip of wasteland where your railroad is. If you want to know how to get no cooperation from me, just threaten my city. That prick doesn't care about the improved neighborhood environments those grants would help us accomplish, or about the new fire equipment they made possible. He only cares about winning something for his Republican friends… in this case Harold Blatchford. I almost think those two hold each other's dicks in the men's room."

I sat for a minute. "Can you help me with this, regardless of Blatchford and Wittenauer?"

He raised his eyebrows and looked at me all over again. "I like that: cut the bullshit, mayor, let's do some business. Pretty good, Walt. Okay. Here's what's on the table as I see it. First, how many jobs are we really looking at here?"

"Like I said, I add up numbers. I don't do the human resources stuff, but I know the numbers. It looks like a solid forty full-time positions. But that's just in-house. There will be work to refurb the railbed – good union jobs – there'll be work on the river, too. The best part as far as Blatchford Steel is concerned is that we'll be able to bid much larger jobs because of the improvements we'll be making to our shop. Whether we'll need the spur in future work, I don't know. Long term job prospects are pretty good for Blatchford. We'll have the capacity only three or four other steel services companies have in the U. S. and Europe. Seems to me it's worth doing on all fronts. So why not?"

"Alright, Walter. That's a good case. Now I'm gonna say something you can't share. Give me your word…"

"Okay," I nodded.

"Somehow, I don't want Wittenauer to get any credit for this. I have some ideas but you'll be on the spot so tell me you'll help me on that score." I nodded again and reached across to shake his hand.

"Good, good, Walt. Now, I have to explain that I don't run the PDC. I do have some influence, but I don't always get what I want, either. It looks to me that that's where I can help you the most."

"Awright, I can see that. But the other fly in the ointment is the Trust. I'm gonna meet Roberta McGillvray at four, but I don't know what drives her in this, at all. I don't even know how they have anything to say about land they don't own, anyway."

"Well, that's kind of interesting, as a matter of fact. The Three Rivers Trust developed out of the first wave of, quote, "renewal" in the fifties. As people tried to fight the federal bulldozers some of the city's elites – especially the wives – tried, little by little, to insert themselves into the urban renewal planning. It took them a while to have much effect, but eventually they gained enough political sway to get candidates to seek it. They had no ownership baggage; they weren't trying to gain development rights – at least not back then – and they began to be asked their opinion on this or that renewal or redevelopment idea. Eventually, if the Trust hated an idea, it would be withdrawn. If they liked it, every politician who could gain something would shout their praises to the rooftops. Supposedly they're non-political, but they're the best politicians in the city."

"So who are the big powers in the Trust. Is it really Dame McGillvray? It looks like everybody kisses her ring."

"Well, she's formidable, make no mistake. You won't be able to go behind her back to her supporters. They won't do anything to thwart her, at least not that you could see. She's a granddaughter of one of the early railroad families, and was married briefly before being widowed. She knows business, she knows money and she's become a damn good power broker. If she's not happy it can be very hard to get a project permitted.

"Over the past fifteen years or so the Trust has brought in some young dreamers who just can't stop turning out pretty renditions of what some piece of land should look like. They file these plans with HUD or with the Pennsylvania Department of Urban Planning and even with the EPA. It's sort of first-come, first-served. The Trust gets some level of approval for the land-use and keeps renewing it. When they get wind of some developer's plans that may abut their plan or include it – and they always do – they sit down with them and offer to grease the skids for their project so long as it includes these other plans that are, as luck would have it, already approved. They form a consulting partnership with the developer, get their dreams turned into reality, and some nice fees for planning and "permit facilitation."

"Lately they have arranged for some land swaps for their political support for projects. Amazingly, they always get financing for whatever they want to do. Mostly they're parks and fountains, sculptures, rock gardens… you know. Different people and foundations donate to them, both land and money. Of course they're non-profit, but if they were a business, they'd be paying taxes.

"So maybe that's your picture of the Trust? If you want to do something with Parcel 840, they're gonna have to agree with what you want to do. Since you're not a developer you don't have plans that intersect with something they've dreamed up, but you also don't need to get construction financing or building permits they usually get paid for. How are you going to bribe them to help you?" McKay steepled his hands and smiled. Our meeting hadn't conflicted with anyone else that I could see, and it had gone on longer than I'd planned. I looked at my watch and was shocked to see that it was already ten minutes of four.

"I don't know, Harry. If I miss my date with Roberta I may never find out. Listen I have to literally run to the Trust's offices. I will speak to you about what I learn this afternoon. And I want to thank you for being so… ahmm… regular, I guess. I decided I liked you when I heard you at lunch. I think I still do."

McKay came around his desk and shook hands with me. I apologized again and scooted out through his outer office and ran to the elevators. It was four o'clock when I hit the sidewalk and took off west, in a jog. Smithfield Street was a block west and two blocks north.

I half ran. I'd pushed to see her and now I was late. Damn, damn and double-damn. I ran more. Three Rivers Trust had a storefront where they displayed dreamy renderings. On cheap easels. Two floors up were the offices. I hustled up the stairs. My breath was coming in gasps when I walked into the reception area. It was empty, but the door was open, so I might still be in luck. I called out.

"Helloo-oo. Mrs. McGillvray! It's Walter Anton. Sorry I'm late!" I could hear some movement but no one came forward. I sat down and waited.

The waiting area was utilitarian. A multi-colored street map of Downtown was framed on the facing wall. To the right were a couple dozen plaques and photos showing Roberta McGillvray cutting a ribbon or holding a shiny shovel with one mayor or another and various important people. I stood and read the legends on the photos. You never knew.

"I'm not married, Mr. Anton," her voice caught me in total surprise. I jumped and turned, almost stumbling. "Please call me Roberta if we meet again." I felt like a grade-school student.

"Yes, ma'am. My apologies. Linda and I have never spoken about the Trust before today. There's a lot I have to learn. Thank you very much for seeing me." I walked toward her.

"It will be a few more minutes, I'm afraid. Please make yourself comfortable. I can let you make yourself some coffee, if you like."

"No, no thanks. I'm fine. Please... take your time. I'm fine."

"I always do. Thank you for waiting." She walked back to a rear office and a door closed. I read some more about the photos and eventually sat down again. By the time Roberta's meeting was over, I was dozing. A door opening and a flurry of words stirred me awake. I stood up to clear the cobwebs. Senator Fahnstahl was still speaking as he walked with Dame McGillvray.

"...when I get back to D. C. Don't commit to anything for a couple of days. We should get some good movement by then. I'll send you a fax as soon as I know."

"I can't be hanging, here. I'll do something by Thursday or the choice will be out of my hands anyway."

"Don't fret. Thanks for the libations. I'll be back to D. C. Sunday. Great to see you again." When he turned he noticed me for the first time and stopped moving for a second. He looked like he'd revealed a state secret. I smiled at him, enjoying his discomfort. I could see he was repeating mentally what I might have heard. Abruptly he put on his campaign face and extended his hand toward me. "And hello, ahh...Mr....umm..."

"Anton, Walter Anton. I saw you at lunch, today." I nodded my head up and down as if to remind him that of course he knew me.

"Oh, of course. Good to see you again, Walter. How ya doin? Everything okay?" He had his other hand on my forearm to emphasize his thrilled-ness. I tried to look just as excited. He gave our hostess a quick hug and kiss on the cheek, half-waved at me and was out the door in one move.

"Well, Mr. Anton. I'm all ears. I hope I'm worth the wait. Actually, I hope you are, too. C'mon." She started back and then stopped and locked the front door. There were two offices and a big room with a table and more easels, a transparency projector and some big pads of drawing paper. We turned left and stepped into a much fancier room that was ordered and neat. Roberta's desk was a thick plate of glass on two marble pillars. Her phone sat on a credenza. Several lateral files along the wall faced her desk. On a round table in the center of the room was a plastic covered model of the Gateway Center with a brass plaque that showed the name of the architects and the date, 1953.

"Okay, Mr. Anton, you wouldn't be here if I didn't know and like Linda so well. What do you, or what does Blatchford, need from me? Are you trying to resurrect Parcel 840?"

"Whoa. You make it sound like it's dead and buried. I am very late to this game and I don't know what you know about what others have tried to do with this land or tried to get you to do or anything else. I'll tell you everything I know but I have a feeling that my role here is as student, not teacher." I wasn't sure what to think about Roberta McGillvray or the Trust.

"You should know up front, Walter, that you aren't going to slip something by us. Who has actually sent you to talk to me?"

She was pushing back before I even made a case. This might not be fun. "In the immediate sense, Roberta, no one..." She started to sit up straighter and raise her hand to argue with that. "...wait a minute... just a minute..." I held up my hands like a traffic cop, "...I said 'in the immediate sense.' Obviously I'm here representing Blatchford Steel Services. I'm not a fool. Maybe it would be more fair if you told me who you are representing."

If you've ever seen a cartoon where the aggrieved blowhard turns red like a thermometer – that's what I was watching. I have to give her credit for not throwing something at me – consequence of a clean desk. "I am the president of the Three Rivers Trust, Mr. Anton. No one tells me what to do." Her words were measured. She could have pounded the table between them.

"You can't come in here and expect to be welcomed with open arms after your bosses did such a dirty job of offending me and the Trust." She leaned onto the glass with both elbows, clasping her hands in front of her. I hoped she didn't have X-ray vision. My heart was beating a mile a minute.

"I am here because I need your help, Roberta. I have a task to accomplish for my employer. If I succeed it will generate forty or more new jobs, expand Blatchford's business into the future, and, I hope, benefit the Trust and the City. From what I've learned in two days, you, Madame President, are the one person that can tell me how that benefit can manifest. So, let's talk."

"Why have they sent you, this time?"

"Actually, nobody told me to come here or anywhere. I wound up with the job of providing the cost estimate for upgrading the rail spur on what I have learned is called 'Parcel 840.' A certain Tom Wittenauer …" McGillvray scrunched her face like she'd spit up into her mouth. "…who you may know, suggested that Blatchford purchase some land to give to the Trust for a park or something, in order to gain your support for our plans. I have had no input in any previous discussions, and hadn't even a hint of them until yesterday morning. Now I have enough authority, since everything else has failed, to get something done and I've even mapped out a price range. Maybe you should tell me what was done already."

"Are you a Republican, Mr. Anton?"

"Yes, but why is that important? You're the second person today to ask me that."

"Really? What did you tell the other one?"

"I told him I wasn't very political...that I was born Republican. He was proud to be a Democrat and we got along just swimmingly. I am not here to..." She held up one hand.

"That sonofabitch, Wittenauer, is Republican and so is the esteemed Hal Blatchford. I need to know if you're trying to win at their game when they couldn't. What is it?"

"What is what? The game? I don't have time for games. I'm here to see what the Trust needs to enable us to use that rail spur. There's nothing else."

"Hmmnnh, you say. Oookaay, let's assume you are as pure as you sound. What are you prepared to do for the Trust?" She leaned back and crossed her legs. I don't think she expected to like my offer.

"I think you're a little too quick to jump to the price, here. I found that this parcel is listed by the PDC, and that it has EPA file numbers on it. Just pleasing the Trust doesn't solve all my problems. Can you tell me what your hopes are for that land? No dark secrets in that, are there?"

"No." She seemed to be considering how much to share with me. She got up and walked to the big room across the hall. I didn't know whether to follow, but that was resolved in a moment.

"In here, Walter." What the Hell.

A cute rendering was spread out on the conference table. If I hadn't looked at the PDC map I wouldn't have recognized that it was Parcel 840. The housing project looked like the most beautiful garden apartments; all of its denizens were slender and well-dressed. Around the building were lots of basketball-trees and green-colored lawns and play areas. It looked like a stone retaining wall snaked along where the bridge interchange ran on the other side of the space. There was a pond I hadn't noticed, with walkways and basketball-trees and a fountain with little kids in it. I didn't see any railroad tracks... none.

"Pretty," I said. "Where is it?"

"Oh, that's your parcel, Walter. We like it better as a people-place. It's a wasteland, now... a filthy, polluted wasteland, and dangerous for children, especially."

"Looks like we're pretty far apart on the use of this land, wouldn't you say?"

"Ohh, many yards, Walter, many, many yards. Your buddies tried to freeze us out of the planning for this parcel. Tried an end run. Trouble was, they stepped out of bounds, so, no touchdown on their play. Not even a field goal. And it was fourth down, Mr. Anton. They turned the ball over! Now it's our turn to score and you want me to reset the clock so you can run another play?" She was shaking her head, pursing her lips – everything but wagging her finger at me.

"Madame President, I don't have any pull in this city. I have no powerful interests backing me. I'm not a player... I'm an employee of Blatchford Steel Services. We make steel girders and prefabricated steel components for a host of purposes. To do this we employee almost one hundred people – taxpayers, homeowners, parents, all. Good folks doing valuable work. We have an opportunity that our contract negotiators have been working on for three years. It involves making custom designed steel arches for the King Frederik Bridge in Denmark. We have won out over four larger fabricators. To not lose our five and a half million bid bond, we must commit to perform under the contract by July first, just forty-four days from now. If we can make that commitment we will begin hiring upwards of forty new employees and purchasing a lot of new hardware and refitting our shop. There is only one element of our ability to grow with this contract, that we have no control over. And for that I must appeal to you and to the Trust."

"I'm very flattered that you think we are so important to your success, Mr. Anton. You heard me at lunch when I explained our mission. We have no secrets. If something happens to Parcel 840 the Trust is determined that it will not remain a blight on the cityscape, that it will not remain a wasteland. You want it to be a railroad and you're probably perfectly happy to have it remain a wasteland as long as your choo-choo trains can run through it. Our goals are different."

I kept quiet for a few minutes and studied the drawing. It looked like it had been done on the same basic plot plan I had a copy of. The outlines were all the same. The railbed was simply whited out along with the few poles and culverts associated with it. The colorful rendering didn't completely obliterate the original building lines. I looked at it for another minute. "We have some money to commit to our end of this effort, Roberta. It seems to me that with our resources and your planning we ought to be able to both use this land. Can you see this as possible... at all?" Her head had been turning from side to side just a little, while I spoke.

"I don't. How can we have a railroad track, of all things, cutting a scar through the middle of this potentially beautiful park? You'll be cutting off half of the space from access by neighbors and children. That is a very, very high price to pay for this neighborhood. Do you realize that children in these buildings have to cross two busy streets to get to play areas?"

I shook my head. "I think I've kept you long enough, Roberta, and you have been very generous to give me this time. All I ask is that you meet with me at least once more. Can we do that?"

I stood, waiting, as she started to take short steps toward the hallway. Her head was down and she was thinking, evidently, about what to do with me. At least I hoped that's what she was thinking.

"I will have to buy a lot of what you're trying to sell me, but, yes, I will meet with you again. You should know that we have preliminary approval on our design for Parcel 840, from Pennsylvania Urban Planning. There's also the EPA problem. We don't know how costly that will be." She turned the tumbler to unlock the door. "Until next time, then, Mr. Anton?" She held out her hand. It could have been to kiss or shake. I shook.

"Thanks, again, Roberta. You haven't wasted this time and I won't waste your time the next time, either." She just smiled. I turned to the stairs. It was after five o'clock.

***

"Hank, it's Roberta. What do we have on Blatchford Steel? And while you're at it, see if there's something on a guy named Walter Anton. He works there. His wife works for *englishclass publishing*. Thanks. Fax it over if you get something we can use. Okay. You too. Bye."

Roberta McGillvray closed the office of the Trust. Lights off, door locked. She rode the elevator to the garage level. Her Mercedes was waiting just two spaces from the elevator. She pressed a button and the motor started. Not new, the S-Class 450 was in immaculate condition. In nine years it had accumulated twenty-six thousand miles. She placed her bag on the passenger seat and looked at all three mirrors before backing. Slowly she pulled up the ramp to Oliver Avenue, turned left onto Wood and onto the Penn-Lincoln heading east. Three miles later she ramped right, before the Squirrel Hill Tunnel and then a short way along Beechwood Boulevard. Within eighteen minutes of leaving her office she pushed the button on her dash to open a simple gate. When the yellow light came on she pulled through. As soon as the car passed a treadle the gate began to roll back. She drove up to the brownstone house.

As she ascended the steps to the spotless front door, it opened and a well-dressed man came out to greet her. "Good evening, madam. Dinner will be ready at six. Your tray is in the solarium."

"Thank you, Wallace." She walked through the foyer and down two steps to a rear hallway. Her steps were soundless on the long carpet runner. On a narrow table in the angular solarium were her glass of merlot, a folded napkin and a small dish of bon-bons. She sat on a tightly upholstered love seat that faced west toward the city, where the tallest buildings were just visible.

Wallace Hoagland drove the Mercedes to the car barn. He took a few swipes at some dust on the lower part of the fenders. From the small cabinet just to the left of the white, swinging doors, he took a small brush and carefully brushed the driver's seat, all in one direction. Then he took a bottle of window cleaner and a clean wipe and cleaned the mirrors and the driver's window and the windshield. He stowed the cleaning materials, shut the two doors and walked briskly to the kitchen door, where he dropped the car keys onto the morning tray and resumed preparations for the dinner he would serve on time, at six.

***

I took my time back to my car. Had I gained anything? I didn't think I had displayed the sinking fear I felt when Roberta showed me the Trust's idea of Parcel 840 with no track in it. At least I knew how wide the gulf was. The color rendering was dated three years earlier. The Trust had been sitting on its grand design for a while. The more I thought about it the more logical it became that the Trust was not about to put out its own money to transform Parcel 840. Nor would they buy that land because it probably had no commercial or residential resale value. Plus, the EPA problems would make any charitable desire to beautify some acreage too costly to realize. If I were cagey I might have figured how to take advantage of Parcel 840's uselessness.

The sun was getting low when I arrived at my car. Stuck in the rubbery seal of the driver's window was a warning from *Iron-Clad Security, Inc.* that the lot was for University business only and that my license plate had been recorded so that any subsequent unauthorized use of this or other parking facilities on the campus would result in the vehicle being towed. Any questions could be directed to Campus Security in room 12b of the Public Safety Building on Stevenson Street. Thank you for visiting Duquesne University. I scrunched the small paper and tossed it on the floor. I would mooch parking somewhere else.

I drove through the campus, past the Public Safety Building, and around the edge of the huge property. It's nice to be able to drive home in the light. There's some day left and I have more energy later into the evening. The tough part is having the sun setting right in the mirrors. I tend to stay in the two right lanes on the interstates. If there are only two lanes, I'm in the right one. So I couldn't figure the guy who kept tight up behind me, driving like I was the main impediment to the rest of his evening. There was no lane farther right. From time to time I pulled left to let cars merge.

Just east of exit two to Pitt, I completed a left shift and pulled back into the right lane only to find the same pickup tucking in behind me in the right lane. I heard a horn farther back. He was tailgating so closely I couldn't see his grill emblem. I kept moving my eyes to look in the rearview mirror and he hung tight behind me. I couldn't see his face. He was glued to me through the Squirrel Hill.

Fortunately I don't have a long ride. I started signaling a half-mile before Rodi Road to make sure the idiot wouldn't be surprised. For all I knew, he couldn't see my taillights. When I started to shift toward the ramp the bastard started honking at me and even drifted right as if he were taking the same ramp. I sped up a little to pull away from him but he accelerated, too. At the last second he zipped left to miss the divider. Drivers honked as he wedged his way back into the line of cars. I slowed quickly as the ramp sloped to a stop sign.

What the Hell was that all about? I didn't cut anyone off. I mentally kicked myself for not getting the plate. At the very least someone should report him... could've caused a bad crash in that traffic. But the day's worries were melting away, including a crappy driver. In a few minutes I looped up onto Jefferson to our little Cape on Mapleledge.

I parked next to Linda. A light was on over the kitchen sink. I flipped on the hall light and noticed a piece of wrapping paper on the little half-round. "Dinner at Elly's" was written in Magic Marker. I quickly changed out of my suit and put on chinos and a soft long-sleeve pullover. I grabbed a bottle of red wine and crossed to the Maxwells. Every light was on.

"Hi, Honey!" Linda called as I raised my hand to knock on the screen door. She met me with a kiss and called out, "Okay, Elly, Walt's here!" She seemed bouncy and excited. I decided to rev up my own mood and shuck off the weight of a weird day.

"Well, this is a nice surprise! I was thinking we could flip a coin for frozen pizza or some restaurant. This is much nicer." I gave her a big hug and lifted her off the floor. She licked my face. "Oh, hi, Elly! Thanks for having us over."

Elly Maxwell sashayed over to us and gave us both a quick kiss and hug. There were wonderful smells emanating from her kitchen. A little salt, plenty of garlic, onions and celery and... umm, let's see...anise, I thought. She dished out perfect steamed rice. There was salad with slivered almonds, grape tomatoes, broccoli florets, spinach and arugula. Finally she removed a standing rack of lamb. I sniffed deeply.

"Elly, is that anise?"

"Yes, do you like it? I had it once and I thought I'd try it. I was worried you might think it out of place."

"No, it's great. I'm gonna use it someday. I'm starved. Mmmnnh, mmm, mmnh." I set the salad on her dining room table and went back to help remove the roast. It was on a wire rack with lots of juice in the pan. She had a strainer on a sauce pan. I took the roaster with oven mitts and poured the liquid through.

To that she added a cup of port wine, some cornstarch and a teaspoon of raw honey. This was brought to a quick simmer. I stirred it constantly with a whisk. I took a tiny taste and the anise overtone was just enough to announce itself – a master touch. Elly opened the wine and poured some water for each of us. A cruet held fresh Italian dressing.

We sat down and I carved. The lamb was done to a crusty pink medium. I cut us each a rib chop and we served ourselves rice and salad. There was garlic bread with pesto. I was in Heaven.

Linda sat next to me with Elly about directly across. As we ate I evaluated Elly's comfy-looking bosom. The more I looked, the more she had no brassiere. I couldn't make out nipples, but the breasts were not as firm as usual. I wondered how they didn't sag. Worth some study.

I couldn't really see Linda's chest, beside me, without being completely obtuse. I glanced, fruitlessly. For some reason, I began to picture both women with tops and no bottoms. I wondered how the creases at Elly's hips would compare to Linda's. As I imagined details I ended up staring at the center of the table as if I could see through it. I wondered if she shaved, too. Did women talk about things like that? I knew men didn't, or not to me, anyway. But I could imagine men talking about women's shaving. I forgot I was eating.

"Walt! Walt. Earth to Walt… come in please!" Linda poked me in the side.

"Huh? Whasamatta?" I jerked upright and looked around. Elly looked up through her bangs and smiled. Linda giggled and asked, "Where did you drift off to? Aren't you hungry?"

"What? No, of course! This meal is terrific." I resumed chewing.

"Well, then, the meat on your fork will be cold." I had zoned out with a bite of Elly's lamb hanging in mid-air.

"Jeez, I'm sorry. It's been a tough one. I already had a hard day before we met at lunch time. After that I had two tough meetings. Why, it's lucky I made it home! I hope you're both glad to see me!" I smiled… leered… at both of them.

"You'll have to tell me about it, Honey," Linda sighed. "But show your hostess some gratitude."

"I'm eating, I'm eating," I mumbled with lamb in my mouth.

"Don't rush, Walter," protested Elly. "Whatever's left will keep. Sip a little wine… it's good for the digestion." Elly leaned back sipping her own wine, her nipples more present. I am often surprised by my ability – willingness – to multi-task.

Finally, I couldn't finish. My eyes were closing. It was only seven. The past two days were the hardest I'd had for as long as I could remember. I walked around the table and gave Elly a little peck on the cheek. Linda hugged me hard at the door. "I'm going to shower and see if it wakes me up."

"I'm going to finish up with Elly, Walt. I'll be along."

As I backed toward the front door I got a good look at Linda's chest, too. No nipples, but definitely a softer outline. I suppose that bras are uncomfortable. No sense wearing them if you don't have to. I shuffled back to our Cape and shucked my shoes, then the rest of my clothes. I hung things up, mostly, and slipped into the shower and started to review the day. I'd met people I'd never bothered with and things felt different. At the same time, a lot of people had met me, too, and were going to have to deal with me for the first time... should I manage to figure out what action to take. Man, I was bushed.

I was zonked when Linda came in. I hadn't bothered with underwear. I may have heard her in the bathroom but was asleep again when she slid under the covers. She hadn't bothered with any underwear either, I could tell. She leaned on my shoulder and kissed me, at which point I decided being awake would be all right. I started to raise myself up on one elbow but she pushed me back down.

"Don't do a thing, Honey. I'll take care of you this time."

SATURDAY, MAY 18, 1985

It was cloudy… misty. Visibility was low, everything dripping wet, yet not raining. A front had moved in with cooler, humid air. We often had this when fronts moved up the slopes in the Alleghenies: the midst of a cloud.

Linda had made-from-scratch hotcakes, grilled leftover ham, pan-fries with onions and dropped eggs. The smells lifted me, pulled me into my bathrobe and slippers, and dragged me into the kitchen. I sat with coffee in the little nook opposite the stove. Lindy preferred the chair, anyway, in case of drafts. This was one of those Saturday mornings that brokers used for selling houses with small kitchens. I felt good. Every problem I'd dragged from work into Friday night, seemed containable, even solvable. I turned the pages of the Gazette.

"How ya doin, Sweetie?" Linda called over her shoulder as she manipulated pans and spoons. I couldn't believe I'd sat without hugging her.

"Fabulous, my little cherubim," said W. C. Fields, as I embraced her from behind, grabbing a pleasant feel as I did so. I kissed her neck. "Baby, you're the greatest!" Now, Jackie Gleason.

"Well sit, sit. This is just… about… ready." She held a dinner plate with two hotcakes, ham and potatoes opposite, and a cup with two dropped eggs in between. A few seconds later she placed a carafe of warm syrup.

"Wow! Perfect. I'm not touching it until you're here, too."

"Just a sec." And a minute later she had a plate of smaller amounts in front of her as she smiled one of those smiles that makes me feel better about everything. Indescribable. I managed to eat.

Within minutes we worked our way to the hotcakes, which were more than either of us needed. They were good. I couldn't push them away. Linda shifted her position from sitting with one leg under her to sitting with one knee under her chin and she reached around to get bites of hotcake. It was more than enticing. Her multi-layer wrap fell open revealingly. Plus, her leg was bare. I was forgetting the flavors in my mouth.

"What did you do after we split, yesterday? Did you meet with Roberta?" She picked at her plate; her eyes were down. "How did that go? Do you like her?"

"I like you. I know that much." This got her to look up and observe that my eyes were fixed on her breasts. She pulled the cloth around her.

"Can't you control yourself?"

"I am... we're still sitting here." I took a bite.

Linda hopped up and brought the coffee over to the table. She poured with one hand, holding her robe tight. "Listen, I really want to help with the Trust, but I need to know where you're at. What progress have you made or what's your roadblock ... that's what I'm asking."

"Hey! It's Saturday, Sweetie. Why don't we just get naked and talk business sometime after that?" I gave her my best eyebrow raising. Deep down it was wishfulness. Linda never let something go once she focused on it.

"There's a time for everything, mister. I thought you were up against a tight timeline. I did some homework, yesterday, too. I want to see where we are, so far. C'mon, now."

"Okay, all right." I held up my hands in defeat. "I tell you mine if you tell me yours... and you don't have to wear any more than you are right now, deal?"

"Maybe. Okay. I know you were seeing Roberta, but did you get to see the mayor?" From someplace she produced a pad of lined paper.

"Yeah, I did. And you know? I kinda like him! He seemed genuine and we got along for more than an hour. He really believes in Pittsburgh, and he wants what he thinks is good for the city." I poured coffee. "Or else I'm a sucker for political propaganda. But I think he was genuine."

"What is he going to do for you? Did you ask him to do anything specific?"

I raised my voice at that. "How the Hell should I know? I don't know what to ask any of these people to do!... I don't know. Shit." I was shaking my head, holding it in both hands. "Aw, jeez. I'm sorry, Lindy. It got so late and I had to meet Roberta. But I got sucked in to this and I don't know what to do. I act like I do, but I don't."

"I know, I know, but that's okay. That might be an advantage. People will let things drop in front of you. They're used to dealing with real estate sharpies, big-time developers who are always playing people. Everyone's looking for some political angle. You haven't got a political bone in your body. I think it could be a big advantage, anyway." She made two columns: one labeled "Plus," the other, simply "Minus."

"Okay, then," she said, adjusting her butt on the chair and preparing to do serious mental work, "since yesterday morning, what do you think was negative and what seems to be heading towards a solution to... to what, exactly?"

I shifted around, myself. "Well, the main goal is to upgrade the railbed and tracks that run through what is designated as

Parcel 840, so that Blatchford can use that run for about a year. The simplest way to do that is what would be best, overall."

"Okay. So what was the first negative thing that happened?" Linda had her pencil poised for my powerful thoughts.

"That's easy. The most negative was that I got pulled in on a meeting where I got handed the primary responsibility for obtaining just those permissions or licenses or whatever, with absolutely no preparation, knowledge of previous attempts or even who the players are. I thought I was helping Jack Jackson look good when all the time he was part of slipping this hot potato into my pocket! Bastard."

She made a few notes; looked like single words, from my angle. "Maybe there are two efforts going on here. Do you think there is a specific attempt to hurt you or force you out of your job?"

I slumped back in my seat. That never occurred to me. I thought about what Jack Jackson said, Blatchford and others. The more I thought, it didn't look like I was actually a target. "It's not aimed at me. I think the big bosses think I'll make a good patsy and because of your presence on the Trust... that I would finagle that somehow – take advantage of you, in effect. In a way, they were right, because I have and I'm not very happy about that. I'm sorry."

"Well, I'm not really bothered by that, Honey. Really. It's sort of neat to be working with you on a problem. You never talk about work and now we can work together. I like it. It's sexy!" She had that old grin from dating days and keeping secrets from her parents. It was sexy. "So, let's think about this from your angle. Who actually produced the knife they stabbed you with?"

"What? No, it's not like that. They weren't after me, exactly. I don't think." I sat still, puzzled.

"Maybe not, Walt, but somehow a bad situation got shoveled onto your plate, you said so, yourself. Somebody provided that shovel… that's all I'm saying. Think about it."

"Jackson. When you put it that way, it was Jack Jackson. And If I manage – if WE manage – to pull this off, he'll look like a hero, and I think he was part of how it got screwed up before it was dumped on me. That'll suck. I gave him what-for yesterday morning. He knows I was irked." Linda was clarifying all the things I hadn't given much thought to. I was interested in what she came up with next.

"There ought to be a way to make you more powerful at work if you succeed in this." Linda was chewing her pencil. I could tell she was cooking on all four burners.

"So, what are you thinking?" I asked after a minute.

"Well, I'm not sure, yet. But you should deliver your victory directly to Blatchford… not go through any managers in between. What do you think?"

"Hey! I'd be happy to do that, but I don't know how to get there from what I've got."

"Let's not worry about that. Just figure that when you see light at the end of the tunnel, the end game should play out to your benefit. Now what else looks negative?"

"Mainly it was meeting with Roberta. The Trust has drawings of a park with fountains and things on that parcel, and no railroad tracks. The only thing positive was Roberta's agreeing to speak with me at least once more. But she didn't think the Trust could compromise on what it sees for that land."

'Well, listen. I'm only a seat-warmer. But, I do know things are never what they seem with them… maybe nothing is. All we have is influence. We don't control much land. We get paid to, quote, 'facilitate' permitting for developers. We also get numerous in-kind benefits like nearly free rent on our offices, nearly free insurance, nearly free accounting, sponsorships for our banquets... things like that. I think we are able to function because Roberta and her friends have chosen the right enemies, politically."

"Enemies?"

"Oh, you're helpless, you know that? Roberta McGillvray is from old, old money – railroad money. Her grand-daddy smoked cigars with Andrew Carnegie. She's got connections with Mellons, Shoenbergers, and Goulds. Somewhere in just about any developer's deal, Roberta has a string to pull. She really loves the city and thinks the Three Rivers Trust is the only group that has the true rebirth of Pittsburgh at heart. Everyone else... including Walter Anton, probably... is mired in evil politics that will destroy Pittsburgh for tawdry profit. You can't impress her with either money or political connections. So, there. You've got one negative from yesterday, but, you may have a positive, too." Linda made entries under both columns. She was probably right, but I still didn't know what to do.

"Now, what else have you got from the first two days?" Linda was beaming at me, ready to write.

"Well, I think our esteemed congressman, Tom Wittenauer, is a negative. Roberta seems to hate him. He managed to really piss her off somehow. And I don't think Mayor McKay has much use for him, either, and not just because he's a Republican. Something Wittenauer has done... maybe several things... has made Blatchford a negative, too, at least with Roberta. So he's a negative. But I think the Mayor can be a positive. He wants jobs and federal money for his city. He loves the city, too, but pictures it a little differently than the Trust does. And people making profits doesn't bother him. I'm not sure how to parlay his friendship into help with this deal. I don't see her hating the mayor like the congressman, do you?"

Linda shook her head vigorously. "No, I don't, not that I'm her confidant, but she seems to get along with the mayor when necessary. That doesn't hold for everyone who works for the city. I may be able to learn who she trusts and who she doesn't. I'll see."

"Lindy, I think that's enough for one Saturday morning. It's time for a shower, I think. I may find it hard to go in there by myself," I chuckled.

"Can't you control yourself? You have a hard life." She was smiling.

"Your life is tough, too, especially when you're all sticky with maple syrup…" I tossed a syrup-soaked chunk of cold pancake down the front of her thin robe. Bullseye! I tossed another while she was reaching between her breasts to scrape the sticky wad off her skin. Another good shot. I'd been thinking of those for thirty minutes.

She threw the glob of pancake back at me and scored a hit on the little depression below my Adam's apple. "That's it," I said, "you've done it now, lady. You've forced me to rinse you off, bodily." I was coming around the table to grab her, but she was too quick for me.

"Oh, no you don't, you big galoot," she squealed. She ran toward the bathroom. I gave chase and almost reached her when she jumped through the door and tried to slam it. Painfully, I was too fast for her. I had one leg and one hand into the bathroom when the door swung sharply against them.

"Ow! Hey! That hurts. Now I'm injured!" I used my most injured voice and the most pitiful puppy sounds. She took pity on me and opened the door with an accentuated sorrowful pout.

"Oh, you poor thing. Did ooo get a boo-boo?"

"Yes. This leg got a big bump and this one, here, is only partly straight. Oh, oh, oh."

"Oh my goodness. Let's see if I can kiss it and make it better." Linda grabbed my incipient boner and gave it a couple of soft pats. She leaned over and kissed the tip of it. "There, there. I think it's getting better, already!"

I picked her up and set her on the faux stone countertop between the two sinks.

"Hey! That's cold, buddy!" She wiggled more cloth under her cheeks.

"I'll fix that," I promised. I put my hands under her butt and lifted her and pulled her toward me. I spun around and leaned against the edge. She slipped over me as smooth as maple syrup, my sore shin forgotten. She doesn't enjoy that position as much as I do, but she enjoyed the shower, afterwards.

Eventually we were side-by-side at the two sinks. I shaved, by accident. I usually don't on Saturdays, but my mind was swimming and I started my regular after-shower routine. While I shaved Linda dried her hair, alternately leaning way over to let it hang loose, blowing it with hot air and brushing it with a round, spiky brush.

"You know, Sweetheart," I started, "the other day I was going to ask how you decided to shave yourself… you know… down there. I like it. For sure. But, it was a surprise and it must have been awkward, no? What made you do that?" She kept the blower going and turned it to a higher speed. I finished shaving.

She killed the blower and looked at me in the mirror, I looked back inquiringly. "Well, I thought you'd like it, you know?"

"Oh I sure do, like I said. But you're so smooth, you must have used my razor with the dual blades and… and It must be awkward, especially the first time. I mean… there's lots of nooks and crannies, you might say." She was pinning her hair up, still looking at me in the mirror.

"Don't you want me to do it anymore? I'll let it grow."

That's what I didn't want. "No, no, no. I mean, I really like you… like *it* that way. In fact, I'll help you the next time. In faa-act, I would really dig that. That's a date I am really looking forward to. Whaddaya think?"

"If you say so. We can try it, I suppose. Okay." She seemed relieved. Maybe shaving her vagina was one of those non-subjects I couldn't understand. And maybe I didn't, but it tended to wake up Ol' Useless.

"I have a problem… maybe you can help me with." I stepped back a bit and waggled my boner up and down. She stared down at it and grabbed it with one hand.

"I suppose it's hard to control yourself."

"I am controlling myself." I squeezed my butt and made it pulse in a way she couldn't fail to feel. "It's a problem only you can solve."

She pulled me into the bedroom.

MONDAY, MAY 20, 1985

Jackson was subdued. But, everyone was: Cincinnati had beat "our" Pirates by six runs. Maybe it was me. I believed I had to have my Parcel 840 problem solved in these five days. If it went any longer I'd be as much of a failure as the bozo's who had screwed it up. Worse, if I didn't get it done it might not be doable, which would hurt a lot of people along with Blatchford Steel. It *was* just me.

When I left, Lindy confirmed her mission to find out about Anna Shriver, and any connection to Brightman founder, Aaron Brightman. Now it was up to me to find out more about what Blatchford had done that failed, and what Wittenauer did to cause enmity with Roberta McGillvray. What a mess.

I looked at the Plus and Minus list over coffee. The solution wasn't there, at least not yet, but it did show what doors were open and which were closed. How to open more doors? I was a babe in the woods.

I still had mid-month reports to wrap up. I couldn't concentrate though, and I'm a poor multi-tasker. I would start a column of dollars and cents and find myself daydreaming about what Roberta and said or about what belonged in Plus or Minus on Linda's list. Then some sound outside my sort-of office would jar me and I'd find my place again.

I wasn't the one who entered invoices into the bookkeeping system, nor the purchase requisitions. I imagine I could figure out how to create a report on the IBM machine that only our white-coated computer-priest could actually touch. But I much preferred to look at every original, and then list it by hand. Then, when my mark was on the invoice one of the clerks Jack Jackson oversaw could enter it into the bookeeping software. The same was true with requisitions. I would list them on a projected-cost report and then pass them along to the purchasing manager. He always tried to beat the projected total – made him look good. With both of us looking at them we never got caught paying too much for regular items, and we would kick back items that had never been purchased before. The shop managers would have to justify new items. This is also how I got sucked in to the rail spur problem.

About quarter of twelve I was within sight of completing the mid-months. A sharp click interrupted me and I looked at the in-boxes that hang inside my cubicle. Invoices go into one and reqs into the other. Messages go in either one. I thought about getting it, but I stayed at the reports. It was almost quarter past when I totaled and confirmed them for the second time.

I pushed back and reached for the message. It was from "Dieter F." There was a lunch reservation at the Marriott, Chatham Center for three, at eleven-forty the next day. Wow! Those guys know how to live. I made a note to cash a check on the way home. I'd need it for this lunch. Whatever, I'd expense it on the real estate problem.

I took my fourteen by seventeens to engineering where they had an Ozalid copier for big drawings. Basically the machine shined light through my sheets and exposed the negative paper to a shadow of the lines and writing, and then developed it with ammonia. It had a huge stovepipe for the exhaust. I was glad I didn't smell it every day. I took my copies and originals down to Jack Jackson.

I tapped on the door, though I expected he was at lunch. He was there. He grunted to acknowledge that the reports were done. It may have been a pleasant grunt. I backed out to leave and he called me. "Hey, ahh... Walt! Did you... ahh get to talk to my ah... my... ahhmm... my friend Roberta McGillvray? How'd that go?"

I stopped in mid step. "Yeah, Jack. I did. She seems pleasant enough, huh?"

"Really?" now he turned around and looked over his glasses. "I mean, uh... really. Yeah, she is. What happened?"

"Oh we chatted in her office and went over some plans for the parcel. It was cool working with her." I was driving him crazy.

"Oh, ahh... well, great. Keep it up. Let me know what happens, okay?" He was blushing, I thought.

"Okay. I'm off to the City, now. Talk to you later." More grunts ushered me out.

I went to the quays where we hoped our welded girders would soon be transferred to barges. There were some good lunches down here and I wanted to talk to shippers or even just dockmen. I knew nothing about river shipping or what the costs might be to handle girders like ours. I knew roughly what they weighed and it interested me. Plus, I wanted to see the signal bridge we'd have to modify.

I walked in to Mid-Waters Freight & Navigation. Their place looked professional and surprisingly pleasant. A woman greeted me and asked who I needed.

"Don't know. I'm researching shipping of very large items and it's my job to project what the costs will be."

"Oh. Let me see if Mr. Newhall has a minute. Who did you say you are with?" She stood and had her hand on a doorknob.

"Blatchford. Blatchford Steel. We're just a few blocks from here, actually."

"Oh," she nodded, "I'll tell him. Just a minute." She disappeared. I looked at photos of barges and tow-boats with a "Mid-Waters" logo that looked like knotted ropes.

Shipping on the Ohio and then on the Mississippi is unlike other kinds of water-borne freight. Huge barges with a variety of deck equipment carry everything from modern containers to oil, coal grain, iron ore, pig iron and anything else that can be properly poured in, piled on or lashed to specialized barges. Long strings of barges may be guided fifteen hundred miles from the heartland, indeed from above Pittsburgh, to New Orleans where the loads transfer to freighters or bigger barges for worldwide shipment. Photos showed Mid-Waters transferring huge G. E. diesel railroad engines, whole aircraft fuselages, Abrams tanks and everything in between. A casual observer might assume that pieces of the future King Frederik Bridge were within their purview.

"If you would come this way, Mr. Blatchford..."

"Huh? Oh, sorry. And I'm not Blatchford, I'm Anton."

"Oh, well... I'm sorry, Mr. Anton..."

"Walter Anton. Thanks." I slipped into the hallway that led past two office doors to a huge industrial shed.

The first door was open. I could see lettering that said "Angus Newhall" and the words "General Manager."

"I appreciate your seeing me, Mr. Newhall. With no appointment, I feel lucky." I held out my hand and Angus Newhall, whose hand was two of mine, enveloped it and pumped firmly.

"Have a seat, laddie. Whatcha shippin t'day?" He leaned back in a huge pilot's chair with big arms. It didn't look like office furniture.

"Today? Nothing. But I'm putting together figures for a series of large steel girders for Denmark. If all goes as planned they're gonna come down that old spur over behind us..." I gestured in the direction of Parcel 840. He seemed to know what I was referring to, "...and get hoisted over to a barge somewhere around here – this being the biggest river in town – and shipped down to New Orleans, onto a freighter or something, and over to Denmark. I don't know if that's with you. I'm here to learn." Now I sat and folded my hands over my own belly.

"That's pretty intrestin business, it is. A person in the riverboat business would need to know how big your girders are, what they weigh...intrestin shit like that." He squinted over his ample cheeks toward the rube from Blatchford Steel.

"Exact weights I can't quite give you. I do know we're going to buy a special balancing winch for our crane that can handle a hundred and fifty tons. I can tell you that the maximum width is fifty-point-four feet and two hundred and ten, point seventy-two feet in length. That's why we're using the spur; we can't move these things on the regular tracks."

Laddie," he was talking to a child, now, "ye ain't moving em down that spur, neither. Won't make it tru' your signals."

This old buck knew his stuff. "Right you are, Mr. Newhall. Pretty good! We are gonna modify that to get our pieces through. We have to move a couple of wires, too." I was smiling broadly. He was smiling too, enjoying recognition.

"Okay, then. Yer gettin the bloody things to my dock. What then?"

"Well, you take em down to New Orleans, right? What's that cost?"

"New Orleans is a Hell of a way from Denmark, laddie. They goin on vacation?" Now he was bugging me.

"Well, we have to take them across the ocean and New Orleans is close to the ocean. What am I missing, here?"

"I'm just sayin that Montreal is a Hell of a lot closer to Denmark. How many of these things are ya shippin?"

"Forty" He raised his eyebrows and pursed his lips. His mouth said "forty" soundlessly.

"How many at a time?"

"Ahh...um, well, I don't really know, but I will know by the end of lunch, tomorrow. Let me find out those other parameters. Can I call you then?"

"I'd be happy to hear it, lad. I don't know which is the most cost-effective way to get these things to Denmark. But, if you like, and not for free, I will test some routes for you. At some point over the years we've shipped with almost everyone."

"What will that cost?"

"A thousand. I'll credit it on your billing if we get the freight."

"I'll do that. Now, part of my mission, today, is to get a good lunch. Got any advice close by?"

"If ye ain't a specialist o' some sort, go to *Marko's*."

"Listen, Mr. Newhall, if you haven't had lunch yet, I'm happy to buy. Whaddaya say?"

Angus Newhall regarded me from his deep-set eyes. "Okay, laddie. I'll come wit' ye, thank you very much. But ye'll have to call me Angus. C'mon then." He pulled himself up and came around the desk and put one hand on my shoulder. "Follow me."

Angus told his secretary he'd be at *Marko's* if anyone needed him. He turned me leftward and we walked past a couple of closed-up buildings, an empty lot and a diesel engine repair shop. Less than a block from Mid-Waters we came to *Marko's*, a place I'd have missed. *Marko's* windows were high in the wall. The worn image on the door showed a man in a chef's hat riding a towboat like a bucking bronco. The name, "Marko's," appeared underneath the graphic but didn't say either "restaurant" or "lunch."

Every table was full. Waitresses, trays over their heads, threaded their way with arrays of sandwiches and hot dinners.

I saw sausage hoagies, steaming stew, triple-decker sandwiches and fried foods of several kinds. It smelled wonderful.

"Wow, we came too late! They're packed!" I shouted into Angus' ear. He pinched the cloth of my shirt and pulled me through the melee toward a set of stairs that descended against the far back wall. Downstairs there were seats at long tables. We sat facing each other. A couple of waitresses were hurrying back and forth here, too.

"This is interesting," I said. Surprisingly, I didn't have to raise my voice to be heard. Upstairs was a din. Everyone on this level seemed to be speaking at normal levels, probably an adaptation to three walls of concrete and a fourth of windows.

"Food's just as good, if that's what ye've come for." Angus knew half the people in the room, it seemed, as they waved a finger or said, "Hey, Angus," or "Good day to ya Angus."

"Well, everyone knows who you are," I observed pointlessly.

"No shit?" he replied. "I used to lash barges with some of these guys, before pilot school. My dad owned the boats and I worked. It's the only way to get respect among this crew. I got the best labor relations of all the shippers on the river. I been there. It's a tough life and they earn their pay. You push freight to St. Louis in January and you'll understand." I nodded in what I thought was a sympathetic way, but I had never worked as hard as these guys.

"Do you still run a towboat, or are you in the office, now?" We leaned away as the waitress gave us ice-water and rolled-up utensils.

"I'll have the catfish and a bowl of salad. Thanks." The waitress turned to me.

"The same, I guess. Sounds good." She nodded and backed away with the order in her head.

"Yuh. Three or four trips a year."

"What?" I asked.

"You asked if I still rode the river."

"Oh, yeah. What's it like?"

Angus did the squinting thing, again. "It's a different schedule. Every river has moods. The water swirls one way when its low, another when its running full. An easy turn in Summer can be very tricky after a few thunderstorms. You have to pace your sleep schedule for when you can be relieved by someone less experienced. Going through the locks I have to be there, too. It's different. We don't stop much heading down and time is money.

"And, it's expensive down or up without a good load. So we have to keep our connections live all the time so that we push at least a couple of pieces upstream."

"Huh," I replied in total lack of understanding.

"Here ya go boys. Anything else right now?" Our waitress gave us about four seconds to answer, then headed off.

"I hope you like it, laddie. Best catfish around." Angus attacked fresh bread, hot fried catfish and the enormous salad. His was not a habit of eating and talking. I couldn't keep up. *Marko's* had a brown, spicy sauce for catfish that was out of this world.

"You up for coffee, too, Honey?" our waitress asked. She had a big mug already poured and set before Angus Newhall. The mug said "ANGUS" in raised blue letters.

"Sure. I'm all the way with big A." She gave me a funny look but poured me a coffee in a smaller mug that said "Marko's" in black paint. Angus squinted at me.

"So what's next, lad? You're gonna tell me how many pieces will go at once and I'm gonna find the lowest cost for the whole trip... that right?" He raised one finger for my task, another for his.

"I will do that by tomorrow lunch. Meanwhile I've still got to settle with the Pittsburgh Development Commission and the

Three Rivers Trust so that we can actually use that little piece of railroad."

"No shit? The Three Rivers Trust? I got lines on that barge, laddie."

"Really? You know how to get them to move?"

"Now I didn't say that, boy, but we, ahh, use the same bank, you might say. If I get some serious freight out of this I might mention how valuable it would be to ol' Angus, here. Might help, if it's awright wit' you."

"I can use all the help I can get, Angus. All I can get. I will make it clear to our traffic manager that Mid-Waters is the company selected for shipping these damned girders. Your help will be much appreciated."

"Time for work, laddie. Let me know numbers." Angus turned into his office and I climbed into my car. Everyone knew about the Trust except me, but I felt like I was going to show everybody how to get something done in Pittsburgh. At least I hoped so. I took the Birmingham downtown.

As I approached Duquesne I thought of all the contacts I'd made and realized that I had nothing planned to actually do, that afternoon. I pulled over and sat. I had no appointments with any of the players and I couldn't keep showing up and pushing my way in on people. Linda had tried to organize my thinking and I hadn't added anything since Saturday morning. Pluses and minuses. Since nothing had yet happened, all I had was some information, nothing more. I had to learn who the action-makers were and what each could do. No one had told me that. I decided I'd accomplish more from my office.

I saw Big Blatchford's car in its space and it hit me to try to see him. He obviously knew what Wittenauer had done and even more, what he had asked the congressman to do. It was worth a shot.

I walked by the guard desk. The afternoon lady had begun her shift and she didn't look at people very much, nor did I want to look at Jackson. I checked my inboxes and pink messages. Nothing from Brightman, yet. I closed my door softly and went upstairs.

For all his bluster, Harold Blatchford was relatively accessible. He had a secretary in the outer office, but his door was sometimes open and if he saw you he might wave you in. The unwritten rules, however, fairly well limited who should take it upon him or her self to actually show up at his secretary's desk. Most of his meeting was done with the top managers, his board members and his lawyer or CPA. Big customers were introduced to him, or invited to lunch. Naturally.

I had seen him a couple of times prior to Thursday… just to answer some question Jackson couldn't. Now, though... now I felt I was on a sufficiently crucial level that he ought to talk to me when I wanted to see him. At least that's how I planned to act. It worked with Brightman and the mayor, however little there was to show for it.

"Hi, Kelly," I offered in as jaunty a style as I could, "I need to see the boss."

"Well, you can see his door is closed, right now. Can I tell him what it's about?" Kelly Galvin was what you might call perky, though nearing forty. She maintained a youthful demeanor and style of dress. Her hair was a dark russet brown, not quite Irish red, probably because she was more Polish than Irish. Somehow the mix of genes left her pleasant face out of proportion and not as pretty as her personality deserved. She tended to dote on the elder Blatchford. I don't think she had an enemy in the world.

"Just tell him it's about the King Frederik project… that should do it." I stood clasping my hands behind my back, nonthreatening and innocent enough to keep her talons sheathed.

"Okay, then. Just a minute, Walter. Have a seat if you like." She pushed one of the many button on her phone and Blatchford must have picked up because she told him I was waiting to see him about the King Frederik Bridge. "All right, then, Mr. Blatchford. Thank you." She turned back to me.

"He said for you to wait. He wants to see you." She smiled her efficient little quirk and I replied with my sunniest beam.

Kelly turned to her IBM Selectric and started typing something lengthy, perhaps to avoid speaking with someone sitting ten feet away. I looked out over the shop floor where some curved I-beams were being carefully measured and fitted with gusset plates, soon to carry cars on an urban Interstate where space disallowed a straight overpass. Blatchford-modified steel shipped all over North America. There were Blatchford beams in the World Trade Center, beams that had turned Blatchford from a small job shop into a heavy shop, ultimately financing the costs of moving to the foundry building. I watched the lateral crane roll toward my window. A special rig held a big plate of what looked like two-inch steel in a gravity pincer clamp. The mechanism stopped precisely and small tensioning cables dampened the swing. When perfectly still the operator lowered it deftly into the slot of a hydraulic handler that could tilt it to any angle or lay it flat safely, and almost soundlessly. I leaned over to watch two workers position the multi-ton piece of steel...

"You can go in now, Walter." Kelly stood to point the way toward Blatchford's lair. It was entered through the only double doors framed by faux pillars in the room, but I smiled thanks for the guidance.

Blatchford was watching the same operation. The rear wall had floor-to-ceiling windows covered by drapes except for a narrow opening he peered through, now. I walked in about halfway to his broad desk.

"You've been busy, I hear," he said in a slight rasp.

"You do?" I replied, "Uhh, yes, yes I have been and I need your help to go further, I think."

He didn't say anything for a minute. Then he pressed a button and the drapes closed as he faced me. "Siddown, Anton. Let's have it." The words were brusque. He didn't seem angry, but, I didn't meet with him often enough to know. Touching his desk was a long, highly-polished table, like the leg of a "T." Swivel chairs surrounded it and I sat in one of those.

"There's not a lot of 'IT' to give you, sir. I can report on where I've been and who I've met. But I think I need to get a better feel for what happened before I was, ahh... blessed with this project, you might say." He looked directly at me, showing neither anger nor amusement. His face was loose, sort of, almost floppy, but not fat. He was a little over six feet and in decent shape for sixty-something. But his face seemed not as tightly tethered to his bones as the rest of his skin. I think he avoided jerky motions. He had bluish-gray eyes and a full shock of sandy hair turning white.

"Blessed? More like screwed, it must feel." Still the bland expression.

I smiled at that. "I've used words to that effect. Maybe we could start there: why me?"

Now he frowned ever so slightly. "Fair question. I'll admit I wouldn't have picked you. Although you seem to have placed some determination on the task, so it's okay. But, no, you weren't in line for real estate negotiating with the fucking jackals that run this town." He looked down at some papers, one of which was rolled up like the plot plan I'd had copied. In fact they looked like the copies I'd had made on Thursday.

"You took the steps you needed to... to get started." He held up the pages I recognized. "I like that. I got these from John Schumann... you know him."

"Yeah, sure. I met…"

Blatchford kept talking. "He was impressed at how serious you were and that you insisted on an agency relationship. Schumann has fucked around with this piece of land before, you know."

I shook my head and kept my mouth shut.

"He's a good diplomat and tried to get the Trust to ease up but the old bitch won't move. Tom Wittenauer tells me your *wife* is on that Trust? When I asked Jackson he said you'd never mentioned it so I told him to bring you to the meeting and see if you bit when Tommy mentioned buying some land to bribe em with. I didn't believe you didn't know she was part of it but, maybe you didn't?" I started to blush. When he laid it out like that it did sound pretty stupid. I just shook my head.

"No… ahh, actually we had never discussed it. You see, she works for…" Blatchford waved his hand to deflect my comments.

"Doesn't matter. Obviously you talked about it since and then you spoke to McGillvray." Blatchford looked away as if he could see through the drapes. "She doesn't like me."

"I got that impression, but no details. She seems to connect her dislike of Wittenauer to you, as well."

"Does she, now? Old battle-ax." He scowled toward the draperies.

"Actually, Mr. Blatchford, that's why I wanted to speak with you…"

"What? About Dame Roberta? Whose side are you on?" Now he was looking over his shoulder at me. Funny reaction.

"It's not about sides, sir; it's about success in getting that spur. We won't get what we need if we piss her off even more, it looks to me."

He swung back to face me as in a real business meeting. He started to speak with one hand up to make a point, but then settled back, regarding me with an open expression. "Tell me what you've got."

Finally I thought I might gain something. "Mr. Blatchford, I have met with Schumann, visited the PDC, met with Mayor McKay..." He raised his eyes at mention of the mayor. "...and with Roberta McGillvray. I also had lunch with a fellow named Angus Newhall who runs a river freight company..."

"How many goddam jobs are you trying to do, here, Anton?"

"Actually I went down to the quay to see about the signal bridge we have to modify... er, pay to modify. I want to pin that cost down, too. I stopped in to Mid-Waters Freight and Navigation and Angus is the owner. We had lunch and I learned a little of what's important for shipping by barge. Turns out he has some connections to the Three Rivers Trust and he said he'd see if he could help us with them if I thought he might get the freight. He also offered to research the most cost-effective route to get our girders to Denmark, for a small fee."

"How small?" Blatchford was listening to my rendition with some care.

"A creditable $1,000."

"You authorized this?" His eyebrows were up.

"Yes, but I still have to get him some details, so I can quash it if you want." I used my most serious tone of voice, as if we had these discussions every day.

"Umm, no, ahh... no; it's early, but go ahead and let me know what he says, will you?"

"Okay. But let's discuss what happened before I got the mission, can we?"

"Well, uh, I suppose so. What can I tell you?"

"What was Wittenauer trying to do?"

"Oh, well. Tommy was... the Congressman was in a position to facilitate some use of that strip of land because of the EPA problems. You do realize we have a pollution problem there?"

"Yes, I do, although no one has said what that pollution is."

"Doesn't matter, does it? Nobody can do anything until it's cleaned up unless they are willing to pay for cleanup themselves. Goddam ridiculous. If Tommy hadn't found out about that EPA file we'd have been facing whatever millions in cleanup costs." Blatchford shook his head and puffed out his cheeks with a silent whistle. "I like that kid. He watches out for business and employers. Not like those bleeding hearts who think we have nothing better to do than powder our workers' asses. Bullshit!"

I nodded in agreement. "You and Mr. Wittenauer have been close for a while, I guess?"

"Yeah. I've supported him for years. His dad was a friend of mine. Used to work for U. S. Steel and actually helped me get started in steel services. I've always helped him."

I nodded some more. "So he approached the City? Or the Trust? How was he going to get access to that parcel? I need to know how he managed to irritate Roberta so much... if you know. She has agreed to meet with me again, but if she digs her heels in we could be frozen on this."

"As far as I know he spoke to Brightman and they tried to get a simple temporary surface use permit. Sounded like a good idea. We aren't going to build anything or even remove any soil or run any water or any of the things that get you into trouble."

"It does sound simple. How did he manage... I mean, what went wrong with who?"

"I don't know... Jesus! He was covering all the bases but someone spilled it to the Trust and ol' Roberta got her knickers in a knot and everything stopped. Why don't you ask Wittenauer?"

"Okay. I think I will. Alright to use your name?" Blatchford waved an okay. "Now, it seems like there's history between Roberta and the congressman, and maybe involving you, as well, boss. She didn't tell me any tales, but she sure wanted to know if I was a Republican. Can you help me with that?"

"You're a pushy sonofabitch, you know that?"

"That's the second time I've been called that. I don't think I like the real estate business. But you should know that I am determined to bring this together. I don't know why I feel so strongly. You want to go with someone else, be my guest. The whole thing is a pain in the butt!" I showed the frustration I felt and I didn't much care if he took me off the project.

"Oh, keep your pants on. We're running out of time. This project can transform this company in a big way. That's good for everyone. You have at least some communication with the Trust. Just don't blow it... please."

I heard plaintiveness in his words. The old bastard needed me on this and didn't have too many options, once his U. S. Rep golden boy bombed out. I went for broke.

"Mr. Blatchford, I don't..."

"Call me Hal, for chrissakes, already."

"Thanks... Hal. Look, I don't want to hold off if I think I can make something happen. Do I have your authority to do what will move this project to the goal line?"

"You already act like you do. I'll say yes, but there's a price tag on everything. Tommy thinks we need to buy a piece of land to pay off the Trust with. You told Jackson it might be three million?"

"Schumann's number on a different piece of land. It's all I had."

"Well don't go spending any millions until you talk with me." He turned back toward the drapes and pushed the button that opened them a little. The shop was nearly empty but the old man looked at it rather than at me. I got up to leave.

"Thanks, Hal. I'll keep you informed. I appreciate your trust." He didn't change his position. I let myself out, nodded at Kelly

Galvin and returned to my desk. Jackson didn't spot me, if he was in. I looked through my inboxes and decided it all could wait till morning. I found Linda's list and looked at it with fresh eyes. It was after three thirty.

The list of plusses and minuses wasn't long, on either side. My new authority from Hal Blatchford was a plus. Wittenauer was definitely a negative. Blatchford loved him, but I was sensing that Wittenauer loved only himself. He must be taking advantage of the old man in some way. It's what those people did.

The EPA filing was a negative, too... obviously. The only person who had offered to solve that problem was Wittenauer, himself. I wrote, "Get an appointment with TomW."

Blatchford had the pages and the plot plan that I'd left with Schumann at Brightman partners. Plus, he had told me that Schumann had tried to do something with this land once before. I wondered what. Then it bothered me that he hadn't said anything about that to me. To be fair, he didn't know me. That whole Brightman Partners thing was a head scratcher.

Linda had told me about a possible connection of her boss with Brightman. Now if Brightman, and Schumann, were people Roberta McGillvray didn't like… and there seemed to be a number of those, then why was Anna Shriver so interested to keep a connection to the Trust board? Maybe Linda could shed some light tonight. Brightman bugged me. I made a call.

"Brightman partners," sang the receptionist, "how may we help you?" Couldn't have sounded nicer.

"Yes, it's Walter Anton. I need to speak with John Schumann. Thank you." I waited.

"Can I tell him what this is about, Mr. Anton?"

"No. He knows full well. Thanks." I waited again.

"I will see if Mr. Schumann is available, Mr. Anton." She'd stopped singing.

During the third crappy 'Muzak" melody the receptionist broke in.

"Please hold, Mr. Anton. John Schumann will take your call."

"Well whoop-dee-do," I replied, but the former singer had clicked off. I didn't hum when the Muzak came back.

"This is John Schumann. Good to hear from you, Walter. What can I do…"

I was steaming up a little, by now. "Why didn't you call me back, John? Did you give the answer I needed to Hal Blatchford?"

"Whoa, whoa, waitaminit, Walter. What's all that about?"

"I came to you, or, rather, to Brightman partners because your firm had been of important service to Blatchford Steel when we moved in to Pittsburgh. I spoke with you because I was saddled with a tough problem that is within your realm of expertise. Are you telling me I made a mistake in coming to you? Did you give Blatchford copies of the documents I dug up because I was bothering you?"

"One thing at a time, Mr. Anton, please. First of all we are proud to have been of service to Blatchford and we hope to be again. Please don't misunderstand that. I frankly didn't know you and I wanted to check with Harold Blatchford before I did any business with you on his behalf. You can understand that, can't you?" I had to think about that. He had a point, there.

"You have a point, John. I'd have done the same thing. What did he say, anyway?"

"Well he told me you had his complete confidence and that whatever I could do to help you he would appreciate very much."

"Huh." I was kind of dumbfounded.

"Walter?" Schumann inquired.

"Ahh, yeah. Thanks for that, John. That's interesting. May I… ahh… can I ask when you spoke with him?"

"Around one-fifteen, one-thirty, I think. Why?"

"I've been frustrated, here, and I was ready to accuse you of holding out on me. My apologies."

"None required, I assure you."

"Thanks. But now... now let's talk about how to make this move or about what you know that is the main impediment. Can we do that?"

"Well, I can help a little, so far. Have you met with Roberta McGillvray yet?"

"Why, yes... I have. Fascinating lady."

"She showed you her full-color rendering of your Parcel 840 parkland?"

"Yeah. She did. And what is that all about? I mean, they don't own this land."

"It's the game, Walter. They come up with a plan full of sweetness and light, and become indispensable to whoever wants to develop that land or land next to it. The developer then finds it easier to get permitted if the Trust agrees with the changes. That only happens if there is, indeed, an increase of sweetness and light. There's creative bullshit, but the politics are real and people who need votes tend to please the Trust, agree or not."

"Well, Blatchford is certainly in favor of sweetness and light. He'd tell you that. Now the EPA thing..."

"Save that till last, Walter. At least I would. You could spend a lot of energy on that and still have nothing if the Trust isn't backing your new plans. The EPA isn't your problem. You wanna know what is?"

"Sure, tell me."

"You're not building anything. There's no building permits, no foundations being poured, no big developer dollars, no graft. I mean, who really cares about helping you? There's no project in your project! You think this renewed use of the tracks is logical and good for business. Well, so do I. So does the mayor, I'll bet. But there's no big millions moving on this! Nobody can get paid off without being actually... paid off. No insulation. See?"

I sat back and let a big sigh escape in a woosh. "Son of a bitch, John. That makes a logical, perverse sense. How the Hell can I fix that? We don't need to build anything!" I was floored. Having said it made the gulf between poor little Walter Anton and his problems a mile wide.

"I've been thinking about this, Walter. Buying a piece of future park land isn't going to move the Trust. So, I don't have the answer... yet. Doesn't mean there isn't one. We're just going to have to skull it out. We hope to have a suggestion by tomorrow afternoon."

"What? From hopeless to a suggestion in twenty-four hours? What the Hell…?"

"Walter, don't ask. There's always a way in real estate. Be patient."

I took a breath. "Alright, John. I'll be patient, but at least give me a way to help."

"There's one area where our information could be improved. If we knew about other projects that Dame Roberta is highly interested in, that could help. We have worked with the Trust, but it was always when some money was going to be spent. I don't know what you can do, but something along those lines could help."

"I do know people who might help,there, John. Just maybe. I'll call if so."

"Okay. Same here. And don't worry about Brightman. We're your agents."

"Okay, then. Thanks, John. My apologies again. Let's talk tomorrow."

"That's a deal. Bye." He rang off. I felt like Don Quixote. The targets I'd been shooting at were never there. Chimeras. The story of real estate wasn't the "location, location and location." It was really, "money, money and money."

I heard the office clearing out. No look-in from Jackson. Blatchford hadn't said anything about Jack's role in handing me the Parcel 840 project. Maybe I was blaming him for too much. Maybe Linda had some progress to report.

I locked my almost-office and walked past the guard. The evening shift lady gave me a bored look. She was well stacked, I noticed. The coarse cloth and necktie of her uniform shirt didn't excite, but she filled it out. Her waist wasn't fat, from my cursory stare. Too bad she didn't bowl.

I was happy to be heading home. I looked forward to any insights Linda had on the Trust. And I wanted to tell her what John Schumann had taught me. Plus, she might be horny. Could happen.

***

I pulled in and caught the smell of cookout. Oddly there hadn't been a neighborhood cookout all Spring. "Hey, kiddo, your hunk of love is ho-ome!"

Nothing. When I closed the door I found her note: "cook-out at the Maxwells change if you want." In a couple of minutes I had chinos, a soft shirt and leather sandals. I walked toward the talking and found Elly Maxwell, my Linda, Axel Johnson, Henry Buckley, who I hadn't seen for months, the Simpsons, Penny and Bob, and Elly's virtual stepchildren, Teddy and Ronnie. We hadn't seen the boys for a while… the last time it snowed, in fact. They looked like they'd each grown six inches.

I greeted Hank Buckley more effusively than the others. "What's up, Henry? Haven't seen you since the last cookout!"

"No, jeez, I know it. I had a long posting to Saint Louis around Columbus Day and I seemed to be traveling every other week until a couple months ago. Shame on me, I should have brought you an airport knick-knack so you'd know I hadn't forgotten you." He smiled broadly.

I laughed, too. "Quite all right, Henry. But in the off chance… stuffed animals." We chuckled and I clapped his back.

"Hi, Honey. What a Monday, huh?" She gave me a nice juicy kiss and turned me toward the boys. "Hiya, Ronnie; hiya, Ted. How's school? Almost done?"

"Yeah," said Ronnie, the younger brother, anticipating his thirteenth birthday. "Ten days and twelve days, Mr. Anton."

"Ten days and twelve days what, Ronnie?"

"Ten days to my birthday and twelve days till school's out," he nodded actively.

"Those are the main things, Mr. Anton," affirmed Teddy, who turned fifteen right after they moved with their dad.

"So, tell me, Ted, you working this summer? Have you been looking?"

"I hope so, Mr. Anton. I told my Mom that I would help her in the garden and she offered to pay me. And I might work at Klein's Nursery, too. I like doing that."

"No kidding? Pretty good, Teddy. Listen, anytime you and Ronnie are visiting I'll be happy to pay you for some yard work, too. Anytime. Just let me know you're coming, okay?"

Teddy nodded with a straw in his mouth, and made some affirmative "mmmnnhh" sounds. Ronnie just looked at his brother, and headed to the hot dogs.

I shook hands with Axel and we compared weather notes, and I gave Elly a quick hug and peck on the cheek. She was nicely made up and wore loose shorts that weren't too short, and a comfortable man's style shirt, belted with a woven tie. She always looked nice.

Everyone brought a dish. Elly was doing burgers and hot dogs and there were a couple of fresh sausages in case. Linda had a big salad with healthy stuff; Penny Simpson had brought a pasta salad and a bean salad, a guess based on the unfamiliarity of the stoneware. Axel Johnson seemed responsible for a fruit salad he was still holding. There were cookies under Saran wrap and some brownies. A couple of coolers beckoned to the thirsty. I was hungry enough to be a good cookout guest.

For a few minutes we accumulated salads, burgers or dogs on thick paper plates. One cooler held Coke and ginger-ale; the other, Bud and Heineken. Nobody bereft.

I sat near the Simpsons. Bob and I had never spoken much, and I was interested in what he did. Henry Buckley sat on their other side. After some discussion about Bob's work for U. S. Air and complaints about airlines and airports, Penny changed seats to talk with Linda and Elly. Penny appeared a little pregnant. Buckley didn't notice, possibly. I knew enough to not ask.

By eight the boys were ensconced in front of Elly's big Sony. Pittsburgh was playing the Astros at Three Rivers. The sky was darkening and mosquitos were feasting. Axel Johnson had joined 'the men,' talking about air travel, the strengths and weaknesses of several sports teams, and especially the Steelers. It was unusually relaxing. I could have napped.

"Hey, listen, guys, we need to get more regular about cookouts, huh?" Axel, Hank and Bob all nodded.

"I mean, you know I like to cook, right?" More nodding. "I can whip up a London Broil on the grill that will beat any restaurant. When can we get together?"

After some guesstimating of calendars we settled on a week from the coming Friday, at the Antons. I promised a meal they wouldn't forget and further that Linda or I would be in touch for what to bring. Hank Buckley shook hands with Bob, Axel and me and waved at the girls as he headed off. I stretched and walked over toward the ladies. "Well, we settled the problems that face the world," I announced, "what's could be taking time for the three of you?"

"Oh, you," said Linda. "We have much more important things to talk about than smelly old football players and lost luggage." Penny and Elly murmured agreement. "We've been figuring out when to have a surprise shower for Penny's new baby!"

"Oh, wow! Congratulations, Penny," I said. "How did that happen?"

Linda threw a piece of cookie at me, which I managed to catch and eat. Bob Simpson had come up to stand right behind me. "The usual way," he laughed, and somebaby's mommy needs to not get overtired, I think. We oughta go, Sweetie," he said toward Penny. She nodded slightly and stood up, holding Bob's hand.

Elly and Linda stood up and gave Penny a hug, first, and then Bob. "We'll keep in touch and get together for tea. Maybe a weekly."

"I'll love that," Penny smiled. She and Bob headed home. Elly stacked up leftovers and utensils. Linda got the paper goods, rolls and chips. Axel and I re-set the chairs and table. We gathered trash and Axel lifted out the bag and tied it off. I dumped the cold ashes. Elly and Linda were just finishing washing utensils and a few bowls as Axel waited to wash his hands and I lined up behind him.

Finally we said our goodbyes. I popped in to say goodnight to the boys. Teddy was watching the game, but Ronnie was asleep. Axel had a fresh coffee.

"So," I wondered after some deep, deep thought, "Axel must have some squeaky pipes to lubricate, or something?" We walked with our arms around each other.

"Noooo, silly. I don't think so. He's nice, that's all. Don't you think? Besides, the boys are there, tonight."

"Well, they'll be asleep soon, I would think. Hey! I'm just sayin'... you got two sexy people, what the Hell?"

"You think she's sexy, do you?" Linda poked me in the side.

"She's nicely put together, yeah. I mean... it's none of my business."

"You got that right, mister. Fix the squeaks in your own house."

"I like the sound of that. Got any squeaks I can... lubricate?" She poked me again. "By the way... um, does Elly shave the way you do? Do you talk about stuff like that?" We were at our front door.

"What a question! And what difference does that make? It's none of your business, you horn-dog." Her tone had me wondering if I had screwed up my screwing. She turned her back on me and pushed the front door. What did I do? I took a breath and followed, forcing a good mood.

"Hey, Linda? Can we talk for a few minutes?"

"About what?" Now I was sure she was pissed.

"I'm dying to know if you found out anything about your president and the Trust. I can really use your help, as I can explain better, now. So, can we?"

Linda stood for a moment and looked at my feet. She twisted her mouth I thought to avoid smiling. Then, looking as sternly stern as she could, nodded. "I do have some news," she admitted, "and I do want to help. So let's see where we are. Do you have that plus and minus list?" I smiled, then.

"I'm getting some hot water," I told her. What can I get you?"

"Hot water?"

"Yeah...with lemon. Settles the stomach. Want some tea? Hot chocolate?"

"Okay… make me some camomile tea with honey in it. That'd be nice." Well, she's with me this much. There may be a shower in my future.

"You got it." I boiled and poured and met her in the living room.

"Okay," I said, "you first. I'll take notes."

Linda pulled both feet under her. Her loose skirt pulled tightly over her thighs. For the cookout she had worn that jersey top with no bra. She looked awfully good.

"I nosed around today and learned a bit about Anna Brightman Shriver. She meets with Roberta McGillvray sometimes... non-meeting days. Fortunately, I also found out no one uses her middle name before I dropped it at a Trust meeting. I never gave it a thought, before."

"What kind of meetings? Are they friends?"

"Well, they were growing up and it seems like they still are. The Shrivers were close to Roberta's grandparents in the years round the turn of the century. Her father, Jim McGillvray, was forty-four when Roberta was born in 1937. He'd married the sister of the owner of an early soft-coal mine, and she was the only child who survived past age ten. Jim's father was a partner in a shortline railroad that served only two mines, bringing coal to the Thomson works.

"Jim's wife, Abigail, was never strong and she passed away when Roberta was only fourteen. Jim sent Roberta to the Sisters of Charity. Abigail's father, Ellis, had left his holdings to his children. Her brother had no children and was in the process of selling out to Graceton Coke when he died of black lung, evidently. Abby inherited the fortune. Jim worked his way up in U. S. Steel under Harry Frick. When he quit he took a managing position with The Monongahela Connecting Railroad. Before Abigail died he commissioned a big stone house in the hills hoping the cleaner air would be good for her. She died not long after they moved. Roberta lived with her father and a staff of servants. One by one they left or died, until just Wallace Hoagland is left.

"Roberta married Mark Tatum, born 'Tattleman,' who worked for Mellon. They lived in the big house. The in-laws never visited their son in that house. Roberta was barely accepted and she grew to resent Jews far beyond the normal suspicion she grew up with. When Mark was killed in Vietnam his parents almost froze Roberta out of their mourning and her feelings about Jewish things grew deeper. So, she was rich, single, alone and resentful. Many developers in Pittsburgh were Jewish. The people gaining the most power and influence in Roberta's hometown were Jews and she let her resentment attach to all of them. After Mark died, she always used her maiden name and no one ever uses 'Tatum.'

"Roberta's friend, Anna Shriver, knew of Roberta's parochial-school suspicions about Jews. So she never shared her Brightman heritage. Anna learned how Roberta had been treated by the Tatums and though she and Roberta remained acquaintances, they weren't as close as grade-school days and Anna left Jewishness a non-subject. If Roberta knew of Anna's connection with the Brightmans, she never said. She had little other social connection with anyone except through the Trust or the Chamber of Commerce.

"Roberta is always happy to get together with Anna and Anna maintains an active interest in Pittsburgh's renewal and that's the basis of their friendship today.

"The Three Rivers Trust is a good tool for Roberta to 'keep the Jews in check,' as she sees it, at least a little. Every time they stood to make millions on this or that project, she was able to force them to accommodate what she wanted.

"McGillvray money was always in a Protestant bank, as there were no 'Catholic' banks... never in a 'Jewish' bank. One of Roberta's problems with Tom Wittenauer is that he kowtows too much to Jewish interests. It makes him suspect, and so much so that whatever initiative he might take she distrusts. Every sly or shady deal he's made is interpreted as being corrupted by Jews, somehow. When she learned of his attempt to make a deal with the city on Blatchford's behalf, she must have hit the roof. And that's it: 'The Roberta McGillvray story.'"

I was shaking my head. "You're fabulous, you know that?"

"Well, I try." Her skirt was looser and had ridden up quite a bit. Inevitably I tried to look all the way up. I couldn't see panties but it was dark. "What have you got?" Linda asked.

"Today was kinda interesting, actually. I met with a river freight company, *Mid Waters*, and the owner of it turns out to have some kind of connection to the Trust through his bank, at least he says so, Did you ever hear of Angus Newhall?" She shook her head and adjusted herself on the couch, now with one leg stretched out.

"Well Angus is going to map out the least costly way to ship our girders. And he offered to put in a word for our project with his bank, which he says the Trust also uses... Western Penn?"

"Yes! That is our bank. Hmmn, that's interesting. Maybe you should ask him to hold off saying anything until we know he'll have the best effect... just so you don't act at cross purposes."

I made a note. Linda was good at stating the logical. It never occurred to me to ask Angus to wait. Smart.

"Your list is getting longer, now. You're on there as a plus. Roberta is still a negative, as I see it. But I got a big plus today."

She raised her eyebrows.

"I met with Hal Blatchford this afternoon. I asked him directly about what had been done before I got the project. He gave me full authority to take whatever steps I saw fit to make the project go. That's pretty good, right?"

"Well, it should be. It might also have cemented you to this effort. If it fails you could be in a real bad spot. Just thinking of possibilities."

"Oh, crap. I didn't think of that, although I guess it was nagging me. I think I knew I was going to give my all to this, so it doesn't change anything..." I frowned as I thought of my changed status. I could call the old man "Hal," now, but I also had to answer to him for failure, if that's what happened. Then I remembered the call with Schumann.

"Ahh, wait, though! I got some good insight from John Schumann and some good reinforcement, too. He told me that Blatchford had confirmed his confidence in me before I met with him. He told him to work with me because I had his complete confidence. That was a pick-me-up let me tell you."

"You know, Honey, you have been sort of paddling a row-boat to no place over there. I never say anything because you seem happy. But you're showing that you could be a key player. Part of your plan for all of this stuff should be to get a better position, more money and so forth, don't you think?" She now had both legs in front of her and was pushing down her skirt tightly between them. I started thinking about panties and shaving, again.

"Walt?" I jerked my head up. "What's the big insight? It's time for bed."

Oh, yeah. That. Well I was talking to Schumann... at Brightman Partners?" She nodded impatiently. "He told me why I hadn't gotten any action out of anyone yet. It was an eye-opener for me, anyway."

"And...?"

"He explained that our problem is we aren't building anything on that parcel! Isn't that something? Without a construction project there's no money involved. Nobody can get a payday or a pay-off. Why should they care about this idea to fix the railbed? There's no money. And that goes for the Trust, too. Clear as a bell, huh?"

For once I had her speechless. She looked at me with her lips parted. "I'll be damned," she said. She must have felt hot because she took the hem of her skirt and flipped it up to make a breeze. I got the distinct impression that she did not, in fact, have any panties on. Interesting cookout get-up, and then some.

"Well, let's think on that while we strip and get slippery," I suggested. Linda blushed a little and held her skirt down tightly. I walked to her and held out my hand. Old Useless was pushing at the stable door.

"Can't you control yourself?" she giggled. I was feeling better about my chances.

"I am controlling myself. Let's go. If it's a race you'll win."

She skittered away into the bedroom. When I got there she had already lost the skirt and was sliding the stretchy top thingy over her head. She was naked but for socks. Now I had to be careful not to injure myself. She helped and we did the wonderful right on top of the bedspread. I was soft again in minutes.

"You didn't need much encouraging," she said.

"You either," I panted out.

"Well I'm taking a solo shower, now. It's way past bedtime for a worknight." I pouted a little and she leaned over to kiss me, holding her breasts from swinging. I needed a shower, too, so I stood to avoid falling asleep.

TUESDAY, MAY 21, 1985

Over coffee we plused and minused. I had so many crossing arrows that Linda made a fresh sheet.

"Let's change the headings. The information we have either helps get to a... what? A close? Certain things will help us 'close' a deal that permits use of the railroad. Certain ones are neutral, at this point. Some seem to be more difficult hurdles. So far you don't seem to have encountered anyone who has declared adamant opposition."

"Well, no... I haven't. The only person who has opposing plans is Roberta. And Schumann is fairly clear on what it may take to get her on our side: money from some other project."

"How's that? What other project?" Linda leaned back.

"I didn't get around to Schumann's plan, did I?" I recalled. "Schumann wants me... us, to find out what other projects Roberta is interested in. Armed with that info we might be able to connect them with an injection of Blatchford money and buy her off that way. She gets a payday for Three Rivers Trust and we get our railroad. I suspect that if we facilitate her winning somewhere else, she'll practically cut the ribbon when we run the first flatcars to the river."

Linda was really thinking. Her pencil tapped against her cheek between doodles on the yellow pad. Finally she blew out a long breath. Decision time. "If I can find out about this other project you need, you've got to manipulate things so that it's good for Walter Anton, too… not just for Blatchford. Right? Agreed?" She pointed the eraser at my heart.

"Well, yeah. Sure. I guess. How do I do that? I think I'll win plenty if I close this for Blatchford. Why not?" I crossed my arms, gripping both biceps. I shook my head. "I'll be happy if I can do that."

"Lot's of people have a straw in this milkshake, honey… I just made up that metaphor... but it's true. You've got the mayor, the congressman, Roberta, John Schumann – lots of people. You told me that."

"It's true that the mayor asked me to not let the deal be any help to Wittenauer. I said I wouldn't, but I had no idea how the deal was going to happen at that point."

"Well, Walter Anton has a straw in there, too. This needs to help you. Your bosses put your career at risk with this, Walt. When you know you can get this done, you've got to bargain with it to get some valuable advantage. Don't you think so?"

"Well, let's see where we get. If we can get a lead on another project, then we can see if I can score along with Blatchford. I won't drop the bomb until we discuss it. Is that okay?"

She sighed and put her hands on mine. "Okay, Sweetie. I'm not trying to put more pressure. Let me see what I can find today. Which way are you headed?"

"To the office. There's a ton of stuff in my in-boxes. Then I'm going to lunch with the two guys who pulled in this project for Blatchford."

"Why?" She cocked her head in genuine confusion. "How can they help? I mean you can lunch with whomever you want. I'm sorry... none of my business. Never mind."

"No, that's okay. These guys know details about why Blatchford is the number one choice for these girders. I want to know who was number two. What gives us the advantage? It's like talking to the riverboat guy. There may be some insights or factors that don't seem important but may help me… us. I have a feeling. Trust me."

"Okay. I do, Walt... I do. What else?"

Wow, you're like Jackson, today. Part of what I talked about with Blatchford – did I tell you he wants me to call him Hal? Cool, huh?" I nodded a little and she bobbed with me.

"Congratulations, Honey. What do you think?"

"Doesn't matter, but I feel good about it. He's depending on me to resolve this. I like being in this position. Anyway, I told him I needed to speak with our fair-haired congressman and I asked him if I could use his name for access and he agreed to it. He's tight with him and was with his father. I have to be careful not to make an enemy while I find out how he managed to anger Roberta." I shrugged.

"So that's my other effort, today, to get an appointment with him."

Linda nodded. "Sounds like our days are full. Let's report back here at oh-eighteen-hundred hours." She saluted me and then we embraced. A little kissing took place, but we had to get to work. We were out in three minutes... Linda first. Elly Maxwell stepped onto her front stoop and waved. I gave a little honk and her arm came up for me, too. I turned on KDKA and rode in with "John Cigna's Good Morning."

As I waited for a co-worker to take the next closest parking space, I noticed Jack Jackson loitering by the big block of granite that marked where another building once stood, which space was now Blatchford's parking lot. I finished parking and walked to him with a smile on my face.

"Jack," I nodded.

"I'm glad I caught you, Walter. Can we talk?"

Yeah, sure." I kept walking, but he pulled my sleeve.

"No... out here."

I attached an elbow to my own corner of the granite. "Shoot," I said.

"I ahh... what have you gotten done on this rail spur thing? I see you running around but you haven't shared anything."

"You know, Jack, that's a very good point. I really haven't been told who to report to on this. I did speak with..." I thought about rubbing his nose in 'Hal,' but decided it wasn't necessary. "... old man Blatchford but he just wanted to make sure I wasn't spending any money, heh, heh." This seemed to brighten Jack a bit.

"I know what you mean, Walt. Oh, boy," he rolled his eyes. "Hal can be a bear on the bucks." He shook his head. I wondered why he had to use 'Hal' just then. Apparently he knew I'd met with Blatchford and felt threatened. That's what this little ambush was for.

"Listen, Jack, I owe you an apology, today, because I haven't had time to make a special meal. I'll make it up to you, I promise." I started up the walkway to the glass doors where our trusty guard, Pauly waited. Jack took a couple of quick steps and caught up to me. We entered together.

"Nothing to worry about, Walter," he assured me, "I can't say I won't miss it, but I know how your schedule has been chopped up with this project."

"Oh, thanks, Jack. Lemme know what you'd like for next week. Gourmet to you is what I do," I sing-songed. He gave me a little punch in the arm. Suddenly we were buddies.

"Morning, Pauly," I called out. He had a hearing aid, I noticed.

"Mornin Mr. Walter. Find it hard getting up this morning?" Pauly was chuckling and his shoulders were bumping up and down with his "heh, heh, heh."

"I used to, Paul; I used to. But now I've got one o' them cock radios. No more problems!" I laughed with him and kept moving.

"I 'member that one, Mr. Walter. I sure will." He was still chuckling as we passed into the offices.

"Jack," I said, "I do have a sticky problem. Okay if I come in when I've got the piles whittled down?" He seemed glad I needed him.

"Absolutely, Walt. My door is open for you – you know that."

"Thanks, Jack. 'Preciate that. Gimme an hour."

"You got it. See ya." I think he would have whistled, but I don't know if he could. I hung my sportcoat on the wooden coat-tree that came with the building… and my desk.

I breezed through the two stacks. One was invoices. Colleen Walsh had written on each that it agreed with the Purchase Order and that it referenced the right P. O. number. Those were easy to "OK" for payment, but I also entered the amounts on my second-half-of-the-month cost report. One of them she noted did not agree, and she had clipped the P. O. to it. That one I'd take to purchasing and find out why. The system was cumbersome, but it kept the buyers and the vendors on their toes. Once in a while we would pay only what was on the P. O. and the quotes would be tighter from then on. When I gave a semi-monthly cost projection report it had better be pretty damn close to what the eventual expenditures actually were.

The other pile was Requisitions and most of these were standard goods. These came from purchasing directly, and the particular buyer would make a note about whether we were filling inventory or buying a new item for stock or a brand new tool. We looked at those things and if the amount was large, I'd talk to Jack about it and he'd take it further to make sure of the need and source and all the happy horseshit that kept costs in check. Engineers always needed the latest gizmo; the shop guys, too. Again, cumbersome, but everyone knew that lots of eyes were going to see their 'reqs' and that there had better be a good reason to spend new dollars. There were a lot of proposed new dollars on the King Frederik project, which is how I got onto it way back when... five days ago.

Around ten I tapped on Jack's door and he told whoever I was to come in. He looked up and his very first expression was one of... I don't know: anger, perhaps, or fear. In a split second he waved me to a chair. "Howzitgoin Walt?" he asked. "Bewithya in a sec." Jack was never that casual, so I figured he was working hard to be buds.

I sat and feigned interest in the one framed diploma on the wall: a Masters in Accounting. I'd never given it much thought. Smart guy. The sheepskin was from University of Pittsburgh and they don't just hand them out. It made me think that Jack was a local guy who'd never left home. Didn't matter; he was still a dink. Yet, he had a masters and I barely earned a BA in history, which means a little knowledge about several things and a decent ability to pass tests. Finally Jack was finished whatever he was slaving over.

"They want me to project monthly expenses for a full year assuming we get the King Frederik nailed down, and I've got to explain them. It's a bitch and half guesswork. Thank God your projections are thorough. They make it possible to extrapolate with at least some confidence." He slapped both palms on the blotter in front of him and picked up the small pile of papers and set them to one side. "Let me ask you a couple things you may have an idea on. Okay?"

"Sure, Jack. We all want this bridge thing to work out for Blatchford Steel. And I think it ultimately will."

"Really? You got a report?" He sat forward and his hands started to fidget.

"Well, I can report that I think I've found the path or at least the direction where success lies. There are a lot of steps to go and I haven't gathered all the information, but it is coming in. It's very stressful."

"Well, what have you got? Anything we can put a number on?" He seemed nervous. "Do you have a hard price on the land?"

"No-ooo," I laughed, "I promised Mr. Blatchford I wouldn't spend any millions without asking him, but right now the steps to create a deal that permits that spur are still not known. We know the kinds of steps. I might have a plan by tomorrow morning but I have to depend on other people."

Jack was trying to smile and look agreeable as I rambled on, but I could see that he was as confused as when I started. "So, ahh… what do you, um… have, exactly?"

I shook my head as if my student were simply failing to learn. "Jack, if I tried to tell you what I've done and what might happen because of it, you still wouldn't have anything you could report on. You've no idea how friggin complicated this whole mess is. It'll make quite a story if I'm successful. Right now it's pieces. Linda's digging for leverage, I am, John Schumann is, too. What have we got? Right this minute, nothing. With luck I'll know by tonight. If this works, it should be done in a few days. I think if it doesn't happen that quickly it's not going to. My next few days are going to be stressful, but I have made some progress fixing up what Wittenauer did to mess it up. That's one of my tasks for the next day or so."

Jack recoiled at "Wittenauer," but he didn't say anything.

"Jack, let's speak again tomorrow. I'll try to have some good news." I stood up. "I have a lunch meeting on that score and I've got to clear the decks. Don't worry. Things are in motion." I reached out to shake hands. Jack stared at my hand hanging over his desk, realized what it was and stood to shake it.

"Okay, Walt. Tomorrow's good. Thanks." I backed out of his office and returned to my desk. I thought for a minute about what that conversation was really about. Jack was nervous. Either he needed to be my reporter or if he wasn't, he might lose his job. I couldn't imagine that. It was a puzzle for another day. It was eleven-fifteen.

***

I went to Contracts and looked for Dieter and Casimir. I heard talking and found them in Casey's cubicle, drinking coffee. That's the definition of a sales team: three wise-asses and a coffee pot.

"Hey guys. Time to get going?"

I'd caught them by surprise. "Holy shit! Yeah. Hi Walter. Let's go, Case. Our reservation is at quarter-of. Walter, ride with us!"

I shook my head. "I've got to keep moving, Dieter. I'll follow you."

"Okay, then. Let's roll." The three of us trooped out. Late morning wasn't a bad time to get around the city and we got to the Marriott with about five minutes to spare. The hostess seated us at eleven forty-five. I felt out of place, but to my two hosts it was a Denny's. We ordered small filets with steak fries and salads. Our waitress brought us fresh rolls with butter in little Marriott "m's" and water with lemon slices. Despite other diners the high ceiling, drapes and carpet softened everything. It wasn't *Marko's*.

Dieter and Casey had beer – Saint Pauli Girl, imported from Germany. I stuck with water.

"Well, then, Walter, here ve are. Do you like it?"

I nodded. "I never come here for lunch, but I can see the attraction for two top salesmen. Is this a good place for clients?" I looked around energetically.

"Oh, yah. We had the Danes here and this is the hotel we arranged for them."

"The Danes were here? I didn't know that. Who were they?"

"The chief engineer on the King Frederik and the architect's partner. They both came over. Had to see if we have what it takes, you know?"

Dieter was nodding and I nodded along with him. "So, they saw the shop and liked what we have?"

"Pretty much, pretty much. We told them the new equipment we were ordering for the bridge project, and they liked that, but mostly it was the precision welding capabilities we have and, it was probably our three class-A welders, themselves, who made the biggest difference." They both took a sip of beer and looked at me. I wasn't sure which question would make me look smart.

"Who did you… did we, beat out for this?" I sipped my water. My question surprised them.

"Uhhh… there were five bids, besides Blatchford. One was Norwegian, a big shipyard, and they seemed the strongest to us. I don't really know why they didn't win," said Dieter, who did the talking, evidently. "They've handled similar stuff and they are a Hell of a lot closer! There's obviously a reason. It's not our job to tell the designers they made a mistake selecting us."

"They made a mistake? You don't believe that!"

Casey and Dieter looked at each other. What thoughts they shared I had no idea, but it was weird waiting for this answer.

Casey spoke. "We never expected to win this, Mr. Anton, not really. We're lucky to even be considered. Submitting a bid on this was good for Blatchford's resume… you know what I mean?"

I did know what he meant. Still weird. Blatchford was probably ready to do this project, but we had no similar work to point to. We did have some phenomenal welders, though; I'd heard that.

"So, then, fellas," I looked at them in turn, "what was the magic? Whose hat had the rabbit in it?" Casey looked puzzled.

Dieter explained, "It's like when a magician pulls birds and things from his sleeve. We say 'pull a rabbit out of your hat' because sometimes magicians do that, too. You know?" Casey smiled and rattled off something in German and Dieter nodded enthusiastically. "Ja, ja, ja!" he said.

"I don't think there was any magic, like you say, Valter. We made a serious proposal with minute detail. We played up our facility and our three welders, like I said. When we invited them to visit us we had our fingers crossed. When they accepted we felt that it was a possibility for the first time. Funny how it works." He took a long pull on his beer.

"Who else was bidding? You said there were five?"

"Ya, yes. Five. The Germans were also a proven shop – ship builders, in Bremen. But I think the Danes would have only used them at half price, if you get me. They hated the idea of doing business with a former Nazi industry. There was a Japanese bid, too. They are usually pretty good but after the initial opening we didn't hear any more about them. Same with the Koreans… South Koreans. Hyundai Heavy Industries could handle the job as well as anyone, we thought. Actually they are doing a big piece of it, just not this part."

"And the fifth bidder?" I raised my eyebrows to accentuate my curiosity.

"General Dynamics. Our nuclear sub builder. They have facilities and skills galore. I don't think the Danes wanted to deal with any military contractors, period. Funny."

Our entrees came. Our petite filets had holes through them the long way. I had expected them to be grilled but there were no grill or grating marks on them, and they were done perfectly. I filed that away. We ate.

Finally I took a breather from chewing and swallowing. "It almost sounds like Blatchford was the least capable bidder. Would that be fair to say?"

"Well, not too loud, we think!" Dieter poked Casimir in the arm and they both nodded and smiled. "Really, Walter, we can do the job and Casey, here, is the one who proved that. We submitted a dozen sample welds on a series of joint geometries and our guys aced every test. I know we can do this. But we haven't sent our commitment, have we?" They were both looking at me. That commitment was on my head... alone.

"No. We haven't. You guys should know that I've been on this project for only three and a half days. You know that, right?" They looked at each other.

"What do you mean, Walter... three and a half days? You've worked for Blatchford longer than us." They were genuinely confused about my position. I wondered how much I should tell them about our fucked-up real estate dealings.

"In effect," I began, "I got called in to smooth out some difficulties we'd run into on use of a piece of railroad that is crucial to shipping the long pieces... you know the ones." They both nodded. Their elbows were on the table as they leaned closer to me. "As I understand it our famous congressman, Wittenauer, got some people ahhh... irritated, you could say, over getting permits for that short piece of railroad track." Both men sat back and became agitated at the mention of Wittenauer's name.

"Are you sure it was Wittenauer who caused the problem, Walt?" Dieter asked.

"Well, yeah. So what?"

"We couldn't have gotten this far without his help, that's so what. He's been with us all along." Dieter was frowning and appeared angry. Casey sat back with his arms folded, expressionless. I realized I was inches away from stepping in something I knew nothing about. It was the story of this whole goddamned project.

"Hold your welded joints, boys," I advised as I gestured with my hands to stop. "I only know what I know. This is why we are having this lunch. So, tell me what he's done for the project. I need to know, if we are ultimately going to win this thing."

Dieter ran his hand through his straight blond hair and looked out the windows towards the South Shore. He was breathing audibly. Casimir clasped his hands between his knees and was leaning down, studying the floor. Finally Dieter, the explainer, wiped his eyes and put his elbows back on the table.

"Walter, you don't seem to know too much about what it has taken to win this selection." His face was blank; Casey's head was shaking back and forth. I could see his bald spot.

"Listen, Dieter, right now I'm all you've got. Don't give me a hard time. I'm doing my damnedest with very limited information. I'm picking up pieces without knowing who dropped them. Tell me about Wittenauer so I don't go make a mistake that wastes all your work."

"Wittenauer got us the Ex-Im bank agreement on financing, without which we had nothing. Then he got the State Department to smooth some issues with the Danish government – something we're going to purchase from Denmark that is important to them, big contract, I think. Then I heard he was even working on this railroad of yours. We'd be dead in the water if he hadn't been there every step of the way. He met the Danes when they came over to see the shop. Really made them feel wanted, introduced them to Terry Bradshaw, Franco Harris and a couple of the other guys. Shit we could never do. Like I said: dead in the water."

"Wow. Well, okay. I never heard any of that. I knew he was tight with Blatchford. I know he has offered to help with a pollution problem – work with the EPA for us. I heard that at a meeting. But," and I held up one finger, "and it's a big 'but,' he also has some enemies in town, here and they don't want him to succeed at anything and I have to make those people happy enough to let us run your girders down that little track. So it's not all pink marshmallow fluff."

"What?" they both said.

"Just a saying, that's all. One of his non-admirers said that the good congressman thinks he shits pink marshmallow fluff." They both laughed and I felt on par with them, again.

Dieter said, "I have to say we know what you mean about that." They were both smiling and shaking their heads. "He's a politician, after all, right?" I nodded and shook my head, too.

"Look," I said, "you two have provided me with some crucial insights that may have prevented a blow-up with Wittenauer, and that's a big deal. He has pissed some people off. Right now there is no clear path for permitting us to use that railroad and no practical way to get the damn things to barges without it. That's what I have to do: get that permitted. There are multiple games being played and I'm still learning them. When the ball is finally in my hands I'll probably have only one chance to score. Anything you think of that Wittenauer told you or that you have heard someplace that might affect me – my efforts – call me. We can meet again. Whatever. It's coming to a head in a few days, I expect."

"What can *you*," he emphasized, "actually *do* when the time comes? What power does a... do you have?"

"I've got Hal's full support to take action when it's needed. I can spend a lot of money to make it happen. If either of you have friends in the City who might help with the mayor or with the Three Rivers Trust or with the Development Commission, tell me. We need to attack on all fronts." They looked at each other blankly, then back at me. They held their hands palms up.

"Don't know people like that, I don't think. Never heard of em."

"Well, wait a minute. Haven't we ever sold fabrications for bridges or something here in Pittsburgh? We must have."

Dieter's mouth hung open. Casey looked at him. He started to nod slowly. "I think Blatchford has steel in Three Rivers Stadium and not long ago in some new ramps and overpasses on the Point. Probably some other stuff, too." They both nodded a little.

"Well, there must be someone you can talk to who has influence..." Dieter shook his head.

"Not our deals. I can find out maybe."

I nodded vigorously. "Please. Real estate in Pittsburgh is a real nightmare. Any advantage is crucial. Anything, okay?"

"All right. We'll see what we can find." The two salesmen stood and Casey signaled for the check. I reached for it, but Dieter pulled it to his chest, firmly. "I can get this, Walter. This was interesting, I think, no?"

"Very much. I appreciate your time."

"We are all swimming together, I think you say?" I looked at him blankly.

"You mean, 'it's sink or swim.' I guess you could say we better swim together or we'll sink separately; something like that."

"Ya, ya!" He laughed. She brought him his credit card slip and we walked out together, me still trailing. The Beemer was already running. As they climbed in I remembered what I needed to find out for Mid Waters.

"Dieter, Dieter! Wait a second." I scooted over to his window. He rolled it down.

"What is it?"

"I need to know how many girders will we ship at one time? How many will go together?" Dieter looked over at Casey as if to ask what kind of a numb-nut are we dealing with?

"Eight. Eight at a time; five shipments. Three weeks apart. Like clockwork. It's in the contract." He squinted up at me, still wondering how little I knew.

"And each one weighs what?"

"What for? Forty-four tons."

"To calculate shipping costs. Shipping costs. But," I paused for a few seconds, "can we build them that fast?"

"I think we are having two meetings for the price of one, eh?" Dieter was irked that his air-conditioning was escaping. "We are going to run two long shifts or three shifts some of those weeks. You'll have to ask someone in Personnel. We sell em, that's all." He started his window rolling up.

"Thanks," I half-shouted. "Thanks for lunch, huh?" I waved and then leaned down to wave more to make sure they both saw my appreciation as their car backed out and pulled away – tight-assed pricks though they were.

I sat in my car letting the oven cool before starting the engine and the American air-conditioning that my car had. I flipped a sheet on Linda's Plus and Minus pad and I wrote down what the two contract men had told me.

Probably the main thing was Wittenauer's role up to now. Why hadn't Blatchford said anything? Maybe he really thought the two puzzles were unconnected... compartmentalized. I was determined to speak with our Rep but I would have been a lot more hostile if I hadn't met with Dieter and Casimir. His good works for Blatchford didn't cause me to trust him, but at least I wouldn't be the reason he scuttled us.

Dieter and Casey were unfriendly and I couldn't figure why the meeting ended on a negative note. They didn't seem to think I was on the same team, pulling for the same result. Strange. I better ask more questions, but of whom?

I pulled onto the Crosstown Boulevard, swung under the Allies and onto 376 east. From there I took the Birmingham to East Carson and to the quay where Mid Waters' cranes stood waiting. I said hello to Angus Newhall's secretary, Sally Routsis.

"Ahhh… Sally, I told Angus I'd have his information after lunch, today, and here I am. Can he see me for a minute?" I smiled my waiting room smile.

"He is here, Mr Anton," she assured me, remembering my name. "I'll check."

"Send him in, Sally!" boomed out Angus. We heard him standing up.

She opened the door and Angus was standing in his doorway.

"There you are, laddie! Good to see ya!" He clapped his big hand on my shoulder and guided me to sit while he resumed command from the pilot's chair. "So, have ye been busy, then, lad? Whatcha got?"

"Well, Angus, I have been busy. I now know how many of these big curved girders we'll be shipping at once. That's something."

"Right you are, Walter. Right you are. So… uhh… what?"

"Huh? Oh! Yeah. Eight at once, Angus. Eight pieces around forty-four tons each."

"Humph. Eight, huh? Eight. Well I was thinking about two at once just to see what we might have to do. Kinda intrestin.

You got, say, ninety ton. We need to weld up some racks to set these things in. We'll ride em low to keep em stable, but to pick em up we'll need two cranes, and that's a tricky transfer. I been thinkin about this job."

"Two cranes. Wow. Why?" I shook my head, reflecting complete ignorance.

"One crane can handle thirty-eight ton; one crane can do twenty-five. So we've got to balance fifty-fifty. We've already figured out how we might practice before we get one of the actual pieces." Angus sat back with a supremely confident smile and clasped his hands. I was impressed.

"What were you able to find out on the route... and cost?"

"Ahh, yes. The r-root." Angus leaned way over to reach a file folder from a cabinet behind him. Bulging with papers, it dropped onto his desk with a loud "slap."

"There ye be, lad. Dig in and ye'll find it." He was chuckling. I looked at the folder and then at him.

"Not what I'd expect for a thousand."

"Aww, c'mon, lad. I'm playing wit' ye. You should appreciate you can't find it in the Yellow Pages."

"I guess not, but what is it?" I leaned forward with my arms crossed.

"I'll tell ye I worked this in multiple ways, Walter. I worked it alone and with some standard bulk loads... coal, gravel, wheat... stuff like that. I looked at going North, then I figured it for the Mississippi and for the Ten-Tom. They got some deals working to ship on the Ten-Tom so I'm lookin very hard at that."

"What's a Ten-Tom?" I tried to see the papers he had, but I doubt they'd have made much sense.

"Ohh, God, laddie. I wasn't charging for an education but I'm includin one, eh?"

I shrugged.

"The Ten-Tom is a barge route that uses the Tennessee River and the Tombigbee River and some canals the Army built for us. It starts at Paducah and winds up in Mobile Bay. Right now it's cheaper than the Miss and faster. I'm thinking that's our route. Save ye quite a bit, I'm figurin."

"If I can stipulate that there are savings… and I believe you, Angus… can you tell me what it will cost to take eight of these things to Mobile?"

"Aye. Aboot twelve thousand…," I raised my eyebrows. "Each." I stood up.

"Siddown, lad. It sounds like a lot but that's because you have no idea what a lot is when it comes to river shipping, do ya?"

I had to agree, but it sounded like a lot. "All right. Let's say that's all fine. What will the rest of the trip cost… to Denmark?"

"Don't want much, do ye? I can price the trip south, Walter, but the trip north and east is another kettle o' fish. Probably not up to you guys, anyway."

"And why not?" That didn't sound right.

"Usually, I would think the builders are going to dictate who brings the pieces. There's lots of factors, Walter. I can't control them. If you want me to contract for the ocean leg, I can do that. I can do that. I've done that. I'm just thinkin the buyer has a lot to say aboot that part. You ask them first, okay? You'll be happier."

I was smiling as he leaned back in the pilot chair. "Looks like good work, Angus. I'll need a written description of how you handle them and the cost. Include your invoice for $1,000 and I'll get it paid promptly."

"Right here, laddie." He handed me a bulky envelope and clapped me on the back. "Anything else now?"

I stopped and whipped around, scaring Angus back a step. "Angus!" I practically shouted, "I do have something else!"

"Well, ease off boy. Ye'll bust a hawser. What, pray tell?" I gestured for him to sit down.

"Yesterday you said you shared the bank or something with the Three Rivers Trust, didn't you?" He looked back, blank for a moment.

"The Trust? Yeah. I said sumtin like that. What of it?"

"I may need help with the Trust, Angus, but I don't want to be at cross purposes with how you might influence them. Do you see what I mean? I need the Trust… which means I need for Roberta McGillvray, herself, to accept our use of that little railroad. I don't know what your ability to help is. I guess that's what I need to know, Angus. How can you encourage the Trust to back our railroad and your added business?"

Angus Newhall turned back and forth in little quarter turns on his pilot's chair. He looked at me with a little squint, his hands folded on his belly. "Truth to tell, lad, I been thinking aboot that question since we talked. I may be able to help… I just may, I just may. I'm not sure exactly how to move on it. Maybe we can set up a couple shots and see where the balls go, eh?"

"I thought I was in the deep woods... and you're asking *me* for directions?"

"Well, Laddie, you're the one who knows where he needs to get to, ain't ye?" He leaned forward like a cat – too fat to pounce but dreaming of the day.

"Okay, I guess I am, so let's see. First, you mentioned the bank. What's that got to do with it?"

"Yeah, right. The only bank she's felt comfortable in is Western Pennsylvania Trust. You can look em up. Got their start in the '80's… the last '80's. Two Scots and a Lutheran started it with coal and railroad money. No Jews have held an office, there, by coincidence I'm sure. Now, way back when I have relatives from those Scots so I've always banked there and they've always been fair with me. Roberta banks there because it's not Jewish, I believe. Ask someone else. I do know she puts a lot of stock into what the President of Western Penn has to say about investments and such. I'm thinking I could encourage him... to encourage her... to favor your plans. Maybe you know better."

"I don't know, Angus. You and I are trying to use logic cause it's good for business. Logic doesn't move Roberta McGillvray. If it's okay, let's keep your influence in our quiver to use at a vital time. I can see where her banker could tip the balance… if she's on the balance point, sort of. Make sense?"

"It's your game, Laddie. I'll play along wit' ye." He stood and stretched. "Time for work, now. I'll see ya later."

We shook and I left. It seemed like it was time to contact Wittenauer, which could be interesting. He maintained his largest District office in the Gateway Center, near the Point. The Gateway was the first big urban renewal project, undertaken in the late 1950's. Railroad yards, warehouses, rows of tenements and old business structures were razed… everything but the tiny remnants of Fort Pitt. The Gateway Center rose from those ruins to put a shiny, stainless steel and glass face on the new Pittsburgh. The congressman's budget provided for a suite that looked over his electoral fiefdom. I drove over the Fort Pitt Bridge and into a big parking garage off Commonwealth.

The elevator doors opened facing a cute black receptionist who appeared too tiny for her console. I saw no reference to Thomas Wittenauer, Representative in Congress, Fourteenth Pennsylvania District. The receptionist said, "Congressman Wittenauer's office?"

I nodded "yes" and started to speak. She continued, "through the double glass doors behind you, all the way to the end of the hall and turn right." She didn't look up as she repeated directions for the thousandth time.

"Thanks," I said to the top of her head.

No one was guarding the fancy wood door into the great one's office, but I could hear people talking inside, and I saw people walking back and forth. I started into the inner sanctum of congressional services and wasteful spending. Behind me the outer door closed and a soft-spoken man asked, "I can help you, please?" I processed his statement and took a couple steps back in to the anteroom.

"You must be seeking Mr. Wittenauer, the Congressman?" I felt like answering, "No, Mr. Wittenauer the dick-wad," but I nodded and replied with a pleasant "Yes, thanks." Still, how many Wittenauers worked here?

"Do we know you are expected to see Mr. Wittenauer?" I decided I didn't like the way the slender man spoke, looked or acted.

"We aren't sure. I represent Hal Blatchford and I am following up on our meeting of last Thursday at Blatchford Steel. I'm sure he'll know why I'm here. Thanks very much."

The young man, whose name I could see was Devlin, stayed standing, fussing with some papers, piling them just a bit more neatly. "Well, uhhm... sir, we have a very tight schedule here, in the District. I'm not sure the congressman is here. We should have your visit on the calendar. Why don't you seat yourself in one of the leather chairs."

There were three chairs, all leather. I wondered why Devlin needed to describe the upholstery. I stood. Devlin turned half way in each direction as if seeking some crucial item. If I would wait a moment he would see what *we* could do, holding his hands up as if telling me to "stay." He backed through the door and took a full step backwards, facing me, before he turned toward a pair of staffers outlined in a window. He came back and closed the door to the inner rooms.

"Congressman Wittenauer is in Washington, I'm afraid. Is there some sort of problem that we can help you with?" Devlin made his papers still neater, alternately looking up, his head cocked. He moved as though his hips and backbone were all one.

"Perhaps, ahh... Devlin, I was not speaking clearly. I am personally following up on a meeting I had with your boss. He has been working on a project for my boss, Harold Blatchford, an old, old friend of your boss." I stopped speaking to see if the slender functionary had changed his expression. He had his hands on his hips and was looking at me wide-eyed, waiting for a point.

"Please tell me, young man, if I have said something you don't understand." I waited.

He shook his head, moving it only a couple inches each way.

"Okay. Now I will ask you a question. Are you ready?" I brightened my face and looked as happy as I could, even nodding slightly, hoping he would answer in the affirmative. He seemed ready. "Awright, Devlin, here it is: Why did you think I had a problem that you or anyone besides the congressman, could help me with? Do you understand the question?"

He nodded. I thought he might tear up. "I... I just... um, we always try to, ahh, help everyone who comes in. We, ahh, well... we're supposed to."

"Okay, then. We're getting somewhere. I'm gonna ask another one. Ready?"

He nodded again.

"Since I really need to speak to Mr. Wittenauer and since he really needs to speak to me, do you think you could arrange a meeting for me?" I nodded and nodded, "with the great and powerful Wittenauer?" More nodding from me and a tight pout from Devlin.

"You could have just said that, mister... ahm, mister what's-your-name."

"You are a real prize, Devlin. I will share my observation that your boss is lucky to have you here, helping everyone. When can I see him?"

"Well, I'll have to see if we can fit you in to the calendar, won't we?" I'd never seen such a smug look of self-realized power.

"What do you mean, 'we,' Devlin?"

"Huh?" He was slow on the uptake.

"Not, 'we,' Devlin. It's you. As in, you should pick up the Bat-Phone, there, hidden on your big desk. Then you can hit the button that connects you to the Washington office and demand an appointment with Congressman Wittenauer. You have done that before, yes?"

He opened and closed his mouth without a sound. "I'm a busy man, Devlin. Tell me which button does that and I'll make the call. How's that?" I stepped to the edge of the desk and started to pick up the phone. Finally he moved and grabbed the phone from my hand.

"If you'll sit down, mister, I'll call. Who am I calling for? You never said your name." His tone was tight and without inflection.

"Walter Anton. I am here representing Hal Blatchford. I know that's two names. Can you keep them straight?"

"Yes. Please be seated." He gestured the phone toward the chairs.

"In one of these leather chairs, here?" I swept my hand toward the three chairs. Devlin glared at me, but at least he had the phone clamped to his cheek, dialing.

"Yes," Devlin said, "I know, but there is a man who insists that we fit him in. He says he's associated with Blatchford." He kept his eyes on the desk and turned halfway away from me. There were a few grunts, "hmmns" and partial words. Then, "If you can." He changed expressions and fidgeted with his free hand, checking his nails, then he nodded, probably unheard. Finally he wrote on pink message paper. "Okay, then. Yes, I'll tell him. Yes. Uh-huh. If that's all you have. No." At this point he looked at me and nodded, again. "Thanks, Naomi. Yes, I know. You're wonderful, girl. Thank you!" He ended in a little sing-song.

I stepped closer to the desk. "Well?"

"He can see you tomorrow at ten o'clock. They are in session but he is making time for you." I stood there, dumbfounded. I had about eighteen hours to make it. In a way it was fine, but I knew I was supposed to be angry, then. Devlin pulled out a poor photocopy of a map of Capital Hill. He leaned close to me and began to point out how to find Wittenauer in the Rayburn Building.

I snapped the paper from his hand and moved back a step. He was too close. I'd been to D. C. a couple of times and the map was not hard to read. I took the elevator back to the lobby.

I stewed over the visit. The next-morning game was probably employed when they really hoped the visit would never be made. For me, it was awkward, but not impossible. If I moved quickly I could make it to room 2332, Rayburn, in time. I took a couple of rights, Liberty to Commonwealth and onto the Penn-Lincoln and home.

***

"Where?" Linda squeaked.

"To Washington, D. C., it's not that far."

"That's crazy, Walter. There's no parking. What if you get tired?"

"It's less than two hundred and fifty miles. I take the Pike to Exit 161 and then I-70 to the Beltway. There's a Hyatt on the Hill. I get in before midnight, get a decent night's sleep and the whole appointment will be only a half-hour, if that, and I'm back for supper. Simple."

"Tomorrow is Wednesday. Don't you have league?" I hesitated. I never missed league. Worse, I was dying to speak to Katy Mellon for the first time since Thursday's meeting. I thought I could make it for seven if I left D. C. no later than noon.

"I can make it with no problem. If I miss it, we still have four to bowl. So, no disaster." Linda shook her head.

"Well, let's pack, then." She went to the bedroom, resignedly. In minutes she had packed underwear, socks, a fresh white shirt, and two ties to choose from. On a wooden hanger she had my really good suit with two buttons fastened. In a separate, plastic-lined bag she had a full man's kit, with a brand-new toothbrush. By the time I had brushed my teeth she had made a reservation for that night. Amazing.

I topped-off the gas at Penn Hills Shell at 5:20. In fewer than ten minutes I was on the Turnpike. KDKA was on and stayed with me until the signal faded. My Jeep had a tape player. Sinatra and I cruised together for sixty miles.

WEDNESDAY, MAY 22, 1985

About five miles before the Beltway I leaned my head out the window to see the monuments through only air. It meant something... always has. At twelve-thirty the Hyatt attendant took my car; a bellman took my bags. Within minutes I entered an elevator. A robot confirmed my wake-up call. The bed was comfortable.

The room was $209 a night. It seemed worth it to get our project moving. To be early to Wittenauer's office, I paid the crazy $18.95 for the "buffet" breakfast. For that price my waffle had a mountain of strawberries, the o.j. was fresh-squeezed and the coffee genuinely good. I scooped a "Post" and ate alone, doing my best to look like I did this all the time.

Packed again, I headed to the bell stand. A big man named Jamal greeted me warmly. "Jamal," I asked, "can I leave my bag with you for a couple of hours?"

"Absolutely, Mr. Anton. The charge is five dollars. Here's your claim check. How else can I help you, today?"

"Well, I'm going to visit my congressman... naturally, right?" We both nodded. "I was hoping I could leave my car, too. Is that possible?"

"Well, yes it is, for guests. There's no big event, today, so I can hold your car, but that's twenty-five dollars and only until five P. M. If that works for you then just show me the money!" He laughed as I paid that, too.

"I gotta warn ya, Mr. Anton, if your car is here later than that you either check in for another night or it'll cost you a hundred to get the car back. They're pretty strict on that."

"Oh, I'll be back in a couple hours or less."

"Then you have a fine time up on the Hill, then. Your keys will be here; just give one of us the claim number."

At nine-twenty I stepped into a cab and told the driver, "Rayburn, please." I figured that's the way cool Washingtonians gave directions. It may have been, but he pulled up before an array of square columns on Independence Avenue without a word. I gave him ten-sixty-five and a two-dollar tip and he pulled away with no wish for a good day or future contact, perhaps recognizing that what cool Washington-important people did had not impacted me. I could see the damn Hyatt from the taxi stand.

In Washington, at least for those edifices touched by Congress' careful budgeting, no building is worth entering unless one climbs broad granite steps. I did my part and pushed through into cool darkness.

Wittenauer's office was 2332 but only after passing through a metal detector. Nothing I had worried the pleasant, black Capital Officer. I asked her, "2332?" and she told me to take the elevator to the right and turn right when I got off. It was about ten doors from there, on the left. I'd see the numbers or the nameplate. I followed directions and marveled about being in the same place as famous congressmen and women. Two of them even walked past me on the third floor. I didn't stare. Coolly important Washingtonians would walk down the hall the way I was at that very moment, knowing where I was going, unimpressed by their surroundings. I found Room 2332 at nine-fifty.

It wasn't all that fancy. It looked like a steno pool with a half-dozen men and women typing, calling, photo-copying and moving papers. The closest drone came over to me after a short wait. "Can I get you some coffee?" she asked.

"No, thanks. I have a ten o'clock with Tom," I said Washington coolly, "and I'm supposed to ask for Naomi." The youngish woman looked me up and down and asked, "Wittenauer?"

"Huh?" was my cool reply.

"Did you mean Tom Wittenauer, the Congressman, himself?"

"Oh, sorry. I didn't think there might be two Toms. Yes. The appointment was made just, ahh, eighteen hours ago. From Pittsburgh." She widened her eyes.

"I'll check with Naomi. Why don't you have a seat?" She pointed to the chairs. "I'll just be a minute, Mr..."

"Anton. Walter Anton." I sat and she disappeared. I picked up the Post and found where I had left off in a story about the mayor. My greeter came back.

"Naomi wants to know who you spoke to in Pittsburgh." The plump brunette smiled toward my feet.

"Why? Does she think I would drive here without an appointment? What sort of opera ..."

"No, please, Mr. Anton," brunette pleaded with her hands. "The only confirmation we have is your saying who you spoke with in Pittsburgh. Please." She really had a delightfully cheery face. I took a breath.

"I believe the sweet young fellow was named Devlin. Does that work?"

"Yes, thank you, sir. Please come with me." She opened the big door and I pondered her fluid butt as we walked.

Again, an anteroom where the big cheese could be seen only by pleasing a door-mouse. One end of the room was full of files and stacks of newspapers and a table covered with cut up newspapers – filtered daily, evidently. I could imagine that positive and negative articles, photos and editorials were collated and presented with summaries to the great man so that appropriate, politically useful responses or amplifications could be quickly made.

To my left was a nice desk, the realm of Naomi. There were two plain chairs and she gestured for me to sit. She didn't bother standing.

"I apologize for the little quiz, Mr. Anton, but we get a lot of people waltzing in who think we can disrupt our schedules. Devlin did call me and the Congressman is looking forward to speaking with you. The chairman of Natural Resources just dropped in and he's in with the Congressman, now. Can we get you some coffee? Something stronger?" She waited for my choice of beverage. I could imagine that people chose option two.

"Holy cow," I exclaimed, "coffee is plenty strong for this time of day. I'd love some. Thanks." I smiled back at her. She must have touched a button because brunette showed up with half-decent coffee moments later. I slid my chair back from Naomi's desk and sipped as unobtrusively as I could. A wall clock said ten-twenty.

At ten-thirty-two Naomi's phone buzzed. "Yes Congressman, he is," she said. "About a half-hour or so. Yes. Yesterday, that's right. Are you... ahh, ..." She made a couple of agreeable humming sounds, hung up and stood up. Choreography.

The door to the inner sanctum opened with Wittenauer and an older, heavier man stepping through. Naomi held the door. Wittenauer said, "Jim, again, it's no problem. I think Sam and Carolyn are with us and we should be okay. I'll see ya at lunch. Thanks a lot." They walked through Naomi's realm and to the outer door, making no attempt to hide their conversation or to acknowledge me.

"I think you're right, Tom," the older man said. "And no more amendments would be best, too."

"I'll make sure of it, Jim. In an hour, huh?" Jim may have answered but the door closed ending the banter. Wittenauer practically bounded into the small anteroom with his hand held out. I stood up and accepted it.

"Great to see you, Walter. Feels like we were just together. Smooth ride down?" He ended the handshake by clamping his other hand on my shoulder and pushing me into his big, living-room office.

"So," he said, "how's my friend Hal Blatchford?"

"Well, Tom… may I call you Tom?" After a pause the great and powerful Tom nodded and flipped his hand for me to continue. "Thank you, Tom. I appreciate that. You know, I've been a Republican since I was born, I think…" I was chuckling and the congressman joined in.

"Best way to do it, Walter. Saves time and worry, doesn't it?" His voice rose with the question and I agreed that it surely did. A weird plan was forming as I thought about the next meaningless statement or question.

"On that note, though, I think Hal is doing fine… at least he looks good. I know he's got a good mad building up though. That's why I'm busting my ass on this Parcel 840 business."

"The what? Parcel what?" Wittenauer had his hands steepled in front of his chin. Maybe he thought he'd be protected from splashing bullshit.

"Where that little piece of railroad track is, you know? We were talking about trying to get a permit to upgrade it, last Thursday." I finished my statement as flat as I could. I looked past his face to the outside scene. His office faced the inside court of the Rayburn, not toward the Capital. I tried to appear unconcerned.

"Oh yes, yes. You know, I tried my damnedest to get the city to move on that silly thing. Has there been any movement? Anything at all?"

I shook my head and started to speak but he was a faster deflector than I was a shoveler.

"You'd think the mayor there... McKay, right? You'd think he could see that letting us run a few flatcars down that spur was good for business and good for jobs. Christ, I told him that Blatchford was ready to hire up to a hundred new employees. What the Hell's the matter with him, do you wonder?"

"Boy, you're right about that, Tom," I lied. "I tried talking to him but all we could agree on was Old Overholt whiskey. Funny."

Wittenauer shook his head as if to commiserate with me. His fingers were drumming on the desk. Must be something he'd rather do.

"One of the reasons I needed to go over this problem with you, Tom, was to see what you might be able to do to help us with the Three Rivers Trust. They seem to be a brick wall; maybe you know what I'm talking about." More head shaking on my part. He was smiling a funny little tight-lipped grimace.

"Well, Walt, I do. The real power in that agency is a woman named Roberta McGillvray. I don't know if you heard of her?"

"I have, Tom, but I don't have any special sway with her, that's for sure. In fact, my wife, Linda, actually goes to their meetings and I never even knew it. That's something, huh?"

"No shit, Walter? Who'd have guessed? That's a fine how do ya do. Can't she help you with Roberta?" He was smiling and shaking his head, too.

"Well, not so's you'd notice, apparently. I got an introduction but no encouragement about using that piece of land. Not a bit. That's where you can help Hal... and me, too, actually. What will turn Roberta on in our favor, Tom? You've known her a lot longer than we have. What can you share with me that will provide some leverage?" I gave him my best helpless bumpkin look.

"Wow, that's a tall order, Walt, you know that?" His head was shaking in shorter little jerks, now. "What makes you think I have that sort of sway?"

"I can only judge from that luncheon she had at Duquesne on Monday. If I had to guess, she was looking daggers at you and fawning over Senator Fahnstahl. I figured there must be some history there. No?"

"Oh, jeez, Walt. I think she just doesn't like Republicans, is all. I mean, that's about it, honestly." I pursed my lips and nodded.

"Well, that's just something I'll have to work on, I guess. Now, before I go, let me ask you about that EPA problem. Just take a few minutes, I think."

"Fire away. That's one I probably can help you with."

"Well, I know that Hal really appreciates your alerting us to that problem. Absolutely." Wittenauer was grinning, maybe a little more than necessary.

"Walt, I was gonna be damned if I could let Blatchford be injured buying that land and getting screwed on someone else's pollution. Hell no!" His congressional dudgeon was sky high. You had to love his concern for business and for his old friend, Hal.

"I know how you feel, Tom. Damn straight. Listen, you had mentioned that there might be a way to get EPA to work with us. What can you do to get that settled? If I get anywhere on the land I'm going to have to move quickly, so every minute matters. We have to resolve our committment to the Danes on that bridge within a couple of weeks. I understand you've been right out front in helping Blatchford get as far as we have. Pretty good!"

Wittenauer tried to diminish his prideful role with his body language and gestures. "I'd do it for any business that has a chance to grow with just a little help, especially on international stuff. That's one reason I'm here. I'm glad it has worked out so far." I had to steer him back to doing something we really needed NOW.

"Now we need you for this EPA stuff. I mean, we know nothing about getting through that kind of red tape. But, let me tell you how I see it and you correct me." I looked up at him, wide-eyed.

For his part, the congressman used his best 'I'm the expert, here and you are right to acknowledge my leadership' face. "Don't even try, Walt. They'll tie you up for months. Look, give me your personal numbers and I'll get this moving and let you know..."

I interrupted. "Yes, but first, what about this, Tom? We aren't building anything and we're barely going to even disturb the soil. Shouldn't that help our case? I mean, we're going to lease the land and turn it back in its current condition, right? I mean, won't that be important in all this?"

Wittenauer played along. "Wow, Walt. You may be right-on with that." He made a flourish of writing some notes as if my ideas mattered. "I will push this today, in fact. Don't you worry any further. I'll get it done." He stood up, ending my overnight jaunt, he seemed sure. He stepped around his desk to shake my hand.

"Walter, anytime you're in the city, come on by and see me, okay?"

"Sure, Tom. Thanks very much for that. Listen..." I stopped and turned toward him and he recoiled as from a cobra. "Is it alright to call you if I haven't heard by Friday? We're really getting close, you know?" He relaxed visibly.

"Sure, Walt. You do that. If I'm not available I'll make sure Naomi has your information. How will that be?" He pushed my shoulder toward the outer office. I went with it.

"Gee you've been just great on all this, Tom. I really appreciate your seeing me on short notice, like this."

"Hey, anything I can do, my friend. And you tell Hal I was asking for him, won't you?" I'd never seen such a wide smile.

"Will do, Tom. And it's been great to meet you, Naomi, too. Much better to have a face to go with the voice. Thanks, again!" I shook her hand for a moment, too. She smiled at me while her eyes flicked back and forth to Wittenauer's. He turned abruptly and headed back into his office. I asked Naomi for her card and felt better the farther away I was.

I sat near the elevator. I had index cards for notes but nothing was noteworthy. I took a couple and wrote down that I found almost everything he had said to be not true. I jotted down "Roberta" and noted that he acted like he didn't know her much. I jotted down "mayor" next to that and "same crap."

I'd just wasted a day on this stupid trip to D. C. If I tried to push Tom Wittenauer on the TRT I would have no more than I did. I did learn how disingenuous he was, but I had surmised that. Of course, I might have been wrong and he could have opened up, but when he acted like "Parcel 840" was not familiar, I knew where I stood.

If the congressman was that untrustworthy it made sense that Blatchford shouldn't trust him either. I neither liked nor disliked the owner of my company, but I began to feel a need to expose whatever might hurt him… including Wittenauer. So, what was his game with that meeting last week? I thought and thought with my pen poised over the index cards. I began to wonder about the EPA filings that only Wittenauer had discovered. If we couldn't clear the EPA it wouldn't matter what else I accomplished. Our Rep was pretty fast to promise a deal with the EPA on our behalf. I didn't know whether the EPA actually made deals. I wrote EPA on a card in different sizes.

Sitting there at the East end of the Mall, the EPA wasn't far away. I had copies of the PDC pages, including the EPA file numbers. I decided going to the EPA was worth more than making league. I got in the elevator with a handful of others and tried to see if anyone famous was with me. How the Hell would I know?

The Rayburn Office Building is about midway between Capital South and Federal Center Metro stations. I asked the lady who'd screened me in which station she would go. Her opinion was Federal Center because you didn't have to climb the hill. Sounded good to me. As I walked to the door I spun around and called out to her, "which station for the EPA?"

"Honey, take a cab. Too many changes by subway. There's cabs out front now… it's lunchtime."

"Thanks! 'Preciate it!" I waved and took the steps two at a time. A green and white "DC" cab was first in line. I told him I needed to go to the EPA. I hoped he thought I knew the route.

It wasn't far. The building looked nice but this part of "M" street was a little trashy... not safe after dark.

I spotted a deli with outdoor tables, and it struck me there were probably EPA employees right in front of me. Maybe one could speed me through a federal bureaucracy. It was worth a shot with only four hours to get my car.

I ordered coffee and a sweet roll and went outside. I tried to look lost. Finally, a small miracle. Two women at a table for four spotted me and the older of the two pointed next to her. I replied with my coffee cup, sidestepped through and smiled as I set my things down. "Wow! Thank you for rescuing me!"

"Oh, well. We've both been there." They nodded at one another. "You'll be much more comfortable sitting and we're almost finished anyway." More nodding.

"Well, I appreciate it. Listen, and don't take this the wrong way... can I ask if either of you work at the EPA?" They compared raised eyebrows.

"Neither of us, but Ann knows someone." Ann looked irked.

"Look, please don't worry. I'm not a Washingtonian and I have a problem to ask the EPA about. I was hoping I could find someone there to see if he or she might get me a quick answer. It's a small issue. Do you really know someone there?"

Ann finally spoke. "I do have a best friend there. I can call her."

"That'd be great, Ann. Do you have a waiting area at your office?" She nodded as she sipped some kind of frozen drink.

She glanced at her watch wide-eyed. "I have to be back in five minutes, so you'll have to finish fast if you want me to call."

"I'm with you. You're a life-saver." I smiled at the older woman who seemed a little miffed with her young friend when it was she who had invited me over. "I'm afraid I haven't introduced myself. Please forgive me," I aimed at the older lady, "I'm Walter Anton… from Pittsburgh. Came down last night."

She held her hand out and I held it for a moment. "Kathy, with a 'K' Simonetti. I work at a law firm. I've known Ann, here, since she was about ten. Her mother and I are old friends.

"So, you're both from the Washington area?" I gulped my coffee.

"Yup. Born and raised in Lewisdale, just a few miles into Maryland. My husband and I still live there."

All I could do is nod at how delightful Lewisdale must be. Ann had gathered up her wrappers and drink cup.

"Okay," I said. I shook Kathy's hand and thanked her again. Then I ran to catch up with Ann... a fast walker. Her office was on the second floor of a restored brick row-house, and she took the stairs, climbing nicely.

She turned into an office labeled Koenig and Roudenbush, PC, swiped her card in an electronic lock, and disappeared. There were newspapers and the Yale Law Review and the Bar Association Journal on a low glass table. I sat.

Ann was back two minutes later. "What kind of problem, Mr. Anton?"

"Oh... ahh, I guess it's just, umm, what kind of pollution is connected to a file number. I have the number with me." She nodded and held up one finger and backed inside.

About a minute later she returned. "Mr. Anton, if you go across to the EPA and tell the guard you're seeing Amaya Raines, she'll get you in. Third floor, knock on door three-oh-six, and she'll greet you. She thinks she can answer your question. I hope this helps."

"You've been wonderful, Ann, part of my lucky day, I think. I wish I could repay you somehow."

"No! No... ah, thanks. No. I hope it works out." The door swung closed and I headed downstairs.

I'd barely tapped the door at 306 when it popped open and a strikingly beautiful Hispanic woman beckoned me in. "I'm Amaya, Mr. Anton. I can give you a few minutes. What is the file number?" All business. She led me to her desk and sat me at a barren one next to it. I felt the need for quiet.

I handed her the page listing the EPA file numbers. She looked at it with a frown, turning it over and back again. She shrugged and slid a keyboard out. She tapped some keys and looked at a yellowish screen. She made sounds of frustration and started the sequence again.

She picked up the PDC page and asked me, "Where did these numbers come from, again?"

"The Pittsburgh Development Commission." I know they're the right numbers because I took pictures of the little signs on the property. Those are the numbers."

She was shaking her head. She handed me the page. "Let's try this again, sir. I may be misreading them. You read them to me as I enter them.

"Okay," she said, "slowly and clearly, if you will."

Carefully I read off the digits, letters and dashes. Amaya repeated each one as she keyed it in, her head shaking a "no" with each stroke.

"Mr. Anton, I don't know what you are doing, but these are not valid file numbers. Why would you think you could make up numbers?" Her expression was not that of a friendly public servant.

"Wait just a goddam minute. The use of the land these numbers are posted on is very serious business for me and my employer. I haven't made up a damn thing! How in Hell could the EPA post these numbers if they're no damn good?" I was seething and I didn't mind her knowing it. She was as much of the EPA as I'd ever met.

She stood up. "There is nothing else I can do for you, Mr. Anton. You'll have to leave."

"Wait a second. I… I'm sorry for being angry but you have no idea what a serious problem having a filing on this land is for us. I've told you only what I could. What should I do? The city obviously thinks the EPA posted these." Her face was like granite.

"Maybe you could check with the EPA field office in Pittsburgh. They have a good-sized staff." She walked over to the door and opened it.

As I walked past her I tried to shake hands but she ignored me. I thanked her anyway. I shuffled down stairs, holding the PDC page like a prescription for awful-tasting medicine.

I bought another coffee. I hadn't called Linda, yet. The cashier suggested the Metro had pay phones.

"Hi, sweetie," I said when Linda picked up at *englishclass*. "I'm sorry I didn't get to call this morning. I've been on the go. How are you?"

"Fine. It has been twenty hours, but I'm fine. How'd it go with the congressman?"

"I made some notes… mostly about what a liar he is. But, listen, I visited the EPA while I was here, you know? I mean, what the Hell? I was right down the street. You won't believe this."

"What, Walter? What are you talking about?"

"The EPA… the Environmental Protection Agency. They have a file on that land Blatchford needs to use. If we can't clear that hurdle nothing else matters. Wittenauer was claiming he could resolve that but I thought it wouldn't hurt to find out what kind of pollution there is, see?"

"Well, maybe he will take care of it. He's Blatchford's friend, you said. Now you're late for bowling. You'll be late, period, won't you?"

"Yeah, pro'bly. But listen! The EPA says they aren't valid file numbers! What about that?"

"Are you sure you have them right, Honey?"

"Positive. I even have the PDC pages. A lady at EPA tried to enter them and they wouldn't register. She got mad at me for making up numbers and told me to talk to the EPA in Pittsburgh. There's something funny about the whole thing."

"Well, you can't do any more there, can you? When are you coming home?"

"I'll be getting a subway in a few minutes. I should be on the road in a half hour."

"Well, you just drive safely, huh? I'll break your arm and both legs if you get into an accident. Or maybe not, but don't, okay?"

"I can't wait to get back, lover. And I'll be showering as soon as I get back. No bathing till I get there, promise?"

"Okay, Napoleon. I love you."

"Love you too. See you in a few."

Tony Bennett guided me out of D. C. and past the Beltway and almost to the Pennsylvania line on Route 70. I stopped at a McDonald's. I ate fries from the bag and thought about the EPA. How was Wittenauer going to resolve our "EPA problem" when the file numbers weren't even correct? Maybe there was no problem and it was all a big mistake. But the little signs were there. It was a puzzle.

Talking to Wittenauer was a waste. I suppose I wasn't surprised, but if he'd been willing to share a little I could have gained some background on the Trust and on Roberta. I had no more than I had yesterday. But the EPA was interesting. It would be doubly so when I found out what Pittsburgh knew about the numbers and the little signs. Bennett finished and I selected blindly from my stash of tapes. I came up with Linda Ronstadt and sang along with "What's New?"

It was after ten when I killed the engine at our Cape with the raised roof. Lights were on and I was really, really looking forward to hugging my Lindy with no clothes. I shook my arms and legs, took some deep breaths, rolled my head and neck and licked my lips.

Linda was right inside the door, wearing her filmy housecoat. I dropped everything and lifted her up a few inches with an enveloping embrace. "Ohhh… you must be exhausted," she said beside my ear.

I turned her left to right in a big "no." "Not too bad," I breathed. "I made good time and I stopped and walked around a couple of times." I held her at arm's length. "Boy, you look good to a tired traveler!" I kissed her. "I actually learned some interesting stuff. We'll have to go over our situation with this new info I got… or non-info, I guess."

"Yuh, that's interesting, but it's time for bed. Let's get you cleaned up."

"Well, if you're going to help, I'm for it."

"It's late, Honey, I think sleep is number one right now." She hung up my sportcoat and slacks and stowed my shoes. While I brushed my teeth she ran water to get the temperature right. To my delight she shucked her wrap and stepped into the shower before me. I finished up with mouthwash and stepped in right behind her.

I wrapped my arms around her. I was standing at attention and she could feel it.

"Walt, this is the wrong time of the month. I'm willing if you want to get involved with that, but nothing too elaborate." She held my boner with one hand, up against her belly.

"We're in the perfect place, aren't we? You can see I'm ready."

She raised one leg and guided me toward the promised land. Soon, we were washing each other, which was a good part of after-sex. She dried while I rinsed. She had panties on by the time I got to bed. We spooned and slept.

THURSDAY, MAY 23, 1985

Jackson looked up with a scowl. "You certainly had a low profile, yesterday," he grumbled. His eyes returned to his papers.

"That's what I want to explain, Jack. I took a run down to D. C. overnight." Now he looked up.

"You what? Washington? What on Earth for?" He pushed his papers away. "What kind of a plan is that? What'll that do for us? Jesus!"

"Easy, big fella," I tried to joke. "I got some insight that is going to affect our real estate problem big time. Being there made that happen. Not a waste at all."

"Speaking of real estate, Captain Marvel, your buddy Schumann called yesterday, but, since I had no way to reach you," he glared, "all I could do was tell him you'd call. I hope it wasn't time-sensitive. He didn't give details." Jack's face had a tight, pissed-off look.

"I'll call him. I have to go downtown, today, but I'll get my paperwork up to date first."

"That'd be nice." His eyes were back on his papers. I was dismissed.

"Yeah, fine." I headed to my almost-office, inspired and invigorated by my boss. What a leader.

The piles were deeper than usual. Both in-baskets were full, thanks to two contracts we had for a monster tunnel project in Boston. I had handed off a lot to Colleen. She was as good as

I am. I barely had to correct any judgement she made. I might have been worried but little by little I was forming an image of myself doing something more valuable in the future... based on railroad success, of course.

Is was eleven when I tried Schumann. "Good morning, John. Sorry I couldn't call yesterday. I was out of town..."

"So I heard. In D. C.?"

"You knew I was in D. C.? How'd you find that out?" I was thunderstruck.

"Oh, Jackson told me. Were you visiting Wittenauer?"

How in Hell did Jackson know that? I was dumbstruck.

"Walter? Is this a bad time?"

"Oh, sorry John. You had me wondering there. Yeah, listen, meeting with Wittenauer was a big waste, but I went over to the EPA and that was really interesting."

"Really," Schumann blurted out. Sounded like "rilly." "What did you learn; is it going to help us?"

"I think it might, but I have to check with EPA's office here in town. Tell you the truth, I think there's something funny with the whole business. I'll definitely let you know."

"Well, okay, good. Let me tell you why I called. I think there's a project in Larimer that could work as a swap opportunity. It's worth about two million and I know there's some UDAG money available and some other HUD dollars that might fit if the right paperwork is submitted."

"What can I do about it?"

"I'm coming to that. Liberty Bank wants to be involved in the project; it affects a minority community and they like to look good and make money, too. They could be an ally."

"I've met that guy! Baker or Walker or something like that. An odd name, I recall."

"Well, you've gotten around," Schumann observed. "It's Forrest Akers... sounds like a housing development all by himself, doesn't he?"

"Yeah, that's the guy... Forrest. Good-looking wife, too. Hummnh, that's interesting. I hope Roberta likes him... or his bank, anyway."

"Good. Okay. Now, look, here's what we need: we need to find out if the Trust is interested in this project. Do they have any pretty renderings of the site? Stuff like that. Do you think you could find that out? Could your wife help us?"

"Well, probably. She's very interested to see this work out. I will speak with her by lunchtime. I'm gonna go downtown and follow up on the EPA here, locally. I don't want to wait on any of this if I can make forward progress."

"No, good idea. Umm... "

"John, can I ask you a question?"

"Sure. Shoot!"

"When I first met with Roberta McGillvray I got her to agree to meet with me at least once more. Should I use that option now or what?"

"Ahh, well... um, I would say let's keep that in the bank. Let's see if we get some information on this Larimer project. That's parcel number LAR488-dash-8, by the way. If the Trust has given some thought to this parcel they'll have filed something, somewhere, and probably have a rendering of it, too. If Linda can find out any of that it will be a big help."

"I will see what she can do, John." I was ready to ring off when another question struck me. "John?"

"Yuh!"

"John, does this new project have a direct financial impact on Blatchford?" There was silence. I could hear a deep sigh.

"I wasn't going to get in to that until we knew more about feasability, Walt. I have to make full disclosure, here: Brightman would make money on the overall deal. I have to disclose our position. Right now I don't know how much Blatchford money will be needed. It depends on subsequent HUD funding and whether Liberty Bank is going to be a real investor or lender or just symbolic. I can't put those pegs in the right holes yet. I know you're always projecting costs. Let's put a number on Hal's table that would be my best guess on the maximum that might be involved. That would be about one million."

Now I blew out a breath. "Well. Okay, then. What would Blatchford own or be able to write off, in that worst case?"

"As far as I can see... and what I would frankly advise Blatchford to do, is to donate whatever is required. Straight out donate and do it in such a way that the Three Rivers Trust looks like heroes and champions of the downtrodden, etcetera, etcetera. You follow me?"

"I do. Actually it sounds like a basis for our planning. If we can get the Trust's blessing on our use of the railspur, I think Hal will see the investment as worthwhile. But, John, we've got only about five weeks, now. Can this come together in that little time?"

"It's not impossible. We'll need some breaks and some luck, but it's possible. Maybe your new buddy, Wittenauer can help us with HUD like he says he will with EPA." I felt like a cold, cold stone had landed in my stomach. I distrusted Wittenauer so much that I hated the thought of relying on him in any way.

"That's a tall order, John. I don't trust him. Maybe his connection to Blatchford is strong enough to get him do what's needed. I'll be careful with what I say to either of them."

"That's smart, Walt. You sound like an old hand at putting deals together."

"Hmmnnh, but I haven't put one together, yet. Listen, John, I'll let you know about the EPA filing. Thanks for your work so far."

"No problem. It's just business for us. You're a good client. It will be kind of special to see this work out, though. Talk to you soon." I sat back and mused about this real possibility of progress. Linda and I hadn't talked about pluses and minuses that morning. I said I'd call at lunch. I cleared the rest of the immediate invoices and made piles of requests, then got coffee.

Casimir, Dieter's sales partner, was sipping tea in the kitchenette. "Hey, Casey, how ya doin?"

Casey tipped his cup toward me. "Pretty good, Walter. You?"

"On the go every day. Pieces of that shipping problem are looking better and better." We both nodded at that useless commentary.

"Vell, dat's good. See you." I looked at an empty coffee pot and bought a soda.

I called Linda at *englishclass*. She was out. I got to the 'beep.' "Hi, Lindy. Give me a buzz back, will you? I'll be downtown. So, never mind. I'll stop in to see you. See ya."

I figured I could find a sandwich. I took a quick look in the in-baskets and locked my office. In an envelope were the PDC pages and one of my Polaroids of the EPA signs.

The Yellow Pages said the EPA had offices at Gateway-1. Handy for our congressman, I thought, and easy for me to find, including parking in the same garage. I asked the attendant for a lunch place. She thought I'd do better about two blocks toward Heinz Hall – lots to pick from over there. Dark clouds were building to the northwest. Potent thunderstorms often run right up the Ohio. I guessed I'd have time to eat before the rain hit, but I'm a better cook than a meteorologist. It started pelting down in teaspoon-sized drops as I chewed a Philly Steak at a bar along the windows, and within a minute of its first "hello" the storm blanked out my view. I could see only shapes of cars as everything turned blurry. Maybe it would blow over as fast as it came in. Every few seconds bright flashes heralded thunder that shook the building. I ordered a beer, something I never do at lunch.

Of course I had no umbrella. The sky lightened and the rain lessened. The thunder grew distant. I could get a cab, but that seemed ridiculous for two and a half blocks. Maybe staying close to buildings and awnings would be drier. What the Hell; I stepped out and walked quickly. I was only moderately wet after a block, but there was no cover at the Gateway. What the Hell, again. I wouldn't shrink. I walked at a faster-than-normal pace until I got within fifty feet of tower one and then jogged as if it helped. Between the doors, I was dripping. In the lobby my feet squished with each step. At a big stone planter I rolled up my coat and set it on the moss. Then I dumped water from my shoes. Squishy socks didn't make sense, either. What the Hell, a third time. I squeezed them and left them with the shoes and coat. My envelope of evidence was inside my shirt.

The EPA was two floors below Wittenauer's office. One guy rode up with me and he gave me but a single glance. I wondered how I'd react to being alone with a barefoot, wet idiot in an elevator. Ignoring him was probably best.

We both exited at 3. An arrow pointed toward the Environmental Protection Agency. I turned that way as did my polite fellow passenger. When he saw I was going his way he turned around. *For perfectly good reasons,* I figured.

Government offices see all kinds, but my entry into the EPA's lobby stretched the envelope for the ladies who ruled the long angular desk. I pulled the package with the PDC pages and my photograph from my shirt, set it on their console and buttoned up. They might have thought *what's the point?* but I believe in doing business in buttoned shirts, damn it. I had a tie on... what did they expect? It dripped periodically, but the knot was perfect.

Both women regarded me but neither jumped to ask how I might be helped. Perhaps they'd judged whatever they were trained to do would fall short. I gave them my most business-like demeanor.

"Hi," I opened, "my name is Walter Anton and I need to discuss a filing on a piece of land in the South Side Flats."

"Of course," the closer one replied. "Please sign in and I'll see if anyone can... deal with you." She pushed a large notebook closer. It had a ballpoint pen on a chain, fastened with a rivet. Theft prevention. I signed as representing Blatchford Steel Services and looked up; the same lady told me "Two-oh-five, sir." I entered that and looked up. "Just wait over there and someone will be out to help you," she sympathized.

She hadn't suggested I sit. Couldn't blame her – didn't want to. I stood by a rack of official-looking EPA publications, monographs on cleanup procedures and other exciting materials, occasionally feeling a trickle of water down my legs and butt. Now and then a drip hit the carpet. I pretended I dressed this way when I visited federal agencies. Good grief.

In a few minutes a pleasant-looking young woman stepped through a door. "Mr. Anton?" she called out. I looked around and I was still the only one there.

"Must be me," I replied. I smiled to allay her natural concerns. She seemed to concentrate on my feet. I admit they aren't photo quality but I don't have toe-fungus. I looked at them and up at her. She finally met my eyes and snapped to.

"Yes, Mr. Anton, how may we, ahh... help you today?" She was looking at my feet again.

"Well, it's my feet, you see? I notice you all have those coverings on yours."

"What?" She sounded dry.

"Look, I'm kidding. My shoes were full of water and this just seemed better. They're downstairs. I really do have a problem with an EPA filing. Here are the numbers." I held out the package to make my point.

Relief washed over her. The shoeless idiot was cogent. "We should have any information you need... ah, Mr. Anton, is it?" I nodded.

"Okay. Umm, maybe you should, ahm... no, that's fine. Follow me, why don't you?" She held the door and I used my best this-is-how-I-visit-government-offices walk. Thanks to cubicle culture, few people saw me or my feet. My savior led me into a small meeting room. I was squishing less, so I sat.

"What filings are you concerned about, Mr. Anton?" She seemed genuinely interested in being helpful. I felt better. I handed her the PDC pages and the Polaroid.

"You can see the numbers match with the pages I copied, there?" She nodded.

"I tried to track these down in Washington the other day." Her eyebrows went up and she started to say something, but held back and made a note on the margin of one of the copies.

"You say you tried to track these down. Why couldn't they help you?"

"Well, I guess the main problem was the lady I spoke with accused me of making up numbers. She got a little hot, I would say." More eyebrow action.

"Making up numbers. Hmnph." She flipped through the pages, checking them with the photo. Finally she stood up, holding the Polaroid. "Mr. Anton, I'm going to check our system for these. These numbers look like ours. I'm not familiar with them all. I'll be right back. Would you like coffee? Or a soft drink?"

"Actually some coffee would be nice. Thanks."

"It's right next door. You can make it yourself and I'll be right back."

I was reaching for the next door when I spotted two guys coming the other way. They took me in with one glance, and stopped. "Don't worry, fellas; no shoes, but I won't spit in the coffee." I went into the canteen room.

"Follow my lead, Barry," one said, "I'll give him a head fake and you tackle him. I'll call 9-1-1." They were laughing and I grinned back. I explained my crazy, rain-soaked arrival. "No problem, buddy," the squad leader said, "we've seen worse... and they work here!" We shared another laugh. My lady was heading back from the other side of the office, leading a taller man. I nodded goodbye and padded to the meeting room.

"Mr Anton, this is Henry Brill, my supervisor. Oh, and I'm Emily Szepanik." She held out her hand and I shook it and then Henry's.

"I didn't mean to cause trouble, here..."

"Well, you have, it looks, but not through any fault of your own. This photo looks as though there are actually signs posted on this ahhh... Parcel 840. Right?" Henry was looking alternately at me, the pages and the photo, ending up on me.

"I work for Blatchford Steel Services... do you know of us?" They looked at each other. "We ship a lot of steel fabrications. We're in a building that used to be part of J & L, in the South Side Flats." They nodded like Blatchford mattered.

"Anyway, we need to use the tracks that are in the middle of that parcel. I was tasked with finding out how to please everyone in the city and the Three Rivers Trust who might need to approve it all. When I found your signs and the PDC papers, it seemed like I would have to please the EPA, too." They looked like they were following me.

"Fortunately, Tom Wittenauer, your upstairs neighbor, told my boss that he could clear up our EPA problems, but I haven't heard anything. After I met with him, yesterday, I went over to your headquarters in D. C. and that's why I came here. They couldn't find the numbers and thought I should talk to the Pittsburgh office." I shrugged and plopped my hands on my knees.

"Aw, shit," was Brill's reply. Emily looked like she was as far out of the loop as I was.

"Please don't say anything about this to anyone besides Emily and me. At least for a few days, Mr. Anton. Okay?" Brill was standing.

"Well, I guess okay. But I need to find out how to resolve the pollution there so that we can make some other deals. I can't just stand still on that railroad spur. You can see that."

"This won't take long, ahhm, can I call you Walter?" I nodded. "Just sit tight for, umm, a day, let's say. Can we agree on that? It's important."

"For a day, I'm okay. But should I call Wittenauer and have him speak to you?" Brill blanched visibly. He was nervous.

"Ahhm, no! No. Not necessary. I'm sure we can figure this out without any help. I appreciate your bringing this to our attention. Emily will show you back to the lobby.

Be sure she has your number." He held out his hand and I shook it, but it was cold, now. He left… with my copies and the Polaroid.

I had barely touched the coffee. I took a gulp. Too cold to finish. Emily looked apologetic. "I guess we'll head back, now," she said.

"Yes. This seems to have wrapped up." I had nothing. "Is there something wrong with the numbers?"

"Oh, well, nothing serious, I'm sure," she replied over her shoulder. She was smiling; I wasn't.

In the lobby I asked her if she'd seen anything like this before.

"Oh, no, not me. I don't usually deal with the cases, themselves." She wasn't looking right at me.

"Sooo… what do I do now? I have to report above me, you know."

"Henry's a top case man. He manages a lot of what goes on with the mill sites. You can rest assured he'll have the straight information when he calls you. Which reminds me, give me your number and extension." I wrote everything on a file card.

"Thank you for helping me, no shoes and all." She smiled and said I'd hear from Henry Brill, and retreated. The reception ladies didn't even look up. I rode down alone and padded to my favorite shoe-tree. I held the socks and put on just the shoes. It was only a hundred yards.

I'd told Linda I'd drop in. It was late but we needed to catch up on developments.

englishclass publishing occupied the second floor of a crummy-looking building on Forbes Avenue, across from Duquesne. There had been a used-book shop in the storefront, but it was empty. *englishclass'* space, though, was very nice. Old brick walls were interspersed with plastered sections. Parts of the ceiling were tinplate panels; others suspended with grids that mimicked wood. High-intensity lamps hung from both, aimed at built-in workspaces.

I was in an open space. I could see out three sides of the building. A few people were working at word-processors, a couple had those new Macintosh computers, but I didn't see Lindy. Finally someone came over.

"Are you here to meet someone?" She was a thin, older version of the blue-jeaned students who populated the other side of the street.

"Yes, thanks. Linda Anton?"

"Oh! Mrs. Anton. Why don't you sit here," she pulled out a pedestal chair by a workstation, "and I will find her. Are you her husband?"

"Yes, I…" but she was gone.

The chair was formed of heavy plastic and wrapped up and around so that I felt safe. One had to wonder what sort of person could work in a chair he couldn't lean back in. I decided it was designed to make an office look good. I ran out of things to wonder about.

"Oh, Walter, you did come!" Linda walked toward me from the end of the building that wasn't open space. We hugged quickly. "You're wet," she said.

"Yeah. Long story. I've got some developments and I didn't want to wait. Are you okay for a few minutes?"

"Sure, come on in." She led me into a beautifully decorated, traditional-looking home of the 1920's. Furniture, carpets, woodwork… everything would have fitted in a home setting. What looked like antique tables served as desk space. It was quiet and staid. Linda slid panelled doors and we entered a sitting room, lined with books. An oak pedestal table centered the space, surrounded by a half-dozen bow-back chairs. I was in my grandmother's dining room, except she didn't have a computer, or a phone. We sat next to each other.

"Wow, Lindy. This is ni-i-ice. I wouldn't mind driving in to work here." I rubbed the arms of my chair and looked around.

"It is pleasant. When we meet with authors or vendors in here, we usually are able to negotiate arrangements that are good for *englishclass*. It puts people in a good mood. But, let's talk."

"Whew… okay. I heard from John Schumann about a project that is of interest to several people. It's in Larimer. Here's the PDC number." I handed her a blank file card and read off the number as she wrote it down. She showed me what she had written and it was correct.

"What kind of project is it?"

"As far as I know it's something about some existing buildings that will be renovated or demolished, and some empty lots as well. It will become a community center with after-school programs and stuff; I don't know all of it. The thing is that there are UDAG funds available and maybe some HUD financing and even the Liberty Bank, you know, that black bank? Well Forrest Akers wants to be involved, too, so there's lots of positives."

Linda filled the card with notes.

"Anyway, we need to find out if the Trust has thought about this project. If there's some interest on Roberta's part then Blatchford could come up with as much as a million to make it work, doing it so that Roberta and the Trust look like the heroes. That's Schumann's recommendation, anyway, and I think I can get Blatchford to go for it if the Trust will allow us to lease Parcel 840 in exchange. It might work."

"Wow. Well, I don't have anything like that. But I'm not sure what you need me to do. I can't just walk in to the Trust's offices and start pawing through their drawings, can I?" she was shaking her head as she contemplated those steps.

"Well, I'm not an expert, so I don't know what to suggest. Maybe let's think about the schedule and see if there's a time you would be there, anyway?"

She shrugged. "I honestly don't know, Walt. Maybe we can dress all in black and break in. Whaddaya think?" She had her eyes at table level and looked side to side like a Ninja surely would.

"Funny you mention that approach. I did actually buy two Ninja outfits in case you wanted to do a break-in..."

"You what?"

"No, no, no, Honey. I'm not fully serious." I tried to laugh it off, shaking my hands from side to side to brush away that silly idea. Although, if there were a way to get that information quickly, I wouldn't worry about how. I hated the real estate business.

"Look, I'll think who I can ask about this. Didn't you say Roberta agreed to meet with you again? Why don't you just ask her straight out?"

I sat, looking at her. Why didn't I, indeed? I was surprised at the response that came to mind. "We need to know that Blatchford's involvement will tip the balance with Roberta. If I tip our hand too soon she might do a deal without us if just to prove her independence of anyone who doesn't agree with parkland on 840. No, we need to have knowledge of her interest so that we can insert ourselves with maximum impact and get the side agreement on 840. Doesn't that make sense?"

"Is this the Walter Anton I married?" Linda was smiling and shaking her head. "You are quite the manipulator these days."

"I don't know about that, but concentrating on this deal makes me think in ways I never had to. Who knows? Maybe I'll become a peace negotiator for Reagan. If this mess works out, he'll hire me."

"Well, I'll go with you if that happens." Her simple statement made me feel powerful and loved. I could take on three Tom Wittenauers with her beside me.

She pointed out that it really was time to leave. "You look like you went swimming in your suit. What happened?"

"Oh, a little rainstorm we had earlier. I cut quite a figure when I visited the EPA at the Gateway Center."

She gave me a funny look as I left.

At home I spread my suit-coat on the hood. It needed the cleaners. Inside I'd stripped off the pants and other wet things in the hall when Linda came in with a bright "Hey, Walter I'm ho… ooh!" She stopped. "Wow. Who the Hell are you?"

I looked at her blankly as if my situation should be clear to the modern female of the species. "I… I just, um, well. I mean you know I was soaked, so…"

"I was thinking of eating out. Don't change if you don't want to. At Burger King we can sit in the car!"

I laughed with her. "Ohh, Walter, I don't know what I expected, but you 'hanging out' in the front hall was not the image I had."

"It wasn't?" I asked.

"Here, give me the slacks. Where's the coat?"

"On my hood. It was rolled up all afternoon. I gotta take it to the cleaners."

"Well, dump the underwear. I'll take the suit while you clean up. I still want to eat out, okay?" I nodded and handed her the pants. "Lucky I wasn't a social worker following up on that sexual abuse complaint."

I shook my head. When she returned I was dressed and reading mail.

"Let's go. We can try *BlackKnights* in Turtle Creek, and talk about the *Anton Realty Development Company.* People rave about that place."

"Whatever you like. I gotta tell you about the EPA thing. Am I driving?"

"Sure. Please." As we pulled onto 22 I found myself checking the rearview mirror, but the trip to *BlackKnights* was uneventful.

The lighting was low. Each table had its own little lamp but dark wood and carpeting absorbed its output. Soft leather booths absorbed us.

"Miss," Linda asked the girl pouring us water, "can we get a brighter bulb?"

"I can get you more light, ma'am. Just a moment." She came back with a plain white bulb and a whitish lampshade. "I do this a lot at lunch. Your waitress will be with you in a moment."

We both had salad. Linda ordered prime rib, baked potato and boiled radishes, a rare find. I chose broiled tuna. They offered a spicy red wine sauce I had to try. We chewed greens and got down to business.

"Give me the EPA story, first," Linda commanded.

"Aye, aye," I replied. Linda rolled her eyes. "You'd have appreciated how I walked in to their offices. I was so wet that I left my shoes, socks and suit-coat in a lobby planter and rode up in bare feet, dripping. They're still talking about me."

"I wish I had seen it… in a way that wouldn't have connected me with you. But what's the scoop on the file numbers?"

"I still don't know, but my guess is that they aren't valid. The lady I met brought her supervisor over and he's some big shot on the biggest cleanup sites… like old steel mills."

"Sounds like you're getting somewhere." Lindy pulled out the yellow pad and started making notes. "What's his name?"

"Henry Brill, and a no-nonsense guy. When I told him that I had seen signs posting the file numbers all he said was 'Oh, shit.' Then he told me to not speak to anyone else about them. When I suggested I ask Wittenauer to perform the help he had offered on these filings, he told me in no uncertain terms that he would handle it without Wittenauer and don't worry about it."

Linda was writing.

"But he knows I was worried about it. He told me to wait a day. The lady who met me, Emily something, couldn't answer any questions. All she did was assure me that he was a top guy. There's something funny with those file numbers. We may not have a pollution problem at all. That'd be something, wouldn't it?"

Our entrées arrived. Her beef looked perfect, pink juice puddling on the hot plate, salt-encrusted potato and radishes semi-transparent. She speared a radish and held it out for me. Delicious – almost sweet.

My tuna had been cooked at very high heat, sealing in the juices. It smelled wonderful. The wine sauce was rich, buttery. There was cumin and a sense of curry, and some black pepper. *BlackKnights'* chef had the touch.

I cut into the tuna and it struck me: the filings and the cute little signs – all of it – might be a plot by our congressman. He'd have to finagle it with the local EPA, some ally in that office. I sat staring at the table. Linda finally touched my hand.

"What's wrong, Walt? The fish?"

"Uhhn… no, Honey, no. I just thought of what's going on with the EPA. It's a hoax! The whole problem was made up by Wittenauer. I'm sure of it! Son of a bitch! I know that's what's going on. It all fits! Son of a bitch!" I started breathing harder and held my utensils in a death grip.

"Walt? What's the matter? C'mon. Take a sip of water."

"But, look at what I've been chasing. Wittenauer cooked this up so that he could be Blatchford's hero: solving our 'EPA problem.' Who'd have guessed that?"

"Is that even possible, Honey? I mean, who can get the EPA to do that? What can we do?" Linda placed her hand on mine, guiding it to the table and I relaxed my muscles.

"Linda, this is serious stuff. If we expose a congressman, he'd have to resign or something, right?" I was wide-eyed. I was trying to form sentences but my mind was racing ahead. "Sweetheart, I already stirred up trouble for Wittenauer. What if he goes to Blatchford and gets me fired? Shit!"

Linda put her utensils down and clasped her hands across her lips. I was getting ready to say more and she reached out and put her fingers on my lips. "Let's wait a minute, Walt. This needs careful thought. Take a few bites and then we'll talk. Please... okay? Just a few bites."

I put her hand between both of mine and started nodding. "Okay, I gotcha. I'm gonna eat, now, and then we'll talk." Linda nodded with me.

"Good, good," she said, and to make the right example she picked up her fork to show me how it's done. I matched her moves. We both put bites in our mouths. I smiled at her and chuckled in my throat. She smiled, almost laughing, to the point she had to hold her mouth closed. I put the handle of my fork in one nostril and it hung by itself. She teared up doing her best not to spit. I was turning red as I teared up with her.

Finally I pulled the fork out and put my napkin over my face so that we wouldn't make further eye contact... and wiped tears off my cheeks.

I finished swallowing and lowered the napkin. As soon as my eyes were exposed she stuck her tongue out at me. I peered around the napkin, but she wasn't looking.

"Ohh, God," I said. "Are we going to be able to eat in front of each other?"

"Gosh, I don't know, sir. I eat like an adult, but my table-mate has reverted to seventh grade. I may have to spank him."

Now I was leering at her, but she brought us both down to Earth in a hurry.

"Walt, I've lost my appetite... thinking about what you said. We have to make a plan that protects you… us. It could be happening right now – I don't know what! Let's take this home, huh?"

I nodded and stood up to signal our waitress.

"Is something wrong, folks?" she asked. I can get you something else…"

"The food is fine, great, actually. We suddenly have to get home. I'm sorry," I said. "If you could pack it up?"

"No problem. Back in a sec." We were packed, paid and on our way in about four minutes. We left a nice tip, as much to be allowed back.

For ten minutes, I jabbered non-stop about things Wittenauer had promised to do that only made sense if he had a back-door way to clear the EPA filings. That could work only if the filings never existed. I was alternately mad as Hell and strangely elated at having figured it out. Linda stayed silent.

At Rodi Road traffic was lined up behind a mass of emergency lights, police, ambulance and fire trucks. I put the shift in neutral and turned toward Linda. "What are you thinking, Lin?"

Her head was shaking back and forth. "My first reaction was that you were overstating things and the hoax idea is crazy. But it makes no sense otherwise. That makes me worry… a lot, Honey.

Your job could be threatened. If Wittenauer was prepared to engineer this, he would also be prepared to protect himself. Then I thought of how ruthless someone in his position might be, and then I didn't feel like eating any more." She teared up, then. "Walter, what on Earth can we do? What do you think he'll do?" She grabbed my hands. I could feel her fear.

I shook my head. "I don't know, Lindy. I add up numbers for a living. Other people worry about crap like this. I don't even know who to call, for crissakes." I kissed her hands.

"When we get home we can plan our best move. Maybe you should call Blatchford or Jackson before Wittenauer does. They'll believe you, won't they?"

"I think so, but the question never needed asking. They could react the wrong way and it'll be too late when the truth comes out. I don't have backup in the company. Feels lonely."

"They're starting to move us, Honey." A cop with a red flashlight was waving cars past the accident site. We crawled up the road, turned right and up onto Jefferson and to Mapleledge. It felt like we'd left a week ago.

"Did we leave lights on, Walter? I shut them off, no?" I looked and there were lights on, even upstairs bedroom lights.

"We certainly wouldn't have left those lights on. Dammit!" I jammed on the brakes. "Go to Elly's house and call the police, Lindy. Tell em we think there's an intruder in our house. Go on, now!" She ran in front of the car and up the Maxwell's driveway. I waited until I saw Elly let her in. Then I pulled into our driveway and shut down the motor. I quietly grabbed the tire iron. I didn't know what I would actually do, but it felt better to have something in my hand. I crept around to the left where it was darkest, as unprepared to fight as anyone could be, tire iron bullshit or not. I passed the back door and continued around the house.

"Drop the iron! Hands on your head!" A bright flashlight spotlighted me. The officer's other hand aimed a pistol... at me. Behind him a second officer also held a gun. They looked like drain pipes. I almost wet myself.

"I live here! I live here! I'm Walter Anton. My wife called you! Honest!"

"Very gently, sir, put that iron on the ground and kneel down. Then we'll talk about where you live." I had hung on to the iron as I placed my hands on my head. I kept one hand there and held the iron out and dropped it.

"These are good pants. Can't I just stand here?"

"Keep one hand on your head and pull out your wallet with the other, real slow." I complied with his direction. "Toss it to me." I did that, too.

The officer with the wallet put his gun away while the second one aimed at me. The first one looked at my license and other cards. "What's your social?"

I recited it. Linda came running across the street.

"Walter, Walter! What happened?" The cop with the gun on me stopped her. "That's my husband. This is our house. Why don't you catch the intruder instead?" Linda was pissed.

Both cops relaxed a little. The first one handed back my wallet. "Put that iron away, now, will you, sir?" He and his partner went to the front door and tried it. It had been broken in.

"Stevie?" The second cop told us to go stand behind the police car. Then he drew his gun, ready to follow the first cop into the house.

It was like T.V. One officer pushed in the door calling out "Police Officers! Put down your weapons and come out!" The second one followed him and they checked the whole house. We tried to look into the front hall. Elly Maxwell joined us.

"Ohh, Linda. This is terrible. They must have been here in the past hour. How can they do that? This isn't where this happens! How awful."

One of the cops gestured to us from the door. "Mr. and Mrs. Anton, will you come in here, now?"

Linda turned to Elly and hugged her. "Elly, I'll come over after they're done with us. You go ahead. Thanks."

The intruder – or intruders – may have been looking for something specific, but the result was a pointless sweeping to the floor of everything easily reached. Items close to the floor were disturbed as if by foot; items that required the highest reach were untouched. In the kitchen, glass was broken everywhere. Drinking glasses may have made it to the floor, then were broken by dishes or utensils landing on them. Even the silverware was scattered. The whole "junk" drawer was dumped on the pile.

"Ooohhh, Walter! Why, why, why, why?" She was crying, but because she was angry and, at the moment, powerless. "Walter, who could hate us so much? Oh God, God, God. Dirty bastards..." Her tears flowed freely and I had the presence of mind to not tell her everything would be all right.

In the bedroom things were helter-skelter. Clothes everywhere, sheets and blanket off the bed. They just wanted to make a mess. Linda's perfume and lotions were poured on the pile. I remained tight-lipped.

All the towels, brushes, soaps, toothpaste, the contents of the medicine cabinet, toilet paper and towels from the linen closet were in the tub, in a foot of water. What was the point?

There was little to throw around on the second floor. One bureau was tipped over. Most of the rage was disbursed on the first floor. The two officers were joined by two others, one of whom was taking pictures while the second dusted various surfaces and some of the unbroken glasses for latent prints. "Stevie" was circling the house with his big flashlight shining back and forth among the bushes and flowerbeds. At one point he called "Dennis," the photographer.

Linda started to pick up unbroken pieces from the kitchen but one officer asked her to wait. She sat on the front step, crying. I sat and hugged her to me.

Linda was like her mother in the housekeeping department, which is, very neat. Her kitchen was clean, even to go across the street. We weren't messy, but she did not tolerate disorder. Out would come the cannister vac. Her house would always be clean. I liked it.

Now I could barely empathize, looking at the maelstrom in her home. With her, neatness was ingrained; this assault struck her psyche. I held her while the cops finished.

"Mr. Anton?" Sargent Willett was the lead officer, and he was ready to take a statement.

I stood up, feeling every joint. I was so tired.

"We can see what happened, sir, but I need you to describe how the house was when you left it last."

"We had just come from the city in separate cars. I got soaked in my suit, so Linda took it to the cleaners. We were gonna eat out so I showered. When she got back we left within a few minutes. I locked the door like always."

"What time was that?" I gave him my best estimate and answered the rest of his questions. I held Linda's arm while she answered pretty much the same questions - flat-toned and calm. I felt better when she was crying. Now, her face was colorless, and I felt empty not knowing what her next emotion might be.

In a few more minutes the photos and investigations were over. Sargent Willett came over to us by Linda's car.

"Folks, I've called a crime scene company to secure the front door. You got a key to the back door?"

Linda nodded dumbly.

"Okay, then. You are free to go in and out. There isn't much more we can learn here. You may want to pick out clothes for the next few days. I recommend a hotel, tonight. Most insurances are going to cover at least a couple nights in a case like this. Let me suggest you hire the crime scene people to clean up your house..."

Linda started to object. I held her back and told her to wait till they arrived.

"Ma'am, I know what you're thinking, but I also know how painful the cleanup can be. Just retrieve your valuables and let them do the worst of it. You give them instructions on how to leave things. Honestly, it's infinitely better coming back to a house that is livable. But it's up to you."

Linda was whimpering softly with her face in my chest.

"Mr. Anton, you want to call your insurance agent without delay. Do you have a local agent?"

"Yeah, yeah. Sowitsky Brothers in Monroeville… known em for years. I can reach em, I think."

"Tell em the police have the report. They'll get copies. You should get your key papers out of the house now, though."

I shook his hand. Linda and I went into the house. "Give me some directions, Lin. I'll grab my clothes and you find what you can. What's ruined we can replace. Tell me where the papers and things are…"

We went room by room. I filled a couple pillow-cases. We found our insurance policies, bank books, spare keys and other papers. I sifted through the crap in the kitchen to get some favorite antique knick-knacks. Linda gathered up old books, Bibles and pictures. I found a suit that wasn't spoiled and Linda found some underthings and underwear of mine. The front closet was untouched. I took the Polaroid and snapped a couple of my own shots. We left the coats. Bathroom stuff we gave up on. The "Scene-e-Cure" people had arrived and I decided we could leave them with the house.

"Police told me to secure the door. You want we should start the clean-up? I'll have to sign a contract wich'ya." Linda turned away in defeat. I nodded at the man and he produced a contract with sections for "Special Instructions."

We completed it in a few minutes with most of the conditions covered by sections "A," "B," or "C." I told him who our insurance agent was and that reminded me to call him. Linda sat in the car while I called Sowitsky Brothers and left a message we'd call in the morning, as I wasn't sure which hotel we were going to.

The "Scene-e-Cure" crew was already busy with vacuums and heavy bags for broken glass and other refuse. I thanked the crew boss and gave him my office number. When I got back to the car, Linda was gone. Automatically I looked up at Maxwell's where she was speaking with Elly. I swung in to Elly's driveway. Linda gave her a little hug and walked to the car with a bounce in her step.

"I got us a room at the new Ramada in Monroeville. Let's get settled and figure things out." She flounced around a little and put on her seat belt. I clicked my own and gave a little toot to Elly as we pulled away from the one point of safety and security we'd had that was now neither. Axel once said locks keep only your friends out; your enemies will get in when they want. Clearly one of us had an enemy or more than one. And when he wanted to get in, he did. It felt awful. Linda put on a positive demeanor while I nursed a burning hatred for whoever our "enemy" was.

The Ramada sign was comforting. We left 7 Mapleledge feeling like we had no place to sleep; now we did. We were in our room with two pillow-cases of clothing, in about ten more minutes. Linda flopped down on the bed... unlike her. She unpacked and organized when we traveled. I had nervous energy.

"I'm sorry, Walt. I feel whipped. Completely. I'll straighten things out in a few minutes."

"Don't even think about it, Sweetie. I'll pick up some stuff at the Eckerd's. It'll just take a few minutes. Double-lock the door behind me."

She sat up onto her elbows. "Do you know what to get? We need everything."

"I'll make a list. Help me out." Without hesitating Linda rattled off exactly what we needed, half of which I'd never think of. I listened for her to throw the bolt.

It took more than twenty minutes. I never spend more than five minutes or twenty bucks in a drug store. This order was nearly two hundred. I dropped my three large bags of toiletries, razors, hairdryer, and fifteen soaps, rinses, conditioners, peroxide, alcohol, wipes, bandaids, cotton balls, Tampax, nylons, panties, toothpaste and on and on, into the back seat... even a new clock radio. Next door was a package store. We weren't drinkers, but if there ever were a night; I bought his last, dusty pint of Old Overholt.

I kicked the door but I had to set down the bags and use my key. Linda was asleep. I didn't try to be silent but she purred on softly. After I cleaned up I rustled the bags to find the Listerine.

"Don't lose the receipt," Linda called from the other room. "Insurance."

I made closed-mouth grunts to assure her that I would never lose a receipt like this one. "Good morning," I offered after my rinse. "Sorry about the noise."

"Sokay. I need to be up. We've got things to do! Let me clean up, and we can get to work."

"Work? Hasn't today been long enough?" She held up her finger as she closed the door. I waited on the bed and remembered the Old Overholt, luckily on this side of the door. I unwrapped the two tumblers and poured a little Pennsylvania ambrosia. Linda was right: we were planning our response to the EPA business and lost track with our house and all the rest.

"Who can you call about your Wittenauer problem?" Linda had set her grief aside, and I surely needed her help.

"It's ten-thirty. I don't have people's numbers."

"Your office has an answering machine or something, don't you? I've left messages there."

Right as always. "So, ahh… I'll call my office?"

"Of course! Leave a message for Mr. Blatchford and another one for Mr. Jackson. You know their extensions. You've got to get to them early, don't you think?"

"Okay, let me do that first."

"And, what is this?" Linda asked, swirling the whiskey in her glass.

"That, my little lady, is the world's finest rye whiskey, first made not far from right here. It tastes like the woods smell in Springtime." I took a sip of mine. Linda sniffed hers and tried a little touch to her tongue.

"It does have a different smell. If you don't have any Pinot, I'll settle for this." She took another sip. "Make those calls, mister!"

I called Blatchford's extension, first. "Hal, it's Walter Anton. I'm sitting in a hotel room because our house was broken into tonight and totally trashed. But the reason I need to speak to you right away is I have some interesting developments on the EPA pollution business and I am not sure how to proceed on them. It could be a problem for Tom Wittenauer, himself, and I want to warn you about it. I'll be in as early as I can because I think it's serious. See you in the morning."

"Why did you mention the hotel room? He doesn't care about that." Linda had finished her splash of Overholt and taken a little more.

"I don't know. I thought he would take it seriously if he heard about the break-in." I shrugged.

"Well, call Jackson."

I made that call simpler. At least something was underway, "Now what? If I knew a lawyer I'd call him, to record my suspicions. Isn't that a good idea?"

"Could be. Who would you call?"

"I don't know," I said. "I've never needed a lawyer except to buy the house." More sipping. That mayor had good taste in whiskey.

"What about when your parents died. Who was that?"

"Alan Boudreau. He's gotta be in the phone book... in the city."

She pointed at the phone as she sipped.

Boudreau was on Centre Avenue when the wills were probated... still was. The "night" number rang several times, and a man actually picked up.

"Yes! This Benny?"

"Huh?" I said.

"Isn't this Ben Shaw?"

"It's Walter Anton, Alan. I didn't expect an answer at this hour."

"Oh. I'm waiting for a call from Canada. Who is this, again?"

"You probably don't remember me, Mr. Boudreau, but you did my parents' wills… George and May Anton, from Latrobe?"

"Oh sure, sure. My God, that must have been ten, fifteen years ago, now. How are you, Walter?"

"Pretty good, all things considered. Yeah, my mom was in seventy-three, twelve years now."

"Walter, I can't tie up the line. Is there something I can help you with? Not another will, I hope."

"No, no. Listen, I'll be quick. I work for Blatchford Steel… you know them?"

"I may have heard of them. In the city?"

"In the old J & L site. But my problem is that I've brushed up against congressman Wittenauer on a problem affecting my company. Is he a close friend or anything?"

"Wittenauer? We vote in different booths, I'm pretty sure."

"Okay, good. I want you to be my attorney, here. Can you do that over the phone?"

"I'll send you a bill. Go ahead."

"I won't go into everything, but I think I have exposed something fraudulent that he has done that involves the EPA. I want to put my suspicions on record. Does that make sense?"

"Well, that has limited value, but it could help, I suppose. Why? This affects you, too, I guess?"

"I'm not sure, yet. He's a big buddy of my boss, Hal Blatchford... doesn't matter. If I am right and he is found out, he'll have to resign and someone at the EPA could be investigated, too. Who knows what he might do in that case?"

"You're going to have to give me everything you've got and now is not the time. Can you come to my office… you remember where I am? I'll record you and have it witnessed and all that. Are you free tomorrow?"

"I'm planning to go in early because I need to get to Blatchford before Wittenauer..."

"Please, Walter, what time?"

"Well, seven-thirty, quarter of eight is early for me."

"We should talk first... at least that's my advice to you. I'll meet you at seven if you can do that... before you talk to anyone else, is my recommendation."

"Okay, I'll be there. Do I bring the donuts?"

"Blueberry muffins, Walter, and black with a sugar."

"Huh? Oh, gotcha. I'm lucky I reached you."

"Maybe. See you at seven." He clicked off and I slowly set the phone down.

Linda was writing notes on a small hotel pad. "Feel better?"

"I guess I do. He'll meet me at seven, so he thinks it's serious. What are you writing?"

"I wrote down what I observed and heard tonight, with a timeline. I made notes of what you said on the phone. We may have to testify about it, someday."

"Holy mackerel! How did I get into this kind of trouble?" I sat at the desk, my head down.

"I've got notes on what we've done and said through all your real estate adventures. You still have the plus and minus charts?"

"In the car, I think."

"Good. I'll put everything together in the morning."

"Maybe I should take that with me to show to Boudreau."

"Oh, yeah," Linda reflected, "that makes sense. Make copies and keep the originals. Okay?"

"Yeah, okay. I gotta sleep if I'm meeting Boudreau at seven. What will you do in the morning?"

"I'll get a cab and pick up my car. I want to look around the house, anyway. We need to get organized. I'll call you when I get to the house. If you need anything I can meet you." She went to pee once more. I figured out the alarm and set it for five-thirty. That hurt. She came back and we hugged under the covers.

I was still racing. I thought about my parents and our last road-trip vacation... and calmed down. Linda's breathing slipped into sleep mode. Took me longer.

FRIDAY, MAY 24, 1985

Traffic was building at six-forty, but at a good clip. I took exit 2B and crossed to Centre by way of Kirkpatrick. Boudreau's office was a couple of blocks east of the intersection. He'd prospered. His office was in a Victorian house built together with another next door. Two other lawyers shared the "legal" half. I parked next to a Cadillac coupe that was still warm.

"Well... Walter. I guess I didn't dream your call."

"No. I'm afraid it's real. We had quite a day, yesterday."

"Who's we?" Boudreau was unwrapping one of the blueberry muffins.

"Linda, my wife and I. Our house was vandalized last night and we had to sleep in a hotel." My new attorney raised his eyebrows.

"Is that part of your office problem? Connected to your problem?"

"Oh, gosh, no. I don't think so. They trashed our house but didn't steal anything as far as we know. All our papers were there and stuff. Aww... no, can't be connected..." I was shaking my head as much to convince myself as my lawyer.

"Why are you so certain about that?" Boudreau was stirring his coffee.

"Well, I don't know. Trashing a house hasn't got anything to do with real estate. I've been working on a real estate problem for my boss... trying to solve a pollution problem, actually, and some assholes trashed my house." I grimaced my certainty that there couldn't be a connection. "Naww. No way." I shook my head.

"Okay, then. Be quiet for a second and I'll put a tape in. This triangular thing is a microphone. Just speak in its general direction. I'll sit opposite. I'll make notes but you just keep talking. Okay, now. Start at the beginning. This is Walter Anton who works for Blatchford Steel Services and it's May twenty-fourth, nineteen-eighty-five. And it's seven-eighteen in the morning."

"Wow. Okay. I am a cost accountant at Blatchford Steel Services on Iron Way in the South Side Flats. A week ago, yesterday… I mean, last Thursday, which was, umm, May sixteenth. On that day I was called in to an unusual meeting…" I recounted the story. Boudreau made notes as I talked. Now and then he raised his eyebrows or puffed his cheeks. I was able to tell it all by eight. It was hard to believe it was only seven days.

"You didn't mention the break-in. You say the police have a full report?"

"Yeah, but I think you need to concentrate on the Wittenauer issue, don't you? That's going to come to a head as soon as today, maybe."

"Let the doctor write the prescription, why don't you?" Boudreau shut off the machine and popped the tape out and labeled it.

"What should I do, now?"

"You told your boss you were coming in early to speak to him. Make up an excuse why you're not as early as you intended. The question is, what are you going to tell him?"

I sat for a minute. When I left my message the night before, I thought I knew what I'd say, but a little guidance would help. "I thought I'd tell him my thoughts on what the EPA guy said. No?"

"You could do that. It will create a lot of questions you shouldn't try to answer. Why don't you just tell him the facts without embellishing, if you can. Just the facts, man. Make like you are on the Blatchford team and you want your leader to give you the best guidance. Don't act like you've figured things out. Can you do that?"

"Yuh. I like that. What else?" I was itching to get rolling.

"Don't mention me. Right now you don't know where your enemies are coming from. Talking to a lawyer could be threatening. No need to stir that up."

"Okay. I'm with you. Can I call you later with what happens today?"

"Yeah. Good idea. Hopefully it's all a misunderstanding. Hopefully the vandalism has absolutely nothing to do with Wittenauer or anything else… completely random, right?"

"You don't think so, do you?"

"It's quite a coincidence, but it could be."

"Alright, I'm going. Do I need to give you a check?"

"Give me a couple hundred and we'll see what else we'll need as this develops… if it does."

I wrote the check and took off. Travel was slow, now, and I fidgeted from light to light and parked at quarter of nine. Blatchford's car was there. Pauly Lemay started to engage me but I told him I was sorry I couldn't talk.

I took the front hall to avoid Jackson's office and went upstairs.

"Well there you are, Mr. Anton," observed Kelly Galvin. "Mr. Blatchford has been looking for you… twice. I'll tell him you're finally here."

"Thanks a lot for that." She caught a sense of how I felt about her editorializing and looked up sharply. She waved at the couch, but I stayed where I was.

"Yes, Mr. Blatchford. Your Mr. Anton is here." Now I wasn't Walter, anymore and she and I were barely co-workers.

"Go right in, sir," she directed. Now I was "sir."

"You keep in touch, now, ma'am." I touched my imaginary hat and smiled at Kelly as I strutted toward Blatchford's door. She gave me a strange look.

I entered Blatchford's paneled castle, not quite sure how I felt. My buddy, Hal, was looking right at me. I tried a smile.

"Siddown, Anton." His expression hadn't changed. "What happened to you last night?"

"We're not sure why, boss, but some one or a gang trashed our house so badly we had to move to a hotel. Things were so upset that I couldn't get going at a good time. Linda's pretty upset, as you can imagine."

"The police are on top of this?"

"Oh, yeah. They were taking pictures and fingerprints and stuff. They had a company that secured the house and cleaned it up. I haven't seen it, obviously, but Linda is probably there by now. I shouldn't have mentioned my troubles. Sorry."

"No one wants crap like that to happen to anybody. Too bad. Let me know if I can help, will you?"

"Well, thanks, Hal. We'll get through it and it won't make me late again."

"Okay, good. Now, what's this about Tommy and the EPA? Didn't leave me much info. What were you getting at?" He looked grimmer than usual as he sat back in his chair.

"You know I visited Tom in Washington the other day?"

He nodded impatiently.

"Well I didn't get much out of him except that he would resolve our EPA problem right away if not that day. Since I was not far from the EPA, itself, I went over there and got someone to look up the file numbers, you know? I wanted to find out what kind of pollution was actually there." Blatchford rolled his hand to speed me to a point.

"Anyway, she couldn't find any reference to them. She accused me of making up file numbers so I got a little pissed off and told her how important the information was and why would I do that, and so forth."

"So what to all of that, Walter?" At least he called me Walter.

"At the end she told me to speak to the EPA office here in Pittsburgh. I went there yesterday and things got interesting..." I gave him a quick version of how Brill swore when I told him Wittenauer promised to resolve the problem, and how he admonished me to not mention the matter to anyone else. "It looked like I had stirred up something that angered that guy and it involves Wittenauer. They couldn't find those file numbers here, either. It looks like it might be trouble for Tom and I wanted to alert you to that so that it doesn't reflect on us in some way."

I tried to project my best 'we're on the same team and I'm trying to protect you, Hal' face. I don't know if he noticed.

"That's it?" He gestured as if I had put a pile of street sweepings on the desk for him to consider. "That's what you called about?"

"Well, yes! I didn't want you to get blind-sided in case the fact that Tom was trying to influence the EPA on Blatchford Steel's behalf, gets twisted into something negative that screws up our rail spur. Right?"

"I don't see how that could happen." He hitched his chair closer to his desk.

"Well, let me say one more thing... may I?" He waved at me to get it over with.

"If, and I mean it looks possible, but, if... if there really aren't any EPA filings on that land it's a big plus for us. It removes a big hurdle that we had no way to solve on our own, not even with money. So that's pretty good, yes?"

He paid full attention, now. "Is that possible?"

"It certainly looks like there are no files associated with those numbers, and if there aren't, those signs can be removed and we can move forward. That's my hope. I have some other news, too."

"Let's have it."

"John Schumann is looking at another project in Larimer that might work out to enable us to buy a truce from the Trust. I'll have more on that today or Monday. Things are looking up, perhaps."

"Okay. That's enough for now, then. Keep Jackson up to date, too, will you?" We shook hands and Blatchford's grip was solid and strong. I felt still-wanted and a little respected.

"Thanks, boss," I concluded. I turned and was through the door when he called out.

"Anton!" I stuck my head back in.

"Where'd those goddam EPA signs come from if there are no filings?"

I stepped fully in to his office and shut the door behind me. He looked worried.

"Hal, this isn't something I really want to speculate on. I do have some thoughts and I'll tell you what I think... if you want. It might be a good thing to speak to your attorney if it turns out I am right. Which, I hope I am not."

"Okay. You ought to have some useful observations, so tell me."

"I am sorry to be the one to suggest this but I think it's possible that Tom Wittenauer finagled those signs onto that strip of land. He may have an ally inside the EPA here in Pittsburgh. The only purpose I can see to do that is to portray his ability to resolve the problem for you, specifically. It would make him a hero and that is important enough to him that he would take that risk. My poking around has disturbed this arrangement and it may blow up in Tom's face, which could have very serious repercussions for him. My concern is that it might reflect on you or on Blatchford Steel and that's what I am worried about in all of it." I looked as dejected as I felt. Blatchford was staring at me and was obviously angry. I didn't know if he would explode in my direction.

He spun his chair around and pushed the button to open his drapes, letting him look out over the main shop. I wanted to leave but I weighed the various consequences and decided to stay there, until he reacted. He had slumped in his chair.

A couple of minutes had passed when Kelly Galvin tapped on the door and cracked it open. We both turned. "I'm sorry, Mr. Blatchford, but Mrs. Anton has called a few times and it's an emergency that she needs to reach Mr. Anton about." She stood there nervously, looking from one to the other.

"Go ahead, Walter. Stay in touch." Blatchford was looking at the shop when I followed Kelly out.

"I told her I would have you call right back. I think she is at home. You can use my phone."

"Thank you, Kelly. I'll call from my desk. Thanks for interrupting us." She was still standing when I turned the corner on the stairs.

***

"Hi, Lindy. What's up?"

"Oh, thank God. Walter. I've been calling and calling!"

"I was meeting with Blatchford, Honey. His secretary didn't interrupt. What has you upset?"

"Okay. Okay. I was here at the house. Those men cleaned things up but obviously they weren't going to put things away. Things were in boxes so I figured that's how they do it."

"That's the contract I okayed. I thought you'd rather put things the way you want."

"Yes, yes. So I'm in the kitchen putting away the cooking utensils and I finished one box and I noticed that the café curtains were stained with worcestershire sauce or something."

"Uh-huh."

"So, anyway, I went to pull at the curtains and there was a man's face in the window! I looked right at him! I don't know where he came from or where he ran away. I screamed and screamed. I grabbed a frying pan, can you believe it? I mean it's funny, now, but I really thought I would bonk him if he tried to come in." She stopped speaking and took a couple of breaths.

"Are you alright? Did you call the police? Do you need me home?"

"Yes, yes and no. I'm okay. The police did come and I told them what little I could. They poked around outside and left me their card in case something else happens, but that was about it."

"The same cops from last night?"

"I don't think so, but I didn't pay attention last night. Now, listen, I hope you don't mind. I called Axel Johnson and he said he can repair the door frame by this afternoon if it's okay with you."

I reacted to that. I liked Axel and he's helped me before. But it felt like he was doing what I should have been doing, like I wasn't man enough to fix my own front door "Well, sure, Sweetie. I haven't even thought about that, to tell you the truth. I'm sorry."

"What are you sorry about? You're doing what you have to do. I'm going to finish the kitchen and bedroom. Elly and I are going out for lunch while Axel is here."

"Well, at least we'll be able to keep our friends out." She laughed and that felt better.

"What happened with the lawyer? And what about Blatchford, is he okay?"

I lightly related my two discussions and told her I'd fill her in later and there were no crises.

"Okay, then. I'll call your office if anything comes up and you be careful, too. I love you, Walt." I swallowed, with that.

"I love you too, Linda. Completely. Make sure that bedroom is ready."

"Ooooh, well, maybe I will. Have a good day, Honey... see you tonight!" We rang off and I leaned back and stretched. Jackson appeared.

"What the Hell have you been messing with, Walter? You didn't leave me any details but you think something serious might affect Blatchford Steel? Like what?" Jack was using the pugnacious tool.

"Let's talk in your real office. I'll be right down after I straighten out here and get a coffee." Jackson looked around with his lips compressed, as if noticing for the first time that I didn't have real walls like he did. Right. He went back down the hall.

Both in-baskets were half-full. Colleen's stuff was good. I looked at a dozen of them and she was right on. I quickly flipped through the requisitions and spotted nothing unusual. Colleen's notes were appropriate in every case. I figured I could clear them all by noontime. I went in to the little kitchenette and lucked out with a nearly full pot of today's coffee.

"Have a seat, Walt. One minute." If nothing else Jack was diligent. His accounting pulled everything together for Blatchford Steel. Our CPA's took his stuff every quarter and issued quarterly statements, paid the quarterly taxes and reported to the Board. The figures that came back were essentially what Jack had given them. He was good and I respected that. On the other hand, he was always having to prove his authority. I didn't think we'd ever be friends.

Finally he reached a break and pushed his papers aside.

"You've never left me a message like that before. What is so important?"

"I may have uncovered a little scam that our esteemed congressman was trying to pull off to make himself look good to Blatchford. If it is what it looks like, Wittenauer could get into real trouble and so might some people at the EPA…" Jackson put his hand up to stop me.

"At the EPA? What the fuck have you done?" He'd brought out the profanity leadership tool.

"All I have done is pursue the components of gaining rights to that piece of railroad. Remember that? The real estate costs that 'we,' you and I, if I recall, are supposed to come up with as fast as possible? That?"

"Yeah, yeah. But you are accusing a congressman, here, for Christ's sake! You shouldn't be mixing Blatchford up in bullshit like that. You don't like Wittenauer, that's your business."

I struggled into as calm a face as I could. I didn't say anything. Jack got the idea that I was containing myself and that he may be off-base. I waited.

"Okay, what?" he finally asked. We relaxed a little.

"I have described this to Hal," I started, consciously using "Hal" to make a point, "as a way to warn him about possible consequences that could reflect on Blatchford." Jack turned his head to the side slightly when I said "Hal," but he didn't look surprised.

"Warned him? About what?"

"Jack, as far as I can see those EPA filings are not real. I've got one other step to take that will pin that down, but all I did was ask the EPA what pollution was involved with those file numbers. That's a prudent question. If there were big pollution, none of my efforts would matter. Trouble was, there are no filings with those numbers, at least neither Washington nor Pittsburgh can find them." I shrugged with both hands splayed upwards.

Jackson looked as if he were going to slam me down with more leadership, but he was processing what I'd said and the potential of it all was dawning on him.

"Son of a bitch!" I agreed with him. He was looking around as if a different opinion might lurk in the corners of his office… or on the ceiling.

"What are you going to do, Walt?"

"Well, I'm gonna keep working with Brightman. Schumann thinks he has come up with a project that will work for us and for the Three Rivers Trust. Assuming we really don't have an EPA problem, I think we're gonna get this done. I'll know more this afternoon."

I don't know if Jack was glad I might be succeeding… or not. I'm sure he knew how important Wittenauer's help was on the King Frederik project. The last thing we needed was his enmity. But I couldn't help what I'd found or what he'd done, if I was right.

"Okay, then, Walt. Keep me posted, will you?" I assured him I would and went back to my sort-of office. Colleen Walsh was on the lookout at my door.

"I have some fresh stuff and I thought we could go over it together."

"Sure, Coll, come on in."

For an hour we reviewed the pile of req's she'd already looked at and the ones she brought in. Her judgment was impressive. One req was for a brand-new laser measuring and aligning tool that would adapt to our big cutting table. The laser accuracy would save many minutes per piece and drastically cut down the cost to fix cuts that were just a tiny bit off. As pieces were welded together, like on the King Frederik, those tiny errors multiplied until a custom fix was required. The system cost nearly two hundred thousand dollars. But it sounded wonderful. I called Bucky Dighton, our chief engineer, and asked for a few minutes, which he readily agreed to.

We put on hard hats and climbed up a long flight. The chief engineer's office was a mezzanine with a complete view of the shop, much like Blatchford's. Two big tables dominated, with E-size, D-size and C-size drawings held by plexiglass strips clamped by a long plate in the center. The plexiglas could slide back and forth to hold the edges of drawings so several people could look at them. Colored stickers told the engineers what stage or schedule pertained to each drawing. It was simple, but effective.

Bucky Dighton was at the center table. "This is our King Frederik table," Bucky explained. "The welding tolerances are very tight on these pieces and that is why we've been looking at this laser system. You look at some of the bigger shops and they are advertising laser positioning as part of their capabilities. We need to keep up and we promised the Danes we'd have it. Given the lead times to install and learn, now is the time to order."

Colleen and I got a few more minutes of specifications and the value of one brand over another. We thanked Bucky and went back to my office.

"You would have approved this, wouldn't you?" I asked.

She looked hesitant. Finally she nodded. "I think I grasped what the value is. It just seemed like something a man should approve. I know that's silly."

I shook my head. "Not silly, but something to overcome. It's numbers in one end and numbers out the other. If you adhere to the numbers the toys that engineers want to play with are easily separated from the profitable tools that will make us money. You're okay."

She smiled, delighted to be validated. "Thanks, Mr. Anton. I appreciate your trust in me. I just don't want to make a big expensive mistake."

"Just line up your numbers, Colleen. They'll protect you or they'll expose a different decision. Thanks for taking this burden while I do the other project." She bounced back to her desk, beaming. My job was becoming superfluous. I pulled out the 14 by 17's and started to prepare my columns and categories for a week from Monday. While my job's evolving away was not too bothersome, it struck me that Colleen, or whomever, would be doing these sheets in a computer, and that I was the last one to use these big, awkward pages. What the Hell.

It was after eleven. I called Schumann.

"John Schumann."

"Good morning, John. Sorry to bother you. Life is getting more interesting and I thought I'd fill you in on the EPA."

"What have you got? Will they work with us?"

"They may not have to, John. Right now, if I were a gambling man, I'd bet that there are no filings on that parcel, at all. If I'm right, we can forget about pollution as a problem."

"What? What did you do?"

"I asked questions. The problem is that those file numbers aren't actual file numbers! Remember I thought there was funny business? I think it involves Wittenauer, himself, but I'm asking you to not share that until it comes out, if it does."

"I don't think I understand what you're getting at, Walter, but I'll wait until you tell me. Who else knows there might not be an EPA problem?"

"Hal Blatchford and my wife. And Jack Jackson."

"Jackson? Well, no matter. It's the same as telling Hal. Look, Walter, this might play into our negotiations with the Trust. Let's keep it close."

"I agree. Absolutely. Now, change gears. I've got a connection to Roberta's bank through another depositor, and my wife, Linda, knows Liberty Bank a little. Forrest Akers was at a Trust lunch and I sat at his table. I believe if I went to Hal and told him about the million-dollar donation he would go for it, even if he doesn't jump for joy."

"You make it sound like a done deal. Don't count your chickens and all that."

"I hear ya but we are certainly closer than we have been. What can we do to push it along? What can I do?"

"Sounds like you've done plenty. We still want to find out how interested Roberta might be in that project. Will you hear anything today?"

"Well, I might have but Linda doesn't work today and won't be leaving the house, anyway."

"Oh, got the bug?"

"No, no. Our house was vandalized last night and Linda is straightening out the mess. We had a company do the worst cleaning. It was quite a mess. We went to a hotel last night."

"Holy cow, Walter. That's unbelievable. Any idea who would do that? What do the police think?"

"My lawyer made the assumption…"

"Your what? You went to a lawyer? About a vandalism case?"

"Hold on, John. No. I called an attorney my father used to know because I wanted my suspicions on record. About Wittenauer. If that blows up I want to protect Blatchford and myself, too, I suppose."

"You must be loving the real estate business about now."

"Not yet. Look, I've held you long enough, but I really want to do something. There must be something I can help with. Is there another player I could help you with?"

"I'll know better by Monday. If I were wrapping up a week like yours I'd take the afternoon off. Just see what you might learn about the Trust's interest in LAR-four-eighty-eight. And don't tip your hand."

"Aye, aye, commander. Anton out!" Schumann chuckled and clicked off. I sat there, wondering about the afternoon. All week I'd had some part of my mission to pursue; something that took me out of the office. Now I felt like I had nothing to actually do. But there must be something. I decided on *Marko's*.

I wasn't looking for anyone. I liked *Marko's* for both ambience and food. It was a different world.

This time I ordered "Many-fish Soup," *Marko's* unique chowder of fresh and salt-water fish, mussels, clams and crawfish. The broth was buttery and tangy with cherry-peppers. Thoroughly enjoyable with their fresh bread. I couldn't think of who else I might bring here for a meal, except Linda, naturally. But, I knew I'd be back.

I outlined the 'great railroad real estate deal' I was hopefully coming to the end-game of. For the first time I thought I might have actually accomplished something that would secure the railspur. Bigger shots than Walter Anton had failed at it and little old me was getting it done, whatever that meant.

There were gaps, though. First we needed information on the Trust's interest in LAR-four-eighty-eight, dash eight. I made a note to ask Linda. Maybe she could connect with someone who has a key to Trust offices. Just to take a couple pictures of a drawing.

Then, if we found they were interested, how could we use that without talking to Roberta McGillvray, anyway? I drew a few doodles while I pondered. I had to speak to John Schumann some more.

Then I wrote down "Angus Newhall." How could his influence with Western Penn Trust be put to use? I doubted that a bank officer could call Roberta and tell her to do something. Angus couldn't call her; there'd be no reason. I put a question mark next to "Angus."

I also wrote down "Liberty Bank." There was a very tenuous link to me or to Linda, and possibly even to Roberta, herself. But Forrest Akers was intriguing. Many politicians couldn't do enough for black entrepreneurs… or at least appear to. That might be a job for the mayor. I wrote down "McKay" and drew an arrow to Akers. I'd have to speak to him again. Would he be receptive? I'd think of something. More question marks.

The waitress removed the dishes. "Some dessert, today? Coffee?"

I wasn't ready to stop my pondering. "What kind of pie is there?"

"Apple, blueberry, chocolate cream, banana cream and pecan." She rattled in a hundred-times-a-day monotone.

"I'll do blueberry, and a coffee, black with a Sweet n'Low. Thanks."

"Got it. Thanks." She was back in less than a minute. "We close this room at two, my friend. Just so you know."

I nodded my acknowledgement. I took a bite and a sip and pondered.

My big worry remained Wittenauer. There could be a problem for a U. S. Congressman. I wondered what he knew. Had the EPA or his ally contacted him? Was he already plotting to discredit me? And I realized that that is exactly what he would do. His connection at the EPA would be working just as hard to make the charge of whatever-you'd-call-it that yielded a phony

EPA file number, sound ridiculous. Would Henry Brill become a champion for truth, justice and the American way?

But that Emily… ahh, Emily… um. Oh, geez, I had to have her name if I was going to ask for her. Would they let her talk to me? I had decided to try, I realized. Okay, I wrote that down. I had to get her somwhere we could talk... secret-agent like. I left more than enough money to pay my bill and took one more, huge bite of pie and washed it down.

I needed a pay phone. On East Carson I pulled in to a big Exxon station where there were pay phones each with a phone book, or large parts of one, anyway. I looked through the first and found U. S Government listings and the EPA. I dropped in a quarter and punched the numbers.

"EPA, Pittsburgh division. How may I help you?" I pictured the two women I had seen just the day before. What should I say? I couldn't use my own name, could I?

"Um, yes, ma'am. I'm Angus Newhall and I need to reach Emily, thank you very much."

"In which department, sir?"

I laid on a thick West Virginia twang. "Oh, by golly. I b'lieve she works with Mr. Brill. You know who ah mean?"

"Yes, sir. That's Emily Szepanik. Please hold." Scratchy music came on. I studied the traffic.

"This is Emily Szepanik. Who am I speaking to, please?"

"This is Angus Newhall, ma'am. I spoke with you about some pollution over here on the South Side?"

"I don't recall speaking with you Mr. Newhall. Is there a file number that you can refer to?"

"Well, ma'am, I'll tell you that if you can tell me if these calls are recorded." My twang was slipping.

"No. Why would you ask me that? Maybe you should speak with my supervisor…"

"No! No! NO! Emily! It's me, Walter Anton. Don't hang up!"

"Who?" she almost squeeled.

"Shoeless Walter Anton. Don't say my name out loud."

"Oh, goodness. Mr. An… um… Yes. I don't think I can be of any help to you. I can't really stay on the line, either."

"Emily, do us both a favor, will you? You know the Marriott by the arena?"

"Ye-eh-es. Why? We can't fraternize with anyone who has business before the agency."

"Well, I don't know that I really do, do I? I must speak with you. We can meet in the lobby and talk in the lounge, there. Please say yes."

"Not the Marriott. Some of our people go there. Meet me at the student union at Duquesne... quarter past four. Goodbye." I stared at the phone.

Well, okay. She knows something's up. I sat in my car digesting my sudden rendezvous. Secret agent, indeed. Now what? It was two-ten. I turned around and headed to Blatchford Steel. I had to find out if the old man had spoken to Wittenauer. At the first light I turned right and looped back to the Exxon.

I dropped another quarter and dialed the office. I punched in Blatchford's extension, answered by Kelly Galvin.

"Mr. Blatchford's phone," she sang into my ear.

"Hi. Kelly. It's Walter Anton. Can I ask you a question?"

"I guess so. I can't talk long in case Mr. Blatchford needs me."

"Has he had any calls from Tom Wittenauer, today? We've been working together on this railroad problem, you know."

"Yes, and Mr. Wittenauer's assistant is here, right now. Is there a message?"

"No, thanks, Kelly, you're a peach. I'll get the latest from Mr. Blatchford or from Peter. See you later." I rang off. Son of a bitch. Wittenauer must be in Washington but he sent his man to start explaining. Of course, Hal might have called Wittenauer, himself. I hoped not. That would make me a bigger enemy. What a mess. I drove back to the office as slowly as I could.

Dieter Fuchs was just pulling away in his pretty BMW as I got out of my car. He slowed down and powered his window most of the way down. "So, Valter. Bizzy veek, heh?"

"I do what I can." I started to smile but Dieter's face was sour.

"Well, when you get a free minute, you can go fuck yourself. How vould that be?" His window slid closed and he screeched his tires a little, pulling away. Jesus Christ!

What on Earth happened, there? I'm no enemy of his. What turned him like that? I walked into the office in a daze. Wow.

I sat behind my desk, numb. From thinking an hour earlier that I was on the verge of success, I had descended into doubting everything. Man, I hated the real estate business. What the Hell?

I emptied my in-baskets, to get my mind onto things I understood. In the requisitions pile I found a note – from my German fan, Dieter Fuchs.

"You will fuck up the deal if you ruin things with Wittenauer. Get off that shit!!!!"

Son of a bitch! Wittenauer spoke to Dieter! I held my head and shook it. What did I get into?

I had to think about my situation. As far as I knew, Wittenauer's man was still upstairs with Blatchford. Dieter hated me, and probably Casimir too. If people's feelings could get that hot over something involving Wittenauer, maybe our break-in was connected to my visit to the EPA. Naw. That was still crazy. But, still, who was on my side? Jack Jackson walked in to my almost office.

"You're here."

"Yes. I seem to be… not loved, but present."

"Well, I don't know what that means, but you sure have stirred things up, haven't you?" He sat in one of my chairs. "Blatchford is talking with someone from Wittenauer's office right now. I can't imagine he's making you out to be a whistle-blowing hero."

"I'm sure, Jack, but I couldn't have done anything else. Just the fact that Wittenauer's office is all over this tells me that there is something wrong with what he was doing with the EPA and he's doing damage control. From what Dieter Fuchs just said to me, he's also doing his best to destroy me. All I did was ask a question. I haven't gone public with any charges or anything else. I spoke to you, to Hal and to my attorney. Now Wittenauer is attacking..."

"Your attorney? What the Hell do you need a lawyer for?"

"I wanted to record my suspicions as clearly and as calmly as I could, and have them notarized and all that, before anything became public. Frankly I was worried about what might happen if my suspicions were correct and Wittenauer tried to strike out at me in his own defense. You'd feel the same if you were the target. I'm glad I took that step, now." I was huffing and puffing a little and I could feel my heart beating. I was scaring myself.

"In your defense, Walt, I am going to recommend to Hal that he stand firmly in your corner on this. I believe you have been doing your best to help the company. It will be hard for the old man, though. You hafta know that. He goes way back with Tom."

I nodded. "Thanks, Jack. I feel better that you said that. Much better." I reached across to shake hands. He looked at me for a second, and then shook my hand firmly. I was a little surprised, actually.

"Jack, I've got one more meeting for this week, in about, ahhm... less than an hour. If anything spooky happens I'll leave you a message, again."

He pulled out one of his business cards and wrote another phone number on the back of it. "Call me at home, if you have to."

I turned the card over a couple of times. "Thanks, Jack. I appreciate this very much." I smiled for the first time since lunch. "We're going to come out all right on this."

Jack gave me a quick grin, and headed outside. I wondered what had happened to shift our relationship in the past few hours. Hal's car was still in its spot. Maybe meeting with Emily Szepanik would be genuinely useful. I headed down East Carson to cross over on the Tenth Street Bridge.

I took a "Faculty" spot in a line of them. I doubted any faculty members would be jostling for a spot at four on Friday. What the Hell. I walked up the hill and into the Duquesne Union, past the information desk. A little farther on I watched kids playing pool and wished I had an ID. I looped around and as I came back to the information desk I spotted Emily Szepanik.

"Hi," I began, "I am really, really glad you're here."

"Shoes," she said.

"Huh? Where?"

"On your feet. They suit you."

"Oh! These old things? My velvet boots are at the cobblers." I grinned at her, relieved she had a sense of humor.

"Mine, too." She held out her hand to shake mine. "I've got about twenty minutes. What did you need from me?"

"Let's sit around the corner." We went past the pool room and sat in a cinder-block hallway, decorated with old photos of the city. We faced one another on a backless bench. She was a pleasant-looking woman, maybe five years older than me, dressed neatly in a pant-suit. I liked her.

"From what I observed from Henry Brill's reaction, yesterday, it seems that someone in your office was pulling a little scam with Tom Wittenauer, involving phony EPA file numbers. Tell me I am misinterpreting."

Emily looked at the floor, studying the warp and woof of cheap broadloom. Then she checked the number of holes in the sound-deadening ceiling tiles. "I'll give you my personal opinion, Mr. Anton, nothing more. And I trust you'll never attribute anything to me. I depend on my salary to live."

"I agree with all of that. I need to protect my family. Our house was broken into, last night, and trashed so badly that we had to sleep in a hotel. I don't know if it's related or not. But it has me thinking differently, you know?" She nodded a couple of times. "So, do you think I am on the right track?"

"I can't say exactly what went on, but your questioning got Henry really upset. He was on the phone after you left. I'm guessing, but he may have gone up to the congressman's office. I'm pretty sure he shredded the papers you gave him."

"Huhnnh." I thought for a few moments as Emily studied my face. "What you say makes me more certain of my suspicions. I'm not sure what I can do about it... probably nothing. I will keep you out of it. I can testify to what I saw, only. But your observations make me more confident, in case I ever have to. I appreciate your taking the risk."

"There's no risk meeting here. I'm a Duquesne alum and a couple of my classmates are on staff here, so I come often. A visit here won't stick out."

I nodded. "Okay, that's good."

"But I have more." She looked at me and I stopped trying to stand. "I asked one of our bean counters what this meant, in a generic sense. He's an older man, filling out his time, but he does analyze the financial impact of what is learned about this or that real pollution and proposed mitigation. He's pretty smart about operations over the past fourteen years. I asked him why someone would want false file numbers or to post false numbers on a site."

I raised my eyebrows. She had my total attention. "And…?"

"Apparently he'd seen something like it in Youngstown, also a mill town, in an old coke plant site. A city councilor wanted to stop a developer. I don't know details, but the city councilor lost his position and there was quite a stink. He must have had an insider helping him. My friend transferred to Pittsburgh as part of settling the dust in that deal. He then asked me if something similar had happened, here, and I told him I thought so. He told me to watch out for myself."

"You're safe with me, Emily. I can't thank you enough. Things may be starting to heat up already as a result of my visit with you yesterday. My advice is, don't ask any more questions in your office. Wittenauer's ally was either Brill or someone he's protecting. Don't let him know you have any further interest in the matter. Someone may be scapegoated on this."

"I think I'm safe. I hope you aren't hurt, either." She slapped her hands on her thighs and stood up. "I'm going to visit my girlfriend in the library. Don't call me, I'll call you!"

We chuckled and shook hands at that. I headed out to my car, a couple of steps behind her as she headed across the street to the Gumberg Library.

***

On the second floor of the Gumberg a man took a series of photos with a telephoto lens. Centered in the field were two people, a man and a woman. He worked for Blatchford Steel.

She worked for the EPA at One Gateway Center. He replaced the long lens with a shorter one, and slipped it into a shoulder bag. The camera hung around the man's neck like those of many tourists.

He drove an old Chevy to the corner of Fifth and Smithfield where a 1-hour photo service operated in a large chain pharmacy. He handed over the roll of film and a twenty-dollar bill to the clerk. "I'll wait here to get them, if that's okay?" Which was a request the clerk knew how to fulfill. Fifteen minutes later the half-dozen photos were in a brown envelope on the front seat of an old Chevy as it wound its way to route 79. Forty-five minutes later it exited in Canonsburg, crossed over chartier Creek and drove along West Pike Street. In the litter-strewn parking lot of the *GMC Sportsbar* the Chevy parked next to the only working light pole and waited. Finally a big Dodge pickup pulled in, its brake lights bright red. The driver of the Chevy climbed out with the brown envelope and walked behind the Dodge, checking the West Virginia tags before tapping on the driver's door. The window of the Dodge rolled down and the brown envelope was slipped in. The Chevy retraced its route to Pittsburgh.

***

Number seven, Mapleledge was a welcome sight, recent vandalism notwithstanding. After Dieter's little pick-me-up, nowhere in the city felt very good. I had to give Jackson credit for expressing confidence in me, but I still wasn't sure where I stood. I'd been in the real estate business for just eight days and it felt like a lifetime. At least here, things were comfortable.

I reached for the front door latch and it didn't feel right. It was new. Axel Johnson had been busy. The new latch was centered on a brass plate that covered the area occupied by the old one. The door jamb had new wood neatly fitted in with the rest of the original. I ran my hand over the joints, which were barely discernible. Properly painted the repairs would be invisible.

Inside was a fitted steel plate that would make future break-ins more difficult, but, as I could hear in my mind, only for our friends. I looked into the kitchen and the difference was miraculous. There were deep gouges in the cabinet doors and cuts in the Congoleum and, on the windows Linda had draped beach towels in place of curtains. But everything was clean and nearly normal and I felt tears burning at my eyes as I thought of the labor that Linda had invested for our little family. Humbling.

"Hellooo, Linda?" I set down my briefcase and headed toward the back hallway. Then it became obvious that the living room was also nearly like it had been.

"In here, Walt. The bathroom."

I turned toward her voice. She was scrubbing the floor on her hands and knees wearing… well, blue rubber gloves. My week was coming to a fine end.

"You weren't cleaning like this all day, were you?"

"No," she huffed, scrubbing under the toilet tank, "just since Axel finished. I was at Elly's for most of the time he was here. We went shopping." She backed up on her hands and knees, then swung her head down low and looked up from under one arm. "I don't have much food in the house, though. So after I clean up we can go out for dinner and see if we can start last night over again."

She stood up and wiped the side of her nose with her fore-arm. She did have blue rubber gloves on.

"You look delicious!"

"Ha! This is a very practical way to scrub floors. You're just looking at the lack of clothing… and you can't control yourself."

"Was I supposed to?" In fact, blood was flowing. I could feel it and I'm sure she could see it. "I feel like I've been scrubbing out garbage pails, today, myself. Don't I get to clean up, too?"

"Okay. You can share my shower but it's strictly for clean-up purposes."

"Of course... be right back." Linda packed up her scrub brush and rags as I headed to the bedroom. I was down to floor-scrubbing duds in about ten seconds. The shower was running and Linda was sudsing up with shampoo as I stepped in. I held out my hand and she squirted some shampoo into it. I started shampooing, too.

Linda moved to one side of the tub and gestured for me to step out from under the spray. I acted like we were passing by in a subway car. My boner was straight out and she couldn't help but rub by it as we changed positions. I pretended to not notice. She turned with her back toward the shower spray. I faced her, rubbing bar soap over my glorious, semi-hard body. I washed my feet by holding them up high, one at a time. My knees accidentally pushed up against her breasts, platonically, of course.

"Just wash my back, will you?"

I carefully scrubbed the bar of soap up and down her back, going only so far toward the front, only so far toward the bottom. Then I knelt on one knee and washed her legs and feet. She lifted each foot up in turn and I washed only so far above the knee... and no farther.

She took the soap and washed the top of her legs and, ahh... between them, all while I knelt before her. I figured I'd better stand before delirium set in. I was panting.

Linda turned a couple of times in the spray and gave her hair a final rinse. She looked sideways at me and my towel peg as she started to slide the curtains away to step out. I had had enough. I grabbed her around the waist and picked her up off her feet.

"Oh! No you don't! You brute! I'll scream."

"Well, if you scream, no one will come."

"You brute. What gives the right to take advantage of someone smaller than you?"

"I can't help myself, lady. I'm under attack by a wily temptress." She slid herself around inside my arms, pressing tightly against my hard penis, now clamped between us. She reached her hands to my back, digging in with her nails.

"You're powerless, now, you monster."

Linda signaled a less than firm belief in that statement as she moved her hands a little higher toward my shoulders. In a quick move I lifted her up as high as I needed to get her ensconced on Old Useless. For his part he found his way inside with nary an objection from the owner of that delightful place. Linda wrapped her legs around me and hugged me tightly. I had my hands under her buttocks, moving her up and out just enough to please Old Useless and my beautiful mate. It didn't take long.

"I thought you'd never ask, you bastard."

"Sometimes I'm pretty dense. Your help is greatly appreciated." We stayed like that until our breathing slowed down. Finally I slid her down and we carefully rinsed each other off. The whole week, the break-in, the rain storm and even Dieter's curses all washed down the drain. I was happy again.

This time Linda succeeded in stepping out of the tub as I dried off. She brushed her hair straight back and applied some powder here and there. I combed my hair straight back, too. In ten minutes we were dressed in jeans and shirts. Linda put on woven loafers with no socks. I went sockless in my walking shoes.

"Where do you think? Wanna see if we can finish a meal at *BlackKnights*? That food was good and I'm more relaxed, now."

"I'm fine with that. Did I tell you the house looks fantastic? How could you do so much in one short day?"

"I have to give credit to that cleaning company, because the worst was pretty well contained. Once I got going it went pretty fast with the trash out of the way, although I'm not finished. But thanks. We are sleeping in our own bed, tonight."

"Baby, you're the greatest!" said Ralph Cramden.

***

The same waitress was on at *BlackKnights*. We asked for her table and ordered the same meals. "You must have really liked your dinners. Didn't you take them home last night?"

"Well, we did but we weren't able to finish what we took home. We're reliving last night. Having you serve us is perfect," smiled Linda.

"Same drinks, then?" We nodded. "Okay. Back in a minute."

"Whew," Linda said. "Little by little I'm erasing last night." She gave me one of those grins that have always tied my heart to hers.

"Last night we were worrying about Wittenauer and my job. Today I feel a little less on edge, but the basic problem is still out there. You wanna hear about my day?"

"I'm all ears… let me take notes." She pulled out our yellow pad. The drinks came.

"Okay. You went to see that lawyer. Then what? Will he help you?"

"He took my statement and recorded it. But he also thought the break-in was related to the EPA business. I said I didn't think so but he doesn't believe in coincidences. I don't know."

Linda pointed her pen. "How did trashing our house help anybody? They didn't steal anything. A congressman wouldn't tell somebody to do that. I mean, why?"

"Makes no sense, that's for sure. Alright. Leave that aside. When I got to the office I spoke to the old man. He was unhappy but I made my case for protecting the company in case Wittenauer's shenanigans reflected badly on us. And I told him my suspicions. One of Wittenauer's assistants met with him this afternoon. Something's going on."

Linda flipped the page. "Doesn't sound like a coincidence."

"I also had a couple of meetings with Jack and he expressed his confidence in me and what I was doing. He said he would tell Hal to stand with me. That felt good. But! But! Let me tell you about Dieter Fuchs!" I related why Dieter even mattered and why he cared about the congressman. When I got to the sweet talk he threw at me, Linda got really angry.

"Who does he think he is? What a hateful man!"

"Hey, hey, hey. He's got his straw in the milkshake, too. He's responsible for Blatchford's even having this opportunity. Not many of us could do what he and Casey have to do. You have to see why he'd be worried about losing what's sure to be a big bonus. What bugs me is he's so quick to side with Wittenauer against a fellow employee. There's something stinky about that."

"You're more forgiving than I am. I hope I never meet Dieter what's-his-name." Linda was in full pout with crossed arms.

"Well, our problem is still Wittenauer. And maybe whoever met with Blatchford. We haven't heard the end of this EPA business."

"We can't do anything this weekend. So let's review what's positive before we eat." Linda had made notes, but was back in interview mode.

"Okay, then, Mr. Anton. You say you are going to pull the Three Rivers Trust, the PDC, the mayor, Brightman Partners, Liberty Bank and Blatchford Steel into one big happy development deal that grants you a lease to run your railroad. Do you have any evidence of this wild claim?"

I had to think about how to begin an answer to all of that. "I, ahh... umm, I think there is a project that might fit the bill for a deal, and I, ahh, I think you, madam prosecutor, will be playing a key roll in my success."

"Oh," Linda grinned, "can you back up this new allegation?" She held her spoon like a magnifying glass.

"Yuh, actually, Lin, I think I can, but there's some skulduggery. Are you in?" I held my collar across my mouth, looking as furtive as I knew how.

"Like what?"

"Huh?"

"Like what sort of skulduggery, Clouseau?" I couldn't help my surprise.

"Seriously?"

She shrugged and tapped her pen against her cheek.

"Uh, well, um... what I have in mind is taking some photos of certain colorful renderings that may exist in the offices of the Three Rivers Trust. Maybe you know someone with a key and who might not say anything about your use of that key, especially to one Roberta McGillvray. That's as duggery as I'd like to get. How about you?"

Linda sat back with had both hands on her face, closing off her mouth and nose. I sipped my beer.

Finally her hands came down and she leaned toward me. "I just might," she said quietly.

"Can you reach him over the weekend?"

"It's a her, and I'm pretty sure I can reach her, and I am certain she won't care why I go in there. Can I wear the ninja outfit?" Now we laughed.

"Baby, you're the greatest! Let's figure this out!"

"No. Let's eat. I feel like we just leapt a chasm and we're closer to a win. Makes me hungry."

I gave our waitress a little hand spin and she went into the kitchen. Our meals arrived minutes later.

Linda dug in to her Prime rib, and my tuna was sizzling as Carrie put my plate down. The first bite was ambrosia. We ate without talking. After some agreement on the quality of our meals, we relaxed and slumped into the seats.

"Looks like an interesting weekend." I was famous for discerning the obvious.

"Oh, Walter, do you think so?" Linda mimicked a comedian from a cruise. "I'd like to take another cruise when we're done with this. Alright?"

"That's something to look forward to. Sure!" She smiled. I'd said the right thing. "Right now, though, I can't eat any more. I'm taking this home. You?"

"There's not enough of mine. But take yours. Whew... I'm ready for bed."

I placed my hand on hers. "I don't know how you do so much. I mean it when I say you're the greatest." She smiled again. I said the right thing twice.

I slowed as we pulled close to our house, but there were no lights on or anything out of place. We climbed out like we were carrying dead weights. I unlocked the front door and appreciated again our good neighbor, Axel Johnson. When I flipped on the light in the kitchen I cried out. "Hey! How'd somebody get in here? What the Hell?" A big fresh-fruit dessert thingy was on the counter with a card and a ribbon.

"I think it's Elly, Honey. I gave her a key. You don't mind, do you?"

"No, I suppose not. Just a surprise, that's all. What is this?"

"It's a 'trifle.' I see strawberries, blueberries, kiwi fruit, peaches… yum! Do you want some?"

"No, I'm tired. Is there room in the fridge?"

"It's pretty empty. We can have fruit for breakfast."

I didn't even kid about having sex. We brushed and flushed and fell into bed.

SATURDAY, MAY 25, 1985

Linda rose first, but after nine. Saturday is big breakfast day and kitchen noises woke me. I ambled to the kitchen where I found fresh coffee and the fruit trifle ready and waiting. I hugged my incipient ninja, and leaned against the counter with coffee.

"So, Sweetie, fruit for breakfast?"

"Well, yeah. This won't keep, so we better eat it, if you're okay with that."

"Sure. What else? I know there's a what else."

"Walter?"

"Yes, my little chickadee... yessss." My inner W. C. Fields was expressing himself, my spoon his cigar. Linda shook her head.

"I'm serious, Walt. I've been thinking about our future. We have to give some thought to where we're headed, don't you think?"

"Well, sure. We plan every day." I tried to smile my way out of her serious questions. It felt like a "we're not going to have children" speech.

"C'mon, Walter. Today is like a balance point... past and future. If I get those pictures we could be wrapping this up. Things are gonna change then. Right?"

"Well... yes, sure. I should get more money or a better position, or both. That's what we had talked about."

"You're not seeing my point. This is going to be quite a victory. Look at all you've gone through to get even this far! Have you even started negotiating for what happens when you solve this?"

"Noo…oo. But I mean to. I don't have the victory, yet. Why don't we let's see a deal first?" Linda's cheeks puffed out and her lips fluttered. I was ready to talk about the next step and she was worried about my salary. I had no idea what to say.

"This isn't a test, Wally," she complained, "I don't want you to lose a great opportunity. You bring in this deal for the railroad track and you will have done what was impossible without you. That's worth a Hell of a lot. You see that, don't you?"

"Yeah, yeah, Lin. Of course. But that doesn't motivate me. I want to prove I can do this. I want to prove it to Blatchford, to Jack, even to Dieter Fuchs. I can't worry about myself, right now. How we do it is more crucial... I think."

"Alright, Walt. Let's concentrate on today. Are you coming with me to get the photos?"

"I assumed we'd be together… why not?"

"My source isn't going to actually give me a key. I think she'll just let me in. She works at that building, cleaning on Saturdays. She and I chat and I helped her sister get a job at a printing company. She told me if I ever got stuck she'd let me in. And more than that."

"Sounds like a slam-dunk. What else?"

"Well, the kicker is that Roberta gave her a hard time about the hallway once and wouldn't listen to the fact that she hadn't worked that weekend. I am quite sure she'll keep my secret. So, there!"

"Wow. You're phenomenal. I love you!" That's usually the right thing to say, and it did produce a very nice smile. "You don't think I should come?"

"It's just a couple pictures. It won't take less time with two of us, and this way I don't have to introduce you. Keeps it simple.

No one will notice one person… not like two, anyway." She sat back to end the discussion.

"Guess I'll have to find something to do."

"Go bowling! Can't you call a couple of the guys and catch up on Wednesday? You missed league this week, remember?"

"Well that's a damn good idea. Son of a gun. A couple of em will want to bowl. Thanks, Honey!"

"I do what I can," Linda mused to no one. I dished out another bowl of fruit and topped off my coffee. I felt like humming. In another twenty minutes I had Bobby Campbell set and he was calling Will Guerin. Then I called Tom Kotzinski, over in West Park. His family had plans for the afternoon, but he knew a number for Katie. He said he'd go to the milk store and call her. I didn't pry. We'd meet at one o'clock at the Playmore.

"Well, we're getting our team together. I've got a couple of hours so what do you want done most?"

"Most? We need to get the cabinets refinished. They're all scratched and kind-of old looking, anyway. The kitchen floor is damaged. Maybe talk to someone about that. We've got to put away books in the living room. And, weren't you thinking of refinishing those bookshelves? Upstairs there's damage to the walls and I think a couple of drawers are coming apart so you could glue them or something. We can take down the rest of the storm windows and I can't reach all the windows to wash the outside so while you're up there you could maybe get those. I think I remember you wanted to clear your bench off in the garage and you wanted to get paint ready for some of the trim. Maybe you can find paint that matches the inside trim where it's gouged."

"Well, okay, but I've got two hours," I pointed out. "What about the second hour?"

"I've always wanted to change the shelves in the front hall closet; they just collect things and that would make it more roomy."

"Excellent," I concluded. "I didn't want to be sitting on my hands waiting to leave for bowling." I crossed my arms, looking as serious as I could.

"What? You asked for something to do." She was puzzled.

"I sure did. Think I'll get busy." I got up and stretched and started toward the bedroom.

"Hey. You don't have to do anything, Honey. Just relax. I'll be back from the city in a couple hours and after your bowling we can do something."

"With clothes?"

"Too scratchy. Come up with another plan."

"We could practice right now."

"You'll have to control yourself." She shook her head. "Men."

"I am controlling myself."

"I'm leaving. Give me the camera. Is there film?"

"Yes. I got more. Should be a couple of full ones." I pulled the bag out of the closet, which was messy with stuff collected on the shelves. There were two fresh film-packs. I popped the old pack out of the camera. "You don't want to be changing it when you're in there. No evidence, Agent Ninety-nine!"

"Make sure I have your shoe number, Max," she laughed.

"You know I'm not kidding. Just get the shots and leave no evidence. We're not stealing anything and you don't want someone finding something, that's all."

"Okay, Walt, okay! I know how to be careful. I'm getting my ninja outfit, now."

"I'm getting dressed, too."

"No touching... secret agent mode." I followed her lead, putting on casual clothes that might be work clothes, but could definitely be bowling clothes. She pulled on loose jeans and a gray, long-sleeve pull-over. Sexy, but I controlled myself. We kissed and she was out the door. I kidded about the "mission," but now I felt cold. She was going into an office she'd been in dozens of times, to take Polaroids of renderings she'd probably seen before. What was the danger? Linda pulled away and waved. Simple.

It was only eleven. I dumped my coffee and went upstairs. Linda had put things in place, but I could see deep gouges in the bureaus. A couple of the drawers were not sitting straight. I pulled one and its front pulled away. The corners were dovetailed and on the drawer I held, largely broken off. I tried to figure how to fix it. I carried them both into the garage.

I cleared a space larger than a damaged drawer and set one on the edge with the lip hanging over. A few taps of my hammer finished separating the front panel.

I had to make braces. As I held the sticks I had, I realized I could get by without forty-five-degree braces. That's key to my style of woodwork: flexibility. Early steps in a project often revealed easier ways to continue and only a fool – or a craftsman – would fail to follow those clues. One shock after another.

In any case, and the best part of projects, I needed to go to the hardware store for the exact-length screws and a new countersink bit. There's a big Tru-Valu on the way to Playmore Lanes. It was past noon and the Iron Tigers were assembling at one. I got my hardware and pulled in to Playmore early.

***

"Hey, Bobby! How's it going, man?"

"Good, Walter. You? Trip to Washington, I heard."

"Yeah, went down to talk to our asshole congressman. Waste of time."

"Ahhh, they're all assholes, down there. Can't believe anything they say."

"Seems like, seems like. Who else is coming? Did you reach anyone?"

"Wil is coming and I left a message for Katie. I don't know about Tommy."

"Well even if it's the three of us we can bowl head to head. This'll be good. How'd we do Wednesday?"

"Split all the way. Katie had the highest score. You know she's only a few pins off the highest total on the tigers – for the year?"

"Am I highest?"

"No, that's me," Bobby said. "but you can't make much of it, the way we trade off fourth position. It's just interesting."

"Well let's warm up. I'll tell Nicky two lanes." He fired up 31 and 32 and Bobby and I put our balls on the rails. I took a couple of test slides. There's nothing worse than a hesitation in the slide, swinging a fifteen pound ball. Bobby slid his feet on the wood and lined up to start. Son of a gun rolled a perfect strike ball but the seven stayed up somehow. He collected the spare by moving a few inches left in his approach. The spin took control and straightened out the line just a few feet before the "box." The ball slammed solidly into the lone pin.

Katie Mellon walked in as I got ready. We waved her over. She was carrying a bowling bag. I lined up and made a good approach that resulted in a seven-ten split, an impossible pickup. I stood with my hand over the blower and faced the bench where Katie was putting on her own, new shoes.

"Well, congratulations, I guess! Now you're official."

"Well, a ball that's made for my hand will kick my score up. That's what you guys believe, isn't it?" I nodded and smiled.

"Does it help?" I asked.

"Find out today. First time. Wish me luck."

"You got it. Roll in good health." I turned back to my impossible split and picked up the seven. I hate open frames.

Katie took my lane and placed her ball in the track with the others. She looked as if it might be too dirty for her golden, pearlescent orb.

"Can't be helped, Katie," said Bobby, "the balls get dirty and you have to have a special sling to clean with. Might get scratches on it, too, perish the thought!"

"Yeah, yeah. I know. Still…"

"So, roll, already!" Bobby was standing with his ball, waiting to watch Katie's maiden roll. Katie lined up on her spots, more carefully than ever. Finally she gave a little shrug and made her fluid approach and let the beautiful new ball go. We all watched its progress as though a big gold-plated cup were at stake. In about three seconds it crashed into the pocket between the head-pin and the three. Katie's ball didn't hook, so she got strikes with a more direct hit on the head-pin. Her first roll produced a six-ten leave, which wasn't the strike we'd hoped, but not a gutter ball, either.

"How's it feel? Looked good," I said.

"Well, okay. It fits my hand and fingers. Besides it's better looking than any of yours."

I looked around for Wil or Tom and spotted the big Coca-Cola clock, pointing to one-thirty and remembered that I hadn't heard from Linda for over two hours. What was happening? Did she get in alright? Was her friend working today? Was she hiding somewhere, scared to death? Holy mackerel! I'm here bowling and my wonderful wife is risking her life for me. What a bastard I must be. What could I do? Call the police? *Yes, Police? My wife is breaking in to an office downtown, right near you. Could you check and see if she made it alright?*

"Walt! You bowling, or what?"

"Oh, sorry Bob. I was lost in my thoughts. I sent my wife downtown to break in to an office building and I was just wondering how she's doing, you know how that is?"

"You're a funny dude, Walter. Wife doing a break-in – I love it." I gave him a big shrug and a smile. Inside I was churning.

"Well, c'mon, Walt. You need practice. You're up." Katie was now on the other lane, waiting for me.

"Okay, okay. I'm with ya." I lined up and made my approach without thinking too much about it. A strike. I sat down to compliments, with a big grin on my face. "Your turn, Katie, do the same thing."

She smiled her agreement and made her approach and rolled a sloppy strike, as well – sloppy in the sense that it required some wild knocking around of flying pins to finally flatten the last one. I applauded.

"So, Bobby! How about a triple?" He gave us a thumbs-up and rolled a nine. We sympathized. I switched to lane 32 and rolled again. Wil Guerin showed up. We gabbed for a minute. Wil reminded Katie that he always told her to get her own ball and when her scores went up she could thank him. He got an eye-roll.

We bowled two against two. I bowled with Wil while Katie and Bobby tried to beat us. Our three games took us past three-fifteen. I told Katie I was happy to see her again, since I hadn't seen her since the famous meeting with congressman Wittenauer at Blatchford, and I wanted to ask a couple of questions about that meeting, if that would be all right?

"Now?"

"No, no. At the office. I'll come up to your office or you come down to mine."

"Sure, no problem. I'll see you some time." She walked off and I got in my Jeep.

Behind the wheel I thought about Linda. Maybe she was home already. I went back in to the pay-phones. It rang about ten times. It made me more worried. She could be shopping, her contact might have been late, maybe she stopped over to *english-class*. I got back in the car and pulled onto Buttermilk Hollow Road and turned left, worrying.

Buttermilk runs downhill, basically, to the Monongahela. I usually take Route 837 and cross the river on the Homestead Bridge, then it's uphill to the Squirrel Hill Tunnel. Oddly, I had to pump the pedal a couple times as I passed the first intersection and by the time I headed down the "gulch," I was pumping the pedal four or five times to get significant slowing, just as a black pickup started tailgating.

I wanted to get home. I thought if I pumped the brakes and used the emergency, I could get home. It didn't matter. My tailgater's truck was taller than most; it gave me a sharp push as if I weren't going downhill fast enough. My instinct was to put on the brakes and pull over, but I had to use the emergency brake. In the time lost changing brakes he hit me again, this time pushing for a few seconds. I was screaming at the s.o.b. and why he was taking such risks and it hit me that he wasn't at risk – I was, and my loss of brakes was no accident... except I was wrong about that.

There wasn't time to figure it out. In a second the truck had pushed me straight ahead as the road bent left, flipping my Jeep on its side and ultimately onto its roof as it wedged itself into a tight "V" of rock, its nose in the small creek that followed the road. In the movies these things happen in slow-motion. It's not like that. Everything blurs past your vision and the whole fall takes but a moment. At some point I conked out against the door post.

***

"Can you open it? Huh? Timmy? Open it."

"I'm trying. It's dented."

"Ya gotta shut off the motor, Timmy."

"I know it, asshole. You think you can do better?"

"Is he dead d'ya think? Can you see im? Is he bleedin?"

"Yeah, all over the place. He's breathin."

I could hear the pieces of the conversation as if we were all in a clothes closet, muffled and still. I knew the engine was running but I couldn't do anything about it. My eyes were shut and it felt nice to keep them closed. Timmy whoever finally got in and turned the key. I could smell the heat. I felt Timmy's weight as he pulled out of the window. My face was tightly jammed against upholstery but I couldn't tell where in the car. I slept again.

I heard shouting and a siren.

"Hey, Buddy! Move your hand if you hear me!" I wiggled my fingers. I had pains here and there.

"Okay, okay! Good! Don't move anymore!" He was shouting but it sounded quiet.

"All right, Buddy. Just wiggle those fingers if you understand me." I wiggled.

"We're gonna take some weight off you but I don't want you to try to move. Got me?" I wiggled.

"Good, good. Don't move." I could feel the pressure grow suddenly lighter. "Tony, Tony! Gimme that collar. I can reach him."

"Okay, Buddy. We're taking the weight off you. Don't move!" I wiggled. There was more light. The man slipped a cervical collar under my head and fastened it. "Don't move your head, Buddy. I'm gonna strap a board to you. Don't help. Don't move your head. Nothin to worry about." I wiggled fingers.

In about three minutes he strapped my bent legs to a frame, plus straps around my waist and chest. The strap around my chest pinned my right arm against my body, and that hurt. I moaned but wiggled my fingers when the man near my feet asked if I was alright to keep going. Another fellow, collar-man, was at my head.

"Awright, Tony... we're gonna roll him onto his back. You keep his head moving with the rest of him. I'll make sure the collar is snug."

"Gotcha. Anytime you want." I wiggled my fingers for the Hell of it.

"Okay, Buddy. Don't move yourself. Let us do everything." I wiggled.

"Go," said the first man. In a second I was on my back. I opened my eyes and looked up at the floor of the car where the back seat used to be. Probably my own fault it wasn't latched right. Why was I thinking about it? The man and Tony quickly slid me through a window where two others took over. A cable hooked onto my frame and one of the second pair guided me up the rails of a ladder as he climbed up behind me.

They placed me on a gurney. I tried speaking. "Hey, everybody. Thanks. Don't we want to see if I have any broken bones? Skip the hospital?"

"You blacked out so we're going to the hospital, anyway. Just stay still. They can release you. What's your name?"

"Walter Anton. That's my car."

"Yeah. We checked the plates. If you're up to it the police want to ask you about the accident."

"Sure, but it was no accident."

"Mr. Anton? Officer Arnie Stewart, Pittsburgh Police. Why not an accident?"

"I think my brakes were tampered with and then a guy ran me off the road. I think he meant to kill me."

"Who, sir?"

"I never saw him... just his grill. Big black pickup that was taller than normal."

"See his plate? What make of truck?" Stewart was writing.

"No, I said his truck was taller. I think it had a cross-bar of some kind that he pushed me with. He was right behind me since I left the bowling alley. I couldn't watch him cause I had to be so careful with the brakes. I tried the emergency. How long was I down there?"

"About fifteen minutes. People heard the crash and called us."

"That's all I know, officer. But you check the car for the brakes, okay? You will, won't you?"

"Don't worry. I wrote that down. We'll talk again. Who can I call?"

"Oh! My wife, Linda. She should be home by now." I gave him the number but he said it was the number he'd been trying. "Keep trying though, okay? She's due home."

The ambulance crew was determined to take me someplace so they trundled me in. I was still strapped to the frame. The lights were flashing but no siren. I guessed I wasn't dying.

"Can I straighten my legs?"

The attendant sitting next to me shook her head. "They'll handle that when we get there. Just relax. It's only a couple of minutes."

"Where we goin?"

"Magee Women's." I nodded like I understood but I had never been in an ambulance or an emergency room. A women's hospital? What the Hell?

In a couple minutes we were rolling off the Penn-Lincoln and up to the Magee. We backed into the receiving area and they had me out and in the hallway in one deft move. I watched people moving back and forth and listened to conversations. I heard my keepers arranging to transfer me so they could have their frame back. A doctor looked at me. He waved a light at my eyes and told me to follow his finger.

"Has he had breathing problems?"

"What about this blood, here?" He touched my head and it was tender. "Doesn't seem fractured." He moved to the other end of me and squeezed my knees and calves. "Is that painful Mr. Anton?" I assured him it was not. "I don't see bleeding or bruising here. Let's take these off." The ambulance lady unlatched the straps and gathered them up. "Okay, Mr. Anton, try to straighten your legs."

"Oh that feels good. Thank you."

"Okay, fine. You can take the other straps but keep his head still." Ambulance lady stood at my head and held me with both hands. I could look up over her breasts and into her nostrils. She was kinda cute in a nostrilly sort of way. In a few seconds I was free. Somehow there were several sets of hands under me. With nostril lady holding my head they slipped the backboard out in a quick move. Next thing I knew they'd slung me off the ambulance gurney onto a hospital version. Nostril lady was gone and I was flat on my back with the collar around my neck.

"Mr. Anton we're going to take a quick X-ray of your neck before we take that collar off. The nurse will wash that cut on your head. I'll see you in a few minutes."

Apparently I crashed at a good time. Not too many accidents or births on Saturday afternoon. They had me X-rayed, cleaned up and sitting in "my" curtain-defined room in about twenty minutes. The doctor who had checked me in came by and gave me a simple examination.

"You put a strain on your neck but no real damage I can see. Your head must have taken a whack that caused that bleeding, but that's not serious. Pretty lucky, it looks. You were knocked out – get extra rest for a couple days. If you don't have to go to work, don't. And don't drive. If you feel dizzy, lie down. You don't want another knock by falling. Other than that you're free to go. Is someone coming to get you?"

"I don't know if my wife even knows I'm here, yet. The police were calling the house."

"You can make a call from my phone."

"Thanks, doctor. I'll take you up on that." I stood up and wavered for a few seconds. "My head aches," I said.

"You can have these Tylenols. Nothing stronger. If the pain gets worse you've got to get back here."

I swallowed the pills with water as I stayed standing. "Okay. Lead on, doc." We walked slowly toward a crowded desk, past the curtain walls. He handed me a phone and dialed our number. It had rung maybe three times when Linda came through a door further down the hall.

"Walter! My God! You're walking!" She hugged me. I handed back the receiver. Linda was teary as she stroked my arms and touched my cheek near the head wound. I held her.

"Could have been bad, Honey, but all in all not much... couple of knocks."

The ER doctor, 'Kravitz,' broke in. "Mrs. Anton, he did have a slight concussion but nothing's broken. I want him to rest and not drive for a few days. If he can stay home from work he should. He took some Tylenol but nothing stronger. We need to see him if his headache gets worse, or if he throws up or gets dizzy. Bring him right back if you see those symptoms, okay?" Linda agreed and agreed.

"Walter, I have to do some paperwork. It's this way." I thanked Dr. Kravitz and let Linda guide me out to a turquoise chair while she did admissions business. Then she guided me to her Camry.

"Boy, would I like a beer right now," I said. "I am so dry."

"I'll getch'a soda first chance I can. Tell me what happened." She pulled out to Forbes and headed East to the Penn-Lincoln. I recounted the brakes and the pickup and getting rescued. Then I remembered my worries about her.

"But, what about you? I was worried all day and I couldn't reach you, I mean the police couldn't reach you…"

"Well they finally did. The phone was ringing when I got home. When they said it was the police I almost dropped the phone. How could they have found me out? But they were calling about you and so I came right down. I thought they would be there."

"Did you get the pictures?"

"Perfect! The Trust had two different renderings of that site and it was easy to find them. I had no problem and nobody noticed anything as I came and went. Easy as pie. I told you."

"Baby, you're the greatest. I could really use that soda, now." Linda found a corner market and bought a lemonade and a ginger-ale.

"Let's swing by Alan Boudreau's office. If he's there I need to tell him what happened, don't you think? Head back to Forbes and on to Kirkpatrick and take that right… he's right there on Centre."

"You're supposed to rest. Doctor's orders."

"Only take a few minutes. He should know the threats we're under." Linda shook her head. She turned left a couple of blocks later and in minutes we pulled into Boudreau's lot. His Caddy was there.

No receptionist but the door made a chime. I sat on the couch and Linda stood next to me. A minute later Boudreau stuck his head out of an office, said hello and held up a finger and disappeared. Linda sat.

"What'll you tell him?"

"That guy in the pickup was trying to kill me, today. He tampered with the brakes and came along to finish the job. It's too many coincidences. Wittenauer must be connected to the house and the pickup guy."

"We have no proof."

"We need to get our suspicions on record. And get some advice. We need to be sure of where we stand so that we don't mess up some future case. You'll see." I held my head in both hands. It was throbbing.

"Do you need to lie down, Walt?" Linda clamped my arm to her side. I shook my head, slowly.

She leaned her head against my shoulder. We sat like that for a few minutes. Finally there was some chair scraping down the hall. A happy couple came out, shaking hands with Alan Boudreau. Alan walked them to the front door. When it closed he turned to us.

"This is a surprise, Walter. Is this Mrs. Anton? How do you do, ma'am?"

Linda stood to shake hands; I stood more slowly.

"What happened to your head, Walt? Took quite a bump, it looks like. Come in to the conference room. Can I get you something to drink?"

"I'd love a soda," I said.

"Mrs. Anton?" Linda shook her head. He was back with a bottled water for himself and a root beer for me.

"So, what is so important on a Saturday? Boy, Walter, you look tired. Are you okay?"

"We just came from the hospital, Mr. Boudreau," Linda said, "because someone ran Walter off the road."

"Holy shit! Pardon my French, ma'am. Is this connected to the break-in?"

I nodded. "I think so, now. It's too much of a coincidence for two crimes in a matter of days. No?"

"That seems so. What have you told the police?" He reached into the middle of the table and switched on the microphone. Then he looked beneath the table and slipped a tape into the recording system. "We're recording... speak freely."

I explained what little I had told officer Arnie Stewart.

"What details can you recall? When did you see the pickup the first time? What color was it? What brand? What did it sound like? Anything."

I ran through the sequence. I could recall bits and pieces about the truck. The headlights looked square. There was a big pipe with wires around it across the grill. The grill was black, not chrome. The engine had a certain roar I might recognize. It had big wheels. I saw them in my side mirror. The rear fenders stuck out. Boudreau took notes while I spoke.

"That's pretty good. You may think of a few more things. Write em down. And tell the cops everything you said. Don't hold back unless you think you will be implicated in some other charges. If so, call me."

"How should we protect ourselves? We've been threatened twice, now. What do we do to be safe?"

"Well, I suppose you can stay at home and call the cops every time a stranger walks down your street. You probably have to work, though."

"Okay, so, what? I wouldn't know what to do if I got pushed off the road." Linda was pissed.

"Look... folks. I'm just a lawyer. I don't enforce laws. I can't make you safe. Unless you hire a bodyguard or two you won't be any safer, and the police aren't able to do anything until a crime has occurred. You'll be on your own, same as you are today."

"That kinda sucks." I said.

"You'll be safe again when whoever is behind this gets arrested, and all you have now, are suspicions. We can't bring suit or file charges until we connect actual perpetrators to their actions. You don't need me to tell you to be careful. But, be extremely observant. Maybe you'll spot that pickup. If it follows you, drive directly to a police or fire station or draw the attention of a police officer. Hopefully you can find one when you need one." Boudreau shrugged and compressed his lips.

"Look, it's good that your suspicions are on record. At least we can establish a pattern of threats against you. Has anything else happened on the road?"

We shook our heads, but something nagged at me. I knew I'd had that chased feeling before. "I… I was chased another time, not long ago, I think. I can't remember when, but I had that same feeling when the truck was on my tail today. It was after work or, or… late in the day. I think it was after work, though. Yes! The guy followed me through the Squirrel Hill! I remember it! He almost caused an accident at my exit because he had to swerve back into traffic. It was the day we had dinner at Elly's, Lin, a week ago."

"You never mentioned it, Walt."

"I know, I know. It seemed just stupid so I didn't think much of it. But it… ahh, it was before I went to the EPA. It can't be the same thing, can it? I don't think it was the same truck, either. I guess it was nothing." I was excited as the memory came rushing back but I deflated. My head ached and I had no energy. I slumped and Linda put her hand on my arm.

"All right, folks," said Alan Boudreau, "there is nothing more to do, today. If we ever have to file a civil suit we have some basis, at least. Just keep an eye out for that pickup. If he intended to kill you, Walter, he'll probably try again. Not very cheery, I know, but being observant and careful is the best advice I have."

"Thanks, Alan." Linda and I stood up. "Oh. I thought of something else. I'm not sure if it helps, but one of my co-workers who worked with Wittenauer to get the contract to this point, swore at me, Friday, and warned me to get off the Wittenauer business, and one of Wittenauer's assistants met with my boss that afternoon. He must have heard about the EPA problem from the EPA guy, Henry Brill. At least it seems that way to me."

"Okay. I made that note. Let me know anything else that happens along those lines. You better rest. We'll talk another time."

Linda drove home. The house was secure. We went in and I got ready for a shower. Linda got ready and joined me.

"Ohh, boy. This would be terrific if I weren't so beat. I'll take a rain check, if that's okay."

Linda gripped me around my waist. "I'm not trying to do anything, Sweetheart. I just want a hug." That's what we did. I finished rinsing, brushed my teeth and went to bed. Linda joined me then... or later. I don't know.

SUNDAY, MAY 26, 1985

I was stiff, but better. Linda must have shopped. We had pancakes with granola in them. It was quiet. Finally I asked about the big break-in.

"I went in as expected. I found two different renderings and got several shots of each. I didn't look in any cabinets or mess around with papers. No one can tell I was there."

"Let's see em!" Linda retrieved the Polaroids from her purse. "These are great! Nice and clear. I'll call John Schumann in the morning. This should make that deal come together. I love it! I love you!" I leaned over the table and we kissed.

"The way it looks, the Trust wants a play area built as part of the redevelopment of what are two lots. They also have a lot across the street turned into green space."

"Hmmph," I said. "Actually, I don't care what they want so long as we can leverage it into a permit for that rail spur."

"It was exciting, but by the time I left I was calm as can be. I walked to my car and drove home after some shopping. I had no idea you needed me. Must have been awful."

"It was strange, that's for sure. But no long-term harm. I'll need a new car."

"Well, I'll take you, Tuesday. You shouldn't drive, anyway."

"Yeah. If I have to go anywhere I'll call a cab." I finished my coffee. "What do you want to do, today? Work on the house? Do some gardening?"

"Sure, Honey. All of those… none of those. We need some serious hanging around... too much week this week."

"I can do that. Actually, the stuff I bought to fix the bureaus is in the car. We should find the car. My bowling ball is there, too. I'll call."

"Pittsburgh Police, you're being recorded. Are you reporting an emergency?"

"No. I was in an accident yesterday and they towed the car."

"Yes sir. Hold on." I had my jaw set sternly. Something about talking to police.

"Traffic. Sargent Alford. Who am I speaking with?"

"My name is Walter Anton. I live in Penn Hills but I was run off Buttermilk Hollow Road yesterday afternoon."

"Yeah? And what can I help you with?"

"I need to find my car. They sent me to the hospital and I need stuff in the car."

"Well they probably took your car over to city impound under the Fortieth Street Bridge."

"Where? Fortieth what?"

"In the Strip. Take the Crosstown and up the north side of the river on East Ohio. Cross back over on Fortieth. It's underneath that bridge. You'll find it."

We met Nick Sowitsky and followed him. He was all too familiar with the impound lot. I'd have driven past it and past my poor Jeep, too. Hard to recognize, upside-down. He took pictures and told me it was totaled, but I better move it from impound to save City storage charges. He knew a father-son team of insurance investigators who could store it cheaper, and insurance only covered a few days. I said I'd take care of it.

By the same token, insurance covered a rental car for up to two weeks and I thought I'd take advantage of that. What a weekend. Memorial Day was a blessing, this year.

MONDAY, MAY 27, 1985

I forgot about real estate, railroads and auto accidents. I'm not a veteran but my dad was. He served for about ten minutes in World War II and then was called back for Korea where he saw the Yalu River and escaped from the Chosin Reservoir. He'd been wounded I learned after he passed away. My mother had his Purple Heart packed away with letters... from Korea.

Memorial Day we'd visit my parents' graves in Latrobe. We take the Turnpike and hop on to Route 30 near Westmoreland. Thirty goes through Greensburg where I pick up Donohoe Road into Latrobe from the northwest. It's about the prettiest ride in Westmoreland County but more built up every year.

There used to be good industries in our valley, served by the railroad. We had lots of warnings to keep off the tracks. When I was eight a kid was killed when trains came from both directions and he didn't hear the second one. I didn't know him although my buddy's older brother was in junior high with him. Still it was sad to think of a real person who actually died in a place I knew. I think of that kid because his name was Walter, too. Sometimes I think about him being six years older than me, at my birthday – he'd have been thirty-two when I married Linda and he never got to meet his Linda, and all the rest.

My dad died first, after a Memorial Day parade, in 1968. I was fourteen and he had marched as proudly as ever. I loved the parade because he made it important... that and Memorial

Day, itself, Veterans Day, Flag Day and July Fourth. My father could still fit his uniforms and he marched with precision. At "the Legion" he organized the ranks for marching. A few guys would ride in two shined-up cars with flags on the fenders and red, white and blue crepe paper stuck on where it wouldn't hurt the finish. Every year there were the same three World War Two vets who pushed the same three World War One vets in wheelchairs, the whole route.

My father was a task-master about marching and uniforms. But, when his Army guys came by they were eyes front and looking sharp. Mom and I always stood near the reviewing stand at the Post Office where marines set the official flags and the mayor and the City Council members, along with the head of the Chamber of Commerce, and a couple of clergymen, would judge the bands and floats and marching corps.

My dad's group was always right ahead of a Drum and Bugle Corp that kept the cadence. Right at the reviewing stand they would do a little turn-step-turn maneuver that he called a "Flying Dutchman." The judges loved it. After that they marched to the high school and mustered out, with most heading to the Legion for beers. The day he died he had invited me to come with them, for root beer. Minors weren't allowed in the bar, except it was special right after the parade.

There were other kids there, too, with their dads. We stayed at one table while the men cheered each other's marching prowess. At some point an argument started about how the Viet Nam vets were being treated and how Congress was screwing vets on curing diseases they caught over there and other things. I remember my father standing on a chair and pointing his finger at somebody and then stopping his speech and sitting down. I was talking with kids at our table and we didn't notice right away how the room got quieter. "Give him room!" someone shouted.

"Call the ambulance," another voice called out. "Get his kid out of here!"

A couple of men, still in dress uniforms, came to our table and every kid was scared to see their faces, they looked so serious. One of them reached toward me but as I stood up I could see through the crowd that it was my dad who was lying on the floor with somebody pumping on his chest. It was quiet. I screamed, "Dad, Dad, Dad!" because he would always turn toward me if I said his name three times like when I was learning the two-wheeler. But they hustled me out of there no matter how hard I kicked and twisted.

The ambulance came while they held me and I watched them wheel him out with a mask on his face. That was the last I saw of him until the wake when I couldn't bring myself to go near the casket. They said it must have been his heart, but I knew it wasn't the good part… only the part that could fail.

I could see the whole parade, again, as we drove around downtown. Then we looped under the tracks and drove to Unity Cemetery where we parked by the main building and walked in, holding hands. The Boy Scouts had placed a new flag in the bronze holder.

This year I knelt in front of them for a minute. I don't practice much religion, God knows, but I felt closer to them kneeling. I whispered, "Dear God, watch over them." What that accomplished, I'm not sure. Something. As we walked along the oval Linda suggested that maybe we should go to church more than once or twice a year. I agreed that we should. We ate a late lunch at a turkey restaurant, same as every year.

TUESDAY, MAY 28, 1985

"Heya, g'mornin Mistah Anton. Wife drivin you in today? Car in the shop? Heh, heh, heh."

"Oh, yeah, Pauly. Everything's upside-down. I may be renting a car."

"Well, listen, Mr. Anton. My Junior, is working for Alamo, at the airport? I'll have him call you and set it up, if that be awright with you."

"Sure, Pauly. You do that. If I gotta spend it why not with a friend, huh?"

"I thank ya for that, Mistah Anton. Yessir."

"Okay, then, Pauly. That'll be fine." I slapped the counter in front of the hefty guard and headed to my nearly-an-office.

"Hey, Walter, how ya doin? What happened to your head?" Jack Jackson popped in – a rare event.

"Oh this? Got a little bump. I'll tell you about it. Thanks."

I checked my in-baskets and asked Colleen to swing by.

"What have you brought?"

She spread out a handful of invoices and one requisition. We discussed the impact of a new vendor the shop was trying out and spent a few minutes on the req for a new laser cutting device. I called Bucky Dighton and put him on speaker. We talked through the need for the cutting tool. He made a good case. I gestured to Colleen to give our response. She stared at me for a moment and then pointed at herself with a question on her face. I nodded.

"We're going to pass this on, Bucky because you make a good economic case for it. I hope you get it."

I nodded and signed off with the chief engineer. "Very good, Colleen. I'm going to tell Mr. Jackson and Mr. Blatchford how well you do at this."

She was blushingly pleased as she headed back. I cleared as much paper as I could and made sure there was nothing too timely in the pile. I was sitting on my news of the road-rage attack on Saturday. I wanted to ask Katie about her connection to our congressman, and find out from Emily Szepanik if she heard anything more about the upset I started. I'd just leave my number, not my name.

"Environmental Protection Agency, Pittsburgh Division. What department, please?"

"Yes. I need a call back from Emily Szepanik, please. My number is six eight-eight, fifty…"

"Oh, sir, you haven't heard. Miss Szepanik was killed over the weekend. Some kind of car accident. It's been very sad here. I'm sorry. Is there someone else who can help you?"

I sat like a cold stone; the phone clutched in my hand. I couldn't think. I was building up anger and I wanted to hurt somebody.

"Sir? Sir?"

"Yes! Yes! I'm sorry, there. I wasn't expecting that. I'm sorry. Listen, yeah. Let me speak to Henry Brill, If I could." My eyes were teary.

"Mr. Brill left a message he can't be disturbed."

"Really? How interesting. Well you tell him that 'Shoeless Joe' was asking for him and that he's really pissed. Use those exact words. Shoeless Joe is really pissed about the murder of Emily Szepanik. Can you tell him that?"

"Murder? Who is this?"

I shouted, "All I ask is that you tell Henry Brill that Shoeless Joe is really pissed about Emily. Write it down so you don't forget anything!" I slammed the phone on the receiver. The noise carried outside my almost office.

"You okay in there, Walter?"

"Yeah, yeah! Sorry. Got some really bad news."

"What happened, Walt?" Jack Jackson was in my doorway. I grabbed my coffee and walked past him. He followed me to his office. "You gonna tell me what's going on?"

I told him how I'd been run off the road on Saturday, gone to the hospital and that my car was on its roof in the police lot.

He reacted strongly and started to speak. I just held up my hand and took a few breaths. "The issue now is, Jack, that the woman who tried to help me at the EPA was killed in a car accident over the weekend! The same person! What are the chances?"

"Easy, Walter. You don't... I mean... no connection?"

"Yes there is! She met me Friday night at Duquesne so it was safe – she goes there often, but they must have connected her to me!"

"Oh, cripes, Walt. That's all speculation... you know that. Who's 'they,' anyway?"

"I don't know! Do I think it's the congressman? I don't know. But he's the only person who's been stirred up, lately. Kind of a lot of coincidences, don't you think?"

"Jesus Christ."

"Maybe, but the congressman is more likely."

"Huh?" asked Jack. I just glared at him. "Oh. Yeah. Well." We sat there breathing. "What can you do? Go to the police?"

"I have to, anyway. I'm going to find out what the scoop is on Emily's accident."

"Who?"

"Emily Szepanik... worked at the EPA. Nice lady."

"Oh. Umm, not to make light of that, but what about the land deal?" I started to burn but it dissipated.

"I know, I know. Actually, I have made progress that John Schumann needs. We may be very close to the solution."

"Anything to tell Hal?"

"Not yet. I'll let you know when there's something. Don't worry. Listen," I remembered, "will you fill Hal in on my accident and the death of Emily Szepanik?"

"Me? Tell him yourself."

"He doesn't want to hear more crap about Wittenauer from me."

"But, ahhm... well, no. You're right. I'll tell him."

"Thanks, Jack, 'preciate it." I started to leave and remembered Colleen Walsh. "Jack, there is one more thing. I want to tell you how effectively Colleen Walsh is... doing my job, essentially."

"What?" Jack's squeaked. "Your job?"

"Yes. I've been handing off a lot of it, and I have to say she can do everything I've been doing. She's very bright. If you want, tell Hal that you've been grooming someone to take over for me if he has plans for me."

"You want me to get you a better job? What are you talking about?" Now Jack was standing, to reestablish his position.

"No, Jack. But it doesn't seem I'll be doing the same old job if I pull off this railroad deal, does it?"

"Uh, well, I... if you put it like that. What are your plans?"

"Honestly? I don't have any. Stay alive, I guess." We shook hands firmly.

"I gotta rent a car. I'll be in my cubicle for a while."

"Okay. I'll talk to Hal, too." I detoured out to see Pauly Lemay.

"Hey, Pauly. Can you have your son call me, now?"

"Oh I gotcha covered on that one, Mr. Anton. All he needs is the word from me and he'll be here with the car in twenty minutes."

"Well, now's the time. What kind of a car did you tell him?"

"Well, I figure you're practical, Mr. Walter, but you don't like those little raisin-cake cars. I tol' him a Chevy Impala, but I didn't tell him any special color… that way you're sure you get the right model."

"You're right on, there, Pauly. Give him that call!"

"I'm dialin right now, Mr. Anton. Right now."

I went to my desk. I had every intention of meeting with Katie Mellon, but I was at loose ends. Emily Szepanik was a nice woman. Knowing next to nothing about her, I guessed her only sin was meeting me at Duquesne. What a shitty reason to literally get bumped off. I pulled out a clean sheet and made a list for the day.

One, Talk to the police, hopefully to Arnie Stewart. He didn't have to be a detective to see the similarity of my accident and Emily's. I also had to ask about moving the car to Carson Engineers.

Two, talk to John Schumann about the really big information Linda had obtained. We might actually get the main job done.

Three, tell Alan Boudreau about Emily's death, but learn what I could from the cops, first; tell Linda, too.

Four, I really was pissed at Henry Brill. I didn't like him from the start. Of all the people I'd dealt with recently, I distrusted Brill the most. Only Wittenauer was greasier. Somewhere among Wittenauer, Brill and whoever else was involved, an asshole was ordered to run me off the road, and probably Emily Szepanik, too. That was my theory and I was stuck with it.

I called Schumann. It was eleven-fifteen.

"Brightman Partners. How can I help you?" The question was pleasantly sung into the phone.

"Yes. You can help me. I need to reach John Schumann. This is Walter Anton."

"Good morning, Mr. Anton. I'll see if I can find him for you." I said thanks to Muzak.

"John Schumann. How are you, Walter?"

"Well, all in all not bad… a little sore and achy. I'll tell ya about it when we get together."

"So, what have you got for me? Anything that moves us toward the goal line?"

"I think so, John. I'd like to catch up with you and show you what I have about that Larimer project."

"Oh! Really. When can you get here?"

"As soon as my rental comes I'm headed over to Zone Four… the police. I'd like to come down after that, if that works."

"I'll make it work. I've spoken to Forrest Akers. We can do this deal, I believe. What time do you think?"

"Probably about two."

"Good. I'll be here. See what you can find out about Blatchford's readiness to spend some dough, if you can."

I looked at the old clock: about twenty before twelve. "Okay. I've got to move fast for that. I'll see you at two." I rang off and grabbed for my keys, except I no longer had that car. I trotted to the stairs and took them two at a time to Kelly Galvin's desk. She was not very happy to see me.

"Yes, Mr. Anton. You want to see Mr. Blatchford, I suppose?"

I nodded. "Yes, Kelly, and it's crucial." I stood closer than she likes. She froze for a moment. "Please, Kelly?" She finally pushed the button to flash the big man.

Kelly held up one finger to me after announcing me. "Yes, sir. No. He said 'crucial.'" She set the phone down. "He'll speak with you but you're interrupting a meeting, Mr. Anton. It's a wonder he gets any work done between you and Mr. Jackson."

I hoped she might see that I commiserated with her. I don't think she did.

"This way, please," she indicated as she stepped toward the fancy door. She made a light tap and Blatchford's gruff "Yup!" could be heard by both of us. She opened the door wide enough to slip through, so important thoughts couldn't leak out.

It took a second to adjust to the light. Seated by Blatchford's desk, was an older man I didn't know. He looked at me like a lion might regard a rabbit. Hal Blatchford looked at me like I carried diseases. "Whaddayawant, Anton?" he asked cheerily.

"I want to know if real estate issues can be discussed here, right now." I thought the old man was going to turn purple but to his credit he kept sufficiently cool to regard me differently. He looked at his guest and back at me. Finally he came around the desk and pushed me through the door to the outer office.

"Okay, kid. What's so crucial?"

"I'm gonna talk to John Schumann in a couple hours and I may have the piece he's waiting for to move a project the Three Rivers Trust really wants to do. If we set the hook properly Roberta will acquiesce to our lease of the rail-spur in exchange. I want you to understand where your money needs to go."

He had been looking at the floor while I spoke, but he looked at me, now. "How much money?"

"Maybe a million." His eyebrows went up.

"You want me to spend a million bucks standing in my secretary's office?"

I shook my head. "No, Hal. But this is the only way to make this happen in a short time. Before I talk to Schumann, I need to be able to tell him the deal can be done. The money won't move for a little while."

"What do we get for the million?" He was all business.

"Your million will be injected at the right time in the form of a donation."

"A what?" he asked quietly.

"It's to push the Trust over the edge. The project is for minority, community benefit. Blatchford, indeed, you, yourself, will look like a hero for adding the crucial few hundred thousand or so – no more than needed – that gets the project done. As part of that agreement, the Trust drops its opposition to our leasing the railroad parcel from the city. It's Schumann's plan and I think we can make it happen. I have to tell him that you're behind the concept. I'll have more info tonight or tomorrow."

He was back to staring at the floor and I could almost hear the gears turning. He made a couple of "humph" sounds as he debated the idea. He turned to me with the hint of a smile. "The three million number is not going to add to this later, is it?"

"No." I looked him in the eye with my arms crossed. I could see Kelly Galvin listening without appearing to. She wasn't typing.

"Okay, you hot shit. See where it takes you and let me know everything. I'm talking with a guy from the U. S. Attorney's office… a guy who got his job through Tommy. You're making things difficult for me, but I understand, I think… the car business and everything."

We shook hands and he went back into his office. For the first time in several days I felt like a million bucks. Kelly was staring at me as Blatchford closed his door. Whatever she was thinking, her look was unlike the one she greeted me with. "Thanks, Kelly," I said as I walked to the wide stairs. She remained quiet.

At my office I saw a young black man leaning on my door. "Are you Mister Anton?" he asked.

"Yes. You must be Paul's son."

"Yessir, and I've got your car." He gestured outside and I walked with him.

"Here I go, Pauly," I said as we passed his desk. His son smiled. Pauly grinned like he'd won something.

"You drive carefully, now, Mr. Walter. Hear?"

"Absolutely, Pauly. Won't put a scratch on it." I waved at him.

"No scratches on you, neither, Mr. Walter!" I waved again.

"Here you are, Mr. Anton. Do you like it?" He had his hand on the fender of a deep green Chevrolet Impala SE. It had some nice appearance features, all sorts of electric gizmos and leather seats.

"It looks wonderful, Paul. Isn't this extra cost?"

"No, sir. I got you an upgrade. Same as the regular sedan. I need to see your license and get some signatures and your credit card." He spread the papers out and I signed the triplicate form. He wrote down my license information and the credit-card stuff. "You're all set, sir. I appreciate the chance to do business with you."

"Very good, Paul. This is great service. Do you need a ride to the airport?"

"Nope. All set." He nodded at a white compact, idling a few slots away. "Here's your copy."

I took the paper and shook the young man's hand. "I may need this for a week, maybe more."

"Just let me know, Mr. Anton. Whatever you need." He took off toward the compact. I slid into the seat and moved my hand across the dash. There was something about a new car, and this one was certainly new to me. What a lift. I checked the mirrors, found the wipers and headlights and took another look around before I started the engine. I backed out testing the brakes, shifted into drive and turned right to get to East Carson.

If you're not in uniform you really don't like visiting the police department. If you're not one of them, you're a suspect. The desk was caged in bulletproof glass, where you spoke through a round hole that was shielded inside with a disk of thick plastic.

"Arnie Stewart, please."

The heavy black officer was as disinterested in me as he was in the noisy upstairs neighbor of the Latino ahead of me.

"He expecting you? What's your name?"

"My name is Walter Anton and he is investigating my accident where I was run off the road on Saturday. I have more information for him."

"Fill out this visitor's sheet and I'll see if he's available. You can sit ahh…" he looked at the benches on both sides of the room, already occupied by odd-looking characters. "… or stand. Shouldn't take long." I handed in the blue form, and leaned against the soda machine.

After the Latino man had been in there for a while, the desk officer leaned close to the round opening and called out "Walter Anton." I walked over to the hole. "I'll buzz you in, sir. Go through the metal detector."

A muted buzzer unlatched the door to a short passage ending at a metal detector. I didn't have much metal. I put my new keys and some change in a little basin and walked through. A woman handed me my things and I turned toward the innards of the building without knowing where to go. I was turning back just as my name was called.

"In here, Mr. Anton." Arnie Stewart was three doors down the hall. I trotted to meet him.

"I got a few minutes, Mr. Anton. What's up, today? No more accidents, I trust."

"Well, yes there was. I think it's connected to mine. Maybe you don't know about it."

"Do you mean... here, let's sit in here." He opened the door to a smaller room and pulled up a metal chair for me. He sat across a table from me.

"What? Am I being interrogated?" I was uncomfortable.

"No, no, not exactly. You say you have information and I need to ask questions about that. I'm ready to listen. You don't mind if it's recorded, do you?"

"Wow, I don't know. I'll tell you what I think is true, so I guess not. It's creepy, though."

"Don't worry about it. You're not on trial." He turned on a small recorder and set it on the table. "Just state your name for the record. And the date, too."

I did. And waited. He looked at me with his lips pursed together. Finally he gestured toward the recorder as if to get me started.

"You want me to just start blabbing?"

"If blabbing is why you came, sure." He clasped his hands together and looked at me.

"I came to ask if you have investigated the brakes on my car. Have you?"

"Should I?"

"Of course! Jesus Christ! Don't you remember what I said? That my brakes had failed suddenly? That it was probably the guy who ran me off the road?"

"You think your brakes had been tampered with? You were driving home, you said. You wouldn't do that if your brakes were failing, would you?"

"It's not like that... the way you say it. I was pumping the brakes, taking it easy and using the emergency brake. I could have made it home."

"Sounds pretty dangerous, to me. Maybe you lost control and went over the edge."

I jumped up. "What the Hell is this? I'm a good driver. Traffic was light and I was being careful. The garage I use is near my house. I coulda made it!"

Stewart sat still, looking at me. I suddenly felt stupid. He'd made me feel guilty when I hadn't done anything. I consciously calmed down. I sat and looked back at him. He looked at his watch.

"I came here to find out what your investigation had uncovered. It sounds like nothing. I was hoping you might have obtained some paint from the guy's truck. I was hoping you'd found where the brakes were tampered with. Then I was hoping we could talk about the other accident. Now I don't know." His demeanor finally changed when I mentioned the other accident.

"What accident is that, Mr. Anton?" He now had a small notebook in front of him.

"Are you aware of a traffic fatality over the weekend concerning an Emily Szepanik, who worked at the EPA?"

"Who is she?"

You mean 'was,' officer. Who was she? She was a person who tried to help me at the EPA. Because of me she found out about a fraud going on there. She met with me on Friday evening and now she's dead. That's who she is... was."

Officer Stewart had made notes as I spoke.

"What kind of business did you have with her?"

"It wasn't with her. My business had to do with EPA filings on a piece of land but they are apparently fraudulent. She happened to be the person that came out to the lobby when I went there on Thursday, just a couple days ago."

"Why were the filings fraudulent, Mr. Anton?"

"As far as I know it's involved with political activities by Congressman Tom Wittenauer. I'm not sure how bad the consequences might be for Wittenauer, if and when the fraud gets exposed. I don't know if someone could get killed over it, but I was run off the road and Emily is dead. You'll have to figure it out. I'm just a cost accountant at Blatchford Steel."

Stewart finished writing and lifted his head up to look at me. "You are accusing the congressman of killing Miss Szepanik?"

"I am suspicious, but you're the detective. All I'm trying to do is buy some land for Blatchford. There have been some unusual things happening as we get closer to completing that land contract, and one of them involves Tom Wittenauer and these fraudulent EPA filings. As far as I can see, he is the only person who will be hurt being involved with a fraud. So I suspect his involvement, yes. Now that someone has been killed it deserves a real investigation. Don't you think so, officer?"

"I do think, Mr. Anton, that you have every reason to be upset because you believe some other vehicle forced you off the road. I also think I have no proof that's what happened. We looked at the pavement where you went into the gully and there were no tire marks like we expect if you have been stepping on the brakes when that, quote, 'big black pickup truck' forced you off the road. Frankly it looks like you weren't paying attention and drove straight over the edge when you should have been turning left. So far nobody else has seen that truck you say was tailgating you, nor has anyone come forward to say they saw a truck push you off the road." Officer Stewart slapped his little notebook down on the table as if the last word on the matter had just been uttered, by him.

I did my best to not show anger at Stewart's viewpoint. The sad truth was that his version of events made more sense than mine. Traffic was light and the whole pushing thing took only a few seconds. But I knew what I knew. There had to be a way to prove what happened. I pondered.

"Officer Stewart, I understand why you see things like that. However, I also know what precisely happened. I'm not a bad driver and I don't spend time trying to duck my responsibilities. My Jeep was never in bad repair. Let me ask you if you were able to accept my version of events, and if another accident had happened on the same day, that was very similar, to someone who only the day before had connected with me for twenty minutes... if you could accept that possibility... what would be your next move in proving if the two accidents were connected?"

Stewart smiled and gave a little "humph." He looked at me, poker-faced.

"Let's say things happened as you say and that I was sufficiently suspicious of that possibility. I suppose I would want to get the details of this other accident and look for outward similarities, wouldn't I?"

I nodded as if considering the weight of his words. "You definitely would, officer. And I believe you could ascertain those similarities in no more than a few minutes. In fact," I held up my finger, "I think we are in the very building where that determination could be made in the *next* few minutes. What do you think?"

"I think you're right about the building part. I could make a call and get a copy of that accident report on my desk by the time I got back to it. In fact, if I were reviewing that report it might help if I could ask you a question or two, if any questions occurred to me."

I didn't know if he had just invited me or not. I stood up. "You know the way." Happily, he led me out of the ugly little room.

"That report is already on your desk, isn't it?"

"Maybe." He looked at me out of the corner of his eye and led me into the squad room. There were small desks against one wall. Stewart gestured to another metal chair. I pulled it around to read with him but he kept me against the wall. "I'll ask you what seems pertinent. If there are the similarities you think there are, I'll get a new case number on it. Fair enough?"

"Fair enough… if you agree with me." He just glared, then opened a folder he'd been carrying. I gave my own "humph."

"This accident happened at one-seventeen pee-em, Saturday afternoon on Lincoln Road, just past the turn off to Verona – in Penn Hills, actually. I had to ask for the record. She was pushed into a rocky "V" where a recent accident had taken out the guard-rail. Maybe he scouted out the area. We don't have a description of a pickup truck, but there was a vehicle tailgating, according to a plumber a few car-lengths behind. He stopped to see if he could help the victim, one Emily Szepanik. He radioed his office and they called it in. The tailgater took off so no plate. Apparently firefighters responded within six minutes. The first guys down to the wreck confirmed that the occupant was dead at the scene. She was driving a Dodge Intrepid, white with a vinyl roof."

"Good grief. I told you," I said. "He got both of us on the same day."

"That the name of the lady you were talking about?"

"Yes. She worked for the EPA, right?"

"It does say that. We have informed her mother and sister. Apparently she wasn't married." He was flipping back and forth among several papers. "How well did you know Miss Szepanik? Were you in some sort of relationship?"

"What? Relationship? No… oh. I met her for the first time on Thursday afternoon, right after that big thunderstorm we had. Do you remember it?"

"What does that have to do with your relationship?"

"There was no relationship! Why are you asking me that?"

"Might have been your wife or her boyfriend who had it in for you. That whole Wittenauer business could just be a smoke-screen."

I shook my head as I leaned over. "You are a piece of work, Stewart." I sat back up. Stewart was looking at me with total skepticism.

"How did you know Miss Szepanik was dead?" he asked.

"I called the EPA to ask her if there had been any repercussions from Wittenauer's office. The lady who answered told me she had died in a car accident over the weekend. I guessed that it had been Saturday because of what happened to me. You confirmed that it was on Saturday." Stewart's notebook was back out.

"What repercussions were you afraid of?"

"It's a long story, officer."

"I'm ready. Go ahead."

I shrugged and started recounting the previous two weeks. From time to time Stewart would stop me and make me repeat a portion of the convoluted story. As I recited the events it seemed fantastic. Couldn't be helped.

"You say you have a conflict with this Roberta McGillvray, as well?"

"Strictly business, strictly business. She wants a parcel of land to be used one way and Blatchford would like to use it another way. I think we are getting closer to a resolution of our differences. Strictly business."

"And there's a problem with the EPA? You seem to have spent the last two weeks making enemies, Mr. Anton."

"More like I stumbled across them – enemies I didn't even know two weeks ago. There were EPA signs on the land we want to use. Everybody thought we couldn't do anything because of some kind of pollution, there. All I did was ask the EPA what that pollution is? That's when I learned the signs were fraudulent. This was connected to a deal between congressman Wittenauer and somebody inside the EPA here in Pittsburgh. All I did was ask the questions. Emily Szepanik was totally peripheral to all of that. But you should talk to a guy named Henry Brill at the EPA. He's the one who got really upset when I asked about those little signs and the fake file numbers."

"B-R-I-L-L?"

"I think so. He told me not to talk to anyone else about the matter. When I met Emily Friday afternoon, she said she thought he had gone right up to Wittenauer's office after I left on Thursday. You gotta talk to him."

"If I decide all this shit is connected, I might."

"What else do you need? I gave you everything that ties it together. Christ!"

"I'm going to talk to the commander and ask for some help if he agrees with me... and with you. We'll have to see how it plays out. I'm sure we'll be in touch. Don't leave the area, okay?"

"Are you going to inspect my car for the brakes and paint residue?"

"Well! Thanks for that, Sherlock. I'll let you know." He stood and guided my elbow out of the squad room and to the front desk. He stuck out his hand and we shook. "You may have something in all this, Mr. Anton. I'll be in touch."

"Thanks, officer. If anything new happens, I'll call you, too. Meanwhile, though, we want to move the car out of the impound lot… ahh, because of the cost. Let me know when we can do that?" He looked at me and nodded slowly, and then shrugged. It was already after one-thirty. I hustled to the rental and drove too fast to Brightman Partners. Ten bucks to park.

"John Schumann is expecting me."

"Can I tell him who is here?"

"Just say Walter Anton." The cute girl looked at me for a second and turned to her zone of silence and called inside. Schumann appeared.

"Hi, Walter. What happened to your head?"

"Well, in simple terms, I got run off the road; landed upside down."

"Run off? On purpose? Holy mackerel!"

"I think on purpose. It's making me love the real estate business more each day."

We were back at the conference table. "You think it's related to this deal?"

"It is, at least, related to that phony EPA problem. I'm pretty sure of that." Schumann shook his head with a worried frown before proceeding.

"Well, tell me what you've got for us. Something about the Trust's interest in LAR488-dash-8, I hope?" Schumann was almost salivating as I opened my thin satchel. I pulled out an envelope with the Polaroids.

"Linda made a, shall we say, 'quiet' visit to the Trust. She photographed renderings of this parcel. Let's not reference that visit, of course."

"Of course. We'll use this information to know when to agree with what the Trust wants and, more effective, I think, when to take their side in pushing for some feature or another. This will help us be allies. You'll have to be the bad cop. We'll steer things so that the deal can only be made if Blatchford's money is added. You'll have to be the son of a bitch who holds back that money unless you get what you want for your railroad. Can you be that person?"

"Sure. She thinks I am, anyway. It'll fit."

"What you'll want to do is have the city all lined up to lease you that parcel for your uses. Might be time to meet with the mayor again."

"Okay. We got along pretty good. I'll bring him some Old Overholt. He likes that."

"Don't wait. We have to get moving. I want to be the one who alerts the Trust to the possibility of something happening with LAR488. It'll help in the whole relationship." John sat back and laid his hands flat on the big table. I'd seen that before.

"Anything else, Walt?"

"No. No, let's get going. I'll keep you posted; you do the same for me."

"Done." He stood up and reached out to shake my hand. I told him I could find my way. He went out one door and I left through the lobby. The same little cutie was at the desk.

"Excuse me, Miss. Can you make a call for me? It's to the mayor's office."

She looked back at me with big doe-eyes. She didn't pick up the phone. I waited, looking at her. "The mayor of Pittsburgh?"

I nodded with bright agreement. "That would be excellent. If possible, when you reach them, I'd like to speak to him. Would that be okay?"

"Yes, sir. I can switch the call to that phone by the couch." I looked where she indicated.

"Okay, then. When they answer just tell whoever it is that you have Mr. Anton calling for Harry McKay. If they say we'll have to call later, or if they want to take a message, just say that you're calling from Brightman Partners and that it's crucial I speak with him. Can you do that?"

She looked at me like I had two heads.

"Great," I said, "you're the greatest." She liked that part. I went over to the sectional and waited.

I looked at the city. I could see the rivers through buildings near the Point. I day-dreamed about possibly finishing the marathon I was in. What was I going to do afterwards?

"Mr. Anton?"

"Huh? Yes? What?" I turned abruptly.

"Mr. Schumann has approved your call. I'll make it now." Her face projected smug dominance. She was entitled. I'd apologize to John Schumann later.

"Okay, Mr. Anton. She asked me to hold for Mr. McKay." I nodded. The phone next to me warbled. I sat down and waited on hold.

"This is Harry McKay. Walter Anton? I only got a minute." I jumped when he spoke.

"Hello, Mr. Mayor. I am remembering our sharing of some Overholt a couple weeks ago..."

"Yes, that was very nice. Whaddayuwant?"

"That project we spoke of is coming to a head and your input is suddenly crucial. I need to see you for a few minutes. I think I can grant your wish about Wittenauer, too."

"I'm not sure I know what you're getting at, Anton. I've got a tough schedule. When do you want to meet?"

"I'd like to meet now, Harry. Things are moving quickly and you will come out of this event looking very good, I think. You'll be glad."

"Jesus Christ! You always this pushy? You were last time, I recall."

"No, that was two weeks ago Walter. My therapist has changed me into a puff ball."

"A fuckin comedian, now. Okay. Better be good." He clicked off.

I walked past the little girl at the desk and patted the countertop as I did. "Thanks a lot! You are very good!" She looked at me but stifled a smile that was tugging her lips. I hit the "1" button repeatedly to drop the elevator faster.

It was only a couple of blocks. I trotted to the city-county building and speed-walked to the mayor's suite. I said hello to the perky young thing who had blocked me a couple of weeks earlier. She barely flicked her eyes in my direction. I said, "He's expecting me, right now." I was already headed to Maureen Bailey's domain. The receptionist waved in that direction.

Maureen, was polite and welcoming. "He'll see you in a minute or so, Mr. Anton. Can I get you some coffee?" I told her no. "I'm afraid there's no chair." She turned to her paperwork. I leaned.

I was nearly nodding off when the heavy door opened with a bang. "C'mon, Anton. I ain't got all day."

I jumped and followed McKay back into his office, taking it upon myself to close the blond wood door behind me. He turned around in front of his desk and I stopped where I was. His arms were crossed.

"This is twice I've let you make your own schedule with my office," he complained. "You better have something useful."

"I think so. I'd like to tell you how we're going to solve Blatchford's railroad problem, get past the Trust's roadblocks and screw Wittenauer to the nearest billboard… and make Harry McKay look like a hero. But I understand if you're too busy."

"Why do you have to be such a prick? Can't other people have a schedule, too? Jesus!"

"You're right, but let's sit down, can we?" McKay stepped over to an oblong table. He pushed some papers aside and I sat close to him. "Here," I said, "I managed to get a shot of a rendering that the Trust has on a potential project in Larimer. I know it's small, but can you see which one it is? Are you familiar with it at all?"

"I'm not sure of the address. I recognize the way the streets are. What is it?"

"I'm not sure of all the details; Brightman is working on it with Liberty Bank. You know, Forrest Akers."

"Uh-huh."

"It's some sort of minority community services building with a day care and the Trust's trademark of green space, parkland and play area."

"Okay, I see that. So what?"

"Well, it's heating up. If the Trust's interest is what we hope, Brightman will bring Roberta in on this and I'm sure the rendering will pop up. She'll push to get her way and John Schumann will accommodate her bit by bit. At the right moment Blatchford, meaning me, will ride to the rescue with a pile of cash to make the whole thing possible, provided only that she agrees to allow the city to lease 1983-840 to us for, say, two years. We get to move our girders. What do you think?"

"I don't see where I get anything out of this."

"That's one reason I wanted to speak to you before we take another step." I'd thought quickly on that one. Wow. "We need you to be some sort of mediator in this. You put out the press releases and things like that. How will it play best for you?"

"Let me think on that. We'll skull that out and I'll call you by eight-thirty tomorrow. What about Wittenauer, you said...?"

"Apparently he's involved with those little EPA signs on the land. They aren't real. Some kind of little game he was playing to be a hero to Blatchford. But the shit is hitting the fan on that one. It's possible there's even been a murder connected to it. You'll hear more soon, I would think."

"A murder? Are we on it?"

"I think so. I've spoken to the police and as of this morning, at least, there is a multi-pronged investigation."

The mayor turned toward the corner windows, deep in thought. I sat quietly. If his clock ticked we'd have heard it. I walked over to read some framed newspaper reprints about his political ascendancy.

"Want a shot?" he asked without turning around. "It's in the sideboard there. I'll take one, too."

I didn't hesitate to pull out the Old Overholt and two rocks glasses. I poured a couple fingers of the tasty liquid in both. I walked over to Harry and handed him his glass, but he was still looking out the windows. I lifted my glass and wished him "Salut." He lifted his an inch or so back at me.

"Harry, I've got to ask you a couple of questions." He shifted in his chair, puffed his cheeks out and turned back toward me as he released air from his mouth

"Yeah. Go ahead."

"First, what is the mechanism for executing a two-year lease on that parcel?"

"Ah, well. First we get the PDC to convey the parcel to Parks and Recreation. Then Parks and Rec can lease it to you. We'll have to negotiate a good profitable rate that helps our programs for kids, city pools, stuff like that. I can't give you a figure on that right this minute."

"You're making me nervous about that rate. We can't finance everything with one contract." I steepled my fingers together and looked over them at the mayor. "Do you have an idea where you think that lease will be?"

"When Wittenauer was finagling this he offered a million bucks a year. I kinda liked that number."

"I see. You know, of course, Mr. Mayor, that Wittenauer was pulling a fast one on everybody. Blatchford is very interested in putting these pieces together, but we now have to pay some big bucks to help finance the Larimer project, which is also good for the city and certain of its well-known leaders. And there are other benefits as we expand to produce these girders and actually make and ship them."

"So, you're offering what? I only hear whining." He gestured with both hands, indicating that I offer something concrete we'd be willing to pay.

"Harry, I don't want anything to slow this down. I think all I can ask is that you keep the amount somewhere below a million a year... maybe seven-fifty. I can get that past Hal Blatchford. He may be going for a million on the other project and we've got about a quarter-million to spend on the track itself and other changes to move those girders. Say yes."

"We may think about numbers in that realm, but I don't know, yet, what Parks and Rec really needs. I'll find that out and let you know where you need to be."

I puzzled over his words. I looked at the carpet. If I could put this in some set form I'd have something. I lifted my head to face him.

"What about an approach like this? You go to Parks and tell them you're working a deal that will expand their budget by three-quarters of a million for this year and next. Tell them you want some ideas of how they could invest the windfall that will make things better for years to come. That could work." McKay stood up.

"I'll let you know how we're going to take advantage of the Larimer announcement." He guided me out a side door. "You'll hear from me." The door closed. I stood there wondering what happened. I was in a narrow hallway that opened out on the main hallway to the atrium. McKay hadn't quite kicked my butt, but he'd heard enough. I had to assume the annual tab would be below a million. He didn't want to admit I had a better idea on Parks and Recreation. It wasn't my administration. I headed back to the office.

***

The afternoon guard-lady barely glanced at me. Luckily, I worked here. I checked my desk and the in-baskets. The baskets were light, thanks to Colleen Walsh. I called up to Kelly Galvin.

"Mr. Blatchford's office." She was a lady who had never wasted a word that I'd heard.

"Kelly, it's me, Walter. Can you see if I can speak with him for a few minutes?"

"So nice of you to call ahead, Mr. Anton. Hold on, please." Zing. Good for her: never forget a slight... it might come in handy.

"He says to come up." Click. No waste. I started up when a flash of an idea hit me. I called John Schumann.

Brightman's receptionist was as fast as ever. Finally Schumann picked up.

"John Schumann."

"John. I met with Harry McKay a little while ago. He is pondering how to look best in this Larimer announcement."

Schumann responded with an odd tone. "Ahh, yes... ahh, what… ahh, sort of announcement?"

I hadn't expected that question. "Well, when the deal gets put together, I mean. We need the mayor's help with the leasing of our parcel. The way to get it is for him to look like a hero. I kind-of assured him that is what would happen."

"Well, that's understandable, I guess. There's nothing to announce yet. I'm having dinner with Forrest Akers tonight. He needs to look good, too."

"As does Hal Blatchford."

"Right, right. And I don't know how much press the Trust… or Roberta, herself, is going to want. She usually doesn't worry about it if she gets her way."

"I'll need to know how much Blatchford has to put up. I think the city is going to be looking for eight hundred thousand a year to lease the spur."

"Ouch! Is that what McKay said?"

"Not too specifically, but he tacitly accepted that it would be well under a million a year. Apparently that asshole, Wittenauer, had tossed a million around."

"I see. What are you asking?"

"You can probably figure out how to let the mayor make a splash better than I can. I picture a little stage with bunting on it and the mayor speaking first with all the players on stage behind him. Crazy, I suppose."

"Maybe not. You've given me an idea, though. The key is who's on stage. I'll get back to you."

"Thanks, John. I'm gonna speak to Hal right now."

"Good luck." He rang off. I trotted up to Kelly's desk.

"Finally," she observed. I stayed mum. "You can go right in, Mr. Anton." I guess bright and chipper Kelly was off if I showed up.

I tapped on the door as it opened. Blatchford was overlooking the shop. "Take a look, here, Anton."

I stepped over to him. It was almost four and activity was winding down. "Yes, sir," I said.

"I don't know if you have ever appreciated how efficiently we operate down there."

"Well, honestly, no. I know how tightly we control costs, so it makes sense that we would."

"No, it doesn't. There are lots of cost-conscious people in this business. None of them makes as much per man-hour as we do. You probably think I waste my time looking at the shop. Some do."

"I've always figured it was helpful to you. I never worried about it. You're the boss."

"Humnph. It isn't easy to get the best people and we've got a lot of them. When I decide on a key hire it's because I can picture him or her fitting into a production flow, like on the floor. We have a damn good workflow in the shop. Damn good. It helps us win business. Looking at operations there I can visualize operations behind the scenes, too. People have to fit the flow. Watching the shop is my decision engine. Helps me quite a bit, as you suspected."

"Yes, sir." I was afraid to say the wrong thing. He had never spoken to me with any intimacy before.

"What do you see? Down there." I was almost trembling, now.

"I think I'm looking at results of all of our efforts. I've always been glad to be a cog in the machine that enables what the shop does. I've never thought of it as a model of management process, but I see that it is. I don't know if that's what you're looking for."

"That's employee thinking, Walter. Think like a leader, not a manager. Managers hire people who need management – makes em feel important. Mostly a waste of time. Jackson told me you are grooming Colleen Walsh to do what you do. Let her spread her wings."

"Well, yes I have. I've been on this railroad project and she has shown her ability. Frankly, I don't see myself approving requisitions for the next ten years if I manage to get this deal done. Someone needed to be doing my job; I wasn't trying to force your hand."

"You showed a little leadership, there, in case you didn't know. You've shown some leadership on this land deal. When I think of your activities I try to imagine the workflow that's taking place and where everything fits. So far, I'm impressed. Your success will make my judgements right or wrong, in the final analysis. Why do you need me, now?"

I had to calm myself. Heady comments. "I met with the mayor today. I told him we wanted the land for two years and that we could accept seven hundred and fifty a year, and that we would make sure the whole deal made him look good. Schumann's working on that as we speak. At the same time Blatchford Steel is going to look good and the president of a black bank, Liberty Bank, also wants good publicity for his bank's financing of the project. The announcement might be more complicated than the deal."

"What other costs are we looking at?"

"Up to now it has looked like about two hundred thousand to upgrade the track and make some other fixes to get the girders to the river. As far as the chunk we'll have to throw in on the Larimer project, it could be less than a million, too. We might get everything for less than the original three million."

"And the EPA?"

"I'm convinced there is no actual pollution problem, but we hafta make that official. I'll figure that out. The police are investigating the accidents, which will eventually lead into the EPA office, but I'll find a way to get the signs off that parcel quicker than that."

"You have a way?" I could see why Kelly's austere verbiage was pleasing, up here.

"No. But I have some ideas. I'll start moving on it as soon as we're done."

"Okay, then. Go ahead. Let's talk tomorrow or the next day." He pressed the button that closed the curtains. Some lights brightened. I reached out to shake his hand and he took it, firmly.

Outside, Kelly was poised at her desk but doing nothing that I could see. She followed me with her eyes. "He's naming me vice-president and assigning you to me," I said in a calm, evidently believable tone. Kelly's eyes widened and her face flushed a bright red. Tears were pooling in her eyes. I was trying to joke about the absolutely wrong thing. "I'm kidding, Kelly. Kidding. I'm sorry."

She looked daggers at me. I had crossed a line. I apologized again and left as quickly as I could. Boy, had I stepped in it. I needed a dramatic apology. Linda would know how to fix this. Whew!

At my desk I looked up senator Fahnstahl's office. I didn't think he cared a whit about the fortunes of Tom Wittenauer, judging from the Trust luncheon. The phone rang several times.

"Senator Fahnstahl's office. This is Georgette. May I help you?"

"Yes. Thanks, Georgette. My name is Walter Anton and the senator and I met at the Three River's Trust luncheon a couple of weeks ago and then we had some business together at the Trust's offices later that same day. He asked me to call."

"He's not here, of course, Mr. Anton. Why don't you tell me what this is about?"

"Well, because I can't, Georgette. It's connected to some federal crimes and has a rather extreme political effect that he needs to be aware of. It's best to tell me when I can speak with him in person. Thanks."

"I can't respond to your request without more information, sir. Lots of people need to see the senator. I can't let everyone who has something important to say to him take his time. He'd never get his work done. I'm sure you understand. Is there anything else we can do for you?"

"Apparently you don't want to be helpful. I'm going to say two words. Do you have pencil and paper?"

"What?"

"Something to write on and something to write with. Pencil and paper?"

"Being snide doesn't help, Mister Anton. What do you want?"

Now the steam was seeping out of my ears. I spoke very deliberately. "I-want-you-to-write-down-my-phone-number-and-these-two-words-that-I-am-going-to-say. Tell-me-when-you-are-ready."

"Uhh. This isn't funny, sir."

I stated my home phone and then said, "Tom Wittenauer. Got it?"

"Tom Wittenauer. Got it. Who's he?"

I laughed. The whole day had been accumulating emotion. Now her lack of recognition of the congressman triggered a silliness I couldn't control. I laughed in her ear to the point she must have thought me in need of restraint. I coughed to get control. "Ohh, geez. Miss, I'm sorry for laughing. It's been an unusual day. I mean no offense." I contained some internal guffaws and coughed again. "I… I'm very sorry. I must not have been clear. Wittenauer is our congressman. Do you recognize him now?"

"Yes. Thank you Mister Know-it-all. I'll pass your stupid message on to the senator. Goodbye." She was gone and I couldn't blame her. I hoped my message got delivered. If so, I expected Fahnstahl would call. There was nothing else I could accomplish this day. I stopped by Jack Jackson on my way out.

"How'd your day go, Jack?"

"Huh? Oh… hi, Walt. A lot of the same old stuff, I guess. You? Close a railroad deal yet?" Jack hadn't moved more than to look up at me. He looked like a fixture of the building in which I'd first met him. I thought about what Hal Blatchford had said to me about leadership and I felt some melancholy in Jack's reaction to my question.

"Actually, Jack, there's been a lot of progress today. There are only a couple more pieces to pin down and I think we'll get our railroad. Became pretty complicated, but it's fitting together, now. I don't know what kind of a celebration we'll have on that day." Jack gave a little grunt.

"But, I definitely want you to have a prominent role, whatever that celebration is, Jack. You are the one who taught me cost accounting, truth be told. I owe everything to you. I know I've been a pain in the ass, but you have been my mentor. I want you to know I know it. Thank you." I was surprised I'd said all that. I did appreciate his instruction over the years and I'd never given it a moment's thought or Jack a moment's consideration. I felt a little sad. "Well, I'm heading out, Jack. I'll see you in the morning, huh?"

"Yeah, Walt. Sure. See you." He stood up to shake hands and was back at his papers when I left.

***

Linda's Toyota was home but she wasn't. I automatically looked across to Elly's but could see no activity. I changed out of my suit and grabbed a cold Miller's to assist me in my drawer repairs. I cut all the rest of the pieces for the other five drawers and prepped them for reconstruction. I had cleared room on the bench for two of them at a time and I was considering what I'd do with them as I finished screwing them back together when Linda came down the two steps into the garage and wrapped her arms around me from behind.

"I was afraid when I saw a strange car. I was visiting with Elly."

"Oh, yeah. My rental. Nice, huh?" I crossed my hands over hers, then I reached around backwards and tried to grab her butt. She wriggled against me to keep my hands away but I was stronger. I spun around and picked her up, planting a big smooch on her lips. She wriggled some more and I could feel her breasts sliding across my tee-shirt. She felt a little sweaty and that is interesting.

"You feel like you've been working hard. Let's take a shower."

"Now or later?" she asked with a little frown.

"Ohhh… oh, right now. Absolutely."

"You're up for this?"

"Sure am. Just feel." I moved her hand over my zipper, already bulging out.

"Can't you control yourself?" she giggled.

"I am controlling myself… or you'd be covered in sawdust."

I was still carrying her when we got to the bedroom. It took seconds, for us to get naked. Weirdly, I began thinking about talking to her about Blatchford and my police interview. I controlled myself. We almost tripped each other getting to the bathtub. Showers had become fantastic. I had only one idea when we climbed in together.

This idea was my best yet. We coupled more completely than we ever did in bed.

Watching her dry off made me start to stiffen again. "Can't you control yourself?" she asked.

"I am, I tell you."

"You'll have to wait, this time. I can't do that again for a while." I resigned myself.

"How about we eat out? I've got lots of news and I'm hungry."

"Sure! I can eat. I had wine and cheese with Elly, but not a meal."

"Okay. Let's go back to *Fishwives*."

Linda set her lips and gestured for me to lead on. We took my "new" car. "Well, this is nice, hmmnh?" She slid her hands over the leather. "Is this what you want next time?"

"I don't know. I liked the Jeep. It is pleasant to drive, though. Why? Do you want one?"

"For me? No. I'm happy with mine. There's nothing wrong with it. Why change?"

"No special reason. If you'd be happier with something new, we can afford it."

"You know what would make me happy?" My antennae went up.

"I'll have to pull over, but I thought you couldn't do it for a while."

"Oh, you bastard! I'm not talking about that. I'm talking about children!"

Luckily I had prepared myself for a shock and didn't hit a tree. I should have known the whole no-children thing was not final. Women need to be mothers. I think being a father with her as the mother would be pretty special and I wasn't sorry the subject had come up again. But I had no idea where we were headed, now.

"Okay. I'm happy to talk about that. Very much. I love you and I'm with you."

"I know." She said resignedly, quietly. I hadn't heard that voice before. I placed my hand on her thigh and she put hers on top of mine. I stayed mum until we pulled into *Fishwives*. I jumped out, opened the door for her and we held hands into the restaurant. "A booth please," she told the hostess. She seated us apart from other diners. *Fishwives* is noisy at best, but tonight was slower – good for serious talk about futures and babies and stuff like that.

"Do you want to order first or just get a drink?"

"I'll have some wine, I guess. You have what you want."

I waved to our waiter. "She'll have a Pinot and I'll have a cabernet."

"The House okay?"

"Yeah," I nodded. He left. I sat silently wondering how to get into the conversation. I felt better pushing on mayors and congressmen. With Linda I was almost wordless. I decided to ask.

"What do you want to do, Lin?" She gave a big sigh and looked out the window. Finally she turned to me, looking at her hands. I waited.

"I haven't really decided what to do, Walt. It's not like I agonize every day over this, but I can't completely forget about being a mother. When you asked me about buying a car to make myself happy I just couldn't help the rush of feelings about truly being happy with a baby in my arms, nursing at my breast. I couldn't help it. I don't want you to feel bad. I don't."

I wanted to hug her and hold her. I took both her hands in mine. My eyes were tearing up as she freed one hand and dabbed at her eyes with her napkin. "I'm with you, Sweetie. I always have been. Give me some direction, here."

"I've been editing a study on adoptees. Most have good lives. Mostly the study is on the effects of finding their natural parents. How the adoptive parents deal with that process proves to be crucial... which doesn't matter, now, of course. It just got me thinking, reading about childless couples who adopt and how it made them happy." She was looking at me and her hands, alternately. "It's a crazy idea. Crazy."

"No it isn't, Honey. Not at all. We..." Our drinks arrived and we both sat back while 'Alain' set them before us.

"Just give me the high sign when you want to order, okay?" I nodded and thanked him.

"What I was gonna say is that we should start thinking and planning. I can love a baby with you. I can be a father to any child you love. I'm with you. I love you." We were clasping hands, again. She looked right at me, her head nodding in little motions.

"Okay. I love you, too, Wally. That'll never change. I feel good now and I know you have plenty to talk about, too. So, let's file adoption in the 'active' drawer and see what happens." Now she put her hands on mine. "Thanks, Walt… really."

"Never thank me for loving you. I should thank you." She gave me her phenomenal wedding day smile that told me there was a good life ahead of us. We sipped for a while. I thought about adjusting to a child or children in our house and our lives. The idea was sliding in under the edges of my selfishness where I'd been existing, sharing my good fortune with only one other. Maybe I had more love than I expressed for Linda. It wasn't a bad line of thinking. I took a deep breath and signaled to our waiter.

"All right," Linda began, as she shifted her little butt on the bench seat, preparing for a new path of discussion, "what have you been up to?"

I related my discomfort at the police station, being grilled by Arnold Stewart, eventually discussing the similarities between my accident and Emily Szepanik's.

"Who's Emily Szepanik?" I realized I'd never mentioned her or her death.

"She worked at the EPA here in Pittsburgh. When I visited their office on Thursday she's the one who came out to the lobby and led me into a meeting with her boss, Henry Brill. Friday, I met her for a few minutes at the Duquesne Student Union because we couldn't talk on her office phone. I think that meeting, even though she often visited a friend there, is why she was killed on Saturday…"

"What?" Linda almost shrieked. She lowered her voice to a hoarse whisper. "Someone was killed connected to you? You didn't tell me that!"

"Hey, hey, hey." I held up my hands. "I didn't find out till this morning when I called to see if there was any news since I opened up things with Wittenauer. That's when they told me she'd been killed in a car accident over the weekend. Officer Stewart confirmed the similarity of her accident to mine. She was run off the road by a tailgater."

"Good God, Walter. That's a little important, don't you think?" She had her 'dammit' expression.

"I'm sorry, Lindy. I went from the police to talking about the deal with John Schumann, then to a meeting with the mayor, then I met with Hal Blatchford and finally a call with Senator Fahnstahl's office." I thought I was leaving something out but I couldn't place it. "I just needed to get my thoughts together, Honey."

"I know, Walt. But, can't you see how scary this is? Whoever ran you over the edge really intended to kill you! Gracious! It makes me cold." Linda wrapped her arms around herself and shivered. I did know what she meant and I felt guilty for being a target.

"I know this is serious stuff, Lin. The investigation is under way. My interview with Officer Stewart, did result in his agreeing that the Szepanik accident and mine are related. He said he'd get on it and that they would examine my car for the brakes. So things are moving on that front. I think that's good, yes?"

Linda set her jaw to a firm image of a smile. "Yes, I suppose they'll figure that out, but look at how vulnerable we are… you are! I don't feel safe." She sat back and folded her arms.

Before I could say more our waiter tapped my shoulder. "Excuse me, sir. You came in a new green Chevy, didn't you?"

"Yea…sss. What of it?" I was half rising and feeling both protective of Linda and intensely pissed off. "What's wrong?" I stood up, a little taller than the waiter.

"The hostess noticed a guy hanging around your car and thought you'd want to know."

"Still there?"

"He was when I came over."

I looked around the dining room for something to have in my hand. There was a fireplace in one corner with utensils. I asked Alain if there was a back door I could use. He said he'd show me. "Let's walk by the fireplace, okay?" Alain shrugged and wove his way through the mostly empty tables, toward the fireplace. I grabbed the poker and told him to lead me to the back.

Linda had followed our motions. Now she stood and called to me, "What the Hell are you doing, Walter?" She sounded like a school-teacher.

"Stay here and don't bother me!" I growled at her. She dropped, shocked.

I followed Alain past the cooking area and through a stock-room that opened outside. "Do you want me to come with you, mister?" he asked. I shook my head and glared at him to stay where he was. I couldn't believe they'd figured out I had a new car already and could follow me all the way to Monroeville. I held the poker down against my leg and edged up to a bushy juniper by the corner of the building. I could see a man in denim clothes on his hands and knees by my rear wheel. I walked quickly to that row of cars. The guy couldn't see me, kneeling, but he certainly would when he stood up.

I walked quietly. I hadn't thought through how to confront him, but I was mad enough to slug him with the poker. Crazy. I looked around for a black pickup. There were a few pickups, not all facing me so I couldn't see if there were a bar across a grill. By now I was standing a couple of feet from my trunk and the crouching man must have realized my footsteps had ceased. He tried to stand and move toward the front of the car at the same time but he stumbled and wound up sitting solidly. I gestured with the poker and moved to the space between the cars, about four feet away from him. He didn't look scared in the slightest.

"What the fuck are you doing, you shithead?" I slapped the poker into my left hand as if experienced in poker-fighting.

"Nothin. Just checking out the car, ya know?"

"Why this particular car, huh? Some special interest in my car?" His eyes flicked off mine. He was sliding his ass across the hot-top to get away from me. I took a step toward him. "Where's your car? Is it a pickup truck?"

He almost nodded, but caught himself. Suddenly he rolled around and crawled rapidly toward the front of the car and pulled himself up. I was now half-way toward the front of the car, myself. He was looking past me and I figured his vehicle was behind me. In a second he started to move right at me and I backed up. I raised the poker.

"What are ya doin, asshole. You gonna whack *me*?" He emphasized "me." He was within three feet and I realized he intended to take the poker unless I did something.

I swung at him crazily. He automatically held his hand up and the poker caught it a glancing blow that make a sharp sound before it ricocheted off and into the roof of the Impala, leaving a sharp hole in the metal. He was now backing up, holding the injured hand, looking like a stuck bull.

Half a dozen employees of *Fishwives* had lined up about a car-length away. A handful of customers were watching, too, mostly new arrivals. Linda was standing behind them.

The stranger looked at the small crowd and ran to one side and through the line of cars. I followed his path, madder than ever. I turned as if to follow him. "WALTER!" Linda screamed at me. I hesitated. Then I moved again in the man's direction. About a hundred feet down the lot, close to the exit, he jumped into a big Dodge. I still couldn't see the grill, but the truck was big enough. I ran toward it as he peeled out of the lot, squealing the tires and throwing back pebbles. At the last second I thought of getting his plate number, but all I could see were West Virginia colors.

I turned and walked back with the poker hanging at my side. I walked past the rental and ran my hand over the hole in the roof. That would be interesting to explain to Pauly's son. Linda had come up to me and was holding my empty hand and arm. "What on Earth were you thinking? Running after a thug like that?" Her voice was low. She took the poker from my hand and handed it to our waiter, Alain. He had a puzzled look.

"Are you… ahh, you folks still having dinner?" He gestured toward the front door with the poker.

I smiled and assured him we were. We followed him back toward the restaurant but a police cruiser pulled up and a cop called out, "You, there with the poker! Please put it down, now!" He pointed at Alain who dropped the poker with a clang and started to raise his hands.

I stepped over to the officer. "Officer! I'm the guy who had the poker."

"And who are you, sir?" He still had his hand out toward Alain as he turned to face me.

"My name is Walter Anton and I swung at a guy who was trying to sabotage my brakes."

"Hold on a minute," said the officer. "Sir," he directed toward poor Alain, "please give me the poker. Thanks very much. You're free to go." Alain happily entered the restaurant. Linda stayed near me as an even larger audience surrounded us.

"Folks!" the officer called out, "Show's over. Go on about your business." People slowly split off, some to enter the restaurant, others leaving. "Mr. Anton, if you would step over by the car." He gestured toward his cruiser. "Maybe you can explain why you think this guy was sabotaging your brakes?"

I gave him a brief description of being run off the road and another colleague's being killed the same way on the same day. He stopped me and pulled out his note-pad. "How can I confirm this, ahhm… story?"

"I'll refer you to Officer Arnie Stewart of the Pittsburgh Police. He's investigating the two accidents. The thing is, it was a guy in a black pickup in my case, and I know my brakes were tampered-with the first time, and here's this guy I don't know kneeling by my back wheel. I kinda lost it, I admit. But I bet we'll find evidence he was screwing with the brake line on that Chevy."

"And if we don't?"

"Then I look pretty stupid, I guess. I'm willing to look, though. I'm pretty sure what was going on, here."

"Well, let's, then." The cop and I headed for the Chevy. Linda stood still, undecided whether to enter the restaurant or come with us. Finally she stepped off the curb and trotted up to us.

"What's going on, Walt?"

"We're gonna see what that bastard was doing to the brakes."

"You can do that?" Linda stood by the trunk as the officer and I knelt by the tire.

"There should be some evidence if he had time to do anything." I reached behind the tire and felt along the ground. There was a small triangular file there. Without saying anything I stood up and pulled out the keys. I slipped into the driver's seat and pulled forward about six feet. I killed the engine and stepped out. The police officer was holding the file. It was new. I asked Linda if she had a mirror. It was in the restaurant.

"Do you have a jack, Mr. Anton?"

"Must have, although I've never seen it." I opened the trunk to rummage around. There wasn't much rummaging to do, since the trunk was empty. I pushed a tool kit back and forth in its little plastic valise. The cop told me to not bother. He called the company that Monroeville used to clear accidents. We talked about my accident until a wrecker pulled up.

"You're not towing me, are you?" I was getting upset again.

"Hold your horses, sir. We're going to lift the car more safely." During the delay he had produced a camera, and a battery lantern. "Just stand back, please."

Together we watched the tow jockey put his plates around the rear wheels. Then he engaged some hydraulics and the car's rear end rose up about eighteen inches. The officer signaled to hold it there. Then he positioned the lantern where it illuminated the wheel and the rear axle. He checked his camera lens and lay down on his back and hitched himself under the car.

I was damned if I was going to miss this. I lay down and did the same, out of his way. I wasn't sure what to look at, but he was. He ran his fingers across a metal tube that was shaped to fit over the axle, attaching to a mechanism inside the wheel. As he flashed a half-dozen shots I was able to see where the file had scored the metal tube. It hadn't quite cut through. I owed the waiter a big debt of gratitude.

"Do we have proof?"

"Yes, Mr. Anton, it seems that we do." He set his camera out from under the car, slid the light out and then hitched himself out. "Stay right here, Mr. Anton, if you would." He stood and took the tow operator aside and spoke to him for a few minutes, then he came back to where I was standing with Linda.

"You realize I have a lot of questions for you, now?" We both nodded. "Are you still going to have dinner?"

I looked at Linda and she shrugged and nodded. "Yeah. We'll be here for a while, I guess. Why?"

"I'd like your permission to have that brake line replaced… right now. It can be done in an hour, they figure, and then we'll have the line for evidence. You will be billed for that but I suspect you have some sort of insurance that covers the rental? And the tow?"

"Ahh… well, I umm… I don't really know. I never did ask if I had emergency brake-line and towing coverage after criminal vandalism on a car I might be renting. But I'll get it covered or I'll pay for it."

"Okay, good. Go ahead, Jerry." The operator climbed in to his cab, revved up the motor and pulled out of the space where I had been parked. After he straightened out he stopped and came around to the car and finished chaining it to the rack that held it up, and drove off. Or, he could be stealing it and the cop was a sham, too. What the Hell?

"May I ask you both a question?" The officer looked from Linda to me. We nodded.

"You'll be here, eating, and I wondered if I could join you and ask my questions at the same time?" Linda and I agreed again. "Thank you. Very much. I'd be pulling into a diner for my break about now." We walked in together. I signaled to Alain that now we'd be three and he rushed to bring another set-up.

Our new guest was Officer Jason Marx. He ordered coffee. Alain brought Linda and me fresh wines. Linda and I ordered our favorites and Officer Jason ordered a turkey club and some clam chowder. "I'll be done long before you are," he said, "and outa your hair." He pulled out the notebook and clicked his ballpoint.

"You say the waiter alerted you to the suspect 'hanging around' your car?" I answered and corrected as best I could. After about five minutes our meals came, which was rocket-fast for *Fishwives*. We kept answering. No, I had never seen the guy before but, yes, I would recognize him easily, now. Yes, I did connect with the poker and my opinion was I broke a bone in his left hand. Did I get his plate number? No, but I did see that it was a West Virginia plate. It was a black truck. Why, again, did I have the rental? I gave a brief rundown. Jason wrote and wrote.

True to his word he finished his questions, his chowder and half his sandwich in fairly short order. He asked Alain for some foil and wrapped the other half. We offered to pay his tab but he said he couldn't allow that. He settled with Alain and left.

"Wow," I said. "Sorry about that."

'Well, it was scary, all right. But you don't have to apologize for anything. It was sort of exciting. I never saw you fight anyone."

"It was pretty stupid, actually. He could have used that thing on me. I'm lucky I actually hit him. I was so angry... it wasn't smart. And I'm really, really glad that there's evidence of what he was doing."

She put her hands over mine. "You're my hero, anyway. You've got me all excited, again, if you know what I mean." I did know. Her fascinating grin told me everything.

"We better eat faster, then."

"Just control yourself. You have no car, anyway."

"I am controlling myself. Listen, while we're waiting, I have even more news. Your photos are already helping the effort..." I continued on to fill in what I thought I had accomplished within my several meetings. Then I remembered my last meeting, with Jack Jackson.

"You know, when I was leaving the office, today, I stopped by Jack's office, too. He was laboring along and I barely interrupted him. Blatchford had praised me earlier for what he said was 'leadership,' and I was struck with how my role has been changing with this project and Jack's has not. I thanked him for defending me and mentoring me for the past several years. I hadn't really felt that strongly about it but I wound up feeling a little sad for him. Funny."

"He's been there a long time."

"Yeah... and he's pretty close to Hal Blatchford, too. Many times I've thought he was trying to keep me in my place, in a sense, vis á vis the old man. It has to be hard for him to see me dealing with the boss on my own. I don't know how I'd feel."

"I think it was good to thank him." I hummed an agreement with that. I started to think about how I would get from today to the closing ceremony Schumann and I had speculated about. I asked Linda to lay out a new schedule of positives and negatives, emphasizing things that will help conclude the deal. The more we debated which elements were mostly positive and which negative we agreed that legal issues surrounding the accidents and the guy I hit with the poker, should be kept separate from the real deal. There'd be time to chase criminals after we got the lease secured.

I was debating another wine when the hostess came to our table and informed me that the car was back. Linda picked up her purse-satchel thing and we met Alain at the hostess station. I gave him a twenty-dollar tip.

The car was driven by an elderly beanpole of a man. I invited him to drive back to the garage and Linda and I sat in back. He told us his name was Zachariah Abbot. I asked if his son owned the garage and he replied that it was his *grandson* who signed his checks. I congratulated him.

Linda then asked, "have you lived in Monroeville your whole life?"

He looked up into the mirror and replied, "Oh, I hope not!" We laughed. He went on to explain that he'd operated the garage and tow service starting in nineteen-fifty, when there was very little of what we could see, here. His garage was an outgrowth of an ability to fix farm equipment, and he had farmed as late as nineteen-seventy. By then, though, houses and business parks were springing up, and his son had expanded to three repair bays as well as the towing services.

"Well, that's all the history for now," Zachariah told us, "we're here." He pulled into a large, expanded "Gulf" station and stopped gently. "If you'll just sign a couple of things and let me have your credit card, you'll be on your way."

I marveled at his erect stance and obvious clear wit. I signed the credit-card slip and the repair order for replacing the brake line… and for the tow. I had no idea how I stood with Alamo regarding charges like these. We'd figure it out.

"That's enough for one day, I think." Linda nodded agreement.

"Bed will feel awfully good." She had her head back against the seat and was looking languidly at me.

"You know this ain't my car, little lady," I explained in my best John Wayne. "Ahh have ta be real careful-like with it. So there ain't gonna be no feeling up on the rahd home, ya hear?"

"Okay, sheriff." We smiled together and kept our eyes peeled for black pickups.

Home did look pleasant. We unlocked our new front lock and Linda keyed in the alarm code. As interested as man-to-man conflict may have made her earlier, we were asleep in record time.

WEDNESDAY, MAY 29, 1985

There was a cruiser in the parking lot. Officer Arnie Stewart stepped out as I walked toward the building.

"Hey! Morning, Arnie," I called out like we were old friends.

"What? We're buddies, now?" He smiled. "Before you go inside I was hoping we could talk for a few minutes?"

"Sure, okay. Out here?"

"Won't take long. We can sit in the cruiser, or not." I answered by firmly leaning on the rear quarter with my back to the sun. Stewart had his notebook out.

"I was surprised to hear from the Monroeville PD last night. I guess trouble follows you wherever you go."

"It was a surprise, but I think I scared him off."

"Yeah? Tell me about that." I ran over the events of the previous evening.

"What the Hell possessed you to take a poker to someone? Military experience?"

I shook my head. "I was so angry that this bastard would try to kill me and actually kill Emily Szepanik, and then show up to try again! But I wasn't hot, you know? I was cold, if that makes any sense. When he was coming at me I was scared and I swung at him. I'm lucky I hit him. If I missed he'd a been on top of me."

"Luck is a good description. If you can find a few minutes in your busy day come by the station and take a look at a few photos. When I heard it was a West Virginia plate I was led to a group of known thugs you should take a look at."

"Yeah, sure. I'll come down. After lunch all right?" He nodded as he made notes in his book. He tapped his pencil on the binder.

"You thought you did some damage to the man's hand?" I nodded. "But he drove away at high speed?"

"Yeeahh." I didn't know where he was going with his questions.

"Do you have an appropriate respect for the danger he poses to you?" The hefty officer held his head down and looked sideways at me.

"Well… I suppose so. You feel he'll try again?" I hesitated for a moment before answering that silly question. "Obviously."

"Like a wounded predator. He either has been paid to get you or won't get paid unless he does. One way or the other he has to finish the job and you're his only target, as far as we know. He clearly knows what you're driving and the greatest likelihood is that he will change vehicles. You won't see him coming. I would take cabs wherever you go. Just a word of advice. Do things differently, different routes – by cab." His tone of voice was downright grim and unsettling. But I put on my game face and tried to act unconcerned.

"Okay, if you think it's that serious. I'll take your advice."

"Good. See you later." In a quick move he slid into the driver's seat and started his engine. I stepped away and gave a simple wave as he drove off. I was motionless, unsure of my next move. I knew it was inside the big building behind me, so I walked that way. Pauly Lemay tried to gin up some laughter but I moved past him like a zombie. I could hear him worrying that, "Mistah Anton don't look to be feelin too good t'day… no siree." I made it to my office.

A cloud of dread was inhibiting every move. For the past few days I had been carrying on without grasping the actual threat. Thanks to Arnie Stewart, I was now thoroughly discombobulated. Someone was actively trying to kill me. My immediate death served someone's serious purpose. It was hard to set those thoughts aside to read invoices and requisitions. I had to do something normal to get out of the 'woe is me' rut. That meant coffee.

Katie Mellon was in the little kitchenette making tea. "Hey, Katie. Good morning."

"Oh. Hi, Walter. How's it going this fine Wednesday?" She was dressed somewhat casually, office presentable. I didn't care. I really was in a funk.

"Well, I'm happy to be here! You?"

"I got through Tuesday. I believe I'll make it the rest of the week. Looking forward to league, tonight. We face the "Big Macks" for first place, you know." I was still a little sluggish in processing the world around me.

"Ohh. Yeah. It's been a while since we faced them. That'll be interesting, all right."

Katie looked at me with her head tilted. I know I wasn't acting normally. But, I did have a real thought.

"You remember I was hoping we could have coffee at some point?" She nodded. "Do you have some time, now? It may be important."

"Whatever you need, Walt. We can sit in my office. I have until ten." I followed her up to her office, around the corner from Bucky Dighton's. We sat at a small round table.

"So… what's so crucial?" She sipped her tea and looked over the rim.

"Okay. No sense dancing around. That Thursday morning when we met in Hal's office with Tom Wittenauer, you sat next to him and, it seemed to me, were keeping notes on his behalf. Am I wrong?" She turned light pink.

She looked from side to side and finally took a big breath and straightened up, tightening her blouse. "I've known the congressman for a long time. We're friends. Mr. Blatchford always asks me to make him welcome and help him if I can. We've dated a few times, not that it's any business of yours."

That last was ice-cold. I felt rotten. But I was facing a murderer outside the building; I had to press on. "Katie, I am not trying to pry into your life. It's not my business and I know that. But there is more to Wittenauer than you may know. It may be a matter of life and death. No, no," I protested as her expression flared, "that is not an overstatement. I'll explain."

Her face, normally ready to smile, now looked like she was ready to tell me to go fuck myself. To her credit, she just folded her arms.

"Thanks," I said. Then I gave her a quick timeline of the Walter Anton real-estate juggernaut and the phony EPA file numbers. She took notes. When I mentioned Henry Brill she gasped, but quickly resumed her stoic demeanor. I wrapped it up with being run off the road and then learning that Brill's associate had been run off the road and killed, which turned her face pink again. Tears were waiting in the corners of her eyes. At last I told her that a second attempt had been made on my life and that I had received a firm warning from the police this morning, regarding that attempt. She finished her notes and sat back again, looking at my hands, not wanting or willing to meet my eyes.

I tried to sit with as open body language as I could. I waited. Katie sipped cool tea, I sipped cool coffee.

"Why have you told me this?" Katie was still not looking at my face.

I hadn't expected that question, it seemed self-evident. I debated what tack to take. After a minute I said, "Katie, I like you. I like bowling with you. You're a happy moment whenever I see you."

"I know you like checking me out. But why would you be different from other men?" Now she was looking directly at me again.

"Yeah, I do. I should apologize for that. You deserve the utmost respect and I have taken visual advantage. I'm not sure I can stop. You're very attractive and I am like other men. But that's not the point. I am a little afraid for you and I want to warn you about being close to Wittenauer, just now."

"Oh for Christ's sake, Walter. You really believe Tom is involved with this attempt on your life? Come on, now." Her facial expression said everything.

"I'm afraid it is real. I can't see another explanation that explains what's happened. I hope I'm wrong. But, Tom is involved in these phony EPA signs. Henry Brill was quite agitated about the matter. His employee is truly dead and I am not, by luck alone. How else can we explain the sequence of events?"

"Maybe you pissed someone else off and they're trying to kill you. Maybe you told the wrong person you knew oral sex?" She could have smiled then, but carefully did not. I blushingly felt the stupidity of that night all over again.

"For that I am truly sorry. Please accept my apologies. It was awfully stupid and you were more than fair to not throw a bowling ball at my head."

She was working hard to not smile. I wasn't.

"You're a funny man. I can't imagine Tommy being connected to anything so stupid. But you may consider me forewarned." She shook her head a little and frowned. "So, how are we going to beat those Big Macks?"

Now I smiled a little. "Best strategy is to distract them with a pretty bowler," I said, deadpan. She smiled in return. I stood to leave and held out my hand to shake hers. She did, and I figured we were okay.

As I reached the doorway, though, she spoke harshly, "This wasn't some goddam plan to make me ask Tommy about this whole business, was it? Was it? Damn it!"

I spun around and stepped back toward her. "No! No! No! Whatever you do, don't say a word about it. Nothing. Do-you-understand?" I was more brutal than I expected, but her question exposed a huge threat to her own safety. She seemed taken aback by my hard tone.

"Okay, okay. Jee-zus! You really think he's involved. You'll find out you're wrong, you know, but I won't say anything. Really. I won't."

"Okay. Sorry. Look, the only person to speak to about this is probably Mr. Blatchford and me. Be sure you don't mention it to Dieter Fuchs or to Casimir in contracts. They're on edge enough as it is. Promise?"

"Okay, I said. Okay. Stop worrying. That's it. Goodbye." She looked down at her papers. I left.

I stopped at Colleen Walsh's desk. She brought things from her "Walter" tray and followed me back. In less than half an hour we reviewed her decisions. After a little 'what-if' questioning, she changed her opinion on one requisition, not killing it, but to obtain more information from Ginny Makepeace, in purchasing. I told her my office would be unlocked and that she should take everything in my in-baskets and check them through and pass them along as appropriate. If she had any questions she could save them to ask me or do some research and make decisions. It must have been blush-day, because she was a little pinker when we finished, too. But she was proud of my trust and it was well-placed.

I picked up the phone to call Schumann only to find someone asking if it was me on my end.

"Who's this?" I asked.

"Arnie Stewart, Mr. Anton… got a sec?"

"I guess so. What's up?" I was a little irritated to hear from him again.

"Have you done any driving or traveling this morning?"

"Uhh, lemme think. Nope!"

"Okay, listen. I've been reviewing things with a couple of criminal guys down here and we've got a good idea who we're dealing with and I thought it fair to warn you about some things. Got a sec?"

"Yeah, yeah! What?"

"Are you listening to me?" Somehow he had transformed his voice into a stone I couldn't lift. I told him he had my attention.

"This case is now involved with the FBI. That's not why I called, but you should know it's interstate and involves a federal official. The point is, your brakes man has a record of assault with a dangerous weapon…"

"No shit. A black pickup truck."

"No, shit, a military issue forty-five. With real bullets." I could feel that crappy, lost feeling coming back.

"I'm listening," I said.

"Thought you might. He shot a guy in a brawl in Follansbee, West Virginia about three years ago. Claimed self-defense. The other guy did have a knife and the gun was licensed. He got probation with some 'don't get into any more trouble' bullshit. Second time he flashed the gun but no shots were fired. Since it was within his 'be a good boy' period he spent a few days in the lockup in Archer Heights. But the gun was returned to him and charges were dismissed. He pretends to be an Army Vet. His father was... Viet Nam. The point is, now that you wounded him he may be ready to just shoot you rather than fucking around with traffic accidents. Do you hear what I'm telling you?"

I was a little numb. He could just shoot Linda, too. "Yuh. I hear ya."

"Be sure you take that cab when you come down, huh?" It almost sounded like he cared about me.

"Yeah. I got it. Thanks, Arnie." He rang off. A little nag in the back of my mind was telling me to order in and go nowhere that afternoon. The rest of me was just pissed enough to challenge the son of a bitch to try something. I started to imagine some of the great chase sequences in the movies. I'd be Bullit, tricking the bad guys, getting behind them, driving them crazy until they crashed and burned. Right. I called S & S Taxi and asked for a cab at twelve-thirty. For an extra tip I'd get him to drive through a McDonalds on my way to see Stewart. It was almost eleven-thirty. I called John Schumann.

Moments after the pleasantness I heard, "John Schumann."

"Hi, John. It's Walter Anton. How ya doin?"

"I'm good, thanks. You?"

"Well, aside from a second attempt on my life, pretty good, I think."

"What happened? Holy Cow!"

"Well, we caught him trying to cut my brake lines, but he got away. I may have broken his hand with a fireplace poker, though. This real estate stuff's getting dangerous."

"Jeez-us. You're a different kind of cost accountant." There was a little pause before he went on. "You're looking for an update, I guess. I got to speak to Forrest Akers again last night. We met for a drink and wound up having dinner at a 'soul' place near the project site. He's really plugged in to his community. Probably a dozen people interrupted us to say hello to him."

"That sounds positive for our project." I needed something good to hold on to.

"Well, I'd say it is. He's anxious to be part of it, but it also presents something to think about."

"He wants to be the hero?"

"Not that, exactly. His needs are simpler, but much greater than good 'p-r.' Put your thinking cap on, now." I made some noises opening and closing the old desk's drawers.

"Okay. Got it."

"Yeah. Listen. Liberty Bank is a small, niche bank. Akers' dream is to be taken seriously in Allegheny County as a serious development bank. He's tight with a segment of the black population, including a lot of their businesses. People love him but he hasn't broken in to serious capitalization. He is aware... because I told him, that Blatchford is prepared to push this project over the goal line..."

"Is he to be trusted, John? We can't have our involvement bandied about. I mean, you know that. I'm sorry. But what about Akers, himself?"

"Look, Walt, I've known Akers for years – not intimately, but he has handled himself carefully and cordially. I keep an ear to the ground and I've no prior hint that he has tried to play on racial stuff or sympathy or anything else. After discussing things with him, I am certain of his circumspection. So, yes, he is trustworthy. His gain will not come from bragging about how important the other people in the deal may be."

"Okay. You say it, it's good enough for me... for us, at Blatchford. But I guess I'm still wondering, so what?"

"Where does Blatchford do its banking?"

"What? Banking? Mostly at Mellon, so far as I know. We have accounts at PNC and at National City, too. I'm pretty sure the largest balances are with Mellon. And what on Earth does that have to do with anything?"

"Maybe nothing, but maybe everything. Let me ask you a question, now. Keep in mind that it's only a question and not necessarily tied to our deal. It's a question Akers asked me and I told him I'd ask it, too. But it's not a frivolous one."

"So ask, already." I had an eye on the clock.

"What would it take to get Blatchford to bank with Liberty?"

"What?" I squeaked. "Move from Mellon Bank? To a black bank? Is Akers holding us hostage, here?" I was thunderstruck: confused and angry at the same time. After everything I had gone through to get within hailing distance of this deal, this demand from way out in left field could ground everything. I was lost.

"Walter?"

"What?" I snarled.

"It's not a demand," Schumann said gently, "and I need to know you understand that." I could hear him sighing. I let him wait while I calmed down.

"I hear you, John. You understand my upset."

"Yes I do... I expected it, yet I couldn't think of a way to ask the question any better. But, it is a question and an idea. Put on a different hat and think about it. It's your job, I guess, to broach the idea to Hal Blatchford. Hopefully you'll do it more smoothly. And there will be questions you can anticipate, I imagine. Things like how Blatchford will *profit* from the change. You can think of others."

"John," I queried carefully, "does this question have to be answered before the deal is done?"

"No," he answered firmly. "Akers is ready to roll on LAR-488."

"All right, then. Lemme think about the banking thing while we proceed, okay?"

"Sure. Akers is ready but we need to think about how you'll approach Roberta McGillvray. And, what about the mayor and your lease of the parcel?"

"I did meet with him, yesterday. He kind-of got onto the idea that he would find out from Parks and Recreation how much money they needed to change the face of western civilization and that the lease amount would be based on that. I was trying to keep the amount under a million a year, maybe seven-fifty a year. When he started down the open-ended path I'm afraid I suggested a better approach and he was not pleased to hear it. He didn't say no, but he ushered me out unceremoniously. Could you call him, perhaps? I am close to wearing out his patience."

"I don't mind calling. But, you should send him a laudatory note. Could help yourself quite a bit."

"Mmnhh. Okay. I'll give it a shot. How are you making out with UDAG money?"

"Pretty well, I think. We've tried working with Fahnstahl and with Wittenauer's office, and see more progress working with Wittenauer. There was an old application filed through him on this parcel and by resurrecting that we've got a real shot of completing this within ten days."

"He doesn't know of our involvement, does he?"

"I haven't mentioned it. His people seem anxious for good press and a minority project will suit them just fine. You're gonna hafta be doubly coy to slip your support in for this so that Roberta agrees and the congressman doesn't screw it up."

"What about Akers? He doesn't know why we're secretive, does he?"

"I don't think so. I'll get that message to him."

"We'd better get Roberta going on this so that the Trust can get some billing out of it. Maybe have Akers do that appeal."

"Great idea! You're a natural. I'll get him moving on that and help him create a non-specific assurance on the rest of the financing."

"Okay. I am glad you're on this, John. I have to go over to Zone Four, now, to look at mug shots, believe it or not."

"That rates another 'holy cow.' Let's talk in the morning."

"Okay. Thanks for everything. I'll have some ideas on the banking thing by then." We rang off and I headed out to the entrance, expecting my cab to be there momentarily.

"Morning, Pauly. How ya doin?"

"Well, for an old black man, pretty well, I figure, Mr. Walter. Pretty well. You in a much bettah mood, seems like. Feelin bettah?"

"Oh, yeah. Sorry about that, Paul. Really had my worries going full tilt this morning." A horn toot had both of us looking around. A blue and white cab was at the curb.

"What's the matter with the Chevy, Mr. Walter? I'll have Junior take care of it!"

"No, no problem, Pauly. Parking problems, is all. See ya later."

I climbed in the back seat and told the driver to swing by a drive-through restaurant on the way to the Zone Four Station on Northumberland. Before he could ask, I told him I'd buy him a lunch, too, if he wanted. He smiled and assured me he knew the right place. I think he was from Jamaica or another warm, beautiful island that big white ships visit. His name was Micah. He knew his way around more of Pittsburgh than I did.

"You eena hoory sah?" I thought about the sounds he'd made and figured out an answer.

"Not specially. We've got time."

"Okay, sah. We goin fren'a mine. Gone like it." I sat back and closed my eyes. If I didn't eat anything for lunch I could get through the day.

Soon we're driving up Kirkpatrick to a neighborhood I'd been near but never in. Stores and restaurants had odd names and here and there men had dashikis and "Ebeneezer" was in the name of the last church we passed. I was watching, but I'd never find the place we were heading to.

Abruptly Micah took a sharp right and parked tight to the curb, next to a three-legged postal box. The car ahead of us was in front of the hydrant. I doubted we'd be bothered.

I gulped dryly. "We're here?"

"Yas sah. You want dey brings it to you. But the man happy fo you comin in."

Ah, what the Hell? My life was already under threat. I opened the door to spicy smoke and barbecue. I could eat a little something. When my eyes adjusted to the light I saw that we were in a neat, narrow restaurant with a half-dozen tables. Three had black men at them, eating barbecue. The place was clean, although no money had been wasted on decorations. They had a license for beer. Three other coolers held various sodas, non-alcoholic beers and malt liquors. Unknown labels were on the sodas and I grabbed what might taste good: "Alan's Birch Beer."

"Where do we order?" I asked in a low voice.

"You want, we sit outside." I shrugged agreement. We stepped through the back door to a shady little garden-like space with a handful of tables, all different. To one side there were two half-drum grills tended by brown men with beaded braids. A heavy-set woman tended to some pots at one end. Every table had people already seated. There were benches with no tables; a few people ate on those.

Micah caught the eye of one of the barbecuers and got a nod to the two fingers he held up. There was no menu. You came to… wherever we were, and you got 'lunch.' In about a minute one of the cooks came over with two large plastic plates piled with enough food for three, each.

Along with ribs there was a chunk of brisket, and roasted kernel corn with some kind of leafy vegetable mixed in. Underneath the pile was a rounded cornbread lump, soaking up the juices. Between us he'd set a bowl of a pungent sauce, that was similar to that dripping off the ribs, a little bucket of water and a stack of brown napkins. No utensils.

Micah had torn off a piece of the cornbread and was using the crust to slurp the roasted corn mixture into his mouth. I tucked a couple of napkins into my collar and tried the same procedure. The mixture was sweet and bitter. I had to find out what was in it. Everyone was eating meat with their fingers.

We basically kept eating until we couldn't. We dumped the leftovers into a barrel and delivered the water pail and the two plastic plates to a bin near the open grills.

"Fantastic," was all I could think of to say. The woman smiled broadly, remaining teeth gleaming. The grillmen just nodded, acknowledging my simple truth. One of them grabbed Micah's hand and wrist in a sort of secret handshake. I was wondering how we would pay for our meals as we passed back inside. A young woman met us and asked if the number was just two. When I said that was right she told me, "Twenty."

I asked, "Each?"

She shook her head and held out her hand. I quickly handed over a twenty and a five, which she pocketed.

Then I remembered to ask about the beverages, and gestured that I would give her more money. She shook her finger at me and I said thanks, again. Micah was already out the door. He started rolling and after a few turns we were on Centre Avenue and minutes later at Zone Four. I paid Micah his meter and offered an extra ten. He refused it.

"C'mon, Micah. You did everything I asked and didn't waste any time. Take it."

"No sah. My lunch makin me berry happy, sah. We set, now." I figured I'd ask for Micah what's-his-name if I ever took a cab again. I walked up the low ramp. Inside, the desk officer took my name and asked, "Stewart?"

I didn't like being a regular.

Stewart came out and I followed when he turned around. He had three mug books already opened.

"Start at the open page and go about eight pages. Put one of these sticky-notes on the faces you think it might be. Don't say anything until you're done."

The photos were numbered. I looked at the three open pages just to see if there were any differences in the types of men in each book: none I could see. I did put one sticky thing on a picture on the first page of the third book, left to right. He looked similar, unshaven and heavier, but similar. I pulled off another sticky note and turned the page of book One.

Nothing. A lot of grim characters, but definitely not the man I swung at just last night. I moved to the middle book and turned the page. "Holy shit!" I said under my breath. The man was staring at me from the top row, right corner – younger, but the very man I'd encountered. I looked back at the first picture with the sticky note on it. He could have been a brother, or his father, but I took that sticky and moved it to the picture in the top right corner.

"Okay, officer," I called. "He's here."

"Already?" Arnie exclaimed. "You're dead-certain?"

"No question. I was able to look at him for about a minute. This shot is a little to the side, but there's no question."

"All right. Close the book and I'm going to show you another photo. It's a fax but you should be able to tell." He waited until the book was closed and then held a folded paper that showed the same man coming out of a doorway of what might have been a gas station mini-mart.

"That's the guy."

"Okay, read off the number under the photo you chose."

"One six eight. One sixty-eight."

He wrote that down and then picked up the three books. He thumbed through the middle one to the sticky note and left the book open there. "Your man is named Gary Sindledecker. He was born in Washington, Pee-A and grew up in the Wheeling area. His father died in Viet-Nam, but never married his mother. She got no benefits and wasn't very smart about applying on Gary's behalf. She moved around. Somehow Gary got through high school. The army rejected him because of minor arrests. He usually works and makes a score of some kind from time to time, hence the big Dodge pickup, which he actually owns.

"I don't know, yet, what connects him to the congressman or to anyone at the EPA, but I will. It appears that he's working on another big score that may be connected with your death, if that's any comfort."

"Not that I can tell, no. Is he the guy you were describing to me this morning?"

"The very same. Always close to trouble but nothing like a murder before this. You have every reason to be afraid of him."

"Arnie, if I can call you that," to which he shrugged, "when is Emily Szepanik going to be buried?"

"Tomorrow. Saint John's in Southside – not far from your office, I believe. Why?"

"I'm gonna go to the service and maybe to the cemetery. This Gary asshole might show up, too. Whaddya think?"

"Now you're Mickey Spillane? I can't stop you from going to the service or the cemetery. It sounds stupid, frankly. We'll be there, but we won't be there to protect *you*."

"And if your guys get into hot water, I won't be there to bail them out, either," I retorted.

"Thanks for your help, today, Mr. Anton. Don't let the door hitcha in the ass."

Stewart was already studying papers. I walked the length of the dingy hallway and went out. The Hell with him, I thought to myself. I supposed that I was a pain in his ass. At some level, I still didn't take the murder thing completely seriously. I thought Gary Sindledecker was more of a jerk than a hitman. I stood in front of the old granite building and debated my next move. I had a moment of worry, realizing that I had no one else to bother that afternoon. I had handed off my workload to Colleen Walsh and there was no strong reason to be at the office. That was scarier than Gary the Hitman.

I thought of places to go. I could take a bus to Linda's office, but there was no reason. I could take a cab or the bus to Alan Boudreau's office, where I could catch him up on my harrowing days, but I could do that anytime. I'd already pissed-off the mayor and I couldn't dredge up a valuable reason to visit John Schumann, either.

Then it hit me. I could take a cab to the Gateway and see if Henry Brill had come back to work, yet. At no level did that move make any business sense, but, it would be immensely satisfying, I thought, so I dropped a quarter and off I went to tweak the nose of the lion... in his den.

***

I had to wait to announce myself this time. About ten well-dressed Japanese or Korean men were standing at the reception counter. It took me a minute to realize that none was actually speaking to a receptionist. I sidled around the pod and gave a little wave to get one of the ladies' attention. As soon as the group realized what I was doing it moved away from the counter like a school of fish, no audible.

"I need to see Henry Brill, please."

"Who is asking for him, please?" The woman had a headset and appeared ready to push a button.

"Tell him 'Alan Boudreau'" She hadn't said he wasn't in, but if I had told her 'Walter Anton,' I doubt he'd have come out. I kept my back toward the door he would enter from. It took only a couple of minutes. The Japanese Koreans were still huddled on one side of the lobby when Brill entered.

"Yes, Marion, which, ah, who...?"

I turned quickly and stuck out my hand. "Henry! You old son of a gun. Great to see you again so soon!"

Brill automatically held his hand out, too and I pumped it firmly, grasping his wrist with my left hand. He had not recognized me at first and visibly hardened as he realized who I was. We were right next to the counter, which, as I had hoped, kept him from punching me in the nose. He hadn't said anything.

"I know we have a lot to catch up on, Hank. Let's see if we can clear those Parcel 1983 dash 840 filings while we do that."

"Uhh... I don't think we're gonna be able to do that today, WALTER!" Brill's jaw was straining.

"Oh, but today would be an ideal time to wrap it all up, what with Emily's services coming up tomorrow, Henry." I flashed my best Cheshire. Brill started to color. He grabbed my bicep firmly and directed me toward the door – the one Emily had walked me through five days earlier.

As the door closed Brill shoved me up the hallway between the cubicles. I stumbled but kept my footing. I looked back at him and he was walking toward me like I held a red cape. If steam could actually come out of a man's ears, it would have from his.

"Watch that carpet, Walter. We really need to get that fixed." He grabbed my arm again and marched me silently into his office. I was a lot less certain about what I was doing than I had been in the lobby. Still, I didn't think he'd do anything to me here.

The door slammed behind us and he pushed me again in the general direction of the two plush chairs that faced his desk. I stayed standing. Brill was a good three inches taller; there was no way I was sitting.

"What the fuck do you want?" he snarled.

"I want a document that states that there is no known pollution problem interfering with projected uses of Parcel 1983-840. Then our business, yours and mine, will be done. The rest of your troubles I can't solve."

"Why do you think I can do that?"

"Well, it seems like there are no filings on that parcel… or do you have legitimate filings, now?"

"Fuck you."

"Later, Hank. Right now it would seem like a wise move to get me to stop caring about the EPA and Henry Brill's reaction to the false filings being found out… it would seem."

Brill sat behind his desk. His face was as dark as a thundercloud. He appeared to be considering how he could produce a document that wouldn't connect him to the fraud. I was coming to the realization that good old Henry was not all that clever.

"Why are you…? You can't…" Brill held his head in his hands and shook it slowly side to side. When he looked up at me, again, his eyes looked tired and dark. "Just wait twenty-four hours. I'll fix it but there will be no forms or signatures." Abruptly he stood up.

"I'm done fucking around with this. That's it, take it or leave it. Watch your step on the way out." I thought I'd find my way out alone, but he pushed my back as we left his office, and followed me closely back to the lobby.

"Don't ever come back, Walter." I wasn't planning to. I looked over toward the receptionists. The closer of the two was watching my exit. I was starting through their fancy door when I heard Brill growl, "asshole." I stormed back into the lobby.

"Hey, Brill!" He spun around.

"Next time you call me an asshole, don't wait till my back is turned, huh? You fix those filings or I will be back! Hear me?"

Brill was struck dumb, but his blood was boiling. For the first time he looked around at the receptionists and realized what I was doing. He was trapped. "I will kill you," he mouthed at me. I knew what he said. I turned around and walked out the double doors. I waved at the receptionists, both of whom were watching the little scene.

I got into the elevator and slumped against the railings, my heart beating a mile a minute. I was still shaking as I left the atrium. Outside I sat on a retaining wall. What had I done? I had surely poked the angry lion. Had I just scuttled everything? I had to think. I was afraid of encountering Brill outside the building, so I walked quickly to the garage and wandered around for a few minutes before remembering that I had no car to find. Shit. There were pay phones in the Gateway buildings. I jogged over to Gateway-2 and called S & S Taxi. I asked for Micah. He was going off shift in a few minutes. The man would ask. "Okay," he said. Micah was anxious to help me. I hoped he wasn't looking for dinner.

Micah cruised into the garage ramp in minutes. "Where we goin sah?"

I told him I wasn't sure. Maybe he could find a coffee place? Yes, sah, he knew just the place. He crossed over to Southside and headed East on West Carson. I had never pulled in to "Spikes." I gave Micah a ten-spot and told him to get what he wanted and a large decaf for me, black with a sweetener. He looked at me a little funny, but he brought me what I asked for. For himself he had a frozen coffee thing with whipped cream. I waved at the change for him to keep it and asked him to wait there a few minutes.

If my little scene at the EPA had been part of a well thought-out plan, it might have been a good move. As a spur of the moment outburst, it likely created a lot of unneeded trouble for me and for the project. I had to think of a way to defend myself from Brill's vengeance. For all I knew, Brill was behind Gary Sindledecker.

Little by little I devised an outline of my next best moves. First I would speak with Alan Boudreau, again. I wanted everything on record. Then I had to speak to Arnie Stewart. Maybe Brill could be caught removing those little signs. Maybe he wasn't worried about them, anymore and was just going to kill me. I sipped and contemplated.

Micah finished his frozen drink with a "sluck." He looked at me in the mirror. "We still be sittin, sah?"

"No, thanks, Micah. Let's go to my work. Thanks." I wasn't really drinking my coffee. I'd pretty-much decided to drive my rental, come Hell or high water. Let em take their best shot. I also didn't think there would be a third attempt. Micah cruised up Carson, West to East, and pulled around Saint John's Church taking me through the other end of Iron Way and into Blatchford's lot. I paid the meter and gave him another ten. He protested, slightly, and I assured him I wanted him to take it. He smiled and gave me one of his cards.

"Call fo me anytime, sah!" He pulled away. I walked over to the rental and looked around the wheels for any evidence of scuffing or iron filings. Forensics finished, I ran my hand over the hole the poker had made. It was a clean puncture at the end of a groove. I headed in to see if anyone had duct tape.

I went straight to Maintenance. They had it up to six inches wide. I snipped off a six-inch square. To clean the area the tape must stick to, I asked afternoon guard-lady for a tissue. She handed me a napkin from her lunch, or Pauly's. I thanked her, but she was unmoved. I did the bodywork and dropped the napkin in her wastebasket.

My desk was clear. Colleen had passed through only a half-dozen questioned requisitions, God bless her. I ignored them as I placed a call to Alan Boudreau.

"This is Alan Boudreau."

"Alan, it's Walter Anton. How ya doing?"

"Fine, fine. But I'm afraid to ask after you. What's happened now?"

"Well, nothing physical, but I think I'd better get the rest of this story on one of your recordings. There are a lot of new, ahhmm… details, I guess."

"I am fascinated, I've gotta admit, Walter. When do you want to come in?"

"Now?"

"May as well. I'm here."

"I appreciate your doing this with no notice, Alan. I think I'm coming up to needing some advice." I was surprised at the odd relief I felt at the opportunity to talk about the threads of my days.

Then I called Zone Four and asked for Arnie Stewart. He was off schedule. They would pass my number along and he might call me if he thought it important. I left my home number.

Finally I left a message for Schumann. Things were going to happen in the next day or two. I wanted the players to know what I knew. The more I contemplated it, I couldn't think of anything that had to be shared with Hal Blatchford.

***

I popped the Tab that Boudreau handed me and took a long draught.

"It records for sixty minutes, Walt, so just carry on. Don't filter out details. Do you feel okay?" I nodded. "Okay. Collect your thoughts. Do you want to write some things down?"

"No. This is all top of mind, believe me." I breathed deeply a couple of times and gave the tape machine a rambling rendition of my battle with Gary Sindledecker and discussions with Officer Stewart and my verbal challenge to Henry Brill, including his mouthed threat to kill me. Boudreau was shaking his head.

"You're a Hell of a scrapper, aren't you?" He pulled the tape from the machine and wrote on the label.

"Well, I never have looked at myself that way, but since I got onto this real estate project, I seem to be pushier than ever."

"You have skirted the edge, now, twice. First by taking up a weapon against this Sindledecker guy and now by challenging Brill on his own turf. I will point out that he has not yet given you anything substantive that you can accuse him of."

"Well, I can't get over the feeling that he is involved in the attacks on me, on Emily and maybe even on my house. It's just a feeling."

"Can't advise you on feelings. This Officer Stewart seems to be pursuing the actual perpetrator. Leave that stuff to the cops, Walter, honestly. Concentrate on prosecuting this real estate thing and lay low on everything else. That's probably not the advice you were going to ask for."

"No. I'm not sure what advice I wanted. I will consider it, though."

I stared at the tabletop. Boudreau sat looking at me. "You're on the clock, Walt."

"Yuh. Yeah. I know. Alan, let me ask you something way off base."

He gestured with both hands, inviting me to throw it at him.

"Do you know anything about adoption?"

His eyes widened. "Adoption!"

"Yeah, Alan. It's something that Linda and I are thinking about. I know it's not as simple as it sounds."

"I have helped some people who adopted overseas. One couple adopted in China. But I was only helping with the State Department and INS paperwork. I haven't ever dealt directly with an adoption agency."

"Can you make a recommendation? I don't know where to start and I want to take some action, if only to show Linda that I am with her on this."

"I do know some people. I'll call you." Boudreau stood up and took my Tab can. He came back and straightened up a few items on the side table, without sitting down. "What else can I do, Walter? You didn't really ask me for any advice regarding your brushes with big trouble."

"Alan, I can't feel safe. I know things are percolating and I can barely influence them. It's an awful position to be in. The main thrust of the past two weeks has been to get permission to use a piece of land – not even buy it! We're getting close to finally executing a complex deal in Larimer..."

"Who's 'we?'"

"Well, it's Blatchford Steel... and me, you'd have to say, but the action is in the hands of everybody else involved. That's mainly Brightman Partners..."

"Brightman! I know those guys. Aaron Brightman? You working with him?"

"No, John Schumann. Pretty capable guy as far as I can see."

"That's good. Schumann's solid. What's the problem?"

"There's just so many pieces to it. Schumann is juggling UDAG money with Senator Fahnstahl, grants the city controls, which means Mayor McKay, and Liberty Bank who wants to..."

"Forrest Akers!"

"Ha! You know everybody? Yeah, Liberty Bank. The project is a benefit to minorities and he wants to be there. Plus the Three Rivers Trust is going to be involved. They already have plans on file with the state." I could see Boudreau getting ready to exclaim, "Roberta McGilvray!" and I held up my hands.

"Roberta McGilvray!" I shouted. He looked irked for a moment and then laughed.

"Roberta," I explained, "is a major part of the complexity in this deal. She is the reason Blatchford even cares about a development project in Larimer."

"How is that?" Boudreau was seated again, paying close attention.

"We are basically bribing the Trust by helping finance a project they care about in one place, to get their agreement on allowing us to lease a parcel for a couple of years, in another place. Simple, huh?"

"I still don't get the whole picture, Walt. Are you working with Western Penn? They could swing some weight with the Trust."

"Really? I met a guy who banks there and he thought he could sway the Trust because of that, somehow. I told him to hold off until it might do some good, which I still don't know how it might."

"And Forrest Akers, you say? I've done some estate planning for customers of his. He likes being involved… not like most bankers. How'd you meet him?"

"He was at a Trust luncheon a couple weeks ago. I sat at his table but we didn't speak much. I think Roberta likes him well enough. He wants to take his bank to the next level of capitalization so it can be a major development player."

"Does he, now? I should find a way to have a chat with him. How would I have found out about his interest in greater capitalization?"

"Well, not from me, that's for sure. It's something he alluded to in a conversation with John Schumann. Make up your own way to broach the subject, if you please."

Boudreau waved his hands to dispel any fear of exposure. "Don't worry." He turned his hands upwards and raised his eyebrows: was there anything else?

"I'm going, I guess. I just feel so unsettled. I'll deal with it."

"And, Walter," he waited until he had my attention, "no more poking at the wounded animals, huh? Their reactions could spill over onto Linda or others. Just lay low."

I nodded and clamped my lips together. "Thanks, Alan. Listen, let me know if you come across a way to advance my baby project, will you?" He nodded and I left. I sat in the rental for a couple of minutes before pulling away. I had no control over the success of what I'd been handed. I'd gone from obscurity to aggravating some people, collaborating with others, to threatening some of the most powerful politicians. In return I'd received death threats, vandalism, injuries and now, it seemed, helplessness. And a rental car.

***

Linda was planting flowers under the kitchen window.

"Officer Stewart called you, Honey!" she called to me. I stepped carefully over to her and kissed her. She was pleasantly sweaty.

"Yeah. I left him a message. Thanks." I called Stewart from the kitchen phone.

"What's up, Anton?" Nothing warm or fuzzy came across.

"I stopped in to see Henry Brill this afternoon."

"Brill? What's the... the guy from the EPA? Henry Brill?"

"Yup... the very same. He doesn't like me."

"No shit?" That Stewart was efficient with words. "What the Hell for?"

"I was curious, for one thing, but I also wanted him to certify that there were no pollution problems on Parcel 1983-840. I did have fun..." I went on to describe my challenge and his silent threat to kill me.

"Sounds kinda stupid, to me, Mr. Anton. What do I care about it?" Stewart had had enough of me for one day.

"Well, I don't know how he can clear this matter without getting rid of those signs. He might actually go take those signs away, himself. Maybe he could be caught. Whadda you think?"

"You're crazy. That's a long shot, it sounds like. And don't you start doing stake-outs, either."

"But what if we... you, I mean, could catch him in the act?"

"In the act of what, Anton? Picking up signs that aren't officially anything? Forget it."

"Well, I... umm, it seemed like you could catch him, that's all." It was a great idea to me.

"Our efforts are on finding Sindledecker. And we will. I'll call you when we've got something. Just be extremely careful until we do. Do you hear what I'm saying?"

"Yeah, yeah... I got it. Thanks." I hung up mechanically. Linda stacked her gardening things in the breezeway.

"Everything okay?" she asked.

"Yeah, sort of." I told her what had happened at the EPA office... without the death threat part. "I wanted the cops to stake out the EPA signs to see if Brill came to take them. Sounded good to me. Stewart told me it was crazy."

"You think he would do that?"

"I... well, he said he'd take care of it but there would be no documents. What else can he do?"

"It won't solve your problem if there's no document. The pages you got from the Development Commission still have those numbers, right?"

She was so good at seeing things clearly. How could I prove to the Trust the filings were meaningless? Give her my word? Could I get her to ignore what she thought she knew about that parcel? I asked Linda those same questions.

"What power does the Trust have to stop you from leasing the parcel from the city?"

"Political, mainly, but I think they could really tie things up by bringing in the state environmental people. That delay would ruin what Blatchford needs the spur for and Roberta knows that. No. We have to get her to leave us alone on the lease. I've got to have proof of no EPA filings to guarantee that the state can't hold us up."

"Do you have someone else at EPA who can provide a document?" Linda was holding her pad of paper.

"No. If we try to obtain that proof from someone else, Brill could delay things, himself. He has absolutely no reason to expedite anything. I'm stuck."

"Who will know how to force their hand? There must be a way. Let's think about who."

"You know? I was at Alan Boudreau's office before I came home. I couldn't express what was worrying me. Everything felt out of my control. This is probably what was nagging at me and you've helped me, again. I'm gonna call Boudreau on this."

"I'll make a salad. You go ahead."

"This is Alan Boudreau… who's this?" I thought too late that I had probably interrupted his supper.

"Alan, I'm sorry. It's Walter Anton. Would you rather I call later?"

"I assume it's important, Walter. What?"

"I need a way to force the EPA to confirm that there are no filings on our parcel. Brill refused a document, for obvious reasons. I don't have a connection with anyone else there. How can we force them to produce a document? That's the question."

"You could bring suit… in federal court. Takes several weeks. I could file that if you want."

"We don't have that much time, I'm afraid. I have to have everything wrapped up in a matter of a week or two at the very most. What can you do in a matter of days?"

"Lemme think on that one, Walter. I'll call you."

At least there was something underway. I was able to eat supper and even relax a little. Linda pulled out some fancy Italian pastries with rum-flavored filling. Things that were so unsettled earlier now felt somewhat controlled. We watched Magyver fix the unfixable and went to bed around ten. It was all good.

THURSDAY, MAY 30, 1985

We had heard thunder in the wee hours, but it hadn't rained. That happens in the mountains. We hear thunder from far off, echoing between the ridges. Linda was dressed impeccably.

"Special meetings today? You look fantastic."

"Well, thank you very much, Mr. Anton. I am going to a symposium, in fact, on urban planning. One of the speakers is Andres Doany, who doesn't come to many of these things. Another is Ed Logue, who had a huge impact on Boston, among other places. e*nglishclass* always has a presence at these gatherings because there are always some papers and authors that need publishing." Linda checked herself in the front hall mirror. "What about you?"

"Oh, drivel, details, delirium… same as most days. I should hear from Boudreau about forcing EPA's hand. It was suggested to me that I send a note to the mayor, who I seem to have irritated last time we spoke…"

"Use a courier, Sweetie... works wonders."

"And don't mail it you mean?"

"Yes. I did that once when I said the wrong thing about a professor's odd writing style. He got all upset. I picked out a card, wrote a simple apology and had it hand-delivered by a bicycle courier. He was flabbergasted and we kept the contract. Try it."

"Okay. I can do that. I hope everything goes well for you. Drive gently." She hugged me firmly and gave me a glancing kiss that couldn't smudge anything, and was out the door.

KDKA was reporting that the city was already getting rained on. When I came out of the Squirrel Hill Tunnel, I was in it too. I turned on wipers and headlights and stayed in the right lane.

At a newsstand on East Carson I picked out a card that had a stylized image of a pen and pencil desk set and no message. I knew what I wanted to say.

When I hung my damp sport coat on the coat-tree I noticed a clean folded paper sitting in the center of my blotter. On it was the message: "Senator Fahnstahl's office called." Aha! Progress… at least I hoped that was the case. I had to call John Schumann, first.

"John Schumann, Brightman Partners."

"John. Walter. I've gotta ask you about Fahnstahl."

"Wow. Okay. I'm fine, thanks. I hope you are. And it's good to hear from you, too, Walter."

"Sorry, John. I'm keyed up about the details. I had placed a call to Fahnstahl to see if he could help us, but now I need to ask him if he can help us get proof of no EPA issues on our parcel. But I think you were going to speak with him, also, and I don't want to screw that up."

Schumann was quiet for a few moments. "I have placed a call to Fahnstahl. No one has called me back. I want to solicit his help with Block Grant monies. As far as I can discern, the UDAG dollars are committed and it's up to the mayor and the PDC to disburse them. The minority neighborhood impact of our project fits some of the UDAG purposes. I don't know yet how many dollars are coming from UDAG… around a half-million. What are you asking him?"

"Well, yesterday I tried to get a document out of Henry Brill that confirmed the lack of EPA filings on our parcel. By the time I got out of there Brill had threatened to kill me. But, he wouldn't sign anything. I have spoken to my attorney about how to force the EPA to confirm its, ahh… non-interest in our parcel. He might call me back this morning, but I think Fahnstahl's office could probably shake that confirmation out of EPA. We'll need it before you can close. Roberta could bring in the state based on those filings and tie us up for weeks, which kills everything for us."

Again I didn't hear anything from Schumann's end.

"John?"

"Yeah. Sorry, Walter. I admit that I hadn't thought much about those filings since you found out they were phonies. You've got me worrying, now."

"Sorry. What do you want me to do?"

"I don't know, Walt. Trying Fahnstahl is probably a good move. But call me after you speak to them… or to him, if you're lucky."

"Okay, John. I should be back to you shortly."

"Good. Thanks, Walt. Talk to you later." We signed off and I sat back for a couple of minutes. Sure of what I wanted Fahnstahl to do, I dialed his office.

"Good morning!" his receptionist sang. "Senator Fahnstahl's office. How may I help you?"

"Yes, good morning. This is Walter Anton and I am returning his call."

"Oh," she replied. The single word sounded like a pile of swim-team towels being dropped into a laundry bin. "I will see if he is ready to speak with you." Muzak.

She must have been the girl I was snide to. Served me right. I was glad she didn't hang up.

Suddenly she clicked back on the line. "The Senator will speak with you now." I jumped and felt like the King of Siam was granting an audience. He was only a damned Senator.

"Walter! How are you?" Sounded like he knew me.

"Very well, Senator. Thanks for asking. I hope you received my message."

"I don't understand it, Walter. I really don't. What do I have to do with Representative Wittenauer?"

"It's an odd story, Senator, but after hearing you at the Trust luncheon the other day, it sounded to me like you were the person to trust in all of this."

"In all of what, Walter. I can't chat all day." So far he sounded businesslike and interested. I decided to go for broke.

"You've heard about this funny business at the EPA? It appears that Wittenauer is in the middle of it so I can't ask for his help, can I?"

"Ahh, yes, the EPA stuff. Why do you think Tom Wittenauer is mixed up in it?" He was quick on the uptake.

"Well, Senator, Congressman Wittenauer was the first one to mention those phony filings to us at Blatchford Steel Services, and he was the one who said he could get our, quote, unquote, EPA problems resolved. But there really were no problems. Even the EPA in Washington confirms that the file numbers on the parcel we need, were not ever in the system. That's certainly strange, don't you think so?"

"Well it certainly sounded that way. But I don't see how I can help. It's up to the F. B. I."

"You're absolutely right, there, Senator. Absolutely. Here's where your help is indispensable, though. I don't want to complicate things for you so let me explain why your help is so crucial. Blatchford is getting ready to hire fifty to a hundred new employees once we secure a big contract with Denmark. You have heard of the King Frederik Bridge?"

"Yes, sure. I understand there's an Ex-Im Bank loan available on that. You don't need my help on that."

"No, you're right. Absolutely. What we do need… desperately, in fact, is an official acknowledgement from EPA here in Pittsburgh that there are no filings on the parcel of land in question. When I asked the question at the EPA, yesterday, they stonewalled us and we won't be able to secure that contract without the use of that parcel of land. Everyone I asked thought that you were the one honest office-holder who could get that done. That's what we are really asking."

"Huh. I see."

"Now there is one more issue you need to be aware of, and I hate to worry you about it, but it's only fair to you, I think. You can tell me where I'm wrong."

"Well, go ahead, Walter."

"When you speak with the EPA, the part that Wittenauer has played in this scheme with the phony file numbers… well, it's bound to hurt the congressman's reputation. I have thought and thought, but I don't see how you can contain that part of it. What do you think?"

"Well, Walter, I really can't go in to how we do our work. I'm sure you understand."

"Oh, I do, sir. Absolutely. I won't ask again. May I ask one last thing?"

"Okay, but then I have to go."

"Thank you very much, Senator. I'm so glad we can truly count on at least one federal official to help us in Pittsburgh. When do you think you might speak with EPA? Our drop-dead date on this big contract is June twentieth. When may I contact you?"

"I will have Margo call you, Walter. You said June twenty? I should expect that you'll hear something in two or three days… certainly by Friday. How's that?"

"I knew you were the one, Senator. Friday is more than I'd hoped. You're our hero, you really are. Thanks again!"

"Well, let's see what I can do, shall we? Let me know whenever I can be of service." The phone clicked to silence and I let out the rest of my breath. His reaction was what I'd hoped for. I pumped my hand in the air. Time for coffee.

Dieter Fuchs was pouring coffee as I entered. I doubted it was a pot he'd made, but it was fresh. I put on my best mask.

"Hey, Dieter, how's everything going?" I smiled at him as brightly as I could. He kept stirring his cup. Slowly his expression slid into a sneer. I ignored it.

"We're about to put that deal together so we can commit on the King Frederik. That's good news, huh?" I grinned right at him, which he must have perceived as threatening.

"Vell, that's just great, Valter. Just great. I hope it happens before you fuck it up. That would be great, too. Casey and I haf our fingers crossed on dat vun." I stood holding the pot in one hand and my cup in the other, staring after him.

There was more involved than pissing off Wittenauer. Dieter and I would never be pals. What I couldn't decide was why he wouldn't see progress as good news. Funny.

I dialed Brightman Partners again.

"Yes, Walter?" Schumann started.

"Yuh, listen, I spoke with Fahnstahl, a few minutes ago. I laid it on thick and assured him that he's the one honest man Pittsburgh can count on. I told him I hated to bring up the possibility that our congressman might be involved in a problem at the EPA. Ultimately he promised his office would be in touch on the matter of confirming EPA had no filings no later than Friday. I think that was the most I could get."

"Sounds like you did well, Walt. Sounds like you'll hear more in the next few days. Could be interesting."

"I'll let you know when I do."

"Fair enough. Same here. Do you have anything on that bank question?"

"No. I have thought about it, but not enough to ask the question. I'll ask today, I promise."

"Whatever you can do, Walt, thanks."

"Okay. I'm sure we'll talk soon." I hung up and actually reviewed some papers for my real job. There weren't many. I made a few notations and sat back with a pad of paper. Switching banks to a minority, community bank. What kind of a question was that? From me? And it's awfully left field. Why should Hal take it seriously? Would he take me seriously afterwards? That was a real question.

I doodled on the pad among the few notes I'd made about the bank question. Sometimes I outlined words or sentences repeatedly until the line was smooth. Sometimes I'd draw boxes and put wheels on them and then other embellishments. I took an internal call from Colleen and we chatted about a couple of requisitions and a mismatched invoice. Then Jackson called and we talked about the next mid-months and whether any King Frederik expenses were going to be on them. As had become habit lately, he ruminated on the difficulties of the real estate deal and was there anything new?

I shared what I could. There was no straightforward way to catch him up on all the angles. But he still consumed twenty minutes. I finally turned back to my desk and opened the card I'd bought earlier.

"Dear Harry, just want to thank you for the help you have provided to me and to Blatchford. I know I was obtuse the other day and your restraint and good sense are admirable. Thanks doubly, for that. I am looking forward to hearing the praise directed toward you for making the Larimer project come together. You and I know how well-deserved it will be. Walter Anton."

I read it a few times and decided it was suitably expressive. Hopeful, too. I looked in the yellow pages and called City Cyclists – good alliteration. Twenty minutes was their estimate for pick-up, and nine-dollars was the fee. I wrote "Mayor McKay, City Hall" on the front of the envelope and sealed it. I gave it to Paul LeMay and gave him a ten and a five.

"Give him the whole thing, Pauly," I said. "Maybe it'll get there faster with a big tip."

"Heh, heh, heh, Mr. Walter. You should go wit' da flowers. Dey always work fo me. But maybe a card, with a courier and all. Never tried that."

"It's not what you think, Pauly. This is for the mayor and he sure ain't expecting flowers from the likes of me!"

"Huh. Oh, yeah. I see the name, now. Well, either way, I hope it works fo ya."

"Me too, Pauly. Me, too." It was after ten o'clock.

I stopped in my tracks and slapped my forehead. Emily's funeral! It was scheduled around now. A secretary walked into me and stepped back, apologizing. After my own apologies I ran to my office. No way I was going to miss this.

Saint John the Baptist Ukranian was all of four hundred yards from Blatchford Steel. I still drove. There were few parked cars and only a half-dozen in the procession, lined up behind the hearse. One man from the funeral home stood outside the big center doors. I trotted up the steps and he guided me to a side door and let me in.

I sat a few rows back and tried to pick out who was who. I could tell who her parents and, apparently, two grandparents, were. A younger woman was obviously Emily's sister. Two young men also sat in the family row. One appeared distraught.

Across the aisle were four women I guessed were co-workers. It took me a few minutes to recognize one of the receptionists, all dressed up and hair-do'd. No one looked back at me. I looked behind me, hoping to see Sindledecker or Henry Brill. No luck.

Growing up in Latrobe my family attended the Presbyterian church and I always had some skepticism about the odd rituals Catholics supposedly endured in their churches – a key reason I went to Bucknell and not to Saint Vincent's right there in Latrobe. But it was the same God, I'd heard, so I looked for similarities.

The sanctuary was bright and colorful, covered with Byzantine portraits of Saints, Apostles, and the Holy Family. I'd never seen so many pictures in church. The stained-glass windows replicated some of the iconic paintings. Every visage had wide, wise eyes displaying a challenging clarity of thought. They all were asking me why I didn't allow myself to see things as clearly as they. I stared.

The altar was elaborate. An inlaid wooden screen stood halfway between a small marble table and the rear wall of the rounded nave. Bright colors and gold leaf defined heaven on the curved wall with intricate Byzantine crosses, clouds and Jesus with a wise-eyed Lamb. It all seemed so, well... important. I took being there more seriously than expected. When the priest entered with his incense burner on a long gold chain, clad in his elaborate garments and tall boxy hat, I thought how these people really believed in the story the images represented.

Unfamiliar with a real Mass. I stood when others did, and knelt when they did, avoiding as much outsiderness as possible. Emily's sister spoke about growing up together and celebrating the big events in Emily's life and how proud they all were when she started her job at the EPA. I teared up in conjunction with the sobbing that came from everyone else. When I looked around I spotted Arnie Stewart. He was looking at me but made no gesture or expression. There were a couple of strangers farther back.

Finally everyone up front had been served communion, the priest coming to each in turn. He spoke in Ukranian and in English. The censer smoked liberally around the coffin as he prayed. The somber funeral home people wheeled the coffin down the aisle with the priest and two assistants following it. The attendees followed in grim procession. I found myself genuinely choked up, yet I'd known Emily Szepanik for all of thirty hours. I was angry again. I stepped in behind the family and co-workers and walked past Officer Stewart whose eyes betrayed his wondering what the Hell I was trying to prove. I wasn't sure.

Outside I shook the priest's hand and thanked him for the ceremony. He noted that he did not know me.

"I'm not Catholic, Father. I knew Emily slightly and she was very nice to deal with."

"Were the two of you serious?"

"Huh? Serious? Uhh... no, nothing like that. No, no. She helped me with some EPA issues, that's all." I nodded and shook my head to make sure he understood.

"Are you Walter?" he asked quietly. I almost stumbled from shaking knees.

I nodded. "You... you know my name?" I couldn't swallow.

"Yes. One of her co-workers said she had some trouble because of a funny man named Walter. I guessed it might be you." The priest's eyes bore into me and I looked away. Farther down the walk Arnie Stewart watched our conversation.

"It was a strange situation, Father, and the first time I met her I had no shoes on and we had a good laugh over that. I met her once more at Duquesne, a day later, and then she was killed the next day, Saturday. I didn't get to know her much, actually."

"Killed? You think on purpose?" The tall priest looked at me blankly.

"I think so, yes. There have been attempts on my life, too." I looked directly at him, now. "Since we met." I nodded slightly.

"Hence our police visitors." The robed priest gestured toward Arnie Stewart.

I nodded and turned away. The priest called after me, "We can talk whenever you have time, Walter." I turned and waved a sort-of agreement. The priest climbed into a car. The spaces where the hearse and other cars had been, were now empty. I caught up with Stewart.

"Thinking of converting, are you?" He fell into step with me as I walked around the building toward my car.

"No. Interesting church, though."

"Father Shaksvili is a detective, you think?"

"You have good ears. He knew my name, which surprised me. That's about it."

"I see." We arrived at my rental. "We didn't see anyone we didn't expect. The others went along to the burial. I doubt our man will show up."

"Were you able to examine my car?"

"Yeah. I had the boys check it out. Seems like the brake line was filed through. You figured that. Doesn't change our search for Sindledecker. We'll charge him with murder and attempted murder when we get him. He'll show up eventually."

"I've got to get back to Blatchford, Officer." I opened the door and let the puff of oven-baked air come out.

"Yuh," said Stewart. He walked to his unmarked cruiser, got in without hesitation and drove off. I started my engine, lowered all the windows and turned on the fan full blast. I swung my legs in, pulled out into South Seventh Street, and the rental car drove me to *Marko's*.

***

The same waitress I'd met with Angus Newhall was anxious for the order today, too. I ordered baked Great Lakes Pike with a salad and mashed potato. I'd seen it served and the lemon-ginger white sauce it came with was too much to pass up. I had to taste it.

In the farthest corner from where I sat, two well-dressed men faced each other. The one facing me looked like a power broker of some sort, or at least I imagined he was. I couldn't see the man whose back was toward most of the room.

After a few minutes, though, I saw a pattern of those who could see his face looking over toward him from time to time. Must be well-known, I thought. I tried to figure out who it might be who would eat at Marko's. Abruptly a big mitt clapped my shoulder and I almost tipped over. Angus Newhall gave a big guffaw.

"Well, laddie, I see yer got the taste of it, all right. Billy, meet Walter Anton!" The man who was seating himself opposite reached out and we shook hands.

"Billy Warshofsky. Pleased to meetcha."

"My pleasure. You work with Angus, here?" I gestured with my thumb. Billy and Angus laughed at that.

"You might say that, I guess," was Billy's reply.

"Aww," started Angus, "Billy is one o' them customers who gets quotes on big shipments, and then ships em. You might try that, y'self, Walter."

"Hey, wait a minute! We'll be shipping soon. Just a few more real estate details and we'll be in production soon."

"Take it easy, laddie. The river an I will be here when yer ready." Angus gave me another good-natured shove. "Not to worry. Whatcha eatin today?"

"I'm trying the Pike. And a salad."

"Oh, good one." Our waitress arrived with my salad. Angus and Billy both ordered catfish.

"So, laddie, what brings you here?"

"Just being hungry, Angus. Do I need a better reason?"

"Well, I thought maybe ya came in with yer buddy, Harry McKay, but he refused to eat witchya."

"Huh? McKay?" And then I realized who the well-dressed man was. "What… does he come in here much?" I looked past Angus and studied the back of the man's head.

"Oh, we see him now and then. Closer to elections, usually. Maybe he likes the fish." He gestured with his head toward Billy Warshofsky, as if to see if he agreed. Billy just smiled and gestured toward the mayor's table.

"The mayor likes the union boys to see 'im. It's good for his image and doesn't do any harm. He'll glad-hand everybody. You'll see." The waitress came back with all three meals. We busied ourselves. The lemon-ginger sauce was worth the price.

"What do you ship, Billy?" He looked up from his plate where he was mopping up the catfish.

"Junk. Scrap metal. Old cars… in small pieces. Not very glamorous. Keeps Angus in lunch money, though."

"What kind of tonnage?" I asked in my best river-ese.

"Some years close to half a million." He turned back to his plate and dabbled with his remaining salad. If he were trying to make it seem like no big deal, it didn't work.

"A half-million tons? There's so many junk cars? Holy cow!"

Now he was grinning, looking at Angus, next to me.

"Well, it's not all cars. There's old girders and sheet metal. Busted up pipes and things. But I'd say something like five to six thousand cars a month. We have one of the largest de-construction plants in Pennsylvania."

"Wow. Makes my bridge girders seem insignificant."

"You demolish bridges?" Billy was concerned about competition. He gave me a funny look. Angus was unusually quiet.

"No! I mean, no. We will soon be building them… or one, anyway, over in Denmark." Billy was smiling again. I ran down a brief description of the shipping Blatchford would be doing with Mid-Waters.

"Tell me about your railroad, there. You ripping up old rails? We can clear them for you."

"No, at least I don't think so. We'll be upgrading the railbed and some other things, but I haven't heard anything about replacing the rails." He seemed mildly disappointed.

Angus chimed in. "Ye'll be kissing Roberta's feet, before there's any upgrading done, eh laddie?"

Billy Warshofsky perked up at that. "Queen of Pittsburgh, Roberta?" He knew the right Roberta.

"Friend of yours, too?" I watched Billy's face. He had a fresh twinkle to his eyes as he pursed his lips to answer.

"I'm afraid it's a one-sided romance. My passions are excited every time we meet but they are unrequited. The subject of my passion barely knows I exist. It's very hard for me." He looked ready to laugh, but kept a straight face.

"Have you tried flowers, Billy? I'm just asking; I've heard they usually work." Now he put on a much more serious visage.

"Ohh, Walter, I've thought of everything… even hemlock."

I began to run through different kinds of flowers, trying to think of what hemlock blossoms looked like. Then I realized what he'd said, and laughed. "Gee, who carries hemlock bouquets around here?"

"Yeah, I don't know. I think about it, though. How did you fall in love with her?'

"It was love at first sight. I just want to use some land exactly as it has been, run a few flatcars on some tracks that have been there for about fifty years, and pay the city handsomely for the right. Sounded easy, to me."

"Hmmnh... to me too. What happened?"

"It's a long, long story, I'm afraid. The key is that the Trust thinks that land is supposed to..."

"Lemme guess! A park and a playground, right? With a little fountain?"

"Why, Bill Warshofsky, you must be psychic." We laughed more. "Is that what happened to you?"

"Happens, Walt... happens. Every time I renew my salvage license, or pull a permit for a little steel shed or a new roof, the Trust files a complaint about this or that supposed blight, pollution, destruction of viewscape, failure to observe set-backs, insufficient diameter of waste water drain pipes, engaging in manufacture without proper permits. I could list more if you're interested."

"Holy moly. Is any of it legit?"

"They got me once on setbacks. We had to cover a pile of rusting scrap because the slope of the land might cause rain run-off to carry rusty water into the storm drains. We built the goddam thing, put in special drains to capture run-off and then they filed the improper setback complaint. They knew all along we'd be too close when they instigated the run-off complaint. I just love em to death. All I get in return is a visceral hatred of junkyards and, by association, of me. Don't mention me if you get to negotiate with the great lady."

I shook my head. Angus Newhall was itching to get to work. "Ask him where he does his banking," he nodded toward Billy.

I asked, "So, Billy, where... ?"

"Western Penn. Always have. I know Roberta's car so I don't go in at the same time."

"You're an interesting guy. Glad to meetcha." I shook hands as we stood. "But I'm not surprised you're a friend of this interesting guy." I bumped Angus with my elbow.

"Hello, boys!" boomed a familiar voice. Harry McKay was clapping his hand on Angus' back and smiling broadly toward us. "Walter, you have to be careful who you're having lunch with."

"Well, Harry," I pointedly said, "I always am… and here I am. Best lunch on the Mon, I'd say."

"I'd agree with that. And I'd say you chose good table-mates, too." He smiled broadly, but Angus and Billy seemed a little bemused by the greeting.

"Well, they chose me, but, again, here I am. How was your lunch? This one of your favorite places?"

"Yeah. Food's great and there's no fuss. It's good."

I stood and moved closer to McKay. "Harry, may I ask a question about our project?" He reacted, but not too badly. "Have you been able to determine a lease cost if we are able to get to that point?"

"Ahh, sort of. Parks and Recreation is set. That was the easy part. I'll let you know about the PDC. Thanks for your little note, by the way."

I was surprised that he'd already received it but I acted as coolly as I could. "I meant it and you're welcome." Then I raised my voice. "You know both Angus and I are hoping for our use of that little railroad. We both thank you for your efforts!"

"Well, boys," McKay boomed, "I'm with you cause it's good for business and creates more jobs. You can take that to Western Penn Bank!" He winked at that and gestured to his associate to head upstairs.

"Well, Laddie, you got friends in high places now?"

I smiled. "That and eight ninety-five will get you lunch at Marko's."

"The mayor is up on local banking practices, I guess, ain't he?" offered Billy.

"He's up on Roberta McGillvray's habits, I bet, and probably on both of yours too. I don't think much escapes him that's important for the city."

"D'ya think he's a Western Penn customer, so to speak?"

"If he is he'd never let on. I'll bet on that, too. He did work for Mellon Bank, for a while, and he hated it, he told me. So, who knows?"

"All very intrestin, laddie, but it's time for work. Don't you work?"

"Oooh, Angus, that hurts. I have a very good job. I just can't describe it for you." Billy had a funny expression at that, but Angus laughed with me.

"Then ye better get back to it, don'cha think?" Angus turned to go. Billy dropped a twenty and a five. I handed my money to our waitress. Angus' jab rattled me. I did have a job, but I didn't do it anymore.

The conclusion of my real estate odyssey looked to be no more than two weeks away. I knew I'd be busy dealing with that, and there'd be days that would exhaust me, but I felt rootless. I'd been working since I was fourteen, starting with helping the sexton in the Baptist church in Latrobe. The best part was every Saturday morning he and I would climb up the steeple, behind the pipe organ, and look out a small port about fifty feet up. It was the greatest view ever.

Later I washed floors and bagged groceries at a Latrobe supermarket. By the time I graduated from Greater Latrobe Senior High I'd been working for four years and saved up three thousand, eighty-eight dollars and sixty-seven cents, with interest. I was a good kid. On the other hand, nothing I did stood out. No arrests, no drinking parties, no car accidents. When I went to Bucknell College I'm not sure anyone but my mother paid notice or missed me.

And, I've worked ever since, through college, and eight loyal years at Blatchford Steel Services. But now, my very fuzzy job description... well, I didn't like the feeling. When a deal finally got done for "our" railroad, I'd be helping Blatchford earn a new eighteen million, or more, but it felt like I wasn't doing anything. I headed back.

There were no new slips in the in-baskets. I pulled out my yellow pad to update pluses and minuses.

Schumann was a plus and the first one I thought of. I wondered about that for a few moments, but, in fact, he seemed to be the steadiest player in the whole mess.

I thought McKay was a plus. He had a sense of what was positive for his city and that seemed to guide his decision-making. At least he felt genuine to me so long as I didn't piss him off totally. A plus.

I placed Senator Fahnstahl in the plus column, but tentatively. We'd see soon enough.

Forrest Akers was a plus. He wanted in on the project and his interest attracted others. I was glad he was part of it.

Hal Blatchford was a positive, for sure. He was prepared to spend hundreds of thousands to finance Larimer, and then spend hundreds of thousands more to prepare the spur for our use and for the lease. I had new appreciation for him. He was a steady player. I couldn't think of any other plus-type players in the project. There were some 'neutrals' like Angus Newhall, Alan Boudreau and, I finally decided, Officer Arnie Stewart – people I was glad to be associated with in some way, but whose impact on the project I couldn't define.

I placed Gary Sindledecker among the minuses to the degree that should he finally kill me the deal would probably fall apart. Comforting.

Linda was a major plus, and shame on me for not putting her at the top of the list. Of course, I'd also put her in danger. Thank God I had her.

I wrote down "Devlin." I never had learned his last name but he had tried to be a part of my problems and not part of a solution. I stared at the name and tried to figure which list he belonged in. I crossed it out.

Then I started to list names that I couldn't pigeon-hole. I wrote down Dieter Fuchs. I thought he and I were aiming at the same goal but Dieter was not happy we were "swimming together." I put 'Casimir' in parentheses because he did seem peripheral. Fuchs, I wasn't comfortable about.

I kept thinking of Katie Mellon. She had some kind of involvement with Wittenauer. I wrote 'Katie' under Dieter Fuchs. Her flash of anger when I challenged Wittenauer's ethics might represent taking sides.

The page had two loose groups of pluses and minuses and other names that didn't fit in either. Plus I had doodled around the names. It looked like a steep road with a pickup truck driving out of the page. The front of it had angry teeth behind a black iron bar retainer. I hadn't been concentrating on the scene, but the truck looked familiar.

I opened my portfolio and pulled out my notes about asking Hal about the possibility of changing banks. Amongst the doodles was a similar image of the big-toothed grill with the black retainer. I looked around the cubicle for corroboration, but I didn't need it. I could see the similarity and I began to question my memories. Had I seen this grill? On Buttermilk Hollow Road?

The revelation, if it was, was exhausting. I suddenly felt like I couldn't face the rest of the day. The two images were similar... not identical, but similar, with the second one more detailed than the first. I turned the pad over with the previous notes under it. I had to take a break. It was after two.

I checked around my sort-of office. I had nothing to do. I went out to the rental.

As the heat escaped I leaned on top of the door frame. What would really feel good would be a call from John Schumann with news of a deal ready to roll. I was musing on that dream when Colleen Walsh came trotting out toward me, calling my name.

"Whew! I'm glad I caught you. You have..." she stopped to take a breath, "...a call from Mr. Schumann. They told me you had just come out here so I asked him to hold on. Is that okay?"

"Yes, yes, yes, Colleen, that is very okay." I was already running toward the door. I held it for her, but she wasn't wasting any time.

"I'll switch him over to you, Mr. Anton."

"Thanks, Colleen... and it's Walter! None of that 'Mister' stuff!"

In a couple of minutes my phone rang once and I scooped it up. "Walter Anton. Is this John?"

"Yes. Hi, Walter. Glad she caught you. Have you got a few minutes?"

"For you? Absolutely. You sound excited so I'm very interested. Good news?" I pulled a pad of paper under my arm in case I needed to take notes.

"Well, I guess good news. If what I think is in place actually jells, you're gonna have to get ready with Hal Blatchford and the cash he needs to donate. And you'll need your best tactics ready to play Roberta properly to let you run a railroad. Are you ready?"

"Wow, John. That's a tray-full. Assuming that Fahnstahl's office can deliver tomorrow, when will this all take place?" I was trying to think quickly. What had been an amorphous load was suddenly a sack of sharp-cornered bricks I had to build with.

"Hang on a minute, John, I'm actually thinking, here, trying to catch up with you."

"No problem."There was a period of silence, then he came back. "Walt, I'm going to put my end on hold and I'll be right back. Hold on." Brightman's too bright Muzak came on. I set down the receiver where I could hear the sound, and made a few notes to myself.

I wrote down "Blatchford" and drew an arrow to a dollar-sign. Then I went blank. What else did I need to do? Ahh! The lease from the city. I had to have McKay on board, too, ready to sign a lease for two years on parcel 840. And I had to prepare a strategy to bring the good ship McGillvray alongside my stealthy submarine where we could exchange things of value. It was all still a bit fuzzy. Fahnstahl was key, in the immediate sense. I heard Schumann calling my name.

"Sorry, John, I had you right here. What more?"

"Walt, the key seems to be Fahnstahl, right now."

"I have just written that down."

"You seem to be okay with the mayor, am I right?"

"I think so, yes. We're chattin buddies, now and he told me at lunchtime that he's got a settled number from Parks and Recreation. So, yes. That tells me they are ready to sign. But I'm not sure of how to guide Roberta to come alongside us and agree. I have to cogitate on that."

"I may have some thoughts on that. Let's see what comes from the good senator tomorrow and we can talk again."

If everything is perfect, when do you think we'll be sitting down?"

"Could be Wednesday, let's say. Sound good to you?"

Now my heart was pounding. It seemed unbelievable… too good to be true. "It sure does. Listen, I'm going to get busy and tonight I'll skull this out with my chief strategist. Can I meet with you tomorrow, late morning, maybe?"

"I figured as much. Call me before you leave."

"You got it. Wow. I can't believe were finally getting there."

"We're not there. We'll be working non-stop, now, to reach the table with every piece of paper in hand. You will be, too, I imagine. See you tomorrow."

"Okay. Thanks, John. I'll call ya." We hung up. I sat back with a whoosh of air escaping. I tried to focus on the pad of paper but I was picturing a big oval table with all the muckety-mucks signing contracts, one after the other. Finally I stood and walked around. My first move was Hal Blatchford.

I called upstairs to Kelly the gate-keeper. Before she picked up I remembered that I had hurt her feelings the last time I was up there and still hadn't done anything about it. I promised myself...

"Mr. Blatchford's office." She could tell it was my extension. I wondered how pissed she still was.

"Hi, Kelly, it's Walter Anton. I just got news on the King Frederik project and I need to speak with Mr. Blatchford."

"His door is closed. What is it about?" So that's how it was going to be.

"It's about the King Frederik Bridge, Kelly, and it's very important." There was a click as she put me on hold. I tried to make myself feel happy so I would sound happy. My dreams were coming true, weren't they?

She clicked back on. "Ten minutes." The line went dead before the dial tone came on. I slowly cradled the handset. I jumped a foot when it rang before it settled into its cradle.

"Ahh... Walter Anton." My brain was trying to catch up.

"Oh, good! Walter!" Linda exclaimed, "Have you remembered the barbecue tomorrow night? Isn't tomorrow when you said it would be at our house?" She was perfectly chipper. I was lost for a minute.

"Ahh, well… um, sure, I guess I am remembering it right about now. Lucky thing you remembered. Wow. That had slipped right away. Thanks, Honey!"

"Well, Chef, you're very welcome. What can I pick up for you? I can do a salad and pick up some fresh bread from Zappala's on the way home tomorrow. What meats are you getting?"

My ten minutes were almost up. "I was planning to have London Broil, actually. I get it at Bucklers, but I can't talk this second, Lin. I have to go upstairs. I'll call you back. I love you. Bye." I hung up and felt awful, but an appointment upstairs can't be missed. I took off for the wide stairs.

I was puffing when I got to Kelly's desk. She barely looked at me. Her right hand pointed toward the fancy door. I hustled to it and knocked.

"Come in, Anton."

"Hi, boss. Thanks for seeing me."

"I assume you've got something crucial. Let's have it." The big man glared at me with his full attention. I tried to feel confident.

"Yuh, I do, Hal. I just spoke with Schumann and he thinks there is a good shot to get everything signed by Wednesday. That's the earliest, I guess, but it's then or not much later. We need to be ready to commit our quote, unquote, 'donation' by Wednesday. I'll have a better idea on what our number needs to be after I meet Schumann tomorrow, but I think you need to take steps for up to a million dollars liquid."

He raised his eyebrows and leaned back, looking straight at me. I looked straight back.

"I've got things ready to go with a lease on the parcel from the city and Senator Fahnstahl is getting back to me on a full release from those EPA signs, tomorrow morning. I haven't got every step…"

"Okay, okay. I get it, Walter. But I've got to talk about Wittenauer now." He waved at me to stop talking. "Tommy was at my house last night. He was pretty upset and I don't want any of this to leave you and me."

I nodded my commitment to that.

"You know I've been tight with Tommy and his dad before him. I think I'm a pretty good judge of people. I want you to carefully consider what he told me. I think he is truthful about it." Blatchford adjusted his position and sat forward, elbows on his desk.

"Tommy was in his cups, a little, but not out of control. He was crying, believe it or not. You may take some comfort in his admission that he had planned to get rid of those EPA filings and look like a business hero to me." My jaw dropped. "He was struggling to tell me that. It hurt him and it hurt me. The thing is, though, he swore up and down that the signs were put there about two years ago, illegally… illegally, but long before the King Frederik project was even heard of. He knows who was involved in the EPA, at least he thinks he does, but he doesn't know who originally paid him to do it. And his connection there never told him."

Hal poured some water from a carafe and gestured to me if I wanted some, which I took. He was shaking his head. "I can see why finding out about false filings could be attractive in a political sense. I think he was being straight with me about being ashamed of playing that game to impress me. He was a wreck, Walter. I let him sleep in my den. I know you have no use for him, but I'm asking you to consider that he told me the truth about those signs. Can you do that?"

I let out a big breath and slumped back a little. I pursed my lips and thought hard. I wondered, had I been in the room, if I'd accept Wittenauer's story? I have a lot of respect for Hal Blatchford and that's what led me to nod my head. "Hal, I can't overlook your own reaction. I can almost say if it's good enough for you it's good enough for me. But your reaction impresses me so I'll be neutral toward the congressman. Obviously he played a dangerous game and the consequences of being found out are still making waves. One lady is dead and I'm still under some threat. It's been hard. But I'll be with you on this – you've got my word."

Oddly, getting me off Tom Wittenauer's case seemed comforting to the boss. He relaxed a bit.

"What else do I do besides the money?" he asked. His whole tone of voice was softer.

"I think that's it. I'll report back on developments tomorrow."

"That's fine. Thanks, Walter."

I stood and reached out to shake hands and he shook firmly. "Thanks, Hal. I'm glad you're my boss." He smirked and waved me out. I left feeling much, much better. Kelly Galvin looked at me without moving her head. I smiled at her but she wasn't buying it.

Most of the office had left. I called *englishclass*. Linda had left. I was buzzing with energy and needed to share it. I picked up my keys, took a brief look around and closed the door to my three-quarter office. Someday. I pulled out of the lot and headed across the Birmingham to pick up the Penn-Lincoln East.

I got off an exit after mine and headed down the William Penn to Bucklers. I selected three London Broils totaling about eighteen pounds. A lot of my condiments and spices had been messed up in the vandalism so I restocked in that department, too. I had a glimmer of a recipe for London Broil on the grill.

From Bucklers I went to a huge liquor mart for a pint of dry sherry. We'd see how my imaginative grilling worked out. I went home.

"Hi, Honey," called out Linda from the kitchen. "Busy day, I guess!"

"Oh, boy. It never stopped." I slipped my arms around her and slid my hands up to cup her breasts. She snuggled back into my arms. "This is sooo... much... better than the rest of this day. I am glad you reminded me about tomorrow. What a dunce I am."

"Actually, Mr. Empty-head, it was Hank Buckley who called me to find out what to bring. That's when I called you. But I told Hank to bring some shrimp and cocktail sauce and things he thought went with that. So this will be the most elegant cookout in a while."

"Well, that'll be something. Sounds good. Do you know who else is bringing?"

"Well I made a couple calls. Axel had forgotten but immediately said he'll be here. He'll pick up something to bring – fruit or something. Elly is going to surprise us with some of her own veggies and things. I left a message on the Simpson's phone machine but I know Penny had been talking about the cookout with Elly already. I don't know what she's bringing. And anyone who asks tomorrow I'll suggest dessert. Now you've got the meat we just need to get some soda, beer and wine. Simple, no?"

"Simple, yes. Boy, am I glad you're in charge, here!" Linda made a little curtsey. I left my package on the counter and went into the bedroom to change.

"Do you want me to do anything with this steak, Honey?" Linda called.

"No thanks! I've got some ideas for that. Be right there."

I spread out my treasures. I wanted to marinate the beef. I rinsed the three thick strips, dried them and then rubbed them with olive oil, salt and fresh garlic. In the morning I would add some other things. I put them in the refrigerator.

"Well, li'l lady, ahh hope yu'v rustled up some grub," I drawled as I channeled John Wayne.

"Not yet, cowboy. But I might. What's a dusty cowpoke hungry for?"

"Oh, 'cowpoke,' why that's got me thinkin. Maybe we can skip dinner…"

Linda tried to look exasperated. "You just control yourself, there, Tex. Pokin cows is not a nice image at all. Stuff that and tell me what you'd like."

"Well, I'd be happy with a tunafish sandwich, actually." I was sitting in the nook behind the table. Linda opened a beer for me and started to collect what she needed.

"So," she asked with her back to me, "where are you in the real estate marathon?" She washed some celery and split a couple stalks and started chopping as quietly as she could.

"It was a quite a day, now that you ask. The last call I got was from John Schumann and he thinks the whole thing could be signed and sealed next week. I should be jumping for joy about now."

"I guess so. You're not?" She washed a piece of a green pepper and diced that, too.

"No I'm not. We still need to get a clean bill of health from the EPA…"

"EPA? I thought you said there were no real filings!" She was opening one of three cans of tuna.

"There aren't, but we have no documentation. If Roberta wants to tie us up she can just refer the false filings to the Penn State Department of the Environment and nothing will be able to happen for weeks. That's as bad as if there were no deal, at all."

She drained the tuna in the sink and seemed to be thinking about what else to add.

"I got some scallions, Hon. Try those."

"Ouu... sounds good. Okay." She pulled out one stalk and sliced a half-dozen thin disks near the base. She diced these as finely as possible and tossed them in a big glass bowl along with the other chopped veggies. The drained tuna went on top of those and she started breaking it up with a fork.

"Fahnstahl's office is supposed to call me tomorrow."

"What?" She spun around to look at me.

"Fahnstahl... Senator Fahnstahl. He's looking in to getting us a clean report from the EPA."

"Oh, Well that's good, right?" Linda squirted a little ketchup onto the mix, then plopped a big dollop of mayonnaise and started mixing and folding.

"Yeah, but we haven't got it yet. That is the biggest hurdle in all of this and it always has been. I'll do my dancing when we have it."

"Bread?" Linda could change subjects as fast as I could.

"Huh?" I replied smartly. "Bread? Oh... yeah. I don't know. Whacha got?"

"Wheat or sourdough. Toasted?" I took the wheat, toasted. She popped in two sets and sliced a tomato. "I have some romaine."

"Sure." I watched her efficient movements that produced two tuna on wheat, toasted with tomato, in about one minute. It was just pleasant to watch her be domestic. She spun around with the two sandwiches and sat opposite me.

"Wow," I said. She just looked at me with one point of her sandwich ready to be bitten. I smiled and started on my own. Before I finished chomping down she popped up and pulled a bag of chips from someplace and poured an unhealthy pile into a salad bowl. Perfect.

"So tell me about the deal." Linda kept chewing, looking up at me. I swallowed and took a sip of beer.

"I accidentally saw the mayor at lunch and he indicated that the number work for leasing the parcel was done and in line with what I was hoping for. Your friend, Forrest Akers, has come on board in a significant way, evidently, and John Schumann must have the city and the PDC all set for UDAG moneys. I still am not sure how to finagle Roberta to agree on our side of the deal when Blatchford donates the difference that makes it all work. You'll have to help me, there." I took a big bite that finished off half of my sandwich. Linda's eyes grew large watching me fit it in. I made some "mmnnh, mmm, mmmnh" noises to show her I had to do it, it was so good. She shook her head.

"Well, tell me what you thought of and we can expand on that." She started her second half-sandwich.

"Okay, but… I mean, you know her better than I do. I'm trying to make business sense and that doesn't impress her. How do I make her believe I care that what she thinks is important? How would you define what that is?" I shook my head in confusion.

"I wouldn't try to do that, Lover. You can't succeed at that and it's not you, anyway. You've got to make the argument you believe in without getting personal. Her interests and yours are going to coincide only briefly. That's the point you have to be sure you get to at the same time she does. How can you do that?" Linda clasped her hands and looked at me with a confident little smile. I knew right then why *englishclass* paid her well.

"Well," I rubbed my chin, "I really don't care about this neighborhood development project we're fighting for. Maybe I should, but I have no passion for it. It has only one, singular value to me. I'm not even on commission, for crying out loud! Schumann is getting paid, Akers will make something, even Roberta is goin…" I stopped abruptly, like I'd run into something immovable. Linda held her hand to her mouth, holding back from speaking.

"Roberta is going to make money here, isn't she?" Now I was nodding, not shaking. "She, or her Trust, anyway, will benefit financially when the deal is done. How crucial is that for her, Lin? You must have some idea of cash flow over there. How long since they made a good score?"

"Gosh, Wally, you make it sound illegal, or something. The Trust performs a real service for many developers and, they think, for the City of Pittsburgh."

"I understand, Lindy, but it still needs money. It doesn't seem as though they're rolling in cash. Is there any way to get a picture of cash flow and how critical this project, this month, is?" My mind was running full tilt. "When's the last time the TRT made some significant money?" Linda was thinking, concentrating. I'd seen the look before and answers always came from it.

"Truth to tell, I don't spend much time studying Board reports. I have some, though… at my office. But I could see what has happened with the cash balance over the past two or three months. I just can't do it now."

"Baby, you're the greatest!"

"I don't know, Ralph," she said. I gave her a big kiss that wound up in a very nice hug.

"All right, Sweetie, all right. You did it again and I'm feeling like a plan for success is possible." I was leaning against the counter, vibrating with nervous energy. "This just might happen."

Linda was looking up at me. "So, umm… what does that mean you'll do, exactly?"

"Well, if the Trust is a little shy of cash then I'll… ahh, I mean, she'll need to make the deal, right? I'll save the deal at the last minute with Blatchford's cash and she'll agree to my terms! Doesn't seem that complicated." I looked at her with a beaming expression, looking for her agreement. She looked at me blankly. I began to lose confidence. "Right?" I asked.

"It might work that way, I suppose." Her expression hadn't changed. "Shouldn't you have a plan if it doesn't?"

"Well, yeah... sure. I would have a plan. In case she doesn't bite on that. What would you do?" I sat on the other chair, my knees outside hers.

Linda looked at me with her eyes squinted. She put her hands on my knees and looked right into my eyes. I tried to look serious right back at her. "You have no idea, do you?" She shook her head as she spoke.

"Well, I ahh, would say that, umm... no. Nothing. Not a clue. I really need your help." I tried to put my hands on her knees but she picked them off.

"You're okay one on one, Walt, but pulling this off in a complex deal like this is something there is no training for. But, that doesn't mean I have it figured out, either. Maybe you should get this part of the agreement done before the big closing."

I sat back, stunned. How did she do things like that? "How did you do that?"

"What? I didn't do anything." Linda sat up straight, emphasizing her bosom. I struggled to keep my hands on my knees.

"That whole business about solving the Roberta problem before the big closing. It's brilliant."

"Oh. Well, I know how she reacts to being tricked or manipulated. I think you should go to her and politely explain your position and power and how it will help her and answer her concerns... rather than trying to blind-side her at the last minute."

"It makes perfect sense. I will call for an appointment tomorrow and find a way to work things out." I was feeling confident. Then I remembered Brill and Fahnstahl. "So long as I get good news from Senator Fahstahl's office. I am anxious about that."

"What you need is a good night's sleep and something to relax you. Get ready for the big day." She ran her hands up the outside of my thighs. "We could paint the upstairs bedrooms… that would tire you out."

"Just what I was thinking, for sure. Paint the bedrooms. Yes." I ran my hands up the tops of her thighs. "Maybe we could practice our shaving skills…"

Linda turned completely red and pulled her hands away, crossing her arms. "Why… why would you think of that?"

I was completely confused, now. I'd crossed a line I hadn't seen approaching. "Remember I offered to help with your shave the next time? I've been dreaming of that ever since. I mean I was just thinking…"

"Well, I wasn't. Why don't you go make some notes on what you have to do tomorrow. I've got a manuscript I have to read." Linda stood up and headed in to the living room. I leaned back with a frown. Crap. I was looking forward to some severe relaxation one minute, homework, the next: Shinola. I went out to the garage and started straightening up my work bench. Within a few minutes I became engrossed in sorting out screws. I took an old roasting pan and dumped my catch-all into it and lined up three empty plastic coffee jars to receive flathead screws, roundhead screws and machine screws, respectively. Good mindless work.

About twenty minutes later I was making piles of screws that didn't fit the three jars for some evolving and arcane reason. Linda slipped up behind me and put her hands in my pockets.

"I heard there was a Titan rocket preparing to launch in here." Her hands reached toward the launch pad. I'm not slow when it comes to pocket rockets.

"We're just waiting for internal power to take over and guidance to kick in. I think the count-down has begun."

"We'd better examine the outer skin of the rocket before ignition. Right this way." Linda had her hand on my penis, now nearly ready for launch, as she pulled me toward the bedroom. She was dressed only in panties and blouse. I barely managed to switch off the garage lights.

In the bedroom she undid my belt and slid my pants down in seconds. I had my shirt off just as quickly; underwear and socks, too. She pulled me to the bathroom. I leaned over to start the shower and noticed the tub had about three inches of very warm water already in it. An inflatable pillow floated on it.

"What's the water in here for, Hon?"

"It's a comfortable way to get my shaving done... at least I think it will be. You sit at the far end." She handed me a Lady Gillette and a can of "Edge" with aloe vera. "And I'll lie down with the pillow, um, like this, I think..." She put her legs beside me on both sides. Her valley of paradise was right before me, like dessert. I could have made a few adjustments and done the wonderful right there, but I had a job to do and not even an orgasm would keep me from it.

"Okay, now, Doctor," Linda cautioned me, "you have to promise you'll be very, very careful. I'm putting a lot of trust in you right now."

"Oh, yes ma'am. You just relax, now. Everything will be just fine. I'm going to let you stay awake through the procedure so you can tell me if it feels the way it should. How's that?"

"Whatever you say, Doc. But you'll stop if I say so?"

"Oh yes, ma'am. Yes indeedy." I took a big glob of shave gel and shared it evenly on both hands.

Five minutes later I let out a deep breath and set the razor on the side of the tub.

"Oh, wow, Wally. You're done?" she panted.

"Well, the shaving part. Where would you like to go from here?"

"We better stand up and shower, don't you think?" Linda was flushed. She stood up using the wall behind her for support. I flipped around and reached between her legs to lift the stopper thingy. The soapy water drained away. I reached around and adjusted the water temperature and then flipped the lever to "Shower." We both stood there breathing deeply. I wrapped my arms around her. Old Useless was now fat and floppy, having been on 'hard' setting for about fifteen minutes.

"Oh, dear… is it broken?" Linda held Mr. Softee in one hand and stroked it with the other.

"I hope not! Maybe a little air pressure can firm it up."

Lindy applied her lips to the business end and pretended to blow air into it. Lo and behold. I turned to face Linda and lifted her right up. She grabbed me around my neck and wrapped her legs around my waist. In a minute I was completely happy and relaxing by the second. Linda rested her head on my chest as I let her slide down to standing. Slowly I began the washing ritual and she joined in after I finished her hair and back. I loved her more than anything.

FRIDAY, MAY 31, 1985

I was pumped about the day. Linda was going to the office for a short time, so we parted like most mornings. KDKA had me chuckling at their inanities. Even traffic seemed smoother. I almost skipped into Blatchford Steel.

"Hey, Pauly! Weekend's comin."

"Yessah! Happen every week, I notice." He reached out one hand and I high-fived him sideways.

"We're doing a big cookout, tonight, at my house. London broil on the grill. Why doncha come?"

"Why, you mean dat? I'd love to come. Do I bring the missus, too?"

"Absolutely, Pauly. You're welcome at my house." I was thinking quickly, not sure if I'd meant to make the invitation. But, I liked Paul Lemay. "Lemme write down the address for you." I took the back of one of his check-off sheets and wrote down, "7 Mapleledge off Jefferson off Rodi Road opp. Shop. Ctr. Come hungry."

"How's that?"

Paul studied it for a minute and nodded slowly. "I guess we can find that... if you're sure it's okay."

"No question about it, Paul. What's Mrs. Lemay's name?"

"Mrs. Lemay, like you said." Pauly's face was set in stone but his eyes were laughing.

I laughed and asked for her first name.

"Jemay. I calls her Jemmy but she would like if you called her Jemay."

"Okay, then, see you around six-thirty or so?"

Pauly nodded. "Six-thirty," he repeated. I hustled on to my office.

I sat at my nice clear desk with my yellow pad. Notes with the spooky truck picture were on top. I tore the page off and wrote "Friday" on a clean page. Number one was "Fahnstahl" who I hoped had the right answer from the EPA. Any delay, now, was bad. I circled his name a few times.

Two was "Roberta." Linda was absolutely right that I needed to have the Trust satisfied in advance. I studied the old notes, again. Something was missing, it felt to me, but I had nothing to do if the EPA wasn't cleared. I decided I couldn't put off hearing that news any longer.

"Good morning. This is Walter Anton from Blatchford Steel. Is it possible to speak with the senator? He expected me on Friday." I gave it my brightest cheeriness.

"And good morning to you, sir. The senator is not here just now. Can someone else help you?"

"He told me to speak to Margo if he couldn't be reached."

"Okay. One moment please." I heard some clicks and a snatch of music before Margo picked up.

"Margo Jakes."

"Good morning, Margo. This is Walter Anton, from Blatchford Steel?" More brightness.

"Ohh, ah... yes, Mr. Anton. How may I help you?" A hopeless sensation settled in. Maybe she just didn't know how vital the EPA information was.

"Well, Margo, I had a conversation with the senator about the EPA here in Pittsburgh. He promised to look into the problem for us and said you would be getting in touch with me by today. So, umm, I was a little impatient to hear what you have, you know?"

"EPA?" she asked.

My heart was sinking. I tried to sound cheery. "Yuh, the EPA. He was researching some filings that seemed to be in error. Did he, ahhh, pass anything at all to you?"

"I don't have anything right here, Mr. Anton. I'm sorry. Let me speak to the senator in a little bit and call you back. How can I reach you?"

I dictated my office number and extension and we rang off. Maybe the good news was there and Margo just didn't know it. Now I was really grumpy. I went for coffee.

I stared at the list: two items that had to be handled in order. I had nothing. Still, there was going to be a great cookout on Mapleledge that night. An odd idea struck me to invite Hal Blatchford. I called upstairs to Kelly Galvin.

"He said you can come up, now, Mr. Anton." Kelly was as cool and sweet as old coffee. I wrote on the yellow pad to get her a peace offering. She deserved it, for sure.

"Whatcha got Anton? Things happening?" The old man was at his desk with piles of papers, something I'd never seen before. I never pictured him doing drudge work, but I suppose he must have.

"Actually, Boss, I came to invite you to an excellent cookout tonight... if you aren't tied up, I mean... if you're not busy we'd love to have you." He was speechless. I don't know if he ever fraternized with employees – at least, I'd never heard of it. But, I did like him and it would be interesting to know him better. "You know I like to cook, right? Surely Jack has mentioned it?"

"So, I've heard," he nodded. He was smiling a tight little grin.

"Well, tonight is my special London Broil on the grill and a bunch of other delicious stuff. Bunch of neighbors will be there and I'd be proud to introduce you to them. If you can make it."

"Well, I'll see, Anton, I'll see. What else is there on this land donation business?"

I stayed casual and positive. "Right now I'm waiting for Fahnstahl's assistant to call me back on the EPA stuff. Once that is clear I'm going to meet with the Three Rivers Trust to pave the way to get our lease on the land. Schumann is chomping at the bit but he's waiting on me to resolve the EPA and the Trust. I should have a hectic day."

"We are ready to get our cash, but who do we give it to?"

"Ahh! That's why you're in charge. I almost forgot. The key bank on this is Liberty Bank, do you know it?"

"I've heard of it... black bank, right?" Blatchford's hands were clasped before him, arms on his desk.

"That's it. The president, there, is Forrest Akers, a pretty smart guy, too. I met him a couple of weeks ago. Actually, he's hoping to become a significant development bank here in the County. As a black bank, though, he gets a number of advantages for political reasons. Even Blatchford Steel could profit from working with him, strange as that sounds. Not that it's on point with this deal, but you should meet with Akers, see what he has to say." Blatchford started to sit up straighter and was ready to object. I continued my original thought before he could.

"The point really is, though, that the money should be deposited in Liberty in an escrow account. John Schumann trusts Akers completely, by the way."

I could see Hal relax. "Alright, but how much?"

"I'll get that figure today. Listen, I know your banking is none of my business and I'm sorry to try to say anything. But, just so's you know, our taking part in this Larimer deal is already a big boost for Liberty Bank. You might be surprised what Akers' gratitude could be worth to you." I shrugged and raised my eyebrows. Blatchford looked at me with a little squint.

"I'll take that under advisement, Anton." He picked up some of the papers he'd been looking at. My time was up. I thanked him and left. Kelly Galvin kept her head down but watched me over the top of her glasses. I smiled and thanked her for her help. She didn't care.

Within a minute of returning to my sort-of office, the phone rang. It was Margo. I let my hopes shoot up to unreasonable heights.

"This is Walter Anton." I sounded as pumped as I felt.

"Yes, Mr. Anton. I want you to know that I have spoken with the senator, just a few minutes ago."

"Yes?"

"Yes. He appreciated your turning to him for help but unfortunately he has learned that the filings by the EPA are perfectly valid and there really isn't anything he can do. He hopes you understand that his hands are tied."

My unreasonable hopes that had been buoyed by Margo's speaking with her boss were dashed to unspeakable despair in seconds. I didn't know how to respond. I held the phone silently with my mouth hanging open.

"Mr. Anton? This is Margo Jakes. Did you hear what I said? Mr. Anton?"

"Uhh, yuh, Margo. I am thunderstruck by this news. He, ahh… I mean Senator Fahnstahl told you that the filings are legitimate? The EPA said they are?"

"So far as I know, Mr. Anton, yes. He said this to me just minutes ago. I wish there were something I could do but that's all I have." Margo sighed as she finished. "I have other work. You understand."

"Sure, sure, yes. Me too. Of course I understand. Thank you for calling me back, Margo, and tell the Senator thanks, also. I mean that."

"Certainly, sir. Have a good morning."The line clicked dead. I still held my phone half a minute later. I heard her words over and over: "EPA filings legitimate."

The phone started squealing at me. I dropped it like a hot potato.

Somehow I wasn't crying over the news, nor was I steaming mad. The real estate business was getting me to act cool under pressure. I perceived a game being played that could completely upend my efforts to secure the use of our little railroad spur. Yet I knew what the truth was. Emily Szepanik was not dead because the filings were legitimate. I had to think. And I needed another head working on this with me. I was a little surprised at who I thought of, but I felt better and better about it as I called Kelly Galvin's line.

"Yes, Walter, what is it?" Now I was Walter, but that represented a small put-down by Miss Galvin.

"I have to see the boss again, Kelly. Can you clear that for me, please?" I kept my voice level and, I hoped, dominant.

"What is it about, Walter?"

"It's important, Kelly, or I wouldn't bother him. I'll hold." I could imagine Kelly turning pink as she struggled to keep her voice under control with Hal Blatchford. I know I angered her by saying I'd hold. No one told Kelly what would happen except the old man, possibly.

She clicked back to me, icicles on every syllable, "You may come up." The phone went quiet with a click. I didn't wait. I knew the approach to take.

I smiled broadly at Kelly as I tapped on the boss's big door.

"Yeah, come in," he called to me. He was standing by the windows that overlooked the shop. "Big news?" he asked without turning.

"I've bumped up against some funny business, Hal, and we should think it through and maybe recruit Tom Wittenauer to help us." At the mention of Wittenauer he turned and came to the conference table and sat across from me.

"Whatcha got?" His eyes were boring in to mine, reminding me that bullshit wouldn't sell here, no matter what the price.

"I've been giving a lot of thought to the whole Wittenauer business, and after speaking with Senator Fahnstahl's office, I think he's the one who is in position to help us get things done with the EPA. But I want your thoughts on what's happened so that we make the right move."

"Okay, shoot."

"Well, I had appealed to Fahnstahl, personally, to intercede with the EPA here in Pittsburgh to get a clear report that there were no filings on our parcel. I know you see why I had to do that." He nodded and looked away for a moment. I think he wanted to say something but he waved me forward.

"If I can't get that cleared our commitment on the bridge will be delayed, essentially killing it. So, it's as crucial as it could be. Fahnstahl's office came back with the story that the EPA assured them that there *are* filings on parcel 1983-840. At first I was set back but I know the truth about those signs. There's a woman cooling off in her grave and it's not because those file numbers were legitimate. I know Tommy has an in there. What do you think is the way to move next?" There it was, my best alley-oop shot, tossed up on the hope that Hal Blatchford would leap on faith and slam it home.

"Tommy knows those filings are false, too. He didn't cause them to appear, though, I'm sure of that. What would *you* do?"

"If I thought he would work with me after all the trouble I caused, I would ask him to help us and himself by getting those signs and falsehoods cleared – officially – as he originally thought he could. It may not be that simple, though."

"Why not?" Blatchford pressed. He was leaning closer to me. I did my best to hold my own posture.

"Somebody with a lot of pull *did* get someone in the EPA, whether it's just Brill or someone else, to post those phony signs. It's a very risky move if someone like me asks questions. So, it's somebody with some serious push – or pull. Tom is going to have to extend himself to get the filings cleared. There could be some risk to him, too. There is a criminal roving around who has already killed an EPA employee and threatened me twice. The congressman will be poking the same hornet's nest. Do you think he would do that for us?" I sat back.

Blatchford sat back, too. He held one hand over his mouth, still looking at me, then stood and went back toward the windows. "We need to have some real political protection to offer him if he does this. That's his profit: political power. You come up with a way to protect his reputation and maybe make him look even better for having cleaned up this mess at the EPA. That's the path you need to take." He'd turned toward me but was still looking down at the shop floor.

"Thanks, boss. I knew I was asking the right man for direction on this. Big thanks!" I wasn't stupid. I knew when a bit of brilliance revealed itself, especially one I could take advantage of. I decided I'd said enough. "I'll get back to you later today." I headed to the door. "And I do hope you can make the cookout. If Tommy can come, he's welcome, too." The old man gave a grunt of acknowledgement. I stepped through and closed the door.

"He's a Hell of a guy, isn't he, Kelly?" I flashed my twenty-four carat smile. Kelly almost smiled back but remembered who she was dealing with and just nodded. I trotted down the stairs.

Blatchford and my wife had a lot in common. Each could distill quandries into manageable parts far better than I. Find a way to entice Wittenauer with some political advantage: brilliant. My own feelings about dear old Tommy had blinded me. He cut through.

I didn't hurt my standing by asking, either.

Jack Jackson tapped on my three-quarter door. "Got a few minutes, Walt?" Casual.

"Sure, Jack. Today's a big day, I'm starting to think. Good day to catch up. What do you need?" I could do casual.

"Well, I actually did want to get an update on the real estate stuff. I know you've been on a whirlwind but I heard things were getting close. That true?"

I could imagine how he heard that, but what the Hell? He was entitled. "There are always some last-minute hiccups, but John Schumann says things are nearly lined up to close on a carom shot so that the eight-ball drops into our pocket." Jackson looked at me questioningly until what I meant became clear. Then, he nodded.

"I getcha. What exactly is the carom shot?"

I proceeded to outline the Larimer deal as a way to extract the Trust's neutrality towards our use of Parcel 1983-840. His few questions were on details. I answered everything and he left, satisfied he had my confidence. It was an odd switch in roles, I reflected. He knew I met with Hal Blatchford whenever I wanted, and that I no longer took direction from Jack Jackson. It was odd. I wasn't trying to muscle in. I thought about inviting him to the cookout, but decided not to. I made a note to invite him to dinner soon, though. I wasn't trying to make a wedge between him and Hal. Tonight, if Hal and Tom Wittenauer showed up, there would be some serious discussion I'd have to exclude him from, and I didn't want to do that. Another time.

I called Schumann.

"John? Walter. Got a minute?"

"For you, always. What's up?"

"I heard from Fahnstahl's girl this morning – and I had to chase her for the information – about clearing the EPA filings..."

"I hear a 'but' coming..."

"Yeah. The big 'but' was that now the EPA is claiming the filings are legit. How about that?"

"Ohh, shit! I thought you were taking care of that problem! Shit, shit, shit. Now what?" He let out a long "ohhh."

"Take it easy, partner. Let's don't forget that the truth is still what it was. This is an irritating development but it can't stand. I've gone over it with Hal and we're going to work with Tom Wittenauer to finally clear it."

"Wittenauer!" Schumann was steaming. "How does one suddenly work with his mortal enemy... and at the last minute to boot?"

I waited eight, nine, ten seconds. Schumann asked me if I was still there.

"Yes I am, John, and the deal will still get done. I thought you'd be the one to hold my hand and here I am reassuring you."

"The Hell you are! This is terrible news." I waited again.

"John, I know I'm the novice, but this glitch will get squared away soon, I'm sure. We might not make Wednesday, but it won't be pushed back much. You told me that Wednesday might be a little quick, didn't you?"

"Yeah, but we're going nowhere without the EPA off your back. What's the fix on that?"

"Hal is convinced that Wittenauer did not put those signs up, although he was willing to take advantage of them. So now we have an opportunity to help Wittenauer politically if he gets them cleared officially. But that also means someone else hereabouts actually got somebody in the EPA to post those false signs. So, it gets interesting."

"Politically? What are you thinking?" He was sounding more rational.

"I'm still toying with that. Somehow when this gets done we'll announce or cause to be announced how the good solon risked everything to clean out this corruption from the EPA... something along those lines. Whadda you think?"

"Sounds like you're on track. Where'd you learn this stuff?"

"From a guy name John Schumann, powerful real estate magnate in Pittsburgh. You might know him?"

"Very funny. You gave me a heart attack and now you make jokes."

"Anyway, listen. I told Hal that the money we're kicking in is going into an escrow account in Aker's bank. Was I telling the truth?"

"You're a hot shit, you know that? Why didn't I think of that? I will make it true before lunch. In fact, I'll see if the city will deposit its money in that same account. Damn good idea."

"I also suggested that by so doing, Blatchford was helping Akers a lot and that he should meet with Akers and find out how his gratitude could be profitable to Blatchford Steel. He said he'd take it under advisement, but the idea is planted as requested."

"Better than requested. Very smooth." I could hear Schumann's smile in his voice.

"Feel better?"

"Of course. What's next for you?"

"I'll meet with Wittenauer, maybe later today. I'm confident he'll help us. I'm gonna speak to the police, again, too, find out where the criminal investigation is. If I can offer them Wittenauer's assistance inside the EPA, that might help. They've already spoken to the FBI."

"Wow. Well, okay. I'll keep working on loose ends till you give me the word. It's all on you, now."

"I know, I know. I'm going to do everything I can think of and I'll need more ideas from you. Probably, though, things will get done Monday and Tuesday, so you will need to reschedule. I'm sure we'll know a lot more on Monday."

"Okay, boss. Keep me posted..." Schumann started to ring off.

"John! John! Don't hang up yet!" I yelled into the phone.

"Okay, okay, I hear you. What?"

"What's Blatchford's number? I have to give him a figure! I almost forgot."

"Looks like eight hundred and thirty grand. Probably a little less, but I would suggest depositing that much."

"Good. That's a little less than I'd prepared him for. Thanks, John."

"No problem. We'll be in touch." He clicked off.

I held a pen and toyed with my yellow pad. I was again waiting for someone else to do something we were stuck without. I hated it. I stretched my hands over my head. "Don't shoot, don't shoot," I said to myself as I held my hands up. At that point I remembered my desire to speak to my old friend, Arnie Stewart.

"Pittsburgh Police. This call is being recorded. What is the nature of your call?"

"My name is Walter Anton and I'm not calling about an emergency. Can I reach Officer Stewart, please?"

"Stewart? Zone four?"

"Yes, I'm sorry; Zone Four."

She didn't say anything else but after some clicks a masculine voice announced, "Zone Four. This call is being recorded."

"Arnie Stewart, please."

"Is he supposed to be here?"

"Um, well, I guess I really don't know. I was hoping. Can you check?"

More clicks and near silence. "He's out on a call, sir. Do you want to leave your name and number?" I gave him both. My fingers drummed the desktop. It was only eleven-thirty, but I decided to go to lunch.

I skipped *Marko's*. I swung through a *Kentucky Fried Chicken* on West Carson and bought a dark-meat meal with beans and cornbread. I drove over to Parcel 1983-840 SSF and pulled into the grassy gravel as far as I could. The day was cloudy – not yet June hot. I sat on the Chevy with my feet on the bumper and opened my box of Kentucky's best and grabbed the little drumstick with a napkin. It lasted quick.

The old tracks looked the same. I looked left, toward Blatchford's building. We'd have to do some serious work on the turnout that connected the spur with the line that ran past us. I changed position to look more easily at the building and the tracks. I knew the basic dimensions of our huge girders and it struck me that getting them out of the building was going to be pretty tricky. There was a giant overhead door that allowed one flatcar inside. We often shipped out that way and received raw metal that way, too. But the length of these girders would not permit the center point to hit that flatcar in the building. I wondered.

To the right the tracks curved down out of sight. I could see the top of the block signals that we were going to modify. Farther on, a crane over the rooflines. I tried to picture a short string of flatcars being pushed over that little rise with a pair of long, elegantly curved, welded girders sitting proudly on their special cradles, stark against the sky. The more I tried to form that picture the harder it was to picture the damn things actually getting off the shop floor. We needed a crane that extended at least a hundred feet beyond the overhead door.

Nah... they must have thought of that. They wouldn't have gone this far without having a way to put them on the flatcars. Nah. But I made it my business to ask Bucky Dighton how we were doing it.

Some older kids walked along the track, toward the river and Merriman Street. School was almost out and they were skipping class. I might have done the same so many years ago. I licked my fingers and stared at the little tub of chopped cole slaw. It didn't excite.

There was a pink message when I got back. Arnie Stewart. Good. But first I went upstairs to see Bucky Dighton. He was eating lunch at his desk.

"Hi, Buck. Sorry to interrupt your lunch." I felt a little humble entering the lair of engineers.

"No problem, Walt, since I don't really want it, anyway. Doc's got me dieting... cholesterol." He sneered at his Tupperware container. "Bleacchh" he sounded with his tongue stuck out. "Whatta ya got?"

"Well, I was eating some take-out looking at the rail spur we're going to use for the King Frederik girders, you know?"

"Yeh...ess. What about it. I thought you were making progress on that."

"On the railroad, yes. Moving fast right now, in fact. No, my question has to do with our end of the tracks. Those finished girders are over forty feet high and more than two hundred and ten feet long, right?"

"Uh huh. No news, there."

"I know, I know, but I got thinking about actually putting them on the three flatcars we'll use to move them to the river. I mean, you've got some custom racks that will hold them and allow for turns and things, right?"

"Yup. Designed em myself. We'll weld them directly onto the flatcars. Why?"

"Well, maybe I'm just not able to see it, but I don't see how our overhead crane is going to position these things on the center car when we can get only one car into the building. Am I crazy?"

Bucky held a cup of something. It hadn't moved while I asked my question. He looked as if he could just as easily throw it at me. I pursed my lips and looked back as seriously as I could. He cracked a little smile.

"Son of a bitch!" he said.

"Yeah," I said. "Son of a bitch what?"

In answer he slipped the plans for the special transport racks out of a wide flat drawer and went over to one of the drafting tables by the windows that overlooked the shop. The inside portion of the siding was across from where we stood and to the far right corner of the building. He studied them for a couple of minutes. "Son of a bitch," he said again.

I just looked at him blankly. He looked back, clearly upset with somebody, but not me, I hoped.

"I think you did me a big favor, here, Walter. We have all overlooked your point, entirely. Son of a bitch!"

"Listen, Bucky, I am perfectly happy leaving myself out of this. Perfectly."

"I'm not saying that."

"No, but I know I'd rather figure it out myself if I were you, so let's say you did and forget about it." I nodded a little – like a salesman, I thought. He smiled with his lips tightly together.

"If you say so, I'm grateful, Walt."

"Okay. Buy me lunch at *Marko's* sometime. How can you solve it, though? That's what's really interesting."

"Simple answer? We either have heavy-lift capacity outside the big door or we have two cars inside at once. There's nothing else that I can see right now, and both pose tricky handling problems. Right now I can't say which is better."

"Huh. Well. I usually look at costs and I'm no engineer, so let me ask what it would mean to get two flatcars inside the building?"

"Well, here," he stepped aside and gestured for me to look out the same window, "see that big stamping machine against the wall opposite?"

"Yeah. What is it?" I wasn't sure what he meant. The largest machine looked like an iron castle.

"We use the stamper to punch holes in girders and plates. Not its best use but it works great and it came with the building. We've made some custom jigs for common sizes and it's three times faster than using torches on certain jobs. But it takes a lot of space. All in all I'd rather have it here. If we cut the floor for another sixty-five feet of siding we'll have to give up that stamper and a lot of other floor space. We'd have another lift-plate to cover the space, but we wouldn't be able to position equipment on it." He rubbed his chin. "I just talked myself out of that choice. We'd really mess up use of our space. I don't know."

"Okay, I follow that. I can figure the rough costs on cutting the floor and adding some track. How would we add lift outside the building?"

"We could lease a big crane, but those things cost a few thousand dollars a day, among other charges – like an operator, for instance. I don't like that, already."

"Me either."

"We could add some pylons outside and extend our inside overhead crane maybe a hundred feet outside the building. That would require some major reconstruction of the east wall. Truth to tell, I'd love to have that capacity sometimes, but I don't think it can be done in time to help us now. So, I don't have an answer."

"I got one more question, Bucky. Which of these solutions has the most future value, after the King Frederik is done?"

"Extending the overhead, no doubt about it."

"Do you know a construction company if we chose to do that?"

"No, but I know who I'd speak to first."

"Which is… ?"

"Wheeling Crane. They service our crane, now, and they do hundreds of other cranes and mine lifts. They would know."

"That makes sense. Let's talk to them right away and I'll create some line items in my projections for what we'll need to do. I'll tell the old man that it's been my oversight to not include these construction items in the King Frederik projections. But we've got to hear from the crane people first. Can you get someone here tomorrow? Saturday?"

"You're serious, aren't you?"

"There's no time to lose! We have to be able to load these damn things in just over six months. We try to get this done by committee and were sunk. I think if we take some action and find a way to make the deadlines, we'll be forgiven with a cherry on top. I'm sorry about Saturday, but let's find out as soon as we can. You in?"

Bucky was smiling to the point of almost laughing. "I'm in. You're a ballsy guy but you pulled my fat out of the fire, so I'm with you."

"Alright, then! See if your crane guy can bring a designer or architect or whatever they call those people. It's a lot to ask, I know…"

"We pay Wheeling a lot of money and we're going pay them a ton more to retrofit the crane. Mike will come."

"Call me at home… here's my home phone." I wrote it down on an index card. "Call whenever you find out they'll be here. If Mike Whatshisname says the designer has a fee for coming on Saturday, tell him I'll get it covered."

"You got it. This'll be fun. Thanks."

"Hey, fun for me, too. See you later." I hustled back down to my office. It was after two o'clock and I had every intention of leaving early to get ready for the cookout. The message from Arnie Stewart was staring at me. I sat down and called Zone Four.

"Arnie Stewart. Who's calling?"

"It's me, Walter Anton, Officer Stewart. Thanks for calling me back."

"Got a new problem?"

"No, same old, same old, but I was hoping you could tell me something about whether your investigations have reached into the EPA office yet."

"I do believe there have been some interviews done there, but I don't know if there's anything to tell you."

"Oh, okay. But do you know whether they have spoken to a guy named Henry Brill over there?"

"They might have."

"Well, umm... good. You know he's the guy that threatened to kill me. He's in the thick of this thing. He admitted the filings were false and now he told a U. S. Senator that they actually are legitimate. So, he's likely to lie to the police, too."

"Boy oh boy, thanks, Perry."

"Okay, I'm just saying." Arnie Stewart knew how to rile me.

"Look, Anton, these things take time. We're looking for Sindledecker and we're interviewing people of interest. So far we haven't charged anyone with anything. I'll tell you when we do. How's that?"

"Thanks, I appreciate that. I really do. Do you think I'm any safer than I was?"

"Can't say. We've had no sign of your man for about a week, now. He'll pop up sooner or later, but until then be doubly vigilant. That's all I've got." He rang off. I would've said "thanks."

I headed down the hall. Jackson was on the phone. I tried to not listen.

"Hi, Jack! Got a sec?" I used my bright and cheery approach.

His hand was still on the phone in its cradle. "Ahhm, well, yeah, I guess. C'mon in."

"Thanks. Listen, I want to tell you, first, before I say anything to Hal." Jack's expression changed to dark suspicion.

"About what?"

"About the King Frederik expenses. The crane problem?" As if he'd certainly know what I meant.

"Oh, yeah? What about it?" As if.

"It's all my fault, I think. I've ignored those expenses. I don't know why I didn't recognize them as connected to the King Frederik. In the process I didn't put them anywhere and I'm sorry about that. I don't want it to reflect on you."

"Well,... ahh, I mean, how big are they?"

"I think we're in the tens of thousands. I bumped into Bucky Dighton and he happened to ask me if there'd been any push-back on his approach, because of the costs, naturally."

"Approach to what, Walter, retrofitting the crane? You had those in there."

"No, not those. The costs for extending the crane outside. It's a bit of a construction job."

Jack looked at me like a second head had sprouted behind my ear. "Extending the crane? What the Hell are you talking about?"

"To load the damn girders on the flatcars! There's only room for one car inside and we're using three cars to move em. We've got to either dig up the shop or extend the crane. It's not all that unusual but we have to move fast. I don't know why this hadn't come up, but if I'd included those costs earlier it would have, that's for sure."

"Why tell me today?" Jack had his sly look.

"I told Bucky to get his crane guy in here tomorrow so we could put some numbers on this and act as though it was just a slipup somewhere along the line, including me. We can resolve this in time to meet the contract, but we need to move fast. Turns out the extension will have a lot of profitable value down the road, too. I'll sell it to the boss."

"You're sure we have to do this?"

"It's either this or we lease a big crane for months, with an operator. That will actually cost more than the extension." I sat back in confidence. Jack was stewing over how he'd look. "You know what? I'll tell Hal you've been bugging me for the preliminaries and take the blame for being pulled in too many directions at once, and that I screwed up on them. I think that's the best approach. We have to do it."

"Why didn't we think of this before?" Jack was finally considering the problem instead of being pissed off.

"I don't know, honestly. It never crossed my mind until Bucky asked if I'd heard anything. He probably figured things were moving along. I don't know." I gave my "what do I know?" shrug. Jack was leaning back deep in thought. I pressed forward.

"We have just enough time to get the modifications done, it looks like. That's why we're meeting tomorrow instead of waiting."

"You're no engineer. What the hell do you know about overhead cranes?" He was pissed, again.

"Why don't you meet with us, tomorrow? We don't have to know how to do the construction to at least get the costs. We can't ship these girders without putting them on flatcars. Doesn't it seem better to get things moving toward a solution the board can sign off on?"

Jack was clearly uneasy. I felt like the wise guy encouraging his buddies to steal candy bars. "I don't know, Walt."

"Look, Jack, sooner or later you and I have to make the case for the costs. No matter when we do that some bigwigs are going to be upset that they hadn't heard of this expense. We can't help that. Ask yourself: Are we better off dumping the problem in their laps, or laying the solution before them, with the costs quantified? I think its better to be associated with the solution, don't you?"

"You make sense when it's put like that, I guess."

"Okay, then. Now, has Blatchford worked with any big contractors before?"

"None I can think of. We poured the shop floor, but, we didn't have to do much to the building itself. I'd remember any big expenses. So, no."

"Alright. Let's pick the brain of the crane guy. Bucky's asking him to bring a designer or an architect with him. We can investigate the contractors they like so that there won't be time lost once we present this. And we've got to present it fast – two, three days. We have our work ahead of us." I was doing the nodding thing. Jack nodded, too.

"Okay. Listen, Bucky's going to call me with the time to meet tomorrow. I'll call you, then, right?"

"Absolutely. We've got to learn as quickly as we can. I'll be there."

"Dyn-o-mite! See you tomorrow, then. I have to leave. I'll call you when Bucky tells me."

We shook hands. "Thanks, Walter. Glad we caught this in time."

"Me, too," I nodded. "Talk to ya." I left and headed outdoors. For the Hell of it I drove to the far end of the lot and parked again. I slipped between the chain-link fence and the building and stepped out next to the siding that ran under the huge roll-up door. The East end had no windows and a trucker's door up a few steps. To the left was a smaller roll-up where trailer trucks backed in.

The roof slanted up from the left to a clerestory that faced South, then a little peaked roof with a taller flat wall facing North. The masonry wall was about forty feet high. A newer steel-clad wall extended up to the roof, which peaked about eighteen feet above the roll-up. The girders curved about forty feet, so we'd have to have some way to utilize the height above the roll-up. I'd be sure to ask about that.

To bring the crane outside we'd have to have a lower masonry wall and a good way to seal up around the opening in the wall. It would be very interesting to hear what the crane engineer said about that. I headed home.

***

Linda was organized, God bless her. There was barely a breeze, and paper goods, utensils and things were lined up on a folding table. Elly Maxwell had brought two tables. Amongst us we had enough beach and sports chairs to seat everyone.

In the kitchen were bowls of potato, bean, macaroni and green salad. And chips. Outside were dressings, sauces, mustard and two kinds of Heinz ketchup. The refrigerator held sliced tomatoes, cucumbers, onions, summer squash, and zucchini. We had maybe fifteen people coming and food for thirty.

My beef was covered with Saran wrap. I'd added some sherry and flavors that morning. I sliced off a tiny medallion of steak and grilled it in a pan. It smelled good and the taste was not too strong. I decided to baste two of them with chili marinade.

Linda had wine and beer in one cooler, soft drinks and lemonade in another. There were thick hamburgers, separated by wax paper. And, if anyone wanted a hot dog, she had a package of the fat ones.

"Who else have you heard from?"

"Well, everyone who was at Elly's last time, plus Penny and Bob are bringing her mother, who's visiting. Hank Buckley, of course, maybe with a doctor lady-friend."

"Ooo, la, la!"

Linda rolled her eyes. "Seems like eleven or twelve. We've got plenty."

Well, I gotta tell you that I invited a couple of folks, too. Hal Blatchford and Pauly Lemay, who's one of the guards at Blatchford – really nice guy, and his wife, Jemay. I rented the Chevy from his son, who works at the airport, too."

"Thanks for telling me." She might have been upset – had every right to be.

"I met twice with Hal Blatchford, today, and there's more things to discuss, plus he and I had a good skull session on our very sticky EPA problem. It just sort of spilled out and I don't know if he's really coming. I think he was pleased that I thought to ask, at all."

"Well, I hope he comes. It will be nice to meet him away from the factory."

"Yeah. It looks like we might be able to make use of Tom Wittenauer to resolve it. How about that turn-about?"

"Wittenauer? I thought he was trying to kill you!"

"More and more it doesn't seem like that. That guy, Brill, he deals with at the EPA apparently flew off the handle when they discussed what I was questioning. Blatchford is convinced he didn't set those false signs. I'm almost convinced. Besides, he's all we've got."

"I certainly hope you know what you're doing." She was shaking her head as she added some veggies to her greens.

"You and me, both, Sweetie. Everything hinges on his helping us." I hovered over her, looking for something I might do. "Oh, and Wittenauer might come tonight, too." I tried to let it slip out, but she didn't buy it.

"He what?! That, that… scoundrel is invited here? Dammit, Walter!" She stood with her hands on the counter, staring into the greens. I stood back, shifting my weight from side to side.

"I sure am glad we're partners in life, Walt, you know that? Able to share everything, talk things out. You know, stuff like that!" I was in deep with no grappling hooks. I felt awful.

"I'm sorry, Lin, I really am. I haven't had a chance to explain my day. I'm sorry." I went into the back yard and puttered around setting up chairs, moving bottles of condiments a few inches one way, then another. Finally I sat down, facing the back of the yard, afraid to catch Linda's eye. My hands were clasped, hanging between my knees. I let my head hang, too. Son of a bitch.

I sat there, reviewing my day. Everything depended on everything else. Everything justified inviting Blatchford, didn't it? And his inviting Wittenauer? Seemed to me. I stewed. I could hear little prep noises coming from the house. Little by little I cleared my selfishness and, in little bits, came around to recognize that the most important person in my life had been ignored as I tried to cope with work. I had ignored her so easily. How could I be so arrogant?

The prep noises came up behind me. I started to cry. Linda's hand found my neck where she massaged me a little.

"I am so, so sorry, Lin. I get caught up in my own importance. I could have called… should have called. You save me from myself so many times." I shook my hanging head.

"Well, I can be more trusting, too, Wally. I should at least assume you have a good reason to do something unusual. So, I'm sorry, too." She picked up my chin and sat down across my legs. I hugged her to me. She wiped the tears.

"I've decided this could be an interesting evening. I hope they both come. Maybe you could catch me up on the congressman?"

I gave her a synopsis of how Blatchford had come to believe in him, again, and that the EPA was now claiming the filings were legit… at least they told the senator that. And how Wittenauer was our last best hope, so long as we could turn his help to his own political advantage.

"How can you do that? You're no politician." She moved the condiments back where she'd had them.

"Well, I haven't figured that out, completely, but if we can publicize his part in rooting out corruption at the Pittsburgh EPA, that might do it." I let out a long breath. "Your ability to cut through my nonsense would be a big help, there. I think."

"Let's see what happens. Are you ready to start baking the beef?"

"Yeah. I'll wrap em and put them on the shelf above the grill. I only want them in there for an hour."

"Okay, get them going and go take a shower. You'll feel better."

I started the charcoal, including a layer of applewood briquets. Each strip of steak was wrapped in heavy foil. I positioned them on the shelf about six inches higher than the grill grating. I lowered the cover and set the airflow to keep the coals low. Linda was sitting in the breezeway between the garage and house, with a glass of wine. I kissed the top of her head and went in to shower.

***

Elly arrived first, although she'd been over twice already. Her sleeveless dress molded to her bosom rather nicely. The front was a square scoop and when she bent over the view was tantalizing. I determined to be careful with that. The ice was thin.

She'd brought us the cukes, zukes and tomatoes. Now she had an ice-cream cake that Linda made room for. There was writing on it.

"Somebody's birthday?"

"Two somebodies."

I gave Elly a quick hug and an air kiss. She turned to the counter where Linda was wrapping her green salad in Saran, and gave her a sideways hug, too. When I turned I almost bumped into Teddy Maxwell, who stepped back and bumped into his brother, Ronnie.

"Hiya, fellas. How ya doin?"

"Good, Mr. Anton. School's out and Ronnie turned thirteen." Teddie was the spokesman.

"Wow! So you're fifteen and Ronnie is thirteen." They both nodded solemnly. I was out of teenager conversation. "Howsabout a game of frisbee?" Teddie looked at Ronnie, who shrugged his enthusiasm. I crossed to the garage and pawed through my frisbee repository.

We formed a triangle and started throwing gently. Right away, Ronnie tried to outdo his brother. When he threw to me, the disc sailed over my head. I kept switching who I threw to. Ronnie spotted a garter snake.

"Hey, Teddie, catch it... catch it!" In moments the inseparable brothers had escaped frisbee. I looked at my watch. The London Broil had been in the grill for almost an hour. I took the three strips off the grill shelf and unwrapped them. With a small knife I cut into one of them and tested the temperature at the center: warm, but not cooked. I would finish them on the grill, proper. I carried them into the kitchen, covered with the aluminum foil. I took some olive oil, lemon juice, finely chopped chili pepper and honey and swirled them all together, then I twisted the pepper mill over the mixture. That was enough. I dumped it all in the blender.

Hank Buckley was next with a big bowl of fruits that he must have cut and mixed himself, but no doctor on his arm. Axel Johnson was right behind him. He had a big plate of cheeses and a basket with fancy crackers. We left it in the kitchen. Hank, Axel and I went out back and cracked some beers. We talked about trips, work and home repairs. I complimented Axel on the quality of his repair of our front door.

"It'll keep your friends out," he nodded.

Teddie and Ronnie sidled up to our table. "Did you guys catch that snake?" I asked.

"I had it in my hands," said Ted, "but I couldn't hang on to him and he got away."

"Well, better wash your hands, and we'll start snacking, I'm sure." They headed into the house. As if on cue, Linda and Elly appeared with the cheese platter and crackers fanned out in the basket. Elly had one of the salads. We helped ourselves to some crackers and cheese. In a couple of trips the girls had everything spread out over the three tables. I fired up the small grill and added some more applewood briquets to the big one. I would start grilling in about twenty minutes.

"Hellooo!" someone called. "Hello, Mr. Walter?" I recognized Paul Lemay's voice.

"Out here, Pauly!" I trotted around the garage to find Paul and his wife heading toward me. Jemay Lemay was a round woman with energy. She rocked over to me well ahead of her husband. "I'm so glad you could come. It's a pleasure to meet you," I said. "How ya doin, there, Pauly?" I reached out to shake hands and we did a manly half-hug. "C'mon, c'mon. I want you to meet some of the neighbors." I took Jemay's arm and led them around the tables. I ran through the introductions, coming at last to Teddie and Ronnie Maxwell.

"No kiddin? I used to work with a Maxwell. His name was Jack, though." Pauly was smiling but Teddie and Ronnie displayed a sense of horror. From a few steps away, Elly Maxwell looked over toward the boys. Pauly looked at me.

"That's a real coincidence, Paul. Their Dad's name is Jack. I think you surprised them."

"Oh, yeah. So I see. Look fellas, there's lots of Jack Maxwells. The guy I knew was kind of a crazy guy and nowhere as good lookin as you two." The boys weren't convinced, but looked less horrified.

Linda and Jemay hugged. She accepted a wrapped basket Jemay was carrying, and almost dropped it. "Goodness, it's so heavy! What's in it?"

"Well, Mrs. Anton, I always serve my special baked beans when we have guests, so I thought I'd bring some. You don't have to serve them if you don't want." Jemay's smile was about five hundred watts.

"Oh, no! I wouldn't think of not serving this. This is wonderful. Thank you." They unwrapped the basket and Linda placed the earthenware pot on the table near the grills. "I'll be surprised if there are any left! Mmm-nnhh." Linda lifted the lid and breathed in the aroma. Suddenly we all could smell it. I decided to start grilling.

I brought out the platter of meat and some of the burgers and hot dogs. I opened a couple of the vents in my big grill and lay the three strips on the grate. They sizzled loudly. I lathered up two with my special sauce and went back to my beer. Pauly Lemay was sipping one, too, as he got to know Axel and Hank.

Little by little we all talked about our jobs. Axel had the least to say while Hank talked about his constant travel. I gave some low-key descriptions of how Blatchford was setting up for a big international bridge project. But Pauly Lemay talked mostly about his previous job, working for the University of Pittsburgh, where he had briefly been second in command for campus security. The more he talked the more intelligent he sounded. I was glad I'd been friendly with him. An old memory nagged me about Pitt.

I got up to check the meat. It was starting to look crispy. I rolled them over with tongs and liberally basted the two. For the one I wasn't basting I sprayed it with some Worcestershire sauce. I figured about ten more minutes and then second-guessed myself and went inside and grabbed my big chef's knife and my cutting board.

Sometimes the safest thing to do is just cut into the meat and take a look. It makes no sense to pay good money for beef and over-cook it. I sliced into the very center of the non-basted strip and I was glad I did. It was perfect. I grabbed the other two and plopped em on the board. "Dinner is served!" I shouted out. I got London Broil, plain and kinda spicy. Grab a plate!"

Penny and Bob appeared with her mother and a fruit-layered trifle in a big glass stem bowl they'd finally found a use for. Little by little they met everyone as they walked toward the back of the line. I don't really grasp these things, but Penny seemed more pregnant than even two weeks ago. Far be it from me...

The boys preferred burgers. "Well, how about one for now and another if you want it." On the grill they went. I dripped some Worcestershire on them, too. "Anyone for dogs?" I called out. Not a hand was raised. The London Broil was a hit.

There was about half of each kind of steak left when I sat down. We started talking about how I prepped it. From the corner of my eye I spotted a man coming around the other corner of the house. It took a double-take but I realized it was Hal Blatchford. I almost spilled drinks jumping up.

"Hey, Hal! You came! I'm really glad you made it. Come meet everybody." We shook hands. He was carrying a bag from a package store. "You didn't have to bring anything." I told him.

"Oh yes. You never go to dinner without bringing a gift to the hostess… but I brought something for you, too." Now I was curious. I introduced him around, asked his preference in beer or wine and offered the two kinds of Broil. He chose spicy. Linda helped him find different salads and Jemay's beans. To his credit he didn't show the slightest surprise to see Pauly, and he specifically asked for her beans, which pleased Jemay mightily.

The old man was dressed better than any of us in what he thought was casual. Everything was spotless, creased and polished. But, casual. In the bag were a red and a white wine and, the pièce de resistance, a full fifth of Old Overholt.

"How'd you know to pick Overholt, Hal? It's fabulous."

"A little bird told me. Like it?"

"Absolutely. I thought only the mayor knew I like that."

"My lips are sealed." Blatchford enjoyed his secret.

"Well, we're opening it after dessert. There's no better way to finish off a perfect Friday night and you can't let it get confused with other flavors."

Hal looked around with a grin. "You say so," he said. I think he was glad he came.

Automatically, the men grouped together as the women wound up in the house. In a sort of round-robin fashion we talked about jobs we had or used to have. Hal described getting into the steel services trade and how he acquired the old J & L foundry building. Bob Simpson checked on his wife a couple of times, who apparently was fine, but it kept him from saying too much about work.

I had never heard Axel Johnson say what he did for a living. He didn't want for much and his schedule, I knew, was pretty flexible. It may have been Hal Blatchford's being with us, but Axel appeared to be about to tell us where he worked when we heard a car pull up. Surprisingly, Blatchford, himself, got up to see who it was, limping slightly around the side of the garage. "Hey, Tommy! Ya made it!" he called out.

Everybody looked at me and I shrugged and said, "I think it's Congressman Wittenauer," with my eyebrows raised. Axel stood up.

"I kinda lost track of the time, Walt. I gotta get back. Thanks for a great time. The steak was fabulous." He was already halfway to the other corner of the house, waving at everyone. He disappeared around the corner as Hal came back with Tom Wittenauer.

When the congressman came around the garage, Blatchford was behind him. Hank, Pauly and Bob now stood up with me. A little silly, but it didn't hurt anybody. Hal walked him around to shake hands coming last to me. "Good to see you again, Tom." We shook hands, too, although I got a long stare.

"You know, dessert is ready. Tom would you like a sip of Old Overholt with us?"

"Only what the law allows, Walter. Sounds good." We trooped in through the kitchen where the girls were setting out fruits, the enormous trifle and some coffee. In the living room Linda had placed folding chairs and a folding table in place of the coffee table. It took a minute before the girls realized Axel had been replaced with another guy.

Linda spoke first, having known what to expect. "Welcome to our home, Congressman. Sorry we're a little cramped tonight."

"Nonsense. Everything is lovely. I heard your house was vandalized and I can't imagine how much work you did to restore it. Thanks for having me."

I made the other two female introductions. For her part, Elly made it clear she wasn't attached as she hugged his arm close to herself. Tom didn't resist, but I don't know if he got the message. I could see why a woman would flirt with him, handsomeness-wise.

Teddie and Ronnie appeared in the hall doorway, silent as church-mice. Wittenauer spotted them and went over to shake their hands. "You guys twins? No?" as they shook their heads. "You look like you could be, ahhm, sixteen, am I right?" Ronnie giggled while Teddie stood as tall as he could.

Teddie gestured with his thumb. "He's thirteen."

"Ohh… I getcha." Tom could see a couple of future voters. "Well, you look older to me!" He started to turn back to the rest of us but stopped and spun back to the boys. "Who's ahead?"

Ronnie answered. "Cardinals, but the Pirates have the bases loaded and Madlock is up."

"Aw right, then."

"He's fifteen." Ronnie made sure the air was clear. Wittenauer guffawed and grinned as he came back in to the main part of the room. People could like the guy.

The boys eased back to the TV. "Those are your boys?" he asked of Elly. She showed a flash of horror and instantly beamed a smile. "Stepsons, but they are wonderful kids."

"Now," said Linda, "before we go any later, lets bring out that ice-cream cake. Elly?" They left and made kitchen noises. Bob and Penny sat together and the rest of us found a seat, with Wittenauer at one side of the fireplace and Blatchford at the other. Hal looked like a proud stepfather, himself.

I excused myself and gathered up some rocks glasses and my new fifth of Old Overholt. "Have you all had this before?" I asked as I waved the bottle.

"I have," said Wittenauer, but no one else.

I repeated word-for-word what Mayor McKay had told me about it. "It's pure Pennsylvania ambrosia," I finished. I set the bottle down and invited them to help themselves while I got some ice and tongs. Paul Lemay sniffed the bottle but didn't take any. We all agreed on the unique qualities of Old Overholt.

Elly walked through the end of the room and soon brought the boys out from the bedroom. Penny delivered some real plates and silverware. Next the lights went out and Linda carried the frozen cake into the living room with a circle of fifteen candles on it – thirteen red and two blue. We sang "Happy Birthday" and the boys crowded in to jointly blow out the candles.

"Boy, I've been worried about that cake. I'm glad you boys came so it didn't go to waste!" Teddie brushed that off with a noise; Ronnie looked at me in case I meant it.

When the little party was over, Penny, her mom and Bob decided she needed her sleep, since she was pregnant in case we hadn't noticed. Hank Buckley was in a discussion with his congressman about some of the new regulations that made things awkward for airlines. There was some issue about approach patterns to Pittsburgh, too, that got the most input from Wittenauer, since he'd apparently worked on that very item. Paul Lemay looked a little uncomfortable. I sat next to him and his wife as we finished our ice-cream cake.

I asked Jemay if she followed politics at all?

"Not me, Mr. Walter. You want politics you need to talk to my Pauly. He got opinions on all of those people. Yes sir. Pauly always makes sure I votes but not for anyone who tells lies."

"Wow, Pauly, I didn't know you followed politics like that."

"I keep my ears open… yes I do. I don't like people telling me that black folk have to vote this way or that way. I like having a job so I looks to see who is gonna help people find jobs.

That means people like Mr. Blatchford have to be doin business. Seems to me."

"We're gonna have to talk more, Pauly. I think your husband is a wise man, Jemay." She shifted her position a bit and gave me a serious nod. "Pauly, I'd like to talk with you about your job at Pitt. Think we could, sometime?"

"Well, my Jemmy is making a shoulder next Saturday. You and Linda are welcome, for sure." He nodded and smiled while Jemay looked away with serene confidence in her cooking abilities.

"You just might have a date, there, Pauly. I'll speak to Linda and let you know."

"I'll be happy to hear, Mr. Walter, yes suh." Paul and Jemay stood up and smoothed their clothing. "An' you and Missus have been very kind. Very kind. That steak was surely tasty. Me and Jemay be getting home now. Gotta get my beauty sleep!" Jemay rolled her expressive eyes. I gave her a little kiss and shook Pauly's hand. Linda hugged them, both. Eventually everybody shook their hands. I was glad they came.

I took a folding chair around to sit closer to Hal Blatchford.

"I got a number out of John Schumann, finally." He snapped to business mode in a heartbeat. "Evidently our 'contribution' will be eight hundred and thirty thousand or a bit less."

"Okay… that's a little less than I feared. You really think this should go to escrow with Liberty Bank?"

You'd have thought that someone had poked Wittenauer with a sharp stick. He heard the term "Liberty Bank" and shifted his attention to Blatchford before he got to the end of the last syllable. Poor Hank Buckley had to follow that shift with no context at all.

"They are real good people, Hal," injected Tom Wittenauer. He was looking only at his mentor. I might have been in another room. Hank and I looked at each other. Hal Blatchford turned more fully toward me.

"When do we need to do this, Walt?"

"I'd suggest holding off as long as possible. There has to be an interest cost to moving it too quickly, no?"

"Very true. You'll let me know when that point comes." He turned again to divide his attention amongst the four of us.

"So," observed Tom, "sounds like you're getting close on that railroad project."

Both Hal and I started to answer. The old man deferred to me. "Yes. It's become more complex but we are close. In fact if you have a few minutes, later, we could use your help."

"Absolutely. Anything you need." Wittenauer's smile seemed too big for a living room. Blatchford gently slapped Tom's knee.

"Who would like more coffee? More ice-cream cake?" Linda's entry was perfect. Elly Maxwell stood behind her with the pot.

Hank Buckley stood up and declared his need to be getting home. "Let me walk out with you, Hank," I said. I asked Hal and Tom to give me a few minutes.

Hank and I stepped out front. "Hank, my apologies for the twist this evening took. Will you come back tomorrow night for another Overholt?"

"Yeah, sure, if you mean that."

"Oh, I do, Hank. I expected Hal Blatchford, but not the congressman. I know why he came, but it's still a little secretive. I'll fill you in when I can."

"Okay, then. I'd like to chat some more. Thanks, Walt."

"The thanks are to you, Hank. I appreciate that you'll come over tomorrow. See ya then." We shook hands. His accepting my apologies reminded me to do something for Kelly Galvin.

In a funny way I was excited about the meeting that was about to unfold. Linda and Elly were chatting with the two men when I came back into the living room.

Linda folded me in seamlessly. "Walt, did you know that Mr. Blatchford went to Bucknell, too?" And I hadn't known that.

"Son of a gun! Probably the only reason he hired me." Hal chuckled. Wittenauer looked at me, expressionless. "And, I'm glad he found a reason!" Smiles all around. Elly stood up and offered her hand to Tom Wittenauer, who also stood. Hal still sat for a few moments and then must have realized the thing to do was stand. In some ways Blatchford knew very little about women. I'd never thought about that part of his life. Funny.

Elly garnered a kiss from her congressman and a handshake from Blatchford. Linda got a little hug and kiss and so did I. Elly went in to the bedroom to rouse Ronnie; Teddie managed to follow the whole Pirates-Cardinals battle. Soon the three were back. Linda hugged them all. I said "Happy Birthday, fellas." The two strange men by the fireplace just waved.

"You guys come back tomorrow if you're looking for work," I offered. Teddie showed some interest, but Ronnie was sleep-walking. Linda walked out with them.

"There's plenty more Overholt, gentlemen…" Both indicated an interest in a little more. I finished pouring just as Linda returned. "Honey?" I gestured with the bottle. Her face passed from "I feel like a fifth wheel here" to "thank you very much for including me, Sweetheart," in half a second. I poured her an inch of ambrosia and put a piece of ice in it.

Linda settled herself on the couch to Blatchford's left. I pulled the long table back a bit and set my chair in front of the two men, slightly favoring Wittenauer's side. "I hope you guys aren't put off by Linda's joining us. She's a phenomenal planner and negotiator and everything is at stake here."

Wittenauer made a stiff smile and held his glass up to her. Blatchford smiled and tipped his glass toward her and said, "If Walter trusts your judgment then so do I." Linda blushed.

"Tom," I said, "we have not had a very smooth relationship. Hal has convinced me of your position with the phony signs. I am sorry for the scrutiny I have brought down on you, but I can't apologize for it. Those signs have had a very negative impact on Blatchford Steel and on Linda and me, personally."

Congressman Tom Wittenauer was looking at Blatchford who nodded back, then he turned toward me. "Those signs were just something I thought I could take advantage of. You have to know I wasn't trying to hurt anyone." He studied the floor.

There was a small period of silence before Linda spoke. "Did you know someone broke into our home the same day Walter met Henry Brill?"

"I heard about that. I don't think I realized that was the day. I'm sorry for you."

"We are trying to believe it was a coincidence. That Saturday, though, some thug named Sindledecker ran Walter off the road after tampering with his brakes and later ran Emily Szepanik, who worked at the EPA – worked for Henry Brill, in fact – off Lincoln Street and killed her. Did you know that?"

Wittenauer looked like he wanted to shake his head. Blatchford looked very uncomfortable.

"I have heard of those events, yes. I hope you don't associate me with either attack." Linda sat forward to challenge him but I warded her off.

"No, Tom," I answered, "I don't think you caused them or ordered them." I looked over to Linda to reassure her. "But someone you have had dealings with at the EPA *did* order them, and..." I held up my hands to stop his attempt to interrupt. "and... I do believe you know a bit more about some kind of retribution toward me than is comfortable for you to admit. There's a reason we are going through this, Tom, a reason that is good for all of us in this room. So…"

"I know how it looks for you, both," he gestured toward Linda and then me, "but there never was any sort of conspiracy to 'get' Walter Anton, despite how it looks." He was doing his best to not succumb to anger. Hal Blatchford was leaning back with his arms crossed, one hand clutching his Overholt. Wittenauer's was gone, but he hadn't asked for another. Linda's was on the table.

"You aren't testifying, here, Tom. We are approaching a point of trust with one another and you need to do most of the work. I will never repeat what is discussed here and I'm sure that's true for everyone." I stared at him. He was tight-lipped, glaring at me.

"What do you want?" he asked.

"I want to know if you know a man named Gary Sindledecker, first of all." He was already shaking his head in short moves but he didn't say "no."

"And he is…?"

"The man who tried to kill me." He raised his eyebrows at that.

"How do… no, never mind. I assume he's been identified. You want to know who ordered him to attack you." It was stated, not asked.

"That's correct, Tom. He has a history of doing assaults for hire, and he's well-known to police agencies. If you didn't… um, wait." I held up one finger and thought before resuming. "How well do you know Henry Brill?" Wittenauer puffed out his cheeks and blew out a long breath.

"Okay. I've known Henry for a number of years, before he transferred to Pittsburgh. He was a couple years ahead of me at Ohio State and I visited him in Canfield. We have coffee now and then and he has been a supporter of mine."

"Did he tell you he'd threatened to kill me?"

"You can't be serious!"

"Said it right to me, face to face. He's a very angry man." Wittenauer just shook his head, now looking up at the ceiling.

I pressed on. "Did you know Emily Szepanik?"

"No, ahh, no, I don't think so. Who is she?"

"She worked for Henry Brill and was run off the road and killed. Late thirties, I think. Very pleasant."

"Oh, Jesus." Tom was upset, now. "Her death is connected to attacks on you?" Linda and I nodded.

Linda stepped in. "Canfield is near Youngstown, isn't it? Did Brill work for the EPA in Youngstown?" I turned toward Linda and she had that confident little smile.

"Yes, as a matter of fact. For a few years, I think."

"Did you know there was a case in Youngstown that involved false EPA filings? Is it possible that Henry Brill was involved with that case, too?" I may have mentioned the Youngstown business after Emily had told me about it, but I didn't remember it. I was amazed Lindy knew about it.

More head shaking, studying the floor. "I don't really know anything about that other case. I do know that I never asked Henry or anyone else to post false signs. I do believe that Henry had something to do with it because he told me they were fake when I asked about the pollution on that land. I didn't press very hard as to why or at who's behest the signs were placed there. I simply tried to take advantage of them. I am completely ashamed of that, believe me."

"So," I picked up from Linda, "it's likely that Brill is involved in something illegal, here and probably was in Youngstown. That makes me think he has a lot at stake if he was found out a second time, maybe even jail time. That would certainly encourage him to eliminate the person threatening him, wouldn't it?"

"I can't believe Henry would hurt anybody." Tom Wittenauer was looking for understanding from Hal, Linda and finally me. No one wants to believe the worst about a friend.

"Can I splash a little more Old Overholt in there for ya?" I poured some for Hal and myself, too. Linda magically produced cheese and crackers. We all nibbled.

Now it was my turn to let out a deep breath. Blatchford had not tried to take part in the conversation to this point. I smiled at him and he made a facial expression that I thought indicated his approval of the conversation so far. I got back to work.

"Monday I asked Senator Fahnstahl to obtain an official statement from the EPA office that would let us go forward on a deal to use that rail spur. Have you heard anything from Brill about that?"

I think Tom was debating the way to answer me. I actually hoped he would be honest. "Yes, as a matter of fact he did tell me about that inquiry. I think he told him the numbers were valid. For whatever reason, Fahnstahl didn't press."

"Thanks for being straight on that answer, Congressman. The thing is that I know what the truth is. So do you. The longer the validity of those signs is accepted, the greater the chance our railroad deal is going to blow up in our faces and this contract will blow up, too. You realize we're going to do everything possible to prevent that?"

He just nodded, looking at me with a squint.

"Our efforts could do a lot of damage to your reputation. Sooner or later the police will find Sindledecker and he doesn't seem sharp enough to resist talking. Then they'll get Brill and your connections with him are bound to come out. None of us wants that to happen to you." I stopped to let him think about the possibilities.

"Now if things turn really crappy and we lose our King Frederik opportunity, you just may appear to be one of the destroyers of our contract and all the economic effects that will have. Feelings could run pretty hot. None of us wants that to happen either." His head was shaking again.

For the first time Hal Blatchford spoke up, slowly.

"What can we do to work things out with Brill, Tom?"

"Geez, Hal, I'm not really sure. Henry did this for someone else, originally. That person must have paid him a lot or has a hold on him somehow, and it must be a big hold to cause him to act like this. I don't know."

Blatchford looked at me. Linda repositioned herself.

I pressed forward. "Here's the way for you to come out ahead on this whole shitty business, Tom. You are here because we need your help at a very critical juncture. The original intentions you had to 'take care of' the EPA filings for us, can now be fulfilled – by you. Are you up for it?"

Now he sat forward with his hands clasped tightly, knuckles showing strain. "What are you thinking?"

"You will have to get that official release from Henry Brill. We're dead in the water without it. That's number one. Nothing else comes close. Can you do that?"

His head was shaking again. "The minute I demand that, I'll be an enemy of his, too. If he decides to ignore my request we still have nothing and I'll have a new enemy. Doesn't seem like a plan to me." He was glad it appeared impossible. His arms crossed again.

"Tom, there is no way for you to remain friends with this piece of shit and stay in Congress. You understand that?" Blatchford guffawed but covered it well with a cough. That little act made a bigger impression on Wittenauer than what I'd said.

"I don't see how I can force him to make the release."

"You will have to ratchet up the pressure without flinching." Linda could really cut through. Her words hung in the air. I had never fully appreciated her negotiating skills. Magnificent.

"From what up to what? What pressure?"

I picked up the thread. "You simply tell him he must provide the release or you will have to go over his head. Obviously higher-ups will work with you. He will be made to understand that once you go to someone else, his goose is cooked and he'll be exposed and prosecuted. And that you are just the one to make sure that happens if he doesn't cooperate. It's gonna take some balls, congressman."

"Well, he should come around and give me the release without all the threats." I was ready to choke him. Blatchford let out a sigh.

"You know you are completely wrong about that, don't you Mr. Wittenauer?" Linda asked what I was thinking, except politely. "He has already shown a willingness to kill over this. Just asking won't impress him. He will only respond to a threat of loss." That analysis sounded just about perfect. I stayed quiet.

Wittenauer was very uncomfortable. He must have been running through scripts in his mind and not liking any of the outcomes. Finally he responded. "This is a game-changer, isn't it?" With his eyes still on the floor, it sounded like he was talking to himself.

Linda started to add to what she'd said but I held out my hand to stop her. We waited.

Wittenauer looked up at Linda and then to Blatchford and finally to me. "I can't escape this."

"You can profit from it, actually," I said quietly. Tom sat up.

"What does that mean?" He was slipping in to tough Tom, the deal-maker.

"Let's make a list of what's going to happen when you act. Honey? Can we do one of your options lists?" Silly me, she had a yellow pad next to her on the couch.

"Okay, then. First, either the easy way or the hard way, Brill is going down for this crime and maybe some others." Linda was writing.

"I agree." Tom sounded better.

"In the process, we will obtain our clean release on our parcel... either from Brill or from someone above him." Linda murmured her agreement and Tom nodded. "Now those are both big positives. Someone... maybe a crusading congressman, is going to be recognized for those accomplishments."

Wittenauer tilted his head and smiled for the first time. "Yes, someone is," he agreed.

I looked toward Linda and she gestured me forward.

"To make sure you," I pointed, "are getting the credit, we should bring the police in on this at your initiative. They are chipping away at this from the other side and if they get to Brill on their own, it's no help to you." Wittenauer was getting in to it and even Blatchford was sitting forward intently. I looked at Linda again. She smiled and nodded.

"Now," I gestured with my hands up, "we also need to find out who really did put Brill up to those false postings, if we can. Makes your crusade that much better. Are you sure you've heard no clue as to who that is?"

He shook his head emphatically. "I'm ashamed but I never asked. I saw an advantage for myself. Henry said he would lift the signs when I gave him the word and then hide behind the fact that a U. S. Congressman demanded it. I didn't ask the next question. Mea culpa." I wasn't completely certain that was the whole truth, but if Tom delivered our clean bill of health I didn't care whether we captured other conspirators. Still, his answer was pretty smooth.

"When?" Tom was sitting back like he'd just finished his spiel at a neighborhood coffee.

"Monday. No later than ten o'clock. And whatever you do, don't speak to Brill before then." Wittenauer suddenly had the look of being greatly offended.

"I'm serious, Tom. He's a friend of yours. Naturally you want to help him. You just can't. You can't! Give us your word." He reacted like I'd struck him.

"Who do you think you are? For Crissakes, I said I would!" His facial expressions were perfect for his high dudgeon.

"Who am I? I'm the guy who can ruin your career, you bastard! If I go the police – and I've been there a lot, lately – and deliver you to them, and then speak to the press about your connection to a fraud at the EPA… things will be unpleasant, don't you think?"

Wittenauer's face was red. He looked over to his friend, Hal Blatchford, but his face was cold steel. That made the message. Tom's shoulders sagged and he looked beaten. I put my hand on his, which shocked him further.

"Tom, let's work on the first scenario, huh? This is hard for all of us, but you most of all. I recognize that… we all do. Now you have to step up and make this your finest hour. We are committed to bringing you the greatest possible positive effects. Cleaning this up and helping Blatchford economically is the right thing to do. Let that sustain you. We'll make you the hero." He replied with a quick smile and stood up.

"We both have everything at stake, don't we?" The three of us expressed our assent. He walked toward the kitchen and leaned against the doorframe. "I'll take scenario one." I smiled and Hal and Linda apparently did, too.

"I'll go with you," Linda said. Smiles turned to shock, particularly for Wittenauer.

"What...? Why do you...?" Wittenauer was flabbergasted. "What do you mean?" he finally got out.

"I can make your meeting with Brill go more easily, that's all. He doesn't know me and you can just introduce me by my first name. Let him worry about who I am. I won't say anything unless he gets off track. Good cop, bad cop, you know?"

"I don't know, Lin. It's one thing if Brill tries to attack Tom..."

"Thanks a lot, Walter," said Wittenauer. "But you're right." He really, seriously did not want Linda there. As I thought about it, Linda's suggestion was brilliant. She'd been calculating Wittenauer's reactions and strengths – or weaknesses. Her presence would make him stronger and she was a tough negotiator in her own right. I found her courage striking... amazing.

I glanced back at Blatchford and he was studying Linda, perhaps revising his first impression. He jinked his head toward her when I caught his eye. Linda was in.

"I don't like it, either, Tom, but it's a damn good idea. You can act more like it's out of your hands while never revealing Linda's position. It'll work."

Wittenauer was unconvinced but he shrugged acceptance. I relaxed a bit. This whole damned real estate project might get done. I stood and shook Wittenauer's hand warmly. "Sorry for the rough start, Tom, but you and I will be friends out of this, at least politically."

"We'll see," he replied. "Here's the toughest negotiator," he reached past me and shook Linda's hand. "I'll see you around nine-thirty Monday, evidently."

"I'll be there. It'll be interesting." Her face was firm and she held eye contact with the tall man.

Blatchford had come up behind me. He gave Linda a little kiss on the cheek, thanking her for a fascinating evening, then he turned to me.

"Walter, it looks like we may succeed at last, thanks to Tom, here."

"I agree, Hal. He's our key to success. Let me thank you in advance, Tom." We shook hands again, all around.

"I'll walk out with you, Tommy," announced Blatchford. Wittenauer looked relieved to get out of our pressure-cooker. Linda and I hugged side-by-side to wave goodbye. I imagined that Hal was confirming the stakes for his favorite congressman. I started shaking. I hadn't rehearsed what to say if Tom showed up. Linda's involvement was superb.

"You are fantastic, Lady." I hugged her off her feet and kissed her everywhere... almost.

"You're not so bad yourself. I'd much rather have sex with you than with him."

I made a face. "Are you sure. I can probably catch him for you…!"

"Put me down! I'll catch him myself." I let her down and then swung her up on my shoulder. "Put me down! I'll scream!" She kicked her legs but I held on.

"If you scream, no one will come," I grunted.

Now she was beating on my back with her fists while her legs flailed up and down. I carried her to the bedroom. "I saaaid… if you scream no one will come!"

"Well," she panted, "IF I scream, someone might come." Hmmnnh, the game wasn't going the right way.

"Okay, then, I'm setting you down." I dropped her on the bed.

"You brute!" she said.

"Moi? I'm just a big horny Teddy Bear. See?" There was evidence, too.

"You should learn to control yourself."

"I am controlling myself. Would you rather share a shower?"

"No! There's a lot to clean up, still. Let's get that done and see how we feel. I'm not ready to relax."

"Okay. Make you a deal: Let's clean up without underwear. I'll help every way you want."

"Hmm. Well, that might be interesting. Okay. Hurry up." We both disrobed and put on minimal clothing without underwear. Linda had a tee-shirt hanging loose over gym shorts. I liked it. I had a tee and a bathing suit.

"Here, spray me with bug stuff." I handed her the Cutter's. We headed out back and got... active.

SATURDAY, JUNE 1, 1985

We slept in. Our after-the-cookout session with Wittenauer was draining. But it felt good. I had some leverage over the EPA and that bastard, Brill. I didn't care if he got arrested; I just wanted a clear path to our railroad. That would be like winning the Masters.

I made breakfast this time. I fried and drained bacon. I added butter to the pan and let it melt on the remaining heat and turned to the rest of my omelette recipe. I settled for canned mushrooms and diced peppers and onions. As the veggies sauteed I shook on some Mrs. Dash and a little garlic salt. When the veggies were just so, I tossed in crumbled bacon and some mushrooms and pulled it off the heat.

Linda slipped into the kitchen with her thin coverlet – neither robe nor nightshirt. I liked it. She gave me a hug from behind. "I poured your juice. Have a seat and I'll be serving momentarily, m'lady." This time she took the bench and crossed her legs.

With as much flair as I could summon, I poured Linda a cup of coffee. "Thanks, Jacques," she said.

I made two fluffy omelettes, with grilled English.

More flair as I plunked one before my princess. A side dish of marmalade completed the presentation. Quickly I repeated the steps for another and joined her.

"So," I asked around a mouthful, "what's new?"

"The paper says that space aliens have abducted several congressmen and replaced them with identical-looking shape-shifters."

"I knew it! The things those people say. It's inhuman."

"And here's a story about a mild-mannered cost accountant who wrestled with a big congressman and pinned him... in Penn Hills."

"Wow! Is he good-looking?"

"The congressman? As a matter of fact he..."

"No! The cost accountant!"

"Oh, him? Says he's very attractive to certain kinds of women in their weaker moments."

"Really? Can he cook?"

"Yes. He's been quoted as saying he's one of the best cost-accountant-cooks in Pennsylvania. That story is unconfirmed, of course."

"Is that so? What does it say about his prowess in bed?"

"It quotes his wife who says... umm, here it is: she said he's the best lay in Allegheny County, although her eyes were crossed at the time."

"Such testimony can't be accepted unless confirmed by further testing, scientists have stated," I proclaimed. I lifted one leg and put a foot between her legs. With her sitting cross-legged, there was little to stop me. She had quick hands, though. She grabbed my foot and did her best to hold it to one side, outside her thigh. I saw my chance and slid my other foot into the breech. With one hand on each foot Linda was fighting a losing battle. I worked my way to the ultimate goal, inch by inch.

Realizing the precariousness of her defenses, Linda made a quick maneuver and wound up with my feet under her legs. I wiggled my toes, but it didn't have the right effect. It was a defensive stand-off.

"One of us is going to have to make a move before we get hungry again." I grabbed the marmalade before she could. "I've got my emergency marmalade. I can outlast you."

"That's what you say," she replied. "It says here that women live longer than men when deprived of marmalade."

"But their longer lives are gray and featureless when deprived of hot, wet sex. Did you think of that?"

"I've been thinking about that, yes. There are people I can call, though."

"Oh, is that so? Well this cook will fight them off. I pinned a congressman, you know."

"Okay, then. Who makes the first move?" Linda was rocking from side to side as I slid my feet back and forth. "Quickly."

"You let me remove my feet and I'll give you a two-second head start. How's that?"

"I'm thinking, I'm thinking." She did her best to keep her balance as I pulled and pushed one foot and then the other.

I realized I had the secret weapon: marmalade. Linda hated being sticky. I kept her busy with my fancy footwork while I scraped the rest of the marmalade into my coffee spoon. At the opportune moment I flipped it precisely to land the big gob in the center of her chest, which was delightfully exposed.

"Ohh, you pig!" she exclaimed. She quickly recovered as much as she could and threw it back at me. My face caught it.

"This is war," I said, "and I'm declaring a cease-fire. You have three seconds, now, to make a retreat. I am also offering to lick the marmalade off your chest… for free!"

"Nice offer. I'm considering it. Now, you pull your feet out, and then start your three-second countdown."

"Alright. First this one," and I slid out the right foot, "and now this one," I pulled the left foot out and set it flat on the floor.

I was figuring how I could grab her around the waist as she tried to escape.

Linda had on her best non-threatening face, all innocent sweetness. I smiled to assure her I had no devious plan to grab her around the waist. The next thing I knew my coffee cup was on its side, a brown tidal wave sliding to my right. I tried to stop it with napkins. Linda took her opportunity to slip to her right and away from my clutches. She giggled her way to the bathroom. I peeled off my tee-shirt and dropped it on the table where it would sop up the river.

The bathroom door was closed, but not locked. Linda was on the toilet.

"Hey! Give a girl some privacy, you brute."

"I won't look," I lied. "Let me draw you a shower, m'lady."

I soon had the temperature just right and stepped in to the shower. I started by shampooing and kept on until I realized that several minutes had gone by. I stuck my head out through the curtain and I was alone. Oooh… this was hardball. I had to lay better plans if I was going to share a shower this weekend. I got out and got dressed.

Linda was in the kitchen, clearing up the breakfast things. "Hey, big guy. Did I tell you how impressed I was with how you handled our two guests last night?"

"Two guests?" I tried to cop a feel but she brushed me away.

"Yuh. Wittenauer and Blatchford. You've become quite the negotiator." She knew how to make me feel taller.

"I didn't do anything with Blatchford. What are you talking about?"

"Well, Blatchford was the carom shot. He was definitely impressed with how you handled things. He's confident in you."

"Well, then, he must be impressed with you, too. You made the key moves, especially that bit about going with Wittenauer Monday morning. That is genius."

"Not really. You and Mr. Blatchford may respect him, but I don't think he has earned anyone's trust, yet, and I doubt he has the courage to push Brill to the edge. That's why I made that suggestion."

"Well, I think it was fabulous. In fact, it's giving me a hard-on and I think we should go into the bedroom." I held out my hand and started toward the hall. Linda just looked at my hand and then at me, smiling slightly.

"You'll have to control yourself. I'm busy, and then I'm going shopping." Uh-oh. This Linda was different. I didn't know which wild and crazy thing would get her to jump into the sack. I found myself completely under control.

"Oh, ahh, well, sure. Okay. I've got plenty to keep me busy. You go ahead." I'd find something to do. Something, whatever. I'd show her.

Fifteen minutes later I had my bowling bag and I told her I was going bowling.

"Oh, okay, Honey. That's a good idea. Drive more carefully this time, promise?"

"Absolutely. Very carefully. You got it." We kissed like we were going to work. I stood in the front entry a few moments, waiting for something to happen but nothing did. I felt discombobulated. As I climbed in the car Linda ran out the front door calling me back in.

"You got a phone call, Honey. 'Bucky,' he said."

Omigod, I had forgotten about meeting Bucky. Someone was watching out for me. "Hey, Bucky, I was just getting ready to head out." Linda gave me a funny look. "When do you want me there?"

The man from Wheeling Crane was fifteen minutes away.

"Okay, that's perfect. I'll meet you there. Do you want me to bring anything?" He suggested a couple of coffee's.

"New bowling team member?" Linda had her head cocked to one side.

"No, geez! I had forgotten about meeting Bucky Dighton at the shop. I thought I'd get to talk to Blatchford about it last night but it slipped my mind. Thank God and thank you for getting that call."

"You're going in on Saturday?"

"Yeah, have to. We overlooked a key part of shipping the bridge parts and I'm helping our chief engineer straighten it out. Whew!"

"You need a better remindery, somehow. Tell me about it when you get back, huh?"

"Absolutely. Baby, you're the greatest." I channeled my best Ralph Cramden and gave her a big kiss. "See ya later!" I took off.

"Drive carefully," she said to herself.

***

The Wheeling truck was already there. It had extra steel wheels that could crank down to drive on railroad tracks. It also had a cherry-picker and there was a guy in the bucket up at the top of the masonry wall, taking photographs. Bucky Dighton was looking up at him and I did the same... I could learn something. In a couple of minutes he was back on Earth. Bucky made the introductions.

"Whaddaya think?" I asked in engineering lingo.

"Pretty short time frame, I hear?" Mike Vanier didn't waste words.

"Six months at most. Can we do it?" Vanier was doing a pencil drawing on his clipboard.

"What you're gonna do is replace that old roll-up with swinging doors, but not where it is." He gestured to Bucky and me and placed his clipboard on the hood of my car. He had drawn a tower attached to the building that extended up to the peak of the existing roof. "All this here can be cinder-block with a simple steel frame to mainly hold up the doors. A good masonry contractor will rough that out in two weeks at most. You may already know someone who can make the steel for you."

"Gotcha covered, there," replied Bucky. I was puzzled how he knew that, until it struck me. Duh!

"Basically you'll have four steel posts set...," he stopped speaking and looked at the roof. "This is ridiculous!"

Why, Mike? Whaddayamean, ridiculous?" For a few minutes I thought I was so smart to have initiated all the crane hullabaloo. Now I was worried.

"Well," he said, "first this would mean rebuilding half your shop, probably screwing up your scheduled production on all your orders for months." He shook his head as Bucky shook his. I started shaking mine, too. What the Hell.

Bucky walked over to the plate covering the short siding in the shop floor. He looked left, right and straight up. "Mike, we still have to move forty of these girders in a span of about three months. What about a construction crane... a crawler. Could we find a way to reach into the shop and pick up these things?"

"You'll still have to modify the end of the building quite a bit." He sketched on his clipboard. "Forty-four tons each, you said?"

"Yuh," said Bucky.

"There's some smaller cranes coming out, now, for handling container freight... cranes you can drive around on tires. We don't deal with em, ourselves, but I'd take a look there. Still a lot of construction..." His voice trailed off.

I finally thought of something sensible to ask. "Who would you call for the construction part, Mike?"

"Leighton-Aulson... architects here in the city... work with em a lot."

"Will you take care of calling them, Bucky?" He nodded.

Mike Vanier was still thinking. "You're gonna want to make a really wide opening in this end of the building – and a tall one. If you get the right unit you'll be able to drive up to the girder when the big crane stands it up, tilt it a little to let the bridge pass by, and then drive it out to your flatcars. Hafta pour a platform along the track for a hundred fifty feet, I'd say."

I had one more question for Mike Vanier. "Mike, can you make any sort of guess about what this might cost?"

"Well, Mr. Blatchford, that ain't really my job. But I'll make a prediction if ya want."

We both nodded.

"A half-mil. That's what I predict. Five hundred gees. Give or take. You see if I'm close." He nodded with a smile. "Plus the cost of the reach-stacker - that's what they're called."

"You're at a million and counting, Mr. Blatchford," Mike estimated.

"I'm not Blatchford, Mike. I'm Walter Anton. I have to explain this to Blatchford."

"Better you than me. You better get that architect in here, pronto." Mike left his card and said his goodbyes. I sat looking at Bucky Dighton.

"This is bad, Bucky."

He looked at me over the rim of his cup. His eyes were tired and angry. "I'm a shop-floor guy. We've never shipped anything that wouldn't fit on a flatcar or boxcar, or on a longbed trailer. Was I supposed to think of this shit?"

"I don't know, Bucky. Who's the logistics manager or shipping manager or freight manager or whatever? Maybe it's his job!"

"We don't really have anyone like that. Skinny Butler arranges for trucking and for the C&O to spot us a car – stuff like that. Purchasing does the rest. But way back when we were all told that we'd be shipping on special cars down a track right to the river, I never worried about it. It seemed like somebody higher up was figuring out the shipping part. I've had my hands full figuring out how to cut it, weld it and handle it inside the shop, mostly horizontal. None of us took it upon himself to figure out the vertical. I'm really sorry, Walt."

"I don't think this is anybody's fault. It's new for all of us. Rather than worry, let's cogitate until Monday. Mike gave us an elegant solution. If I tell Blatchford we overlooked a million bucks of expenses… well, I better have a damn good value for that money, know what I mean?"

Bucky smiled a grimace and shook his head. "How do I start thinking about this. I rely on Mike Vanier."

"Just sleep on it, Bucky. It's not a worry, it's a challenge. We'll figure it out." I hoped I was telling the truth. It probably helped that I wasn't an engineer. Seeing it from outside had revealed the problem. I wondered what outsider-ness meant to the solution.

"This was a good thing, today, Bucky. Good that we met with Mike… the whole thing. I think we have identified a solution, don't you?"

He shrugged and smiled. "I'm glad one of us thinks so. I hope you're right." I shook his hand and thanked him again. We walked out together. I looked upwards as he locked the shop door, as if the answer were hovering there.

***

Linda was still out when I got back. I poured some Old Overholt and picked up a paperback mystery. What the Hell? I started to doze with the book slipping into my lap. The phone woke me up.

"Yeah? This is Walter Anton."

"Sorry to bother on a Saturday, Walter. It's Tom Wittenauer." I woke up.

"Yes, Mr. Congressman. What can I do?"

"Well, if you recall, last night you said I should bring the police in on my own. Not to wait for them to catch up with Brill on their own?"

"Yes, I recall that but then I dropped it. I'm glad you called. You want me to set up something?"

"If that's the best thing to do, then yes." Wittenauer sounded despondent, depressed.

"Tom, calling the police on your own suspicions is the best way to take control for your own advantage. Make the news instead of answering for it. Listen, I'll call my contact, Arnie Stewart. He's been on this the longest. I'll tell him you are going to the EPA Monday morning with an assistant, and that your purpose is to demand a statement from your contact, there, and that will expose a fraud. He'll call you, I'm sure. You can describe your concerns about Brill's willingness to strike out at his enemies and that you think it prudent to have some backup. I'm pretty sure Arnie will do the right thing."

"This is getting complicated." I could hear his sense of resignation.

"Tom, this can't work if you expect to fail. You have to be the pillar that will not bend. Brill has got to see that you expect no compromise. When you are done on Monday, you'll either be a lame duck or cruising to re-election. It's on you, but what a story you'll have."

"I suppose that's right. I'll be ready. But, you'll call the police?"

"Yes, immediately. Don't worry, huh? You'll be great at this." I tried to pump up a twelve-year-old little-leaguer. Just get a hit, Tommy!

"Okay, then. Thanks, Walter. I'll look for that call."

"Don't worry. Talk to you soon." We hung up. I had forgotten to call Arnie, but Wittenauer really didn't have the confidence that he'd need Monday morning.

I walked around the kitchen a few times and opened a diet Coke. I dialed Zone Four.

"Pittsburgh Police, Zone Four. This call is being recorded."

"Ahh, yes. I'm calling for Officer Stewart, please."

"He's off schedule. You have an emergency?"

"No, no, not right now. But I will have one on Monday morning. It involves Congressman Wittenauer. I need Officer Stewart to call him at his earliest convenience."

"How do you know you're gonna have an emergency on Monday?"

"Well, it's hard to explain. It's part of an investigation that Arnie... uhh, Officer Stewart has been involved in already. If you could have him call me, first, he'll know why it's important." I gave him my number and told him I'd be available all weekend. He didn't sound too motivated. I went back to my book.

Minutes later Linda walked in the front door, rustling bags of various materials. She dropped them on the couch next to me.

"Well, that's that!" she said. "What have you been doing?"

"Oh, nothing. I polished the heads of some of my favorite screws... waxed my handtools, things like that."

"Oh, good. We were concerned."

"Oh, yeah." I stood up and received a quick hug and kiss. "I waited before eating. Did you have anything in mind for supper?"

"Well, no, but there is that tunafish and some of your London Broil. You could stir-fry some of that. We have leftover salads, too. You want me to serve it up?" Things were different. It was as if I had to make friends with a new Linda. It was unsettling.

"Listen, Lin, I'm sorry about that marmalade business this morning."

"It washed right off. No problem. The omelettes were very good, too."

"Oh, well then, everything worked out I guess."

"I think so," she sing-songed. She started preparing some food and had things ready in minutes. "C'mon, Walt. Sit and eat. We can catch up on things... get ready for Monday, you know?"

"Monday" gave me a chill. No matter how good a negotiator Linda was, challenging Brill was worrisome and unpredictable. She and Wittenauer would be in a busy office among lots of people. It should be a safe environment.

"Wittenauer called me," I announced, "just a little while ago."

She set down her fork and looked right at me. "What does he think?"

"Well, he called to remind me about involving the police, and I called them after he hung up, but he seemed kind of depressed-sounding, all in all."

"Depressed?"

"Yeah. Despondent, you know? I tried to buck him up... told him he'd be terrific on Monday and what a great reelection story and so on." I leaned back from my plate. "I told him what to tell the police when they called, to set things up so that he would come out of it looking good. I know what I'll tell Arnie Stewart when he calls."

"I'm still going with him. It may be the only way to get what you need." She resumed eating.

"Yes, I know. It is a courageous plan and I am proud of you. Still, it's dangerous."

"Well, won't we be in an office with lots of other people? All he can do is shout at us, right?"

"I hope so. The police will be in the lobby, right there, too."

"They will? How so?"

"Well, that's what I'm gonna suggest to Arnie Stewart and what I recommended to Wittenauer, too. I'll come too, if you want."

"No," she said rather quickly. "We don't want Brill to associate me with you. He hates you. The congressman and I will do fine. It'll only take a few minutes."

I dreaded the whole thing but Linda was pretty tough… and a practiced ninja photographer. I had my own battle over the crane business and I wasn't looking forward to that, either.

"I have to sell the crane expenses we've come up with, on Monday."

"What? You mean what you were meeting about today?" She was evidently pleased to stop talking about her Monday.

"Yeah, the problems I spotted about the length of the girders getting out of the shop are even worse because of the height of them. It's gonna require some serious construction on the building and the purchase of another crane."

"You're making a boat you can't get out of the cellar?"

"Huh? Yeah, pretty much. First I asked Bucky Dighton how we'd get the girders onto the middle car of three flatbed cars when only one car gets into the shop, itself. That was bad enough. The man from the crane company recomended a new kind of drivable crane that can drive into the shop and out, holding the girders. It's looking like a million or more that we'd never considered in the cost projections. Bad."

"Well, at least you solved it." Linda started picking up dishes and leftovers. I got up and helped.

"We don't really know if this is the best solution, yet... or what the total cost is. We have to talk to a specialized architect."

"What's wrong with the solution? A drive-around crane, you said."

"Too many things to go wrong. But I'm no engineer. And, when I get the figures I'll have to tell Hal we overlooked a stray million dollars or more of expenses. I told Bucky I'd take the blame for it."

"You did? Why? It's not your fault! Sounds like somebody closer to Blatchford was supposed to think of that stuff. And Bucky's the engineer, right? Shouldn't he have asked those questions?"

"Well, maybe he should, and he's a damn good engineer. It's easier overall if I say I hadn't included these expenses in my projections by a forgivable oversight, what with all this real estate business. It protects Jackson, too."

Linda looked at me with a funny expression. "You can't take on everything for everybody. What about watching out for yourself sometimes?" She had tears in her eyes. "What is wrong with you?" And the tears started to spill out.

I had nothing to say. The worst thing I ever did was make my Lindy cry and I couldn't stand it. "Aw, c'mon, Honey. I'm okay on this. It'll work out. Please tell me why you're crying."

"I don't know, I don't knoooww," she wailed. I hugged her, and she put her face into my shoulder but her arms were folded up tight against her body. I made what I thought were soothing sounds but she didn't soften at all. Finally she turned to break away and I let her go. She wiped her face with Kleenex and leaned against the counter. "Want some tea?" she asked.

"Yes, sure, I'll have some tea." At least we could share something. She busied herself with the fixings and I finished clearing the table and even loaded the dishwasher. Linda got the cups and saucers ready. The kettle whistled. Her face was grim, although she smiled at me as she sat at the table. I sat in the nook. We fiddled with the teabags together. She sipped first.

I plunged into the deep end. "If you are worried about Monday you don't have to..."

"No, no, no. I'm fine with that. It'll be interesting and it'll help you finish the real estate thing."

"Well, how can I help. What can I do?" She just shook her head slowly.

"I think I'm pregnant, Walter." The words came out simply and with no emotion... flat – a balloon that had exhausted its oomph somewhere near the ceiling and plummeted soundlessly to the floor.

I knew I was supposed to be jubilant but she wasn't. I put my hand on hers and waited.

"Aren't you curious?" she asked me.

"Wow! Of course. This is fabulous! We can decorate and tell your parents and I'll paint the stairs and put those non-skid things on the edges and *englishclass* will let you take leave or maybe you can stay home anyway and I'll..." she put her two hands up and stopped me with more tears streaming down her face.

"Easy cowboy. I don't really know if I'm pregnant. I could be coming down with something. But..."

"But this is great news! Aren't you happy?"

"But," she continued. "I haven't had the test yet. I just started worrying more about people trying to kill you and now you're risking your career to help cover up somebody's mistake and I don't like the new Walter being like that. I want the Walter I married who didn't make me worry about things. I mean... I don't mean I'm not proud of you – I am. You're taking on challenges and succeeding and I am proud of you... so much! But sometimes I worry and today it's making me cry for no reason. That's all. No reason." She squeezed her eyes shut to wring out the last tears and dried them again with a napkin.

"Okay," she said. "I'm good... fine. Let's just get this Blatchford business wrapped up as fast as we can, okay?" Her face was almost normal again.

"You'll forgive me for being excited about having a baby?"

"Wouldn't have it any other way. I wasn't sure about what you'd say and I was going to wait until I saw the doctor, but I just seem to know this is real. We must have found the magic way to do things."

"Well, I guess so. It seemed magical to me and I think we should keep in practice, don't you?"

"That will be nice. But not in the delivery room – too crowded."

"I can control myself, you know." She flashed a perfect Linda grin and my stomach slipped back into its normal location. Breathing improved, too. "And I meant all that about getting ready. This'll be terrific. This'll be great. We can name a boy 'Tom' for our congressman; a girl we can name 'Hayley' for Hal Blatchford... whaddaya think?"

"I'll get back to you on that, buster. Let's confirm my belief, first." She was smiling as she finished her tea. Mine was pretty cool. I looked at it and then just slurped it down in one gulp. Linda stood and cleared the teacups. "So, no more booze for me, and I'm cutting down on coffee... more herb teas. And some vitamins, I'm sure... extra calcium. And I'm going to exercise more. We can take classes, too."

"I'm with you all the way, Lindy. It'll be interesting. At the end of it we'll have a baby to name and teach and grow with. It's fabulous. I love you."

Linda came over to me as I stood up. We hugged warmly. "I love you, too, Honey. I think we'll be good parents."

"Mmmmnn... me too." I brushed her hair back and kissed her. "Of course, helping you shower is a task I will be consistent about, too. Don't you worry."

"Is that so? I suppose your assistance will be handy from time to time."

"Oh, yes. Cleanliness is very, very important. And being clean-shaven. I can help with all of that. Oh, yes."

Linda was smiling, even giggling. I was feeling good about my chances of having some great sex this weekend. Both of our chances. I really wanted to make Linda shudder with a great orgasm. We stood there, wordless.

"Well," I said, "what shall we do for the rest of the weekend?" We stepped apart.

"Oh, I don't know... pick out paint colors and wallpaper?"

"But, we don't know if we should pick boy colors or girl colors."

"That's true. Maybe we should check out bassinets and car seats, safe high-chairs and things like that."

"Sounds exciting. But," I raised my hand to stop her protest, "I promised to be with you all the way. So, if I will be useful checking out high-chairs and things, I'm with you."

"I'll let you know if I need you. Don't worry about it this weekend. On the other hand, what did you have in mind?"

"We could take our clothes off and see what happens. I think that's a good plan."

"Wow, that's funny. I've never heard of such a thing. I'll hafta let you know."

"Please do. Meanwhile, I'm going to shower while you're thinking." Might work, I thought. What the Hell?

And, it did work. Her thinking came around to mine. It was a great shower.

***

We settled in to watch the Pirates and the Cardinals play their second game of the weekend. I remembered that I had encouraged Hank Buckley to come back Saturday night. I told Linda I had done so. It was fine with her if he came. We still weren't following my no-clothes plan. The phone rang.

"Walter Anton; who's calling?"

"Mr. Anton, it's Arnie Stewart. You need to speak to me about Monday?"

"Oh, yes. Thanks for calling, Arnie. There's a couple of things. Has Tom Wittenauer called you?"

"No. Is he supposed to?"

"I think he expects that I'll speak to you first, but you should definitely speak with him. He is preparing to challenge Henry Brill about those false filings at the EPA, Monday morning. It could get sticky and he's hoping you can back him up."

"Wait a minute, here. I thought you said he was in on it. Now he's going to expose it? What kind of bullshit is this?"

"Hold on, now. I know how it looks, but I am convinced that Tom Wittenauer had nothing to do with the false signs themselves. He knew about them, but Brill was a friend of his. He didn't do anything about them, which he is ashamed of. But since these attacks on Emily Szepanik and me he is determined to expose the crime and Brill, too. It could get dangerous and that's where you come in."

"You people are fuckin crazy. You've cooked up this operation and then decided to tell the police? What if we can't be there? Ever think of that?"

"I apologize for that, Arnie, honest. It was only last night around ten thirty or so that we got Wittenauer to agree to this. I called you as soon as possible, don't you see? And it's not till Monday."

"Un-fuckin believable. Alright, Eliot Ness, what's the plan?"

"That's where you've got to speak with Wittenauer. He's become a crusader on this. If Brill attacks him or something, he'll need backup."

"You have reason to expect this in the middle of an office? Isn't this at the Gateway Center?"

"Yes, and no, we don't expect it. If all goes well, Brill should come up with the documentation that says there are no EPA filings on the parcel we care about and Wittenauer and his assistant walk out of the office. But Brill will know that he will soon be charged with a federal crime so he might try to flee. It seems he was involved in something like this in Youngstown, too, before this. So he's in big trouble when this comes out."

"Jesus, Christ! You should be talking to the FBI, not me."

"You're right, Arnie. The trouble is we need to get that release from the EPA right away. Wittenauer can get that if anyone can and he feels obligated to do so to make up for not reporting the illegal filings. Don't you see?" Linda was standing next to me, listening to my side of the conversation.

"Listen, Eliot, I have to call in the FBI on this. I don't have any choice."

"I understand, but let me ask you something. Can you wait until Monday to call them in?"

"No. Jesus!"

"Well how long can you wait?"

"I can wait until tomorrow afternoon, but I don't feel like it."

"But..."

"No 'buts.' The FBI is a lot more sophisticated than we are and this is a federal crime all the way. We'll be backing *them* up, on this."

"Yeah, but you are investigating assaults here in Pittsburgh, right?"

"Yeah, so what? Unless Sindledecker is going to be at the Gateway, I don't have any business there."

"I don't know where he'll be."

"Okay, then. You were right to call me, but wrong to think you could manage your own police sideshow, Mr. Anton. Give me a number to call Congressman Wittenauer."

I told him the number I had. I asked him to not make a point about calling in the FBI, when he spoke with Wittenauer. Let him think it's just a police backup.

"I don't know what you're worried about, Anton, but I don't have to tell him. If the FBI decide to tell him, it's up to them. They're in charge on this. I'll talk to you later." The line clicked to dial tone.

"You heard most of that?" I asked Linda.

She nodded. "What are you going to do?"

"Not much I can do. Stewart knows the legal end of it and I don't have anything to say about it. Probably screw it up if I try to steer it any further. We have to trust the FBI."

"I'm confident in them. It doesn't make any difference to me for Monday morning. We'll be in and out. We don't care who arrests Brill, do we?"

"No, I guess not. No. And you're right. Your part will only take a short time and you'll be out of there. You still want to do it?"

"Sure. I still don't trust Wittenauer, but now I'm tired. It doesn't seem that Hank is coming. I need someone to caress me after that baby talk. Whew."

"I'm not sure who I can call on such short notice."

"Oh, there are any number of people, but you'll do. At least give it a try."

Things were going better than I hoped. Cranes, babies, caresses.

MONDAY, JUNE 3, 1985

It dawned rainy but with a light sky to the west and unseasonably cool. June third, indeed. I kept flipping between excitement over the solution to the crane business and dread over Linda's meet-up with Wittenauer. I hadn't heard anything from Arnie Stewart, not that he owed me a report. Whatever he and the FBI had planned was out of my hands.

Linda sounded happy. She was humming and 'da-da-da-ing' as she washed and dressed, maybe to avoid worries. Maybe she really was confident. I wasn't going to screw up her attitude. Being upbeat and confident was what Wittenauer would need and what would get Brill to give us our clean record on the parcel. But I kept getting that feeling you get when you almost fall off a ladder. We drank tea.

Linda had her nicest ensemble, I thought, of a blouse, little jacket thing and pleated plaid skirt. She could have been a professor or a student – alluring enough to keep Brill on edge... maybe. She showed me her look with reading glasses – studious and professional. Brill wouldn't know what hit him.

We kissed and hugged and wished each other luck. I waited for Linda to pull away until she turned onto Jefferson, then I backed out and followed her. Her taillights glowed as she headed down to Rodi Road. At the lights at Rodi I was overcome with a desire to see her again. When it turned green I stepped on it, only to be frustrated by traffic. I tried to jockey ahead on the

Penn-Lincoln, which was unlike me. There were dozens of beige Camrys, but none was Linda's. I said a little prayer, also not like me. Fatherhood.

My thoughts were flying a mile a minute and I had to keep refocusing. I greeted Pauly and thanked him for coming on Friday. Jemay was delighted her beans were eaten and I better not forget that shoulder she was fixin for this Saturday. I assured him I hadn't.

I hung my umbrella on the old coat rack in my almost office and noticed a single white sheet that said "Mr. Blatchford wants you." I called Kelly Galvin.

"I'm here, Kelly," I said.

"Come right up, Mr. Anton." The line clicked off as I tried to ask what was up. It was crane stuff... I was sure of it. I grabbed a blank spreadsheet form so that I could draw a diagram, just in case. I rolled it as I went down the hall. Jack Jackson's lights were on but his office was empty. I ran up the stairs two steps at a time. Kelly waved me into the old man's office. Jack was there.

"Good morning Hal, Jack." I stood between the door and the T-table. Blatchford sat on the T, facing Jack Jackson.

"Siddown, Walter," Hal commanded, neither angry nor happy. I complied, sitting next to Jack.

"Jack tells me we have a crane problem that you and he were going to work on Saturday but he never heard from you. Maybe you can illuminate me?"

"Yes, sir, but I do need to apologize to Jack." I turned to him. "Bucky called me at the last minute, Jack, when Wheeling was almost here. I jumped and ran over here on the spot. It was my fault, but I forgot to call you. Please forgive me - but you may have to wait in line." They both gave me puzzled looks.

"Now," I continued, "there is a crane problem. I don't know how I overlooked the expenses and I still would be if Bucky Dighton hadn't asked me about them. It was a shock…"

"Cut the shit, Walter," Blatchford interjected. "Nobody asked you about these expenses because nobody thought of them. So stop trying to cover for other people. I appreciate what you're doing, but this time you can't. Let's talk."

I let out my breath.

***

Linda swung into the parking garage on the corner of Fort Duquesne Boulevard. It was part of the Allegheny Towers but not far from the Gateway and she was not familiar enough with the area to look for another spot. She held her umbrella and debated before stepping out of the stairwell. The rain was now a heavy mist, but able to make you wet. She opened the canopy and started out. No sense getting damp in good clothes.

On the big directory of engraved plastic signs, most were dark gray and white but "Congressional District Office, Hon. Thomas Wittenauer" was blue. She looked for the EPA: also blue. Okay, ride up to the fifth floor for the congressman, then down to the third for the EPA. Easy. She pushed 'up.' By the time the car arrived about ten more people had joined her. She called out "five" and a man replied, "yeah."

Only one person got off before the fifth floor and three got off, there. As Linda walked toward the district office the man who'd pushed 5 fell into step with her.

"Visiting your congressman?" he asked.

Linda nodded. "He's going to help me with an EPA problem. You?"

"Just some interagency business."

The man held the door as Linda stepped through. No one was at the front desk. Some sort of signal must have alerted people in the back offices because very quickly a thin young man came forward. "I can help you, please!" He announced.

The man advanced ahead of Linda, which seemed odd, and passed the young man his card. The young man, whose desk sign said "Devlin Wakefield," changed his demeanor in a flash and immediately called someone else by phone.

"Just go right in and speak to Wendy. Thank you," he singsonged. The man went into the back, closing the door. Linda finally received the young man's attention and looked into his eyes for the first time. She got the strangest feeling of recognition. She tried to study his face but he kept looking away.

"And what can we do for you, madam? Do we have an appointment, today?"

"We?" Linda asked. Devlin looked up at the ceiling, rolling his eyes.

"No, madam. Do *you* have an appointment with the congressman?"

"Yes. Just tell him Linda is here, would you?"

"Fine, then. You may be seated in one of those leather chairs." He waved Linda toward the three seats. She sat as he called in.

"Well," said Devlin, hand on hip, "He really is expecting you. It's straight back and to the right." He flailed his fingers toward the door. Linda stopped by the desk and waited a few seconds for Devlin to look her way.

"Devlin, I get the strongest feeling that we have met elsewhere, don't you?" Linda tried to get him to look straight at her but he seemed unable to.

"I suppose it's possible, Madam, but I don't think it's so." He then busied himself with his back to her.

Linda went through the door, straight back and to the right.

"Good morning, Linda!" Wittenauer's best campaign smile greeted her as he reached an arm around her shoulders and guided her to a seat. "You look very, very nice, Linda, I must say. Henry will be unable to resist, eh?"

"We can hope." Seated next to Linda was the man she had entered the office with.

"Let me introduce Special agent Mark Tallman. Linda Anton, Mark Tallman." They stood to shake hands. Wittenauer rolled an office chair over to them and sat facing them.

"Let's just review what's happening downstairs, this morning, shall we?"

Agent Tallman took over the meeting. "This meeting at the EPA is intended to obtain a statement from Henry Brill. Am I right?"

Wittenauer and Linda looked at each other. Tom gestured for Linda to speak.

"Agent Tallman, what do you know about why we are meeting with Brill?"

"I believe Mr. Brill is suspected of fraudulent activity and may attempt to flee as a result of your meeting. Beyond that I am not at liberty to discuss."

Linda nodded. Wittenauer was happy to let her keep speaking. "Are you aware that Henry Brill is also suspected of hiring a thug to kill my husband and a woman who worked here at EPA? And that, in fact, the woman, Emily Szepanik, was killed?" Tallman was trained to keep secrets, but his face briefly revealed that the murder business was news.

"Those are under the jurisdiction of local police, I believe. I am here only because Mr. Brill is a federal employee. Mr. Wittenauer has asked for backup in case Brill attempts to flee."

"Who else is with you, agent, if I may ask?" Linda was becoming irate to learn that Wittenauer's "backup" was only partly aware of the situation.

"I'm the one on site, which is standard op for white-collar crime situations, particularly where we don't yet know if a crime has been committed. I have my radio to call for both federal or local support. I don't think there is much to worry about. I'm here as a favor to Congressman Wittenauer, primarily."

Linda studied his face without emotion. After a few moments the agent became uneasy and shifted his gaze to the congressman and to various items in the large office.

"Agent Tallman," she resumed, "will you make one call to have at least one more person here before we go downstairs?"

Tallman shook his head slightly and looked at Wittenauer. The congressman smiled tight-lipped and gave a little shrug, demonstrating his lack of concern about what might happen but... but, if the little lady was that worried... Linda watched all this and felt the steam start to build. She stifled it. Being upset might totally screw up the drama they were about to take part in. She applied a sweet smile.

"Well, if you two men are not worried, let's just get going, hmmn?" What could Brill do in the middle of the office, for Heaven's sake?

"Okay, Congressman?" Tallman stood and adjusted his suitcoat. Linda could see that he probably had a shoulder holster, but doubted his presence would matter if Brill flew off the handle.

"I'll just get my coat. I'm set," Wittnauer said as he shrugged it onto his shoulders and smoothed it out. "Linda?" she stepped forward and led the trio out through the door to the waiting area. Devlin stood up when Wittenauer entered. Linda managed to get a full-faced look at him and her unease about knowing him sharpened. She shook it off. They marched out into the hall and to the elevator by the fancy law firm.

***

"Okay, Hal. I apologize. I do feel as though I should have thought of the crane expenses before this. It seems so obvious now that I see it. I don't know who else might have thought of it and I didn't want to get Bucky in trouble..."

"All right, all right. It really pisses me off that none of us thought of this. However, I am really glad that someone did. If that was you, then thanks. Now, you have given this some thought, where are you on it?" Jack was silent next to me. I looked at him before I answered.

"At first I thought only of the inability to position the girders upright on three flatcars when only one car fits in the building, you know?" Blatchford harrumphed his understanding. Jack just said "Hmmn."

"Then, as we're talking to Mike Vanier from Wheeling Crane, it kind of became obvious to all of us that the forty-foot height of the things can't pass under our crane. So even if we get em on the cars by extending the crane outdoors, we still have a problem. That's where the dollar signs really started to show up."

"Like what, Walt," asked Jack Jackson. I was surprised but Hal didn't react.

"Until we talk to the architect, it's mostly guesswork, but on Saturday we pretty quickly slid from a hundred thousand or so to a half-million to more than a million. Scary stuff, if you ask me."

"What makes it so costly?" Jackson, again.

"Well, at first the guy from Wheeling Crane was trying to figure out how to extend our overhead crane outside and all the construction required for that. He changed his mind in the middle of it, though." I took a breath.

Blatchford, now, "But you think you have a better solution? Like what?"

"A mobile crane called a 'reach-stacker' that can be driven inside and outside of the shop."

"Jesus Christ, Anton." Blatchford stood up and pressed the button to open the drapes overlooking the shop floor. "Son of a bitch, Anton." I sat still. Jack had written "New drivable crane" and an "=" sign. Blatchford was looking intently at the crane and at the peaked ceiling and clerestory above it. He shook his head as he came back to the table.

"How the fuck is this gonna work?"

I spent the next half-hour drawing the end of the building and how large a platform we'd have to pour along the siding, outside. I promised to get some specs on "reach-stackers," and their costs. I explained that the extra lift capacity would have substantial future value, not just for the King Frederik. The best point was that part of the extra cost to upgrade our present crane would be available to defray costs on the new crane. Jack Jackson made copious notes.

"When is that architect coming?" asked Hal Blatchford.

"Today, I believe. I may have a message from them waiting for me. They're a local outfit, highly recommended by Wheeling Crane."

"I think we're in two million country, here, gentlemen. But I don't see a smart way to ship these things otherwise. We're not going backwards, now, so let's do this step intelligently, hummn?" Jack and I agreed, actively.

"And Walter, if you want to stay on this, too, go ahead. Tell Jack, here, every day what has happened on it. Jack, you nursemaid this. We'll need reports on every change that has to be made inside the shop, especially. Get Bucky Dighton's input at every turn, both of you. Got it?" We nodded. "Okay, then."

***

Agent Tallman held the door as Linda and Wittenauer entered. The tall representative walked directly to the reception desk and spoke to one of the women. She smiled and started to dial the extension for Henry Brill.

"He's here. Should only be a minute," he explained. Linda walked in small circles forcing her worries into the background. Agent Tallman stood apart from the congressman and his "assistant."

Moments later, Brill, himself, stepped into the lobby. When he saw his old friend, Tom, he broke into a wide smile, clasping his hand and arm. "What's up, Tom?"

"I got a couple things you can help me with, Hank, if you can take a minute. This is my, um… assistant, Linda."

Brill ran his eyes up and down Linda's small frame, virtually taking inventory. "Well, yes, very pleased to meet you, Linda." He smiled and winked at her. "So! C'mon in folks." He held the side door and they disappeared into the offices.

FBI Special Agent, Mark Tallman, stood by the one outside window. He studied every part of the lobby and flashed a smile when he caught the eye of the receptionists.

"Is there someone I can call for you, sir?" the one whose sign said 'Jean,' asked the agent.

"No thanks," Tallman answered.

"Ahh, well, sir, is there some reason you are waiting here?"

Tallman stepped up to the counter and showed Jean his FBI badge. Her eyes widened into saucers. "I am simply waiting for the end of the congressman's meeting. Nothing to be concerned about, at all, ma'am."

"Oh... okay, umm, Mr. ahh... special agent, I guess."

"Yes, ma'am," smiled the tall, manly FBI agent.

Tallman resumed his post by the window, eyes roving the rest of the room from trained habit. Jean McArdle returned to answering calls and connecting callers. After a few minutes she told her partner that she was going to the ladies' room. Tallman took no notice.

After a bit Jean returned to her post, carefully watching for any suspicions on the part of the handsome FBI man. The minutes ticked away while Tallman grew more and more interested in what was visible outside the window.

***

"Let's get a fresh coffee before we start." Brill led his two guests to the same kitchenette Walter Anton had visited in bare feet. Linda stayed bored, deferring in little ways to Tom Wittenauer. Brill was overly solicitous of everyone's delight with his or her coffee. "Right this way, lady and gentleman, to my palatial office and my majestic view of... the rest of the office!" He and Wittenauer chuckled. Linda stayed demure, looking bored.

Brill beamed as he looked from Tom to Linda and back to the congressman. "What can I do for you, Tom? Somebody irked about pollution?"

"Oh, I guess there's always somebody irked about something, hey?" Tom was still smiling with his friend,

"So, what can I do? I'm not in a rush, or anything, but there is a big-deal meeting at eleven. So?"

"Well, Hank, you remember those filings on that stupid parcel eight-forty in Southside?"

"Oh, not again. I'm starting to hate that parcel. Did you know that Senator… uh, Tom, is this discussion okay with…" He gestured toward the assistant, Linda.

"Oh, no problem, Hank. Linda is with me, just making sure I don't screw up my own schedule, you know? You'll see, if I stay too long, she'll be making sure I keep moving. Best thing I ever did. Totally okay."

"Yeah, heh, heh, I'll bet, Tom. Wish I had one."

"Oh yeah." Tom gave Brill a syrupy, smug look. Linda choked back the disgust she felt for the two lecherous dopes in whom she now feigned disinterest.

"Anyway, Tom. What about those filings?"

"I really need to get them lifted, now, Hank. Hal Blatchford is putting unbelievable pressure on me to deliver. I mean whatever you can do, you know?"

"We need a clean document of some kind, Congressman," Linda piped up.

Brill looked at her as if she were suddenly despoiling his office. From lecherous winks to a sneer, Brill's face could display a disturbing range of emotions. Linda looked at him with her best innocence, a tight smile on her lips.

"Almost forgot," Wittenauer shook his head with a smile. "She's right as usual. I gotta bring back a statement of some kind to fend off the Three Rivers Trust, evidently."

"This making you nervous, Tom?" Brill asked the question quietly, his eyes like black pearls.

"Uhh, why… no, Hank. Should I be nervous? Huh, huh, huh." Tom stood and placed his hands on his back, under his suitcoat, and looked out over the cubicles. "I'm just in a Hell of a bind over these filings. You understand, right? I promised big Blatchford I would resolve these signs on the parcel he needs. Now he expects me to deliver, so I have to turn to my friend Hank, don't I?"

"I was gonna tell you, Tom, how our friend Fahnstahl was asking about the same fuckin signs just a few days ago. Hell of a coincidence you coming in like this to ask about those things. Could make a person wonder just what the Hell is going on, don't you think?"

Tom had his hands up, waving off any possibility of coincidence, as an aide tapped on Brill's office door. Perhaps welcoming the interruption, Brill waved her in. She looked tentative as she walked between the congressman and her boss. "Tracie! Have you met your congressman? Tom Wittenauer? Tom? Meet Tracie McKittrick, one of the best!" Wittenauer shook the young woman's hand. She smiled and made a hint of a curtsey. For a few seconds no one moved and then Tracie remembered her mission and passed a folded note to Henry Brill and left. Everyone sat down again.

Brill glanced at the note and slipped it into his center desk drawer. "I am finding this meeting rather strange, Tom. I'm concerned, I really am. You and I both know I don't control those filings or the signs, either. It will take some serious time to get things resolved through the levels of management – you know how it is. We haven't even finished our determination of what is in the ground over there. I understand that the State environment people are starting to look at that parcel, too. So it isn't moving fast." Brill sat back looking very serious about the steps of procedure EPA filings engendered.

Wittenauer sat facing Brill, mouth open to speak but saying nothing. Finally he managed to wet his lips. "Are you… I, ah, think this sounds like you are saying the filings are, um… real?"

Brill looked at his old friend as if he were suffering some kind of breakdown. "Real, Tom? I'll tell you what's real…"

Linda jumped in. "Mr. Brill, wouldn't it be a lot simpler to give Mr. Wittenauer the release statement rather than have us go over your head to get it?" Brill's head snapped around like a snake, his face lowered as he looked up at Linda.

"Is that a threat you two had prepared to make me do what you want?" He looked from Linda to the congressman repeatedly. No one answered his question. "This is really rich, Tommy," Brill snarled, still looking up across his brow. "First that prick, Walter Anton," he sing-songed the name, "comes in here threatening me and embarrassing me, and now his fuckin wife slides in here with you, Tom Wittenauer, my old friend from Ohio State." He slid his reptilian eyes over toward Linda, again.

"You think I could be so easily fooled, LINDA?! Linda Anton! Miss cutesy tightass?"

"Shut up, Henry!" Linda looked quickly toward the congressman, surprised at the sound of his indignation. Brill sat up straighter, staring daggers at Wittenauer. "Give me the release and things will go much better for you. I will go all the way up if you refuse."

Brill sat back, his hand on the edge of his center drawer. "Tom, this doesn't sound like you. You just want the release or else? And maybe a check for the campaign? How would that be?" He sounded weirdly cheerful.

Linda stood and moved over next to the taller Wittenauer. "Tom, it's time for plan B, don't you think?"

Brill stood as well, sliding a small automatic pistol from his desk drawer. "This is plan B, Linda. I call it plan 'bullet.' There are plenty in the clip. You can both go to Heaven, you see? That's way over my head, huh? A pistol this size won't be loud enough to alert your Special Agent in the lobby, do you think? Oh, how silly. You've never heard it go off, have you? Take my word for it. I'll pull the blinds so that you won't be disturbing the many hard-working EPA drones doing their important work. I'll go out the back way and it'll probably be fifteen or twenty minutes before FBI-man gets suspicious. So, let's execute plan B, shall we?"

Wittenauer launched himself directly at Brill. "Run, Linda!" Brill's pistol went off, muffled by Wittenauer's body. The momentum carried Brill into the wall behind his desk, partly pinning him. Linda stood in shock momentarily. Brill struggled to get his gun free to shoot again. No one seemed to pay attention in the rest of the office. Linda dashed out, disoriented. She knew how to get to the coffee room.

***

"Jack, let's meet every day on this crane and construction stuff, okay?" We stood at Jack's real office door.

"I think we should, too, Walt. This change is going to be exciting and I'm glad to be part of it, as I imagine you are."

I wondered how Jack expected our meetings would go. What parts would we play? Would we really accomplish anything jointly? Within all this, Hal Blatchford had a plan for the two of us and I wasn't clear on it. We'd find out.

"Yeah, I am. We've got our work cut out for us to pull this off in six months. The next thing is the architect, obviously."

"Yeah. I called them first thing this morning."

"You did? Who?"

"Leyton-Aulson." He saw my raised eyebrows. "I asked Bucky." I kept my reaction small.

"Good. When can they come?"

"Any minute, now, I expect. I'll buzz ya."

"All right. Thanks. Right now I gotta call our congressman to find out how he made out with the EPA." Now Jack's eyebrows shot up. I didn't elaborate. "I'll see you with the architect."

"Yeah, yeah." Jack finally went in to his office. I hustled to mine and picked up the phone.

"District Office, Congressman Wittenauer. How may we help you?" I recognized sweet Devlin.

"Why, good morning, Devlin. It's me, Walter Anton. Remember me?"

The cheerful greeting switched to a flat, nasaly tone. "Yes, I remember, Mr. Anton. What do you want?" Wow, what a petulant little prick.

"I need to speak to your boss, Devlin. He is absolutely expecting my call."

"Hold on." The line clicked and then delivered Muzak. I tuned it out and thought about the morning so far. I jerked back to full alert when Devlin cut in.

"He's at a meeting elsewhere in the building, I'm afraid. I will give him your message when he comes back. I'm afraid that's it, mister." He hung up. I stared at the phone for a moment.

The meeting with Brill had to have started thirty or more minutes earlier. How could it still be going on? Then I thought of the probability that Linda would call me as soon as they were out of there. I hadn't heard from her so maybe they started later. Must be that. I called Schumann.

"John Schumann."

"John? It's Walter Anton. How ya doin?"

"Ahh, Walter. Just the man I need. Tell me you've got a plan for those EPA filings."

"Funny you should ask about that, John. Wittenauer and my wife are meeting with Henry Brill right now, as a matter of fact. How about that?"

"Your wife? Why is she involved?"

"Long, long story, John. Let me just say that both Wittenauer and Hal Blatchford came to a cookout at my house, Friday night, and this is the plan that emerged from that. I'll tell you about it."

"Well, sounds interesting. Let's say you get your releases. You say Hal is ready to deposit his escrow?"

"Yup, but not until he has to."

"Wouldn't expect otherwise. Listen, we are practically set. Akers is in for three hundred. He formed a Trust with an agreement with the PDC, to purchase the buildings and land and to redevelop the space. His money is in escrow and the city is ready to make a double signature deposit in the same account, subject to the PDC's approval. Those grants come to almost seven hundred. Blatchford's donation may only need to be seven-fifty because there's still some negotiable leeway."

"What about Roberta?"

"Ahh… best part. Forrest informed her about the potential action on this project. She was very appreciative. I think they've had a little bit of a dry spell, tell you the truth. She pulled out her renderings and Akers let her advise him on how to structure a contract with the PDC for beautification of the land in that complex intersection. She feels in charge but doesn't have the picture on the financing. She does have preliminary approval for her design and the traffic pattern, with the County. It will actually save us some time and avoid last-minute…" He stopped speaking and I could hear a woman's voice in the background. He came back to me.

"Wow, Walter! This is weird. My secretary tells me there was a shooting at the Gateway One building. Isn't that where the EPA is?"

***

Linda crouched below window level in the coffee room. There were no unusual sounds coming from the rest of the office. So far no one had noticed the shooting, nor had they noticed Linda scurrying past their cubicles. Maybe I should just tell someone to call the police, she thought. Brill has probably made his escape. How bad is Wittenauer? He needs medical help! I've got to get to a phone! She stood up and looked around the corner of the door frame.

Looking left and right, Linda tried to see the closest cubicle opening. All seemed solid until there was a wide opening into the main part of the office. Along the coffee-room wall it looked like office doors. To the right was a conference room. What was the next room to the left? Would she know how to use the phone? She had to try. She took a breath and started down the hall to the next office. She heard some commotion.

"Lindaaa!" It sounded like Brill. "Lindaaaa, where are you?" His voice was varying like a child calling for his lost mom. Behind him came a scream. Linda froze. Then came a shot and more screams.

"Get out! Get out!" Suddenly there was a cacophony of movement, bumps, screams and chatter. Over it all she could hear, "Lindaaa!" She ducked back into the coffee room. She needed somewhere to hide. The only possibility was the cupboard under the sink, double the width of the others. Linda switched off the lights. The windowless room became dim, but not dark. Linda crawled silently across the floor and opened the cupboard. Inside were bottles of dish soap and airspray, a roll of paper towels and stacks of foam coffee cups. Carefully, she moved it all to one corner. She could fit.

The office was much quieter. A few doors slammed. Someone ran past the coffee room toward the front. Another shot rang out, a man cried out. Linda backed into the black space and pulled the doors closed.

"Lindaaa. We're alone now. Come out, come out wherever you are! Lindaaaa..." He seemed to be only a few yards away.

Linda shrank back, under the sink, her feet pressed against the back panel.

"Linnnn-daaaaa! Walter is very worried about you! Come out now and we can call him so he won't worry. Linda?"

What is the matter with me, she thought. I should be throwing things at this jerk, and escaping, not cowering like a child. She heard Brill whispering hoarsely.

"Lindaaa. We are still friends, you and I. I won't mind giving the release to you. Just say the word and we can wrap this up in a few minutes. I'm sure my friend, Tommy, won't mind if we negotiate while he's on his back."

She shrank back in a tight little ball. The panel behind her moved and abruptly popped backwards with a sharp, scraping sound. Her feet hung into the space behind the sink unit.

"Why, thank you, Mrs. Anton. You do want to work things out, eh? Just make one more little sound and we can be meeting face to face. If you don't want to say anything, I understand. Just scrape something, again. That'll work for me. Will that work for you? We can conclude our business and get out of here in time for lunch. Is that a plan, Linda?" He seemed to be right at the door of the coffee room, perhaps at the cubicle wall waiting to hear which room to enter. Linda tried to feel what was behind her by reaching out one foot as far as she could. It edged back until her knee was touching her ankle and her foot was touching the panel that had popped out. It seemed to be leaning back.

***

I ran out of the office and jumped into the rental. I flicked on the radio and punched 1410 AM, the all-news station in Pittsburgh.

"... still not known where the shots were fired but a small crowd has gathered outside the building. A few minutes ago we asked police on the scene if anyone has been injured or sent to a hospital. Here's what we were told:

"the situation is still very fluid, and we are issuing no statements at this time."

"Are the people who are standing outside the building workers from that building? Can you just answer that?"

"Yes, Mary, they are employees. They will be moved away very shortly."

"Alex, we don't have any more than that... oh, okay, there they go. Everyone in the plaza and in the lobby is being moved into the parking garage as we speak. Officers are now positioned on every level of the garage, itself. Oh, ahh, it looks like, well, Alex, there are at least four ambulances pulling in to the plaza. Police are keeping them in the shadow of the parking garage entrance. We will keep rolling on this event. For now, Alex, back to you in the studio."

I sat for a moment, breathing in gasps, more frightened than I could remember. I slammed the car door as I ran back in to the office.

"What's upsettin you, t'day, Mr. Walter...?" Pauly asked. I was through his entry room before he could finish. I grabbed my desk phone and called Arnie Stewart from memory.

"Pittsburgh Police, Zone Four. This call is being recorded. Do you have an emergency?"

"Yes!" I shouted. "I absolutely do! I need Arnie Stewart."

"Officer Stewart is out on a call, sir. Let me take your information. Where are you...?"

"Never mind that! My wife was meeting at the Gateway One building! Do you know who has been shot?"

"Take it easy, sir. Who is your wife?"

"Anton – a-n-t-o-n. Linda is the first name. Do you know...?"

"No sir, not any details. So far as I know one man, an FBI agent, has been wounded and he's being treated at the scene before being moved. There has been no mention of a woman."

"Thank you, I'm sorry for shouting."

"Yes sir. What shall I tell Officer Stewart?"

"Tell him I've gone down to the Gateway building. Thanks!" I slammed the phone down and ran.

This time Paul Lemay stood in the way. "Hold on, Mr. Anton, hold on." He held me by both arms, and with surprising strength. "Just stop fo a minute!"

"Pauly," I panted, "Linda might be shot down at the Gateway..."

"I hear ya, Mr. Walter. I hear ya." He still held me with vise-like grips.

"You think you're gonna jump in that car and tear down the street and speed like a demon to the Gateway. I can't let you do that. Theys no point at all to you killin yo'self trying to help your Linda who may not be hurt a bit. You know what I'm sayin is true."

I took a couple of breaths. "You are right, Paul. I'm okay. I'll drive well and make sure I am fully alive when I arrive."

"There you go, then, suh. Now we both feel better. Now get goin and say a prayer. That's what I'm gonna do."

"Thanks, Pauly. I'll talk to you later." I waved and hustled out to the Chevy, carefully started the motor and turned on the AC. I backed out smoothly and pulled away. Pauly stood on the granite step, watching.

I had to calm myself as I drove. I took the Birmingham and then the Penn-Lincoln downtown, swinging off on Commonwealth and into the Gateway Center near the Allegheny Tower. The rest of the entrances were blocked with cruisers. I parked illegally and ran toward the police line. There were more reporters than bystanders, and more police than anything. Police kept me from getting closer than about a hundred yards.

I finally got an officer to answer my entreaties. "Look, officer, my wife is in there. Can you just tell me what office the shootings were in?"

"What is your name, sir?"

"Anton, Walter Anton. My wife's name is Linda. She was in a meeting at the EPA!"

"Hold on a minute, sir. Stay right here." I stood where he directed as he walked over to a superior officer. A reporter stuck a microphone in my face.

"Sir, is it true your wife is one of the victims in there?"

"Holy shit!" I snarled. "Can't you wait until I find that out myself? For crissakes!"

"You told the officer your wife was at the EPA where the shootings were. Can you verify...?"

I turned fully around. "What? You know it was at the EPA? The shootings?"

"That has been mentioned, although nothing official. Was she there with an FBI agent?"

"Yeah, maybe. And with Congressman Wittenauer. What have you heard about him?"

She held up one finger for me to wait, as she reported back to the station that Congressman Wittenauer may have been involved in events at the EPA.

***

"Lindaahaaa! I need you to help me with this statement of release. I think that together we can help Walter run his railroad, don't you? It will take only a few minutes, Lindaaaa. Let me know where you are so we can, um, get down to real business. What do you think of that, Lindaaaa?"

Brill seemed closer, but it might just be my fear, thought Linda. Suddenly the light in the coffee room clicked on. Maybe he had only reached in to flip the switch. She reached back a little farther to see if there were more floor. The toe of her shoe rubbed against what felt like cement. She wished she'd taken her heels off first. Now she had to make sure one didn't fall off. She held completely still and breathed through her open mouth. Calm, calm, calm, she told herself. She willed herself to relax. Somewhere she'd read that tense muscles make jumpy movements. That could create a noise. Can't have any noise, she thought.

Brill called her name again, but he seemed to be in the doorway of the next room. Linda let her extended leg bend until her knee reached the concrete floor. She slowly, agonizingly slipped her other leg back, back, back. Her shoe fell off. The noise was tiny. She stopped moving.

"Lindaaaa! Linnnnnnda! Are you afraid of me? That's very silly, Linda. I don't have any anger for you, Linda. None whatsoever. You have never betrayed my trust, have you? No, of course not! You and I can work things out. But we'll need to be face to face, isn't that right?"

Brill was definitely next door. Linda tried moving again. Why haven't the police come to capture him? Everyone was screaming, they must have told the FBI agent what was going on. What was taking so long? Slowly she moved her leg until her second knee was on the cement floor in the darkness behind her. She had to angle her legs to one side to keep from pushing the panel again. Bit by bit she shifted more weight onto her knees and off her hands. Soon her hands were on the edge of the shelf under the sink. Suddenly there was a shout.

"Henry! Henry Brill! Pittsburgh Police! Throw your gun down the hall toward the rest rooms. Then walk this way, hands on your head!" Silence.

Linda heard a soft swishing sound and then nothing. She stayed frozen. The light in the coffee room went dark. Then a boom like a cannon!

"Get the fuck out! I'll come when I'm fuckin ready!" Another shot! It was answered by a yelp and some furniture falling over and then, "Ahh, shit! I'm shot!" There were more shouts and some commotion. Linda hadn't moved. Carefully she tried to calm herself, again.

The space she had backed into seemed to be about three feet deep. She had kept her head down as she backed out from under the sink. Now she stretched a little as she raised her head. There was the dimmest change in the darkness. Still, only black shapes in the almost-black. If Brill followed her in here she'd be trapped. He could shoot blindly and hit her.

***

I tried to signal to another officer but even those who saw me, ignored me. The radio lady was asking me questions from a couple steps away. I pretended to not hear her. I was frantic. Each time my eyes fell on the reporter, she pressed harder to get me to talk. I concentrated on the cops.

The officer I had given my name to was coming back. "If you will come with me, Mr. Anton." We walked to the parking garage.

"There are still some people on the upper floors, sir, but we are bringing them down in groups. Let's walk through the people here and you'll spot your wife. Here we go."

We walked down one row of cars and up the other side. Unhappy people were sitting on fenders, leaning against cars, leaning against concrete posts. There were no more than a dozen office and folding chairs. The oldest workers had those. There were now about five hundred people who had been working just twenty minutes earlier. Some were from Wittenauer's office. I recognized Devlin, who ignored me. Linda was not there.

"Are you sure, sir?"

"Am I sure? Of course I'm sure. If I hadn't seen her she'd have spotted me! She's not here!"

"Hold on a few minutes, sir." He started to walk away. I looked at his back.

"Hey!" I shouted, "hey, hey, hey, officer!" He stopped and faced me. "That means she's still in there, doesn't it? She's in the EPA office! Who's shooting? Is it Henry Brill? That's it, isn't it?" I was totally pissed off.

"Sir, please. We're trying to get to the bottom of this. She may have left before the crowd and is on her way home, you don't know."

"Oh, yes I do. You gotta tell me what's happening up there!"

"All right, sir. Come with me." We started to walk toward a staircase when a woman's voice called out to me.

"Mister, mister. You met Emily!" I stopped and grabbed the sleeve of the officer's uniform. We turned toward the voice. It was the lady I'd spoken to at the EPA front desk. She'd seen me with no shoes and probably at Emily's church services.

"Yes, yes, hi! You saw my wife this morning?" She was a fairly large woman and panting as she approached.

"I think so. A pretty woman with a plaid skirt!"

"Yes, yes, a plaid skirt. That's right! What happened?"

The cop held his hand up to hold her off. "Ma'am, you work at the EPA?"

"Yes, at the reception desk. She came in with the congressman and an FBI man. The FBI man was shot first, right in the doorway. We hid behind the counter. Then when everybody came out screaming we left as fast as we could."

"Ma'am, why don't you come with me. I'd like you to speak to my captain." The receptionist was pleased to be part of events. The three of us went down one flight and into the lobby of the building. It looked like a full S.W.A.T. team was deployed in the lobby. One black-clad trooper stood next to the door we came through, four more stood in the space between the two banks of elevators, and others were guarding other doors. A half-dozen Pittsburgh uniforms stood near the empty guard station to our left. A knot of suits were huddled by the tree planters near the doors to the plaza. I looked twice and realized that Axel Johnson was among them. Might explain his odd schedule. I looked for the officer who had led us in and spotted him walking toward us. He peeled away from the group and went to Axel's group. Axel, himself, came over.

"Axel!" I called, "why are you here?"

He showed me his FBI badge. "Just business, Walt. I'm very sorry it has to involve you and Linda."

"What do you know about where she might be?"

His head was shaking. "Nothing, right now, Walt. People who left the EPA don't recall seeing her leave. Only a couple of them saw her come in. She was with Wittenauer, you know."

"Oh, boy, do I know. We planned it out Friday night!"

"You what? At the cookout?"

"Yeah. At the cookout you left in a hurry."

"Walt, I… I couldn't be there with Tom Wittenauer. I can't explain that. It just would have been, umm… awkward. Might have screwed things up for you, too."

"Are you investigating him?" He held his hands up to ward off more questions.

"Right now our interest is Brill, upstairs. He's managed to shoot Wittenauer, the special Agent who was in the EPA lobby, and a local officer. So far we have no information about whether he, ah, may have wounded Linda, too. No news is good news, I think."

I moved to ask him for more but he turned and gestured to one of the local officers who wanted to talk to the receptionist and me. We followed him to the guard station where there were some chairs. A few of us sat.

"Walter Anton?" An officer was scanning our faces. I raised my hand.

"Right here!"

"Okay, Mr. Anton. I know you are worried and we want to do everything we can without endangering Mrs. Anton, so please bear with us for a coupla minutes, okay?"

There was damn little I could do. I nodded.

"You're familiar with our officer Arnie Stewart, yes?"

"Yuh! We have spoken about problems here at EPA, before."

"Arnie sustained a bullet wound upstairs just a few minutes ago. He's not seriously injured…" he held up his hands as some people murmured their concerns, myself included. He tried to get the suspect to toss out his weapon and was answered by a couple of shots, one of which penetrated the cubicle and hit him. Apparently the suspect is using a small caliber automatic. Officer Stewart is still on site being treated by EMT's. He recommended we contact you but, obviously, you contacted us."

"Where is Mrs. Anton?" I asked.

"We don't know, to be honest. She hasn't contacted us or made any noises we can use to find her. We are operating on the assumption that she is in hiding or being held by the suspect. You say that she planned to be here this morning with Congressman Wittenauer? Who were they meeting with?"

"Henry Brill. Is that who you are calling the suspect?" The receptionist who had recognized me touched my arm and whispered loudly that she had already told them it was Henry Brill. I nodded at her and patted her hand to thank her.

"Right now we aren't certain, but Congressman Wittenauer was found shot in Mr. Brill's office. FBI Agent, Mark Tallman was shot by a man who may have been Henry Brill, also. When

Arnie Stewart was shot he had called out Henry Brill's name. We are proceeding on the premise that Henry Brill is our perpetrator."

"Well," I said, feeling the heat build up in my gut, "how are you going to get him and save my wife? Let's talk about that, why don't we?" I was standing, now.

"Yes, sir. First I want to know if anyone else has anything to add to our information about Mr. Brill?" The heavy-set receptionist was ready.

"Well I certainly do!" she declared. She moved around as if planning to stand, but finally remained seated. "I know he has threatened Mr. Anton, here. He's a hateful man!"

"Okay, ma'am, please give your statement to Officer Deloury, here." Another officer came to sit next to her.

"Mr. Anton, if you would answer some other questions, please." I moved up behind the guard console.

"Why was Mrs. Anton meeting with Brill?" I told them a brief version. "And you had spoken with Arnie Stewart about these matters?"

"In general. He was investigating an attempt on my life and its similarity to the death of one of Brill's co-workers."

"Okay, he said something like that. How was Brill involved in the attempt on your life?" Another story session. I was getting antsy.

"When are we going to get this bastard and save my wife?"

"Look, Mr. Anton…"

"Walter or Walt, please!"

Okay. Look, Walt, these S.W.A.T. people are itching to make some sort of assault on the EPA. The FBI would like nothing more. However, until we know where your wife is, we are not going in with guns blazing. I hope you see the wisdom of that."

I had to agree but it didn't make me feel better. "So how can you find that out, first?"

"Right now we have a team trying to slip a fiber-optic camera through the ceiling to see where Brill and your wife are. He hasn't claimed she's a hostage. He is still in there, we are sure. All the doors are guarded. So far the camera hasn't gotten in."

"Well, listen, if anyone is hated by Brill, it's me. Maybe I can get him to react and we can learn something."

"That's a risky step, but one we were going to suggest."

"Then, let's go. Time's a-wasting." I looked at all of them in turn. They looked at each other until all eyes rested on Captain J. Collins. Collins nodded.

"All right, then. Three of us are going with you, and we're going up the stairs as quietly as possible." Suddenly there was a little commotion at the front lobby doors. EMT's were wheeling a patient into the lobby.

"C'mon, you guys. I can walk faster than this! F'crissakes!" It was Arnie Stewart. They wheeled him over to where we were standing. "Anton! Good, they found you, huh?"

"Well, I found them, I guess."

"You goin up? That's what I would do. He'll react to you, I think."

"Just about to. Why aren't you in a hospital?"

"Ahh, by the time the bullet got to me it could barely get through my belt. Bled a lot, though. They patched me up but it's not too serious. I demanded they let me see the end of this." I reached out and shook his hand.

"I'm really glad you're here. Really glad."

"Yeah, yeah. Go see if you can flush him out." He was almost sitting up on the gurney, the head of it angled as steeply as possible. "I feel silly sittin on this thing."

"We'll be right back. I'll talk to you then." The three officers and I started up, careful to not clink equipment. Everything was quiet as we got above the lobby level, three double flights.

"There are microphones on all the doors," one of the officers whispered. I nodded my understanding. Quietly we arrived at the third floor. The door was wedged open and we entered the EPA. A plainclothes officer signaled there was no sound inside.

Behind us another officer puffed up the stairs. His face was red and he was breathing heavily. The lead officer, Captain Collins, gestured with a shrug, "What's up?"

The flushed officer whispered in his ear. Collins opened his eyes wider and trotted toward the men's and ladies' rooms near the reception counter. He signaled to the detective with the microphone on the door. He ran over to where he was and they whispered together for a few seconds and then he grabbed his equipment and ran back to the ladies' room and applied his mic. After a couple of minutes he shook his head. Then they moved over to the mens' room door and repeated the operation. The lead officer gestured to the other two and whispered to them briefly. Each went into a rest room.

I gestured to the officer who'd run up the stairs, now a more normal color. He put his mouth next to my ear.

"Restrooms open both ways," he whispered. I looked at him blankly and he pointed at the office door I knew so well. Then I got it. Two more potential exits.

Captain Collins came back after posting his guards. He crooked a finger at me and we went past the restrooms and through another door into a hallway between the EPA and other tenants. Twenty yards along was a plain, metal door. A detective was listening there, too. He pointed at the earphones and shook his head. Collins gestured to me to come to the door. He had a key.

"I'm going to open this as quietly as I can. You keep behind it until I tell you to come around. I'll give you a microphone. What are you gonna say?"

I shrugged. He shook his head. He leaned toward me again. "Say what you think will get a reaction."

He opened the door. It made a scraping noise, but the two officers held it hard against the hinges. We heard no reaction. Collins gestured to me. He handed me a microphone while he held a small bullhorn unit over his head, aimed into the cubicle-filled room. He nodded.

"Hey Henry, you asshole! Man to man, Henry! It's me, Walter!" He signaled to me to stop. We all crouched down and waited.

***

"Lindaaaa," Brill whispered, now in the coffee room door. "They're coming for us Linda. They want to save you from the mean old man, Linda. Isn't that good?"

Linda managed to stand up. Everything was dusty. She started to wipe her hands on her skirt and decided it was a waste of time. Little by little she could pick out lighter and darker areas. The access space she was in appeared to end a little way to her right as she faced the blacker opening under the sink. She could feel the panel that had fallen out. It was regular in shape except for a slot for pipes. She slid it back along the bundle of pipes and inched it back to the hole leading to the sink. It scraped the floor. She froze.

"Liiiinnndaaa! I hear you." He whispered just loud enough.

***

Collins reached down suddenly to his vibrating beeper. A single digit displayed. "Wait here," he whispered. He took off at a trot. A few minutes later he returned.

More whispering. "The man at the back exit heard Brill whispering to Linda like he doesn't know exactly where she is."

I relaxed measurably. If Brill wasn't holding her hostage after all this time it meant she was outsmarting him and probably not hurt.

***

After the scrape sound Linda had to decide whether to slip farther back in the access corridor or finish propping the panel back in place. She waited for Brill to do something. Nothing. She slipped the panel the last few inches and felt around the edges. Nothing held it. It was just pressboard that fit a hole in the drywall. She took two bobby-pins from her hair and jammed them into the gypsum board, tightly against the pressboard. If Brill pushed at it, it would seem firm. She stood back up.

Far up to her left she could see a grayer area. Where she was she could make out only dark and darker. She slipped sideways along the passageway. Here and there were pipes of various kinds coming up from holes in the floor. Between the pipes and the wall there was enough room for a normal sized man to fit. She kicked a piece of pipe on the floor and it rolled off in the dark, clanking and banging until it came to rest. She froze again. The noise had lasted long enough for Brill to zero in on her location. She heard him plunk a paper cup against the wall opposite where she was.

"I can hear you, Linda," he said in a low voice. "It's just you and me, now. It's only wallboard between us, Mrs. Anton. I could shoot right through it, you know? But you could help me and I can protect you. Walter sounded very angry, didn't he? If you and I are together then I won't get hurt and I can guarantee that you won't get hurt either. Isn't that a good plan, Linda?" She heard the cup slide along the wall. "Just say 'hello,' Linda."

She found it hard to think when she couldn't focus on her surroundings in the dark. She bent over and felt around her feet. Where she would have next placed her foot she found a bent piece of thin metal tubing. Now that she had it she couldn't think of how to get rid of it. She tucked it into her belt and slid her shoeless foot along the floor farther away from the coffee room. She managed a couple of steps silently and started to lose her balance. She reached her hand to the wall with the pipes. It closed on a horizontal pipe and she steadied herself. No discernible sound.

Horizontal pipe? At shoulder level? She slid her hand along the pipe and came to a vertical pipe, welded to it. A ladder? She felt for the next rung and found one above and below the first. Maybe a way out.

***

Collins led me back to the EPA lobby. Two other uniforms were there, plus the man who'd been listening at the lobby door. We weren't whispering, now.

"Our man at the rear exit heard Brill talking to the walls as if Linda were hidden someplace. We have a construction drawing coming up in a minute. At this point, then, I would say your wife is safe, Mr. Anton, but hiding. Evidently, Brill is focusing on the rooms at the far end of the space from where we are. Mrs. Anton is probably hiding somewhere back there, too. We are still not going to start shooting. The walls are thin and the cubicles provide dozens of hiding places. Our plan is not to kill him if we can help it. He is armed but nothing high-powered."

Nobody said anything. I decided to ask what I wanted to know. "So, your plan is to rescue Linda first?"

Collins looked at me for a second. "Uhh, well, yes, I guess it is. When we get that floor plan we'll know better how to do that, or at least make sure that Brill is separated from her, enabling us to capture him safely. If the opportunity presents itself to do that we will not hesitate, hopefully with no one else being shot." Collins visibly relaxed now that a plan had been stated. One of the other officers asked a question.

"Uhh, Captain, is this a S.W.A.T. move or do we handle it?"

Collins puffed out his cheeks. "I'm gonna call down when we get the building plans. They'll be looking at the same thing. Then we'll find out if this is the battle of the bulge or good police work. Everybody downstairs wants a piece of this. The TV stations are looking for big news and everyone's itchy. You know how it is. I'd rather handle it small. The FBI guys want their revenge for Tallman. Stewart says Brill is the subject of a murder investigation, so PPD wants him. But, the apprehension is in federal office space and involves a crime against a congressman, for crying out loud. So..." He shrugged his shoulders.

***

Linda placed one foot on the ladder. Reaching up she pulled herself onto the ladder and climbed up two steps. A couple more rungs and she would be above Brill's firing level. She climbed slowly. Her panty-hosed feet were slippery on the rungs. With one arm hooked on the ladder, Linda carefully peeled the panty-hose down her legs. One foot at a time she pulled her legs free and let the hose fall to the floor. Two more rungs. She could just discern the ladder against the gray concrete. Locking her arm, again, she looked around. She could see islands of light: ceiling fixtures in the offices. Her stomach sank. They made her realize that she had climbed about eight feet above the floor. She hated anything higher than a kitchen stool.

"Lindaaa! You're not talking to me, Linda. That's very hurtful, you know. We still have some work to do, you and I. Just say you're sorry and we can both leave alive. You'd like that, Linda, I know you would."

Linda smiled for the first time. She reached down and took the piece of pipe in her left hand. There must be a way to divert Brill's attention. She tried to gauge the distance to one of the light fixtures she could see. It sat in an opening in a blanket of insulation that covered everything else. Very small target even if she weren't trying to throw from a ladder. Her stomach did another flip-flop as she thought about that. She tucked it back into her waistband.

The light was grayer at this level. Linda looked upwards and could see the ceiling, with a darker patch right over the ladder. The concrete block wall extended about the same distance further the way she had come, as it did to its end just past the sink opening. Only three more steps to reach the ceiling. What if she couldn't open the hatch when she got up there... way the Hell up there? She closed her eyes and fought to slow her breathing. If she did get through the hatch up there she'd be at floor level again, but at the floor level of what? Could she get out of there? There had to be a way, didn't there? Even if she had to find a sink panel, she would find a way.

***

Two FBI agents delivered the floor plan. Collins spread it out on the lobby table where the Japanese Koreans had stood. One of the special Agents did the talking.

"Behind those rooms on the far end of the offices you can see a service area about three feet deep. We believe Mrs. Anton is in there somewhere. Brill has heard some sounds and seems to still be in that area."

"I don't see a door to get in there," Collins observed.

"Not on this floor, but there is a panel in the hall area on floor four."

"What good is a service space you can't get in to?" one of the PPD officers asked.

The FBI-er pointed to an "H" in a circle by the wall. "We think this is a ladder. There is some sort of firestop door closing off the floor, apparently."

"Won't that be heavy?" I asked, which earned me a flat stare from the FBI man.

"I'm sure it weighs something, sir, yes." Arrogant prick. The more I thought about it, the more unlikely it seemed that Linda would climb up twelve feet if her life depended on it. Which it did. Maybe she had found the ladder.

"Are there lights in there?" Again the FBI-er stared at me.

"Who do you represent here, sir?"

"My wife! The person you're supposedly saving, that's who!"

"Easy, now, Mr. Anton," said Captain Collins. "But that is a very good question, Agent. Why can't we turn on some lights in there?" They all looked at each other. Collins went on, "Let's get to that panel upstairs and see if there's a switch, why don't we?"

The talkative FBI agent gestured to his associate to go ahead up there. Collins sent two of his men to go with him.

***

Linda climbed another rung. This was very high up! She controlled her breathing, again. After some seconds her heart rate slowed. This time she hooked her arm around the next rung before stepping up one more. Look at the wall... look at the wall, she thought.

Below her she could hear Brill moving something, but off to the sink-panel side. She took the bent pipe again and tossed it farther away from the sink opening. It clattered loudly, then silence. She got ready to move up one more step. Suddenly lights snapped on, bare bulbs in little wire cages hanging from the ceiling, one within a couple feet of her head. Her eyes hurt, but she got a quick look at the distance down to the trash-littered floor, far, far below... and screamed.

Above her the two uniforms hustled to the firestop panel. It was hinged away from the ladder with a recessed ring handle, but latched. One officer turned at it and pulled on the door until it broke free, swinging up and away and releasing a cascade of grit down on Linda's head.

"Sorry, ma'am," he said. "If you can reach your hand up I can have you up here in a jiffy."

Below them, Linda heard Brill kicking the panel free behind the sink. "Linda? I heard you scream," he shouted. I'm coming to save you!" Remarkably quickly for a big man, Brill slid through the opening on his back and twisted around to face toward the ladder where Linda looked down from almost twelve feet up.

"I see your friends, Linda. I can't let them interfere. I hope you understand, Linda!" He shot toward the opening above Linda's head. Linda screamed again and wrapped both arms around the ladder. One of the officers shot toward Brill, aiming to hit near his head. The other reached down from his position lying on the floor, and reached Linda's right arm.

Brill had ducked and now stood tight to the cement block wall. Pipes partly hid him. Linda was yanked through the opening, landing on top of the prone officer. The other officer fired again toward Brill, keeping him pinned against the wall. His partner, now on hands and knees, lowered the firestop to close the opening with a loud "thunk." Brill was trapped.

The two officers and Linda made their way to the end of the work space and out into the hall where the FBI man radioed the news downstairs. For the first time, Linda worried about how she looked. "Let me go to the Ladies room?" The cops shrugged. Linda found the door and disappeared inside.

When she returned she had rinsed her hair and washed her feet. The warm air dryers did an awful job on hairstyles, but at least the grit was gone. Together they took the elevator to the third floor.

***

I couldn't hug her enough. We kissed and kissed as tears rolled down my cheeks. "I was so scared, Linda, and I couldn't talk to you! I knew you were scared, too. Now you are here. I can't explain why I'm crying." We hugged with our faces side by side. Finally I held her back where I could look at her again, and the tears were flowing from her eyes, too. I don't know when I'd ever been so happy. The cops stood off to one side until we stopped. They had a hundred questions, but the interviews would be on the ground floor. In the few minutes we had been reunited some fifteen additional police officers of various kinds had gathered in the EPA lobby. Brill was going down when they made the decision to go in and get him. Two officers, Linda and I took the elevator down to the main lobby.

I introduced Linda to Arnie Stewart. It had been about twenty minutes since I'd gone up to the EPA, but it felt like hours. Now everybody was relaxed and smiling. Linda gave her statement to the PPD detectives. I could feel for how she felt at every stage of her retreat into the service space and, most terrifyingly, as she climbed a ladder higher up than she'd ever done before, culminating in Brill's shot at the cops. My eyes were watering again as she finished.

An FBI agent led us over to a group of EPA employees, including some suits. Malcolm Porter was the Executive Director, Allegheny Region, and he asked me to explain the underlying issue that had led up to today's meeting with Wittenauer and Brill. It took several minutes. Linda seemed happy to let me get through it all. Finally he understood and started to thank me for inadvertently exposing the basic fraud and the perpetrator, Henry Brill. I reiterated that a person or persons unknown had originally induced Brill to have the false signs posted, maybe with money. In any event, the rest of the perpetrators were not captured or even identified, as of yet. Porter seemed to grasp this; the FBI agent took notes of everything I said. I reminded him that Arnie Stuart of the PPD was in the middle of investigating Brill's connection to the murder of Emily Szepanik and to the attempted murder of me and, now, of my wife.

I had to ask. "Director Porter, can you sign a release stating the absence of any known pollution on parcel 1983-840 SSF, with reference to the desire of Blatchford Steel to obtain a lease for use of the parcel without significant alteration or construction, excavation or change in existing drainage?"

"Anton, you sound like a staff attorney. I should be able to do that when things get back to normal around here. When do you need it?"

"This afternoon. I will happily come back and pick it up. It is what we have literally risked our lives for." He looked at me like a bug, but there were too many witnesses to refuse me. I had the feeling that he generally knew as little as necessary about the operations of his case managers. I smiled broadly as we shook on the deal. Linda smiled and so did some law enforcement types.

"Okay for us to go?" I asked of the group. Everybody looked at everyone else and their consensus was that we were free to go. Linda and I went back to say thanks, again, to Arnie Stewart, but he had been taken to the emergency room. I'd catch up with him later. We walked out the front doors and I finally took note of her lack of shoes. "Come here shoeless often?" I asked.

"No, but my husband recommends it, so I thought I'd try it."

"You want me to carry you?"

"No. I'll stick to the grass, though. I parked in that tower," she pointed.

"My car is right there, too. So..." she took my arm and we walked like teenagers to retrieve our cars. The TV and radio people hadn't recognized me and were now running to take part in a hastily convened public statement with police and FBI brass. I realized, then, that I had forgotten about the continued hunt for Henry Brill and, now that I remembered, didn't much care. We drove home, carefully. It was just after noon.

***

Linda took a shower the minute we got home. I left her alone. She brushed and fluffed and finally presented herself as beautifully as ever, in slacks, blouse and three-quarter sweater vest. "Wow!" I said, which made her giggle a little.

"Look okay?" she spun around, pulling at her slacks like a skirt.

"Absolutely delicious. Aren't you staying home?" She shook her head in tight little motions.

"I'm still going to work, just a little later than I expected. No sense brooding over what happened. I wasn't hurt."

I stood there, speechless. "A guy almost kills you and you can brush it off?"

"I still have a job I'm responsible for… same as you. You're planning to go to the office again… I can see it in your face."

She was right. I tried to come up with how my going to work was different, what with the architect coming for the crane stuff and going to pick up the release from the EPA. After all, I, ahh,… what I had to get done was so, um… There was no difference. I just had a stupider look trying to find one.

"You are right, as always. I wasn't trying to minimize your work, honestly. I thought you deserved a rest after what I put you through. That's all."

"My own idea to go, this morning… you know that." She was looking downward and was quiet for a few moments. "Tom Wittenauer threw himself at Brill while he was pointing a gun at both of us. He really did act courageously, Walt. We've got to get that part of the story out." More silence. "Where did they take him, anyway? I hope he's okay."

"I was just thinking the same thing. I've gotta go see him and that FBI guy, Tallman, too. He went in alone. So did Arnie Stewart. Something, huh?"

Linda came to me and hugged me. It felt wonderful. "They all broke the rules of engagement. Pretty brave, all of them." We stood there for a couple of minutes.

"I'm cool with standing here until much later. You?" I asked.

She pulled away. "No, I do have work at *englishclass*. Let's go and get back early. We can eat ice-cream with no clothes on." She gave me that fabulous, devilish grin that ensnared me when we were dating.

"I'll be here!" I thought about the menu. "Chocolate syrup?"

"We don't have any, but you pass a store, don't you?" I laughed with her as we turned to leave. A weird day and I still hadn't had lunch.

I drove carefully to Blatchford. It was odd. I had things I would have rushed to on another day, but I felt as though everything could just damn-well wait for me. Pauly was just getting off his shift. He came around the counter and gave me a hug, which was kind-of funny, but I appreciated it. The late-shift lady stood at her station, looking uncomfortable without embracing.

"I sure am glad you and Mrs. Anton is okay, Mr. Walter. Yes sir, I am. That was terrible news to be watching. Terrible. We were all keepin our eyes on what was happening down there. I even saw you for a little bit right on the TV. How come you didn't have a big interview like they do?"

"Just lucky, I guess. Thanks, Pauly, but I have to keep moving. I'll tell you all about it. Saturday, right?"

"Huh? Oh yeah, that's right. Fresh shoulder this week, Mr. Walter." I patted his shoulder and headed to my office. There were several messages sitting on my desk. Most said, "glad you're okay," or words to that effect. Jack Jackson's said to come to his office when I saw the note. I decided to get that out of the way.

"Hey, Jack. Some day, huh?"

"Wow, Walt! Is Linda okay? We were all watching the news! Siddown! Tell me about it!" He was half-standing behind his desk as we shook hands. "You want some coffee?"

"Yes and, ahm… no."

"What?" Jack was looking at me, smiling.

"Yes, Linda is just fine… went to work actually. And I don't need any coffee."

"Oh, yeah. Well, okay, what happened?"

"It's a long, long story, Jack. The shooter never actually held her hostage. She managed to escape and hide in a crawl space until the police freed her. I assume they captured the asshole. I haven't listened to any news."

"No! He's dead, I heard. You didn't know this?"

"Nope. Linda is okay and that is all I cared about. Who shot him?"

"He shot himself. Good riddance, I say, huh?"

"Hmm, shot himself. Well, it's a good end for him. Weird." I was a little set back by that news. In a way I had been looking forward to talking to him again. Hopefully Arnie Stewart could fill me in. He'd have the story.

Jack was still smiling, which was not like him. "So, tell me about the architect. Did he give you any figures?"

"Oh, yeah... no. He took some pictures and I think I gave him the right dimensions of things. Bucky Dighton talked to him a lot. He promised to get back with preliminaries tomorrow."

"Tomorrow? That's really quick. That's great..." I ran out of things to say. My thoughts were swirling in too many directions. "Jack, I'm gonna get my primary mission done, this afternoon, then I can relax a little and clear my thoughts."

He looked at me questioningly.

"My EPA release. I got Brill's boss to agree to give it to me when we met with the cops. I'm going down there in a few minutes."

"Really? You could take the rest of the day off if you want."

"Never more sure about anything, Jack. My whole family has risked its life to get the damn thing. If someone down there will hand it over, I'm going. Right now I have a few calls and then I'm heading downtown. Tomorrow will be an important day, too. But thanks for the offer. I'll see ya." I shook his hand again and headed to my almost-office.

"John?" I asked when the phone picked up, "it's Walter Anton."

"Walter! Holy cow, Walter! Are you all right? Is Linda all right? I can't believe it!"

"Everybody's okay, John… that is everyone who wasn't shot, anyway. It was very interesting for a while, but we're okay. Thanks."

"Why aren't you home, after this?"

"Actually, and you'll be proud of me for this, I'm going back downtown to get our release from the EPA!"

"What? Now? Are they even there?"

"So far as I know, they're there. I got a guy named Malcolm Porter who is the top dog in Pittsburgh, to agree to give me that document this afternoon. He wasn't thrilled, from all appearances, but he agreed to do it in front of lots of witnesses. And I really, really want that God-damn release."

"Oh man, that'll be fantastic. That makes everything possible. I mean, I hate what's happened to you and Linda, you know I mean that, but it'll be like Christmas getting that one piece of paper." Schumann's excitement was real and frankly, I felt the same way.

"When I have it, John, what do I check it for?"

"Huh? Oh, yes. You want to see terms that state something like: 'no evidence of any pollution requiring a filing on that site,' or something that says, 'no restrictions on any of the proposed uses for parcel 1983-840 SSF.' You are right to read it carefully. It has to be our defense against action by Pennsylvania Environmental Affairs. Very good to be careful when you accept it." I decided right then to call Alan Boudreau to see if he could go with me.

"Awright, John, I'm heading out. I thought you'd be happy to hear the news, though."

"You are making my day infinitely better, Walt, that's for sure. Call me, okay?"

"Will do." We rang off and I started moving before I remembered to call Boudreau. He picked up. I explained the stage we were at without mentioning the news. He must not have been watching because he didn't ask me about Linda. He almost jumped at my request that he meet me at the EPA.

I was sailing as I drove downtown, enjoying a strange euphoria. It seemed that Linda and I had navigated a terrible obstacle course. It's the first time I'd felt that way since Parcel 1983-840 SSF was dumped on me. Today I was unbeatable.

Things looked normal at Gateway One. One TV truck was still on site sending live shots back to home base every half-hour. Unfortunately the reporter recognized me. In a second she was challenging me to a duel with her microphone. I stepped around her but she appealed to me to provide first-hand information that Pittsburgh was yearning for. I stopped and faced her.

"You were in the EPA today while your wife was trapped, is that right?"

"Yes, but I didn't play a role – the police were the professionals, there. My hat's off to them." Alan Boudreau walked up and called my name as he did.

"Alan, thanks for coming down. Wanna be on TV?"

"No thanks, Walt. I'll wait." He stepped well behind the camera.

"But, Mr. Anton, wasn't it your wife whose life was threatened by the alleged gunman?"

"That's true. She outsmarted Brill and even though hiding in a dark service area, kept him from finding her until the police could get to him. I am very proud of her."

Now I was ready to keep going and tried to walk around her again. She wasn't done with me.

"What was it that originally brought your wife to the EPA with Congressman Wittenauer this morning? Does she help the congressman politically?"

"No, no," I shook my head emphatically. "She was visiting this office to help with a prob… with some business I have with the EPA and our congressman had agreed to help us. He was the big hero, today. He literally threw himself at the shooter to save my wife. That is real courage."

"Do you know how badly wounded he is? Have you been to the hospital to see him yet?"

"No, but I will be going over there immediately when I leave here. Do you have any news on his condition?"

"It's being reported as serious."

"Thanks for that. I do have to go. Sorry." This time I didn't stop despite her appeals. Alan joined me and we took the elevator up to 3 and into a nearly normal EPA lobby.

"Hello, ahh, Marion," I said. "I feel like we're old friends, now."

"It is good to see you, Mr. Anton." She looked at Alan Boudreau but didn't ask who he was. "Who are you here to see?"

"We're here to see Malcolm Porter. I'm pretty sure he's expecting me." I smiled.

"Just a moment, then." She smiled back at me. I turned to wait by the table when I noticed a plainclothes officer standing near the window. I was pretty sure the horse had left, but I appreciated the effort.

"Mr. Anton? He said to send you in."

"Oh, okay. Where...?" She told me the turns to take and to watch for the office with the dark blue drapes. I thanked her and we stepped through the door for, I hoped, the next to last time.

Porter wasn't outside his office to welcome us. I tapped on the metal doorframe and he called me in. At least he stood to shake hands. "How are you doing, Mr. Anton?" he asked with all the concern he could muster, "and who is this?"

"I am on top of the world, Malcolm," I replied. I got an internal blip of joy noticing his discomfort at my use of his first name. Maybe I just liked poking at big shots. "My wife is safe and everything I have risked everything for, is about to be made possible... thanks to you... and I do thank you, very much, for following through on this." I smiled at him. "Oh, this is my attorney, Alan Boudreau."

"I have to tell you, Walter, Mr. Boudreau," he pointedly said, "that I have done my due diligence on this false filings business and it appears that there really are no issues with that parcel and, therefore, as you alleged, there is no reason to not provide a statement to that effect. I have it here, in fact." He held up a nine by twelve white envelope with official EPA logo and address. I could almost smell it.

"I think the wording will meet what you need, but you have to know that we always reserve the right to post filings in the event pollution is discovered later." He still held it close to himself. I gestured for him to pass it over.

"We'd like to just make a quick review of the wording, if you don't mind." I held my hand out and stared at him. He slowly brought it closer to me and I plucked it from his fingers.

The envelope held a thin piece of cardstock and the letter, signed by Malcolm Porter, Allegheny Regional Director, U. S. Environmental Protection Agency. He must have thought it suitable for framing. I handed it to Alan.

"So, you had a worrisome morning, I guess, huh?" Porter wanted to be buds, now. I just nodded and gestured over towards Alan, such that I wanted to let him study the words in peace. Porter was getting pissed, but he looked around and didn't say anything else. I was Mr. Patience.

Alan read it for the third time. He wrote something on it and read it again. At last he was ready.

"If you'll permit me, Mr. Porter." He placed the letter where Porter could see it and Alan could still read it upside-down. "You say that, quote, 'to the best of our knowledge there is no reason at this time to prohibit the described uses of Parcel 1983-840 SSF.'" He pointed at the line with his pen.

"Yeah. I see that." Porter's face was stony.

"Can you see what I have written above that line? Can you read my writing, there?" Porter nodded and mumbled that he could. "It says that, quote, 'the EPA has discovered no reasons to prohibit or inhibit Blatchford Steel Services' intended uses for Parcel 1983-840 SSF,' period." I think if you can replace that sentence we'll be good to go." Now Boudreau smiled at Porter and waited for his capitulation. Short wait. Boudreau never lost his hint of a smile. Porter took the letter and stepped out to his assistant's office. I started to say something but Alan gestured for me to stifle it.

Within a couple of minutes Porter was back, looking like his lunch had backed up. "I believe you will find this satisfactory, Mr. Boudreau," he said while looking at me. Cripes, what had I ever done to him? Aside from the police activity and embarrassment to the agency and a load of grief internally, what, actually? I couldn't wait for Boudreau's agreement to the letter. He was rereading it very carefully.

"I think we can work with this, Mr. Porter. Thank you very much," Boudreau said in his most lawyerly voice. He slipped the letter into the large envelope and handed it to me. I started to get up but Alan remained seated, staring at the front of Porter's desk.

"Alan?" I asked. He flicked his fingers at me. His face was very serious-looking. Porter was still standing since returning with the modified letter. I sat down. Boudreau slipped the letter back out, turning it over. Finally, he looked at Malcolm Porter.

"Mr. Porter, is there a file in one of your cabinets, here, on this Parcel 1983-840 SSF?"

Porter looked like he'd been hit with a cream pie. Now he sat. "What..umm, what do you mean?"

"Some sort of Pendaflex folder with a little plastic tab on top, or maybe just a manila folder, somewhere, specific to this parcel?"

"Well, I imagine we do. What of it?"

"Bear with me for a moment, sir, if possible," said Boudreau. "When documents are filed in any of these folders are they somehow identified by date or other indicia based on when they were filed?"

"Maybe. Listen, you got your letter. Our business is done."

As if he hadn't heard what Porter had replied, Alan continued in the same tone. "And, in fact, aren't they marked by the initial of someone here at the EPA showing that the document belongs in that folder and has been reviewed by somebody? Indeed, you have special stamps made to so mark documents, do you not?" It was a cross-examination.

"What do you want, here, Mr. Boudreau?"

"Well sir, just a couple more answers. Did you keep an official copy of this letter," now waving at the end of Boudreau's arm, "so that it will be officially filed in that folder you say you have?"

Porter's mouth dropped. His eyes looked like bullets. He was moving his mouth and jaw but had not yet, evidently, decided which words to emit.

"Let's just resolve this problem by taking a look at that folder that pertains to Parcel 1983-840 SSF. Since there is no litigation the records you have are public. Shall we?" Boudreau stood and gestured for us all to leave Porter's office.

"What? You can't order me around. Take your fucking letter and get out!"

"I'm afraid that I can't do that without seeing that this letter is an official copy of a bona-fide EPA document and record. Surely you are not objecting to establishing provenance for this official letter, are you?"

Porter was flummoxed. I knew enough to keep my mouth shut as I enjoyed every Boudreau moment.

"Just wait here a minute," he snarled and stalked off.

"Alan," I whispered, "I absolutely did the right thing to ask you to come. Bill Blatchford directly at your corporate rate, if you have one." Boudreau was getting a 'plus' slot.

Porter came steaming back with a young man in tow. "Follow us," he commanded. Boudreau smiled at me and let me precede him as we followed Porter and the young clerk.

After no more than thirty steps we stopped at a numbered cabinet among many. The young man opened the bottom drawer and after a checking a few folders, pulled out a dark green Pendaflex with several thinner folders inside it. Ultimately he pulled out a single manila folder with a label on it that included the correct parcel number. Boudreau had written down every identifier he could see that formed a path leading to the particular folder we cared about. There were five or six sheets of paper already there. Boudreau asked to see them. The clerk looked to Porter who nodded grimly.

Boudreau looked at the kinds of identifiers on each page. "Would you stamp this letter the same way, please?" He handed over the Porter letter. Again the young man looked for authority from Porter, who again nodded. Soon the letter was stamped and identified like other pages. As Boudreau stared, again, Porter put his initials in the appropriate little square, as the original filer.

"That's very good, Mr. Porter, and I do thank you for indulging my old-fashioned quirks. Now I just need to ask for one more step. Let's just Xerox these pages as a group and you can initial our copy of this official letter so that we can get out of your hair. I appreciate that."

Porter told the young man to go make the copies. He started to head off to do it when Boudreau called out, "Wait!" The youngster stopped and turned around. Porter almost jumped out of his skin.

"Does your copier put numbers on the pages?" That answer was "no."

"That's fine. We can handle it another way. Let's all go to the copier, shall we?" He smiled broadly. It was fortunate that Porter, himself, wasn't armed.

Once the seven pages had collected in the bin, Alan fanned them out so that they under-lapped by half an inch. Then he asked for a red pen and one was produced by the clerk. Alan drew two lines across the fanned sheets so that each one had two red lines that extended off their edges. When that was done he asked Porter to initial each page right over the red lines. Steaming, Porter did so.

"Are you happy, now, Mr. Boudreau?" Porter was really angry. His clerk gathered the originals and slunk away to re-file them, where it was safer.

"I am very happy, Malcolm," Alan replied with a grin. "You have done a very good thing, here, today. Your help is extremely important to some very valuable taxpayers. I know I am thanking you on all of their behalf." He reached out his hand and waited for Porter to finally shake it.

I stuck my hand out, too, and it was shaken in turn. "I'd be lying if I said I wouldn't be happy to never cross your path again… either of you." The young clerk was trying to walk past us, unseen. "Here, Jacob, show these men to the lobby, will you?"

"Yes sir," the young man said. We stayed tight-lipped until the door closed behind us.

I stepped over to the receptionists. "Thanks for everything, Marion," I said. I looked for the other lady's name plate, which said "Jean." I thanked her, too. "I probably won't have any further business with the EPA, after this," I told them. "I am only sorry that I won't see you two again." They smiled and wished me luck. Marion said she was glad things worked out that morning.

Down in the main lobby Alan handed me the envelope with the copies in it. "You may have been alright with Porter's letter, Walter, but it could have been very sticky if they simply denied ever issuing such a letter. You are better off to have a copy of an official document with Porter's initials on it."

"I would have kissed the back of his hand and danced all the way to my car if you hadn't been here. Thanks." I shook hands with my attorney. He acknowledged my thanks and expressed his appreciation for the business. We parted, smiling. I practically hugged the envelope to my chest as I walked to my rental. At one moment I felt like a successful entrepreneur, accomplished in business; at another I felt like a kid who had a chit for a sundae from his dentist. I couldn't wait to get to the office.

I headed west on the Boulevard with a heightened sense of responsibility now that I was in possession of the magic letter. It was like moving my life savings at age thirteen, in cash, from one bank to another a block and a half away. I gripped my two hundred and eighty dollars with my fist inside my pocket as I walked. Now, I gripped the letter.

I had a firm grasp on the envelope. I dropped it on my desk and slid the seven Xerox copies into the light. You'd have thought I was rubbing a pile of gold bars, but it was just a thin stack of pages. I studied the letter Boudreau had engineered to be genuinely useful to Blatchford Steel. How easily I would have accepted whatever Porter handed over. Thank God for Boudreau. I had a permanent smile on my face as I called Schumann.

The phone rang and rang at Brightman. It was four o'clock, after all. Finally, with a couple of bumps someone picked up. "Brightman Partners. This is Aaron."

I hesitated. I'd never spoken to Aaron Brightman. Still, he had to wipe his ass the same as the rest of us. "Yes! Hi, Aaron. It's Walter Anton. Howya doing?"

"Oh, well, okay, I guess. I hope that's true for you as well."

"Yes, thanks. Listen, I've got some very important news for John and it's burning a hole in my throat until I can share it. Can I still reach him?"

"I believe he is due back momentarily. I'll have him call, if you like."

I felt deflated but gave Aaron my number.

"Very good, then, Walter. He'll call shortly, I'm sure."

Now I wanted to show my treasure to Blatchford, and not miss Schumann. I looked over the other pages. Two of those were letters, too. One from the PDC referencing the parcel with a reduced section of map printed onto it. Another was from Jones and Laughlin describing their uses of the land and the rail-spur that bisected it. In that letter J & L claimed that no significant spills had ever occurred along the track since it was laid down during World War Two. Another page described the parcel, named the parcels it abutted and listed the dimensions in degrees and minutes of direction and feet and inches of dimension. Still another was a chart of test samples that had been drilled out of the parcel... bunch of numbers that didn't say much to me. The phone rang.

"Hey, Walter! Is the big news about finally obtaining the release, I hope?" It was Schumann and I could feel his excitement.

"Yes, my friend. We have it. People have risked their lives to get the damn thing, and I have it in my hot little hands. My attorney, Alan Boudreau went with me and probably saved my bacon by insisting on certain wording and archiving standards that I'd have ignored completely. I think we have the exact statement we need, as a result."

"That is fabulous, Walter. Even Linda's life was threatened to obtain it. What a story!"

We both were quiet for a few seconds. Schumann spoke again. "I am giddy over your success, Walt, but you now must set things up with Roberta McGillvray, don't forget. I can't really schedule the big day until you know things are all going your way."

I came back to Earth. "Yeah, you're right of course, John. I'm gonna make some copies of the letter... which is a copy, itself, and then show it to Hal..."

"It's only a copy?" Schumann was exhibiting a much different tone of voice. "Where the Hell's the original?"

"Oh, it's still at the EPA. What we have here is an authenticated copy, engineered by Alan Boudreau. When I bring it over you'll see why this is better than the original. Trust me."

"Well, maybe. I like originals. It's what we do in real estate." Now he sounded downright grumpy.

"John, I thought I'd be cheering you up. Don't worry about the letter, will you? It's as good and valid as I told you. You'll see."

"Okay, I guess. We've come all this way. Bring it over as early as you can, okay?"

"You got it. I'll call ahead." We rang off. I took the packet and headed toward the stairs, stopping at our own copier to make two more sets. With the still-warm copies filling out the envelope, I headed upstairs.

Kelly Galvin was putting odds and ends into her pocketbook, standing by her desk, obviously ready to leave. She gave me a grimace.

"Is he here?" I gestured toward the fancy door.

She nodded. "But he's not expecting you," she declared, emphasis on 'you.'

"I bet you're right, Kelly, but he'll be glad to see me." She started to pick up her phone. "Don't bother, I know the route." I knocked on Blatchford's door to Kelly's shocked horror.

"Kelly?" he called out.

"No, boss. It's Walter Anton if you've got a minute." Silence.

"Come ahead," he said. I turned and smiled at Kelly and gave her a big wink. She turned and walked away, very irked.

"Thanks for seeing me, Hal. I apologize for not making an appointment but I've had a strange day."

"I heard. Linda okay?"

"Excellent, actually. She even went to work afterwards. Pretty tough."

"Good for her." He stood up and moved to one of the six chairs on the "T." "Whatcha got?"

"I've got the magic letter from the EPA... what we have been striving for since this whole thing started." I held up the envelope. He stared at it.

I took the "original" copies out first and then the two copies I'd just made. I turned the red-marked pages toward him with the letter on top.

"What is all this?" he gestured toward the red markings and initials. I told him how I'd taken Boudreau with me and that he had probably saved us from potential problems down the road. "What's he charge?"

"Tell you the truth, I told him to bill Blatchford Steel directly at his highest corporate rate. I don't know what that is."

"Are you always such a fuckin jokester, Anton?"

"I'm not joking, boss. What Alan Boudreau did for us this afternoon is worth a fortune."

"You think so."

"Absolutely, Hal. I absolutely do." I wasn't sounding at all lighthearted. He looked at me and nodded after a few seconds.

"Okay. Now what?"

"Now I have to prepare the Three Rivers Trust to do the right thing when your money hits the table. I believe I'll succeed at that and then John Schumann can schedule the closing and the public event. We are just a few days away from getting our railroad."

"You really are a hot shit, kid. So far it seems like good work. Just bring it home for us, now. Bring it home."

"Will do, boss. Listen, have you got a few seconds more?" He leaned in.

"Do you know the whole story about Wittenauer, today?"

"I think so. He called me, you know."

"Was he operated on already?"

"He called before they took him in, I think. Sounded pretty logy. Couldn't really tell me much."

"He was a real hero in there. He threw himself at Brill while Brill had his gun on both Linda and him. Pretty gutsy move… enabled Linda to get away and hide. That's when he got shot – real close range."

"No shit? I guess we don't have to make anything up to promote him in this." The old man was smiling.

"No, sir. I don't think we can say enough about what he did. When the chips were down he came through like a hero. The whole event is what made getting the letter possible, it turned out, so we all owe him for finally coming through with the EPA, just not quite like he wanted. Surprising."

"You're right on that. Okay, then, what's with the copies?" I explained how I was going to use them and that the "original" copies should be kept very, very safe.

"I'll take one copy and the red-marked copy of the letter with me to bring to Schumann, but the marked one will come back to you for safe-keeping. The other copies we should file with documents pertaining to this whole project."

"All right. Now, have you spoken to Jackson about the architect?"

"He tells me we'll get figures tomorrow. That's pretty fast."

"Okay. Keep me posted." We shook hands and I left with the two copies I needed for Schumann. I went directly to the rental and hopped in, heat and all. I couldn't wait to get home.

***

Linda had made a salad with romaine, endive and some of Elly's cucumbers and zucchini. The very red tomatoes must have come from Elly, too. Jack's legacy of compost was paying a nice dividend, his only good quality. Along with the salad she had cold cuts and cheeses and sliced London Broil, a feast. As I hugged her and kissed her neck we heard a tap on the front door.

"I invited Elly to eat with us, if that's okay? The boys are here, too."

"Sure! Makes a party. I'll get the door." Elly Maxwell had yet another bag of something with her. She let the boys enter first. I solemnly shook hands with both of them. "Come right in, everybody. Come right in."

I let Linda have most of the conversation, her's the best story. Elly's concern for her was shown in every question, while I added words emphasizing Linda's courage. I could see that Teddy Maxwell was itching to say something and waiting politely for a break in the story. Ronnie watched his brother but would have preferred the ball game. When the break came I took advantage.

"So, Teddy, how much work are you getting this summer?" His face brightened.

"I got my working papers, Mr. Anton, and I got a real schedule at Klein's Nursery! He pays me $4.25 an hour and I already got my first check."

Elly looked at him. "Well, you're excited about working, aren't you?"

"Yes, ma'am." Teddy had a tight smile, but he was looking at me. He wanted a man's approval of this big event.

"Teddy, I think that's pretty good! You know, when I got my first job I was just a few months younger than you are, right now. But it wasn't as good a job as you have." I was shaking my head. "My first job was washing floors at a church and they only paid me a buck-seventy an hour! I wish I'd had a neat job like yours. Whadaya have to do?"

"Oh, yeah! Well... when I first get to work I sweep around all the outside pots and planters and I take that stuff to a compost pile they have. Then I have to water the outside pots and raised beds and only so much water based on the square feet of each bed and so many seconds for each pot. I have to be careful or things will rot. After that I have to check on every person in case they need something from the shed where they keep all the supplies. Then I pick up in the store area and empty the trash barrels, but I have to separate things that could go on the compost pile and dump the trash in the dumpster. When I'm done with that I have to count how many bags of mulch there are of each color and fill enough bags to have the right number ready to go. Sometimes I have to go get bags of limestone chips or spreadable limestone and I bring them around and help people put them in their cars but I don't handle the cash registers and I can't tell people what they should buy. If I work there next year or maybe during Christmas season I might be able to work in the store and not just in the yard. But Mrs. Klein asks me to do things in the store and I always do what she asks because…" I held up my hands and waved for him to stop.

"Wow, Ted. I can't believe you've already learned so many steps to your job. That's fantastic. You must be proud." He nodded and was still smiling. I looked at Elly and she was still taken aback by how talkative Teddy was about his job. Ronnie had already headed to the living room and the Pirates, having heard the job story already, maybe twice.

"Well, Walter," Elly began, "you have had quite a month since you got the real estate assignment."

"And we're finally coming to the end of the whole damn thing. And despite everything, I've met some very interesting people and learned a lot about Pittsburgh. Now I'm even helping solve a construction problem at the plant."

I started to tell her about Axel Johnson being in the FBI but thought twice about it. Maybe Axel was in an official capacity when he was fixing squeaks. He hadn't said anything about keeping his job secret but had apparently been doing exactly that.

"Did Linda tell you about what our congressman did today?"

"No! Linda, are you holding back the best parts? He was shot they said."

"Well, no, I didn't mean to. I thought I mentioned it. It was very dramatic. I just wasn't thinking of it, I guess. I mean, he saved my life by jumping onto the man with the gun. He shouted at me to run and that's what I did. Nothing very brave about me."

I studied Linda for the first time. She wasn't sounding like the Linda I knew… no confidence, or firmness in the telling. It was funny. It didn't make sense for her to forget the most dramatic event. I felt badly that I hadn't insisted on staying home and talking about the morning's events with her. Yet, she had wanted to go to work right afterwards. And I'd let her! I let her put herself in danger and then glossed over the morning and let her leave the house. What a fool I was. She hadn't asked me any questions over dinner, not even whether I'd obtained the letter or about anything else since we'd split up at midday.

"Elly, I'm afraid we're going to make this an early one. We've had a wrenching day. Please forgive us. I'm glad you were here for dinner, though. Let's do it again in a couple of days."

"Of course, Walter. Make sure Linda gets some rest. C'mon boys – time to go. Let's go, now!" Elly stood by the front door and the two teenagers joined her. She blew us kisses and left. Teddy gave me a little wave before he ducked out.

I stepped to Linda at the sink and put my arms around her from behind. "How ya doin Lindy?" I murmured against her neck.

"Ohh… okay, I guess. It just all seemed to catch up with me all of a sudden, you know?" She let out a long breath.

"I never should have left you, today. It was too much to go back to work so quickly. We should go to bed now, I think." She nodded.

"I have to finish the kitchen."

I took her hands and pulled her toward the living room and then to the back hall. "I'll finish up. We can worry about perfection tomorrow. Go on, now." I kissed her. She nodded and headed to the bathroom. I went back in the kitchen and neatened things up a little. All the cold things were wrapped and refrigerated. I wiped the counters and put things in the dishwasher, checked the doors, shut off lights. It was still light out but we'd sleep easily. I got to the bathroom as Linda finished brushing her teeth.

"Okay?" I asked.

"Yes, Walter. I'm doing very well, thank you for asking." It was an okay statement but she said it as though I were a potential customer of *englishclass*.. It sounded odd. She didn't look at me or reach out to hug me or kiss me. I looked at her in the mirror with toothpaste suds spilling out of my mouth. She was standing by the door but not leaning on it... just standing. I finished my ablutions quickly and took her hand and basically led her to the bedroom.

"You must be wanting to have sex by now," she said. "Don't you want to have sex with me?"

"I always want to have sex with you, Linda, but tonight we have to get some extra rest. Let's look forward to tomorrow night, eh?"

"Oh, that's a good idea, Honey," she said. "We can drive in together tomorrow in case you're busy."

Now she wasn't making sense. I laid her down and pulled the sheet over her and shut off the table lamp on her side. I shut off my light and then sat on my side. I waited until her breathing slipped into sleep mode. In the kitchen I found Linda's address book. Her gynecologist was listed on a slip tucked in the front, with an appointment scheduled for the following Monday. I dialed the number.

The answering machine gave me a number to call in case of an emergency. I called twice to get the number right.

"Doctor Gemmelman's answering service. Are you calling about an emergency?" I said I was. "What seems to be the problem, sir?"

"I believe my wife is in shock. She isn't talking right. She had a life-threatening experience today. She's pregnant."

"Hold on, sir." I drummed my fingers as the phone clicked a few times. I heard another phone ringing.

"This is Doctor Zachary. Who am I speaking with, please?" I told him who I was, why I called and why I thought Linda was in shock – psychological shock. He asked me for some details and seemed to agree with me. I asked him if I could bring Linda to the office in the morning.

"Here or to Dr. Gemmelman's?" I wasn't sure what to say. I asked which seemed better to him?

"Well, my partner is a trained psychologist. Dr. Gemmelman would probably refer your wife to her, and she is a woman, which will help, in any case." I got his address, which was right in Squirrel Hill. Linda's suggestion that we drive in together was coming true.

I slipped back into the bedroom but it took a long time to fall asleep.

TUESDAY, JUNE 4, 1985

I told Jackson I'd be late because of a doctor's appointment. Couldn't be helped. I think he was unsure of why I called on this morning and not others. Linda and I drove directly to Drs. Zachary and Waitz, Womens' Health Center. It was funny to be sitting in the waiting room of a womens' doctor's office, but after the once-over, everyone kept her eyes on her own magazine.

Dr. Waitz was a prophet. I caught up on my Time, People and National Geographics. What a relief. In fact I was glad she was affording so much time for Linda. She'd been perfectly functional getting ready, but had yet to talk about Monday. I'd have read Cosmopolitan if necessary.

At the end of the appointment she had me come in. Yes, she could go to work if she wanted to; no, there was no way to force her to talk about anything she didn't bring up herself; yes, she might burst into tears at some point but probably wouldn't. It was surprising that Linda could hear us talking about her without objecting. She did seem pretty chipper as we left. I promised not to push her into any sort of discussion she didn't initiate. We went home.

Linda called *englishclass* to finagle a late start, and went shopping, instead. I went to Blatchford after a lot of hugging and a promise from Linda to call if she got upset or anything.

I gave Pauly a little patter but wasted no time. I had to face Roberta... today. This would take some thoughtful preparation...

with coffee. It was cooked dry again, and I appreciated mindless washing and brewing. Fresh cup in hand, I returned to my ostensible office. With Colleen Walsh doing my work, I could do some cogitating.

As far as we knew, the Trust was a little shy of cash and nothing significant was coming up in June. Roberta ought to be receptive to a deal like Larimer and, therefore, willing to bargain on 1983-840 SSF. Schumann had made it sound like her response to Forrest Akers indicated the same thing. It was all I had – that, and her promise to see me again. I called her office.

Roberta would have started her virtual machinery to wrangle a nice facilitation fee for smoothing regulatory hurdles and for her already-approved plans for green space. The phone rang until I thought I'd get a machine, but she finally picked up.

"This is Roberta McGillvray."

"Well! Good morning Roberta! I hope you're well. This is Walter Anton. Remember me?"

"You are impossible to forget, Mr. Anton. What do you need me for?" No more snide than expected… a positive sign.

"I am hoping you recall your willingness to meet with me one more time." I had my full cheeriness running.

"I suppose I do. What for?"

"I have a couple of ideas on that railroad parcel that I'd like to place before you, if possible, and, since our deadline is getting closer, I am appealing to you for your earliest possible appointment." Absolutely bubbly.

"I don't have a lot of time to waste on ideas I don't like. There are other, more positive projects going forward, you know." Crisp and un-encouraging. But I had to see her.

"I do appreciate your time, very much. I can be brief, but I do have some new … ahm, what you'd call 'angles' on this that might just convince you. I have to try. You understand, don't you?" I could hear her sighing in resignation.

"When did you have in mind, Mr. Anton?"

"If you can fit me in today that would be my ultimate dream. If not, can we do it very first thing tomorrow?"

"How about right before lunch hour, then? You'll have your afternoon free." Ouch!

"At eleven, Roberta. I think you'll be pleased."

"We'll see, won't we? Eleven then." The phone clicked dead. One down. I called the mayor's office.

"Mayor McKay's Office. May I help you?"

"Yes! Good morning. This is Walter Anton and I need to speak with the mayor, please."

"He's in a meeting." No "I'm sorries," just, "he's in a meeting." I decided the 'meeting' business was stock for almost everyone.

"Yes, thanks. He told me that's what I'd hear when I called, but I'm pretty sure he'll take this call. Just tell him Walter Anton and use the word 'important.' Thanks."

I didn't hear anything for a few seconds. Maybe she was asking someone else. Then, some clicks. "Hold on, Mr. Anton." More silence.

"For Christ's sake, Anton. I hope we're coming to the end of my having to talk to you!"

"Good morning to you, too, Harry. I hope you're well."

"Whadda ya want?" After yesterday I didn't care how he felt.

"I want you to know that I have an official release from the EPA regarding our proposed use of parcel 840. After a few more details I'm working on we'll be ready to lease it. Can you have Parks and Recreation prepare the lease agreement?"

"Forgive me for not asking how your wife is doing, Walter. My apologies."

"She's amazingly strong, I've found, as well as beautiful and smart. She came through the ordeal very well and even went to work in the afternoon! Thank you."

"Listen, I'll get the city attorney to draft a lease agreement. It'll be simple. Anything else?"

"Yeah, actually. We still need your ideas on how to stage the announcement. I promised you you'd look good coming out of this but we are novices at these things."

"I have an assistant who does protocol and PR stuff. I'll have her call... ah, who?"

"I guess John Schumann. He'll know what to do."

"Yeah. Okay. Well, if there's nothing else..."

"Thanks, Harry. Someday you'll want to talk to me... maybe." I started to hang up

"Walter! Walter!" I heard faintly. I pulled the phone back to my ear.

"Yes? I hear you."

"What about the Trust? Are you saying Roberta is ready to go on this?"

"No, not quite, but I am meeting with her in a few minutes, actually."

"Let me know how that goes, will you? That's your real test, I think."

"I agree. I'll have to call you, though."

"What? Oh, for crissakes. You are a pain in the ass." And that did end the call.

***

I paid to park. It was already a few minutes past eleven. I ran up the stairs. When I stepped into the Trust offices a chime went off. That was new. "Back here, Walter!" Wow. She must have a camera, too. Interesting.

I stuck my head around the doorframe. She looked right at me and waved me in. "Good morning, Mr. Anton. To what do I owe the pleasure?"

"Well, good morning back at you, Roberta. And I think you will be pleased at what I hope is a good solution for both of us." She just raised her eyebrow at me.

We sat facing each other for a moment. She looked up at her wall clock pointedly. "It's your dime, Mr. Anton."

"Actually, it's my hundreds of thousands, Roberta. It strikes me that if it's used for both of our benefits we can make a deal."

"What changes have you made on your use of that parcel? Is it still going to be ugly?"

"Well, for a couple of years it will still be, um… industrial, I guess I'd say." Her head was shaking as I spoke.

"Our view of the best use of that land hasn't changed. Why should I do something different today that I would not have done a month ago?"

"Let's take a broader view of changes in the city, can we?"

"Like what?" Not a very happy response. Ah, what the Hell?

"Like Larimer LAR488-dash-8. I have heard that project is of interest to you and Forrest Akers and others." I gave her my most neutral visage, and waited. At first she looked straight at me and I watched her face go from mild surprise to hardened anger, maybe hatred.

"What of it?" She really was pissed. "We are here to talk about your Southside parcel. Larimer and my interest in it is none of your business."

"Actually, madam, it is. I have authority to donate several hundred thousand dollars to enable that project to fly. It's going nowhere until I do. Do you understand what that means?"

Her attitude was now to belittle. "What on Earth are you talking about? Blatchford has no interest in Larimer 488. That would be a waste of money."

"I think you don't understand. Whether Larimer goes forward is really up to you, Roberta. That project is eight-hundred grand shy on financing. You may not have known that. I can write that check. But, I need something from you, in return. You can do all the facilitating you want but you can't make that lead balloon fly without my eight hundred. That's what I am offering. Now, do you understand?"

Her face had the look of horror. She stood and turned her back. She was the one who twisted events to her own benefit. No one twists her for theirs. She may have been hiding tears... I couldn't tell. I got up and wandered over to the model of the Gateway and pretended to be interested in it. You could have heard a pin drop.

"I should throw you out of here." She'd turned but was still standing behind her desk.

"But not when a deal is so close to being consummated?" Her face could have been carved into Coal Hill.

"I knew I didn't like you when Linda introduced you." I didn't react.

"Tell me what you want, now." She was looking over at the Gateway model, not at me.

"A cup of coffee, if that's possible. And some tea for yourself, I believe?" Her reaction was almost a laugh but she held it back. She waved me toward the kitchenette. Either she had decided that a deal was unavoidable or she was going to refuse and it didn't matter what I did. I took my time heating water in her microwave. I put instant coffee in mine and chamomile tea in hers, then put both cups on saucers, grabbed two spoons, and carried them back into her office. She was seated again, shuffling papers.

I set the cups down and stirred my black coffee a few turns, then clanked the spoon into the saucer. She looked at her tea and then pulled out the bag and squeezed it in the spoon. She sipped, looking at me over the cup.

"You know I have resolved my EPA problem, don't you?"

"You had quite a day, yesterday. I hope Linda is okay?"

"Yes, thanks for asking. I'll relay your concern. Henry Brill's boss gave me the release late yesterday." She was nodding very slightly. "We're good to go with the city as soon as you and I agree."

"Again, then, what do you want?"

"I want you to step aside on 1983-840 SSF. No objections, comments, actions of any kind. That frees us to lease the parcel for two years. We aren't going to do any construction or affect drainage or anything else except to upgrade the railbed. Its subsequent use will be identical to its original use. In turn, Blatchford will donate sufficient funds to complete financing of Larimer. That's it, simple."

I don't know if I wanted an immediate reaction or thoughtful consideration, but her dead silence was hard to take. I sipped coffee and pretended to be calm. After a bit she got up and left the office, perhaps to the restroom. I sat and reviewed what I'd said. I thought I was on firm ground. A good ten minutes ticked by. She came back into the room like she'd found a new direction and purpose.

"I think we'll get along without your money, Mr. Anton. Thank you very much for coming in today. I'm sorry we couldn't come to an agreement." She remained standing, expecting me to leave. I resolved to not let her feel like she'd won, but I had been counting on the logic of my position to bring her to the table.

For the ten minutes she'd been out of the room, she must have been trying to find someone else to put up the eight-hundred thousand. Could she have found someone? Who the Hell else would donate that kind of dough? No one else could profit from Larimer aside from Liberty Bank, could he? Or they? I pondered what game she was playing. What the Hell?

"Well, then, Roberta, if that is finally it, can you answer a question or two for me?"

She sat down in a more relaxed demeanor. "What do you want to know, Mr. Anton?"

"Please, call me Walter, won't you? I feel like we are now able to be friendly."

"Okay, Walter. Ask away."

I smiled and sipped cold coffee. "I have to ask why you feel we can't make this deal? It seemed like a win-win to me."

"Truthfully? It seems a bit deceptive to me. You have been working with Schumann and Brightman on this scheme long before you came to me. You have to see how distasteful that would appear."

I nodded my agreement. "You may not believe me, Roberta, but I do see that, but may I suggest that a very slight adjustment in perspective also shows the great value to the Trust and to the city that *you* can bring about by extracting Blatchford's donation on behalf of the Larimer project."

"I suspect it is a great value to those two… um, real estate people you are working with, too."

"To Brightman and Schumann, you mean?" She nodded carefully with her lips pushed out, a smile playing at the corners of her eyes. What hatred she must harbor for Jews, I thought.

"I was hoping you might also be swayed by the great value to a lot of workers at Blatchford, at Mid-Waters Shipping, on the railroad and for Wheeling Crane and the contractors who will rebuild the tracks. That is a lot of benefit at no cost to the Trust, don't you think?"

She was quiet. Maybe I had tilted the scale a little. Eventually, though, she started shaking her head again. "I still feel blind-sided."

So, it was mostly personal, coupled with her hatred for Brightman's heritage. But something wasn't calculating. I was more certain, now, there was no one else coughing up most of a million for the Larimer community center. She was willing to hurt everybody and forego a payday for the Trust, just to put me in my place. Wow. I couldn't give it up.

"Earlier you asked about Linda. Did you know her life was threatened by Henry Brill, yesterday?" A look flashed across her face when I mentioned Brill's name. She quickly returned to a sort of interested concern.

"We think he was involved with an attempt on my life, too. You may not have known that."

"You appear to have survived. What is that misfortune supposed to mean to this deal?"

"Well, nothing, I suppose, except to say that we have risked our lives to put this little railspur back into use for only a couple of years. After Blatchford is done with this contract and our city lease is up, you'll be able to insist once again on certain modifications to the parcel."

"I understand all that, Walter. But if I hold my ground, I can insist on modifications to the parcel right now. Your uses of it don't interest me."

I could have become despondent at that point, but I still felt that something wasn't adding up.

"Did you know that Tom Wittenauer saved Linda's life, yesterday? He was there to pressure Brill to relinquish that clean bill of health for the parcel. It was very heroic of him to throw himself in front of Linda while Brill held a gun on her. That Brill was a bit crazy, I guess. He shot himself before they could arrest him. Strange."

"I don't like Wittenauer very much." She must have reflected on how that sounded because she continued immediately, "But, I am glad he wasn't killed."

"We still aren't sure how Sindledecker got involved in everything." Roberta coughed and stood up, almost gagging. She stepped into the little pantry and drank some water. When she came back she appeared to have had enough of our discussion.

"Well, Walter. Today seems to have not gone the way you wanted. Another time, perhaps."

"It is disappointing, that's for sure. I just hope Gary will lay off, now."

"Yes. Well, drive carefully, Mr. Anton." She ushered me out. I was heading to the parking garage as I realized how she reacted to "Gary" with advice to drive carefully.

No, that was just something to say: "Drive carefully." But did she know Gary? I had mentioned Sindledecker but I was pretty sure I hadn't used his first name. Did that mean she knew Gary Sindledecker? And Brill, too? Did she know of the attacks?

I got the rental and sat dumbfounded. Being turned down made me extra suspicious. But I should run things by Arnie Stewart. I decided to visit him and Wittenauer. They were both at Mercy.

***

I found Stewart sitting in a chair. Another cop was chatting with him. "Uhh, sorry. I'll wait down the hall." I backed out of the doorway.

"C'mon in, Anton!" called Stewart. I poked my head back in. "Anything you say is okay to tell my partner, Marty Calnan. Marty… Walter Anton." We shook hands, then I shook Arnie's hand, too.

"You look good, Officer. What are ya hangin around here for?"

"Ahh, doctors. They want to bill out one more night to the city, I guess. Christ... I could've jogged over here yesterday! They want me to 'rest.'" He made air-quotes.

"Maybe that's good, Arnie. You know... infection and things. The city needs you healthy, right Marty?" We nodded.

"You know Gary Sindledecker is still out there somewhere. You should be the one to nail him, seems to me." Stewart looked at his partner.

"Marty and I were just talking about that son of a bitch. He's a piece of work." He shifted his body up a little higher in the chair. There obviously was still some pain where they'd sewn him up. "What about your buddy, Wittenauer. Are you still gunning for him?"

"Ohh, you mean Tommy?! We're big buds, now. At least since he threw himself between Brill and my wife. He was damn heroic yesterday. But there is a story there."

"Well, I ain't goin anywhere." I told them how Wittenauer's role in the phony filings was peripheral; how he had been a long-time friend of Brill's; how the person who originally enticed Brill to post those signs is still unknown. Marty Calnan was taking notes.

"That is a story, for sure. You got any suspicions who the conspirator is? Brill never said anything to your wife?" I shook my head.

"Tell you the truth, I haven't had a detailed conversation about what she went through. She's in a form of mild shock, I think. Traumatic stress... something like that. So I haven't pressed her to talk about it. Doc says she'll come out of it."

"We really do need to talk with her, Mr. Anton. Arnie told me to hold off or I would have been at your house already."

"I appreciate that. Thanks. But I am nervous about Sindledecker. Should I be? Is he likely to fade away without Brill or more likely to strike at me? Would he strike at my wife? Should we be hiding?"

"Whoa, whoa, whoa," Arnie said. "Marty, here, has been tracking him down, step by step. We've interviewed known associates, here and in West Vee. You may want to keep taking cabs for a while, but I doubt he'll be free for long."

"Did that cop in Monroeville speak with you? He kept some evidence from that time... the brake line, I think."

"Yeah, we got his report and copies of his photos. You don't have to worry about his being convicted. When we bring him in he'll stay in."

"Well, good. What do I actually do, though? I hate being helpless."

"If you insist on driving around there is one thing you should do."

"Yes?"

"Practice routes to police stations and fire stations. No matter where you are you need to know the shortest route to police, especially. If Sindledecker tries anything in his truck or some other vehicle, get to the police... period! Memorize the phone number to reach the police in Pittsburgh and surrounding towns. You see something or feel threatened, you can't be looking up the number or looking for a phone book. Make sense?"

"Yes, daddy." I stuck my lip out like a little kid.

Stewart rolled his eyes and Marty smiled. "You're a son of a bitch yourself, Anton. Get out of here and be careful. And Marty can't avoid an interview much longer. See if you can prepare Linda for that, will you?"

I saluted to an eye-roll. We shook hands and I split to find Wittenauer.

The nurses near Stewart didn't know. They sent me to the ICU, up two floors. To the right of the elevator were regular beds; to the left were closed doors and instructions to check in before leaving the waiting area. I went through those.

The ICU is a circle. The wall opposite the two doors included big windows. The nurses' station was in the center with a view into 3-sided, curtained "rooms." On a small desk was a book to sign and a phone with instructions to press "3." I heard a phone ring and the nurse that picked up looked at me.

"Do you have a relative here in ICU?"

"No, just a friend. Tom Wittenauer."

"Mr. Wittenauer is still very sick, sir. We are limiting visitors, so... "

"He saved my wife's life yesterday. It's why he was shot. I'll be only a couple of minutes." She left me hanging for a bit while she spoke to someone else.

"Just come in to the desk where I am." Click. She buzzed me in.

"Mr. Anton, the congressman is in serious condition. He is mildly sedated but he should be able to come around when you speak to him but please, please, nothing exciting and only a couple of minutes. I will remove you if you are in too long. He's right behind you."

I turned and walked softly into the three-curtained bay where a man lay in bed, his head slightly elevated. A half-dozen machines were hooked up to him, either dripping into him or counting events. Right behind me came a nurse who checked a beeping sound and asked the man if he was thirsty, to which he must have indicated "no." She wrote down a few things on the chart and gave me the once-over as she left. I was almost afraid to disturb the man who was, purportedly,

Tom Wittenauer, tall, virile congressman from Pennsylvania Fourteen... nearly unrecognizable.

I had last seen him on Friday, four days earlier. Now his cheeks were hollow and his color was pale to gray. The stubble of his beard and disheveled hair added twenty years. I felt terrible for having involved him in the shooting.

"Tom? They tell me you can chat for a couple minutes. Do you feel like it?" Talk about feeling helpless.

"Hiwalter."

"Hi, yourself, congressman. Howyadoin?"

"Been better. Never shot before. Hurts."

"I have been telling everyone how brave you were to throw yourself onto Brill like that. You saved Linda's life, for sure."

"She got away?"

"After a while. She was hiding, thanks to you. Brill shot himself."

"I heard that. Get the docs?"

"Yeah, actually, Brill's boss gave it to us. He was mad but we got it. That's thanks to you, too."

"I told Hal I would."

"And you did. We are all very grateful to you. I take back all my doubts. I don't know who else could have done what you did."

"Hummnh."

"Well, it takes more than a bullet to stop Tom Wittenauer, I guess. They tell me you'll be making speeches again soon."

"Linda and I are praying for you, Tom."

"Thanks, Walter. Not the way to get re-elected."

"Well, I hope you are re-elected, and I mean that. You deserve every success."

"Thanks, Walt. Gotta sleep now."

I took his hand, carefully because of the IV lines. "I'll see you again. Get well, Tommy."

His eyes had tears in them as I left. Drugs, probably. I went home and nobody ran me off the road.

***

Linda was upstairs prettying up the bedroom to the right of the stairs. She was humming.

"Hi, Sweetie," I called to her. She smiled vividly when she turned to me.

"Welcome home, Honey. Do you like it?" She swept her arm toward the matching drapes and bedspread.

"It's beautiful. We may need a crib, though, at first."

"I know, I know. I ordered one and they'll ship it to us. It's extra safe and made so that babies can't choke themselves. Some cribs are dangerous, you know."

"Okay. Good. You wanna eat out? I'd like to go to *Fishwives* if you're up to it."

"Sure, Wally. I'd like that. Just give me a few minutes." I gave her my best fully-clothed kiss and held her hand behind me as I went down ahead of her.

"I'll just catch a little news, Lindy. You take whatever time you want." I flicked on the TV and watched WTAE's News at Five.

All I learned from "First News at 5" was that some news and tomorrow's weather was coming up right after these messages, whereupon Lindy bounced into the living room and declared her readiness. There wasn't anything wrong with what she said or did, but it was somehow off-target. Maybe it was that everything was too perfect. How could I complain? But there was something.

We asked for Alain. We had liked *Fishwives* for a long time, but it held a special place after the Sindledecker affair. And the food was good. We placed our orders and got some sparkling grape juice and sat quietly for a couple of minutes.

"How are you feeling, Lin?"

"Oh, pretty good. I'm going in to work tomorrow. I'd rather be busy."

"Would you like to visit Tom Wittenauer in the hospital?" I had thought long and hard about asking that question. I could see her eyes tear up as soon as I asked it.

"He's in the hospital?" Uh-oh. She wasn't kidding.

"Yes, from the shooting."

"I heard shooting when I was up the ladder. But I don't see how Tom was hurt by that. He wasn't there." She was looking up and to my left, focusing on something far away.

"Lin," I tried to begin as softly as I could, "do you know what happened yesterday?"

"Well, I guess I do. I was hiding in the dark and that man was trying to find me but I climbed a ladder and the policeman pulled me on top of him while they were shooting at us."

"Who was that man you were hiding from?" I kept my hand on top of hers, which she seemed to find comfortable.

"He worked there, I think. He wanted me to help him escape. I don't like him. He wasn't very honest." She was thinking seriously, now. "He shot a gun at the policeman in the ceiling. He told me he could shoot me, too. I don't like him."

"That man was Henry Brill, Honey, the man you went to see at the EPA." She looked at me with her head tilted as if to make the crooked parts appear straight.

"Mr. Wittenauer's friend?"

I nodded and smiled, squeezing her hand a little tighter as I spoke. "That's right, Lindy. Henry Brill was Tom's friend. Do you know what happened to Tom, yesterday?"

"Aren't we going to eat, Walt? I'm getting hungry." She pulled her hand away to clasp it with the other, on the edge of the table. She hadn't reached a point.

"Sure, let's eat. What are you thinking of?"

"Fried food, can you believe it? I want some clams... shrimp, too."

She always avoided fried stuff. Must be pregnant. "Then let's order a Fisherman's Platter. It's got all that stuff and more. We can split one, I think. I'll ask." I twisted around to catch Alain's eye. He must have been watching for my sign. We ordered with an extra plate. I wasn't ready to let Monday go, though.

"It must have been scary climbing that ladder, especially in the dark, huh?" She nodded and sipped her juice before answering. At least on this she appeared to be animated.

"Oh, Walter, you know I hate heights. I don't even like stepladders." I nodded with her. "But I had to get out of the line of fire, you know?" More nodding.

"That man, Brill, you said?" A quick nod. "He had told me he could shoot right through the wall if he wanted. So I wanted to get above the wall... in the dark. When the lights came on I saw how high it was and I screamed. That... that was the scary time."

"Was there a way out at the top of the ladder?"

"I... I... I don't knooooow. That's a good question. Because that man came into the dark place when the lights came on. But the police were there just then! Wasn't that lucky?"

"I guess so-o! they were able to open the door above you and save you."

"Yes. I should really thank the man who pulled me up and out of the gunfire. Did, um... did they shoot the man with the gun?"

"No. that was Henry Brill… you know that, right?" Linda rocked her head from left to right.

"The Henry Brill that I met with, yes?"

"That's right, Henry Brill. He turned out to be a very bad man. Later, after you were safe, he shot himself when the police were coming after him."

"Oh, how awful! His poor family. What is happening to them?"

"Honestly, Honey, I never heard he was even married. I don't think he had children, but we can ask Tom Wittenauer when we visit him."

"Oh, Tom? Is he sick?" Immediately her hands went to her face and she tucked her arms tight against her bosom. She wasn't looking right at me.

"Do you want to hear what happened to Tom?"

"Not now, Wally. Our dinner is here." Alain carefully placed the mountain of seafood between us and gave us each a plate to serve on. He refilled our waters and made sure we had what we needed.

We dug in to the steaming-hot shellfish, whitefish, fries and rings and helped ourselves from the fresh cole slaw *Fishwives* was famous for. In the end we couldn't finish, but the good stuff was gone.

"Whew, Lindy, that was a great feast. Good idea."

"Yes. I don't know what struck me to order that, but it was good. I'll have to watch out I don't blow up like a balloon."

"Let's head home, then. This week has already been hard. Do you want tea?"

"No. I make tea at home." I agreed and signaled Alain. I made sure my beautiful Linda was secure in her seatbelt before climbing in behind the wheel. I was really liking the Impala. It had power and comfort. I'd yet to find the top speed, but I knew it could accelerate sharply onto the Interstate. We backed out and took the Old William Penn Highway. Sometimes after a big meal I liked to drive gently. We could pick up the East end of Jefferson without getting on 376.

After a few sets of lights we crossed under the Interstate and I reached to my right and grabbed Linda's arm. She sat up with a jolt.

"What, Wally! What?"

"We have our old friend behind us, Lin," I said coldly. "I think he intends to kill us." She whipped around and looked straight back where a black Dodge pickup with a bar across the grill, was keeping pace with us, twenty feet away.

"What are you going to do?" Her voice was shaky but not fearful. I had a stone-cold understanding that it was my job to defend the three of us. I did not, in fact, know what I was going to do. I kept driving at a steady rate. The Dodge moved a little closer but didn't bump us. I was trying different plans in my head.

We couldn't stop and run away. He was probably armed. I might have been able to outrun him, but I couldn't lead him home or put others in danger. I hadn't yet figured out the fastest way to get to the Police Station in Monroeville, but it certainly wasn't the way we were headed. I had to trick him. Finally a wild plan.

"Linda, at some point I'm gonna spin the car around. It will stop for a second and you will jump out and run away from the road into some woods."

"No, I want to stay in the car!"

"Do what I tell you and don't question me when I stop. Be ready!" I sped up a little. The Dodge hung tight with us. I eased up over fifty, close to sixty. I was looking for just the right spot.

"Walter! You're scaring me! Slow down!"

"Shutup! When I say jump… jump! Keep your hand on the belt release! Get ready!" She believed me. Her left hand rested over the release button while her right shielded her eyes, her head down.

The Dodge bumped our bumper at almost sixty miles an hour. The moment it did I accelerated. Linda was moaning softly beside me. As we crossed under the Interstate again the road curved left, downhill. Houses were far apart, no other cars coming at us… it felt right. With the dodge just inches away I stepped on the gas, steered left and stepped on the brakes with my left foot, cutting the wheel hard over left. The pickup zoomed past us as the Chevy cried and skidded around the front wheels. As it aligned with the other side of the road I pushed Linda to get out.

"Now, now, now. Get out. Hide in the brush! I'll be back!" Crying she released her belt and stumbled out. "Hide, hide, hide! Get going!" She ran down the shoulder toward the gully. I couldn't wait. She was smart. I stepped on it, the passenger door still hanging open. I whipped left and right and made it slam shut. A hundred yards behind me the Dodge was screaming up the hill. I didn't accelerate too fast. I needed him to follow.

I passed under the Interstate again looking for a route that wouldn't be congested. As he closed on me I took a wicked left and took a local road back under the highway and then left again. My better acceleration kept him well behind me after each turn. As I careered down Evergreen back to the Old William Penn a homeowner had to stop sharply to avoid being hit. I honked at him and kept honking and flashing my headlights. Maybe he'd call the cops.

I took the right back onto the old highway, close to where I hoped Linda was hiding. I stomped on it and took off with the Dodge racing to catch up. We were doing eighty and ninety paralleling the Interstate. Every time he got close I always seemed to have just a little bit of oomph that helped me pull away. I loved the Impala.

When I popped out of the viaduct at Thompson Run, I used the brakes-gas thing and turned right before the Dodge could react. He shrieked his brakes and did a donut to complete the right. I made sure he could see my taillights before I accelerated away. I let him catch up as I zigged over the tracks. I could see the flashing lights of a cruiser. I knew I'd be all right. The dips and rises made it fun. I could slow down heading downhill because I could leave him behind going up hill. Somehow I had to stop the road-race, get Sindledecker arrested, and Linda recovered. There were bad curves on this road. The time to stop things was now.

A few hundred yards past the tracks the drop on the left, became more gentle. I looked for where I could try another whip-around. I spotted a slope where the trees were back from the road. I started my maneuver but Sindledecker was ready for it. He braked hard and steered into the left curve of my car's track. The big Dodge struck me behind the driver's seat. It spun the Chevy down into a thicket of brush. The Dodge backed up and the driver's window rolled down. I was shaken but I could still react to the sight of a gun aiming at me.

I ducked right. A shot exploded. My left arm felt suddenly hot, and heavy. I passed out. Within seconds I came to and listened as two more shots were fired. "Police! Put down your weapon and put your hands on your head where we can see em!"

"Fuck you!" Another shot. Then quiet. Sindledecker was close, evidently taking shelter behind the Chevy, next to me. When he shouted it was if he were in the car.

"We make a deal or the next bullet's in his brain!" I was confused. Did he have such a bead on a cop that he could make that threat? What kind of a deal? He was right outside my car.

Maybe he was dealing over my brain. Holy shit! That was it! And he was perfectly happy to shoot my brain, wasn't he? Too late to play dead, I guessed.

My left arm felt like concrete, now. I couldn't move to hold it. I could only lie still. Clearly there were more cops there. I heard radios.

"Gary!" one called out, "this is Chief Spencer. I need to know that Anton is alive before we deal." Sindledecker shifted his bulk around and opened the passenger door by my head.

"Alright, asshole. I'll help you up and you tell em how happy you are to be here. No fuckin around." We were on the same page there. He grabbed my hair and pulled my head up. I yelped from pain. "Tell em," he growled.

"I… I'm hurt! I'm okay! I…"

"That's enough, asshole." He shoved me down and gave an extra thump on my arm. It throbbed hot again.

"Here's the deal!" he shouted. "Me an' Anton are gonna walk to my truck. Nobody gets hurt, see? One cruiser escorts me to the Pike and I disappear into the sunset and you all forget about me. The rest of you all move back, fast!"

Silence. Did this shithead really think cops would fall for this? Must be, it sounded. Once we drove off, I was dead... even I knew that. They'd never go for it.

"Relax and hold on, Gary!" Oh, no. They wouldn't. And there was nothing I could do. I dreaded hearing the next words from either side.

"I ain't got all day, chief." Must have someone to run off the road west of here, I thought.

"Okay, Gary. You see we pulled back. We're ready on the escort. You got enough gas?" What the Hell? This can't be happening. I'm gonna die tonight. I could see blue sky but we were in deep shadow. What are they thinking?

"Okay!" Sindledecker shouted, making me jump. "We're gonna walk, now. Anybody moves and Anton gets it! Some a' you, too!"

"Not to worry, kid! No one needs to get hurt, here! Just take it easy. Nobody make a move!" *This was bullshit! Those damned cops were letting him get away with murder. I was gonna die. I couldn't even see Linda's face before I went. Aww shit*!

Sindledecker pulled me off the seat of the Chevy and held me tightly around the chest until I got my footing. My arm was killing me and I was dizzy. He leaned me against the car with his big forty-five jammed into my armpit. "We're moving! Stay back like you promised!"

"Okay! Everybody! Stand down now!"

We stumbled up the slope. Gary was stopping every couple of steps, looking around like a cat. I doubt I could have walked without him. It was odd to depend on his strength. We took several steps in a row, closing in on the pickup.

"Alright, Chief! I'm going to open the truck door. Nobody move!"

"Okay, Gary. You're the boss!" Crap. He was getting away with it. I don't think I even heard the shot, but the next moment we were pitching forward. I tried to brace myself but I must have conked my head.

THURSDAY, JUNE 6, 1985

"He looks innocent when he's sleeping, doesn't he?" I knew the voice but it was too much work to associate it with a person. There were a few people, but pretending to sleep was so pleasant. And, why did they care about my sleeping? Besides, they must be standing cheek to jowl in our little bedroom. Why doesn't Linda get rid of these people? She must be home from… from… she must be back from the woods by now. That's it! She was in the woods and surely she's home by now. Hey! Linda! Can't you get rid of these people? Linda?...

"Linda!"

"I'm here, Sweetie! He's awake! Get the doctor!"

I could feel her hands on part of my face. I was wearing a hat because I couldn't feel her hands. I was forced to open my eyes.

"Okay! Here goes." I opened my eyes and immediately had to squint against the light. Just as I thought it would be nice to look right at Linda, some bastard shone a flashlight right into my eyes. I jerked my head away.

"Hey!" I called out. "That's bright, all right?" But I kept my eyes open this time, looking back and forth for Linda's face. When I finally found it, up near the end of her arm, I smiled a big silly grin. "Found you!"

"Oh Wally," she replied, "we've been waiting for you! You're in the hospital, you know?"

"Sounded like a party. Why is everyone here?"

"Everyone is worried about you, Honey. You've been sleeping for two days."

"Really? Why? I thought we were going out to dinner."

"We did, we did. We had fried clams, remember?"

"That's right. Mmmn. I'm hungry, too. And you were up a ladder." I could feel the bed rising up.

"How's that, Mr. Anton? Dizzy?"

I shook my head and the dizziness set right in. "When I shake my head, yeah."

"Well, stay still and we'll let you sit up for a while, okay?" I nodded, slowly. A doctor was speaking. Now he took my blood pressure. I looked around. My left side was in a cast. I couldn't move my arm or shoulder.

Linda stood to my right. Elly Maxwell was behind her and Axel Johnson stood back, near the door. "Wow! What happened?"

Piece by piece, Linda told me what she had learned. When she related how I had spun the car around and kicked her out I remembered exactly that event. "I was racing that truck, right? The black pickup?"

She nodded and went on with the police report, how she'd seen me speed by, how they found us off the road on Thompson Run Road. I remembered details, shooting. A nurse brought my meal tray in.

"You guys want to share this?" It looked like enough for four people.

"You eat, Honey. It's been two days." I started on mashed potatoes with canned gravy. Heavenly.

"Ohh, boy, that's good." There was crumbly meatloaf, carrots and a roll. Lots of starches but who's counting? I got help spreading butter. There was milk and a plastic glass of apple juice. Another dish held red Jello; an apple stood alone. I chewed slowly. Good when breaking a fast, I'd heard.

"I never came back for you!"

"I hid for a while after the truck chased you by. Finally I walked the same way. I saw the tow truck from that same garage? The one with the nice old man?" I nodded, chewing.

"I flagged him down and asked where he was headed and I got a ride with him. I think he was the man who came to *Fishwives* that time, remember?"

"The first time we met Sindledecker."

"Right. He recognized me. But, you were gone in an ambulance. There were lots of cops. I just sat in the truck and rode back to the garage with the wreck. You'll have to tell the rental company that story."

"But you got home alright?"

"The Monroeville police gave me a ride. They were very nice."

"What hospital is this?"

"Forbes Metro." I must have looked puzzled.

"Near Frick Park." I shrugged.

"Elly, it's nice of you to visit, too. And Axel? This is really above and beyond."

"Someone had to drive who knew the way. I'm glad you're okay. Maybe I could ask a question or two?"

"I don't know much that can help you. Ask away… I'm done stuffing myself." He placed a little recorder on my tray table, and pulled out a small book.

What followed was questioning about Tom Wittenauer and about Gary Sindledecker. I couldn't tell him much. He already knew Wittenauer's relationship with Brill. I couldn't recall hearing Sindledecker's name from either of those men and Sindledecker never mentioned either of them. Why didn't Axel ask Sindledecker?

"He was killed Tuesday when you got hurt."

"Oh, yeah? Cool. I don't miss him already."

"Few do, but it's unfortunate we can't question him."

"I guess. We didn't do small talk."

"Well, we need to find who hired him or who got Brill to hire him. And who created those false postings. Still a lot to do."

His words reminded me that I still had a lot to do, too. It was depressing. "Do I have a phone, here?"

"I'll set it up for you, Sweetie," Linda answered. "They told me you're here til Monday. What else?"

"Just a pad of paper… and you, Kiddo."

"Well, now that I know the way..."

"This is your first visit?" That didn't sound good.

"Of course not. I took cabs. Axel explained the turns. Now I can get here on my own." I smiled broadly.

"Good!" I reached for the apple.

"They'll have to visit later, now," said the Gestapo-nurse person. "You have some tests."

"Alright, Honey. I'll be back tonight." Linda leaned down and gave me a big kiss. Elly leaned down and gave me quick peck on the cheek and a nice look down her blouse, not that I cared at this serious time. Axel shook hands. A couple minutes after they left the nurse was back with the doctor, at least he acted like a doctor.

They were concerned about my concussion; they'd kept me under for more than a day. My arm was shattered above the elbow. They'd pinned the bones successfully, they thought, but the brain had to heal itself. So far, so good, but they had to watch my reactions for a couple more days. I passed this test, evidently, but when I shook my head the pain was sharp. They advised me to not do that. I asked them if I had a TV in my room. They said they'd arrange it. I wondered if Linda had set up the phone before she left. Didn't matter. When the doctor went out, I did, too.

I woke up around three-thirty. There was a phone on my tray table. It had a tone. A sticker said dial "8" for outside. I had the mayor's number. What the Hell?

"Mayor McKay's office. Who is calling, please?"

"Yes! It's Walter Anton. I survived an attempt on my life and I think he'll want to speak to me."

"Is he expecting this call, sir?"

"I doubt it, but he won't be surprised. Thank you." I waited.

"Hold on, please." No Muzak, today. I had nowhere to go.

"Hold for Mayor McKay, please." Click.

"Is this Walter Anton? What's up this time?"

"Nice to speak to you, too, Harry."

"Okay. Howyadoin?"

"I'm in a cast at Forbes Metropolitan. You?"

"No shit? What happened to you?"

I gave him a quick run-down.

"Jesus Christ, Anton! Does trouble just look for you?"

"Well, it finds me, but at least the guy who was gunning for me is dead. And it's all related to that lease on that little railroad spur, and that's why I called."

"I thought we were all set, waiting for you to make a deal with the Trust."

I told him what had happened on Tuesday.

"So that's it? No deal, no big announcement, nothin?"

"Well, I'm not sure of the rest of it, but why can't Blatchford lease the parcel from the city? I know you'll have to buck Roberta. Are you able to do that?"

"I'll have to think about that. I like the idea of that Larimer project getting done."

"I understand, I guess. It's a means to an end, to me. No offense."

"Well, you don't see it like I do. That project is good for Pittsburgh for lots of reasons, and it's good for me. The Sun doesn't spin around Walter Anton, you know."

"No, no, Harry. I know that, honestly. It's just that, umm… I mean, both Linda's and my lives have been threatened to get this finally completed, I can't let it go."

"Okay, I get you, Walter, but you have to work with me, too. After all, what difference does it make who you're bribing to get your way?"

"Huh? What do you mean?"

"Well, weren't you kicking in on the Larimer deal just to get Roberta to say you could lease the parcel?"

"Yeah. So?"

"Hey, I don't blame you. Now you want to cut her out. Why not chip in so that Harry McKay signs off on the lease? What difference does it make?"

"I get ya. I suppose none. It'll be an end-run around the Trust, though. Are you up for that?"

"I am, yeah... whew! I guess I am. And you? All set with EPA, right?"

"We're covered, there."

"Alright, then. Let's get this moving."

"I'll get things moving. But, you know I can't let Blatchford's money move without a signed lease agreement. He'd shoot me himself if we didn't get what we have been after."

"That shit works both ways, bub."

"I agree. We're going to put our money in escrow with Liberty Bank. I can give the go-ahead by phone from your office. Will that work?"

"I'll make it work. Square it with everybody else and let me know."

"Will do. Thanks for this, Harry. I'll get it done." We rang off. I slumped back, exhausted and feeling great. Fuck Roberta

McGillvray. We got it done without her... without her! I nodded off.

***

Linda woke me around six-thirty. She'd had them take my meal back until she called for it. Now they brought up a cold plate with cut up fruit.

"I talked to the mayor, Lin."

"About the deal?"

"Yeah. He's willing to go forward regardless of Roberta. How about that?"

"Why would you do that? Won't that cause problems?" I realized we had yet to talk about my Tuesday meeting at the Trust.

"I never told you about my meeting with her, did I?"

She shook her head, her face blank.

"Yeah. I told Roberta I could write a check to make the Larimer project go. She turned stone cold and said, basically, she didn't need Blatchford's money, see you later! I couldn't believe it!"

"She didn't bend at all?"

"Nope. All we wanted was for her to not object to a two-year use of our parcel on Southside. I thought it was a big win for her but she wouldn't see the positives at all."

"So, what can you do without her?"

"Well, we've got our release from the EPA. It's all legal and registered. We can make our deal and not worry about her. Now the mayor wants Blatchford to kick in the money to get him – the mayor – to make that lease for use of that railspur."

"Why, that's some kind of holdup, isn't it?"

"I guess so, but like McKay says, what difference does it make who we bribe for that lease?" Linda had no quick reply; I stuffed my mouth with fruit.

Eventually she started to nod. "I guess you were offering a bribe to the Trust. Now it's just to benefit the city. It isn't very different."

"How are you doing, Lover?" We held hands on the side of the bed.

"Better, I think. I had a big cry after your accident. I called Elly and she came and cried with me. I told her the story of Wittenauer jumping in front of Brill, how I hid in the dark. Everything. After that I was able to sleep. I was in a fog there, for a couple of days."

"I am so glad you figured out everything, Honey. I was worried about you. You were in shock, I think."

She nodded and gripped my hand more tightly. "It's amazing he's doing well, at all."

"So, you visited him?"

"Yes. He said you visited, too. I saw him Wednesday and they had him sitting up in bed and he said he was going to be walking that afternoon. That's wonderful!"

"He impresses me, now," I said.

"Very brave." We were quiet again.

"He saved your life and the life of Hillary… or Harold, there inside you."

"Where'd you get those names?"

"In honor of Hal Blatchford, of course." I was mostly kidding, I think.

"Then they should be Tom or Tomasina"

I was shaking my head. "Let's consider family names." Linda sat back, having won that round. Arnie Stewart tapped and stuck his head in.

"Hi, folks. May I?" I waved him in. He shook my hand and Linda's and sat in the other chair.

"You're out late, aren't you? Shouldn't you be recuperating?"

"Ahh, nah. I tried that for a couple days. Doesn't suit me. I only had a flesh wound… and plenty of flesh to have it in. I'm okay."

"You're on the job?"

"At my desk, but I heard about your latest accident and I insisted, so the Captain said I could stay on this case until the doc says I'm fully okay."

"Well, good, then."

"Yeah. By the way, the world thinks your buddy Sindledecker is in the ICU, fighting for his life."

"But, he's…"

"Oh, yes. But he was working for somebody, probably outside of the EPA, but we're still investigating them, too."

"I guess that makes sense. You think his connection will show himself or contact the patient?"

"I do. Someone should be very nervous that an idiot like Sindledecker is in custody. What could he say? So, yeah, I think the contractor is going to get to him to either pay off his silence or maybe kill him. One or the other. So far, no one even called to ask about him."

"Wow, that makes sense. What can you do?"

"Well, I don't have much budget. Headquarters agreed to a rent-a-cop with a radio who will keep up appearances. The average person will assume he's PPD. But it's only a week. I'm hoping this moves fast."

"We're still in danger, then?" Linda asked.

"Pretty slight, I would think. The only threat to the unknown contractor is Gary, himself. Unless Sindledecker told you who it is, you can't harm the unsub."

"Who?"

"UNSUB: unknown subject."

"Oh... gotcha. What can I do to help?"

Stewart immediately waved me off. "Nothing! For God's sake, nothing! Just live a simple life and mind your business. I'll do the worrying on this, please!"

"I like that idea," Linda chimed in. Arnie nodded to her.

"I got nothin to do with this," I stated, "just gotta wrap up my real estate career. This is the last you'll hear from me, Arnie." I finished with a one-handed flourish.

"Let's hope. You've certainly been interesting. Don't forget the person who paid Gary is a murderer, also. Stay far away, at least until the cast comes off... two months, I bet."

"Deal." He shook my hand and held Linda's in his big paw for a second.

"Please don't find any reason to visit me." We laughed.

"I hope his deception works, hmmnh?" Linda was stroking my head.

"Yeah. It's a good idea, sounds like." I answered her with a big yawn.

"It's almost nine, Wally. I'm going home and you can sleep."

I nodded and pulled her down closer to get a kiss, helping myself to a nice breast-feel at the same time. "You gotta pick up that book, Sweetie."

"What book is that?" she asked as she swung her breasts.

"Fourteen Positions With a Left Side Cast."

"I'll definitely look for it, but we can improvise if I don't find it. You just have to get home."

"I'll convince them to let me out Saturday. How's that?"

"As long as the doctor thinks you're okay. No showers though. We'll have to think of something." She gave me a quick feel, too, and there was something to feel, I was happy to learn.

"You could sleep over."

"Fraid not, Valentino!" The night nurse pushed in with her cart. "Visiting's over. I gave you as much time as I could."

Linda thanked her and waved goodbye. I got ready for pills, bedpan and tooth-brushing into a little steel dish. Aw, shit.

FRIDAY, JUNE 7, 1985

Monday would be the tenth. Only twenty days to the drop-dead on our contract. I woke up before five and couldn't get back to sleep. I tried the TV controller, finally finding the network morning show. What the Hell? I wasn't going anywhere, although I really wanted to stand up and get off the back of my ass.

They still had hoses on my left hand. I didn't want to fall with tubes in me. But, boy, would it feel good to stand up for a minute.

"Hold your horses, buster," the day nurse said as she entered. "No standing quite yet. Maybe after the doctor sees you."

How did she know what I was thinking? "Good morning, nurse!" I spouted cheerfully.

"Good morning yourself, sir. Any headache today?"

I shook my head. Not bad. "Not too bad... a little when I shake my head. Maybe if I stood up for a few minutes...?"

"Forget it. Whaddaya want for breakfast?"

"I got choices?"

"What a country, huh? Hard-cooked eggs or scrambled. Ham or sausage patty. Toast or English muffin."

"Okay. Scrambled, ham, whole-wheat toast. Can I do that?"

"I'll see to it." I turned back to the TV. While I was out, the Cardinals had beaten the Pirates twice. My breakfast came and, with perfect timing, the doctor.

"Can I eat while you do your thing?"

"You can try. Here, let's get this out of the way," he said as he swung my breakfast from under my fork. "Nurse," he nodded. She took the needle out of the plumbing on my hand. Suddenly the doctor was pulling on my feet and sitting me up straight on the edge of the bed. "Alright, then… up you go!" And I was standing up and watching the room spin around.

"Whoa, Trigger!" I said. "Wow, doc, I'm spinning."

"That's okay. Just hold onto me and stay up for a minute. It'll subside."

I forced my eyes open and tried to concentrate on trees across the street. The doctor and the nurse started me walking. He was holding my arm and shoulder on the right while she had her hand on my back and a grip on the big cast that enveloped my left arm and shoulder. It was a lot more bulky and uncomfortable, standing. I had to keep countering its weight. "Stand up as straight as you can, Walter," the doctor insisted. Pretty soon we had made three circuits of the room. My head wasn't spinning any more and I was sweating, which surprised me. All I'd done was walk about eighty feet… with help!

"You know what this means, Walter?"

"No. something good, I hope."

"Oh, yes, indeed. You'll be able to go to the bathroom." He guided me to an adjustable chair and the nurse dropped a couple of pillows behind me. Then she wheeled the tray-table over to the chair with my breakfast still a bit warm. Didn't matter. I was looking forward to the toilet.

The doctor wrote a bunch of stuff on my chart. "Okay, then. Don't try standing up from this chair on your own. Hit the call button. One of my rules is no falling in the hospital, got it?"

"I fully agree, doc. What else?"

"You can probably stand on your own in the john. There's a grip bar on the wall but there's also a call button. Don't push too far too fast. You will get tired. If you feel like sleeping, go ahead, but nap in the chair. Don't try bed on your own. Call button." He pointed and I pointed with him and mouthed the words, "call-button."

"Alright, then. The key is to walk as much as you can, today. Any headache and you've got to tell the nurse, okay? Don't hide it because the consequences can be very serious. You had a real concussion. It's not a minor thing. Okay, then?" He unwrapped the gauze from my head, looked at the swelling and dropped the bandage in a pop-top wastebasket.

"It's Friday, right?" The nurse and doctor both agreed that it was.

"If I make the right progress you think I'll go home tomorrow?"

"Possibly. I'll see you later." I thanked him and got busy with breakfast. I was starving. All in all, a great morning.

Breakfast done, I knew I could have a bowel movement, in hospital lingo. A good dump would feel great. I couldn't relax on a bed pan. Call button.

A different nurse answered and helped me to my feet. I told her my plan and she kept her hand on my cast as I slide-stepped to the lavatory. She showed me the call button if I had any trouble at all. I agreed and closed the door. I slipped the pajamas down and plopped my ass on the throne. This was fabulous.

***

"John Schumann."

"John! It's Walter Anton!"

"Walter! Wow. What has happened to you? Can I visit?"

"Yeah, sure. Be great to see you. You know where I am?"

"Hal told me but they said you were in a coma or something. You sound pretty good."

"Yeah. I woke up yesterday and been doin great ever since. I took a crap by myself, this morning."

"Oh, well, then! I'm coming right over."

"Hey, you're always welcome. Listen, I even have some big news."

"On the deal?"

"Yup. Two things. One is that release from the EPA… I told you I had that."

"Yeah. Monday afternoon."

"Okay, but I don't think I told you Roberta refused to accept the deal, absolutely?"

"She what? We're screwed, anyways?"

"Not exactly. It's funny, but when she refused to be sensible I was relieved. Funny. I didn't get to do anything about it until I spoke to the mayor, yesterday."

"The mayor? Don't you know enough to take it easy?"

"I am taking it easy. It's just that when I woke up I had all these things figured out, like."

"Okay, so… good. What can he do?"

"He's willing to grant the lease without her! Cool, huh?"

"He is? No Trust approval?"

"That's right." I was waiting for the implication of that to sink in. It was quiet. "John?"

"Walter, that sounds like Larimer is up the creek… that's a real-estate term."

"Well, it isn't, John, but it might have been. A little full-disclosure?"

"Shoot."

"If McKay had agreed to our lease without Larimer, I'd have taken that deal and saved Blatchford's cash. I'd have felt bad about your deal, but my client, if you will, is Blatchford."

"I can understand that. But what do you mean that the deal isn't up the creek?"

"McKay wants that Larimer project to happen… simple as that. If I want my railroad Blatchford still has to kick in as expected." I could hear Schumann breath.

"Whew, Walter. No more heart attacks, huh? You'll have to sell this again to Hal Blatchford, won't you?"

"I don't think so, actually. Like McKay asked: what difference does it make who you're bribing?"

"True enough, I suppose. You're ready to buck Roberta head on? That could be sticky. The mayor says he's ready for that?"

"I guess he is. We worked out how he'd sign the lease and I would release the money from Liberty's escrow. He's as ready as possible."

"Hmmnh. You know, I never thought I'd see the day Roberta came in second."

"I think she needs the mayor more than he needs her. That's how it looks, anyway."

"She'll still be involved in the execution of the deal, you know. The Trust will still get paid. She will try to block you, somehow."

"I think our EPA letter will hold off Pennsylvania DEP. What else can she try?"

"I don't know, but be assured there's something. She never surrenders."

"I'll check what I can with the mayor. At this point, we have to try to make it go. I'm glad your deal will happen. I'll do what I can to keep that Termagant from messing it up."

"Alright, then. I'll get everyone ready. I'll let you know when to do what. I have to tell you, too, that if I found a way to do Larimer and Blatchford's money wasn't needed, I'd go ahead and do it. Full disclosure."

"I understand. I'd be surprised otherwise," I said.

"Okay, then. Talk to you later." Interesting. Obviously I had more prep to do with the city. Now that we were bribing McKay directly, maybe I could get all my permits in advance. Fuck Roberta McGillvray. I figured I oughta check in with my office.

"Good morning Kelly. Is he in?"

"Yes. Who can I say… Is this Walter?" She actually sounded happy to hear from me for a second.

"The very same. How are you this fine morning?"

"Fine, thank you. I… I'm glad you're okay, Walter."

"Thank you, Kelly, that means a lot to me… really. If he's not too tied up, though, I do have some news for him."

"Sure. Hold on." Wow, I felt good hearing Kelly this way. I definitely was going to get her a nice peace offering of some sort, after the way I'd treated her.

"Good morning, Anton. It's good to hear your voice."

"Thank you, sir."

"Yeah, yeah. I really have been worried about you, Walter. What happened?" I gave him a rendition of Tuesday afternoon and evening. I told him also how Roberta McGillvray had refused our offer.

"So all this bullshit is for nothing? Jesus Christ, Anton, you've almost been killed, your wife was almost killed...!"

"Hold on, Hal. That's not the story! I worked it out with Mayor McKay to do the lease whether she likes it or not."

"You did? Really? Okay, I take it back. We save our eight hundred?"

"Well, no. That part's the same. McKay wants that Larimer project to get done, so if we want our lease we still have to take part in that. Sorry."

"Well, I'm not surprised, I guess. Who cares who gets the bribe? Shit."

"I think you've summed it up exactly, sir."

"So, tell me nothing else can go wrong."

"John Schumann alerted me to a couple things to prepare for, but I think we've got a deal, boss."

"Okay. Good. Let me know when things will happen. When are you coming in?"

"I may get out tomorrow, if I'm real good, so that's my goal. I'll have some more crap to clear up, Monday… the car and so on. I'll have to figure out how to drive with this ridiculous cast. That's a multi-week deal."

"Okay," the old man grumbled, "stop up and see me when you get here."

"Will do. Thanks."

"Time for me to thank you, I think. Let me know when the big day comes." Click… silence.

"Up and at em, tiger," announced the day nurse. "You need exercise, buster. Phone calls don't count. C'mon, now, here we go." She was surprisingly strong. I was standing in two seconds and off we went.

It was about a hundred and fifty feet to a solarium at the far end of the hall. She stayed with me all the way and then walked behind me coming back. I figured I would now be sitting down, but that was wrong.

"Keep going, Mr. Anton. Is your head aching?" I shook it in answer and in test. There was no ache. "Dizziness?" she asked. Again, not yet.

"Okay, then. A couple more routes. You can have lunch in the solarium if you want, or in your room. Keep walking."

I did as I was told. Third time back from the solarium Linda was coming toward us. She gave me a quick hug and a kiss.

"That is a large cast, Honey." She walked at my pace.

"Tell me about it. I balance it, now, but I can't forget about it, that's sure. Are you staying for lunch?"

"I thought I might. There's a deli on the ground floor. Can you come down there?"

"I'll ask the boss." I asked 'M. Callahan.' She told me I could go, but I might want to put on clothes… my choice. Linda followed me to my room and helped me put on slacks, but there wasn't much I could do around the cast. I left my robe on and Linda tied the belt below the cast. Good enough. And I got to ride the elevator.

Linda bought sandwiches, half-sours and chips. It was wonderful. I wasn't the only prisoner eating there.

"So," Linda began. "did the doctor give you hope?"

"Yeah! Good chance to leave tomorrow if I'm headache free and doing well otherwise. I haven't been dizzy and even shaking my head I get no pain. I imagine I'll be able to leave in the morning, so end the party early."

"Oh, silly. I want to share the bed again. And cook for you. I got a call from Nick Sowitsky. He says you have some coverage for a rental vehicle but he couldn't say that it covered everything. He also wanted to know if there was a reason to hold your Jeep. It's totaled, of course."

"Nobody will ever insure me. I guess there's no reason to hold it. I'll have to get a new one. I don't know how I'll explain to Pauly, Jr. why his Chevy was modified. Did the garage say it's drivable?"

"No, I'll call them. I suppose you spoke to Mr. Blatchford. Is your deal going ahead?"

"Apparently. I spoke to the mayor and to John Schumann, too. I think we will get our lease, the mayor will make a speech announcing the Larimer development, Schumann gets his commission and even Roberta gets fees for 'facilitating.' And I'll get to relax and see what the future holds. Should be fun."

"Well, I do hope it all works out. No more upsets as we prepare to be parents."

I nodded. "By the way, did you find that book? Fourteen positions…?"

"No, actually, but it's okay cause I've been *thinking* about fourteen positions. So, put your thinking cap on and we'll see if your fourteen are the same."

"I am absolutely getting out tomorrow."

"Well, until then I'm going to work... making up for Monday and Tuesday." We kissed and gave each other a little feel. Definitely tomorrow. I walked her to the elevator and then on to the solarium and back until I had the route down cold.

SATURDAY, JUNE 8, 1985

"I think you'll be all right going home, Walter," the doctor declared. "It's very important that he doesn't have a fall," he aimed at Linda. "And you'll have to help with bathing because this cast has got to stay dry. Terri, here, can give you some ideas on covering up the cast with plastic wrap or plastic sheets, but if it gets wet get him back here so we can replace it. Getting moisture under there won't allow it to last long enough. It's important."

Linda made copious notes. "What about work or driving?"

"What do you do, Walter?"

"I have an office job, actually, but in the next week or so I do have to get around quite a bit. It's the culmination of what landed me here in the first place. I have to complete the project."

"And that means driving?"

"I certainly hope so. I don't know how I'll function without driving."

"Then I want you wearing a cervical collar. It will help keep your head from bouncing around if you have an accident, and it will make you think twice about things. You are not healed because you're going home, you know."

I agreed to everything he suggested. I'd have agreed to eat turnip to get home and get laid as quickly as possible. Linda and Nurse Terri Whatshername applied plastic wrap to my unshirted torso and taped it down with not-too-painful tape. I thanked the doctor sincerely and Nurse Terri, too. Once she and Linda were satisfied and I had my goodie-bag, we were free.

I rode out in a wheelchair. What did I take all those trips to the solarium for? It also felt silly to have an old sweatshirt cut apart and taped to the cast. I had no idea how I'd dress for business. Once outside I stepped over to Linda's Camry and managed to sit, pivot in and even pull the door closed.

Linda secured the seatbelt behind me to keep pressure off the cast. Off we went, slowly.

It was a wonderful feeling to be on Mapleledge. I managed to unlatch the seatbelt and stand up on my own. Still, I let Linda guide me up the steps and through the door. I stood in the living room while she bustled around putting things away. She brought me a kitchen chair.

"Are you hungry, Honey? I've got some salad and cold cuts and some nice roast beef, sliced thin the way you like it. Want a sandwich?"

"Well, yes if you make it with no underwear on... lettuce alone with no dressing?"

"You're awful. Can't you control yourself?"

"I am controlling myself. If I didn't have this damned cast I'd have thrown you over my shoulder already!"

She turned and faced me and pointed the knife. "Do you want the sandwich or not?"

"Yes, Mummy. Roast beef would be very nice. Any Swiss cheese?"

At the kitchen table Linda took the nook and I sat on a chair. Lots to get used to.

"The garage says the Chevy is drivable, although it doesn't look good. They're going to deliver it in a while."

"Oh, good. I need to practice getting in and out of it."

"Well, not till I pick up a spare collar for you. Won't take much of a bump to land you back in the hospital, you know."

"Well, then, maybe you can help me sleep before you go shopping. I'd hate to try napping all excited… like I am." Linda leaned over to see the excitement.

"I suppose you're controlling yourself?"

"I am, I am!"

"At least let me clean the kitchen then I'll help you get undressed."

I had no choice. I got up and went to the bathroom. I brushed my teeth with no falls. I used the toilet and washed my parts with a washcloth. It's good to be ready. I sat on the bed until Linda joined me. She had some skin lotion that she applied to my shoulder, neck and back. That felt good. While she massaged I was able to pull her blouse out of her slacks and even reached up to fiddle with her bra hook, unsuccessfully.

"You're gonna have to switch to Velcro, sweetheart. I can do only so much, one-handed."

"You can do only what I want. Never forget that."

"I promise," I swore with my best Boy Scout salute. "Now I want you to strip and hop on board. Cast on top is position thirteen. Takes practice."

"What if the car comes at the wrong time?"

"I think we're talking about sixty to ninety seconds. Let em wait."

"Oh, no we're not! Do I have to train you all over again?"

"If you think so, I'm good with that."

"Well, put a cork in it until they deliver the car. I promise you'll be relaxed."

She threw a sheet over me as I lay back. I pouted but she went back to the kitchen and I, unfortunately, fell asleep.

***

I awoke to conversation. It sounded like Axel and Elly talking about Jack Maxwell. I carefully rolled to a sitting position and then to standing. I found some sweat pants and a pajama top that fit around the cast. I slipped on my running shoes without tying them and made my way to the kitchen.

"Well, you're a Hell of a sight!" Linda slid a chair over for me. I shook hands with Axel and with Elly, who were both in the nook. That was cozy.

"Trouble has surely found you this past month," observed Axel.

"I think it's over as far as that's concerned. My two enemies are dead. I should be safe… Linda, too."

Elly was shaking her head. "I couldn't believe it when Linda told me you were hospitalized a second time. I am glad you're walking around!"

"In the flesh!" I said, holding one hand up in the air. "And thirsty. Can I have a soda, Lin?" She poured me a lemonade.

"So, why the visit? I mean, I'm always happy to see you, separately or together. Today seems like… um, together?"

Elly spoke. "We are happily together, yes. It's a long story, actually. Axel, you tell him."

Axel shifted around and gathered his thoughts as if reporting to the Chief of Station. "You know I'm with the FBI. I kept quiet because I was investigating Jack Maxwell. Being the handyman made it easy to get close to Jack, and... to Elly, which is a difficult place for an unattached man." Elly poked him and they touched heads for a second. It was nice.

"My wife passed away from an uncontrolled infection. She was gone in two days. That was six years ago and I buried myself in the FBI. The kids were on their way in school or work by then. It was coincidental that an investigation developed on Jack and

I lived on his street and, most significantly, he didn't know I was FBI. So it became my case."

"Wow. Can I ask what the, umm… 'case' consists of?" I looked from one to the other. Elly just looked at the table. Axel had to think some more.

"Remember the other night when your friend Paul Lemay said he used to work with a Jack Maxwell?" I nodded.

"It was the same Jack Maxwell. They worked at Pitt. Lemay was about to become director of campus security, a key promotion. Maxwell was working a scam through campus purchasing and Lemay was working on exposing it without realizing that Maxwell was in the thick of it. Maxwell undercut Lemay with some phony charges that he made look real enough. Lemay was no longer considered for the job. He left with a promise to not discuss why, and a severance. He went to work with Pittsburgh-Allegheny Security and that's how he met you." That was the name of the guard service? Shame on me.

"So Jack Maxwell, who always seemed a little too closed off, really was a bad guy?"

"Is, Walt… is a bad guy. I haven't roped him in yet but the noose is tightening. The good part is that I got to know Elly better and better and I decided to stop fighting my feelings and... here we are."

"Well, hear, hear! Congratulations to you, both. It seems perfect."

"Thanks. It's still not broadcast news because I don't want Jack to hide himself from Elly. The boys know I visit but we've been pretty careful, I think."

Elly nodded. "I'll be happy to have them back, and Jack has been leaving them a lot anyway. Maybe you can keep them busy while you're in a cast?"

"Sure, sure. I got some jobs for them. That'll be great, I think."

"And you ran in to a bad actor, too?" Axel seemed very interested.

"Oh, yeah. The son of a bitch has been trying to kill me. All tied to that guy who shot himself… the one who wanted to take Linda hostage on Monday."

"Brill. We were watching his connection to Wittenauer. I've interviewed the congressman at Mercy. What can you tell me about his involvement?"

"Not much. Right up front I'll tell you I don't harbor any negative thoughts toward him. He took a bullet to save Linda's life."

"But, you had warned Arnie Stewart about him, didn't you? Thought he was trying to kill you?"

"Keep in mind that I never met the guy until twenty-three days ago, nor did I grasp his involvement with the EPA signs until some days after that. I jumped to logical conclusions, but there's somebody behind Brill who is the real problem, there."

"Any ideas?"

I shook my head as he asked. "His boss, Malcolm Porter, was pretty sour when he relinquished the letter we needed, but I don't know him at all."

"Look, I didn't mean to interrogate, here. Habit. We just want to share our news and see how you were doing. Umm, your Chevy's back. Looks a little worn."

"I can imagine how it looks. It's not even mine. It's a rental!"

"I guess you got some 'splainin' to do." Axel was laughing as he eased from behind the table, Elly behind him. He stuck out his hand and I was happy to shake it. I gave Elly a little peck and they both hugged Linda. It was kinda nice. Still, as they crossed the street, Axel peeled off to his house and Elly greeted the boys, who'd been doing yard work.

"That's nice, don't you think?" Linda asked. "You were right all along."

"That Axel is no fool. He doesn't get to sleep with you, but he's no fool just the same."

"Well, you *look* like a fool in that get-up. We're going to have to figure out some outfits that won't look too gross."

"Guys don't wear outfits."

"Fine. But you still need something to button with a necktie. You're bound to have meetings coming up." I half-shrugged. I had to wear something.

The cast made me feel like a turtle. A strap kept it secure against me, and there was no way to put a sleeve over it. I sat still while Linda walked around me and held shirts and tee-shirts up to my body.

She stopped abruptly with four of my good shirts laid out on the couch and a greater number of tees.

"Okay. We can make it work. Now I have some shopping but I promised you relaxation. I always keep my word. Are you still firm in your intentions?"

"Yes, see?" Evidence was popping up.

"You must be controlling yourself, huh?" I nodded and tried to grab a feel. "Careful, pardner, I'm putting that strap around you so we don't do any damage. C'mon." I followed her like a puppy… with a hard-on, but puppy-like.

It was different. Linda crouched over me with her breasts brushing my lips. I managed to suck them until they stood out. Then she eased herself onto Old Useless and carefully rocked back and forth. I fought and fought to hold on but it was too much for me. Off I went, which caused her to concentrate really hard as she carefully rolled back and forth, trying to catch up. I thought as hard as I could to keep some erection going, but it was dissipating. She finally had to stop as I slipped out, truly useless.

"Ohhh," she moaned. You owe me for that. No fair."

"I'm sorry, Honey. I tried not to but you felt awfully good... well, I'll do better next time, and the sooner the better, too. Maybe we can figure out a sponge-bath routine and I can help you shower. Just the thought of it is already working. See?"

"Ohh, men. Makes me appreciate zucchinis."

"Whaaat?"

"They stay hard all week!"

"Is that a fact? They can't fix furniture!" Linda thought about that, still astride me. I thought about it, too and began to perk up in the produce department. Linda wriggled just so and we were back in business. I swelled nicely and she resumed her special swirl-push-swirl motion with her lower lip sucked between her teeth. All right. This debt might get paid soon.

About forty-five seconds after full-zucchini she gave a delighted yelp and collapsed on my good side, my right arm cradling her. I got a second little jolt in there, too and was almost falling asleep by the time she sat back and climbed off. Then it was cold. I grabbed the towel and carefully rolled upright. She was already in the shower. This might be tricky.

I pulled out the plastic basin from the linen closet. I don't know why we had it. My mother had one in case someone was sick. Linda's mother probably did, too. I had soap and a washcloth and a small step-stool ready. Linda switched the shower to faucet and stepped out in her beautiful glory. I put the stool in the tub.

I was able to wash the lower areas but I needed help with the upper body. Linda carefully washed my back and shoulders and wiped them off as she went. I guess I was clean. I hung my head sideways, down as low as I could, and she washed my hair and liberally rinsed it with a wet cloth. Then she dried me. I stood up out of the tub and she dried my legs and various parts. We were going to need some specialized hardware. When she left she had a list of things for sit-down bathing.

It was still light, but I went to bed.

MONDAY, JUNE 10, 1985

Linda had expanded four white shirts with pieces of four new ones. I don't know how she knew what to do. Now I was able to put a shirt on that could button at the neck and still cover the cast. I didn't feel too weird, anyway. I answered inevitable questions. Pauly Lemay deserved some minutes because we had to miss Saturday shoulder and beans. I was happy to reschedule that one.

I took time with Jack Jackson, too. He'd been dealing with the architect and construction people without me. A full rendering and simple design sheets for the concrete platform and changes to the building were due later today. He caught me up on their discussions and seemed oddly pleased that I thought what he'd done was great. I called Kelly Galvin from my office. She said Hal had left instructions for me to come up when I got in. I went up straightaway.

Kelly looked at me very intently as I walked toward her desk. "You look uncomfortable, Walter. How are you doing?" I smiled warmly in reaction to her concern. It was nice.

"All in all, pretty well. It's just difficult washing up and dressing is awkward, but Linda fixed up some special shirts for me." I spun around for her to see the latest fashion for cast-wearers.

"Very good. Tell her I'm impressed. He's waiting." She smiled again Maybe getting shot had balanced the scales. I still intended to get her something nice.

"Morning, Hal."

This time he got up and came around to meet me. He shook my hand and led me to one of the chairs at the 'T' in front of his desk.

"How you doin son?" he asked me. It caught me off-guard. "Son?"

"Pretty well, sir, actually. The rental car's drivable and Linda figured out how to dress me. Could be much worse, so I'm thankful. And my big nemesis is dead."

"Good, good. I was just commenting to Jackson that you've gone through a lot in, what, four weeks?"

"Four weeks this Thursday if I'm not mistaken. Feels like a lifetime. No one could have predicted it."

"And you've succeeded at what seemed impossible."

"It appears that the deal can be done, yes. I have to pin down a couple of city permits to make sure the Trust can't trip us up at the last minute." I looked at him as he appeared to be seeing me for the first time, a half-smile on his lips. "Have you seen Tom in the past couple of days?"

"Yes, yes. He's not in the ICU, now and he was sitting up when I saw him on Saturday. Amazing!"

"Oh, that's good news. Maybe he'll be able to attend the big announcement. I think that would be appropriate."

"So do I, Walt. Tommy really came through for all of us, didn't he? And, you know who else has been visiting him on a daily basis?"

"Katie Mellon." I was smiling, almost laughing.

"Oh... okay. You're up on that."

"I did discuss Wittenauer with Katie when I was afraid for her being too close." I shrugged. "She was very defensive and said they'd dated. Got angry with me, actually. I'm happy for them."

"I tried to encourage them together, you know. Tommy's marriage was never a very good match."

I smiled. "Who would suspect you were a matchmaker?" For a moment Hal smiled with me and then resumed his stern countenance.

"Needn't be publicized, Anton." I zipped my lips... as if no one knew, already.

"Well, I'm not quite as flexible as I was," I gestured with the cast, "but I can still get my work done. I have to get all the ducks in a row for our signing with the city. If it's okay, I'll get on that and report back."

"Okay, good. We'll talk later. You know, I'm sorry I got you involved in all that has happened to you. I really am."

"Well, I'm sorry for the injuries and stuff, but in a way, I wouldn't have missed this for anything. Strange." I sat, shaking my head. "So, please don't regret this assignment… I don't, really."

"Thanks, Walter. Now go ahead." He waved me out with a smile. Our relationship had changed again.

"Thanks, Kelly," I said as I walked passed her desk. She mouthed, "You're welcome" in reply. If I could have bounced down the stairs, I would have.

I called the mayor's office. "Mayor McKay's office. Who is calling, please?"

"Yes, good morning! Can you tell him it's Walter Anton?"

"Oh, yes, Mr. Anton. I'll see if he is available." Wow. I'm a regular with the mayor's office.

"Walter!" the mayor boomed out, "How are you?"

I told him I was doing well and still hard at work on the deal of the century.

"I thought we were in agreement on that. Something wrong?"

"I don't think so, Harry, but I do have a couple of worries. John Schumann reminded me of some permitting steps the Trust might interfere with. I'm not sure of them all and I am hoping you could direct me to someone who can get everything pre-approved so that the lease on '840' won't be interrupted."

"Ahh, well. Are you able to get around?"

"Oh, yeah. I'm driving... carefully."

"C'mon down after lunch, then. We'll meet a couple of folks and I think we can button everything up."

"Thank you very much, Harry. Meeting you is the best part of this whole adventure, I think."

"Walt?"

"Yuh?"

"Don't bullshit a bullshitter. Important lesson." I laughed, but he didn't.

I sat quietly, nothing on my desk. I looked around the old-fashioned, half-office with its wooden coat tree, oak desk, oak file cabinet and plain oak table. I looked at the empty in-baskets. Where would I be, after this? I hoped I was going to work for Blatchford, because I was becoming truly fond of him. But, doing what? It was bittersweet to be so close to victory on the lease... with nothing else certain. Thank God for Linda. She was certain.

I pulled out the yellow pad and made notes for the rest of Monday and the week, itself. Today I'd meet the mayor and wrap up those permit details. Then what? I tried to make a list of steps to get to the close.

The mayor was item one. I sat for a second wondering what the permits were Schumann referred to. I wrote down 1, 2 and 3, but had nothing next to them. Item two was Blatchford's escrow deposit. Under that I wrote that I'd have to set things up with Forrest Akers to only release the Blatchford money when I told him to. The deal with the mayor had to click smoothly.

Item three seemed to involve Roberta McGillvray despite my hopes that I had prepared a good end run. I had no idea what to prepare for. She would be angry, for sure, and would lash out. How could I counter without knowing what she'd do? I was getting grumpy.

I pulled out an old list of pluses and minuses. All the players were listed, although a couple were now dead. I circled Tom Wittenauer's name repeatedly. He was recovering, but not in a position to do anything, particularly. But he had influence. I resolved to visit him again.

I added a blank for the unknown contractor behind Brill and Sindledecker. Would that person try something as we approached the big announcement? I jotted down a string of question marks. Interestingly, Alan Boudreau's name popped into mind. He had shown me the depth of his thinking when we went to the EPA the previous Monday. Worth talking to him, certainly. I made that note and called it '4', but he was not really in the list of steps to the announcement and close. But he was a comfort for me. I would definitely speak with him as soon as I could.

I made a box near the bottom of the sheet and wrote "Alamo" and "P. Lemay, Jr." in it. I had to resolve the virtual destruction of his Impala. It was nearly noon and I was starving - thinking about that barbecue that Micah took me to. I called S & S Taxi and asked for him. The dispatcher said he'd be to Blatchford in about ten minutes. I walked out to tell Pauly Lemay to call me when the cab arrived, and to call his son at Alamo and ask him to swing by.

"I'll be takin care of those things, Mr. Walter. You just relax yourself."

"Thanks, Pauly. I appreciate your help."

I sat back at my desk to wait. For the Hell of it I called Alan Boudreau… he sometimes had an odd schedule. I let it ring until his answering machine picked up. I left my number. Now what? I leaned back and closed my eyes. It felt very nice.

When my phone gave the internal ring I almost fell off the chair. I pushed myself to stand and woke up as fast I could. It was Pauly, telling me that some kind of Jamaican was here for me. I told him not to worry and hurried to the guard room.

Micah was standing next to the door looking uncomfortable. I shook hands with him and introduced him to Pauly Lemay. "Micah, I want to pay you to go to that barbecue place and bring me a lunch." He looked at me with an odd expression. "And I want you to get a lunch and get a third one for Pauly, here." Pauly perked up on "barbecue."

"I carried my lunch, Mr. Walter. You don't need to do that." I assured him I wanted to and that he'd thank me. Micah was doing some mental calculations.

"You be gibin me thirty dollars, sah, and it's ten fo the trip. You okay on dat?"

"I'll be givin you fifty, Micah, so there's a tip for the barbecue and for you. How's that?" He smiled broadly and said he'd be right back and not to worry... sah!

"You didn't have to buy me lunch, Mr. Walter. Why you go and do that?"

"You're a good friend, Pauly. And this ain't lunch... it's an experience. You'll be happy. Just let me know when he gets back."

I started toward my office when Pauly called to me. His son was there.

"Hiya, Mr. Anton. You have some trouble with the car? Wow, what happened to your side?" I wasn't looking forward to the conversation.

"No, actually, I had an accident, Paul. The cast is connected to it but it isn't directly due to the accident. However, we have to figure out where I stand with your contract. Take a look."

We walked out to the Chevy. He was quiet as he walked around, touching the dents and scrapes. "What's the duct tape for, sir?"

"Oh, that. I was in a fight with a guy who tried to murder me and the fireplace poker I was using deflected off his wrist and punched a hole in the roof."

"Okay, okay, I get it. But what really happened? Something fall on it or you drove under something?" I realized how ridiculous what I'd said sounded and I started laughing. Young Pauly rubbed his fingers across and around the depression under the tape. He looked at me in disbelief and started laughing, too.

"I am sorry for the condition of the car, Paul. But that hole in the roof is the only part I am really responsible for. And how it got there is exactly as I described. You can check with the Monroeville Police Department. We were in the parking lot of *Fishwives Restaurant.*" Paul stopped laughing and peeled the tape away from part of the hole. He looked at it and at me and shook his head.

"And the smash-in on the driver's side?" he asked.

"That was just last Tuesday when I led the same murderer on a road chase until the police could catch up to us. When I pulled a stop-and-pivot maneuver he managed to drive his truck into the car, which pushed me off the road. That's when he shot me and how I got this cast. Simple."

If there were a perfect look of incredulity, Paul Junior had it. He took another turn around the car, making notes and sketches on the back of the contract. "But it's drivable, right?" He made another note when I assured him it was. He opened the passenger door and sat on the seat with his feet on the ground. He pulled another form out of his clipboard and wrote extensively on it. I felt bad about the work I was causing. When he finished he came around the car and handed the second form to me. It was a detailed description of damages including diagrams on a generic car outline. I had to sign it.

"What am I signing here, Paul?"

"Basically you're agreeing to my description of the damages, but, since you didn't buy the daily insurance, you are also agreeing to responsibility for repairs that aren't covered in some other way. You understand, right?"

"I'm afraid I do. What happened, happened while I was renting… and driving the car. So, now what do we do?"

"Well, Mr. Anton, I'm pretty much hamstrung to do anything not in the contract, now. If you want to keep renting this car you have to take it to the insurance company's drive-in claims center. There are two of them. The addresses are on the form, there." He pointed and I nodded. "They'll give you a written estimate of damages and repairs. You can decide what to do after you see their figures."

"What to do what?"

"Well, you can get another estimate if your own body shop does the work and the adjusters will come to terms with them. Or you can decide to purchase the car from Alamo if the costs are close to the selling price. Then you could trade it in for something new, maybe… I don't know." The kid was nothing but business, now. "I'll fax you the sales offer if you have a fax machine. Do you?"

There was a new facsimile machine in the purchasing department. I asked him for his fax number and said I'd fax him ours so he could send it. He agreed to be on the lookout for it and stuck out his hand. We shook.

"Look, Paul, I'm sorry about what's happened to your beautiful Impala. We'll straighten it all out, somehow."

"I'm sorry for your injuries, Mr. Anton. I still can't believe everything you said, but whatever it was that got you hurt, I'm glad to see you're doing better." I gestured to him to follow me. I opened the driver's door and pointed to an elongated hole in the leather above where my shoulder had been.

"Bullet hole," I said. He looked at me wide-eyed and then at the cast. The bullet had deflected off my left humerus and into the back of the seat, shattering the bone on its journey.

"I hope it heals up quick, Mr. Anton."

"Thanks, Pauly. I'll send that fax number over." We shook again and he left in his compact. The timing was perfect as Micah arrived with a couple of boxes with foil-wrapped plates in them. I could smell it when the door opened.

"Ev'thing come out just right, sah. We all set, now." Big Pauly came out of the building to help me, and carried both boxes back inside. I thanked Micah and followed my pungent lunch. The rest of this lunch hour promised to be a lot more palatable than dealing with a damaged car. Pauly got lunch and dinner from his.

***

The mayor's office couldn't have been kinder. I was now an invalid and they clicked into perception mode. The mayor knew how to treat the unfortunate. I still had to wait for him, but I could have had six coffees or sodas.

"C'mon in, Walter. Boy you look a sight! What the Hell happened?" He sat me right down and sat next to me at his polished table. I gave him the basic blow-by-blow rundown. He commiserated appropriately. Finally, "How can I help?"

"When I spoke with John Schumann this morning, he advised me to be sure that any other permits we might need for use of Parcel 840, were granted prior to our pulling the trigger on the lease and the money. I don't even know what to ask for. Who should I see? What might trip us up?"

"Hummnh," McKay mused. "I suppose we should look at our permitting agencies and see who applies." He punched the intercom.

"Janet, could you come in and bring the list. Thanks." In a minute she tapped on the door and let herself in. After the introductions she sat across from us and spread out a double notebook. Lots of agencies.

"What is the nature of the business?" She looked from the mayor to me and back again.

"We fabricate steel. Raw materials come in to us, we put holes in it, cut it, weld it and then ship it out to our clients. That's why we need the rail spur."

"Rail spur?" she flipped a page. "You want to lay track in the city limits?"

"No!" She looked up. "I mean, no… it's already there. We just want to use it."

"Who owns the track now?" And on it went. Little by little we pared the possibly affected agencies down to five: Health, Public Safety, Water and Sewer, Transportation and Engineering and the Zoning Board of Adjustment. It was after two when she left us. McKay had been looking at his watch for fifteen minutes.

"You okay getting around on your own, Walter?"

"I'm okay. No problem. Are the places I need in this building?"

"Not all of them. Ask at the guard desk on the first floor. They'll be able to direct you to where they all are. If you have a problem, call Janet's extension and she'll smooth the way for you. That's all I can do right now. Good to see you're on the mend."

Our meeting was over. I'd received more help than I'd have expected. I'd vote for McKay the next time he ran… if I lived in the city. As I opened the door I turned back and told McKay that the closing on Larimer could happen in a few days.

"Call me when it's set, Walt, and we can close our deal right here." I thanked him, again, and headed to the elevator.

The afternoon saw me through three departments. None could find anything that would keep us from upgrading the existing rails and ties, although we'd have to have an inspection before the first cars were pushed to the river. I'd have to visit the DPW and Public Safety Wednesday morning. I went home.

Linda was later than I was. I drifted through my getting-home steps without her sunny presence to define my orbit. I turned on the early news and poured some lemonade. The sound of her brakes was delightful.

"Late, today. Busy?"

"No, actually. Your Officer Stewart called and both he and his partner, Marty, interviewed me for more than forty minutes. I guess it's what they do, but their questions ranged pretty widely, I thought."

"You mean," I asked as we hugged, "they weren't talking only about last Monday?"

"Well, that, of course, but also about my job and *englishclass* and about being on the board of the Trust. How well did I know Roberta? Did she ever pressure me for information about you or about Blatchford?"

"Really? Wonder what good that is?"

"I couldn't see what they were after and I kept asking why they wanted to know this or that, but they didn't reveal their grand purposes. But at least that's done with. And you?"

"I finished up some niggling details at City Hall and the mayor was very nice to me, today." Linda thought that was nice and went off to change. I followed after her.

"Oh, and one other thing?"

"Yes?"

"I met with Paul Lemay's son about the car. I have to decide whether to pay for repairs or buy the thing and trade it for something else. I didn't purchase insurance and now I have to pay the price."

"Ouch! What will it cost?"

"I have to send Paul the fax number for Blatchford's machine and he'll send me Alamo's offer for sale of the car. If I decide to keep renting the car I have to drive through their claims place. Either way, I pay. Maybe I'll sue Gary Sindledecker." She gave me a look.

"Everybody else, though, recommended that I have sex as much as possible to prepare for the big closing and announcement."

"I hope nobody walks in on you."

"Huh? What?" Sometimes it took a while for the light to shine, but eventually...

"I meant with you, Sweetie. You know that."

"Oooohh...okay," she nodded and winked. "Hungry?"

"Not so terribly. I had a big lunch, today."

"You went out for lunch with your cast?"

"Nope. Although I visited the mayor after lunch and other city departments. But lunch I sent out for. Bought lunch for Pauly Lemay, too. It was great." I told her about my new cabbie friend and the fascinating lunch place he'd introduced me to. I promised to take her there, but I'd have to find it.

In minutes, Linda had whipped together cold cuts, bread and salad fixings. It was nice.

"Are you set for closing on the railroad?" Linda chewed and looked at me for an answer.

"Almost. I have to talk to Public Safety and Engineering to have all the permits before Roberta can trip us up. The mayor's office is helping me. McKay is a pretty good guy."

"Any more skullduggery I can help you with?" she grinned.

"No, it's kinda straightforward from here on, I think. You're going to come to the big announcement shindig, aren't you?"

"I don't know. When?"

"I have to find that out from John Schumann. Could be the end of this week... I hope."

"It's hard to imagine when you weren't fighting this battle." She was smiling at me, but tears were welling up, too. "And I don't like it one bit." She sniffled and wiped away tears with a napkin. "So make it as soon as you can. We can take a little road trip on the weekend to celebrate."

"I'll be working toward that," I agreed. "We can go somewhere we don't have to get dressed."

"We'll see, won't we?" I was already thinking about removing her clothes for her, but with one hand I'd have to talk her into it... out of it... them. Maybe chocolate since she wasn't drinking. Which reminded me...

"Did you go to the doctor today? You said you were going today, right?"

"Yes!" She was staring at me. I caught a sense of things.

"And she tested you for pregnancy?" I shouted.

"Yes, she did!" Linda's eyes were bright and moist.

"And she told you you are pregnant?" I was on my feet.

"Yeeessss!" she screamed as she jumped up into my arm. She was vibrating with excitement and wriggling in my partial embrace.

"Why didn't you tell me? Or call me? Or launch a balloon or something?"

"I don't know how much longer I could have waited. I'm ready to explode. I suppose that wasn't fair. I actually forgot about it myself at work, today, and then got excited about telling you coming home. When you didn't ask me that question first I decided to play a little game of how-long-before-he-asks. Another ten minutes and I would have conked you with a two-by-four."

"Whew! I don't know what I'd do with two casts. We'd have to get another manual for one arm and one head in casts."

She punched me in my good arm. "I wouldn't leave any evidence, silly. The original manual will be fine."

"Oh, okay. Let's celebrate with more sex before we forget how!"

"Well, what about your cast. You must be tired." I started pulling her toward the bedroom.

"I'll use pure willpower to find the energy to help you."

"Oh how nice of you. Do you mean you'll generate your own boner or do I have to do that, too?"

"I'm not sure," I replied as we sat on the bed. "I might need some help, there, although I started working on it, already, see?" There was evidence that I wasn't debilitated.

"Will this help?" she asked as she performed a little strip-tease.

"It's working, it's working!" More evidence. Even without the mythical manual, we figured out a position. This time I had enough control to make sure she was well-satisfied before I let go. It was wonderful. Not shower quality, but wonderful.

TUESDAY, JUNE 11, 1985

I cleaned up with help. We now have a slip-proof, rubber-footed seat, safe on porcelain. Naturally I became more than a little aroused as she gently soaped and rinsed.

"You'll just have to wait, cowboy. I'll read another chapter in the manual while you do your important, serious work. Don't forget our weekend plans."

I could have had morning sex and still thought of the weekend. She helped me dress with one of her miraculous shirts. I was starting to envy people who drove cars that weren't banged up. I made a mental note to get over to the claims adjusters and spent the rest of the trip thinking out my day.

I barely touched the office, said hello to Jack, begged off a discussion about what the architect had presented, and went to see the DPW and Public Safety. The Transportation and Engineering office at the DPW only cared about grade crossings and new rail intersections with existing track. We didn't need any of those. They wanted the courtesy of an inspection before we rolled, also.

Public Safety, aside from a ridiculous wait, wanted to know if we were going to modify any grade-crossing signals, pass over any public ways on bridges or trestles, or interfere with existing easements for surface traffic over the leased land. I think I could sum up their concerns as mainly wondering why I'd bothered them. It was late morning. I called John Schumann from Public

Safety and asked about lunch at *Marko's*. It didn't take much. He asked if he could ride with me and I thought of some additional business we could get done if he came to the office. I picked him up.

Apparently Schumann had never been to *Marko's*, although he claimed to have heard of it. I felt like a regular, taking him downstairs to the long tables. I let him look over the specials and then recommended the pike with the lemon-ginger sauce. He was happy with that. I went back to catfish and salad.

"Do you have plans set for the big announcement?" I sipped my iced tea.

"Well," he answered somewhat edgily, "I know where we're going to have it!" His eyes were smiling as he spoke. "I haven't spent a lot of time on it, truthfully. The main concern is the sequence of speakers and who's on stage. I have checked on the staging. There's a company I've worked with before who rents em and sets em up. I'll call the papers when I have the date and time."

"Oh. It sounded more complicated than that." Our waitress appeared and plunked down our meals. We dug in for a few minutes.

"So, once the participants are pinned down, it sort-of falls into place?"

"Just about. Why?"

"Well, I thought we could take a few minutes to talk to Hal Blatchford, if you have time. Get him set for this."

Schumann nodded. "I'd like that. I don't really know him."

"Okay. After lunch let's hit the office for a few minutes. We can talk to Hal and then make a few calls and get everyone lined up, if it's alright with you."

"Uhh, well, okay. Is there some reason we need to do it today?" Now he was squinting at me.

"I am hoping we can do this by Friday." I finished the last few crumbs of my fish and washed it down with the last of my tea. Schumann's lips were pursed.

"Friday, huh? I guess we could. Sure. I'll have to do some dancing, but most everything is in place. Friday. Okay."

I started to look for our waitress but she was on her way, anyway. "Something else, today, fellas?" We said "no" and she laid our check down and left with the dishes. I started to pull out money but Schumann waved me off and dropped a twenty and a five on the slip and put the salt and pepper on top of it.

"Thanks, John. I thought I had invited you."

"You are going to make me a commission in the next few days. I owe you," he said as we climbed the stairs to street-level.

I called Kelly Galvin. I told her I had a special guest to meet Mr. Blatchford and could she get me in? I definitely had to get her a nice apology gift. She came on the line and said to come up.

"Hal, you've met John Schumann." Smiles and hand-shaking and then we sat.

"What can I do for you boys?" Hal asked.

"Well, boss, we need to take the final steps for the big transaction. It's time to put your cash into escrow at Liberty Bank, and I thought if you had some questions about Liberty, or about Forrest Akers, John could answer them. And we need to plan for the announcement ceremony, itself." Schumann nodded next to me.

"Okay on the escrow, but what do I have to do with your ceremonies?"

I answered with a blank look and turned to Schumann for answers.

"Weellll," he began, "you're one of the heroes of this whole effort, Hal, you see? I think you deserve proper recognition and

Blatchford Steel should get the goodwill and good press your contribution to Larimer deserves. It's good for everybody else, why not for you, too?" Now I was nodding.

"What does it mean? What do I do?" Hal was sitting well back, looking from John to me and back again. Neither of us jumped to answer. Finally I gestured and answered his question.

"You need to make a statement... not a long speech, but something positive about being proud of Pittsburgh and how honored you are to be part of its turn-around. Something like that." Blatchford moved his lips and rolled his eyes.

Schumann grinned widely. "What did you say your job is? That was perfect."

Blatchford's eyes widened. I replied, "Really? What else would you say?"

"Nothing!" Schumann said. "That's the point." He turned toward the old man. "Just say what Walter said, Hal. In your own words."

"Humph. If you think it's important." Schumann assured him it was.

"When is this shindig?"

"I'm planning for Friday, actually. We think everything is in place... there's no point in waiting."

"Glad to hear it, glad to hear it. It's been quite a road you've traveled, Walter. You've done the impossible. Are you making a speech, too?"

"I'm a back-grounder, boss. I'll be happy to watch." He nodded. Schumann looked at the table. "And don't mention my name, either!"

Hal sat back, surprised. Schumann guffawed before he caught himself.

"You say so," said Blatchford. "What else?"

"I have an agreement with the mayor that the money won't be released from escrow until the lease is signed for the parcel. When you convey the money, reiterate to Akers that that is how it's supposed to work. I'll be in touch with him again, too, on that."

"Sounds good. And your friend Roberta at the Trust? She's been neutralized?"

"I think so, but my fingers are crossed. She will hate me and probably you, too, but the mayor is willing to sign the lease without her approval. This might mark a sea change in Pittsburgh."

Hal looked toward Schumann at that statement.

"He may be right, Hal. This is the first time I've seen a deal like this go forward without Roberta's approval. I'm kinda interested to see it happen, too."

"All right, then. I'll be ready for Friday… morning, I presume?"

"I hope so," said Schumann, "It's best for the news cycle." We stood and shook hands all around. I thanked Hal for taking the time. Schumann and I went to my office.

"Let's make the calls you need to make."

First was the mayor. Schumann got the run around and a promise the mayor would call back soon. Next he called Forrest Akers, who took his call right away. He told him the Blatchford money was on its way and to plan for Friday. Akers had been hoping for Friday, and said he'd be ready. He would schedule everyone in the community. Great.

Schumann and I chatted about other Pittsburgh issues, car accidents, and how things had transpired with the EPA. I shared with him that Linda was expecting with a due date of March first. I told him he was the only person I had mentioned it to and to not share it until Linda gave the word, but it was a pretty big deal. The phone rang.

"Good afternoon, Mr. Mayor, John Schumann from Brightman Partners. How are you?" I listened to our side. The mayor was a little peeved, it sounded, that we were giving him so little notice. Schumann mollified him. After all, Walter Anton had only finished the details that very morning, and the really important thing was to prepare his speech that would precede the unveiling of an architect's rendering of the new buildings. He, the mayor, could pull the rope to unveil it, before Roberta McGillvray unveiled the renderings she'd been sitting on for years. Top billing must have mitigated other feelings. Before he hung up I asked to speak to him.

"Hi, Harry, Walter Anton. This ceremony will probably be about eleven o'clock," I confirmed that idea with some head-nodding from John Schumann, "so do you want to do our deal around nine o'clock that morning or in the afternoon on Thursday?" In the morning was the answer. Fine, and thanks. One call left.

"John, I don't think you want to mention that Blatchford is still the source of financing for Larimer, do you?"

"You're probably right. I don't need Roberta hating me. I'll be trying to work with her again. What do I say is the source of the additional financing?"

That was a real puzzle. I didn't want her bringing a lot of heat onto the mayor before the ceremony.

"What if you simply say that the money was granted and is already in escrow with Liberty Bank. Then talk about her position immediately after the mayor and unveiling her renderings. Ask her how much time she'll need for her remarks. She might not dwell on the money."

Schumann was thinking, now and then shaking his head. "As soon as she sees Hal Blatchford… or you, there, she'll hit the roof and perceive that I am part of an end run around her, or complicit, at least. I have to think about how that will affect Brightman's business." I had to agree with that analysis.

"What scenario can you think of where she doesn't figure out Blatchford's role? You might tell Hal he *shouldn't* take part in the event... but, if you do, you're on your own." I smiled and elicited a small grin from him, but he was obviously troubled.

"If there were no Blatchford money, we could stay away from the whole issue, I suppose."

I wasn't sure what he meant by that. "Do you have a way to do that?" I wasn't smiling, which he took note of.

His head swung back and forth. "No, not at all. Blatchford has made this deal. We might try to hide it, but Roberta would soon learn of Blatchford's lease of your parcel and improvements you are making to the tracks. She'll be just as mad, if not more angry, to find out that way."

I had to agree. It was coming down to Brightman's courage. "You know, John, the mayor has decided to face up to her. She can make a lot of trouble for him, too. But, he's doing it."

"So, will we stand up against her, too? Do we have the courage?"

I shrugged that maybe those were the questions. "It won't hurt me in the future, or Blatchford. I don't have the same decision to make as you have. I can hope you make it, but I can't help you with it."

"No... no you can't. I think we're doing this deal, and Brightman Partners has to prepare itself for the fallout. I think I need to speak to Aaron before I speak to Roberta McGillvray." And that was the last of what we could do from my office.

"Well, c'mon, then. I'll get you to your office." We were fairly quiet on the way downtown. I asked him if he wanted me to park and come up with him? That merited a sharp head shake.

"Aaron won't do well with a non-partner in the room for a decision like this. Believe me, there's nothing personal. In cruel terms, I could say that you go to the wrong church to be in this particular meeting."

Once again it took a moment, but the lightbulb clicked on. Brightman's Partners all shared one crucial quality. "You'll call me when you decide? Call my house if it's late. Can I offer one thought?" I asked.

"If anyone can, it's you," he said.

"Since there doesn't seem to be a way to do the deal without facing up to the Trust, you will either do the deal or not. If you do the deal, it says something strong about Brightman."

"Yuh," was all he answered.

"I'll await your call, John." He waved and I pulled away. This day had become weird, too. I had the strongest urge to just go home. I was getting a non-concussion headache. More like a bump on the will. I had ridden my determination for a month to get to this very point. Now we could only get to the finish line through the exercise of business courage by people I could neither influence nor speak to. I decided I owed it to Jack Jackson to talk with him about the construction.

We spent half an hour. He showed me the sketches and estimates the architect had given him. He was ready to order the start of construction as soon as we had the lease. We talked about the stages to be followed so that we could take best advantage of the summer weather. The changes to the building would be done first and the pouring of the concrete platform later. So far, it looked like the whole project would be completed by December first. But, it couldn't wait. Neither could the lease. I told Jack I'd tell him the second the last hurdle was crossed and we had our railroad access. When I left I felt like Jack and I could work together.

It was good to head home. Linda had a cooked chicken and made chicken salad, and boiled some eggs for egg salad. With some greens and slices from a small baguette, we picnicked in the back yard and talked about babies.

WEDNESDAY, JUNE 12, 1985

A little rain didn't bother me. Oddly, I wasn't worried about what Brightman Partners would decide to do. Schumann hadn't called, but I wasn't worried. Up until this day it seemed as though I'd had something to worry about every minute since the project landed on me. Today, I just couldn't conjure up the worry machine.

I stopped to chat with Paul Lemay. He asked me what I'd decided to do with the rental car and I told him I hadn't yet gone to the adjusters and still hadn't received a purchase figure from Alamo. I left him with the thought that the people who'd written the manual on sexual positions with a left-arm cast had probably not had a cast. That got a chuckle.

On my desk there was a facsimile message from Alamo. They would sell me the Impala for nine thousand, eight hundred. That was less than full price, but not all that much less, I thought. Still, I had basically wrecked their car. I decided to hit the adjusters before lunch. I also wanted to visit Tom Wittenauer, partly to see if he'd be able to attend the Larimer ceremony. I pulled out my yellow pad and started to list things. I jumped when the phone rang.

"This is Walter Anton."

"Walter, it's John Schumann. How are you this morning?"

"I'm good… and on the edge of my seat. Dare I ask?"

"Well, we had an interesting meeting, I can say that much. I won't say all the things that came up and the opinions that flew around the boardroom. The consensus was, though, that Roberta is an anti-Semite of the first order and after the heat dissipated, no one wants to kow-tow to her any longer."

"That's good, isn't it?" I doodled around Roberta's name.

"I guess so, at least in terms of the deal we want to do. I have the board's instruction to go forward with Larimer. It has financial value to the firm, of course. All in all the partners want financial success and would rather not get into political battles. We need to be cooperative with everyone. Roberta presents a different situation."

"What do I need to do, then, John? Anything different?"

"No, I don't think so. The partners are hoping I can avoid a public conflict with the Trust and, to be honest, some asked if Blatchford would consider not being there, including you, Walt. Now..."

"What the fuck are you talking about?" I was steaming. "My family has gone through Hell for this goddam project and I'm not making any fucking commission for my troubles, either!"

Silence. I looked at the phone, debating whether to slam it down. I spun it in my hand as I regained my composure. Finally, I put it back to my ear and waited.

"Walter?"

"Yes, John. I'm sorry about that." I reviewed what I had said, wishing I could take back parts of it, maybe... mostly.

"I was ready for it, Walt. I am sorry you resent that we are earning a commission, but I understand."

"Oh, jeez, John, I don't, really. I know you deserve to get paid. It's just that I'm looking at nothing but personal expenses throughout all of this. My car was wrecked, I have to pay to fix or buy the rental, I'm in this damned cast, my house was trashed.

It all just kind of blew up in my mind when you said I shouldn't be at the ceremony." Schumann didn't respond right away.

"Anyway, I've had this picture of how the ceremony would look and who would say what and all of that. When I come right down to it, though, it doesn't really matter if I'm there or not. I think if I were there it would only be for sympathy. My ceremony will be in the mayor's office before that. We get our lease and to Hell with the rest of it. I think I can get by with not being there."

"That wasn't the outcome, Walt."

"What?"

"After everyone had his say the consensus was that you should be there and on stage." It took me a second to get that.

"Really? Wow." I was smiling.

"That's right. I must say I am proud of our stand. We're good with Hal, too, of course."

"I... I feel humbled by that, John. I'm sorry for my earlier stupidity. I don't know what to say, except thanks."

"Accepted on all counts, Walt. I will be happy to see you on that stage."

"I don't think I'll be up there, though, John. I've re-talked myself out of that. I'll watch and I don't want even my name mentioned, and I'm serious about that. If Hal thinks I've done something good, that's good enough for me."

"Seriously?"

"Very... couldn't be more so."

"Okay, I guess. So long as you're not saying that because of what I told you."

"Nope, not at all. In fact, I feel better about it now. What's more, I'm going to speak to Hal and let him make his own decision. Personally, I hope he goes and makes his comments. But you know he'll ask about what I'm doing and I'm not going to make anything up."

"Okay, but Walter, we…"

"And I am not going to relay everything you told me."

"Oh, good. Okay. If you're sure of your decision, I'm going to make the agenda on that basis."

"That's how it is, John. But, please extend my thanks to your board. You know that includes you."

"Will do, Walt. And I'll see you Friday morning."

"Okay, then. I'll call you if Hal changes anything."

Oh… yeah. Thanks." We rang off and I sat back. If I could have put my hands together I'd have stretched them behind my head. I settled for just one. Fuck Roberta. I'd be happy when this was all behind us. It was almost ten o'clock and I had to get moving. I called up to Kelly Galvin.

"Thanks for giving me a minute, Hal," I said as I closed the door behind me. "I just spoke to John Schumann."

"Has something changed?" Hal stayed at his desk.

"It could have, evidently, but no, there is no change."

"What the Hell are you talking about? Schumann?" Bullshit or the hint of bullshit didn't go very far with Hal Blatchford.

"Brightman Partners was concerned about being part of an insult to Roberta McGillvray. They have to work with her, as you know. But John tells me they decided to go forward with Larimer and with having you on stage with the mayor, Roberta, Forrest Akers and John Schumann. It looks like we've stirred up a major change in the city vis á vis the Three Rivers Trust and dame McGillvray."

"Okay. You didn't need to tell me this if there's no change. What's the point, here?"

"Well, according to Schumann, his partners wanted me to be on stage on Friday. I told him I didn't want to do that, as flattering as it might be. There is the possibility… likelihood, probably, that Roberta will do something when she realizes that it's still your money that's making Larimer work. She'll know the deal she denied to me is going forward. Maybe you want to reconsider being on stage, too?"

He sat back and looked at me. I held eye contact with him. "What did Schumann say about it?"

"Actually, the partners thought you should be there. It's my own decision to not be on stage, but I think you should be there. You have a well-deserved right to make your statement. It's a good project that's going to help a lot of people. Your contribution is a little heroic, if you ask me."

"You know it's just business, Walter."

"Yuh, I do. The best part of self-interest that helps others. You can be proud of it."

"Humph. Maybe. You think I should be up there?"

"Frankly? Strictly for our business purposes, it won't make any difference. The main event for Blatchford Steel will be earlier when McKay signs that lease and I call Forrest Akers. At that point the mayor will have stood up to Roberta and started an inexorable path to a blow-up of some sort. When Schumann introduces you, there, on stage, she will learn that what the mayor told me he'll do, has been done. I can't predict what she'll do, then or later. It's safe to say she'll react. If you aren't there it may delay that, but not avoid it."

"Okay. I understand. Let's continue on the premise that I will be there. If I don't show at the last minute Schumann can cover that over pretty simply. Tell him to not print my name on any programs or press releases, things like that."

"Okay, Hal. I'll take care of that. I'm sorry I can't be of more help."

"Walter, I haven't decided yet what to do about you, but you have been an indescribable help to me and to the company and everyone employed here. Forget the apology shit."

I contained a desire to grin. I thanked him and left. Kelly Galvin watched me as I left. I thanked her for her help, too. I don't think she understood why I said that, nor did I.

At my desk I called Schumann's office. His secretary said he was in a meeting. I replied that he would appreciate being interrupted for this. She put me on hold.

"What is it, Walter?" No "how are you's," but I didn't mind.

"Hal says he'll be there but he doesn't want you to print his name on any fliers or press releases or the agenda."

"Oh, okay. I hadn't thought of that. Good advice. Anything else?"

"No, that's it. Glad I caught you."

"No, okay then. Later." The phone clicked silent. My yellow pad told me to get to the drive-through adjusters.

I'd never been to a drive-through claims place. I showed them my rental contract and the form young Paul filled out on Monday. Did I want some coffee?

"This going to take awhile?" I asked.

"Naw. Ten, twelve minutes. Sit tight." I picked up Tuesday's Post-Gazette while they poked around and then drove it around the block. I had never realized that avocados could be cooked in the oven. Why? I wondered.

Finally another fellow came over with their estimate, exceeding seven thousand dollars. Because I'd been raised properly, I thanked him and left. Seven grand? This was ridiculous. I drove to *Marko's*.

I studied the menu and the specials for something I hadn't tried. They had fried shrimp and a plate of them went by as I was deciding. I asked what kind of shrimp I'd just seen. Those were "thirties," she explained. Thirty to a pound; the plate consisted of about fifteen of them. That's what I ordered, with steamed broccoli and coleslaw so I didn't feel like a pig. Broccoli is good for you.

True to form, Angus Newhall arrived with another friend. He nodded to me from a few places away and then gestured to his associate and they moved to be roughly across from me at one of the long tables. I reached across to shake hands with Angus and then left it extended.

"Meet Roy Gale, Walter. Roy, this is my future customer, Walter Anton."

"Pleasure is all mahne," drawled Roy Gale. He sounded Texan.

"Sounds like you're from far western Pittsburgh, Roy," I offered. Gale laughed.

"I don't really know accents. Is it West Texas or maybe four-Corners area?" I leaned back as my shrimp arrived, aroma first. I uncovered some cocktail and tartar sauce.

"Waahl, those shrimps look pretty good to me," opined Gale. "What about you, Angus?"

"Not me. I'm sticking with catfish and salad." The waitress took their orders. I apologized for not waiting.

"Midland, actually," said Gale. "How'd you get such a naihs cayast?"

I looked at him while I tried to empty my mouth from sweet fried shrimp. "What?" I asked.

"Midland, Texas. That's where I'm from. You made a good guess, Mr. Anton. But that is one serious plaster job. What happened to ya?"

I shook my head a little as I chewed. Those shrimp were m-m-good. "I got run off the road and shot, There's six metal pins in my arm and shoulder. But not bad, all in all. The guy that shot me is dead."

"Yer good at attractin friends everywhere, ain'tcha laddie?" Angus was squinting down his nose at me.

I gave him a sideways look. "They find me, Angus."

Angus seemed to be sizing me up all over again. "Just keep yerself safe until that bridge is finished, then." I nodded and chewed.

"Well, Roy," I shifted, "you're not shipping to Texas on Angus' boats."

"No, not at all. I live in Homestead, now. We ship mud and muck and other dredgings from time to time. Every now and then my prime tow operator buys me lunch… here, at Marko's. I look forward to it. Maybe when you're a customer Angus will buy you lunch."

"Well, that day's a lot closer than it's ever been."

"That so?" asked Angus.

"Yup. In fact we're making a big public announcement on Friday. Everyone is coming out a winner."

"What is there to announce? You're getting a lease on a piece of railroad, right? Aside from you and the city, who really cares? Roberta?"

"Not quite, but, it's, ahh… well, it became much more complicated. Touching a lot more people the way it turned out."

"Maybe I'll come over and watch yer little party, then."

"It's not near us. It's in Larimer." Angus raised his eyebrows at that one.

"Yer railroad's longer than we thought, eh?"

"No, but the story is. I'll tell you about it once we're shipping girders."

"Well, like I said, kid, we've got the river ready for you." Their meals arrived and we all concentrated on the business at hand. I finished first. "Gentlemen, I am very happy we had a chance to eat together, but this is a busy day and week for me. I'm afraid I have to excuse myself."

"Well, I'm afraid you're excused, then, laddie," observed Angus.

"I'm sure we'll have a very special ceremony when we move the first girders, too. You'll be invited to that, Angus."

"Lookin forward to it, lad." I shook hands with Roy Gale and told him I hoped we'd meet again. I paid the waitress and left to visit Tom Wittenauer.

I headed straight to the elevators at Mercy, but stopped and turned to Reception to ask where I'd find Congressman Tom Wittenauer.

After scanning a list the volunteer told me to take the elevators to the left and get off on the third floor and to check in with the nurses' station there. That was good news. It meant that he was on the mend in a regular room. Up I went.

"And you are?" asked the nurse on three.

"Uhh, well, just a friend, I guess. He is very close to my family. He actually got shot protecting my wife. How's that?" The third-floor nurse held up a finger and placed a call. After some back-and-forth she put her hand over the mouthpiece and told me I could go down, then held up the finger again. I waited. She told her correspondent that I was on my way.

"It's all the way to the end of this hall. The door has a plaque that says 'Private.' Just knock." I headed down the hall.

I thought I was knocking at an office rather than a hospital room. An aide opened the door.

"Walter Anton?" I assured him I was that very soul. He stepped aside and let me in. Wittenauer was sitting in bed, half reclined. Three others from his office were there with a folding-table 'desk' complete with phones, IBM typewriters and a facsimile machine. A separate table held a small copier. Three office chairs were near the bed.

"Walter!" he shouted. "C'mon in! Whaddaya think? Quite an operation, huh?"

"Boy, I guess. How are you feeling? You look good."

"Much better, they tell me. Evidently the infection is controlled and there's no bleeding. Those are key, they tell me. I get tired, but I'm feeling nearly normal. They make me exercise and stretch… not my favorite hour, but I can't mind too much."

"Have they threatened to kick you out, yet?"

"With a bit of luck, good testing and various agreements to do some things and not others, maybe Friday, Saturday." I grinned widely.

"Then I have a special invite… for Friday."

"Well, I'll be restricted. What's on the grill this time? Tenderloin? I'm not sure I'll be doing much visiting."

"No, no, nothing like that… although you're perfectly welcome. Give me the word and I'll get the tenderloin. But this is for Friday morning. We're having a big ceremony in Larimer for that project with Liberty Bank. You should be there. Your sacrifice was crucial to its happening. We want you on stage."

"How many stairs?"

"For you? None. We'll have a ramp. If you want to stand at some point, you can, but there's no need. But you really should be there."

One aide, a woman in her mid thirties, was shaking her head off to one side. Wittenauer could see her but seemed to really want to say he'd come, although he couldn't commit.

"Tom," I said as I placed my hand on his arm, "your presence on the stage will be newsworthy and the ideal venue for those comments we promised you. It would be perfect." My facial expression couldn't have been more encouraging… at least I hoped it was.

"Walt, I will aim for it, but it's not up to me." His aide was glaring at him. "And I'll have to explain things to Liz Bucholz, here, who is determined to keep me from over-doing." She glared even harder and tilted her head. "For which I am completely grateful, Liz… really. But we do need to consider this, it's that important."

Liz spoke. "When the doctor comes in… in, ohh, twenty minutes, we can tell him and find out what he thinks." That was the last word on Friday, I could see. I shifted gears.

"Tom, I have not failed to tell people how heroic you were that Monday. You've got to know that Hal Blatchford is as proud of you as anybody could be."

"He came by, actually. I was surprised to see him, He was uncomfortable, I thought, but I was really happy he came to see me. Nice." I nodded with him.

"A lot of people's opinion of you will change after this incident. I'm sorry I got you into this…"

"I got myself into this pickle and you showed me a way out. I didn't like getting shot, but that's not your fault. Stop thinking about it." He smiled. "I'm thanking you, Walt."

I choked up a little and did my best to hide it. "Aw, shucks, Tom. It was nuthin."

"I'm sure. You're the one in a cast. Well, let me see what I can talk the doctors into. I'll call you at Blatchford if I can be there."

"Thanks, Tom. I'll tell John Schumann that it might happen." I stepped over to thank Liz Bucholz for tolerating me.

"We'll see how it goes," she smiled, unhappily. I waved toward Wittenauer and let myself out. It was only three and I owed more time to Blatchford.

I had nothing specific. I thought about being useful. I was within forty-four hours of the success I'd been striving towards for a month or more, and still felt mildly useless. I headed to Jackson's office.

"Ahh, Walter, it's harder and harder to see you these days. Can we go over the architect's plans and cost estimates?" I was glad to do it.

Jack had been busy. He had three sets of drawings that showed the changes to the roof, the side of the building, the new fifty-foot high doors, reach-stacker crane and construction work to change the building and create the outside platform.

Stapled to each page were letter-size sheets with cost estimates for that page. I could see that we were looking at close to two million. As some wise economist once said, "that ain't chicken feed."

"Where is Hal on this, now, Jack?"

"I've shown him the drawings. He demanded page-by-page costs. He wants them presented to the board of directors. With these costs and the railspur expenses, we're going to borrow the bulk of this cost. Do you want to do the board presentation? Maybe the cast will elicit sympathy."

"You think we need it?" We were both smiling.

"Well, I don't know. We could go in together on the presentation, if you're okay with that."

Jack and I had become equals. I genuinely appreciated his grace during the change. I wanted to build him up. He was managing the construction stuff pretty well, as far as I could see.

"It'll probably be harder to shake the resolve of two trusted employees than of one. I'll be proud to back you up." Jack smiled and leaned back with his hands clasped behind his head.

"Then I think we're ready to make the case. You wanna tell Hal?"

"More appropriate if you do, I think." He nodded.

"Yeah. I'll see if he's still here. He needs to call the directors in to have the meeting."

"All right. I'm heading home, then. I'll be here all day, tomorrow." He smiled.

THURSDAY, JUNE 13, 1985

It was like the day before a holiday when no one is expected to be serious about anything. I loafed along getting cleaned up and dressed while Linda was crisp and efficient. I was relaxed and tense at the same time. It was Christmas Eve day and I wanted it to last, holding off the goodies and presents in a fog of delicious anxiety. Finally I decided I'd better get it in gear. I worked for a living.

I kissed Linda, finished my coffee, brushed my teeth and hit the road ten minutes behind her. I'd never had anything to say to the Board of Directors. I expected that Jack would do the talking, in any case, but being there would be interesting. I tried to line up my thoughts on the new crane, the reasons we had to spend the money, how easy it was to overlook this key preparation for shipping these unique girders. Still, I planned to mainly listen and look serious when necessary.

I shared pleasantries with Pauly, but didn't stop. Jackson was sipping tea by my door. I rejected the possibility that he was pregnant. Maybe he liked tea.

"Morning Jack! Interesting day, I guess." I was smiling. He didn't look too grim, but he wasn't jump up and down happy, either.

"Walter, we ought to review our testimony before the meeting."

"Testimony? We're not on trial here, Jack? C'mon."

"It'll feel like it, Walter. We're talking about a lot of money. I don't imagine they'll be tickled about it."

"Just keep in mind that we're presenting a solution and not a problem. Don't apologize for anything… just like Hal tells me. Don't try to cover for the people who should have already planned for this issue. We're the guys with the solution, and we're moving quickly so that we can still fill the contract. That's what they need to know."

Jack looked at me without saying anything. He was studying me. "You could be right, Walt. You have learned to make your case in negotiations, I see." He nodded to himself and stood up decisively. "Then I guess we're ready. Five minutes, okay?"

"Yuh. Let me check my desk. I'll call you if I have to delay." I hustled off to my almost-office. One of these days.

One message, from Schumann. He wanted a call back "when I have the chance." Probably some staging thing. I scanned over my pad and spotted Alan Boudreau's name. I wrote myself a note to ask him if he wanted to watch the big event. Colleen Walsh had clipped some slips together with a note that said 'when you can.' I had nothing that could excuse putting off the board. I took a breath and walked to Jack's real office.

Jack had a bundle of papers and some rolled-up drawings that he couldn't carry very well. I took the drawings from him and suggested he spread out the other papers. In a couple of minutes we separated the kinds of documents into folders. I rolled up the drawings into separate views and purposes so that we had eight separate rolls.

"You'll find, Jack, that they are not even going to ask for most of this stuff because it looks like you know exactly where everything is. They will more likely accept your verbal presentation. Mark my words." Again he seemed to be studying me.

"Let's go," he said. We handled our bundles and headed upstairs. Kelly Galvin actually brightened a bit. She signaled to wait a moment and called in to the big man's office. In a few seconds she gave us a head-fake toward the inner sanctum.

"Good luck," she said. I tried to give her an especially warm smile in return.

Hal Blatchford welcomed us. A second table was pulled up against the "T" table that extended out from his desk. There were a couple of extra chairs along the inner side, and two chairs on the opposite side, facing the small table and Hal's desk. Those were for Jack and me and room to spread out drawings. I huddled with Jack for a second after we'd shaken everyone's hand. Aside from Hal, the only other person I knew there, was his son, Peter, and Jack's boss, the VP of finance. I never had reason to meet these guys. Jack knew them all.

"Jack," I whispered, "start out by asking what they want to know first. That'll shorten the whole thing." I got a worried look.

Hal spoke first. "Gentlemen, thanks to all of you for making some time this morning. You know we've been preparing for this King Frederik project for several months. Jack and Walter Anton, here, have been watching over expenses and expected new expenses that Blatchford will sustain to make ourselves ready to manufacture and ship these rather unique girders."

The board members nodded. Jack and I went along with him, too. Hal continued.

"Unfortunately, amidst all of our in-shop planning and tooling decisions, none of us thought of the problems presented by the finished dimensions of the girders when it came to getting the damn things out of the shop and onto the railroad." Hal was leading the group where he wanted them to go.

"Fortunately!" he went on, gesturing with hands and face, "our two cost men uncovered the gap in our planning in time to resolve the issues. But it will be costly, and we'll have to borrow money before we see the first payment from Denmark. That's why we're here. Jack and Walter can answer your questions." With that he gestured toward us.

Jack appeared to be dumbstruck. In a few seconds it would be awkward. I jumped in.

"Basically, gentlemen, the height of the girders exceeds our existing overhead crane's dimensions. The existing crane can handle up to about thirty-eight-foot tall items. These girders come in forty-foot-tall pieces. So you can see what we bumped in to." I did the nodding thing and everyone looked agreeable, so far.

"The solution to this specific problem has also presented the company with an excellent opportunity for the future. The difficulties and costs associated with modifying our existing crane to essentially 'get out of the way' of the girders, quickly led us to recommend a second crane, altogether: a drivable reach-stacker that can handle over fifty tons." I left it there to see what would happen. Jack was decidedly comfortable with me talking.

"What's the opportunity?" asked Morris Krugman, who had sold his electroplating business to his largest competitor and sat on their board, too.

"The added lift and shipping capacity will enable Blatchford to bid on numerous projects we have never been able to bid before. Many of our in-shop capabilities would have won some large projects like the King Frederik just in the past three years, but we had to stay away from them. I think when we look back on this period, Hal's decision to aggressively go after the King Frederik will be seen as one of great vision, because of the capacities we have been forced to add, now."

Krugman stared at me. I had kept my face stonily resolute, I thought. One of his board-mates raised his hand a few inches and spoke.

"That's some pretty good sucking up, Walter Anton."

"It ain't sucking-up if it's true, Mr. Wallace." I stayed stony. Jack knew better than to interrupt, although he looked uncomfortable. Hal Blatchford had a friendly demeanor, but said nothing. I saw an opportunity.

"Jack has prepared chapter and verse on the projected cost of the construction that's required, and if you want to pore over the drawings, we have all of those here, too." I sat down. The old man kept himself from chuckling. Finally he pulled things back together.

"Gentlemen, I've got two of the best cost accountants in this business watching out for us. Our top engineer and the best crane outfit in the region have developed this. We have to be ready to ship girders by Christmas so we need to pull the trigger right now. What is the pleasure of the Board?"

"Leave the documents, fellas, would you?" asked Krugman. Jack and I spread out the folders and unrolled the drawings, holding them down with the folders, themselves. After a look around I headed out of the meeting. Blatchford nodded to me and asked Jack to hang back for a few minutes. I was finally able to breathe normally as I moved past Kelly's desk.

"Everything okay in there?" she asked.

"Went very well, Kelly. Thanks. Looks like we're going to build a bridge in Denmark. It's all good."

"Well, congratulations, Walter. Mr. Blatchford is very happy with you. You didn't hear that from me." My finger went up to my lips as I grinned. I thanked her and headed down stairs.

***

"Yes, John, what can I do?" I could imagine that Schumann had his hands full with the announcement event, now twenty-four hours away.

"Yeah, Walt, thanks for getting back to me. I want to know about Blatchford's coming to the event and what you know about Congressman Wittenauer, if he can come."

"Well, John, I would say it's a lock that Hal will be there, but I don't know for certain that he'll take the stage. I know that's not much help."

"It sure isn't. Can you pin that down?"

"I'll do my best. Now for Wittenauer, I asked him yesterday, if he'd be allowed to come. He seems to be doing well. When I saw him he had his room set up like an office and three aides were there handling things. It was interesting. But apparently they've had him up and walking around. If he comes, though, he'll be in a wheelchair, so you'll need a ramp of some sort. He might choose to stand but I suspect he'll stay in the wheelchair. It's a great visual, you know?"

"I had the staging people include a ramp, anyway. You never know. Can you make a final confirmation on Wittenauer, too?"

"Be happy to. Who else you got? I know Akers and the Mayor and Roberta."

"Yeah, them, plus a couple of people who will be managing the new community center and a neighborhood leader-organizer. Akers says she should be there. One of the city councilors… represents that district... he'll be there. With Blatchford and Wittenauer there could be ten. And you'd be eleven. I got room."

"Not me. I'll be in the audience. If Hal goes up I doubt Roberta will know it's him until he's introduced. By then it'll be too late to make trouble. You'd better have her speak before Hal is introduced."

"Oh, I thought of that. Of course, she may see you in the audience and figure something's fishy. What do you think?"

"Maybe I should stay out of sight until she's done speaking."

"I don't think that's necessary." I could hear very clearly in that reply that it might make things easier on stage if she didn't see me. Fine with me. I'm no troublemaker.

"John, do you have time for lunch, today?"

"Ahh, wow, that's in like half an hour?"

"Something like that. Ya gotta eat."

"What are you thinking of?"

"*Marko's*, again. We can meet here. I'm gonna invite Jack Jackson, too."

"Well, can't get all that much done from twelve to one, anyway. Sure. I'll be there."

We rang off and I walked down to Jack's office. It was dark. I stuck a note in the door asking him to join me for lunch at *Marko's*. A thought hit me and I went directly up to Katie Mellon's office. Her light was on. I tapped on the door frame.

"Hello! Come in!" she called.

"Hi, Katie. It's me." I stuck my head around the corner first. Her face went from bright to suspicious and back to friendly. She waved me in.

"How are you feeling, Walter? That's a huge cast!"

"Apparently. I was lucky. I've visited Tom a couple of times and he's looking pretty good, too. I assume you've visited him."

"Oh, yeah. Every day."

"You should be very proud of him. He saved Linda's life."

"I know. I can't imagine doing what he did. He could have died."

"Yeah. Amazing." I shook my head and smiled. "Listen, the reason I came up was to tell you I have nothing but admiration for him. I hope you understand why I was so suspicious of him, but that's behind me, now. I hope he gets re-elected."

"So do I. Thanks for that, Walter. Now, how long before you're bowling again?"

"More than a month, I'm told. Then I'll have to do some rehabilitation. Next week I'm going to come keep score."

"That'll be good. I'll wear the right blouse." I looked and she had a little devil in her eyes.

"I'll appreciate that. My Linda is pregnant, now, which we didn't think could happen."

"Well, congratulations to you, both. That's wonderful. Wonderful!"

"Thank you… very much. Why don't you marry Tom and then you can be somebody's mother, too. You'll be a good one."

She turned red, although not angry. "Que sera, sera," she said with finality. I took my cue.

"Well, thanks for chatting with me. I've got a lunch appointment so..."

"Oh, okay. I'll be seeing you." I left and scampered back down to my office.

John Schumann was sitting in front of my desk.

"Pretty fancy, huh?" I swept my arm around the old-fashioned scene.

"No view but it's got ambience."

"Maybe. Let me just check with Jackson." I called his internal number but it wasn't picked up. Maybe he was lunching with the big-shots. That was fine.

"Guess it's just us, John. Let's go. Wanna drive?"

"Sure. Car in the shop?"

"No, but it should be." As we headed toward his Mercedes I explained that there was more than five thousand bucks of damage.

"Why are you still driving it?" he asked.

"I have to decide what to do with the repairs. Alamo's adjusters said over seven grand. If I can get it repaired for less, I'll buy it. I like driving it."

"The outside looks pretty rough."

"I know, but it saved my life. We'll see how it goes."

"Well, tell me the turns," he said as I slid into his Mercedes. I gave him the simple directions and we glided out of the parking lot.

We descended into the quietude that Angus Newhall had first introduced me to.

"You always come here?"

"Yeah, although 'always' means about five times, but it's the best food around."

"Well, I loved the fish. Good for the waistline, you know."

"I guess, if you choose carefully. The specials are over your shoulder. Have at it." We busied ourselves with the offerings. It was easier for me. I went for the pike with the lemon-ginger sauce, broccoli and a salad. Healthy. Schumann finally selected the same thing again.

"Wise choice... good for the waistline." We ordered our food and iced tea.

"This was a good idea, Walt. I would have stayed in the office fretting about tomorrow when there really isn't much more than a few details to pin down. If I didn't pin down any of them the event would go okay." He looked around to see the kinds of people who shared the lower level of *Marko's*.

"Might see the mayor on the right day," I told him.

"Really! Why would he come here?"

"I think he actually likes the food... plus, no one bothers him. I've come to like him, through all this. When we sign that lease tomorrow, my success will be confirmed. With your help

I'll be able to say I got something done." As soon as I said it I realized how smug it sounded.

"Actually," I went on, "I succeeded with the help of a lot of people. I wouldn't be able to claim anything without Wittenauer, or the mayor, or Alan Boudreau, and thanks to you… and Linda, of course. It's been a long, messy, damaging… even fatal trip. I shouldn't take any particular credit for much of anything. I'm actually sorry for a lot of it." I slumped.

Schumann looked at me with a dour expression. I waited for a comment. He moved his hands around and sipped his tea a couple of times, apparently in thought. He let out a big breath.

"That's pretty deep, Walt. You may be misunderstanding what's happened."

I shook my head. Before he could expound our meals arrived. Good timing, I thought.

"This is really good… really good," he declared with his fork providing punctuation. "Hmmnh, mmm, nnnh." He stayed quiet for a couple more bites and then picked up on the original conversation.

"You might want to look at the good you did in a short time, Walt."

I raised my eyebrows.

"Yes. First, you've solved a crucial problem for your company. It's bringing millions into Blatchford and into Pittsburgh. You've made possible new revenue for the city which we hope will have good results, at least. You're going to do significant business with Mid Waters Freight and Navigation and with a crane company. You have precipitated a new project for Larimer which will have wonderful value to that neighborhood and the kids and families impacted… and which will enable a commission for Brightman Partners and me, personally. Even the Three Rivers Trust will benefit." I started to reply but John held up his hand to stop me.

"And don't forget the political benefit to Tom Wittenauer and to the mayor, as I perceive it. How's that?"

"Don't forget that we exposed a problem at the EPA and eliminated a seriously bad man who was after me." I was being facetious, channeling Edward G. Robinson.

"That's what I mean, Walt! You have been the catalyst, if you will, of a lot of good changes. Have some pride, for God's sake. You've been courageous and came out on top. Enjoy it for a few minutes."

I had to consider everything he'd recited. I guess there were some accomplishments along the way. I knew I'd feel better when the lease was signed. I smiled a little.

"Good. You also helped me by showing me *Marko's*. I know I'll come here again. It's exceptional."

I smiled a little more. "Angus Newhall from Mid Waters originally brought me here."

"There, see? One good turn produces another."

"Someday I'll hafta have my taxi-driver, Micah, pick you up and we'll go for the best barbecue I've ever had. It's pork, though."

"I've been known to eat pork under extreme social pressure."

"Then it's a valid threat. I don't know how to get to the place… I'd have to rely on Micah to get me there. I've only been once and had take-out another time. Just be ready for my call."

"Okay. You got it." He checked his watch. "I do need to get back, though."

"Sure. I'm set." I raised my hand and our waitress appeared with the check.

"Some dessert today?" We shook our heads together. I grabbed the check. I set down a ten and a twenty, which allowed for a nice tip, and signaled to her that it was there.

***

My desk chair allowed me to spin around. Linda had made me promise to make sure I came out well at the end of the bridge project. But I hadn't done anything to that end. Nothing. I made sure everyone else was in good shape. Despite what I'd said at lunch, I was churning with pride. It lasted about a minute before I felt down again about Emily Szepanik and the threat to Linda... more than even the shot Wittenauer took... I don't wish for anybody to get shot.

On the other hand, those bullets were a great career move. It was a funny combination of feelings. I kinda liked the big galloot.

None of which musings put any work on my desk. I called over to Colleen Walsh. No, there wasn't anything right now. The two slips she had the day before she'd covered with Mr. Jackson, and how was I feeling with my cast and all?

Fine, thanks, Colleen. I'm glad you're handling things so well. I guess I could add Colleen's new status as something good. Catalytic.

I still felt useless in my not-quite-office. The oak furniture and fixtures could make you imagine adding up impossible columns of hand-written figures with a Clary Totalizing machine in the summer of nineteen fifty-four. It didn't inspire much else. One thing that would be good, after all I'd been through, was a nice office with its own ceiling and, maybe, modern furniture... no matter what I did in it. Which brought back my problem.

What was I going to do? I'd certainly want to be thinking big thoughts and making big decisions. Smart people who knew how to do all sorts of intricate scientific things would be asking for my guidance... by ten o'clock!

It was a daydream. I felt lucky that old man Blatchford wasn't in the habit of checking up on me. If he'd popped in then I couldn't describe how I was helping Blatchford Steel.

I tried to imagine what John Schumann's days consisted of. He didn't have a deal to work on every day. I also knew the time he spent on the deal that was closing the next day. His value wasn't counted in sheets of paper handled. Imagine working that way… winning or losing in bursts, interspersed with tedium. Still, he drove a Mercedes.

I remembered to call Alan Boudreau about coming on Friday. I made a note. That spurred a call to the mayor to confirm my appointment for the next morning. I did that first.

"City of Pittsburgh, Mayor's Office. Who is calling please?"

"Yes, good afternoon. I'm Walter Anton, from Blatchford Steel Services. I have an appointment with the mayor in the morning at nine o'clock. I want to confirm that and, if possible, check on some details with the mayor, himself."

Hold just a moment, please." Muzak.

She came back on the line. "That appointment is on the calendar, sir."

"Is Harry available for a moment?"

"I'm afraid not, sir, but I can pass him a message."

"No, no. That's all right. I'll see him at nine o'clock."

"Yes, sir. Is there anything else?" Such helpfulness.

"No, thanks." I hung up gently. I should be happy.

Boudreau's phone rang until the answering machine began its response, Alan picked up, aplogizing for not picking up faster.

"No apologies, Alan. It's Walter Anton."

"Oh! Hiya, Walter. What's up? No more accidents, I hope."

"Not today, although I have a cast where Sindledecker shot me. But, he's dead, now."

"Jesus Christ! I was kidding! What can I do?"

"Well, you recall all that business about the EPA and Wittenauer?"

"Yes. He's some kind of hero, now?"

"He sure is. But the point is, we're having a big ceremony in Larimer in the morning, for a project that brings my story to a conclusion. I wondered if you wanted to watch it with me?"

"Watch it? What's to see? Don't get me wrong, but what kind of ceremony?"

"Uhh... well, it's speeches, mainly, I suppose. But I risked my life for them... and Linda's life. Wittenauer took a bullet for it, and Emily Szepanik died for it And I really am in a cast from being shot. So, to me it's big. But, mainly, speeches."

"That's quite a backdrop. Maybe I will. I did play a tiny role."

"Far from tiny, Alan. Crucial. In fact, I'm meeting the mayor to sign a lease on our parcel, tomorrow morning. Maybe put an hour on the clock with me. Come make sure I'm not signing something bad, again. Whaddaya think?"

"A lease?"

"Yeah. It's what we've been striving for: use of that parcel with the rail-spur on it for a year or two. The mayor is going forward with it despite Roberta McGillvray's disapproval, so that's kinda neat."

"He is? Does she know?" I could hear his excitement.

"No, I'm pretty sure. In fact Hal Blatchford is still debating going on stage. There'll be some kind of confrontation if she first realizes what's happened right then, during the event. It's why I'm just going to watch, frankly."

"Oh boy. I can't miss this one. You've got all the players in one place and she's been blindsided? I love it. In fact, I'll go to City Hall with you pro bono. How's that?"

"I'm not expecting service for free, Alan, but I'll be pleased to have you with me. You want to meet at Blatchford or City Hall?"

"Let's meet downtown. Thanks for the call. Tomorrow could be very interesting... historic. Ya gotta be there!"

"Done, then. Nine o'clock with the mayor."

"Got it. See you there." My heart was racing. Alan's excitement got me. I felt lucky I invited him to the signing. Luck was a big part of real estate.

Jackson tapped on my doorframe.

"Hi, Jack. What can I do?"

"I thought you might want to hear the results of our meeting this morning."

"Oh, gosh, sure, Jack. My head's been elsewhere. Tell me."

"There were quite a few questions, actually, after you left, but not on what you came up with."

"What I came up with? Mike Vanier told us about reach-stackers."

"Well, you got us here on time and a second crane is the key to this."

"Well, that's fine. What's to question, then?"

"The questions were more about you. They put Hal on the spot why so much was on your shoulders and when were you hired? It was funny, but those guys had never heard of you; they thought Hal hired you to manage the King Frederik. Probably better to not hear it."

"Wow. Humbling, isn't it? I just wanted that lease. My part is done when the mayor signs our lease. Then I can think about what's next. I'm not taking my work back from Colleen. She does a fine job."

"Yeah. I'm impressed with her. But you should have seen Hal's uneasiness when they questioned him about you. He pretty much told them he had his eye on you and the King Frederik was a proving ground for you."

I realized that everyone can sling the b-s when needed. But it was hard to process what Jack had just said. He was slinging it on my behalf? Maybe I'd be all right when this was done. Although I had no idea what these few weeks had prepared me to do… at least for Blatchford.

"That's a little funny, I guess, Jack, Hal in a defensive position."

"Well, they all signed on to the construction and overall design, so hats off to you, I'd say."

"Right back at you, Jack."

"Well, I thought you'd like to know."

"I'm glad, Jack. Really. The lease will be signed early, which is the big deal for me. But I'll go to hear what the mayor says and, hopefully, what Hal says, too. Should be interesting."

"Well, I hope it's all good and, from me to you... I am glad you have managed this thing to its conclusion. Congratulations, Walt." We shook hands and I thanked him again.

"Look, Jack, I know it's only quarter past three, but I'm heading home. I'll see you tomorrow after the announcement. Maybe we'll have a party for ourselves."

Jack looked dumbfounded.

As I climbed into the Chevy I thought about going to a body shop, except I really didn't know one. Maybe I'd ask the garage in Monroeville. I trusted them.

Then, since I was wrapping things up, I plotted a course for a shopping center, which also meant Monroeville, to me.

***

I didn't see grandfather Abbott at the garage, but his descendent, Peter, was helpful.

"Didn't we have that car in here a week ago or so?"

"I'm afraid you did. It's running and I'm recuperating, but now I need to have it estimated by a good body shop."

"Ain't it a rental car? Why'd you want to to fix it?"

"I like the car, and it's gonna cost me quite a bit one way or the other. I got Alamo's estimate."

"They build these things by the thousands, you know. You could get a brand new one."

"I suppose, but if your body shop can make it like new at a reasonable price, I'll buy it from Alamo and be happy. So, who... ?"

"Best I know is *Re-Kar* in Penn Hills. Kerry Allen. She's got the best paint shop and she's a stickler for detail. That's where I'd go… have gone."

"Okay. Can you call her? I'll go right now."

"Wait a sec." He called and chatted for a few minutes, then he nodded at me. I said to tell her I was on my way. After a couple more stories he hung up.

"Busy place, so don't make her wait."

"Can I make a call from here?" He pointed at a payphone on the wall. I changed a dollar and called Linda.

"Hi, Honey. Got a second?"

"Sure, Wally. Something wrong?"

"No, no. I'm getting another estimate on the rental. Can you pick me up there?"

"I'm ready to leave. Where is it?"

"A couple doors east from Main and Salzburg in Penn Hills. It's called *Re-Kar*, with a K."

"Okay. I know where you are. Twenty minutes, with luck."

"Good, good. Then I have some shopping to do and maybe Fishwives, what do you think?"

"Okay. Shopping? You don't shop."

"Just something I have to do and I have no clue."

"All right, Mr. Anton. Less than half an hour. Bye!"

I got the route to *Re-Kar* and took off for what I hoped was my last trip in a wrecked Impala.

I drove past where Linda jumped out and I first pulled the power skid. A half-mile later I turned onto Thompson Run. When I got to the curve I stopped and looked at the scene of Sindledecker's death. Weird.

Re-Kar was remarkably clean and Kerry Allen was all business. Her coveralls had "Re-Kar" embroidered above her breast, not that I look at such things. She might have been in her twenties, from the smoothness of her skin. Maybe paint solvents are good for you.

She took a quick look and prescribed an overnight. She'd check the alignment and the frame after hearing how the damage was done. I expected, now, to have the car fixed and buy it from Alamo. *Re-Kar* had a good feeling.

Linda arrived about two "Newsweeks" later.

"You're leaving it?" she asked.

"Yeah. The garage highly recommended the lady who owns *Re-Kar*. I've decided to fix it up and buy it. It's got only nine thousand miles, and it has meaningfulness, you know what I mean?"

"Okay. You like it. Where's the shopping?"

"I've been meaning to get a gift for Hal's secretary, Kelly Galvin. I joked with her the wrong way and she was hurt. I need to make amends, but I've no idea what to get."

Linda looked at me funny. "What kind of 'joke' was it?"

"Huh? Oh, not what you think, Honey, honestly. Really." It took a minute to think of how to explain. "I once joked that Hal had made me a V-P and assigned her to me. She got quite upset. It sounded real. She's devoted to Mr. Blatchford... more deeply than I'd realized. Lately we've been more cordial, but I owe her."

"How old is she?"

"Oh, jeez. Umm, forty, maybe."

"Does she dress with bright colors? Does she have her hair done?"

"Hair's always in place, but she's not a flashy dresser. Very neat, though… well-detailed I guess you'd say. Everything matches. Does that help?"

She nodded. I stayed quiet, picturing how Kelly looked. Pretty much I'd said what I could think of.

"Okay, last question… or two. Your basic impression of her is what color?"

"Maroon… or brown."

"What color are her eyes." I had to really reflect on that one. I tried to picture her face but I'd never studied it in detail.

"Not brown, I think… maybe sort of hazel, or greenish, but not strikingly so." I was somewhat confident in that half-assessment.

"Okay. I'm thinking." She pulled into the Monroeville Mall and parked by Abercrombie and Fitch. I looked at her but she firmly indicated that I had to come. It took half an hour, and she had three matching leather-trimmed woolen things, including a soft tartan shawl that I would have never bought on my own. It was over a hundred and fifty bucks. I was more apologetic than I realized.

At Fishwives we relaxed again. I felt like a hard maple project had finally been sanded and stained. "Baby, you're the greatest," Ralph Cramden announced. "You helped me solve a problem I've been avoiding for weeks. How can I thank you?"

"Well, you can order dinner, I suppose, and maybe a nice glass of near-wine." She presented a sweet, knowing smile.

I knew how I wanted to say "thanks." If it took eating a delicious dinner before serious thanking could begin, then so be it. "What are you hungry for?"

She checked the menu quickly and ordered her favorite: baked scallops with cheddar cheese, served with rice pilaf and local cucumbers in wine vinegar. I decided on swordfish with twice-stuffed potato and some sliced tomatoes. As far as I was concerned we were celebrating. I was about to get rid of a burden while Linda was preparing to carry one for the next eight and a half months.

We sipped sparkling cider as if it were champagne. Linda looked as complete and satisfied as I felt.

"Tomorrow is all set, then?"

I nodded and smiled. "I'm meeting with the mayor at nine o'clock. Alan Boudreau is meeting me there."

"Your lawyer? Are you expecting trouble?" She flashed a worried look. I waved my hands to erase that thought.

"Not at all. But, he was so good at reviewing the EPA letter I suggested he come with me. I also invited him to the event in Larimer. When I told him Roberta was unaware of Blatchford's involvement and that Hal might speak, he jumped at the chance and offered to meet me for free!"

"My goodness. Does *he* expect trouble?" Worried, again. I smiled reassurance.

"More like car racing. The accident's the best part."

"Well that makes me feel good. Shall I expect to be off the Trust after tomorrow?"

"Maybe. Once she realizes that the mayor went ahead without her approval, she's sure to be irked."

"Not the word I'd use." Linda was now giving serious consideration to the results my success might have.

"And what if she finds out ahead of time?" Linda's look was grim.

"Well, I've prepared all the permitting agencies and departments so that our lease will stand up to almost anything," I smiled.

"I'm sure. That's not the real issue. What if she makes a scene at the ceremony? What if she does something?"

"You think she could possibly... ?" I think my mouth hung open.

"I don't know the extent of her reactions when really irked, as you say. I can imagine she might lash out. You should be prepared."

My regard for Linda's opinions was immense. She always "got" people faster than I did. But I couldn't share worrying about Roberta taking physical action. I just couldn't. Of her ability to express being angry... that I could see. But, taking a swing with her handbag or something, that was just... crazy. I debated with myself and still couldn't see it. I made like I agreed.

"Well, I'll give Hal a heads-up if he decides to be on stage. I'd better warn the mayor and the congressman, too, do you think?"

She shrugged and raised her eyebrows. "I can't say, Walt. It just seems possible, to me. It's always best to prepare, isn't it?"

I smiled as convincingly as I could. "You are right, as always. I'll take extra care and make sure we are all cautious. Meanwhile, the shopping: you were perfect."

"You won't really know that until you give the gift."

"Well, seems perfect to me. I'm sure she'll love it." Linda smiled.

Dinner arrived still sizzling. "Hmmnnh," she hummed.

"Oh, boy. I am ready for this!" I dug in. Linda was happy with hers, although she ate more slowly than usual.

"Something wrong, Sweetie?" Her quick head shake answered me.

"I'm eating more slowly while I'm pregnant. Chew more... helps the digestion and should keep me from overeating. Natural health advice."

"Oh, I guess. Okay. You think I should, too?"

"Well, it's good for you. You do what you want." I immediately slowed down. If I was going to improve the rest of my life and be healthy, it was a swell time to start.

It was only eight when we got home. Linda refused both help and advice on wrapping Kelly's gifts. "Aww. Look, I'll go struggle with my ablutions while you do the wrapping. I'll be waiting in bed in full 'horn,' you might say. How's that?"

"It's a thought. You go get started and I'll catch up." She smiled enigmatically. It was all I could get, for now. If I'd been able to swing her over my shoulder, things would've been different. But, I was cast in a different role. Hmnh, I had to file that line for later.

By the time I was in bed, naked, it was almost nine. The house was quiet. Wrapping would've taken only a few minutes in Linda's precise hands. I tried to anticipate warm, slippery sex any minute. But I kept drifting to meeting with the mayor, and if anything could kill a mood, that was it. Whenever Linda came to bed, it didn't disturb me.

FRIDAY, JUNE 14, 1985

In a rare, barely hoped-for delight, Linda granted me a quickie. It was Flag Day... good enough. Maybe she'd taken pity on me. I loved her and told her so.

"Oh, that's just coming from your penis, so to speak."

"No! It's from both of us!" I was feeling good and even she laughed.

"We need to get moving, though," she reminded me, "especially if I'm dropping you. I'll make breakfast while you shave."

I padded off to the bathroom.

Traffic was heavy for a Friday. Linda's driving was different. I stifled myself and tried to organize my thoughts. I was excited... with a sense of dread lurking on the fringe. It wasn't fear of Roberta or anything else tied to today. I had no moorings. I'd divested my job and made some interesting friends and acquaintances but I had no idea what I'd be doing on Monday, and I didn't like it. Nor could I talk about it. Long ago Linda said to prepare for my own benefit from this project,. I hadn't and I couldn't handle her displeasure on this day.

Linda got off onto Bates Street and went by the Magee and took Fifth Avenue downtown.

"You always do this?"

"Yes. I don't like the turns farther down and this usually flows pretty well."

Looked like a lot of lights, to me, but progress was steady. She dropped me off at the City-County Building at eight-forty, and came around to give me a big hug and a kiss.

"You'll have a big success, today, Honey. I know you will. I'm very proud of you." I felt like a million dollars.

"I think I've prepared for everything. Should be good. And, thanks, Lin." I touched her hair and cheek. I was the luckiest guy in the world. She almost ran back to the driver's door and waved as she drove off. I took a deep breath and headed into the big stone block.

***

"Good morning, sir. Do you have an appointment?"

"Yes. The mayor expects me at nine. I am waiting for an associate to join me, so you need not announce me for a few more minutes, if that's okay."

"That's fine, sir. Would you like some coffee?"

"Yes, if it's not too much trouble. Just black." I sat on the couch that faced the reception desk. An old-looking grandfather's clock ticked its way past eight forty-five. It surprised me how comforting Alan's presence was going to be. My worries transferred to his arrival. I sipped.

At three minutes of nine, Boudreau appeared. I almost teared up I had been so anxious. I stood and shook his hand warmly. He apologized for cutting it close. The receptionist called down to McKay's gate-keeper.

"It will be just a minute, gentlemen. Can I get you some coffee, sir?" she directed toward Boudreau. He declined and we both sat again. He, at least, was relaxed. I tried to adopt his outlook. We chatted about how it was being in a cast, could I drive all right?

I explained that hot weather made it itchy and that was the second-worst part. Otherwise, Linda had adapted some shirts for me so that I could appear in public. I started to ask him where his best clients came from, when the receptionist signaled to us. At the anteroom, we remained standing while Maureen Bailey did a good job of ignoring us. I leaned.

Finally, about quarter past the hour, her phone warbled. She stood up and invited us through the steel-framed door.

"Walter! Son of a bitch. What happened to you?" He came over to both of us, smiling and shaking hands. "Who's this?" I could see he didn't like unexpected guests.

"Oh, I'm sorry, Harry. This is Alan Boudreau, an attorney who has helped me immensely throughout the process, especially at the EPA. He's coming to the announcement ceremony and I kind-of told him I'd introduce him to you. I'm going to ask him to review what I sign on Blatchford's behalf… I'm not very good at legal stuff."

"Oh," he looked at me for a moment while holding Boudreau's handshake. "Sure."

I smiled, Boudreau smiled, and after a few seconds, McKay dropped his angry look.

"Well, we all have a busy morning, it looks like," began the mayor, "so let's get our business out of the way, shall we?" He looked at me and appeared to purposely avoid including Boudreau in his "we."

He opened a folder that was the only paperwork in view. "The lease is fairly simple, Walter, and is for exactly two years, commencing on July first… just a couple of weeks from now. That what you expected?"

"Yuh, sounds good. The questions I have are first, how much per year and how is it payable, and then what limits are there on our uses of the parcel?"

"Okay, here's a copy so that we are looking at the same thing." He pushed a copy over to me. I shifted my chair so that Alan could see it too.

"Okay," I started, "I see that the payment you ask for is eight hundred thousand a year. How is that paid?"

"We'd like it paid at the beginning of each year." I started shaking my head.

"That's how most of these things are handled, Walt. Standard practice."

I began to answer and Alan put his hand on my arm to stop me. "Please excuse me, Mr. Mayor, I have a couple of questions." His voice rose like a question. McKay looked at him like he gave off an odor, but flashed a smile and waved him on.

"Just for my own understanding, here, but what similar leases are you aware of?"

"What? What do you mean?" It was not a question McKay had prepared for.

"Well, who else can you think of that is leasing a parcel of land from the city on a multi-year basis?"

"Well, ahh... there are parking-lot operators who are leasing lots around the city. People like that."

Alan nodded and smiled, now receiving McKay's full attention. "How are they charged for their lots?" Still smiling.

"Ah, well, they pay every month or we close them down."

"That makes good sense. Why wouldn't their type of arrangement be suitable for Blatchford Steel?" McKay had no immediate answer. I looked at the wording that said "...payable annually in advance."

"Those parking outfits are licensed by the City. They perform a public service like taxicabs. It's different." He seemed satisfied with his answer but Boudreau wasn't.

"How about we change this word "annually" to "quarterly" and we can move past the issue?"

McKay started to pick up his phone but hesitated with the handset a few inches above the cradle. He looked from me to Boudreau and back. "I guess the city can live with that. We have to keep our eyes on the big ball, right?" He grinned like he'd proclaimed victory.

Boudreau smiled back. He pulled out a pen and wrote "quarterly" above the word "annually" and put a line through "annually." Then he pushed it toward me and said, "Make a small oval that crosses through both words and put your initials inside the oval." He watched me do as he said. Then he pushed it toward McKay and told him to do the same on both copies. When that was done he took McKay's copy and had me complete the pattern.

"There," he announced, "you'll notice, Mr. Mayor, that we have agreed to your rather high rate for leasing this small parcel."

"We could have asked for a million," McKay replied. His tone implied, "so, don't fuck with me." But I knew how much Boudreau loved to fuck with big shots. I saw an opportunity.

"Actually, Alan, the mayor has helped Blatchford all the way through this. And, Harry, your willingness to let this go quarterly has helped Blatchford avoid a real hardship. Our expenses have gone up over two million dollars to meet the requirements of making and shipping our girders. We appreciate your flexibility on this matter."

McKay nodded but he was watching Boudreau pick through the lease agreement. Alan was reading with a piece of paper under the line. Here and there he made a note on the paper. When he was done he did the same thing with the other copy. McKay looked at his watch and shook his head. It was only nine-forty.

Boudreau spoke up. "Walt, read this paragraph of what you are allowed to do on the parcel and what you can't do. Make sure that you will have the flexibility to make the improvements that are necessary."

I took the two pages of the agreement and started scanning down the page.

"Paragraph five and then six, Walt."

Paragraph five was titled, "Permissions." I read every word. As I got into the legalese I found myself reading more quickly and even grasping it. Blatchford could make improvements to the track and rail-bed that already existed, and make changes or additions to signaling systems that provided for safe railroad operations. We were obligated to fence in the parcel so that unauthorized persons would not be present when our special shipments moved. It was straightforward and I understood it. I moved on to number six, Restrictions.

Firstly, we couldn't sub-let the property or any part of it to any entity not wholly owned and controlled by Blatchford Steel Services. I shrugged at that one. We could not change any drainage patterns for surface water, although we could improve such drainage where it affected the railbed or trackage, subject to inspection by the departments concerned. We couldn't build any structures, temporary or permanent except as were necessary to make permitted improvements to the track or railbed, or to install signals as required for safe railroad operations.

Okay to that. They paid someone to type this stuff. It next said that Blatchford could not advertise or publicize its lease of or use of the parcel. I was puzzled by that. Who really gave a shit? I asked Boudreau about that sentence. He nodded and smiled firmly, took the paper and cleared his throat.

"Mr. Mayor, we are questioning the inclusion of this sentence that restricts Blatchford from advertising or promoting its use of the parcel."

"Yes. What about it?" McKay sat back as if he had the whole agreement memorized.

"What concern is it of the city's whom we display our use of the parcel to?"

"Well, it seems wiser to keep any use of that parcel on the low-key side. There's no reason to upset others who have concerns about that parcel. Since this is only a temporary lease, we'd like to keep it off the front page, if you get my meaning."

Before I could say anything, Alan Boudreau spoke up. "With all due respect, Your Honor, that is an unreasonable restriction on my client's ability to advertise his business success, which is essential to attracting additional sales and profits. We must remove that sentence for this to go forward. No modifications... a complete strike-through." At which point he drew a line through the words of the offending sentence. "Walter, another oval and initials, if you please." He sat back as if *he* had the whole agreement memorized.

McKay was as red as a beet. I'd pissed him off in the past, but this was new. He was as still as granite. No one said anything. I perceived that McKay had had that line inserted. I kept my mouth shut. Boudreau, meanwhile, grabbed the second copy and drew a line through the sentence with a flourish, then passed it to me and made a little oval in the air. I held the pen over the page and looked at McKay. He had cooled down, but he wasn't happy. He waved at me to go ahead. I made the oval and put my initials in it.

McKay took both copies and looked at them for a second and then looked at Boudreau. Boudreau smiled back at him, but his face said he was very serious. McKay cracked a tight smile and put his ovals and initials on the strike-out. "This ought to pretty much put an end to reasons for you to come to my office, shouldn't it?"

"Uhh, well, yeah. I guess it will."

"About fuckin time. Anything else you gotta change?"

I looked at Boudreau and he said the rest of it looked fine, and smiled.

"Good." McKay took his fountain pen and signed both copies and shoved them across to me. I looked at Boudreau and he nodded and then held up his hand to wait. From a small, sort-of half-portfolio thing he extracted his notary stamp. As I signed them in turn he stamped them and wrote his information on them. I'm pretty sure this only made McKay angrier, but it was all perfectly legal. Alan then told the mayor he needed a witness to the notarization and could he have his secretary step in? McKay's face was red but his countenance was like cement. He picked up his phone and hit a button, but didn't say anything. Seconds later Maureen Bailey came in with a worried look on her face. McKay told her to witness the signatures and Alan pointed to where she had to sign. I folded up Blatchford's copy of the lease and tucked it in my inner pocket.

McKay was standing with both hands on his desk, daring someone to try to shake hands with him. I stepped into the breech and stuck my hand out. After a few seconds he took it.

"Harry, you have exercised political courage, today. I know that. I am sorry for the changes we needed, but I am not sorry to have had the chance to work with you. You have impressed me, for whatever that's worth, and you've done a good thing for lots of people. I'm now looking forward to applauding your remarks in, ahh… holy shit, about fifty minutes! Okay. We'll see you shortly. Thanks, again."

Boudreau and I left by the side door I knew so well. Harry was on the phone as we closed it. I thanked Alan Boudreau for watching out for us… again.

"Walt, there are ten more areas I'd have changed, but none was very important. It's my belief that you can never accept a financial contract in its first offered form. It keeps the other parties on their toes, especially when it's government."

"Can I bum a ride to Larimer?"

"Sure. This could be interesting. Is Harold Blatchford coming?"

"Aw, shit. I meant to call him when we were upstairs" I looked around the lobby area. There were some pay phones closer to the other elevators. "Gimme a sec." I dropped in a quarter and called the office. I asked for Kelly Galvin's line.

"Kelly, it's me, Walter. Do you know if Mr. Blatchford has left for the announcement yet?"

"I believe he has, Walter. He told me to tell you he'd see you there and he wants a report on the lease. You know what he's talking about?"

"Oh, do I. We're just leaving the mayor's office, in fact, and we're all set. Thanks, Kelly, you're the best!" I hung up without waiting for her reply.

"Okay, Alan, thanks. We have plenty of time." We retrieved his Caddy. So far, so good, I thought, as he made his way out to the junction of Lincoln and Frankstown.

***

The square at Lincoln and Frankstown was larger than I expected, and forlorn. It was thirty minutes to showtime and a dozen technicians were checking wiring, sound and lights. A crew unfolded chairs on the scarred lot where the stage was set up, covered by a sun-roof. Channel Four's panel truck was parked on Enterprise, pointing its antennas back to the station. A tiny platform stood on the sidewalk about thirty feet from the truck, with a TV camera mounted on it. As I watched, a KDKA, Channel Two truck pulled up on Lowell Street. They had a portable camera.

Alan parked on what looked like a legal spot on Auburn Street, but he hadn't left the front seat. Instead he reclined in it, out of the sun. I walked back to him. I wasn't looking forward to a stint in the sun, either. With luck the clouds would build up.

I watched people straggle in, pick a chair and find some shade. I spotted Channel Four people checking their watches. It was nearing eleven and the key players were still arriving. They did a brief spot with a pretty reporter-lady and then got back under an awning. Next to the stage there were insulated coolers of water set up with tall stacks of clear plastic cups. I ambled that way.

About forty people were seated, holding newspapers for shade. A couple had umbrellas. I shielded my eyes and spotted Hal Blatchford's car near the Channel Two truck. The motor was running the air-conditioning. Hal lowered his window and invited me in the passenger side.

"How'd it go with the mayor?"

"Fine, ultimately. I had Alan Boudreau meet me there and it's fortunate that I did. He forced McKay to change a couple of things that needed changing. They were trying to make us pay annually in advance and he changed it to quarterly. Oh, and the rent is eight hundred a year."

"Hummph. Could have been worse, I guess. Two hundred grand July first. Okay. What else did he change?"

"Well, there was a sentence in there that said we couldn't advertise or promote our use of the parcel. Alan made him strike that out completely. And even better, at the very end of the signing he pulled out his Notary stamp and notarized both copies. The mayor was irked, but I thanked him for his help. You want the document?"

"Oh, ahh, sure. I'll give it to Peter. He'll get it posted with Jackson and filed. Sounds like we're in business, eh?"

"Yes, sir. We are in business."

"You'll have to get busy on getting the rails fixed up and the other changes needed to get the girders to the river."

"Is that what you want me to do?" I looked at him full on.

"Well, yes. Do you want to have someone else do that?" I was surprised at the question.

"Uhh, no, I hadn't thought about it, actually. Don't you think we should talk about what it is you do want me to be doing – going forward?"

Now he turned to face me. "Yes I do. Thought you'd never ask. You can come up this afternoon or maybe we can go have lunch after this circus." I thought about my promise to Linda a month earlier.

"Lunch would be nice," I replied.

"Heh, heh, heh! Good for you, Walt. Good for you. We'll go over to The Rivers Club. I have a few ideas to run by you." He shut off the motor. "Let's see when this shindig is going to get started." We walked together to the stage.

"You going to speak, boss?" I had my hand on his arm without thinking. He seemed to rock side to side and accepted the gesture.

"What do you think? We've got our lease. The Trust can't stop us now, can they?"

"I don't know how. I spoke to every permitting and inspectional office in the city that could stop us for some reason. All of them signed off on what we are going to do. So, no, I don't think it can… which means, I don't think *she* can."

"All right. I'm going to play this for what it's worth. I wrote down what you suggested. We'll see how that goes. You sitting up there?" He head-faked toward the chairs on stage.

"No. I'll sit with Boudreau and watch. No sense poking Roberta in the eye before we have to."

"Okay, kid. Be sure you clap your hand." He was smiling as he walked around to the ramp that zigged up the back of the stage. Forrest Akers was already seated, talking with some neighborhood leaders. John Schumann touched my elbow.

"John! I was just wondering why I hadn't seen you."

"Because you were sitting in Blatchford's car, that's why. Are you going up on stage?"

I shook my head. "Not me, but Hal is… there, he's talking to Forrest Akers."

"Oh, good, good. All right. I'm glad you're here. I assume the lease is all set?"

Yes! Holy smoke! I never called Akers from the mayor's office to tell him the money could be released. Will you tell him that I told you everything's set and it's okay?"

"Okay. You can tell him yourself."

"No, better not. Roberta has arrived and I'm not going to make a spectacle of my presence. I'll be back in a few minutes." I walked quickly to Boudreau's car. I tapped on his window.

Alan stretched and climbed out. "Wow. I think I was asleep. Did I miss everything?"

"No, they're seating the big shots on stage. We oughta find our seats."

Alan reached into the back seat and extracted some newspaper. "Take a few of these to shade your head." The TV people were both doing briefs with pretty women. On stage I saw the mayor glad-handing everybody, including Blatchford. He, McKay and Akers were standing together. They'd tell Akers the deal was a go. I stopped worrying about it.

When McKay got to Roberta McGillvray he gave her a little hug which she accepted stiffly. He spoke with her with a smile on his face. He was smooth, I'd give him that.

John Schumann was the MC. As he stood by the podium, ready to go live, a short ambulance pulled up and let down a ramp near the water coolers. A well-dressed Tom Wittenauer was rolled down in a wheelchair and then up the ramp behind the stage. Some people in the audience and even some on the stage, stood up and applauded as he was wheeled to the front. Hal Blatchford was at his side and even made a slight seating shift so that he'd be seated next to him. Wittenauer waved to everyone and mouthed his "thank you" with as much expression as he could.

The TV crews were both focusing on his arrival and his presence on stage. The pretty women now had a real story, so long as they got the congressman on camera and on mic. Three radio stations had shown up. Tom's image was definitely going to improve as his story was relived and detailed in interviews. John Schumann looked around at his stage-mates and indicated that he was going to get started.

I hadn't noticed them earlier, but a group of robed high-school girls now paraded out front and Schumann asked everyone to rise. Wittenauer stood with everyone else, even putting his hand over his heart.

The girls sang the National Anthem and received excessive applause. Schumann named their school and their faculty leader and thanked them profusely. He then said they'd be back at the end of the program. Nice touch. Finally he launched into introductions.

"Ladies and gentlemen," he boomed out, "thank you for coming out to acknowledge a new start for Larimer and for the Lincoln-Larimer neighborhood. I am proud to be joined, today, by a group of leaders whose vision and commitment to Pittsburgh and Larimer, is unparalleled.

"To my far right, representing the Three Rivers Trust, an organization that is devoted to improvement to every public space and to the life of every neighborhood, please welcome Ms. Roberta McGillvray! Roberta!" He led applause as the grand dame rose and waved.

"To Roberta's immediate left, closer to me, is our esteemed mayor, whose leadership and courage in making this project finally happen can only add to his broad reputation as the mayor who cares deeply for Pittsburgh, the Honorable Harry McKay. Mr. Mayor!" More applause. This wasn't Schumann's first announcement party. Both TV crews had their lights on and were banking tape for the six o'clock news.

"On my far left, and perhaps the real sparkplug for this project that promises to benefit the neighborhood and everyone that ever drives through this amazing intersection, my friend and hero, Forrest Akers, president of Liberty Bank, based right here in Larimer! Forrest!" Again he led the applause. Forrest Akers stood and stepped forward where he could wave at everyone. The majority of those watching the proceedings were of Akers' neighborhood and race. He received the most applause. Schumann was pleased.

"Next to Mr. Akers is a quiet man who has backed this project in support of its neighbors and in support of the city that has helped his company grow and provide good employment to over one hundred of our fellow Pittsburghers, my friend Harold Blatchford of Blatchford Steel Services. Harold!" Schumann applauded firmly, as did Akers and the mayor, while Wittenauer applauded and yelled out "Hear, hear!" On the far left of the stage, Roberta McGillvray sat stonily and red-faced. She brought a handkerchief to her eyes and nose several times. Alan Boudreau elbowed me and told me to watch her. He leaned toward me.

"There's an explosion building up on stage right." I nodded. He shrugged his wonder at what might actually happen. Schumann carried on.

"Finally I have the extraordinary honor of introducing a man who has represented our county and city for the past two years and who, in order to make the financing of this project even possible, was shot as he literally threw himself between a gunman and a woman who was assisting the congressman expose fraudulent activity at a federal agency. Congressman Wittenauer has battled back from life-threatening injuries to be with us, a hero! Tom Wittenauer!" The applause rivaled that for Forrest Akers, with most on stage and in the audience, standing as well. Again Alan elbowed my cast and gestured toward Roberta McGillvray. She appeared to be cramped and leaned over. She turned toward the railing and spoke to a man. In seconds he produced a plastic wastebasket and Roberta appeared to lose her breakfast into it.

"Ye gods!" exclaimed Boudreau. I was astonished. People were sitting again, and few appeared to notice Roberta's discomfort. Those that did had probably never heard of her. The mayor was asking her something but she shook her head. She was sipping water and looked pale. The well-dressed man standing on the ground next to her chair, was speaking with her. She shook her head in response to him, too. Schumann continued.

"The purpose of what has come to be known as the 'Larimer' project, is to consolidate two pieces of property where we'll build a modern community center, including a safe, after-school youth club and an early childhood day-care facility that will make it possible for more families to increase their incomes and provide better for themselves. In addition to the new *Liberty Community Center*, the project will dramatically revamp traffic patterns in the intersection I am facing, behind you. Included in that reconstruction will be green spaces, outdoor game tables and seating, and play areas in the lot directly across from this stage and here, where the stage itself sits. Traffic control, walk lights and clearly marked pedestrian zones will make it possible for people to make use of the new Center and of the park and pedestrian areas. To describe the community center portion of the project, I invite the president of Liberty Bank, Forrest A. Akers, to say a few words. Forrest?" More clapping. Akers stepped up to the podium. Schumann carried a tripod with an architectural rendering covered by a white cloth, closer to where Akers stood.

Akers issued some platitudes and expressed his own and the Bank's commitment to the best possible neighborhood conditions. He then announced that he was looking forward to the fabulous new community center that would soon be rising on this very spot! At that he flipped the cloth over the back of the foam board that held the rendering of a dreamy building with slender neighborhood denizens walking beneath basketball trees. I expected that most of them were smiling. People applauded, looking around trying to picture the siting of the dreamscape depicted on the rendering. People on stage were clapping and standing where they could catch a glimpse of the rendering. John Schumann now carried the tripod back to the rear of the stage for remote marvelling.

Next he introduced Mayor McKay. The mayor acknowledged everybody on stage and expressed his gratitude to those who had played such key roles in making this great day possible. Then he slipped in his trademark description of the three key things the city could and should do. People liked it. He thanked Forrest Akers and Hal Blatchford for their courageous financial contributions, and Tom Wittenauer for his ongoing help with UDAG and other grants at the federal level. Finally he invited everyone present to join him at the ribbon-cutting he was looking forward to. The applause he received was appropriate. As he stepped back to his chair he seemed to study Roberta, who was looking not at his face but at some point behind and below him.

I could see McKay's expression but I don't know if it was sadness or worry. Roberta was in a state.

***

Officer Stewart dialed again. He let it ring. This time it was answered. "*englishclass* publishing. How can we help you?"

Stewart wiped his face with a limp paper towel. "This is the Pittsburgh Police. I really need to speak with Linda Anton. Please tell me she is there."

"I'm sorry, sir, but I don't know if she is here. Can you hold?"

"I'll hold," Stewart replied. Some kind of mixed classical background music came on.

The respondent came back on line. "I'll connect you now, sir." Click... ring.

"This is Linda Anton. This is the police?"

"Yes, Mrs. Anton. It's Arnie Stewart from Zone Four. I met you at the Gateway?"

"Oh, yes, Officer Stewart. What's the matter? Is something wrong with Walter?"

"I don't know, Mrs. Anton. I've called his office and they say he never came in. Do you know where he is?"

"Oh, well, no, he didn't go to the office, he met with the mayor at nine. I dropped him off there. After that there was some kind of big announcement event in Larimer. I'm not sure of the address. Is he in trouble?" Linda was now standing and pacing as far as the cord allowed.

"I'm not sure, like I said, but we've learned some things about the guy that ran him off the road that indicate he may be at risk."

"But that man was killed, wasn't he?"

"Yes, but we've learned that he had a connection to one Roberta McGillvray. You know her."

"Oh my God... oh my God!" Linda sat down, her heart racing. "That's not possible! I know her. I work with her on the Three Rivers Trust!"

"Has she ever been violent that you know of?" Stewart sounded worried.

"Mr. Stewart, Walter is at an event with her right now! What can I do?"

"Don't do anything, Mrs. Anton. Tell me where this event is being held."

"All I know is it's in Larimer. The mayor is there and I think they were trying to get congressman Wittenauer out of the hospital to be there, too."

"All right. I can find it. We'll take care of things, Mrs. Anton. I'll get back to you."

"What are you going to do?" Linda was edging toward panic.

"I'll find him and make sure nothing happens. Don't worry. I'll get back to you. Stay where I can reach you." Stewart hung up and headed to his cruiser. At the front desk he asked the officer to find out where some kind of VIP event was being held in Larimer.

"Maybe we have a detail. The day sarge oughta know."

"Okay, call me in the car when you get an address. And send another cruiser to the same place. Could be trouble!" He was out the door.

He started his cruiser and keyed his mic to ask where the mayor was having the announcement. He peeled out and headed north.

At *englishclass*, Linda walked back and forth, fidgeting with her hands. She tried to work, but couldn't. Stewart was obviously concerned or he wouldn't call. She couldn't just drive around Larimer, an area she knew nothing about.

But she couldn't sit, either. She went out front.

"Tina, have you heard of an event of some kind taking place in Larimer?"

"Sure. It was on TV a minute ago. The mayor was speaking. On Channel Two."

"Where is it, did they say?"

"On Frankstown Road. They have a stage set up. That congressman is there, too. He was in the hospital, did you know that?"

"I did know that. Do you have a map?"

"No, but I live near there. I can tell you turn by turn."

Linda wrote down the directions. "I'll be gone for a while, Tina. Will you tell Anna that I have some Trust business to take care of? You're a peach, thanks, Tina."

Linda half ran to her car. She'd been late this morning and was forced to park on the other side of Duquesne. Every minute added anxiety. There was no way they made it this far only to see something more happen to her husband. She tried to run in her dress shoes. Damn it!

***

Schumann now extolled Roberta McGillvray and her work on the Three Rivers Trust. Her dedication to neighborhoods in Pittsburgh was legendary. We were all fortunate to have her attend this important announcement and to display, for the first time, how the project was going to bring safe parkland and beauty to this square. "Ladies and gentlemen! Roberta McGillvray!" He led the applause, again, which was, at least, polite.

Roberta stalked up to the microphone carrying her handbag which was soft enough to shove into the podium. She looked to make sure Schumann was bringing her rendering forward as he had Akers'. I made sure my head was covered. So far, I didn't think she'd spotted me. The earlier patchy cloud cover had been thickening, but I kept the papers up, hoping to not exacerbate Roberta's anger.

"Thank you, Mr. Schumann!" she exclaimed. "That is, I believe, a *Jewish* name. Like most of you," she gestured to the audience, "I have watched Jews make huge profits on the backs of our neighbors and neighborhoods. It has been our mission at the Three Rivers Trust to make sure that the rape and paving of our city at least includes some measure of improvement to the lives and environments of the *real* people of Pittsburgh. That is what we have done with today's project: made sure that the money-grubbers from one small group of mercenaries can't ride off with their profits while the real citizens of Larimer pay the highest price of all. So, we started almost four… years… ago… planning for the park and play areas that are part of this community center package."

She sipped some water, and looked around as if challenging the others to stop her. She regally walked the couple of steps to her rendering flipped the cloth off of it and onto the stage floor.

"I know you can't all see the details in this picture. When you do, you'll see that ideas like ours are really simple. How can we *improooove* this neighborhood, making it more livable for its residents, and safer for people to use? Safe for their children and better for the values of their property?

"Some in Pittsburgh only see projects like this as ways to profit themselves, like the leader, here, Mr. Shumann… and like the great Harold Blaaatchford, who doesn't give a damn about Larimer, but has, instead, tricked all of us by using his support for our neighborhood to bribe the mayor into granting a lease that benefits only ONE…" here she held up her index finger… "company, Blatchford Steel Services. In the process they have prevented the improvement of a neighborhood near their plant, condemning children who live there to crossing through traffic to reach safe play areas.

"Mr. Mayor, shame on you for being part of that crude game. And shame on your sneaky minion, Walter Anton, who is hiding there in the audience! You can see him, everyone, ducking under his newspapers. He cares not one whit for you or your standard of living. All he wants is to steal some land from the city... our city, with the evil connivance of Mayor McKay and a cabal of wealthy Jews!" She looked around to gauge the effects of her words. Schumann sat with his hands over his face, leaning over his knees. Hal was talking with Tom Wittenauer, who was shaking his head. Finally Hal stood up and walked to the podium. Without thinking of my limited abilities I started toward the stage. From the corner of my eye I saw a police cruiser pull in directly behind the audience and an officer climb out and start running toward me. I kept moving toward the stage.

Hal Blatchford reached Roberta and pulled her arm to pull her away from the podium. She yanked the microphone out of its holder and swung it at his face, catching him firmly on the forehead, making him stumble back. She then pulled her floppy handbag out of the podium shelf and reached into it.

Harry McKay was now on her other side attempting to get hold of her other arm as Blatchford resumed his attempt to do the same. She was too quick. Her hand appeared with an automatic pistol. Her first shot went through the bag and the front of the podium and buried itself in the tarred surface below. Both men paused for just a second, which was enough time for Roberta to lift the gun toward me.

People around me were scattering and impeding the police officer. He struggled over chairs, flattening some and kicking others aside. Another shot exploded over my head and pinged off a metal chair behind me. I ducked after it went off, but it was hard to move with the damned cast. The next thing I knew the officer had tackled me and pulled me down on top of himself and then onto the ground where we were somewhat protected by metal folding chairs.

"Sorry I'm late, Walt," he said. I recognized Arnie Stewart's voice.

"How…? How did you know to come here?"

"Never mind. Stay right here." He jumped up and ran the rest of the way to the stage, where the mayor was wrestling with Roberta's gun hand. She got off another shot into the air. Finally McKay gave up all pretense of gentlemanliness and twisted the struggling woman down onto the stage with his knee holding her arm onto the floor. Hal Blatchford basically sat on her back as the mayor attempted to pry her hand away from the pistol. Arnie Stewart arrived and quickly had both her hands behind her and bound with a plastic tie. She was screaming and grunting.

"You all work for Jews! You're all in this together. Tell Wittenauer I know what he's doing with the Jews." Stewart pulled her to her feet, where she could look right at the congressman. "You should have died, you weasel. I know what you do!"

Stewart yanked her to the ramp and marched her down to ground level where he made her sit. A second cruiser with two cops had arrived and they took her away. The well-dressed man who'd been hovering near her tried to talk to them as they pushed her into the back seat, but they told him to back away. He looked devastated.

I finally made it onto the stage and checked with Hal Blatchford, first. "Boss, you were great out there! I didn't know you knew judo and all that stuff." We both chuckled.

"She caught me pretty good with that mic, I'll tell you. Strong lady." He touched the welt that was puffed up across the top of his forehead.

"I'm sorry I got you up here," I apologized.

"Nonsense," he replied. "I wouldn't have missed this. I can see why you like this business."

John Schumann came over to us. "Harold, I'm sorry she got to conk you like that."

"Not a problem, John. It was my first time on TV!" Schumann looked shocked as he realized that the whole melee had been taped by the two stations.

"I can imagine what their headline is going to be." He shook his head.

I started to interject, but the mayor stepped into the group. He reached out for Blatchford's hand. "Thanks for taking the lead out there. I should have grabbed her sooner. I knew she was pretty upset, but I never thought it would be more than harsh words and back-room retribution of some sort. Clearly she's very troubled."

I looked around for Forrest Akers. He was out front, picking up chairs and straightening the rows. Several friends of his were helping. Schumann was now speaking with the Channel Four people. One of the Channel Two staff joined them. They reached some sort of agreement and Schumann headed back to the stage. Apparently the show was going on. I passed Schumann on the ramp.

"Don't go away," he said. "We're still going to finish the speeches. We can't leave things like this." I wished him luck.

When I got to where Akers was, he was chatting with Alan Boudreau. I introduced myself. Akers shook hands warmly.

"I don't know if I should get too close to you," he smiled. "You've been stirrin up trouble from here to Monroeville, I understand." He jinked his head toward Boudreau.

"Well, it's what I do. Evidently." We all laughed. "When I'm free of this cast I'm going to join the World Wrestling Federation. It's safer."

"They tell me that I'm still going to make my speech, so I hope you'll stay for that."

I looked toward Boudreau and he nodded that he was staying. "Wouldn't miss it, Forrest. I am glad this project has come about for you. My interests, as Roberta screamed out, lie with another parcel, entirely, but I am glad for you and for this neighborhood."

"Look," he answered, "I know how capitalism should be working and that good business is often good for everyone else. This is one of those times. That's what I'm going to say, by the way." I smiled.

The chairs were filling up with the earlier audience, and then some. A few gunshots will draw a crowd. The school bus that delivered the choir girls was gone. A few gunshots will do that, too.

Schumann called to me with the PA system. "Walter, why not take the empty seat up here?" I waved a "no thanks." When we turned to head back to our original seats I saw Linda running toward us.

"Walter, Walter!" She waved as she tried to run in her heels. "What's going on?" She reached Boudreau about the same time I did. He stood to shake her hand. I gave her a quick kiss. She sat with us.

"Your officer Stewart called me to find you. I had to come. Our receptionist... gave me... directions." She was panting.

"Well you missed all the fun. Roberta had a meltdown and tried to shoot people."

"She what?" Her mouth hung open. "Roberta? A gun?" Her voice rose with each question.

"It was something. It'll be on TV, I'm sure. They caught it all."

"Was anybody hurt?" I told her that probably only Roberta, herself was hurt, although Hal took a good bonk on the head. Schumann asked for attention.

"Ladies and gentlemen, thank you for bearing with us, today. Our program is nearly complete, but would not be without hearing from one of the key investors in the Larimer project. I am proud to introduce my friend, and a friend of Pittsburgh's, Harold Blatchford, founder of Blatchford Steel Services! Harold!"

Hal shook Schumann's hand as he approached the podium. He looked confident. I'd never heard him give a speech, but he was grinning.

"My name is Harold Blatchford. I'm not a politician or a community leader. I run a company. We have some of the best employees in Pittsburgh. Together, we fashion custom steel products that build bridges, buildings, even baseball stadiums like Three Rivers. We are a profitable business. For some, 'profit' is a dirty word, but being successful enables us to invest in growth and new capacities. We'll be hiring more good people as a result." He sipped some water.

"You may wonder why we have become involved in Larimer. It's a good question. Through a long, strange process, we have agreed to pay a 'bribe,' as it was referred to, to the City of Pittsburgh. It wasn't a bribe to the mayor, although he negotiated it. It's a bribe of over two million dollars that not only makes this project possible, but will boost the budget of the Parks and Recreation Department so that they can prepare, repair and maintain parkland such as that being developed for your neighborhood, right here.

"In exchange, Blatchford can grow and handle a major new project of our own. We are purchasing new equipment, which helps employment at other companies. We are hiring more people for Blatchford Steel. We are even helping local banks, like Liberty. I don't see a downside to any of this, and I'm proud that we are profitable enough to take part. Thank you, John Schumann, Forrest Akers, and Harry McKay and, as much as anyone, Tom Wittenauer, for making all of today possible." He returned to his seat. I stood to applaud as did those on stage. I simply slapped one leg. Most in the audience stayed seated but applauded perhaps more than simple courtesy required. I hoped they understood what Hal had explained.

John Schumann shook Hal's hand again as they passed. He now invited Tom Wittenauer to address the crowd, which was larger than it had been before Roberta's blow-up. He wheeled himself to the podium and set the brakes. Then he slowly pulled himself up to a somewhat bent, yet erect position. His voice was strong.

"My healing goes on," he began, "and so does the healing of our great city. I am in awe of the remarkable vision and energy of Mayor Harry McKay. This project, here, today, is a perfect example of your mayor's vision for the city he loves. I can't take any responsibility for the success this announcement represents. I am proud to have played a small part on behalf of my friend Hal Blatchford, and my new friend, Walter Anton. It is businessmen like them who enable all of us to work and pay taxes and raise our families. What I mean to say is that there is plenty of credit to share for this wonderful improvement to this neighborhood and to Pittsburgh. I can't take anything away from the mayor, from Hal Blatchford, from John Schumann who I know has sweated to put this whole deal together, and especially from today's hero, Forrest Akers, of Liberty Bank. Thanks to you all!" He waved and sat down heavily. People stood and applauded him, more for his taking of a bullet, I suspect, than for his silver tongue. Still, he was very gracious. It was good.

Schumann now walked up to the podium with Forrest Akers, who helped Wittenauer to roll back to his spot. Schumann simply shouted out, "Ladies and gentlemen, Forrest Akers!"

Now, the audience stood and cheered. Akers was the right color. No matter what the others had said, they weren't, and he was clearly the one people stayed to hear. He stood at the podium like a revered celebrity, both arms raised and smiling widely. Little by little he encouraged everyone to sit down, almost a little embarrassed by their reaction. When I turned around I was surprised to see how the crowd had grown. I spotted the black city councilor that had been at Roberta's luncheon, standing with some other well-dressed black men. I turned to Linda to tell her how huge the crowd now was.

"The event has already been on TV, Walter. They must have broadcast the shooting, too."

Akers began to speak. "Ladies and gentlemen, I can't begin to thank you for that warm welcome. And," he swept his arm out toward the crowd, "it is great to see so many of you expressing interest in our little community center, here in Larimer." He laughed a bit. "I can imagine that when you heard they were shooting at people over here that maybe the black guy was the target!" The crowd made some noise at that. "Well, he wasn't! The shots were aimed at a white guy, Walter Anton, a friend of mine and of yours. He's right out there in the audience. Walter, in the big cast, there, please stand up!" He motioned for me to rise.

"The reason Mr. Anton has that cast on is because he was already shot..." his voice rose up dramatically, "as he strove to complete the deal that has borne fruit for our neighborhood, here today! Today, thank God, the bullets were not well aimed. I'm proud to have worked with Walter in making today come true, and to have met and worked with his boss, Harold Blatchford for the same reasons. Now I may be the only black man to speak, today, but I'm here with my friends, who have all shown friendship to you, too. You just heard from our congressman,

Tom Wittenauer. Let me explain that he, too, was shot on the same mission to make this day come true! I've worked with Mayor McKay who has cleared the way for the Larimer Project. He is a friend of yours. And I'm glad you have a chance to meet my friend John Schumann, the man who coordinated all the parts and pieces that brought us all together for the purpose of improving this neighborhood.

"So, my friends and neighbors, this hasn't been simple and it hasn't been easy, but it has always been the right thing to do. I can take credit only for making the tiny little snowball and starting it off down the hill where it gained support and the all-important financing that will finally build our center and provide the park and play areas we'll all enjoy. It took every one of your new friends, up here, today, and more, all willing to work with our community and neighborhood. Give yourselves a round of applause!" He led the clapping with his arms raised high. The audience stood, again. Even Wittenauer stood up. You'd think the Steelers had won the Superbowl and Lynn Swan was speaking. It took a couple of minutes.

Linda was hugging my arm tight to her body. I didn't want to sit down. She was proud of me. Almost everyone who had helped me on my odyssey to run a little over a quarter mile of railroad, was here. Even Arnie Stewart had hung around. I'd have thought he'd have to go give a statement, but everything that happened was on videotape.

I didn't have to sit down. Schumann had come up to stand with Forrest Akers and within moments the mayor, Hal Blatchford and Tom Wittenauer were up front with him, as well. John Schumann simply thanked everyone for celebrating this new day for Larimer, and that everyone there should be able to clearly see why Pittsburgh was such a great city and had a bright future. And that was it. More than I'd expected and now it was over.

I shook hands with Alan Boudreau and thanked him for his vital help over the past month. He said he was glad I'd involved him and that he wouldn't have missed it. I asked him if he wanted to come up to the stage? After all I could now introduce him to everyone up there.

"It's enough for me to tell people 'I know Walter Anton,' if you know what I mean."

"I do and I don't," I replied. "I'll get a ride from Linda, but, listen, Hal Blatchford invited me to lunch and I'm sure you're welcome."

"No, I do have to work at least a little while every day. But, thanks. We can do lunch another time. Or, invite me to one of your ribbon-cuttings." He waved as he trotted to his Caddy.

"I am so glad you're here," I said as I kissed Linda's ear. "You had to see this to believe it."

"I'm very proud to be a friend of Walter's." Linda swung my arm widely. "Am I invited to lunch, too?"

"If you aren't, then I'm not going!" She looked at me. "But I had a nice little chat with the old man before things got started, this morning. That's when he asked me to go with him to that new Rivers Club. I think we're going to have an interesting discussion… about the future, I mean."

"Are you ready to decide on what you want to do? Do you want to stay…" She stopped speaking as we climbed the ramp up to the stage.

"John, this is my wife, Linda, who really made this project work." Schumann greeted her with a beaming smile.

"I am very happy to meet you, at last. Walter has told me more than once how you have helped him think through the best steps to take. And, he's right that we might not have made it here without you… to the point of risking your life. So, thank you very, very much."

Linda was beaming, too, and had turned a pleasant pink. I introduced her to Forrest Akers. "That was a Hell of a wrap-up, Forrest. You gave me too much credit, but otherwise a very good speech."

Akers gave Linda a tiny peck on the cheek. "You picked out quite a guy, Mrs. Anton."

"Well, that may be true, Mr. Akers, but it's better if Walter never hears that. He's more manageable if I keep him in the dark." We all chuckled.

"Well, I know what he went through, and you do, certainly. And I learned today what you did with Tom Wittenauer at the EPA. You both impress me. Thanks to you, both."

Wittenauer, himself, rolled over to where we were and stuck his hand out to Linda. "Thanks for visiting the hospital," he said.

"I am so pleased that you're doing so well, Congressman. It's amazing."

"I'm not able to go home, and they're lining up to take me back..." He gestured to two of his aides and the EMT's who had just arrived. "So, I'm in for a few more days, I guess. But I am feeling much better and they took such quick care of me that I avoided the worst infection. I'll be jogging to your next celebration."

"I hope that happens," I said as Linda told him her own version of that sentiment. "It was fabulous that you were here."

"My pleasure, for sure, but I've got to go, now." His aides wheeled him down to the tarmac where the EMT's took over. In a minute they were rolling.

The mayor broke away from some reporters and stuck his hand out toward me. "And this is the incredible Linda?" He gave her a little hug. "I understand you've been the real key to our being here, today."

Linda turned pink, again, and shook her head. "Not true, but thanks for thinking so. Walter is your hero in this struggle."

"We've had our ups and downs, but I have to say he was always moving the project forward and watching out for his company. And, here we are!" He was grinning, but if it hadn't been Linda standing with me, I know he would have described me with different vocabulary. At that moment, I didn't give a damn. I told the mayor I was glad to have had the opportunity to work with him. He liked it. I pulled Linda over to see Hal Blatchford.

"Hello, again, Linda," He said as they hugged quickly. "It's been quite a coupla weeks, hasn't it?"

"Never to be repeated, I hope."

"I'm with you. How did you, ahhm... I mean, it was on TV?"

"The police called me looking for Walter and one of my coworkers knew how to get here. There was no way I could sit still."

"If you have time, today, Walter and I were going for lunch. You will be a good addition to the discussion. We're going to The Rivers Club at the Oxford Center. What do you say?"

"If you're sure it's okay, I'd love to come." She looked at me and I gave her a little hug. She was the perfect person to be with me when the serious discussions began. I thanked Schumann, again, but he immediately turned the thanks back on me and on Blatchford. It was becoming sickly sweet. I couldn't get out fast enough. The TV cameras were gone, anyway.

***

Lunch at the Marriott with Deiter and Casimir was impressive, but I could afford to go there. Going to the Rivers Club was attractive, but uncomfortably beyond my budget. Linda would figure that we had both earned a treat, but I always wanted to be able to pay, even if I didn't. What the Hell?

"Uhh, Hal," I asked, "am I dressed well enough to go to the Rivers Club?"

"You're fine for lunch. Don't even think about it. Let's go. There's plenty of parking there."

Linda followed Hal's Cadillac on the short ride to the Oxford Center, off Grant. Stepping into the elevator felt like we were changing our reality. I was going to be on vacation for however long lunch took at the Rivers.

The place was elegant, for sure, and quiet. Everyone knew Hal and seemed to know us, too, once we were introduced to the maitre d´. The menus had no prices and were printed fresh each day. Today's chef's special had no coffee stains on it. Nor were any of the items emphasized over others. All were described glowingly. I chose a small steak, Linda picked a Cobb salad and Hal had chunk crabmeat on a salad. But it was clear that food wasn't primary.

"Walter, I have done some thinking since you took on this little project for us. I imagine that you have, too. In fact, I'll bet that Linda has been pushing you to look out for yourself."

I nodded and set down my fork and took a sip of water. For some reason I didn't say anything. It's a good plan to let the aggressor keep talking, not that we were at odds, but Hal held the cards. Maybe I had learned something about negotiating. Linda put her hand on my leg.

"You do spend too much energy, I think, trying to make things easier for others, or taking on tasks others can handle. On the other hand, your shifting of responsibility to Colleen Walsh was masterful. I have enjoyed seeing you work with Jack Jackson more. He has taken charge of the new construction in a way I didn't expect, and it has something to do with your leadership. What do you think of the past few weeks?" Uh-oh. I couldn't let him do the talking, now. I had to say something smart.

"I didn't start out thinking this way, boss, but at some point I began to think of the *mission*, if you know what I mean? Instead of doing what had to be done to get through the day or the week, I had to accomplish the many steps by a certain date, and I had to work with a lot of people who had no particular reason to help me. In the past I basically didn't care how well others did their jobs, but now I do, and I had to ask for many people's help, inside and outside of the company. That was new for me."

"You even asked for my help and involved me in public speaking, for God's sake. All part of the mission, I suppose."

"What you said, this morning, was perfect. They should play that clip in Pitt's MBA program. Where'd you get the degree that taught you what to say, like that?"

"I should say 'Bucknell,' right?" We shared a chuckle. "But the truths I repeated this morning aren't learnable in some classroom. Blatchford Steel is my mission, if you like, and having that attitude causes you to think of a greater good, mutual benefits, shared goals. Sounds like feel-good stuff, but it's how the best organizations run, it seems to me."

He leaned back, gathering his thoughts. Our waiter popped up to ask if we wanted fresh coffee. I said yes, and Hal gestured toward his cup, too. Linda asked for herbal tea.

Hal leaned forward, again. "You said something about not doing cost accounting reports, anymore, after this project was finished. What did you have in mind?" Ahh, the big question… the one Linda would rather answer for me. What did I want?

"I actually gave some thought to working like John Schumann does. Not necessarily at Brightman, but they do seem to make a pretty nice living. But I really couldn't make myself comfortable with the vagaries of his days. So I've rejected that." Our coffees and tea arrived – not poured onto the old, all fresh service. That was nice. It spurred a thought for me.

"I have enjoyed being on a mission, Hal. It's been painful and risky, but always having the big goal in mind made most of the steps obvious. Better thinking than I grew up with. I believe I can do a lot more in a day, week, month or year, than I did before. I'm not sure I have all the skills to apply that desire to other projects, though.

"I'm not sure that other projects will permit the kind of on-the-job training that this one did, either." Hal was studying me intently. I could tell that Linda had something to offer, but I didn't feel as though now was the time. I had to speak for myself.

"I should take some advanced business administration courses… maybe get an MBA, as part of the immediate future. There is likely to be more at stake with my future decisions." I could feel Linda relax a bit.

For his part, Blatchford sat back again, sipping his coffee. I sipped, too, thinking I'd said the right thing. Linda made a point of prepping her tea with a little honey, clattering her spoon and sipping the hot liquid with a little flair. I decided to pre-empt Hal's response.

"What would you like for me to do for Blatchford Steel, Hal?" He made that enigmatic smile I'd seen a couple of times, recently. Finally, he sat forward hands clasped together, still looking straight at me.

"I think you should run the place," he said without inflection. For whatever perverse reason, I blushed like a kid caught playing with himself. I covered my mouth and coughed as quietly as I could. Linda changed her posture but stayed silent. I sipped some water, finding myself dry in the mouth.

"As some kind of Vice President, or manager? I have to tell you I was not prepared to hear that." I drank some more water. I was almost angry to be put on the spot this way. Linda patted my knee and I turned to face her. She smiled like the Mona Lisa, the way my mother used to do whenever she heard a compliment aimed at me.

"We'll have to transition, obviously. Probably take two years, maybe more, but you should be president, in my book." He again spoke softly and wasn't trying to pump me up after achieving the lease on the parcel. He was talking serious business, seriously. In fact, he had never had a more serious piece of business to discuss, that I could imagine. I was feeling cold and calm, for the first time that day, as I had sometimes felt during negotiations. Indeed, as I had felt facing Sindledecker when I put that hole in the rental. I almost glared back at him.

"I don't understand this, Hal," I said coldly. My face was frozen.

Linda quietly said, "Walter?"

I turned my head to her and smiled briefly. "Just a minute, Hon." Blatchford was calmly watching me.

"In a company as big as Blatchford Steel, Walt, transition of management is absolutely critical. Competitors and larger customers and, more crucially, potential large customers, watch these things very carefully as they decide how to deal with us. We are now on a path, financed by Denmark, thanks to you, to where we can do some very large projects. Blatchford is going to grow and management has to grow with it. Why do you think I put up with all your crap over the past month?"

I sat back as if pushed by a big hand. It took me a second to digest his words, then I started to laugh… not a derisive laugh, but a genuine, enjoyment laugh. Hal began laughing with me. Even Linda laughed, it was so contagious. I stilled myself and put my hand on Hal's. The dining room was almost empty.

"We have a lot to talk about."

Hal nodded at me.

"One question I have to ask right now, though."

"Shoot," he said.

"What about Peter? I am not interested in being part of that kind of battle. You understand."

"There is no battle, Walt. Peter knows he's not going to be president. In fact, he has made it clear that he doesn't want it. His education was more toward law and political science. He's smart… don't get me wrong. He scares me with his knowledge of history and political insights. I expect he will do great things on that score. Great things. He has told me twice in the past few weeks that I should be thinking of bringing you into management. I believe he'll be delighted in what I've decided. You'll have to agree, of course."

Linda excused herself for the ladies' room. I leaned toward Hal and told him that I needed the weekend to properly respond. He seemed to be taken aback, having just offered me everything he had. I explained to him that accepting his wondrous offer was a life-changing decision, and would change the life of not only me, but of Linda and our expected baby, too. And it was going to affect the lives of others at Blatchford, and I had to consider all of those things and more. Then I told him something I am not sure I ever fully explained to my father.

"I have always looked up to you, Hal, but never on a truly personal level. I have been honored to work with you and share your mission a little bit. Your trust has changed me for the better. I am most proud of having pleased you. When I tell you I will do what it takes to grow your company and make you proud of me, I have to be certain in my own heart that I not only can do it, but that, if I am successful at it, I will remain motivated to do more and be happy doing it. It's worth a couple days of thought." Linda was standing a little behind me where I hadn't seen her. I wasn't sure what she had heard.

"I'm good with all of that, Walter. I'm glad it is that important to you and I can respect that." I stood for Linda's retaking her seat. She looked like she had been crying but had composed herself beautifully. I looked at her questioningly but her smile told me not to worry. I was finally relaxed.

"Now," continued Blatchford, "tell me what's going on with your car." I was surprised again.

"Well, I rented a car after my first accident and I'm having that fixed, I think, and then I was going to buy it from Alamo Car Rental. I'm getting an estimate on it this afternoon."

"Well, I'd like to suggest you don't buy it or fix it. And give me every expense you have had on this project. And don't misunderstand this… it's not a bribe, it's justice. Blatchford Steel is going to replace your car. Pick out what you think is a fair replacement. Get a good price on it and pass the proposal to Jack Jackson. This will happen no matter what you tell me on Monday. Just so you know." He smiled gently but was all business.

I was shaking my head. "You know, I was planning to ask for some help on these expenses when I got everything figured out. We're expecting a settlement on the Jeep, so that's a factor, too. I'll be happy to provide the accounting."

"All right, then. I think our lunch business is complete. I'm heading back to the office and I'm sure you have a lot to take care of, so if I don't see you later, I hope you have a very good and reflective weekend." He stuck his hand out and I was glad to shake it. Linda gave him a warm hug and thanked him for letting her join us for lunch.

"I'm trying to repay you for that cookout. So far I still haven't."

"I hope you come to another, real soon. Walter does like to cook, you know."

"I'll be there. Walter, I'll see you when I see you. Let's go."

We rode the elevator together and said more goodbyes as we found our cars. I let Linda drive. I was so nervous, my knees were shaking. I had to come back down to Earth before operating large machinery.

***

Linda didn't besiege me with questions or even discussion, of what just happened. I had never given a lot of thought to Hal's age so it never occurred to me that he would ever not be running Blatchford Steel. Obviously he felt that day was coming and as he had explained, the best business wisdom would make sure of the continuation of a company, if, indeed, its continuation was intended. Blatchford Steel was an institution, in my mind. It did a lot of business, was apparently profitable, and was led and defined by Harold Blatchford. I hadn't planned on any change in that.

When we pulled up in our empty driveway, Linda shut down the motor and grabbed my hand and kissed the palm. She was crying again, just a little. "Hey, kiddo…" I started but she had climbed out and was coming around to my door. She opened my door and reached in to undo the seatbelt. I kissed her neck as she did.

"Keep that thought," she said. She hugged my arm as we walked to the front door where we found a note from a courier service. It said a package was outside the back door. That was thoughtful of them.

"I'll see what's there," I said. Fortunately I looked first. There was a huge gift basket. I left the door unlocked and walked around the house to retrieve it. I could lift it, but it weighed more than twenty pounds. I thunked it on the kitchen table.

"My gracious! Who is *that* from?" Linda asked as if its very size were an affront to normal people. I held a thick envelope that had been taped to the cellophane.

"John Schumann." I read the message he'd written over both pages. Half of the note was directed to Linda. "He's in love with you, it says here. Maybe I wasn't supposed to see this."

"Gimme that, you oaf." She took the note as I dangled it between my thumb and forefinger. She read it a couple of times. Now she was tearing up, again.

"What's the matter, Lin?"

"Nothing, really. This is very high praise and sometimes when people express admiration of you I feel like crying. You got a problem with that, mister?"

I wrapped her in my good arm. She cried silently for a couple of minutes and slipped away to wipe her face. "He's very wordy when it comes to you."

"I don't know how to respond to this. You'll have to help me, okay?"

"You'll think of something. Let's unpack it in case it should be refrigerated." She filled two Tupperware bowls with the choicest fruits, and stacked up boxes of fancy cashews, almonds, whole walnuts and candied pecans. We found Lindt chocolates, English preserves, including my favorite, ginger, and at the bottom was a wooden box of three kinds of cheese.

"I feel like I should be giving a basket to John... not the other way around. He must have made a pretty good commission on that deal."

"He's telling you he couldn't have made it without you, Sweetie. Weren't you listening to those speeches? Lots of people benefited from your success... just about everyone except Roberta McGillvray..." Linda stopped, a sad look on her face.

"Let's go visit her, Walt."

"In jail? Is that possible?" I was confused at first, but I thought about it. "Okay," I said.

"Now, do you think?"

"I'll call the Department and see if it's possible." I called and first asked if Arnie Stewart was still on schedule. He wasn't, but when I asked about visiting a prisoner the person I'd reached asked for the name and then whether I was family or an attorney. I tried to explain that we were co-workers and therefore, just friends. The first answer to the request was, "no."

I asked if a supervisor could be spoken to, since the lady really had no family. "Hold, please," he said.

After about ten minutes on hold there were a series of clicks and someone else came on. "This is Captain Collins," he said.

"Oh, good!" I said. "Captain, this is Walter Anton. You let me help at the Gateway when my wife was in danger at the EPA."

"Oh, for Christ's sake. How are you doing, Mr. Anton? Arnie told me you'd had another accident."

"Yeah, I've got quite a cast, now, but I'm doing fine. You obviously know about today?"

"I've watched the video and we've reviewed the audios. Stewart was there."

"He sure was, and he ultimately secured the prisoner, I think you say. That's the prisoner we want to visit."

"Why? She took a shot at you, didn't she?"

"Yes, but I have a great deal of sympathy for why she did, despite her comments. My wife served on the Trust with her. We'd like her to know that we don't hate her and that we care about her. That's all."

"Well, I can tell the Warden that you have PPD permission, but he will only allow a visit if the prisoner agrees to see you, and then only through the glass, most likely."

"You mean with the phone thing?"

"I expect so. I don't think he'll permit an open visit. You can ask, but I doubt it. She hasn't even been arraigned yet, that I know of. Call him in about ten minutes. I'll call him now."

"I really appreciate it, Captain. It's good to speak with you again."

"Okay... same to you." The phone clicked off.

"Well, Honey, that was the Captain who helped rescue you at the EPA. He's calling the warden but it's up to Roberta. I'm supposed to call in ten minutes."

"I'll prepare something for supper we can put away if the answer is yes." She started to assemble salad-makings. I put my things away and changed into sweat pants and a thin sports jersey. I came back into the kitchen so Linda could help me get it over the cast... and tie my sneakers. I collapsed into my favorite chair and switched to Channel Two. It was too early for the "early" news, but they had a couple of trailers during commercial breaks showing the gun coming up above the podium, in one, and Mayor McKay and Hal Blatchford wrestling Roberta to the ground in the other.

"Stay tuned for the early news when we show you how the mayor and a businessman kept a gun-toting dowager from shooting somebody at the Larimer announcement!" You wouldn't want to miss it.

When Linda reminded me to call the warden, I was almost asleep. She had the white pages opened to the jail number. I shook my head and called. The assistant warden had already asked Roberta if she would accept a pair of visitors, and she would. I asked him how she was doing, and he replied that she was lonely, and had made no effort to speak to any of the other female inmates. I asked him if we could visit at a table. To my surprise he said we could. Roberta had been preliminarily evaluated as not a violent threat. If we felt safe doing it, he would arrange for it. We couldn't visit any later than five-thirty, however.

"Honey, we can visit if we leave right now and make excellent time."

In about fifteen seconds she had everything put away. We entered the visitors' door at ten past five. It was creepy. We had to leave Linda's purse with a guard, and go through a metal detector. My cast had two metal rods in it, plus the plates and screws holding my bones together. They checked me three times.

The first two doors locked behind us. We followed a tape pathway to the visitors' room. God forbid we step outside the lines. The visitor-room door locked behind us, too. The atmosphere wasn't bad. There were several tables attached to the floor, but it was bright, with big printed scenes locked behind Plexiglass on the walls. If you squinted you might have been somewhere else.

Roberta was led in from another door. The guard who came with her stayed at a counter in one corner. A half-dozen couples were visiting at other tables. Roberta sat across from us and had a neutral expression.

"It's nice to see you, Linda," she said. I apologize for the décor." But she was looking at me. "Why are you in a cast?" she asked.

"I am glad you let us visit," replied Linda. "How are you doing?"

"It's not very comfortable, is it?" Roberta said, "and my room is not pleasant, at all. Can't be helped, I suppose." She was looking at me, again. Her face had virtually no emotion, which was more unnerving than the imperious distaste she'd worn the last time.

"I was shot by a man who ran me off the road," I answered to her first question.

"I'm sorry. What?" She placed one hand on Linda's wrist as she looked at me, bewildered.

"You asked about the cast. Your friend, Gary Sindledecker, tried to kill me, for some reason."

"He wasn't really a friend. His father was with my late husband when he died… in Vietnam. Did you know my husband died there?"

"Yes. I did. I'm sorry for your loss."

"It was a long time ago. His father never liked me." I didn't want to think of anything in response

"Is there anything we can do for you, Roberta?" asked Linda.

"I don't think they will allow gifts. If I am still here on Monday, it would be nice to see you again."

"Sure. I'll find out if you are."

"You're Walter Anton, aren't you?" Roberta tilted her head and seemed truly mystified.

"Yes. I still am."

"I am surprised you would come to see me."

"I don't hold onto my angers for long. I am sorry you had to be put here."

"I'm sorry, too. Were you at the big announcement, today?"

"Yes, in the audience."

"My butler, Wallace Hoagland, was with me, there. Can... you... get in touch... with him and tell him... tell him how to visit me?" She was crying soundlessly.

"What phone number will he answer?" Linda now had her hand on Roberta's. Roberta gave her the private number.

"I'll take care of it, Roberta. Is there anything at the office you want me to follow up or answer for you?"

The old dame was lost in thought for a minute. "Why not call Liz Chiemelski and have her meet you at the office. If there's anything you can bring it here if you have time, or tell Elizabeth how to visit me. That would be very nice."

Linda gave Roberta a little hug. I shook her hand and received an odd look for it. The guard led us out a few minutes after visiting hours ended.

"Thank you," I said to him, "and thank the Warden too, if you will."

"Yes sir." We recovered Linda's purse and went back to her car.

"That whole thing is so sad," Linda said. She pulled out of the lot slowly to get back to the Interstate. "What is going to happen to her?"

"She'll be arraigned before a judge, Monday morning. He or she will order a thorough psych evaluation. Maybe two days later there will be a dangerousness hearing and at that point the judge might set bail or deny bail and order her held over until trial. Probably she'll get out on bail."

"What an awful experience. Maybe you could drop the charges."

"But, I didn't press any charges, Lin. She was a threat to the public. Her arrest doesn't have anything to do with me, specifically."

"Oh. Well, it still seems so sad for someone like that to be in jail." Her face looked drained of energy.

"Let's not forget that it was she who connected with Brill and Gary Sindledecker, a thug and a murderer. It was she who connected with Henry Brill to post those phony EPA signs. It was she who was basically behind everything that happened to me... and almost to you! It's time we changed our opinion of her, don't you think?" Linda looked over at me momentarily. I couldn't tell if she was angry or just sad.

"I don't feel good," she said.

"Are you feeling sick, Honey? I can drive." Her head was shaking.

"No, not like that. Just empty." We finished the ride in silence.

SATURDAY, JUNE 15, 1985

We lay in bed. My mission was over. In one sense, the fabulous proposal Hal had offered signaled the end of my known job. There was no juice in my battery. I wasn't convinced I had what it takes to manage a big operation and that made it hard to grab hold of the rest of my life. Nebulous.

Linda seemed to be delaying whatever the next step to life was, too. I reached for her and she snuggled up to me. "How come you're not jumping up?"

She arched her back a little and settled back towards me. "I don't know, Wally. It felt like we were riding a wave of energy right up until we left that prison place. Now I feel cut off from things. You?"

"Sort of. I don't feel the confidence I had yesterday morning, that's for sure." I kissed the back of her neck and she hummed for a moment.

"I'm going to clean up. Whaddayouwant for breakfast?"

"Pancakes... with something interesting in them."

"I'll see what I have, but no food fights... promise."

"I promise. Go on, now. I'll be there in a few minutes." Linda went down the hall. She came back and started dressing. I lumbered down the hall to wash, sitting on my tub bench. By the time I was sitting in the window nook, Linda had the first four pancakes sitting under a cover. In a minute I had coffee, orange juice, pancakes and syrup in front of me. Another minute and

Linda was in front of me, too. I liked these mornings, this one, especially.

"Lin, we have to figure out this president business. It's time for a fresh page on the yellow pad, I think." She just kept eating. "I need your help, Honey. This affects you and junior, too."

"Junior?" finally she looked up at me.

"Well… so to speak, but this much change is worth discussing, don't you think?"

"Sounds like a good change, to me. What should I say? I don't want you to reap the rewards of a phenomenal success after you risked your life for your employer? List reasons you shouldn't become president of Blatchford Steel? What are you asking?"

Now I didn't like this kind of morning. I drank my orange juice – small decision. Deep down I could feel the tingle of irritation, maybe anger. I wanted to talk. I couldn't imagine that Linda didn't, but with rare wisdom, I decided that she always cut through what doesn't matter and she may be doing that now. It created more pressure because she was making me decide for myself what the best course would be. Finally I took a bite of pancakes. Big decision.

"Want more juice?" Linda asked me. "Coffee?" She had finished hers.

"No thanks, Honey. I'm good."

"Yes," she replied, "you are." Her back was to me. I suddenly felt so lucky I teared up. What the Hell was wrong with me? Not very presidential.

"Are you going to have more coffee?" I wanted her to at least listen to me.

"I'm making some tea."

I finished my pancakes while her water boiled. She took my plate and topped off my coffee and sat down with her green tea and honey.

"What do you want to do?"

"I don't want to fail. Blatchford has more faith in me than I do."

"It's a point of view. You can change yours and feel just like him."

Damn her. Now I still had to make the decision. It was easier when she laid it out for me on lined yellow paper. "I think that MBA course is a good idea."

"You can sign up for that Monday... at Pitt?"

"Um, well, yeah. Pitt. Good program."

"Do you think Blatchford will reimburse you for it?"

"I think if I sign up on my own it will put me in a better position to ask for that. Getting an MBA will make me a better candidate for lots of jobs."

She didn't say anything. I wondered if she agreed or disagreed. Either way, I was taking that course. We sipped. I put my hand on her arm and smiled. I loved her.

"What else?" she asked.

Fortunately I had devised my plan. "I'm going to tell him to hold his decision until we ship the first girders, which is about six months. In that time he can bring me in to the decision process and we can learn to work at that level. There'll be plenty of decisions to be made to get everything in line to fabricate and ship girders. We can both get a feel for things during that period. I'll tell him that's how I want to work it, but I do want a raise and a real office."

"I'll be as big as a house by then," she said with her hands on her stomach.

We were counting time differently, now. I smiled at her. Not only did she not object to my line of reasoning, but she'd put it all into the right perspective.

MONDAY, JUNE 17, 1985

I called Jackson and told him I had a few things to wrap up. I was excited and jumpy, tightening my fists and biceps in the thrill of it. I had no job description and a Hell of a future. Linda dropped me at *Re-Kar*. All she said was "good luck," and didn't even ask what I was going to do or say on this day of days. I was sailing.

I asked for my written estimate at the counter. Terry, herself, delivered it.

"I was right about the frame," she began, "but we have a frame machine, so we don't have to send it out. Saves a couple days sometimes. Everything…"

I held up my hand for her to stop. "I want to pay you for the estimating. I'm not going to have it fixed. I'll let Alamo do that. My company is replacing it. But I do need your figures so I'll know I'm not getting screwed. Sorry about that."

"Don't be, Mr. Anton. At least you're paying for our time. Many people get estimates and never do the work and don't pay, either. So I appreciate it. It's a hundred and twenty dollars." She had a register receipt already printed with a total. I wrote her a check and took the yellow. In a few minutes I was rolling down Main Street toward Thompson Run Road.

The wrapped boxes for Kelly Galvin, sat beside me. I was excited about giving them to her. Who knew how we'd be working together from now on? I thought what I would say to Paul

Lemay, Jr., and then I thought about what new car I wanted. Blatchford told me to be fair.

I always liked my Jeep. Not for any special reason but that I was comfortable with it and it was pretty reliable. When I got pushed into the gulch it had something like sixty-four thousand miles on it and had never needed anything major. But did the new car have to make a statement? Did I want to claim some new status with a car? I got the Jeep at Pleasant Hills Chrysler and brought it there for service, sometimes. It was always ready when promised.

The big car news was the new minivans. The Town and Country was attractive. The sales manager recognized me and let me take one out for a ride. It wasn't sporty, but it would be good for Linda when we had our baby. It was definitely more comfortable. I had him write up the order and told him the discount had to be fair, and that I would be back with a corporate check to pay it in full. He'd have it ready when I was.

I took a brochure and the order form, and headed in. It was only ten-thirty; I stopped at Jack Jackson's office. We talked about the lease and the progress on the new crane. I handed him the car proposal. It was less than eighteen thousand. He smiled and told me it was a good choice. I wondered what Hal had told him.

"I had lunch with Hal after the big announcement, Friday."

"I heard," he said. "Sounds like you're going to get a real office." He looked at me, ready to smile.

"I was planning to ask for it."

"Where are you going to be?" He was leaning back, hands clasped behind his head.

I felt like a deer in the headlights. "I, ahh… I don't know. Second floor? I… I don't know."

"No, silly. Where in the hierarchy? What will your title be?" I wanted to be careful because I didn't know that, either.

"I'm sure Hal will put me where I can do the most good. If I find out today I'll tell you Jack. I'm more interested in getting girders through your new doors."

"Oh, well. Good luck, then. I mean that." We shook hands firmly. I went to my sort-of office. There were no papers. I went for coffee. Miracle of miracles, one of the girls was making a pot. I told her the smell was going to be attractive and that she'd better prepare a second pot. I didn't really know her. I introduced myself.

"I'm Walter Anton," I said, holding my hand out. She shook it a couple times.

"You're the only guy here with a big cast, so, I knew that. I'm Arlene Neath. I keep things organized in Contracts. Pleased to meetcha!"

"You work with Dieter and Casey?" She rolled her eyes.

"I sure do. They're good sales people, I guess." She let out a long breath.

"They sure are… this whole King Frederik Bridge deal and all." She gave me a funny look.

"I guess that's right. You were working on that too, I heard."

"Yes. Yes I was. Just finished my part on Friday. But I'm no salesman."

"You got dat right, Valter. Leaf the selling to de experts. That's my motto." Dieter somehow had slipped in and his coffee cup was already filled while I debated whether to engage in conversation. I watched Arlene's eyes. She struggled to look neutral.

"Good to see you this fine Monday, Dieter. Everything is a go for making your girders, now." His look back at me was indecipherable.

"Just in time, I guess, Valter. Good for you." He turned and left.

"Do you know where my office is, Arlene?" She nodded her head.

"How about you stop by when I'm there? Can you do that?"

"Sure. Anything in particular?"

"I have need for some education, that's all. My extension is two-forty." I took my own coffee as a couple more of the caffeine-starved appeared.

I sat and considered my next step. It was time to tell Hal what I wanted to do. I sipped about half of my coffee, reviewing my words. No pandering. I was capable and about to become more so when I went after my MBA. I got things done and I was a good team member. And, I decided, I was loyal to my employer and his company. I had sacrificed for them.

I also needed to find out what Hal's and Peter's roles would be if I did become president. I needed to know and get known by board members. And, did they even know about this offer? Could there be a problem, there? I took a deep breath and called up to Kelly Galvin.

"Mr. Blatchford's office," she answered, despite knowing which extension lit up.

"Yes, this is the real estate coordinator, calling from extension two-four-zero."

"How are you, Walter?" she asked.

"Almost perfect, Kelly. I need to see the boss, but also see you for a moment. Is now a good time?"

"Ahh, well... hold on for a second." The phone clicked to silence. She picked up seconds later.

"Now is good with Mr. Blatchford. I'm always here, as you know."

"I do know that... and it's a good thing. Be right up." I picked up the Abercromie's boxes and speed-walked to the wide stairs. I felt good.

"What on Earth are these?" Kelly was thunderstruck when I placed the boxes on her desk. Her mouth alternately opened, smiled and clamped shut. "Where did you get them? Why give them to me, for Heaven's sake?"

She leaned to one side as she partially opened the top box, perhaps fearing what I might have brought. With the cover completely off she made a wide "oh" and then smiled as she picked up the leather-trimmed gloves. She immediately tried them on and looked at them.

"Why… they're perfect. What else…?" She quickly opened the other two boxes. She tucked her hands into the matching muffler, and pulled the shawl over her shoulders and clipped it together. "Walter, you shouldn't have! They're beautiful."

"I had help. I would never have known the right thing. But I owe you an apology for being rude. The longer it took me, the interest accumulated and I had to do something you'd really like. I am happy that you do. Please wear them in good health."

She actually gave me a quick hug and peck on the cheek. I was the one who blushed.

"Well, thank you very, very much. I love them."

"You are very, very welcome," I smiled back at her. I jinked my head toward the fancy door as she took off the shawl and gloves. She nodded and pushed a button on her phone. A tone came back and she said, "Walter is here."

Blatchford answered, "Yup." I thanked her and headed in.

***

Hal was standing by the windows that overlooked the shop. "Busy morning, I guess, huh?"

"Yes, I'm sorry for being late. I had a couple of errands with the car. Won't happen again."

"I should be giving you a week off. A couple hours is no problem. What did you pick out?"

"One of those Chrysler mini-vans. Not very racy, but comfortable and very handy with children."

He turned and raised his eyebrows. "I thought you'd get an Olds or a Caddy."

"You said to be fair. Replacing the Jeep would have cost the same. Seemed fair to me."

"All right. Good. Let's pick up on our discussions, shall we?" He swept his hand toward the chairs in front of his desk.

"Want coffee or something?"

"No, thanks. I had coffee thinking about this."

"And what did you think?" he asked as he sat opposite me. He had a small pad of paper.

I puffed out my cheeks, let the air out and tried to relax. "I'm not completely comfortable with all the changes to come, but I have thought through what I think is the best timeline. I can't assume people's respect and I can't pretend that I have earned the high status you suggest I should have. I need to come to grips with it, prepare myself for it, and feel right about it. Otherwise I don't think people will accept being led by me."

"Okay."

That's all he said: "okay." Caught me off-guard. After a few seconds he went further.

"So what?" he asked.

"Well, I... ahm. I, um... hmm." I took some time to be sure of what 'what' was going to be.

"I want to work intensively as some sort of manager from now until we ship those first eight girders. You figure out the most suitable title. I want to know everybody better than I do. Most of your employees have never had to deal with me, talk to me or listen to me. I want to know them – all of them, at least a little. So I want a position that makes it reasonable for me to interact with almost everyone. I want some real work to do. Maybe name me 'special projects manager,' or something like that."

"Okay," he said again. I wasn't getting off easily. I pressed on.

"I'm going to sign up for an MBA program at Pitt... nights. But earning that will help me psychologically and with missing skills. If I do become president I want to be reimbursed for that. After we've shipped some girders you should confirm your decision on that presidency offer. And I also want to get a clear picture of our union relations."

"Okay."

"You aren't making it any easier by just saying 'okay,' you know." I looked at him with half a smile on my face. He still looked friendly. "I do want a real office, before I forget that part… not a bigger cubicle."

"Okay," he said again.

"In the interim, which is a full six months, I want to know what your strategic plan is. What kind of sales and profit goals you have. What will your role be after I step up? And what about the rest of the board? I don't know those people and they don't know me, God knows. We need to find out if we can succeed together." I leaned back and crossed my arms, then realized I might be using poor body language, and forced myself to relax and sit forward. "That's what I've been thinking about."

"Okay," he said and immediately held his hands up to fend off my objection to the short answer. "I really didn't think you'd take the job just like that. I appreciate what you say. I've been thinking all weekend, too, although I was pretty sure, making the offer Friday." He shifted around in his seat and put his elbows on the table. "I had to think about what I'd do if you turned me down, and that was a possibility. But your approach is okay with me. I'm not sure whether I like the approach or the fact that you didn't demand a raise, more. If I were you I'd have demanded money, first. Why didn't you?"

I was speechless. Why didn't I? Was that indicative of a bad flaw or weakness in my thinking? A raise. Of course I had reason to ask for a raise; I was taking a higher position. I looked at Hal for a few more seconds before I answered him.

"I have to admit that I was more concerned with how I could handle the change in responsibilities. All in all, I should get a raise, but I'm not ready to make big demands. Right now I'm making about forty thousand plus benefits. I was successful on the lease business and it seems to me that a bonus for that is appropriate. As far as a raise, I think twenty-five percent would be about right… since I'll surely be more valuable as we bring everything together to make and ship those girders. And I'll earn it."

"Okay. I won't argue with any of that. I hope your MBA courses teach you to be a tougher negotiator."

I nodded, and then raised one finger for a chance to respond. "Boss, I surprised myself in negotiations for the lease deal. I do need some skills along those lines, but I'm not without some ability when it comes to what's good for the company."

"Okay!" He looked at me with a twinkle in his eyes and I burst out laughing. He started laughing, too, and we shared it for a few good seconds.

"Hal, let's get the details on my new office squared away. I want to make the shift as quickly as I can and come in tomorrow with my new hat on. I don't care about fancy or new furniture. Just real walls, ceiling and door."

"I agree. Let's take a walk. There's an office next to Bucky Dighton's that should work out well." We walked out of his office and he stopped at Kelly's desk.

"Kelly, ask Jackson to meet us at that office we were looking at Friday. Thanks." We continued on through the back wall of Kelly's space and into an unfinished area that had small, grimy windows overlooking the shop. Room for growth, I thought, and a place in the building I'd never been. We passed through and were at the top of the stairs I'd take to Bucky's office. Jack was coming up.

Together we walked about fifteen more feet and Jack unlocked a door with a frosted glass window, and flipped on the lights. It had been cleaned and dusted. Even the phone handset was clean. There was a steel desk with glass on top of formica. Behind it sat a high-backed executive chair with soft upholstery and five casters. On one wall a two-drawer lateral file. Behind the desk was a matching credenza. A small coat-rack hung on the wall by the door.

"Okay," I said. Jack looked at Hal and then at me.

"I guess this will do, Walt," said Blatchford. "Thanks for handling this, Jack."

"I'm more than pleased. Thanks to you both. What's my extension?"

Jack answered. "It's two forty-four, right now, but I can have it changed to your original number."

I shook my head. "Leave it, Jack. It's fine. Just make sure it's on my business cards correctly."

He looked at Hal, again, who just tightened his chin. "Okay. I'll take care of it." Then he held his hand out to me. "Congratulations, Walt. Well deserved."

I smiled widely. "I wouldn't be here if not for you, Jack. Never forget that." Everyone was smiling and I was starving. "I'll gather some supplies and then we'll have to plan the work you want me to do," I looked toward Hal. He nodded.

"Write out what we talked about earlier." He turned to go back to his office. I caught up with him.

"Thanks, Hal. I appreciate your faith in me." We shook hands and he put his hand on my shoulder. We didn't hug, but we might have.

My own real office, second floor. I looked in all the empty drawers. Maybe the last person with this desk left a couple of Krugerrands or a wad of hundreds... worth a look. I picked up the phone to make sure of a dial tone. Extension 244. I even looked in the file drawers. Those were new. What would I fill them with? I tried to picture the titles on the plastic tabs that would inhabit them. I decided to write down what I could, but there were no materials. I went back downstairs.

I remembered that Arlene was going to call me. I hoped she hadn't while I was upstairs. I called reception and asked for her extension... "two-one-seven, Mr. Anton." I dialed it.

"Contracts. This is Arlene."

"Arlene, hi... it's Walter Anton. I was afraid I'd missed you."

"I did try a call, sir, but I got busy. Sorry. Did you want to see me, now?"

"Now would be good, if you can break away." She could and was at my old door in a minute. I had my friend, the yellow pad with a fresh page exposed. On top of it I wrote "Contracts."

"What can I help you with?" Arlene asked.

"I have a couple of questions, but I think my other office will be better. Do you want some coffee?" She shook her head. "I'm going to grab a cup. Just bear with me and we'll head upstairs."

Arlene accompanied me first to the coffee pot and then up to my honest-to-God office.

"Wow... nice, Mr. Anton. I guess you got a promotion, huh? Congratulations!"

"Thanks, Arlene. I want to talk up here because what I'm asking must remain confidential. Is that clear and can you do that?"

"Yes," she nodded, "I could not keep my job if I didn't keep confidences for the sales people. They all have learned to trust me and you can, too." Her lips were firmly set.

I looked at her and then at the blank yellow page. I had to be sure of what I was going to ask.

"I detected some frustration with Dieter Fuchs when we were in the kitchen. I have had conflict with him that I still don't understand. Maybe you have, too. My new responsibilities are going to touch a lot of what Blatchford does going forward and sales people in our industry don't grow on trees. I really need to know if there is a problem brewing in Contracts. Do you follow me so far?"

With her lips still firmly together, she nodded her head.

"I also value your trustworthiness to others. I don't want you to tell me anything that you believe will break a promise or an expectation of confidence, and that may not be immediately obvious to you, so take your time answering. On the other hand, I don't respect keeping secrets about things that will hurt Blatchford or hurt other employees. You understand this, as well?"

"I think I know the difference, yes, sir."

"All right, then. You obviously know about the King Frederik project? You know how big it is and how important it is to our company?"

"I have prepared most of those documents, sir, so, yes, I grasp the scope of it."

"It's not 'sir,' Arlene. Call me Walt or Walter, okay?"

She nodded and continued. "I have worked with Dieter and Casimir for three years. The last coordinator quit, I think. I heard stories."

"Was it a woman who quit?" I started to make notes.

She nodded. "I actually know where she's working. If, ahh… you know?" Her face had changed. She wasn't comfortable telling more details about hearsay.

"Let's concentrate on how the department works, now, okay?" I could see her relax a little. "Have you seen anything that threatens the King Frederik project? Or other projects?"

Her eyes grew wide. "How did you think of that question?"

I wasn't sure, myself. I was in the right territory, though. Maybe it was instinct, but things were rotten in Denmark, so to speak. "Tell me what it's like working with Dieter, please."

Arlene sat still, no fidgeting, her lips were together but her mouth was moving. Finally she let her shoulders slump and she got ready to speak. "Sometimes it... ahh, feels like Dieter doesn't like anyone he works with and doesn't like the company either."

I let that lie where she'd left it. I expected there was more. She was uncomfortable and probably hoping I would take up the burden, but I couldn't.

"He is always swearing at people, me included, and he treats Casey... I mean, Casimir, like dirt. I think Casey stays with him because he does connect for good commissions, but he hates the way he's treated, believe me. Dieter is always going 'F' this and 'F' that and 'F' this company... junk like that. I'd like to just ask him why he stays here if he hates the company so much, but I need my job, too. So I take it and try to tune it out." She had tears in the corners of her eyes, but her voice hadn't wavered. She wiped her eyes with the backs of her hands.

"You want some water, or something? We can take a break."

"No... no. I can't really add much, probably. I'm okay."

"Others in the department must hear these things, too?'

She nodded. "So far I haven't told a single secret, Mr. Anton."

Now I nodded my understanding. "Has anyone else ever asked you about these things?"

"No. Never. I think because sales are so good no one wants to disturb the guys. I make up monthly projections and things. There's only four guys in contracts. They all make good money and everybody upstairs is happy. The King Frederik is the biggest deal I can remember and you'd think Dieter would be happy, but he seems more angry than ever! He swears at the company more than ever. So, I just don't understand him, I guess."

"This is new for me, obviously, but whom do the sales people report to? Is it a sales manager or someone higher?" She looked stunned. I can imagine hearing someone on the second floor ask who oversaw Contracts would sound pretty stupid. I couldn't help it.

"It's a VP, Mr. Anton. Don't you know him? Arthur Zinn. He helps the guys make contacts and stuff. They often take clients out to lunch or dinner and Mr. Zinn usually goes with them. He went to Denmark with them more than once."

"Well, you have helped me a great deal with this, Arlene. I don't want you to spy on anybody or call me with every new swear word you hear. If something troubles you deeply, however, it might be good to speak with me about it, but I'll let you be the judge of that, okay?" I smiled warmly and waited.

Arlene smiled with me and sat up straighter. I made a quick assessment of her chest, not that it had anything to do with anything. Certainly not. Still, she did impress me with her openness and ability to keep confidences. She'd given me a lot to think about. I knew virtually nothing about sales or the whole Contracts department, but I knew a problem when I saw one. I'd have to think about how to discuss the whole topic with Hal. I couldn't recall meeting Zinn. What would I say to him? I'd need more background. I also was unprepared to ask Dieter almost anything. Man, was I ignorant. "Thanks, very much, Arlene," I said and she stood and left with a little smile.

I resolved to ask Katie for a personnel chart. Blatchford hadn't suggested it. Maybe he was hoping I'd have enough sense to ask for one. I couldn't believe how little I knew about my own environment – the one I could be head of. Wow.

I looked around my damn fine office and tried to think of what I needed. I had a ball-point pen and my yellow pad. I wrote down what I could think of. I also flipped over that page and wrote down a title, "Disc. w/Hal," to remind myself to write up what I had said to him earlier. Then I flipped another page and titled that one with "Major efforts." I wanted to plot out the key areas where Blatchford had or expected work and the pieces of preparation that still had to be completed for shipping girders.

With every plan I made to make further plans, I couldn't help asking myself, "what am I doing here?" Did I really think I knew enough to help Blatchford at this level? And this reminded me to enroll for that MBA at Pitt. I needed more skills and more confidence. I had to take a step. I went to *Marko's*.

My friend, Angus, was already there. I gestured to sit across from him and he waved toward the bench.

"Good to see you, again, Angus," I declared as I reached out to shake hands.

"Likewise, laddie. Looks like you knocked the great lady down a few pegs, eh?" He didn't waste time on weather or traffic.

"Yes, I guess so. Kinda sad, though, when you think about it." That elicited a squinty stare.

"I wouldn't wish jail on anyone," Angus agreed, "unless she tried to kill me three different times."

"I know, I know. My wife and I visited her, Friday night. Pretty grim. She seemed very small."

"Hmmnph," was Angus' response to that. Our waitress arrived and we ordered. I copied his catfish.

"So, laddie, sounds like yer permitted to run the railroad, eh?"

"That we are. Even before Roberta melted down I had convinced the mayor to sign the lease without her approval."

"Did ye now? He's got bigger balls than I thought. What'd it cost ye?"

"What? Oh, the bribe, you mean? One point six million to Parks and Recreation." Angus raised his eyebrows at that one.

"I hope it's all worth it to ye."

"Oh, and another eight hundred to the Lincoln-Larimar project."

"Hmmnph," he replied, again. His head shook negatively.

"It's all part of getting our railroad. Very crucial. This bridge business is well worth it."

Well, you know your business," breathed Angus as our meals appeared before us.

I hope so.

Angus paused between mouthfulls. "Are you back to your real job, then, lad?" He was looking at me, again, with that piercing squint he had.

"Got a new job, now. Bigger office." I kept pace with the eating.

"Oh, well! Congratulations to you, then. Still eatin with commoners, though."

Now my head shook. "Not that big an office," I replied. "In fact, I can't even tell you what my new job entails, but definitely a bigger office."

"And more money, I trust." Angus sat back, his plate clean. He looked at his watch.

I didn't answer. He could take that how he liked.

"Still making your own hours, though, it looks, eh?" He started to stand up.

"Not exactly. But I've got some leeway, today. I'm heading over to Pitt to take some business courses."

"Are ye now? Well, well, well. Won't be eating at *Marko's* much longer then, I'd wager."

"It's got nothing to do with *Marko's*. I'm not changing. I am who I am."

"So ye say, lad, and I hope it's true. I'm always happy to break bread with yuh." He led me up the stairs. The noise level prevented conversation until we stepped outside. A working boat blew a long blast. "Sounds like you'll actually be moving some freight, then."

"Absolutely. We're modifying our building to handle the girders and we'll start working on the tracks in July. You might want to come up to the shop and speak with our chief engineer, Bucky Dighton. I can set that up for you."

"Oh, yeah. That sounds good. I'll make the time."

"Extension 244, when you call."

"Gotcha. See ya later." He waved and I got in my car and headed across to Pitt.

***

Mervis Hall was one of the newest buildings, sheathed in mirror-like glass, at the base of the iconic Pitt tower. I was just happy it had air conditioning. At the angular desk I asked for "Admissions" and a laconic future CEO directed me behind himself to my right. I tapped but no answer. A well-used sign said, "Please Wait – Back in 5 Min." Black metal trays on the desk held prodigious amounts of paper. There were a half-dozen chairs facing the desk and I chose the closest. After a few moments I shifted to the farthest so I could look at brochures and papers on a bulletin board there.

I found a set of stapled pages describing a "Katz Survival Course for Executives." Doofuses like me could come back after a week of "Survival" training and whip corporations into tiptop shape with military lines of authority. I doubted it, unless everyone else took the course in how to behave in corporations led by graduates of the survival course. There were monographs for short-term business refresher courses and exemplary business problem solutions. The door opened behind me and I stood to greet the boss of the Admissions office.

"Oh! Hello. I didn't expect anyone to be here," she apologized. "Are you a student, or…?"

"No. Not yet. I am interested in the MBA program. I got a promotion and…"

She sized me up and down as if I had come for a suit, and finally stepped around the desk and invited me to sit again. "Where did you get your BS?"

"Bucknell," I replied with a tinge of school pride.

"And you just got promoted? To what?" She'd had practice being genuinely concerned and interested.

"Well, I can't say, yet. I completed a crucial project for my company and the CEO wants me to step up to bigger things… like I'm on an executive track, now. Taking the MBA course is my idea but my company will reimburse me."

She nodded and set her glasses back on her nose. She concentrated on her computer monitor for a couple of minutes. I looked at posters that showed mostly slender, good-looking executive-types who were solving crucial problems with decision-maker smiles on their perfect lips. Behind them, out of the frame of the picture, were basket-ball trees, I'm sure. The lady, whose sign said "Deborah Burke," cleared her throat in preparation for guiding my career.

"We really start the MBA program with the Fall semester, you understand."

I nodded executively.

"However!" she exclaimed, "There's a pair of courses you can take this summer that will apply to the MBA!"

I tried to display the correct executive excitement to coincide with hers. I was glad I could start something immediately. "Uhh… which are they?"

"Well! Okay! One is 'Twentieth Century Leadership' which you have to take, anyway. So, that's good!" She shifted left to right on her small secretary's chair. An itch, perhaps. But she was enthused about the availability of "Twentieth Century Leadership." I was enthused, too, but it didn't itch.

"So," I said executively, "what do I do?"

"There are some forms to fill out, of course. And a down payment. The entire program will be at least twenty-four thousand dollars. If you are ready to commit I will need a check for, say, five thousand dollars. And there are books to purchase, of course." She smiled at me. I gulped and wondered if she were on commission.

"Are you on commission?" I asked.

"What? Why… oh, for Heaven's sake. No. Of course not. I just have to make things as easy as possible for our incoming students. You understand." She was uncomfortable, I thought. "What are your scheduling problems?"

"Huh?" I replied in my most serious manner.

"Well, usually, students who return to complete their education in their later years, have important jobs that place demands on their time. You understand."

I thought I did, but "later years?" When had I entered those? "How… ah… late would those be?"

"I'm sorry. What?" She shook her head in little jerky motions as she tried to focus on me.

"I was wondering how late 'later years' might be. You understand." I nodded to help her.

"Oh, yes. Why, well… certainly you're not, um… I mean your years can't be what we'd call 'later,' can they? No, of course not." She smiled.

"Of course not," I solemnly agreed.

"So, do you have demands on your time, too, Mr… ahm, Anton?"

"Oh, not me, but I hope to, one day. Soon, I hope!" I nodded like an idiot, but she bought it.

"Then you will want that MBA, won't you?"

Deborah Burke was ready to close the sale and help my time start making demands.

"I already do, Deborah. I already do. How do I sign up?"

"For the MBA program?" She was staring at me, her glasses about to slip from her nose.

"No, no. Renaissance Literature. What do you think?" Now she was completely confused. She carefully replaced her glasses.

"I would have thought you were a better candidate for the MBA."

"Master of Business Administration? Me? Do you think so?"

"Well, I'm not a career advisor. Perhaps you'd want to start there. I can arrange an appointment for you."

"No, thanks. I have a lot of demands on my time. Let's sign me up for the MBA like you suggested."

"Are you sure, Mr. Anton? I don't want to push you in to anything."

"No, no. That's quite all right, Deborah. I like your idea. Let me have those forms and get this started, huh?" She slipped the packet out of a folder in front of her.

"I'm not busy, today. You can sit right here and do them, if you like. And I'll be able to answer any questions you have."

"Actually, I'd like to find a cup of coffee. Is there somewhere in this buil…?"

"Stay along this wall to the far end. There's a canteen. The coffee is passable, I've heard."

"Okay. Thanks for all your help and advice, Deb. You've been terrific. Really."

She blushed a little and tucked her chin. "It's my job, Mr. Anton, but thank you."

I headed to the canteen, figuring there must be someplace to sit. In fact it was a little lounge area, complete with a handful of college-age denizens… some pretty. I slipped a dollar into the coffee machine and chose the large size, black. I got coffee and a quarter back. What a deal. I sat and spread out my pages.

I read most of them, and the application, itself. Some of it was reprints of articles complimenting the program, including a profile of a guy who didn't look any older than me, who gained a top position with Mellon Bank after completing the Katz MBA Program. This might be better than earning my CDL.

I filled as many fields as I could, but I had to gather hard facts and numbers before I could submit the app. I packed up. As I passed Deborah Burke's office I tapped on the door and pushed it open. She was studying her computer.

"Be with you in a minute. Just take a seat…" She finally looked up. "Oh, it's you, Mr. Anton. How is it going?"

"I have to get a few things at home to finish this up. I'll bring it back tomorrow with a check, if that's all right. I just wanted to thank you, again. I appreciate your help."

"Oh. Well, you're very welcome, of course. This is the place for you, Mr. Anton. I'm sure of it."

***

I parked in my regular spot and went in the same door, but it felt different. Everything I did was a first… new. Scary, but I liked it. I stopped by my old office and grabbed some more office supplies to take upstairs. I piled up an armful before realizing that someone else, probably Colleen Walsh, was going to use the place. I set it back down, except for a few personal things. I went to Colleen's desk.

"Hi, Colleen, can you help me?"

She stood and moved as if to help a crippled person. "What can I do, Mr. Anton? Are you in pain?"

"No, no. I just need some materials. Where can I get office supplies?"

"Oh, supplies? Like what?"

"Some of those hanging folder things for files, and some manila folders. And some plastic things that you can put on the hanging folders, you know?"

In a few minutes she had me set up with office one-oh-one. "Where are you going with all this stuff, Mr. Anton?"

"To my upstairs office," I replied, which was easier for me to say than "bigger office."

"I'm gonna be working on special projects. My office is near Mr. Dighton's." I wasn't sure why I felt apologetic about moving up. I needed to be proud of it and to believe I'd earned it. Perhaps an MBA would fill that gap. I juggled the armload of stuff. Colleen grabbed everything and gestured for me to take the lead.

I pulled out my pad and tried to make a list of things to work on… problems that we had to solve by shipping day. I couldn't list them by priority so I just put little dash lines in front of each one. "Dieter Fuchs, contracts," I wrote first. Then I wrote, "Arthur Zinn, VP." These topics were top of mind, but they weren't necessarily the most crucial.

The rest of the list poured out: Construction, Crane, special cars, modify tracks, Mid Waters, Jackson, MBA at Pitt. Underneath each of those I could imagine a host of sub-topics. I began to think I was not the right person to be trying to set up these files; I just knew I had to be organized. I wrote down another topic and drew circles around it: "Assistant-secretary." I didn't know if I could get one. Just how expansive was Blatchford willing to be? I figured I could build a financial case for an assistant. I wrote that down, too.

I sat for a minute, hands steepled around my nose and mouth. Blatchford had dropped me in a clearing with few boundaries. Perhaps he was waiting to see where I went first. What a cagey bastard, I thought. I had to take action of some kind. I stepped into Bucky Dighton's office. It was only three.

"Walter! To what do I owe the pleasure?" Bucky was standing at one of the big tables along the windows overlooking the shop. "Problems?"

"No, but if you've got a minute…?" He waved me in. I could see that he'd been studying drawings of the special racks for the low-boy flat-cars.

"I was talking to Angus Newhall, he owns Mid-Waters Shipping and is the most logical guy to take these girders down the river. I suggested that he come in and speak with you about the practical issues of handling them."

"Well, that makes sense. When does he want to come in?"

"I told him I'd set it up. When's good for you?"

"Give him my number. So long as he calls when he's coming, almost anytime. Just not before seven-thirty."

"What are you running into with these flat cars?" I gestured toward the table.

"Well, I wouldn't say there's anything we don't know how to handle, it's just that we can't do anything about them because we don't have anywhere to hold the cars until we get that spur."

"Ahhh. Very interesting. Let me see if the city will allow us to get started before July first. That will help a little."

"That'd be great. Let me know and I'll go ahead and order the cars."

"From who? I don't remember a requisition."

Bucky gave me a cold glare, as if I were putting him in his place for not following paperwork rules.

"Hey, hey, Bucky. I don't mean anything by that. I am just surprised it hadn't already come through for cost estimation on the project. Take it easy."

He seemed mollified, but I had to wonder what he thought was the right procedure for this expenditure compared to others. Something to write on the yellow pad. "Are we buying them?"

He looked happier to answer that. "No, that would be too expensive and we'd have to sell em later. We're leasing them from CSX. They don't care if we install our special racks so long as we can remove them. We need em for only nine or ten months, right?"

He made perfect sense. "Okay, but you want to get them now?"

"Yeah. We gotta build our racks for the girders and run a couple of mock-ups down the track to make sure we've cleared the obstacles, right?" He nodded toward me and I nodded in reply. He made sense.

"Okay, then. Be sure you put through a req right away. We won't issue a PO without it. I'll get to Mid-Waters and tell Angus about coming up to see you. He's going to need racks to hold them on his barges, too. Anything else?"

Bucky squinted at me and smiled a little. "That big office going to put you in my hair every day?"

"Maybe. Probably not. I have a number of irons in the fire… or will have. But it's very interesting talking to you, so watch out!"

"Well, then, I'll keep it dull. But you're always welcome. You saved my ass on the cranes and shit. You're welcome, here."

I'd almost forgotten that part. I guess I had been helpful to him, even valuable. "Is there anything holding up the crane stuff?"

He shook his head. "Not yet, but you'll have to check in with Jack Jackson. He's been talking to Wheeling Crane more than I have. And the architects." I had two more sub-topics for my list.

I stuck out my hand and we shook. "It's no further to walk into my office than it is to walk into yours, Bucky. Never sit on a problem, okay?" He agreed but seemed to be suspicious about what I was in a position to do for him.

Back in my office I made some notes and thought about what I might say to Hal Blatchford after this day of path-finding. How could I justify a secretary? What was his relationship with Zinn or with the sales people? I shook my head. I picked up the phone and called Mid-Waters.

His secretary answered sweetly. "Mid-Waters Freight. How can I help you?"

"Hi, ahh, ma'am. It's Walter Anton. Can I reach Angus, please?"

"I'm sorry, Mr. Anton. He's on the river. Can I help you?"

"Well, he needs to meet with our engineers, here at Blatchford Steel. When, um… will he be back?"

"Oh, a couple of days, I expect. He's solving a problem with one of the boats. Do you want me to call him for you?"

"No… no, a couple of days won't matter. Just leave him a message for me, okay?"

"Will do. Anything else?" I assured her that was all and rang off. It was late enough that I could go home but I wanted to ask Blatchford about Zinn.

"Hi, Kelly. Is it okay for me to see him for a couple of minutes?"

"Hold on, Walt." Boy she could be nice. I wished I'd given my peace offering a lot sooner.

"He says that's fine."

"Thanks, Kelly." I took off through the "dungeons" and popped out in the corner of Kelly's space. She waved me on through. I gave her a broad smile.

"How's it going, Walter?" Blatchford asked as soon as I entered. He waved me to a chair.

"Strangely, I have to say," I replied.

"How so?"

"Well, it's not often one is handed a blank slate and told to write something valuable on it. I have tried to list what is most important to do, problems we must solve to ship the first girders. I have become very aware of my ignorance about the various parts of your success-engine. But I suppose you expected that."

He just shrugged. I had to keep talking.

"I encountered a problem, though… one that I doubt you are aware of since I don't think you'd have let it fester." Wow, I thought, that was a strong word, "fester." I looked for his reaction.

He was pissed. "What the Hell do you mean?"

"Contracts," I answered. Hal turned to face me squarely.

"What about it. What have you heard?"

I gave him a little rundown of my interview with Arlene. Then I asked him about Art Zinn.

"That's a big question for you to ask. What are you trying to do?" He was poised and focused on what I would say.

"Do?" I replied, "I'm not sure I'm trying to 'do' anything. I only know that I had conflict with Dieter Fuchs and I didn't know where it came from. I still don't. Now I have learned that he is very sour towards almost everything and that can't be good for the overall sales effort. I know he has worked closely with

Zinn and an attitude like he displays must have become obvious over time and it seems as though Zinn would be aware of it. It doesn't feel right, does it?" I sat back slightly without moving my eyes off of his. "That's all."

Blatchford sank back in his tall chair. He looked at me and then away and then back.

"What would you do?" I was thunderstruck with that question.

I was balanced on a razor that could slice off a desirable appendage with a slight misstep. What did Hal want to hear? I had no idea, but I knew what I wanted to do next.

"I'd like to get to know Mr. Zinn. I don't think I've ever met him, have I?"

"He was here that day you got the real estate pickle. But he travels in different circles. I don't bug him a lot so long as orders, and contracts, come in. You're saying I should have?"

"But, he's a vice-president isn't he?" Another glare.

"Yeah. So what? He comes to meetings when I ask and submits his paperwork, projections and things. He's a highly productive sales manager. I give him his leeway… like you."

Uh-oh. Was he angry, testing or genuinely curious? I put one foot ahead of the other on the thin edge. I decided to ask what I'd been thinking since Dieter had challenged me in the parking lot.

"Do you think Dieter might be trying to work against us by swinging the King Frederik to someone else?"

Blatchford's eyes grew wide as his lips and jaws set together tightly. He pulled a thick folder of papers out from his desk file drawer. "These are Zinn's projections and reports for the past eleven months. Do a little mental work on these and let's talk tomorrow. Meanwhile I'll set up a lunch date with Zinn, you and me. You need to know him." He looked straight at me, challenging me to propose something else. "Go home, now. See you in the morning."

I stood up and took the sheaf of reports. "Okay, boss. See you." I left the big office and headed back to my own, waving good night to Kelly as I passed. I made a few notes on my yellow pad, tucked it under my arm, and switched off my very own lights.

***

Linda was home when I pulled in. For the first time that day I didn't feel alone. I had comfortable boundaries here. I didn't have to impress somebody with everything I did. I plopped my stack of papers on the little table in the hall and announced my arrival.

Linda replied from out back. I divested my business clothes and slipped on sweatpants and slippers. Linda was tilling a square patch she'd dug up. I knelt beside her and kissed her cheek. "What garden is this?" I asked.

"It's Ben's!"

"Ben who?" I wanted to know.

"Ben, your son, of course." She was cultivating with a three-pronged hand tool, as deeply as she could, now and then stopping to chop at a root and pull it out.

"We're having a son? How do you know that? Do you know that? Really?"

"Or, Virginia, your daughter. Whatever. This will be his or her garden and her first fresh food will come from it."

"Well, how about that? And those are the names we'll choose from?"

"I hope so. I like them. Do you?"

"If you do. It's good to know who we're waiting for. But, this is a lot of work. Tell me what you want done, here, and I'll take over."

She sat back on her heels, letting out a big whoosh of breath. "Okay, Honey. I've had enough, for now. What would you like for supper?"

"Something without a lot of work. In fact, let's clean up and go out for dinner to celebrate. I've got news to share." I felt better, contemplating my news. "I'll finish this for you this weekend. Let's go."

"Okay. Are we showering together?"

"I certainly hope so!" I was practically running back into the house. Then I remembered, I couldn't get the cast wet. What was I thinking?

Linda was no slouch when it came to inventing clothing or showering techniques when one player is in a cast. I wound up clean, rinsed and totally satisfied.

So did she. Made me happy and hungry.

BlackKnights is more comfortable for discussing things and the food, fabulous. Linda had sole and I chose the small filet.

"So, Mr. problem-solver, good news or bad?"

"Almost all good. First, I now have a real office with my own ceiling and light switch… that's good, huh?"

"Oh, I was so worried. Thank God."

"Okay, wise-girl, I also got a raise: twenty-five percent." I kept my face calm and emotionless.

"Wow, Walter! That's wonderful! I'm so proud of you. That's more like it." She rose out of her seat and kissed me across the table. "Wonderful!"

She couldn't stop grinning. "What else?" she prodded.

"Well, I picked up the forms for the MBA program and got Blatchford to agree to reimburse me for it. He's in agreement with my timetable for actually taking on the big title, too. I feel good about that."

Again, Linda was happy for me and with me. I'd made her proud. I explained some of the other things I'd delved into with

Contracts. She pushed her lip out and rocked her shoulders. "Well, aren't you the go-to guy?"

"I try," was all I could say. It made me reconsider how I actually did look out for myself. I had a lot to learn.

Our food came and we ate. "Did you visit Roberta again?" I asked.

"No," Linda replied. "I gave the message to her Vice-president, Elizabeth, and I believe she visited her. Wallace, her man-Friday visited, too, I believe."

"I really can't hate her… not like I hated Brill. I feel sorry for her, more than anything."

"Mmmnnh. I don't know what'll happen at the Trust. The newspapers splashed her arrest all over the front page, and TV showed that shooting scene all weekend. It might destroy the Trust."

I swiped up sauce with my last bite. I pointed my fork at her. "Would that be such a tragedy?"

Linda took that hard. She sat back with her arms folded, studying me. I drank some water and began to fidget. Finally, "You don't understand what the Trust has done for Pittsburgh."

I lifted my eyes to hers. I wasn't sure of any legitimate role for the Trust, but I knew that I shouldn't take that stand, just then. "I guess I don't. Except for you, all my dealings with the Trust have led to opposition and injuries."

"I know, Walt, I know. But a lot of the beautiful areas of the city have been affected by the Trust, and by Roberta, personally. We keep more and more of the limited land in the city from being paved over. Roberta has her demons, but she did very positive things. That's all."

"Maybe you should take over for her." I wasn't serious.

"No. I'm completely non-political and I have none of the connections you need… not the way Roberta has. Besides, my job is gonna be 'Mother Anton.' They'll get someone with a political or government background. I really have no idea."

"It'll be interesting to see what happens, like a lot of things in our lives: it'll be interesting."

"Oh, yeah! Tell me about the MBA course. What did you find out?"

"I brought the package home. I can use help with the application. I have to fork over five thousand dollars, too."

"We can handle that. You did say your raise will be twenty-five per-cent, right?"

I nodded.

"What will the whole course cost?"

"Twenty-four thousand, plus a couple of optional courses, if I want to add them. There's a couple I can take this summer."

"And you're going ahead?"

"I think it's important. I need the skills and time to internalize what leading Blatchford will entail. The timeline is acceptable to Hal Blatchford in terms of the commitment. I need the skills. I have a great deal to learn just about Blatchford Steel, itself. I think Hal respects my decision to not jump in without preparation. But you don't?"

"Oh, Walt, sure I do. If you don't feel ready nothing else matters. And that degree is a good part of your resume if you decide to go elsewhere. Do you think you should be president?"

Uh-oh, that wasn't the same as "do you *want* to be president?" I was hoping with all my heart that with my new special projects position and with what I'd learn at Pitt, that in a few months I'd be able to answer Linda's question with an "absolutely." Right now, I was a little depressed.

"Let's go, okay?"

"Sure, Honey. I'm all set."

I paid the bill and tip. We sat for a couple of minutes before I started the motor.

"Walter, I want to help. What can I do?" Linda started. "You have come through an impossible period. Now we're pregnant. And, topping it off, Blatchford tells you he wants you to take over as president. No one could keep his balance through all that. I am impressed you can drive and make love." She was ready to giggle and I grinned. I kissed her.

"Hey, wanna make out?" I asked her. I tried to slip my good hand into her blouse.

"You horn dog! What'll I tell my mother? She'll be able to tell."

"Umm, say you spilled water on yourself and dried off in the ladies' room. That might work." That tall tale had worked a couple of times, although the second time we poured Coke on her shirt to make it plausible.

"I'm not going all the way in some old car. We'll have to get married, first." She crossed her arms over her breasts and pouted the way she did when I tried for too much.

"Take me home," she demanded. "I can't stay in a car alone with you. And you know perfectly well why. I don't know why I keep going out with you."

"Ahh, because you love me? That's what I'm hoping, anyway, because I love you, Linda Miller. Cross my heart and hope to die."

"Well… I guess I love you too, Walter Anton. You just get finished at college so we can get married, okaaaay?"

"That's what I'm doing, Sweetheart. But I need you right now, tonight! I don't know if I can wait any longer."

"Well, you'll just have to. I told you before. I'm not getting pregnant and ruin everything. We'd better get home now."

I started the engine, feeling very much like when Linda and I dated and I had to wait to have sex with the object of my desires. The whole Pitt thing added to that regression. I enjoyed remembering how it felt ten years ago, and I was proud to love my lady just as much today... or more.

"Whatever you say, Lindy. You're worth waiting for... but if you change your mind before we get to your house, just put your hand on my leg, okay?"

"Sure, Sweetie. Don't hold your breath, you'll pass out."

I drove very carefully. Linda was carrying the future of the Antons and of the two of us, as well. I saddened, thinking of my father... and my mother... not seeing this grandchild. I was sad and romantic at the same time. We arrived home tired, comfortable, wondering.

"How tired are you feeling, Hon?" I asked. "I was hoping you could help me with the MBA application."

"Of course... let's see it." I handed over the whole pile and we sat at the kitchen table. She separated the pages, setting the poor copies of laudatory articles on the bench beside her.

"Here," she said, "you take the forms and we'll pull the facts together. I want to read the course description, if you don't mind." I agreed and re-read the questions.

Among other things they wanted to know my title. I had to put something, so I called myself "Special Projects Manager." Fairly descriptive. For current salary range I realized that I could now circle the range that started at fifty thousand dollars. They didn't stipulate that one had to have been at the circled level for more than eight hours. A space was provided for a two- or three-sentence description of what I, the prospective MBA candidate, hoped to achieve. I had to succinctly state my hopes for a return on my financial and hourly investment in the Katz School of Business MBA program. It stopped me in my tracks.

For her part, Linda was rapidly scanning the syllabus for the course, making short notes. It was a skill of a great editor. She looked up as I sat looking at the application. "Something wrong, Honey?"

"Not really. It's asking me for a statement of what I hope to achieve from this course, and it's hard to formulate it."

"Aha. Okay. Can I ask a couple of questions... if it helps?"

I nodded.

"Alright. Number one: Is your first goal improving your management skills?"

"Yeah... well, it's maybe not the number one thing. I know I need those skills. But number one? It's more that I want to prove I can do this." That felt right to me.

"Prove it to whom?" Somehow she was still reading while listening to me.

"Well, I don't know. Maybe to Jack Jackson, to Harold Blatchford, to you, and to myself. And in that order, I guess." I wasn't sure that felt right.

Linda was concentrating on me again. "Will that make you a better manager, Walt?"

"What?"

"Proving things to others. Is that what motivates you?"

"Well, not just that, no. I mean, I want to prove I am capable of running a company. And I want people to respect me."

"Does Mr. Blatchford have an MBA?"

"Not that I know of." This was becoming uncomfortable.

"Do people respect him?"

"Sure. Everyone knows... he's the boss."

"Yes, but do they hate him or respect him?"

"I think most people love him, in a way. He's fair and his guidance of the company is successful, which provides security for their jobs."

"Are you trying to become a better Hal Blatchford than he is?" I started to deny that but checked myself.

"I don't think so, exactly, but all I can think of is becoming president and having everyone compare me to him. I can't help it."

"Sooner or later you're going to take a job that was held by someone else, whether it's president of Blatchford or something else. Inevitably you'll be compared to your predecessor, but that will go away and you'll become someone else's predecessor, and people will compare that person to you. Which just means that the comparison phase will end before you know it and it is you and your ways that people will respond and react to, and, I bet, respect."

"Okay. I get that. But some people are going to just flat-out hate me… like Dieter Fuchs. That's pretty uncomfortable."

"I hate it, too, Walt. But keep in mind that Blatchford asked you to step up, not Dieter and not even his vice-presidents. You will be able to fire Dieter Fuchs, not the other way around. You might already be in that position."

What a lady. Her perspective made me feel like a million bucks. "Okay. Here it is. 'My primary goal for the MBA program is to sharpen my management skills as I assume ever greater levels of responsibility at my company.'" That felt right and it was all I had.

"Okay, good. If you're happy, don't change a word." She was smiling broadly. I smiled with her. "Now, I see that part of the course will be to write a paper on a business problem you are facing or have dealt with. This is perfect, don't you think?"

"What do you mean?"

"You could write up this whole railroad mess you resolved! Think about it! You can state the challenge very easily and then all of the stages you had to get through to produce a complete solution. It's a terrific business problem story and it deserves to be written up. Whaddayu think?"

"Oh, wow. How long does it say the whole course is going to take?"

"Umm, well, you could complete it in one school year or a little less if you do one of these summer courses. That's by going to class twice a week and a lot of homework. The business problem paper is fairly significant, though, from the way it's described. This'll be perfect and I'll be able to help you. Did you know I'm an editor of stuff like that?"

"I did know that. Wow. This could be pretty cool. I'm feeling good, now."

We completed the application, including my social security number, graduation dates from high school and college, non-years of military service and so on. By the time we turned in I had the complete package and a blank check in a manila envelope.

TUESDAY, JUNE 18, 1985

Linda granted me a delightful quickie. I think she had an orgasm, too, but she didn't act concerned... just made me feel terrific.

It may have been because I exhibited a high level of interest, due mainly to a need to pee. However, faced with an opportunity to ejaculate, a man can set aside his urinary pressure. It was wonderful. I finally relieved myself and then sit-washed, keeping my damned cast dry. Boy, I hated that thing.

Otherwise, it was a work day. I would start at the office and drop off my application at lunch time. I had to figure out how to talk about Arthur Zinn, which meant I had to burrow into his reports. That would be job one. I also had to talk to Jack about Colleen Walsh, and maybe catch up on the construction.

I wanted to find out about my new car, too. Try as I might, I still couldn't escape some excitement about driving off in a new Chrysler... even a minivan.

Linda and I finished our tea and coffee and I followed her to the Penn-Lincoln and into the city. It was muggy, promising thundershowers. Thank God for air-conditioning. Linda took exit Two to Forbes; I slotted right, to the Birmingham, and hit Blatchford early.

"Hey, Pauly, I'm still looking forward to that fresh shoulder, you know."

Paul Lemay answered back, "Yeah, you missed out on the best shoulder I ever had, Mr. Walter. I'll have to ask my Jemmie if she thinks she'll be able to come close to that one. Yes, sir."

"I know a little bit about shoulders, myself, Pauly." I turned the cast toward him.

"Well, you just don't get shot at no more, Mr. Walter, and I'll see about the shoulder stuff. How's that?"

"Sounds good to me, Pauly. See you later!" I was bouncing on my feet as I walked past my former, partial office and up the stairs to my real office with a light switch. My phone was ringing.

"This is Walter Anton. How can I help you?" Then I almost dropped it.

"Good morning, Anton, it's Art Zinn. Got a second?" I swallowed twice.

"Yes! Hi, ahh, Art. This is a surprise. What can I do?"

"I don't know, but I was speaking with Hal yesterday and he suggested I run my question by you. I guess we're both wondering what you can do."

"Well, Art, I've been on the second floor for one day, but I sometimes solve problems, if that is what you have."

"Sort of one. You know where my office is?"

"In contracts?"

"Yuh."

"I can find it. Let me have an hour, though, okay?"

"Oh… ahh, well, I had hoped we might meet first thing, if possible." I noted a plaintiveness in his tone, which surprised me. It also convinced me to make him wait.

"Unless there are flames shooting up, I really need this first hour. I won't let anything deter me after that."

"Uhhm, okay, then. In an hour. Thanks." He wrapped up with more assertiveness than he started with.

I retrieved my keys from the door and sat, wondering. I called Colleen.

"This is Colleen," she answered.

"Morning, Colleen, it's Walter Anton. I have a favor to ask."

"Okay."

"I really would love a cup of coffee and I don't want to be seen in the coffee room right at this time. I'll never ask you to do this for me, again."

"Oh, for Heaven's sake. I don't mind. I'll be right there."

"Thanks a million. See you." I really had to think about my meeting with Zinn. In two minutes Colleen was at my door and I waved her in.

"I brought you a Sweet 'n Low, Mr. Anton."

"You're good, Colleen. Has Jack Jackson spoken to you in the past couple of days?"

She shook her head and looked at me questioningly.

"I'll talk to him, then. I want your status defined. How're things going?"

"Pretty good, I think. I've spoken with Mr. Jackson about a few items, like you said. It's been fine."

I smiled and nodded. "I'm not surprised, kiddo. You're gonna do a better job than I ever did. I'm afraid I've got a lot on my desk and I can't chat. Thank you for indulging my coffee lust." I shook her hand. Then I opened the Zinn folder.

Zinn had forty-six projections reports and more than a dozen details reports on the largest contracts. At first glance they were hard to get into. This rep had done this, then that and it resulted in a contract-order for this number of hundreds of thousands in new business. This other rep had visited so-and-so and wrote an order for four hundred more pieces of contracted part number thus-and-such. I took notes but the information didn't illuminate much, except my appreciation for *Contracts*.

With twenty minutes left before I'd meet Zinn, I felt anxious and wondered why. Had Blatchford told him I was concerned? No, I doubted that, but maybe Zinn had a problem and Hal saw an opportunity. I took a few breaths to calm down, and ploughed on with the reports.

The first one referencing "King Frederik" made me pause to re-read it. It explained expenses for a trip to Copenhagen that Zinn had set for Dieter Fuchs. Travel plans had changed at the last minute and Zinn joined Fuchs on the flight and itinerary. There were notes on meeting the architects and with the foreign minister. There was one reference to the Ex-Im Bank and the name, "Wittenauer." That jibed. On the last day there had been some sort of celebratory dinner that mentioned Casimir Tomkiewicz and… and here I sat up straight and read with my finger under the words, a note in the margin that said, "Fuchs home yesterday."

Zinn and Fuchs had traveled to Denmark for crucial meetings; Casimir had been there already, and Fuchs had left the day before the end of the trip! Why? I asked myself. Did he get sent home? Had he decided to come back on his own? Had he left in anger? Did he walk out on the talks?

I quickly leafed through the pages I hadn't read, looking for Dieter's name. There were a half-dozen more reports that mentioned Fuchs and the King Frederik, plus a seventh that referenced Dieter Fuchs and United Technologies in Bridgeport, Connecticut. I turned the "Fuchs" pages sideways and slipped the stack into my desk drawer. I had a few minutes to spare. I headed down to Contracts with a lot more confidence than I'd had an hour earlier. I heated up my coffee on the way.

Arlene pointed me to Zinn's office, which was bigger than mine and had outside windows high on the wall that let in a lot of light. "C'mon in, Walter. It's good to finally talk to you! I guess we all are glad you were able to resolve our transport problems on the King Frederik, eh?"

"Thanks, Art. Shame on me for not reaching out to you. I really was tucked away in the background before I got shot!" I gestured with the cast.

"Yeah. You'll have to tell me that story one day." He looked at me, neutrally, indicating he really didn't give a shit about my injuries. I looked back at him, poker-faced. Finally he continued.

"The reason I wanted to have this little visit is that Hal suggested you might be able to help with a situation here in Contracts. I would normally have dealt with Hal directly on something like this." A few tics in his expression told me that he was more nervous than I was for having been told to bring his problem to me. Interesting.

"Like what?" I found that fewer words on my part could sometimes elicit more from others.

"Huh?" he asked.

"You said 'something like this' and I don't know what 'this' is."

"Oh, yeah. Well, that's the point, isn't it?" He smiled and nodded to get me to agree. I smiled back but carefully didn't nod. Zinn was not comfortable. I waited.

"Okay, then. I know you met with Dieter Fuchs a couple of times on this King Frederik business."

"We had a lunch… with Casey."

"You're not very talkative, are you?"

I just shrugged. "I don't know what we're talking about, yet, Art. But I am certainly interested. You go right ahead."

He was genuinely uncomfortable talking to me. But Hal had told him to. "I've, ahh… I've had some difficulties with Dieter Fuchs over the course of this King Frederik contract." He let out a long breath and shuddered. Abruptly he looked up and checked the outer office.

"Where's your office, Walter?"

"Upstairs near Engineering."

"Uhh, let's continue our meeting up there, huh? You go ahead and I'll come along in a minute." I agreed to his plan and took my cool coffee upstairs.

Zinn was unnerved and, if I were to guess, virtually afraid of his salesman, Dieter Fuchs. I left my door open. An air-conditioner was something I could use. I made a note. Zinn tapped on the glass as he entered.

"Come right in, Arthur. Sorry it's not elegant." He looked around and then at me.

"What is, umm… I guess I don't know what your position is, Walt."

"Well, that's a good one, Mr. Zinn, it really is. I guess you could call me 'manager of special projects.' Hal has blessed me with some responsibility, but no firm boundaries. So it's not been easy for me to settle on a schedule. That's what I'm trying to establish. But I solved some problems for the King Frederik and Hal is hoping I'll solve some others. We'll see. But you seem distressed, and if I can be of help then I think I have the authority to do something about it."

Zinn relaxed a little in the hard chair next to my desk. I told him to hold on. I went into Engineering and found another hard chair and gestured to borrow it. Bucky waved me along. I took it to my office and sat next to Zinn.

"You don't have to do that, Walt."

"Well, Art, I do, actually. I'm not your equal and I'm certainly not 'over' you. There's no way I'm gonna sit in a plush chair while you sit on that old thing. For the time of our work on your problem, we'll sit equally, if that's okay."

Zinn's reaction was momentarily relief and for an instant, horror. He recovered. "Let's get to work," he said.

I had a pad of paper before me. I wrote "Fuchs" on the top of it, and the date. I thought for a second as if I were going to write something else and then I turned to Zinn.

"You are a little fearful of Dieter Fuchs?"

He pursed his lips. "Obvious, I guess. Fuchs has quite a temper. It's why Casimir is the one we sent to work with the engineers in Denmark. Fuchs had made the original connection, and even that is a little suspect. He found out about the bidding through an ally in a competing firm in Germany."

"Was that the shipbuilding company?"

"Shipbuilding? No. It was Bremen Fabrikwerken Schwerindustrie. Do you know them?"

"No, and Dieter failed to name them when I asked who we had beaten-out for the contract. In fact, he specifically told me it was a German shipbuilder who was rejected because of connections to armament manufacturing." Now I shook my head.

"He does lie. But he also produces big business for us. We have all benefited… I have benefited. Truthfully, I have avoided contending with Dieter because of his profitability. But he is a problem and he may cost us some valuable people. That's why I spoke to Hal. I really don't want him to sabotage this King Frederik deal." He had my full attention with that one.

"You actually think Dieter could do that?" I was breathing quickly, and sweating. Everything we had been spending and risking to lease the rail spur, and all the tooling and construction. Ye Gods! Everything would crash down. I didn't even know if Blatchford could handle that financially if we didn't actually build the girders. Christ!

Arthur Zinn's face was drawn, tiredness in his eyes. "He has made some comments here and there that sound as though he would do that if pushed too far. Mostly to Casey, but others have a sense of his mood, right now."

"How could he stop us?" I had gone from hot to cold… and very, very angry.

"By communicating to BFS through his buddy, there. If they got wind of some kind of nefarious dealing they would immediately raise a stink, Bonn would complain to the U. S. and kill the Ex-Im Bank loans. The Danes might pull back so as not to be part of anything shady. Even if we prevailed we'd be out of the running. They'd give the rest to Hyundai Heavy Industries, who's doing the bulk of the erection and assembly."

"What is Dieter's commission on this whole thing?" I was making notes.

"One hundred and thirty thousand when the commitment is accepted… that's any day, now, and another hundred thousand over three years."

"Holy shit! When he gets his first portion he can walk away in damned good shape, even with taxes. If he's going to screw us, that's when, right?"

"Yeah. Casey is quite worried about what Dieter is thinking, actually."

"What's his cut?"

"About a hundred."

"But it sounds like he was the key guy working with the Danes, no?"

"Absolutely, but Dieter brought in the deal, you see?" Zinn sat with his hands in his pockets. "Dieter can really spin a yarn when needed. He was afraid you would unravel it. He started to get really antsy when you got involved with Wittenauer."

Wittenauer, again. "Is Wittenauer part of the story-telling?"

"I doubt it… he's not that clever. He believed Dieter's bullshit and then sold it to the Commerce Department. Fortunately, we really are able to step up to this level of production and quality. Dieter lied our way into this, including use of BFS's confidential bid, but we actually did impress the Danes when they visited. No one questioned much until you started poking around. Somehow Dieter knows you're 'moving up,' as it were, and has been impossible the last few days."

I wrote more notes and stretched. My gut told me to just shoot Dieter.

"Art, I had an inkling of problems brewing around Dieter. Too much swearing at others, swearing about Blatchford Steel... stuff like that. I had spoken to Hal yesterday thinking that you were not on top of things. This is weird. He handed me a folder full of your reports for the past year and I had found a couple of references to Fuchs that had me wondering. I apologize for giving Hal a negative impression, if I did."

"It is bad and has come on quickly since your involvement. I asked Hal to meet with me two weeks ago but he told me to hold off until you finished up with the lease. Now, here we are. What comes to mind?"

"Where's Dieter now?"

"Probably downstairs. He was due in at ten and that's why we're up here. He has quite a hatred for you."

"I guess one can be known as much by his enemies as his friends. I gotta cogitate on this one. Everything is at stake." I pulled my hands across my face. "Oh! When would Dieter and Casey get their commissions?"

"End of July, although the guys often are granted sizable advances. I imagine they would expect that this time, too. Why?"

"Well, the only reason Dieter hasn't done something already is because he hasn't got that big check. At least that's how I would think."

"That's probably right. For all I know he has to pay his crony at BFS."

I mused on that logic. There were so many wrong steps to take it was scary. "Art, if there were no ways for Fuchs to hurt Blatchford, what would you do?"

"I'd fire him, effective today."

"Okay... so would I. And Casey?"

"I'd give him a raise and the big commission. He was the indispensable man."

"Would his loyalty to Fuchs keep him from accepting?"

Zinn was shaking his head dramatically. "I am certain it's loyalty he'll be happy to be free of. Casey's okay."

"Last question: How can we insulate ourselves... our contract, from sabotage?"

"Why... ahh... well, I guess we'd have to be already shipping and receiving payments. I doubt the Danes would mess up a tight schedule once pieces had already been fabricated and, ahhm... they'd have to be delivered, I think."

"I can't imagine there's any way we're going to delay paying Dieter his commission until some time in January." I frowned and held my hand over my mouth.

Zinn looked lost as he recognized the futility of delivering fast enough. "Nooo," he breathed, "I suppose not." Obviously, part of his productive empire was going to undergo some disruptive change and make his job more difficult, if not precarious.

"Art, I don't want to lay this on Hal until we have a solution. What do you think?"

"I can agree with that." Zinn seemed satisfied for a few seconds and just as quickly distressed, again. "But, I don't have a solution! We've got to come up with something." He was looking to me to save him.

"I'm going to devote a lot of time to this, Art, but I won't be spreading this around and you shouldn't, either. Don't make a point of having met with me. If Dieter has a gossip network, he'll find that out, too. If you come up with a suggestion, call me. In fact, here's my home number. Call me at home if you think of something." I pushed the slip of paper over to him.

He stood and reached out to shake my hand. "Thanks, Walt. I'm glad Hal sent me in your direction. It's been hard to hold this close and not be able to discuss it with someone. I'm sure we'll figure something out." I was glad one of us was confident.

It was nearly eleven. I checked over what I'd written. A few things occurred to me that I wanted to warn Art about, already. I waited a couple more minutes and then called his internal number.

"Art Zinn," he declared.

"Art, it's me, Walter Anton. Can you give me a second?"

"Sure. I'm alone."

"Okay, listen. The worst thing we can do is start treating Fuchs or Casey any differently. Are you with me?"

"Well, yeah, of course. What did you think I…?"

"All right, then. Let's put a special July business push on. This will change the subject for you and for everyone else. Summer is slower, usually?"

"Oh, sure. Usually by twenty or thirty percent compared to Spring or Fall. Why?"

"Well, it's a good reason to make a push. I know we've got the King Frederik coming on line, but it's mostly money flowing out for months… far more than the preliminary contract payments. The increased cash flow is important. If there's any way to accelerate re-orders on existing contracts, or offer a deal of some kind to commit to contracts now rather than after Labor Day, it would be a big help. Can you do that?"

"I guess so. I'm used to taking some time off in July, myself, and we usually go to the Jersey shore in August. What are you saying?"

"I'm just saying that what you and I need to do will be done by the end of July, and probably by the third week in July. If you let it be known that you are deferring part of your vacation to help get a boost in July because it's so important… you know what to say, it will enable you to pester Dieter, Casey, and Mark and Pat, as well, for an uptick in activity in July. It will divert questions, I think, and let you interact with Dieter without mentioning the King Frederik. Keep your friends close and your enemies closer, right?"

"Whew! You don't waste any time, do you?"

"Hey, let's give Dieter something different to complain about. And, one more thing. Take this plan to Hal like it's all yours. Don't mention my input. If he asks about our meeting, just say we are going to meet again later in the week. That'll be true. I expect Hal will be impressed with your initiative. Tell him you want to offer some deals to clients and an extra percent of commission to avoid the July valley we always have. He'll go along, I'll bet."

"Well, I like the sound of it. Maybe we should do it every year. I'll calculate a fair formula, year over year. Anything else?"

"When should we be receiving our first step payment from Denmark?"

"By August first. Why?"

"It fits in with a good reason to boost some sales in July. Go for it!"

"Okay, Walt. I'll try it. Just get back to me with a way to solve the big problem, too."

"Will do, Art. Talk to you soon." I rang off and leaned back. It was funny to make sales recommendations to the V. P. of sales. We had to act before Dieter could queer the deal.

I called Pleasant Hills Chrysler, and asked them if it would be possible to meet me with my car at Alamo at Pittsburgh International? My respondent put me on hold for a minute. After a short time the sales manager I knew came on the line.

"Mr. Anton?"

"It's me," I replied.

"You want to pick up the car at the airport? Do I have that right?"

"If you can, yes. I'll have the check and I'll give your man a ride back. I'm returning a rental."

"I gotcha. We can do that. What time?" We batted the time around and made it one-thirty.

I thought about telling someone what I was going to do and where I was going, but there really wasn't anyone to report to. It didn't seem right, but it was so. I'd have to speak to Hal about that at some point. I went down to Jack's office for the check.

I tapped on the door and heard, "Yup! It's open."

"Hi, Jack. Got a minute?"

"Sure. What's up?"

"Oh, well, my morning's been serious, but not momentous. I can't go into it, but we can talk about it when I get back with my new car."

"Oh, yeah. The car. You'll need a check." I nodded. He pulled out a large perforated page. "Bring me a receipt for the amount of the check. Make sure the paperwork is in your own name and not the company's. This is made out for the number quoted on the form you gave me. If you want to add something else, it's up to you."

"Okay. I agree. I'm dropping off my application to Pitt before I get the car at the airport. They're meeting me."

"Pitt? You? Pretty good. MBA program?" I explained what I hoped to do. "Well, best of luck, there, Walt. It's a tough one, but I imagine you'll be fine."

"Thanks, Jack. I've seen yours hanging there and it's always impressed me."

He looked up at it. "I'll be impressed right back."

"Thanks, Jack. I appreciate that, honestly. I'll see you in a couple hours." He waved me off. It felt right to tell someone I was leaving. First to Pitt, where I dropped off my application and the check. I filled out a short form for the Summer course on "Business Conflicts", which would start in a week: two two-hour sessions a week for seven weeks. Then I headed back to the Penn-Lincoln and followed 376 to the airport.

My new car had been there for five minutes. It took a good twenty minutes in Alamo's office as three people took pictures and calculated charges. I knew a quality shop had estimated fifty-five hundred dollars to restore it to new condition. Alamo tried to say it was at least eight grand. I showed them my estimate from *Re-Kar*. It went back and forth. When Paul Junior came back, things settled down and I was able to leave after putting the rental costs on my credit card. I signed forms guaranteeing responsibility for the damages, but I insisted on a stipulated limit on repairs which they finally agreed to, with fifty-five hundred as a basis, plus some penalty costs of a couple hundred more.

I drove the new car back to Pleasant Hills Chrysler, with some short-cut guidance from their man. I signed what I had to, turned over the check and got the receipt. They showed me all the levers and how to open the hood. The rear windows could be opened with plastic knobs in the ceiling. That was cool. And the air-conditioning worked beautifully. I stopped at a sub place: there wasn't time for *Marko's*.

***

Linda liked the Chrysler. She sat in the driver's seat and then stood up… and then sat back in it. "I like the feel of it," she told me. We went for a ride with Linda driving. She found it easy to handle and with great visibility. "I like it," she said again. I'd done a good thing.

We ate salad and cold chicken. I'd brought home my notes and the reports Hal had given me. Linda agreed to help me with my new dilemma.

"If Dieter is such a problem, why wasn't he fired?" I explained the risk of casting him off and the potential loss of the whole King Frederik contract. Within that was how he had lied to get us the original opportunity to bid and to win the bid.

"So this whole contract is based on a deception? On a lie?" Linda frowned.

I hadn't used those clear terms, before. "I guess that's so. We owe our success so far to a lie. Yes."

"Aren't you going to have to clear the air with Denmark somehow?"

I sat back like I'd been pushed, afraid to think through to that conclusion, but there it was. "I can't just call up some Danish Prince and tell him Blatchford cheated to win the contract, can I?"

"Someone should." Linda had that look that told me there was no arguing her point. Unfortunately, the look was right. I couldn't argue it. But I also knew we couldn't admit what had happened without threatening the company's survival. The worst thing was that Dieter Fuchs was probably quite aware of our position.

"I know you're right, Honey, but I don't know if the rightest possible thing can get done without hurting a lot of innocent people. Blatchford is going to deliver the highest quality girders for the quoted price. I'm not sure the company can afford to not complete the contract."

"Well, I don't know how, but I believe... no. Let me rephrase that. I would like to believe that you, Walter Anton, will do the rightest possible thing. Exactly how, I can't say. I think your energies have to be expended on some way to do the right thing. I can't help you continue a deception."

"It could cost us everything, you know?"

She just nodded, looking at me with real sympathy. "Let's end this long day with a nice slowy. We'll sleep better." We did, and we did.

WEDNESDAY, JUNE 19, 1985

Despite Linda's fabulous medicine, I was restless. I had uncomfortable dreams, and if I could remember them, I hadn't slept well. Somehow I was going to broach the topic of coming clean on the contract… with Hal Blatchford and with Arthur Zinn, my new buddy. I didn't know another way to strip Fuchs of his financial threat.

If we didn't clear the air, Fuchs could get pissed off about something months from now, and cause us trouble and possible future lawsuits. If we did clear the air, we had to do so in a way that kept the Danes with us for the full contract. And we'd have some obligation to compensate BFS in Germany, too, or so it seemed. But I had no confidence in any course. I just knew Linda was right.

My first call went to Art Zinn. I explained what seemed like the only two options we had, short of murdering Fuchs. He was not very excited about either continuing to hide the deception and being subject to Fuchs' moods, which also included the risk that he'd take his money and still scuttle us, or of coming clean with the risk we'd lose the contract. Neither was I, but I felt I had to be upbeat and keep Zinn from depression.

I told him I would call if we could meet with Hal right now. Then I called Kelly Galvin and told her I needed to find a few minutes with Mr. Blatchford. She said she'd call me back, and "congratulations, Mr. Anton." I thanked her, but I didn't feel like anything had been won... again. She called and said anytime was fine.

I called Zinn and told him we were on. He sighed when he said he'd be right up. When he came we walked through the dungeons directly into Kelly's office. I was smiling, Zinn was in a funk. Kelly called in to Hal and pointed at the big door.

"Well, good morning, Walter, Arthur." He didn't stand. "I didn't expect results from putting you together quite this fast."

"This is gonna be an odd meeting, Hal. There is a big problem that possibly threatens the King Frederik contract. I won't speak for Arthur." I gestured to Arthur Zinn to speak up. He slowly began to explain the Dieter Fuchs problem.

I didn't need to add anything. Zinn stated the possibilities fairly well. When he finished Hal was standing up. He never did that. He had both hands on his desk. He looked at me for a second as he asked me what I thought, and then looked back at the top of his desk.

I laid out the case for coming clean and eliminating Fuchs' possible ability to sabotage the contract. Zinn looked like he had just thrown up. Blatchford just stared at me. He hadn't bought it.

"I am surprised that you could throw away what you have sacrificed so much to make possible, Walter. Not very business-like."

I'd lost his respect, like falling off a ladder. But I couldn't retreat.

"Hal, I do understand. But you haven't weighed the small number of options we have." His glare could have softened the steel we sold. I kept talking before he blew. He was faster.

"What the fuck are you thinking here? I thought you grasped the scope of this contract, Anton... the financial risk we have! Look at you, injured over this mess! Jesus H. Christ, Walter!" He was turning red and shaking. I could hardly look at him. Finally I hung my head.

We could have heard a pin drop. Hal finally sat, huffing and puffing until his breathing quieted. I looked up to see him turned away toward his drapes.

"I... I'm sorry about that, fellas," he said. A few moments passed, then, "Tell me what you think, Walter."

I had never been so on the spot. I tried to picture how to look; that was weird. I sat up straighter and then stood up, consciously brightening my face. "If we try to keep this funny business under the rug we'll always be at risk of Fuchs blowing up or…" and here I held up a finger and looked at both Zinn and Blatchford in turn, "…or of this turncoat at BFS being so angry at not getting enough money or something that he spoils the deal, himself. I don't think we can fully eliminate either risk with money."

Blatchford swung around again while I stood there, fighting tremors in my legs. I pushed on.

"I don't know the people in Denmark. Arthur has met them and Casimir has worked with them at some length. Probably Casey would have to be part of our approach on this. The only way forward that secures us against future damages, and gets Dieter out of our hair is to fess up to the Danes and offer some kind of compensation to BFS. I can't speak to the details of all that. But if we work something out with Denmark and keep the contract, and then BFS gets wind of the cheating that happened, we could be sued for millions. Maybe we could help BFS get other business in the U. S. and keep them from suing us now or later. We have to mitigate those risks. I don't see how we can sit here and wait to see which shit storm comes our way."

Blatchford reacted to the profanity, but didn't throw anything. He was glaring at Zinn. "How long have you known how Fuchs got this deal?"

Zinn was sweating and fidgety. He must have known for a while. "I have known since the Danes visited us. Dieter bragged of it after a few drinks. Casey knew earlier, I believe, but I have known for about four months." Blatchford was looking at him rather neutrally. I felt badly, watching Zinn shrink.

"I'm not sure what to feel about this," Blatchford intoned. "I know things happen when sales are hyper-competitive. Promises are made that we scramble to keep. But we can control our performance in those instances. Now we're looking at a sea-change for the company and I find us hanging by a thread. We've already spent a lot of money and we're committed to construction and contracts for two million more, all for the King Frederik. I can't fucking believe it." He slumped back as if defeated.

Zinn started to say something, and then thought better of it. He slumped back too. No one spoke. What the Hell?

"We can fix this, Hal." He looked at me like a caged lion.

"Just like that? Pray tell." The thin ice hadn't yet frozen. What was I going to say?

"I know that sounds crazy, but we're smart people and we can at least figure out how to try to fix it. We have to do that, don't we?"

"Well, let's do it before lunch." Blatchford was feeling trapped... and a sore loser.

'What are you talking about, Walter?" Zinn asked.

I had my yellow pad in front of me. "First we have to neutralize Fuchs until we can resolve matters with the Danes." I wrote down "neutralize Fuchs." No one said anything.

"Then I suggest we invite the Danes back to show em the progress we're making, the work on the building, the new tooling, the special flat-car racks ready to carry their girders. We could have Angus Newhall here to talk about barging them to Mobile; we'll have the mayor, Congressman Wittenauer, maybe even Forrest Akers. We'll involve them as much as possible in how much we value this contract and what it means to the whole city… as much as we can, anyway."

"What will all that do?" Blatchford was interested. Art Zinn was just watching.

"We'll make ourselves more like partners in the success of the King Frederik. Then we can have a closed-door meeting and explain that we have had to fire one of our sales people because we have found… no, because we have *heard… heard* that he may have colluded with a traitor at Bremen Fabrikwerken, and that we are investigating this story. Then we ask for their advice on how to proceed, and whether we should say anything to BFS."

Hal was studying me to see if I actually believed what I was saying. I was pretty sure I did. It was all I had and nobody else had anything. At least we could talk about it.

"Arthur?" Hal asked.

Zinn jumped to full seated attention. "Actually, Hal, I've been thinking of a way to corral Dieter. I know we are always slower in July and that our expenditures are taking a big hit as we ramp up for the bridge. I want to put on a special push for accelerated and new business to boost revenues over last year. I have some ideas for some deals we might offer and commission offers for the reps and for the support people. A whole-team effort for July. It will give me a reason to keep Dieter under the microscope with everyone else. You and I also need to figure a way to stretch out his commission payments on the King Frederik so that he doesn't get his big check in July. We're afraid he may bolt if he gets it because he may owe something to his buddy at BFS. At that point he could still scuttle us unless the Danes are already with us."

"I like that. I don't know about this whole thing, Walter. I also know we can't fail to act. I wish I knew how the Danes felt about dealing with BFS in the first place. They don't like armament manufacturers, I heard."

"That's what Dieter told me, but I don't know if that was true. Maybe you could ask Casey, Art. You need to separate their interests a little bit... at least on the King Frederik. Let me know when you're going to speak with him. I'd like to help with that."

Blatchford was watching the two of us. Zinn's face displayed a spectrum of feelings as I spoke, finally registering relief when I suggested helping him with Casimir. I turned toward Blatchford.

"Let's talk again tomorrow on this, both of you," Hal directed. "I want quick action to get things rolling. I'll set up a visit by the Danes. Katy Mellon can coordinate through Wittenauer's office. Don't spread this around." And that ended it. I shook Hal's hand and we left. Kelly wasn't there. We walked through the dungeons to my office.

"Well, Arthur, we're underway. In six weeks we should be clear. But it's fragile. Every step has to work... and in conjunction with the others, yet not always with knowledge of the others. We'll be pretty slick to pull it off. You okay?"

"I guess. What do you think Hal will do to me?"

"To you? I think he appreciates how you got here. The future depends on how we get out of it. Don't waste any mental energy on how we got here. Okay?"

"I don't know where I'd be if this all blew up a month from now. I'm glad you're here, Walt."

"Art, you do stuff I never could. You know how to bring business in and how to keep sales people selling. My hat's off to you. I'm looking from the outside, as it were, although I'm heavily invested." I jinked the cast at him. "I have faith in doing the right thing. We'll be okay."

He left. I made a note about reinforcing his courage. I outlined resolving the Fuchs problem. I needed to get it typed without sharing the information internally. The Yellow Pages listed secretarial services. Six bucks a page. I told them I'd drop it off in a couple hours. I prepared three separate schedules for Art, Hal and myself. Hal seemed willing to let me lead on it.

Fuchs' relationship with Wittenauer might be a problem. I called the congressman's office. Sweet Devlin answered. "We" were still going to help me. I asked if the congressman were in his office and Devlin told me to wait while "we" found out. In a couple of minutes Wittenauer picked up. I told him I had something to go over with him on the King Frederik, in total confidence, and could I come right over? He protested, but gently, and I wrangled my way in.

I started to gather my yellow pad and keys when my phone rang.

"Walter Anton," I said.

"Walt, its me! I know where I met that man from Wittenauer's office… you know, the slim man... the receptionist?" Linda was all excited.

"Oh, I sure do, Hon. I was just speaking to him, as a matter of fact."

"Wally, he's the face in the kitchen window. I'm sure of it!"

"What face?"

"Don't you remember? The day after the break-in I called the police because a man was looking right in the kitchen window at me?"

I did remember. "Him?" My voice rose to a squeak.

"Yes! Absolutely. I saw him when we went to the EPA. He kept turning away, but I know it was him. He tried not to face me. But I'm certain."

"What do you want to do, Lin? I'm headed over to the congressman's office. Do you want me to call the police, or tell Wittenauer? What?" I knew there was a good reason to not like that kid.

"Oh, Walt, I don't know. He ought to pay for the damages, at least. He was trying to defend his boss, I suppose, when you stirred everything up. I don't think arresting him will do much good. Do you?" I already had a strategy.

"What do you think it came to? You know what we spent that night and I know you've had to buy clothes and sheets and things."

"It's over two thousand dollars, Walt. But we have insurance for most of it."

"What about this, Honey? I'll make him pay and you donate the money to a charity. How's that sound? We can't let him off altogether."

"Well, that might work. I know right where to give it. Okay. Do what you can. I am so relieved to remember that."

"I'm on it, double-oh-six!" She laughed. I told her I loved her and that I'd be home early. She said she would prepare a barbecue and maybe invite Elly and the boys. It was all good.

***

Devlin was extra snooty when I walked in. I didn't wait on what I wanted to do. "So, Devlin, do you trash houses once a week, once every two weeks, or just special occasions?"

He turned bright red and started to wet his pants, somehow restraining himself. His mouth moved like a guppy's, but no sound came out. He looked around for someplace to hide as he held his crotch tightly.

"I imagine you'll really piss after this, but first I have some instructions. Do you need to write them down?"

He shook his head in little jerky motions.

"I know you know my address. So, you send me a check for, say, three thousand dollars… when can you do that, by the way?

By Friday? Make it out to 'cash.' Are you following me?" He nodded as tears spilled onto his cheeks.

"If that happens I won't say anything to your boss or to the cops. Deal? Say yes."

Poor Devlin nodded as hard as he could, but was afraid to speak since it might come out moist. He was gripping his dinky even harder.

"I'll let myself in, then. Thanks!" He ran out toward the men's room. I walked in to Tom Wittenauer's office.

Wittenauer had changed to a hard, straight-backed chair. He stood as I entered. "Walter!" He said heartily. "I must have not heard the phone announcing you." We shook hands.

"I think Devlin had to go potty. I let myself in. Sorry." Wittenauer looked at me funny and then waved an "OK."

"What is so gosh-darn important this time, Walter. I'll take a shot only once each election cycle." We shared a smile.

"Tom, we have a problem that concerns the King Frederik contract, and it's due to something Dieter Fuchs has done..."

We spent nearly half an hour going over the ramifications of Dieter's cheating. I told him Katy would be in touch about a visit by the Danes.

"I'll certainly help Hal Blatchford any way I can, Walter. You know that. What do I do if Fuchs contacts me? We worked closely, there, and he would expect some access."

"I can't tell you what to do, Tom. But Dieter is the problem we have to solve, and I think the easiest thing is to avoid him for a few weeks. Our plan is to keep him extra busy until we can drop the hammer, so to speak. And we certainly hope you can be part of our welcoming delegation when the Danes visit."

"When?"

"I don't know, yet. Hal is working that out and wants to use your reputation to help get them to come. Katy will have the details, I'm sure."

"Well, as luck would have it, I had to cancel my mountain-climbing this summer. I'll be around."

"I won't take any more time, Tom, and I thank you for seeing me." I stood and shook his hand. He stood also.

"The docs made me get this chair and said to stand up as often as possible. Seems to help. I'm feeling pretty good, actually."

I told him I was happy to hear that, and I was. I was planning to just say, "Toodle-oo" to Devlin. He had a very serious look.

"Here," he said, handing me an envelope. I checked and it was his check for the three thousand. I was shocked.

"I want to clean this up. Thank you for keeping it quiet." His face was a little red, again. He couldn't look at me.

"Devlin, this is a good thing. It will stay quiet, you have my word."

He nodded. It took me a few minutes to find the rental, until I remembered to look for a Chrysler Town and Country. New-car excitement again.

I stopped at Jack's office before going upstairs. "Hiya, Walt. Busy day?"

"They all are, these days, and today is a humdinger. I'm not supposed to discuss it much, but you can certainly talk with Hal about things. It's shaping up to be an exciting summer, too. And I'm finding my way along."

"I'm glad you're handling things, Walt. I think Hal chose well to move you up."

I thanked him and then he filled me in on the construction projects – drawings to contracts. We looked at the start of the new walls for the tall doors. Crews were already pouring concrete for the external platform.

"You've moved pretty fast, Jack. Impressive."

"Everyone has cooperated and the crane people have been the best. I think we'll test a mock-up shipment by the end of October. We'll ship in January."

"Congratulations!"

"Well, thanks, but it's because we started in the nick of time. I'd say Hal appreciated the fix for the crane almost as much as the lease."

"So long as we win the race. Thanks for the time, Jack."

I started up to my real office and realized we hadn't discussed Colleen. I turned back.

"C'm'in, Walt. What do you need?" I explained that I had been thinking that my old office would be a good spot for Colleen Walsh. We talked about her quality work and how it was easier to work with her than with me. Jack said he'd take care of it.

A note was under my door. I definitely needed access to a secretary. "Come see us – Bucky." What the Hell?

"Here I am, Buck."

"Good, good. Well, I hear you're the go-to guy, now. I gotta get with your barge guy, Angus. He'll need racks to carry our girders and the more I study them, the racks look more and more critical. I want his racks to be identical to ours. If we introduce a twist into the girders... it's a very bad thing."

"Are you making a wooden mock-up to try them on?"

"Not us. I've contracted with an outfit that makes curved beams. They guarantee specs."

"Expensive? What's their quote?"

"A little over twenty grand." Bucky looked at me.

"Can't be helped, I guess. How are they going to get it to us? We can't use normal shipping... I assume they can't either."

"It's coming down the river. Mid-Waters will pick it up and put it on our cars, and we'll pull it up here. Kinda cool, I think."

"And then what? We throw it away?"

"Nope, they'll sell it when we're done. That's returning us over ten thousand!"

He had me smiling. "Will we be ready to receive it… move it?"

"That's why I need Angus as quickly as you can get him here."

"Okay, I'll call his office. That it?"

"That's it. Thanks." I liked Bucky Dighton. No nonsense if he could help it.

Angus was back and more than happy to meet Bucky first thing. I checked and it was all set. Good. I made a few notes on my yellow pad for the morning. One thing was to meet our other VP, Andrew McCullum, the VP of finance. Why hadn't Blatchford suggested it? Probably wanted to see if I did. I switched the lights and went downstairs.

"Jack? Last time, I promise."

He looked up from his papers. "What can I do?" He clasped his hands behind his head.

"I really could use a little secretarial support. Not full-time," I quickly added when his jaw dropped, "but at least some access to someone, here, for typing and messaging. Whadda ya think?"

Jack agreed to figure it out. Then I asked him about his main boss, Andrew McCullum. In a half-hour I had a pretty good picture of Blatchford finances and debt. I still wanted to work here.

EPILOGUE

Hal Blatchford was away in July, which not even Kelly Galvin mentioned. I spoke with her every day, in case messages had to be acted upon.

One day Peter was there talking with her. He asked me to join the conversation when I started to retreat. "You deserve to get this as early as possible," he said to me, not quite smiling.

"What's up?"

"My dad has been at the Mayo Clinic for the past week. You probably thought he was taking time off, but it's more than that."

I hadn't spent any time on Hal's absence. That was, like the company I was loyal to, his business. But Peter's tenor made me realize he was not talking about a vacation. "I am sorry to hear what you are about to tell me, I think."

"I don't mean to make you sad, but my dad has been getting a lot of tests and they have confirmed what stage he's in with 'ALS.' He has been dealing with the early effects for a few months. I believe his offer to you in June was in preparation for his eventual disability. He expects to step down by Christmas."

Kelly Galvin was crying very quietly. She apologized to Peter and, in a soft way, to me. I could have easily cried, myself, but I knew I couldn't… not right then. Kelly loved the old man and had for years. I loved him, too, in ways I hadn't appreciated.

"Peter, you know I have been preparing myself to meet his request. At the same time I have not advertised the fact in the company. Few people are aware of the change. I don't know if even Jack Jackson is. My wife is, but I haven't spoken about it to anyone else."

I continued, "What are you going to do? You're staying on the board, I hope."

"Oh, yes. I haven't had a day-to-day function for some time, just errands for my dad. My interests are in law, politics, government. When I decide to agree, there's a position waiting for me at the Department of Commerce as a trade representative. At some point I may run for office. I hope you'll back me, if I do."

I matched his smile at that comment. "Absolutely. However, for the next few months I would hope you'll be around… a lot. I'm a neophyte."

"I'll be here, but so will my dad. He isn't going to be helpless."

"I don't mean to imply... I don't know what to expect." My head was swimming. The weight of what Peter had told me was just beginning to hit me. I fought the tears… with some success. Kelly looked as though she cared about *my* situation.

***

The Danes agreed to another visit, having planned to schedule something for a couple of their engineers. It worked out. We laid it on thick, how we had geared the whole company up for the contract, how we had arranged for a whole second crane, how important the "bridge" improvements were going to be to the city, overall, and the difference the contract was already making for at least one disadvantaged neighborhood.

I have to give Wittenauer credit for his world-class schmoozing. He even had a top lady from Commerce join us. In a couple of side conversations we learned that Denmark didn't ever intend to award the contract to BFS, but we had to keep that under our hats. It was Hal Blatchford who told our guests we had been forced to fire our main sales representative because he had obtained confidential information from BFS on their bid pricing. They didn't seem particularly concerned and declared their unconcern whether we ever revealed that to BFS. Big sigh of relief on our side of the table.

Casey Tomkiewicz is now our primary rep and clearly enjoying being out from under Dieter's thumb. Art Zinn produced real added business with his July sales boost program and probably saved his job. By the end of August he hired another field man who had engineering experience with Electric Boat. We all felt he'd done well.

By Labor Day, I had Andy McCullum's agreement to name Jack Jackson Controller. He and I have been working buddies since my promotion. I still was operating as Manager of Special Projects, although the story about Hal's condition had reached quite a few people. All the key people knew that I would eventually be president, but I never expressed it when I had to make some sort of decision. I don't know how much managing I did, except to guide others into more productive paths when they encountered a logjam.

I did manage an "A" on my summer course at the Katz School of Business. It took more than a little help from Linda. She has a way of asking me simple questions which fearlessly lead me to better conclusions. I learned to ask her about every new concept. She enjoys the homework more than I do.

The full course kicked in the second Monday in September. By then I was in student mode and weirdly picturing myself as part of the Pitt student body. Linda's obvious motherhood turned on something in my psyche that had me longing to hold her whenever we were apart for more than a few hours. On class nights I wouldn't be home from about seven-thirty in the morning until ten at night. Supper was something from the Student Union. I teetered between looking forward to class and dreading the period between work and class. There was barely time to get home, scarf a meal and get to Pitt, and it was uncomfortable. It's very hard to leave her, once home. It's better going directly from the office.

One guy, Ernie Burman, is an engineer from "Deltrane – River Road," one of the largest bridge builders in Pennsylvania... in the whole Ohio Valley, probably. His bosses had ordered him to attend the MBA course so that he could take over a new division that built river crossings specifically with cable stays. They use a lot of specialized steel and quite by accident I garnered a big new customer for Blatchford. Pumped me up. It felt great to turn the contracting over to Art Zinn and his team.

Tom Wittenauer recovered nicely. Overall his bravery and recovery made him more popular than we'd promised. His '86 campaign looked to be unopposed. He learned to get along with Harry McKay, too. The mayor had reached out while he was recovering. McKay was the key to anyone's generating a strong effort against Wittenauer, and he'd managed to stay fairly neutral.

Losing the cast at the end of July was a true relief. But I needed a lot of rehab on my arm and shoulder. It healed with fascinating scars, but stiff, and weak. I used that excuse to get an above-ground pool and I swam as often as I could, nursing it back to flexibility and some measure of strength. Linda used it to get me to join a gym... with her. She wanted to be in good shape for delivery and thought I should be, too. What the Hell.

Blatchford did, finally, move some money into Liberty Bank. To avoid paperwork delays Liberty gave us a two-million line of credit with very low interest, which Hal thought was a great idea, but he let Andy McCullum think it was his.

By the end of October we had upgraded the railbed and converted the block-signals on the main line to a swing-away design. By scheduling with CSX we could move our girders through that block and immediately onto Mid-Waters' quay. We also had our new reach-stacker... which came by train, and we'd even tested handling the wooden mock-up. Bucky Dighton had his special three-car racks all sized and fabricated. We really are going to ship those damn girders.

November found me hip-deep in night school and that's when I had to turn in outlines of my business problem write-up. Actually writing the whole story, starting with that meeting in May, was easy. Putting everything into a proper outline format took a lot of work on Linda's part, but she managed to teach me the essence of it. That step made it easy to lay out a project timeline, as if it were possible to teach someone else how to do what I had done, the next time. God forbid. It did show that flexibility was pretty important to meeting goals.

Axel Johnson moved in with Elly Maxwell and her two boys, about a week after Jack Maxwell was arrested for defrauding the University of Pittsburgh. They weren't the exact charges Axel had been working on, but they were bad enough to get Jack a few years at SCI Rockview. His gardening skills may have helped him there, but I never visited.

The Three Rivers Trust didn't do much of anything for about two months and then a new president was named from the board. Her husband was a CPA at a big downtown firm and she had good connections through the partners. I guess they were still protecting western civilizations from rapacious developers... John Schumann mentioned them from time to time, but I cared very little about their activities.

Poor Roberta was released on her own recognizance and placed on probation for two years, promising to not get into trouble else she'd wind up at County Prison where she'd already spent forty-two days. She behaved. She did let Linda visit her a couple of times at home. For their part, the Trust kept Roberta as a board member but she didn't attend meetings for a while.

Katy Mellon was kept busy processing paperwork for new hires as we ramped up for intense activity completing the King Frederik. I got her two assistants. The Danes were so impressed with our preparations that they ordered some other, smaller pieces, as well. Casey Tomkiewicz was over there three more times, and he had a BMW of his own.

Katy and Tom Wittenauer finally got engaged, with a wedding date set for right after the election. Everyone was pretty happy about that around Blatchford Steel.

Linda is due in mid-February, causing us to prepare our nest, including two complete paint jobs on the bedroom. I hope *he* likes the color it is now. Linda hopes *she* likes the color it is now. We'll find out. Her parents are coming to stay with us for a few days over Christmas, which is a first. Linda's really looking forward to having them here, and I am too, although I don't let on.

Hal Blatchford didn't retire, exactly, before Christmas. He stepped back from a lot of details and took days off. When he fell on the stairs one morning we were all upset. He finished the climb and stayed in his office with lunch brought in. It comforted him to watch the shop floor and for that reason and because it was his office, I had one of those electric stair-chair things installed and he was good to get up and down for several more months. During that time I had the "dungeons" renovated and made into a pretty nice office for myself and we arranged the phones so that Kelly Galvin could take calls for both of us.

I didn't know when I'd ever feel right working out of Hal's office. Couldn't think of it.

We shipped our first girders on January sixth. That was something to see and we invited everyone and his city councilor to come to our celebration. Bucky Dighton's team had devised a phenomenal brace and bracket system that allowed for lifting by a single crane or, with quick adjustment, by two cranes, which is what Mid Waters used. We sent the description, photos and specs to Denmark and they instructed us to include one of the custom brackets with every girder. It guaranteed perfect geometry of the girders when they arrived in Denmark, and it sped up unloading them.

Our shop was so jammed with fabrication of the huge bow girders that we had to farm out the brackets. Weird, but it worked. The first two, wrapped in Tyvek, looked strange inching down our spur, onto the CSX mainline for about three hundred feet and then onto a siding where Mid Waters' cranes could pluck them off the flat-cars and nestle them, racks and all, into matching spots on the barges.

We had a band, some speeches, a congressman and a senator, Commerce officials and, of course, the mayor. Hal stayed in a wheelchair, but made a little speech of his own, praising his shop and the best metalworkers in Pittsburgh. I stayed off to the side with strong feelings. Shipping those girders was bringing my date for the presidency that much closer. Hal would be Chairman of the Board. It was upsetting and I couldn't have spoken, anyway.

When Hal had a breathing attack that landed him in the hospital, Jack Jackson seemed to be handling the details. When I questioned why, I learned that Jack had been raised as a foster child, side-by-side with Peter. What an eye-opener. That's also when Jack told me to convert Hal's office to a Board Room and training room. I wrote that down but I didn't move too quickly. Hal came back in the office a number of times after that, long after we finished the King Frederik work. I was glad it was comfortable for him, even if he had to travel with a breathing machine.

I finished my text on the business problem by the end of January, and then "submitted" it to my editor. She really is very good at editing and spent a lot of time on it, even though she was as big as a house by then. Of course, I'd included a lot of our exciting, personal stuff: showers, feelings and so forth, for her reading pleasure, which she edited out.

END

Review Requested:

If you loved this book, would you please provide
a review at Amazon.com?

Printed in the USA
CPSIA information can be obtained
at www.ICGtesting.com
CBHW031253070724
11250CB00015B/37

9 781681 816876